JOSHUA
The Journey Home

JOSHUA
The Journey Home

Joshua

Joshua and the Children

Joshua in the Holy Land

Three Bestselling Novels
Complete in One Volume

JOSEPH F. GIRZONE

INSPIRATIONAL PRESS

NEW YORK

Contents

Joshua

Dedicated
to
My Mother and Father

Acknowledgments

I wish to express deep appreciation to my friends and family, whose assistance and suggestions were most valuable.

I am particularly grateful to Maureen Conners Moriarty, Neal Merkel, Peter Ginsberg and Michelle Rapkin for their persistent faith in "Joshua," which was critical in bringing about this present edition.

1

IT WAS A quiet, sultry afternoon in Auburn. People were gathering at Sanders' store for news and the latest gossip. The weather had been sticky and hot for the past few days, just like before a thunderstorm. It was the kind of day that puts people on edge, when mosquitoes and biting flies invade from the nearby woods and annoy everyone in town.

The Persini brothers had given up laying pipe for the day; the ground was too soupy from recent rains and the site was infested with mosquitoes. Why waste time working mud? They had already left the job and were walking toward Sanders' when they met Pat Zumbar, who had also taken the afternoon off.

Pat greeted them with his usual friendly attack: "What the hell are you guys doin' away from the job? When are you gonna finish that pipeline so we can use our sinks? The women are furious you're taking so long."

"Cool off, Pat, it's too hot to work today. You took off, didn't you, and all you do is sit on a bulldozer. You should be in that mudhole, then you'd have something to bellyache about." That was big Tony. He never took much of Pat's guff. And today was no time to horse around. It was too hot and everyone was on edge.

As the men walked along the sidewalk their heavy work boots pounded the wooden planks like rolling thunder. The men liked to hear that noise. It made them feel important. Pat reached Sanders' first. He opened the squeaky screen door and let the

others enter, then followed them as the door slammed behind
him. The noise startled Katherine Sanders, who was cleaning the
counter. "You guys back again? I thought I just got rid of you,"
she said as she continued working.

"It's too hot to work today," Ernie said matter-of-factly. "I
should have gone fishing like I wanted to."

"Never mind your fishing," Katherine shot back, "you better
finish that water main so we can clean up around here."

At that point George Sanders came out of the back room. He
was a mild-mannered man, recently retired from the county
highway department, where he had worked for the past thirty
years. He now spent most of his time around the store, even
though his wife, Katherine, had been running it efficiently for
years without his help.

This wasn't just a store, and these fellows weren't just customers. They had been friends since childhood and knew each other
better than brothers and sisters. There were few secrets among
them. They knew everything there was to know about each
other and they were still friends. The store was the natural meeting place when there was nothing else to do, and even though
the small counter was hardly adequate, the men were content to
just stand around and drink their coffee or eat their sandwiches.
Good-natured banter and needling was ordinary fare, and at this
they were experts.

The current topic of conversation around town was the new
fellow living in the old cottage at the edge of town. No one
knew much about him except that his name was Joshua and he
was a plain man. He kept pretty much to himself, which piqued
everyone's curiosity. Once or twice a week he would walk up the
street to the grocery store and buy food and other things he
needed. He wasn't particularly shy, though he didn't talk much.
He just went about his business and smiled hello to whoever he
met along the way. He dressed simply, wearing khaki pants and
a plain, loose, pullover shirt that was a lighter shade brown than
the pants. The shirt was tucked in at the waist and open at the
neck. In place of a leather belt he wore a belt put together from
carefully braided strings that formed a flat rope about an inch
and a half wide, with a loop and large knots that hooked together in the front.

Joshua looked tall because he was slim and athletic. His long graceful hands were used to hard work and were pleasing to watch when he gestured. His face was thin but with strong, rugged features. His blue-green eyes were striking in the deep feeling they expressed. When he looked at you you had the feeling he was looking into your soul. But the look was not critical. It was filled with compassion and seemed to say "I know all about you and I understand." His walnut-colored hair was thick and wavy, not recently cut, so it gathered about his ears and neck.

Joshua was an object of intense curiosity because no one knew anything about him, and there was no way to learn anything about him. He didn't seem to have a family. He didn't have a job that anyone knew about, yet he didn't seem to be well-off enough to live without working. According to the mailman he wasn't getting any dividend checks or social security checks, no pension checks or government mail. How did he live? That's what had everyone baffled. Whenever he came into town to buy food, what he bought was meager: a loaf of unsliced French or Italian bread, fresh fish, when it was available, pieces of chicken, some fresh ground hamburger, a few cans of sardines, fresh fruits and vegetables. It rarely varied and never amounted to much. Usually after leaving the market he would walk across the street to the liquor store and buy a gallon of table wine. Then, with arms loaded down with packages, he would walk back to his cottage.

But all this revealed little about the man except that he was orderly in his schedule, regular in his diet, and moderately well-disciplined. Beyond that he was still a mystery.

The cottage he lived in was small, not more than three rooms: a kitchen, a living room, and a bedroom. There was a back room off the house that Joshua used as a workshop. In front of the cottage, near the street, was a homemade mailbox. There was nothing like it anywhere. It was made of wood and constructed like an old-fashioned fishing boat in such a way that the keel could be pulled out like a drawer and letters inserted. There was a fish net hanging down the side to collect small packages.

Along the front of the house was a white picket fence, broken by a gate in the middle, which turned at the corners and went partially down along the sides of the property. Joshua had re-moved sections of the fence at the rear of the house so that the backyard opened out into a sprawling meadow, which was part of the nearby farm where sheep and cows grazed. Joshua never had to mow his lawn; a few stray sheep wandered regularly into his yard and did the mowing for him, leaving only clumps of wildflowers here and there which created a natural, attractive setting.

These were the few obvious facts about Joshua that were fa-miliar to the townsfolk—just enough to whet their appetite to learn more about him.

It was George who brought up the subject of Joshua. "That new fellow from the *Little House on the Prairie* came in just before you guys got here. Katherine gets butterflies every time he stops in for a cup of coffee. I think she's got a crush on him," George said, with a big laugh.

Katherine was furious. "That's not true," she retorted sharply. "I just get nervous when he's around. He's not like other people, and I get tongue-tied when I try to talk to him. And George is no different. He just stands there gawking at him like a fool." George just laughed good-humoredly.

"You know, he really is a likable guy once you get to know him. And he's not stupid either," George went on. "I asked him what he thought of the Israelis invading Lebanon, and he an-swered that everyone has a right to live in peace. That was a shrewd answer. He wasn't taking one side, but he took both sides when you think of it. He knew I was feeling him out, and he was polite in answering but didn't reveal a thing about what he really felt."

At that point Moe Sanders came into the store. "All right, you guys, how come the water main's not finished? Everyone's wondering where you went. I tried to help you out, so I told them you probably went fishing. Are they mad! They said they haven't had running water since yesterday afternoon."

"You're a big help," Tony Persini said. "We worked in that hole all morning and couldn't get a thing done with all the mud. The pipe is broken in six different places. If the pump works and it doesn't rain, we may be able to get it finished by tonight."

Changing the subject, Moe remarked that he had just bumped into that new guy, Joshua. "He was leaving the liquor store and was on his way home. I walked over to him and started a conversation with him, and, you know, he's not a bad fellow. He's got a good sense of humor too. He wanted to know who the roly-poly fellow was with the big mouth. I told him he must have been talking about Pat."

"He didn't say that," Pat burst in. "He don't even know who I am."

"He didn't actually use those words," Moe said, "but he did describe you so there was no mistaking who he meant. You do make a big impression on people who don't know you. And there was no way he could have missed you coming down the street. I could hear you all the way around the corner."

"We were just talking about him ourselves before you came in," Tony interjected. "George had been talking to him. He seems like a friendly guy."

Moe agreed and added that Joshua had even invited him over to his house whenever he's free and told him to bring his friends too. "I asked him where he works, and he told me he just repairs things for people, wooden objects and things around the house. It doesn't bring him much income, just enough to pay his bills. He doesn't need much anyway, he said."

"Boy, what a way to live! I wish my life was that simple," Ernie said.

During this exchange George was looking out the window. "Looks like it's going to rain," he said.

Ernie turned and looked out the window. "We'll never get that pipe fixed. I'll see you guys tomorrow," he said as he walked toward the door. One by one the others followed. Katherine took their cups and cleaned the counter as the squeaky door slammed shut.

The main street was quiet. Everyone had gone home to escape the impending storm. There were only a few cars and pickup trucks along the wide street. Auburn was an old town, built around the late 1700s, tucked away in the foothills of the mountains that sprawled out into the distance. The village, with its surrounding fields and hamlets, had kept its own identity. Its six churches attested to the varied backgrounds of the inhabitants, the names on mailboxes graphically pointing up the wide diversity of nationalities, and the antique houses and stores painted a vivid picture of life here two centuries ago.

The people were warm and friendly, once you got to know them. Being off the main flow of highway traffic, the village was isolated and well insulated from the current of change that was sweeping the big city. The people were more true to the old ways, and change came slowly, if at all.

2

THE RAINS CAME hard and furious and finally broke, allowing the Persinis to finish their work. It was a big relief when the sun appeared and blue sky replaced the heavy, leaden clouds. The feel of dampness still clung to one's bones because the long rains had left the ground wet, but it was warm and one could smell summer. The birds started singing and the flowers in everyone's gardens were bursting into bloom. The sweet aroma of lilacs pervaded the whole town, causing delight to some and asthma attacks in others. Customers who came into Sanders' store to transact their daily business were in high spirits, like school kids who are given a day off.

Even Charlie, the testy mailman, was in a cheerful mood and got the courage to knock on Joshua's door one day under the pretext of asking what he should do with any large packages that he might have to deliver. Joshua was so friendly that he caught Charlie off guard. He even invited him inside to have lunch with him, which made Charlie forget why he had gone to Joshua's in the first place. And even though it was against regulations, Charlie couldn't resist. He accepted Joshua's invitation and followed his host into the house, where he eyed everything in sight, cataloguing them and tucking them away in his memory so he could tell every detail to the folks at Sanders'. What Charlie actually saw wasn't much, but the very simplicity of the furnishings was a story in itself, and with Charlie's vivid imagination that would provide enough to create a whole story. Charlie could hardly contain his glee over what he had accomplished.

He followed Joshua through the living room and the little hallway into the kitchen. It was a simple kitchen. The first thing that caught your attention was the handmade, square wooden table in front of the picture window. It was solid and strong, and the top an uncovered two-inch slab of wood. The three chairs around the table were also handmade, and though not fancy, they were sturdy and expressed the personality of the maker. The chair facing the window was the one most used, as that was pulled away from the table while the others sat snugly in place, with a towel draped over one and a rope slung over the other. In front of the table the picture window gave a view that opened out onto the vast meadow, spreading out as far as the eye could see.

Joshua pulled out a chair and offered Charlie a seat. He sat down and continued to eye everything in sight, much to the amusement of Joshua, who knew he was being given a thorough going-over.

"Would you like a bowl of soup?" Joshua asked. "I'm just having lunch, and I'd be happy if you would have some with me."

Charlie was shocked by this casual familiarity of someone who was almost a total stranger. "No, well, yes, I think I will," Charlie stammered as he rubbed his chin and cheek with the palm of his hand.

The aroma of fresh chicken soup filled the kitchen. Joshua took the loaf of bread lying on the counter, cut two thick slices with a sturdy butcher knife, and placed them on the table with no dish. He dished out the soup in two heavy pottery bowls, then took the jug of wine and poured some into two water glasses. Not used to repressing his curiosity, Charlie asked bluntly, "How come you had everything ready? Were you expecting someone?"

Joshua chuckled. "I had a feeling someone might stop by so I thought I'd put on a little extra, just in case."

"You're beautiful," Charlie said in bewilderment as he sipped his soup. "You don't put on airs or act like a snob, and everybody's curious. Would you mind if I brought some of my friends over to visit sometime? You'd like them; they're real people. They're related to practically everybody in town, and if they like you, you're really in, if it means anything to you."

"I'd like that very much," Joshua said with an appreciative smile. Joshua took a piece of bread as Charlie watched. He broke the bread in half and offered a piece to Charlie. The mailman was amazed. How unusual! Here was a total stranger offering a piece of his own bread as if he had been a friend for years. Half embarrassed at the intimacy of the gesture, Charlie took the bread and blurted out, "Thanks, Josh," as if Joshua had given him a hundred-dollar bill.

"Like being a mailman, Charlie?" Joshua asked.

"Most of the time. The pay is good, but the bosses are miserable. They're always on your back for something or other."

"But you make a lot of people happy, and that's a wonderful thing. That's more than you can say for most jobs."

"By the way, Josh, everyone in town is wondering what you do for a living. Do you work?"

"Of course I work. How do you think I feed myself?"

"What do you do?" Charlie asked.

"I make things for people and repair wooden objects like broken chairs and other household items. Sometimes I make toys for little children, nothing grand, just little things. Children like simple things, you know."

"Do you charge much?" Charlie asked bluntly.

Joshua smiled at his simplicity. "Not much, just enough to buy a little food and pay the bills."

"Maybe I'll have you make something for me sometime. Where's your shop?"

"In the back. It's just a small place. I do everything by hand so I don't need much space."

Joshua got up and asked Charlie if he would like to see his shop. Of course he would. He was dying to see it. What a scoop to tell his friends about!

The shop was indeed simple, with tools neatly arranged on nails along the wall. The chisels were set in slots according to size. At the back of the room was a workbench set beneath a wide window that looked out across the field. Sun was pouring through the window and provided all the light needed to work.

On the bench were two or three partially finished objects; one looked like a small wooden wheel for a child's wagon, the other a setting for an antique clock. Lying next to them was a hammer, a chisel, and a small saw. None of the tools were sophisticated, but the workmanship of the pieces was exact and creative. Even Charlie could see that, and he was impressed, more at the ability to make such objects with such simple tools than at the artistic quality of the objects themselves. Charlie was far from being a connoisseur of fine art, but he was genuinely impressed and had more than enough information to take back to the gang. He was getting impatient to leave, not only because he had accomplished his purpose, but also because he was afraid someone might complain about getting their mail late.

Joshua could sense his uneasiness and started walking out, with Charlie behind him.

"That lunch really hit the spot," Charlie said as he shook Joshua's hand, thanked him for his hospitality, and started across the lawn to his jeep. As he was getting into the jeep Joshua yelled out to him, "By the way, Charlie, if I should ever get any big packages, you can just put them here on the porch. They'll be safe enough here."

Charlie scratched his head in bewilderment. He hadn't remembered asking Joshua, and that was why he stopped in the first place. He waved, got into his jeep, and drove off. Joshua watched him and smiled, then went back into the house.

Charlie couldn't wait until he got up to Sanders' store. When he went in with the mail it was lunchtime, just as he had planned it. The whole crew was there: Moe and George and Katherine, as well as the Persini brothers, and Pat Zumbar, the roly-poly character made of solid muscle whose voice could be heard clear across town. Herm Ainutti was there as well as a few others, a formidable lot, but jovial, good-hearted, and totally loyal to each other.

When Charlie appeared in the doorway his figure filled the whole space. He was a huge man. His face was flushed, as it usually was, a few strands of silvery hair hanging over his red forehead. He had unusually large feet, which pointed outward when he stood still. Charlie liked to play cat-and-mouse, and this time he knew everyone was waiting for what he had to tell them. They all knew he had been at Joshua's house, since Pat had seen his jeep parked outside. It was clear from the look on his face that he couldn't wait any longer to tell them about his visit, and no one would give him an opening, so finally he tried for one himself.

"Anything interesting happen today?"

"Nothing," George answered. "Everyone's tired from partying all weekend."

"Hear about Pat winning the daily double?" Herm interjected.

"No," Charlie said. "How much did it pay?"

"A hundred and forty-five dollars," Herm answered.

"Whew, you really hit it good. When you gonna buy us lunch?" Charlie asked, looking at Pat.

"Next Tuesday, right here. So make sure you're all here," Pat said in mock generosity. Everyone knew next Tuesday was a holiday, and the store would be closed.

Finally Katherine slipped and gave Charlie the opening he needed. "What are you having for lunch, Charlie?"

"I already ate lunch," Charlie blurted out. "That new fellow, Joshua, invited me in to eat with him. I had a great time. You should see the inside of his house. Fascinating."

Everyone was curious anyway, so they all shot questions at him. Katherine asked about the furniture. Moe asked about the shop. Herm asked what they had for lunch. Charlie told them everything, then some. You would think he and Joshua had been friends for years. And he told them they were all invited to stop in anytime. He reassured them that Joshua was a nice guy and would fit well in their little club.

This revelation made Charlie the hero for the next few days. He had broken the ice with Joshua, and now the door was open for the rest to visit him and get acquainted.

3

AUBURN SEEMED IMMUNE to the current turmoil in society. It was peaceful and people there lived simply. They owned their own houses, and though not pretentious, they provided security. When bad times hit the economy Auburn was little affected. Its inhabitants were well insulated from the problems that distressed other people. About the most stirring news in town was usually about changes taking place in the various churches.

There were six churches: the Methodist, which had a warm and friendly pastor named Reverend Joe Engman; the Presbyterian, whose minister was a very proper person; the Episcopal, whose pastor was a born actor; the Lutheran, whose pastor was rigid and pompous; the Baptist, which had a simple but likable man for a pastor; and the Catholic, whose pastor was aloof and inflexible.

Major changes in the Catholic Church had affected and shaken that whole congregation loose from the crusty customs and traditions that had shackled them for generations, to say nothing of the prejudices that had marred everyone's social relationships in one way or another. As usual, people were more willing to make the changes than were the clergy. The clergy become insecure when changes are discussed. They may seem brave enough about changes in ceremony, which don't really affect people's public lives, but when it comes to things that affect life-style and people's relationships with other religions, they often get nervous.

Since everyone was supposed to be ecumenically minded, the clergy did get together on occasion. They scheduled interfaith services once or twice a year. They even met for coffee and doughnuts once a month and talked about all kinds of irrelevant topics. But when members of their congregations attended another church, they were highly indignant and, indeed, personally offended that someone would think another church might have more to offer than theirs. In fact, the clergy became upset when they saw their people even socializing too much with members of other congregations. So ecumenism was more window-dressing than a serious attempt to bring the people closer together.

As friendly as the people of Auburn were, they were, by family tradition, clearly marked packages and knew just where they belonged. Occasionally individuals had, over the years, developed strong friendships that went a lot deeper than denominational loyalties, as was the case with the crew who hung around Sanders'. They were all of varied nationalities and religions and formed a veritable ecumenical movement, except they weren't overly interested in religion.

Because relationships were so tightly knit in the village, a stranger had little hope of ever becoming a part of it. And a stranger was anyone who had lived there for less than fifteen years. In Auburn relationships were established in childhood. You grew up together as friends.

Joshua's living in a cottage on the outskirts of town was not just a geographical fact. It was a symbol of where he stood in relation to the community: outside. He was the focus of everyone's attention and his solitude intensified their curiosity. Charlie's uncharacteristic intrusion into his privacy was an expression of the townspeople's curiosity about this quiet man. Most newcomers in a town make desperate attempts to be accepted, but Joshua gave the impression he couldn't care less. He was the talk of the village precisely because they couldn't get to know him.

But now that a beachhead had been established, and Joshua had made everyone welcome, he could expect a steady stream of visitors in the days to come.

Herm Ainutti was the first. The weather had been pleasant, and people were walking around town again, chatting with neighbors. It was not unusual to see Joshua working his vegetable garden in the backyard. Herm had been out to the liquor store to buy his bottle of "medicine," which he needed for his heart. He had to pass Joshua's place the way he was going, though he could have saved three blocks by going the other way. As he passed, he called out to Joshua. Joshua turned and waved. When Herm started to talk to him, Joshua dropped his hoe and walked over to the fence. He was always ready to stop what he was doing and spend a few minutes socializing. It was almost as if that was his real business.

Herm was a friendly fellow. He had a little printing business, which he worked at mostly for his friends now that he was retired. He had taken a liking to Joshua ever since he first saw him walking down the street with his bag of groceries. Like everyone else, he was curious about the newcomer and wondered what he really did with his life. He asked Joshua about his garden, and, as Joshua was quite proud of his little garden, he invited his visitor to come in and take a look at it. It wasn't much, Joshua told him, just big enough to raise a few vegetables for the summer.

Herm was surprised at how orderly the garden was: about four hundred square feet, with everything arranged in mathematically precise rows. It was a work of art, with perfectly straight furrows between each row to provide drainage and aeration. There were rows of tomato plants and different kinds of lettuce. There were beets and radishes and peppers and a few cucumber plants. There were also onions, but they were arranged in a peculiar manner, all along the outside edge of the garden, in two rows and close together. Outside the onions was a perfectly arranged row of miniature marigolds. Herm was fascinated. "How come you got the flowers and the onions planted like that?" he asked.

"For protection," Joshua answered. "Rabbits don't like marigolds and sheep don't like onions, and, as much as I like rabbits and sheep, I don't like them eating my vegetables."

"Clever," Herm remarked with a smile. "I notice that all the plants you have produce in early summer and by the fall they're all dead. How come you didn't plant vegetables that last till the end of the season?"

Joshua looked at him. The look seemed to penetrate right through him and far beyond as he answered simply, "I may be busy then, doing other things, and I don't want to waste the food. It's a gift of God."

Joshua also told Herm that he was welcome to take any vegetables from the garden, even if he wasn't at home. Herm liked that offer very much and thanked him. Then he took his leave and started for the gate. Joshua followed him. That was a nice gesture, which the mailman had also noticed. For someone so obviously strong and manly as Joshua, he seemed remarkably refined. Little gestures like this gave his guests the impression they were really important to him. It made them feel good, as if he was really glad they came to visit him, even if they were unexpected and uninvited.

As the days went by and people became acquainted with Joshua, he rarely had time to himself. People enjoyed visiting with him and just listening to him talk. He was a good talker, not about trivial things, but about things he noticed during the day—interesting things in the lives of the people, or fascinating things he noticed in nature, details that other people were often too busy to notice. More and more people were coming to him with their problems. Joshua proved to have a rare insight into human nature, and those people who took his advice usually fared well. Most people's problems are of their own making, and making people more aware of themselves would frequently provide the key to the solution. Between visits Joshua did his work. He worked fast, so he didn't need much time to finish a job. Most of the jobs were uncomplicated, so they didn't require great imagination or planning. Even when he was busy he was never too busy to sit and visit when someone came to see him. His happiness and pleasant nature seemed to draw people, and his spirit was contagious. When a person left him it was usually with a deep sense of peace and a renewed enthusiasm for life. Joshua's own view of life was so simple and uncomplicated, and his rare understanding of the goals and purpose of life was so healthy, that people would walk away free and lighthearted until they complicated things for themselves all over again. But it was

tiring for Joshua to give so much of himself, and when evening
came he needed to be by himself to recharge his energies.

Joshua looked out across the valley and into the distant hills.
Behind them, through the slight haze, he could see the tops of
tall buildings in the neighboring city. "All these will I give you,
if only you will fall down and worship me" crossed his memory
as if it were only yesterday. He reminisced as his mind crossed
the centuries; buildings change, architecture changes, styles of
dress change from time to time (though women still enjoy wearing the furs of animals), modes of travel become more sophisticated, tools evolve into complex machines and robots, but man
fails to learn much from the lessons of the past. In spite of all the
knowledge that has been amassed through the ages, people
would still rather learn from their own limited experiences so
their responses to life remain just as primitive as those of people
a thousand years ago. Can man change? His memories are only
from his childhood. He has no memories of things that preceded him, yet it is memory that conditions and shapes responses to life and determines patterns of growth. Is man forever doomed to invent ever more sophisticated technology but
never mature sufficiently to comprehend and control his own
inventions?

Joshua thought long and hard, intermittently envisioning his
own place in the long-term plan his Father had laid out for him
eons ago and for the whole complex course through which humanity would evolve. Always optimistic, always positive, always
understanding and patient of what had to be, Joshua maintained
a simple and happy attitude toward life, looking to distant goals
rather than to momentary and immediate satisfactions, realizing
that, in spite of appearances, his Father's will would ultimately
triumph.

The cawing of a crow on a limb above him distracted him. It
was quiet, even more quiet than before. Shadows were deepen-
ing as they stretched farther across the field, and Joshua felt a
twinge of loneliness. As strong and self-reliant as he was, and as
much as he enjoyed being by himself, at times he realized poign-
antly just how different his life was and how separated he was
from the intimacy of other people's lives. They came to him and
enjoyed being with him, and drew inspiration and strength from

his vast and seemingly endless source of wisdom and strength, but they left and went back to their own world of family and friends and life in the village. He was very much alone, and at times like this realized how unhealthy it is to be alone. He wasn't a part of others' lives. He wasn't unhappy about it, it couldn't be any different, but he still could not help but notice how life went on all about him and he stayed very much the stranger. It had always been that way. This time was no different. He was here for a purpose, a clear and carefully delineated objective designed by his Father, and intimacy in the life of the people was not germane to that plan. It would prevent the easy maneuvering that had to be part of his life.

On the bench in the workshop lay a beautifully carved bird. It was difficult to tell what kind of bird it was, since it was not colored, but it looked very much like a sparrow or a finch. It was so perfectly carved that it looked real—it even looked soft to the touch.

Next he took a large block of wood, approximately a foot and a half long and about six inches thick. It was an almost perfect piece of cherry wood. Laying it on the bench under the fluorescent light, he took the hammer and large chisel and began chipping away with quick, easy strokes. He first carved away the upper corners, and gradually worked his way down the sides. After about half an hour the outline of a lamp base began to emerge. It seemed people were fascinated by the unique wood-carved lamps Joshua made, and each day new orders would come in. The orders came and were simply addressed:

> Joshua
> Mountain Road
> Auburn

No state, no zip, nothing else. The mailman knew. The objects Joshua made were cheap enough, fifteen dollars for a lamp base, two dollars to fix a broken chair leg, twenty dollars for a lawn chair. The birds were free. Little children asked for them, and he was delighted to make them. Some were resting, with their heads tucked under a wing; some had wings spread wide as if landing; others held their heads high as if chirping; each was different and each was perfect.

Joshua didn't work late. Shortly after the sun went down he quit for the night, put away his tools, cleaned up the shop, and went to bed. Going to bed was a ritual. He would kneel at his bedside for the longest time talking to God, sometimes silently, sometimes out loud. When he prayed like this it would frequently last far into the night. His position would rarely change, though occasionally he would raise his hands as if pleading. Most of the time his hands would rest on the bed, relaxed, one hand resting on top of the other, his face peaceful, his open eyes looking into the dark as if seeing something no one else could see. To him God was not just a phantom humans concoct to fix their imaginations on, but a real being present before him who responded to every thought and plea. Nor was praying for Joshua drudgery. It was as if he was enjoying a dialogue with a dear friend, with someone he loved intensely, and someone who was intimately involved in his life, who controlled circumstances, made decisions, even decisions with which Joshua sometimes strongly disagreed. It was almost as if he and God planned the next day in every detail.

When Joshua finished praying he was always tired, and this night was like any other night. He knelt, talked to God, then crawled into bed and slept peacefully the whole night through.

The next morning he woke up to the accompaniment of the rising sun and the singing birds. He sat up, stretched, yawned loudly and sensuously, then got up, washed, and went into the kitchen to prepare breakfast. For breakfast he had an orange or a banana, a piece of bread, which he fried in bacon grease, and a cup of black coffee. Lately, as he was becoming acquainted with more people, he would just have a cup of coffee. Then later on, when the coffee shop opened at seven o'clock, he would have breakfast there with some of the men. On those occasions the breakfast would be much heartier, consisting of bacon and eggs or pancakes and sausages, which he seemed to relish most. He mixed in well with the men, even though he was quiet and reserved. Mary, the shop owner, always took care to wait on him herself and was annoyed if one of the other girls got to him first. He seemed to notice how hard the girls worked, and in his own quiet way, when no one noticed, would tell them how much he appreciated their good cooking and their friendly hospitality. A couple of the girls were boisterous, but they were good-hearted and Joshua would laugh at the funny remarks they made. Even when sometimes they were off-color, he'd still smile at their good nature. Joshua was no prude. He genuinely enjoyed people and felt comfortable with the lively banter and earthy ways of these ordinary folk. Nothing would change them, but beneath the exterior was a goodness and a kindliness that covered a multitude of sins. He liked them, and they knew it and responded.

This particular morning Joshua ate at home. He had a busy day ahead, with more than the usual number of orders to get out. People would be stopping to pick up their pieces, and he wanted to have them ready. After breakfast he put on his sandals and went out.

His walk took him past Joe Langford's house. Mary, his wife, had spotted Joshua walking up the road and called out to him, asking him if he'd like to come in and have a cup of coffee. Mary had spoken to Joshua on occasion when he would be taking his early walks, but this was the first time she had gotten enough nerve to invite him in. Joe was just coming back to the house for breakfast. He usually milked the cows before he had his breakfast. This way he worked up a good appetite.

Joe liked Joshua, and showed it by his broad grin as he spotted Joshua walking up the path to the house. "Up early again, I see," Joe yelled over to Joshua.

Joshua smiled and quipped, "I guess I'm just an ol' farmer who'd rather be up and around than sleeping away the most beautiful time of the day."

The two men met at the front steps and Joe held the door open for Joshua to go in first. Joe and Mary's was a quaint brick house, not large, but big enough for their needs.

Mary had breakfast all ready for Joe, and she asked Joshua if he would like to join them.

"Where are you from?" Mary asked Joshua.

"From Bethlehem," Joshua said simply. Since Bethlehem was a nearby town, Mary and Joe thought nothing of it.

"What brings you up this way?" Mary continued. "It's certainly dead enough in Auburn."

"It's quiet here and the people are friendly," Joshua answered. "I am a simple man, and my needs are modest, so whatever I make on my wood carving is sufficient."

"What do you make?" Mary asked him.

"Whatever people like. I made a lamp for a family the other day. I'm making little birds for some children who came to visit me yesterday."

"You'll have to make something for us when you get a chance," Mary said.

"I'd like to."

"Thanks for the coffee," Joshua said as he got up from the table. "You are good neighbors."

"You're welcome anytime," Mary said as she walked him to the door.

Joe and Joshua walked out the back door together, chatted for a few moments in the driveway, then separated.

Joshua was back home in less than fifteen minutes. It was still early, and even though he had stopped off at the Langfords', he was still able to get an early start at his work.

The workshop was bright on sunny mornings as the light shone through the side window, making the room a cheerful place to work. Joshua picked up his tools and began work on the lamp base he had started the night before. He chiseled away bit by bit until, by ten o'clock, he had finished the job. He took it out of the vise, stood it up to see if the base was level, shaved the bottom on one side, then stood it up again. It was perfect. Next he took fine sandpaper and smoothed every detail, felt it with his fingertips, then put it to one side and began work on another piece. You could tell Joshua was proud of his work. By eleven-thirty he had finished his second job for the day.

The next job was more demanding, and, since he didn't have the wood for it, he had to make a trip to the mill on the other side of town. He walked out, not bothering to lock the door behind him.

On the way he met a group of children playing on the sidewalk in front of the candy store. "Hi, Joshua," a little freckle-faced girl called to him. The other children turned, and when they saw it was Joshua, ran over and grabbed his hands. A pretty blond-haired girl looked up at him admiringly and asked him if he finished carving the little birds.

"Yes, they're all finished," he said. "If you come by when I get back from the mill, I'll give them to you." They all let out a cry of glee. "Oh, I can't wait to see mine," one girl said as the others chimed in.

The children went back to playing as Joshua continued walking up the street. The sun was high in the sky, and it was getting hot. Joshua looked handsome in his own rugged way. His skin was turning bronze from his continued exposure to the sun. His hair was a bit tousled, the long curly strands hanging down over his forehead as he walked briskly along, his arms swinging slightly. His slim, elegant figure radiated a carefree grace. It was a pleasure to watch him move. There was no doubt he was different. Watching him, one couldn't help but wonder what he was doing in Auburn. Half the young girls in town already had their eyes on him. Even the married women secretly admired him.

Joshua turned the corner at the end of the main street and arrived at the entrance to the mill, the only real industry in town. Huge trucks rolled through town all day long, bringing logs to be cut into boards for lumber. Joshua was probably their smallest customer, but the manager liked him because he wasn't pushy and he didn't mind waiting until others were waited on.

"Hi, Josh, what's on your mind today?" the manager called out to him.

"Nothing much. I just need a cherry log if you have one. No rush, Phil," Joshua replied.

"Give me five minutes and I'll take care of you myself," Phil shot back as he walked across the yard with a customer.

"Sorry for keeping you waiting, Josh," Phil said when he returned. "What did you say you need?"

"A cherry log about five feet long and twelve inches thick," Joshua told him.

"That's going to be a tough one. Did you see any out in the shed?"

"No."

Phil yelled to one of his assistants, "Do you have a five-foot cherry log twelve inches thick?"

"I don't remember seeing one," the man hollered back across the huge room.

Phil took Joshua out to a pile of logs that had been lying in back of the shed all summer. "Maybe we can find an uncut log that's dried out enough for you to work with." They walked through the pile trying to find the right one.

"How about this one?" Joshua said, pointing to an almost perfect log with hardly a knot in it.

"You sure do have a good eye," Phil said as he sized up the piece of wood. "Let me have the men bring it in and cut it up for you. It'll only take a few minutes." Phil marked the log and he and Joshua went inside.

"My kids really liked the little duck you carved for them last week. It's such a beautiful piece of work, my wife doesn't like to let them play with it. She's afraid they'll break it. How's your business doing, by the way?"

Joshua replied matter-of-factly, "As well as I'd like it to; enough to make a living. I don't need much."

"What are you going to do with that big log? If you're going to carve that, you'll have a job on your hands. That's a lot of wood. And you won't be able to charge no fifteen or twenty dollars, either. The wood itself is going to set you back about fifty dollars."

"This job's a little special. Some Jewish people from the synagogue asked if I would carve a figure of Moses for their social hall," Joshua answered with a smile.

"I didn't know you did jobs that big. That's going to be quite a piece of work. How long will it take you to do it?"

"Actually, it's easier than working on the little birds. There's more detail in the wing of a bird than in the whole five feet of Moses. There's just more wood to be chipped away. It'll probably take me three or four days working steady."

"Will it be cash, Josh, or shall I hold off until the synagogue pays you?"

"I'll pay for it. I've been saving for it, so I should have enough. How much is it, Phil?"

"Fifty-six dollars even."

Joshua took the money out of his pocket, counted the exact amount, and gave it to Phil.

"That log is going to be heavy, Josh. How are you going to get it back to your place?" Phil asked, concerned.

"I'll carry it."

"That's a heavy load. If you don't mind waiting a couple of hours until the truck gets back, I'll drop it off on my way home."

"Thanks anyway, Phil, but I'll be able to carry it," Joshua said appreciatively.

At that point the men brought in the log. It was all cut and planed, a beautiful piece of wood. "I'd like to see that statue when you finish," Phil said as Joshua went to pick up the log.

"Come down Friday morning on your way to work," Joshua told him.

"Okay. See you Friday morning, first thing."

Joshua picked up the log, hoisted it over his right shoulder, and walked toward the door. Through the yard and down the street he went, seemingly unaware and unconcerned about the weight of the heavy log he was carrying. But as he got halfway down the main street he put the log down and rested. It was a hot day, and he was sweating heavily.

One of the men from Sanders' store spotted him and came over. "What d'ya got there, Josh?" he asked.

"Oh, just a cherry log for something I have to make," he answered.

"It looks heavy, want a hand?" the man asked. It was Mike Charis, a quiet young fellow.

"No thanks," Joshua answered, but Mike had already picked up the piece of wood.

"My God, what is this thing made out of, lead? This is heavy," Mike said as he tried to carry it. Then, putting it down, he apologized. "Sorry, Josh, you'll have to carry that yourself. It's a little too heavy for me."

Joshua smiled. "Thanks, anyway, but I'm used to carrying these things. It doesn't bother me."

"You're a lot stronger than you look, fella," Mike said in bewilderment as Joshua picked up the log and put it over his shoulder. The two men walked down the street together.

"What are you going to make with that piece of wood?" Mike asked.

"I've been asked to make a statue of Moses for a synagogue in the city."

"Are you Jewish?"

"My family was, a way back."

"I saw you in church last Sunday. I thought you were Catholic."

"You're right, I am Christian."

"You mean you're a Jew and a Christian too?"

"Jesus was a Jew and a Christian, so were the apostles."

Mike seemed mystified at this latest revelation. He liked Joshua, and even though this bit of information was a surprise, it didn't really affect how he felt about him. Everybody liked Joshua for what he was, and if he happened to be a Jew, that wasn't his fault. He was still a good guy and a good friend.

In no time at all the story got around town about the "three-hundred-pound log" Joshua had carried all the way from the mill as if it were a piece of cardboard. As the story spread the weight of the log increased, and with it Joshua's stature in the eyes of the people, particularly the young men and boys. Their fascination with this likable stranger knew no bounds, and everyone was curious to find out all they could about him.

After Mike left Joshua at his house Joshua carried the log around to the yard, since it was too big to work on in the house. He placed it carefully on the ground and looked it over closely, analyzing the grain in an attempt to determine which side he should use for the front and which side for the back of the figure. After looking at it from different angles, he finally made up his mind and set to work at once. With a heavy black pencil he outlined the figure on the surface of the wood, stood back, looked at the sketch, made a few changes, drew the arms in two sections so he could carve them separately, then, taking a saw, cut those sections off the block and set them aside.

Then he set to work carving the main part of the figure. His hands worked fast, and in no time at all the wooden log was no longer a piece of wood but was beginning to show signs of life. The outline of a head began to appear. The neck was partially formed. The upper portion of the shoulders joining the neck already showed a character of great determination. In his enthusiasm to work on the piece, Joshua forgot lunch and worked straight through the afternoon.

By five o'clock he had made remarkable progress, and you could see the well-delineated figure, with depth and strength of personality emerging more and more with each stroke of the hammer and chisel. But Joshua was growing tired. He had worked all day, ever since he got back from his morning walk.

Finally he stood up, stepped back from the figure, and looked at it critically. He seemed content with the progress he had made and walked toward the cottage, deciding to call it a day.

As he was leaving the workshop to go into the kitchen, there was a knock at the front door. He opened it to see the four little children he had met earlier in the day.

"Joshua," one of the girls said, "you told us to come over this afternoon to pick up the birds you made for us. So here we are."

Joshua laughed. "I was just thinking about you, wondering if you would come. Please come on in."

The children followed Joshua through the living room, the kitchen, and into the workshop. They were all eyes, trying to absorb as much of the inside of Joshua's house as their vivid imaginations and memories could hold. Joshua walked over to the workbench, took the four little birds he had made, and gave them to the children. They gasped their delight. As young as they were, the children still appreciated the beauty of these handmade creations. They looked at them from all sides, fascinated by their gifts. "Oh, thank you so much, Joshua," the freckled brown-haired girl said. The others chimed in, "Thank you, Joshua, they are beautiful." One of the boys looked intently at his, meditating on it for a long time.

Joshua watched them, smiling, with obvious satisfaction at the simplicity of the children's delight. Then, at once, they turned to Joshua, hugged him, and told him how much they loved him. He bent down, put his arms around them, and told them that he loved them too. "Your Father in heaven has given you many presents, just like these little birds, but all alive and free and singing songs for you all day long, and even at night, like the nightingale. You should notice these beautiful creatures and let them remind you of how much your Father loves you."

"Do you know God, Joshua?" the blond-haired girl asked him.

"Yes, I do know him. We are good friends," he replied, then added, "You had better run along now and let Joshua cook his supper."

"Good-bye, Joshua," they all said as they walked out the front door and down the pathway to the street. Joshua watched them as they walked away, talking excitedly about their presents, admiring them and pointing out how each bird was different from the others. Joshua smiled faintly and walked into the house, closing the door behind him.

It was a long time since breakfast, and Joshua was hungry. He thought of a day long ago, when his mother and her relatives were looking for him, concerned about his health. It seemed some gossips had told his mother he was pushing himself. He had been preaching all day long and had not taken time to eat. They got his mother all upset, so she came looking for him. He blushed as he thought of his response. "Who are my mother and my brothers? They who do the will of my Father in heaven are my mother and my brothers and my sisters."

Just before he ate dinner that night he sat for a moment and raised his eyes slowly, as if in deep thought. He did that before each meal. It was brief and casual, nothing showy. One couldn't tell whether he was thinking or praying. But that was the way Joshua was. His rich inner life rarely burst out on the surface, and his intimacy with God was evident only after one got to know him and could interpret the little things that betrayed the intensity of his feelings.

Joshua was not a pious person in the disparaging sense that people tend to associate with individuals who like to show their religion. He showed none of that kind of behavior. It wouldn't even occur to anyone to think of Joshua as a religious person. He was just an ordinary person who radiated an enthusiasm for life and for everything that had life. He loved the beautiful colors in nature. He was fascinated by the animals, and found humor and playfulness even in the most forbidding of the four-legged creatures. But he wasn't a dreamy-eyed nature lover who got himself all disconnected from reality. He was too balanced for that. He was, indeed, a most fascinating kind of person, with an inner beauty that contrasted remarkably with the external simplicity of his life. Even though Joshua was physically attractive, and possessed a grace that was charming, when one came to know him more intimately all that seemed to pale beside the richness and depth of his personality.

It was a rare person who got to know the real Joshua, either because most people didn't have the ability to see beneath the surface or they couldn't capture at one glance all the facets of his rich inner life.

It was getting late, almost eight thirty. The sun was about to settle down behind the hill in the distance, and a cool breeze was blowing in from the hills. Joshua decided to call it a day and retire for the night. He usually went to bed at sunset and rose at sunrise. Maybe this harmony with nature was the secret of his excellent physical condition.

Joshua went inside, and in a few minutes his lights were out.

4

AT ABOUT THE same time as Joshua retired that night a party was just beginning at the Sanders' house. The whole crew was there with their wives. Most of them were not heavy drinkers, probably because they talked so much that they didn't have time to drink. The conversation at these parties usually ran the gamut of everything from world politics to the economy. Eventually, in the late hours, the topics would come around to more local items of interest, like Joshua, for instance. "Has anyone seen him lately?" "We should have invited him over tonight. He's quick-witted and would have been fun."

"Did you see him carrying that big log down Main Street this morning?" George asked. "That guy's strong."

"Mike Charis tried to help him, but could hardly lift the thing," Herm mentioned. "How much do you think that log weighed?"

"Must have weighed at least two hundred fifty, three hundred pounds," Charlie said.

Pat disagreed. "That's impossible. He couldn't carry anything that heavy. He's too fragile."

"You haven't seen that guy," George said. "He may look fragile, but he's as strong as a bull."

"I don't believe it," Pat continued to object.

Then Moe added in his own quiet way, "I don't think the log weighed three hundred pounds, but it had to weigh at least a couple of hundred, and that's still a pretty good size piece of wood."

"I don't know about that guy," Pat said. "I like him, but I can't figure him out. He doesn't have any girlfriends. That's not natural. Do you think he's gay?"

"That's terrible," his wife, Minnie, interrupted. "He's just a quiet person." Pat's wife still, quite miraculously, had a patient disposition even after over forty years of marriage to Pat.

"Well, why doesn't he go out with girls?" Pat continued, pushing his point.

"That doesn't mean a thing," Herm said, annoyed. Herm had liked Joshua ever since their conversation a week ago. And if Herm liked you, you couldn't do any wrong. He'd defend you against his best friend.

"Maybe he just likes to keep to himself," Charlie, the mailman, put in. "Maybe he's divorced, who knows. He seems normal enough to me. Maybe he loves his work, and is content just being alone."

"Sometimes I don't understand you guys," Jim Dicara added. "You come up with the weirdest theories. You find a fellow once in a lifetime like Joshua. He's a nice guy. He's intelligent. He's friendly. He's got everything going for him, and you tag him as a weirdo. To me he's a very normal person. He loves what he does, and he's just content to be by himself. Personally, I envy him."

Since everybody respected Jimmy, that ended the conversation. It was decided that Joshua was a good guy. They also agreed that they would invite him to their next get-together.

The next morning, at the crack of dawn, Joshua woke up to the sound of birds singing outside his window. By the time he had finished breakfast, it was only six o'clock. But today he was so excited about finishing the figure of Moses that he didn't take his daily walk, getting right to work instead.

The wood was wet with the morning dew, which Joshua rubbed off easily with a rag. He stood back for a moment to view the object, then went to work with hammer and chisels.

By eight o'clock he had the outline of the whole figure cut deeply into the wood. Only a master craftsman could work with

the ease and economy with which Joshua plied each stroke.
Every movement had meaning. Each cut with the chisel brought
new life into the dead wood. By eleven o'clock the figure had
been cut free from the block of wood and had its own independent existence. To an untrained eye, it looked finished, but there
was still much work to do.

Joshua picked the figure up off the ground and rested it
against the trunk of the fat maple tree that grew near his workshop. He stepped back, looked at the figure, turned it around
from side to side, stepping back a little farther each time to view
it from a distance. Then he got down on his knees to do the fine
details of the face with a tiny chisel. First he worked on the eyes,
carefully giving them a well-rounded look while setting them
deeply beneath the brow. This was a difficult job, because the
artist had to consider the effect of light from different angles on
the deep-set eyes.

When he finished they looked almost alive, as if they would
blink at any moment. Next he worked on the nose and nostrils.
Soon they began to flare, as if venting great emotion. The lips,
which seemed soft and sensuous, were slightly parted, as if about
to speak. Even the locks of hair, which he worked on next, were
so delicately carved that it seemed the slightest breeze would
blow them free.

By noon Joshua was tired. His hair was hanging down over
his face, which was lined with beads of perspiration. His body
was covered with wood chips. He raised his hand and put it
through his hair, and then stood up, holding the hammer and
chisel in one hand. He enjoyed working on this project. Indeed,
his enthusiasm for it inspired him to work with an intensity that
didn't show when he was working on other pieces. It was as if he
was doing the sculpture of a dear friend and wanted it to be
perfect.

All that was left to do were the arms. Placing the hammer and
chisel on the table near the grill, he went inside, humming a
tune that was totally unfamiliar, and which didn't sound like
anything of our age. But it was joyful and lighthearted, and one
could imagine people dancing to it.

When he came back outside he was carrying a bag and had a
towel thrown over his shoulder. He walked straight past the

sculpture without even looking at it, out into the meadow. Reaching the pond, Joshua stripped and put his clothes in the water to soak. Then, walking into the water, he dived under and disappeared. When he came up he was far out in the middle and swam across the surface heading for the opposite shore. When he reached it he stood up and looked about, just drinking in the beautiful landscape.

Soon Joshua plunged into the water again and swam to the far corner and back. When he finished he went back to his clothes and, with a piece of soap he had brought with him, started washing and scrubbing them. After rinsing them out he hung them on the willow tree to dry in the hot sun. While he waited he went back into the water and swam until he was totally relaxed.

Then he came back to shore, got out of the water, dried himself, and put on his clothes. As he took them off the willow branch the thought of other willows long ago flashed across his memory: "By the willows of Babylon, there we sat and wept, when we remembered you, O Zion. There we hung up our harps; how could we sing in a foreign land?" The thought brought on a melancholy mood as his mind wandered back across the ages thinking of that lonely exile.

Joshua dressed quickly. It felt so good just walking with nothing on, but, then, human beings can't cope with the problems they create, so he adjusted his thinking and realized how good it was to put on fresh, clean clothes that don't stick to your body. The old robes, he thought, were a lot cooler, but their sheer weight was oppressive.

It was almost two o'clock when he headed back across the field. He still had to finish the arms of the statue.

When he reached the cottage he went out into the yard. He worked on the arms for almost two hours, giving them a form and a plastic look that made them appear like real limbs poised for action.

By four-thirty he was finished. He took the two arms, placed them in holes he had carved into the torso, and set the figure in an upright position on the ground. Then he looked at it from various angles. He touched up a few spots here and there with a small chisel, then glued the arms in place. After letting the glue set, he sanded the figure from top to bottom and applied a dark stain. After an hour he applied a second, then a third coat, each time making the figure richer and more beautiful. Even though it took Joshua a short time to complete his work, no one could say it was anything but a masterful, beautiful piece of workmanship. The strength of feeling and conviction in the expression on the face, the taut neck muscles showing the vehemence and insistence of character, the shape and positioning of the hands and fingers, with the left hand partially closed, clutching his breast, and his right hand gesturing with muscles tense made the figure appear alive.

In meditating on the statue one could easily sense the zeal and power of the man, and also the not so quiet desperation as he tried to bend the will of his listeners. The people at the synagogue would either be honored and delighted to possess such a powerful work of art or they would be offended by the message it so graphically delivered. Joshua smiled as he anticipated the various reactions. But it was his intention to deliver a message that could ill afford to be ambiguous: Moses insisting on a way to God that so many of his people resisted.

The figure was now complete except for the wax, which would give the stain a soft sheen. Joshua waited until the stain dried, then rubbed in the wax, making sure every crevice was smooth and clean. Then he picked up the statue, placed it upright on the table, and looked it over. He was proud of his work. He caressed the figure almost affectionately, as if it were the real Moses and not merely a piece of wood. Then, picking up his tools, he took them into the workshop and went out to clean up the yard and rest for a few minutes before preparing his supper.

Joshua's idea of rest was to look over his garden and pull a few weeds. The garden was growing nicely. There had been good growing weather so far, and all the gardens in the neighborhood were lush with healthy growth.

While Joshua was preparing supper a loud knock on the front door interrupted the almost monastic silence of the cottage. Joshua wiped his hands, went to the door, and opened it. There stood Pat and Herm. Joshua grinned as Pat shot out loudly, "Hope we didn't come at a bad time. Herm and I thought we'd stop over to say hello."

"Come right in," Joshua said with a laugh. "It's never a bad time. I was just putting some things on for supper. If you don't mind my cooking, you're more than welcome to have supper with me."

"No, no. Our wives would kill us if we didn't show up for supper," Herm said apologetically but not too convincingly as Joshua proceeded to add more meat and vegetables to the pan. He got out a bottle of wine, a chunk of cheese, and a loaf of bread and prepared a snack while waiting for supper to cook.

"What brings you all the way over here?" Joshua asked the two guests between sips of wine.

"We had a party at Jim's last night," Pat answered, "and your name came up. Herm and I decided to stop over and visit you today. Also the guys wanted us to invite you to our parties from now on. They thought you'd have a good time. They like you for some reason or other. I don't know why," Pat finished good-humoredly.

"That's why we're here," Herm added, "to give you a standing invitation to our parties. We're having one next week, if you'd like to come."

"That's very thoughtful," Joshua replied. "I would be happy to go," but he added with dry humor, "Does Pat always come to the parties?"

Herm picked up the humor and came back quickly, "We invite his wife. She's a nice person, but he always comes along. We make him behave, so he's not much trouble."

Joshua enjoyed the friendly banter between these two men who had been friends since childhood and whose conversation would have been grossly insulting if spoken by someone else. But between these two, and the others in the group, it was just ordinary fun. If one didn't insult the other like this, the other would think he was mad at him. That's what Joshua liked about this whole earthy crew. They were crude at times, hotheaded, always shooting from the hip, but honest men you could trust, never phonies or two-faced, saying one thing to your face and something entirely different behind your back. If they gave you their word, you could count on it. They would stick up for each other against an army, and even if they lost they would at least lose together. Their wives were good women, long-suffering and tolerant to a fault of their husbands' loyalty and total, un-spoken commitment to one another.

By this time they had already half finished their meal, but they were so engrossed in their conversation, as usual, that they hadn't paid much attention to eating.

"You know, Josh," Herm said, "you're a mystery. You've got everybody in town trying to figure you out. What is it about you?"

Before Joshua had a chance to answer, Pat jumped in. "Yeah, everyone thinks you're a real smart guy, and yet all you do is cut wood. It makes everybody wonder. If I'm not prying, were you ever a priest or something like that? You got class and refinement like you might've been a priest."

Joshua became serious. "I'm just God's son," he answered simply, without elaboration. "We're all that," Pat responded, "but there's something different about you. There's more to you than meets the eye, and that's what's got us curious. And yet you're a humble guy, and you act just like the rest of us, and maybe, in your own mind, you're not different from us. And that's what everybody likes about you. You don't have the slightest idea the impression you made the other day when you came walking down the street with that huge log on your shoulder. Everyone's still talking about it. They were not only impressed with the weight of the log, but that you're not afraid to work like the rest of us."

Even Herm was impressed that Pat got out so much of what everybody in town was thinking. He just sat back in his chair eating. Joshua sat on the step with his elbows on his knees. He looked very serious while Pat was talking and listened intently, realizing that Pat's question had struck at the heart of Joshua's identity. He knew there would be some whose simple faith would pierce the mystery surrounding his appearance, but it was important to keep the secrecy of his identity and his mission intact. Joshua didn't like being evasive. It was against his nature, yet he had no right laying bare truths that would not be understood and which were really no one's business. Those who should know would find out in their own simple way. They would gradually come to a realization and would then understand. He also knew there were some who could never understand. They would always be the ones who would, in the end, try to destroy. They could not be content to see goodness and enjoy its presence. They have to twist and distort and see evil in the simplest acts of goodness until, in the end, they have painted such a warped image in their own minds that they are really convinced that what they see is evil and have to purge it from their midst. That has been the fate of many good people throughout history. No, there was no way he could take the chance and tell them the naked truth.

But Joshua still listened to Pat, and when he finished he responded by saying, "Pat, in all truthfulness I am just myself. You will get to know me more and more as the days go by and, in time, you will come to understand what you have seen. And there are others who will understand, but not all. It has never been otherwise. This is because your faith is simple, and so is Herman's, and you see what others cannot see. All I do is bear witness to the goodness and love God has placed in creation."

Joshua had not talked this way before, and both Pat and Herman were taken back by the seriousness of Joshua's answer. But while Joshua was in the mood, they figured they'd ask him some more pointed questions.

"Josh," Herm asked, "what do you think of church and religion?"

"Real religion is in people's hearts, not in buildings. Jesus tried to teach this lesson once before when he told the woman at the well that the time was coming when men would worship neither on Mount Garizim nor in Jerusalem, but would worship the Father in spirit and in truth. Unfortunately, that lesson never caught on. Religious leaders always felt they had to organize people and structure the practice of religion in such a way that they would become the highly respected mediaries with God, and religion then became the practice of doing what religious leaders told one to do and deteriorated into the measurable observance of manmade laws.

"Religion doesn't have to be like that. Jesus taught that people are free, free to enjoy being God's children, free to grow and become the beautiful people God intended. But this is impossible in the presence of rigid authority that needs to control people's thinking and their free expression. Jesus would be very

unhappy over the way many religious leaders enjoy exercising
authority. He tried right up to the end to dispel that tendency
by washing the feet of the apostles, telling them to be humble
and serve rather than dominate and dictate, like pagans enjoy
doing to their subjects.''

Pat and Herm were not ready for all this, and they were quite
surprised at the bluntness of their host. Yet he did not appear
bitter, just honest and straightforward. They both agreed that
what he said was right. Herm went a step further and asked what
he thought about the man who had been their pastor for over
twenty years.

"He's not a bad person," Joshua answered. "He just doesn't
know how to love. He hurts without intending to because he
knows only law and not love. The law is ruthless and unbending,
and breaks people under its weight. A kind shepherd will put
people before the law, like Jesus did. 'The sabbath is made for
people and not people for the sabbath,' is the way Jesus put it.''

When Joshua finished he took another bite and washed it
down with a mouthful of wine. At about that time Joshua's
animal friends appeared near the big tree in the yard, too timid
to come closer. Joshua spotted them, put some food on his
plate, and took it over to them. The two men enjoyed seeing the
friendliness of the animals, how they came over to meet Joshua
and climbed all over him when he bent down to feed them.
"Look at that! Even the animals like him!" Herm said.

"Why wouldn't they? He probably feeds them every night,"
Pat said.

Joshua came back with the empty plate as the animals walked
away. "They're my regular guests," he said as he put the plate
on the table.

"Hey, Josh," Pat said, "Phil said you were making a statue for
the synagogue. Is that true?"

"Not exactly for the synagogue. Statues are not allowed, you
know. I was asked to carve a figure of Moses for their social hall.
In fact, I finished it just before you came. Would you like to see
it?"

"I'd love to," Pat said.

Joshua got up to lead them into the workshop, which they
hadn't seen before.

They were amazed when they went into the shop and saw the figure of Moses standing there. It was so real and lifelike.

"Can I touch it?" Herm asked.

"Go ahead," Joshua told them. They couldn't take their hands off the figure.

"It's beautiful," they both said. "You're a real artist, aren't you?" Herm said almost respectfully and with genuine awe at the masterpiece standing there before them. "You made that out of that big log you were carrying down the street?"

"In only two days?" Pat fired in quick succession and in disbelief.

"Imagine taking an old log like that and turning it into something as beautiful as this!" Herm said thoughtfully. "It's beautiful."

"Hey, look what time it is!" Pat said. "We'd better get home."

The men walked around the side of the house and Joshua accompanied them to the gate.

"I like that mailbox," Pat said as he rubbed his hand over the keel of the boat.

"Yes, it brings back memories," Joshua said almost absentmindedly, then smiled when they both looked at him.

"What do you mean 'memories'? You're hardly forty years old! They didn't make that kind of boat in your lifetime." Then he added in jest, "Maybe when Herm was a kid, but not you." They all laughed.

After they left Joshua went back into the house, not even thinking to lock the door, and after doing the dishes took a walk out in the backyard to relax for a few minutes. It had been a long day. People were getting to know him, and it was becoming increasingly difficult to control his schedule. He was fortunate to have gotten his figure of Moses finished before Pat and Herm came, because no matter how busy he was, he would have stopped everything to visit with them. He believed people were more important than schedules, and he would never make people feel uncomfortable by letting them feel they had come at a bad time. You only treat strangers or people you don't like that way. Friends are welcome anytime, and everybody was a friend to Joshua. That was another reason they felt drawn to him. They sensed he genuinely liked them, and they were flattered.

When Joshua was ready for bed he knelt down at his bedside, with his head in his hands, for the longest time. Tomorrow was to be an historic event, the first such encounter with his people in centuries. It just had to go well this time. Things were different now. They had experienced so much during the passage of time. Their mingling in with Christians, even though they were often treated miserably by them, couldn't help but give them a chance to see the beautiful aspects of Jesus' spirit and love of humanity. It had to rub off. He prayed intensely that things would go well. He hoped they would like his figure of Moses. Things have changed. In the past it would have been unthinkable for Jews to contract for the sculpturing of a statue, even of Moses. Putting it in the social hall rather than in the synagogue was merely a subterfuge to assuage their sensitivity to the commandment forbidding the fashioning of graven images. It was ironic that the prohibition came originally from Moses himself, whose figure they were now setting up in their midst. But perhaps even Moses would be pleased at the change in spirit of his people. As Joshua prayed he could sense the reaction of Moses and Elijah as they anticipated the events of the coming day. Joshua smiled, ended his prayer, and rolled into bed, exhausted but happy.

5

JOSHUA HAD HARDLY finished breakfast when there was a knock at the door. It was only five forty-five. When he went to the door and opened it there stood Phil, the manager at the mill. He had remembered Joshua told him to come on his way to work if he wanted to see the figure he was carving for the synagogue.

"Hope I didn't come too early," Phil apologized. "I was on my way to work and didn't want to miss seeing your masterpiece. I don't think I'd ever get a chance to see it in the synagogue."

Both men went outside and Joshua placed the sculpture on the table near the grill. The sun was filtering through the trees, and its rays looked like inspiration from heaven as they struck the figure. Phil literally gasped. "God, that's beautiful!" he said, picturing in his mind the lifeless log Joshua had carried out of the shop just two days before.

"You carved that from the log you bought the other day?" Phil asked Joshua, still finding it hard to believe.

"Yes, the same piece of wood," Joshua replied.

"You seem so casual and so ordinary, Josh. It's hard to imagine you as a real artist."

"Why should a person act any different just because he can carve a piece of wood? Talent doesn't justify putting on airs. Any ability we have comes from God, and our recognition of it should make us humble, not arrogant. That's the mistake so many scientists make when they think they have created what God has given them the privilege to discover. In their smallness they use their discoveries as reason to question the very existence of the person who gave them their ability. That is the modern unforgivable sin. In their blind pride they put themselves outside the reach of God's saving grace, like the Sadducees and Pharisees of centuries ago."

Phil listened intently as Joshua spoke. He liked to listen to Joshua because there was a depth of wisdom that flowed from him that was rare. Yet he wasn't arrogant or patronizing. He just had a beautiful way of looking at life and everything in it.

"I know what you are saying, Josh, but I would think you'd be proud of a beautiful piece of work like that," Phil said.

"I am," Joshua reassured him, "and I fully enjoy my work, especially the pleasure in people's faces when they see something I made for them. Yes, I'm proud of my work, but I can also appreciate the beauty of soul in a humble person who has no other obvious talent than the humility to stand in awe of the gifts God has given to others. That gift is more precious in the eyes of God than many others, don't you think?"

Phil laughed. "The way you put it, how could I think otherwise? What you say is so kind, you make even me feel good. I have no talent at all, but I have always admired talent in other people."

"You are a good man, Phil. You have the kind of talent a father needs to appreciate his children and help them grow into the persons God intended. You will be proud of your children one day, in spite of all your worry and grief."

"Thanks, Josh. I needed that. Well, I had better get off to work. The men will be waiting for me. I think the statue is remarkable. The members of the synagogue should love it."

"I hope so," Joshua replied as he followed Phil around the house to the front gate. Joshua went back into the yard and brought the statue inside, then went out to take his morning walk.

He walked up the main street and down the side road that led out into the country. About two miles along the road was a patch of run-down shacks that were once houses. A group of poor people lived there, good people, no better, no worse than the rich people he associated with so freely. Some of them had just lost their jobs, others were chronic welfare cases. It made little difference to Joshua. But these poor people loved Joshua, and he particularly liked the children. They were simple and unspoiled, unlike so many children who are spoiled by having too many luxuries too early in life.

When Joshua appeared coming down the road the children would spot him and run out to greet him, grabbing his hands and throwing their arms around him. Usually he brought little things he had made, like yo-yos or little wooden dolls, or toys that rocked, or funny little figurines with comical faces. The children loved them, but they loved Joshua more, and even when he didn't bring anything they were still glad to see him. They loved the stories he told them, stories about life, and about using God's gifts to do good for others, and bringing happiness into others' lives so God could be proud of them. Each of them could be real miracles of God's love by overcoming the hardships of life and making something of their lives. He told them that God had a special love for them because they didn't have all the nice things that others had, and that they should never be envious or bitter because they didn't have a lot. He told them he had nothing and he was very happy because he could enjoy all the beautiful things in nature that belonged to God, like the sunshine and the beautiful skies, and the little birds and animals and flowers in the field. You don't have to possess them to enjoy them. Being free is the secret of peace and happiness. Always be free, and not possessing things is part of being free.

Of course when Joshua talked this way to the little children it was always when the parents were around. He knew they could understand what he was saying better than the children, but the children, too, would remember one day all the things he had told them, and it would affect their lives long into the future.

As Joshua approached the patch of houses a mutt broke the early morning quiet by his harsh, raucous bark. He was tied by an old knotted rope to his dilapidated doghouse, so he couldn't go far. He looked harmless anyway. A screen door squeaked open and a child in undershorts appeared in a doorway at the side of the house. He spotted Joshua and went back inside screaming. In no time there was a crowd pouring through the doorway, some clothed, some partly dressed.

"Joshua, what are you doing up so early? We're just getting out of bed," a little girl called out to him.

"I'm taking my morning walk. Sometimes I take the other road. This morning I thought I'd walk up this way," he responded as he approached.

"Can you come in our house and have breakfast with us?" a sandy-haired boy with one sock on asked Joshua.

Joshua ran his hand freely over the top of the boy's disheveled head. "I've already eaten my breakfast," he replied, but all the children joined in, asking him to come into their house, one pulling on his right hand, another pulling on his left.

A middle-aged man appeared in the doorway. He had obviously just got up too. When he saw the children tugging at Joshua he laughed. "You're not going anyplace," he said. "You might as well resign yourself to having at least a cup of coffee with us. They're certainly not going to let you go."

Joshua laughed and let the children pull him into the house. In the kitchen was an old-fashioned stove, more valuable as an antique than as a heating unit. In the middle of the spacious kitchen was a long homemade wooden table with benches built into either side. The children all ran to their places at the table, the little ones vying with one another to sit next to Joshua, whom the father had directed to sit in his place at the head of the table. He sat on the bench next to Joshua. The children tried to sit near Joshua, but found it too hard to maneuver, so the tiniest one ended up with no seat, crying that he wanted to sit near Joshua. Joshua picked him up and put him on his lap as the child stuck his tongue out at his bigger brother, grinning with glee over his accomplishment.

A young-looking mother came out from another room, pinning up a large strand of her fading blond hair. She looked tired and worn for her young years, but smiled broadly when she spotted Joshua. Walking over to him, she bent over and kissed him. Joshua told her how joyful and radiant she looked so early in the morning. She blushed, but clearly enjoyed the compliment. People in her station don't receive many compliments, and she didn't know quite how to react, so she merely smiled a thank-you, then proceeded to ask if he would like a bowl of raspberries. She and the children had picked them the day before over across the field, and they have been waiting ever since to eat them.

Joshua's eyes widened. "I'd love some," he said.

All the while the children were in turns arguing, pushing, eating, and trying to get Joshua's attention, which was quite impossible while their father was talking to him. Only the little one sitting on Joshua's lap benefited. He kept picking the berries out of Joshua's dish. The father tried to stop him once or twice, but Joshua enjoyed the child doing it so much that he gave up.

"Mommy, I'm still hungry," one of the children cried. Margaret tried to ignore him, but then one of the other children chimed in and she became embarrassed. She apologized to Joshua for the children's rudeness and then told the children they would have to wait until she went to the store. The children knew, and Joshua also realized, they had nothing else in the house. Hank's unemployment check didn't go very far, and it would be another few days before they could get anything else at the store. That was why they went berry picking. They would probably do the same thing today. If the father was lucky, he might be able to get a couple of rabbits or woodchucks for supper for the next few days, which the kids really hated but ate anyway because they were so hungry.

Joshua didn't stay much longer. He wanted to get back home and get to work. He was expecting the people from the synagogue but didn't know what time they would come. He thanked the couple profusely for their generosity, kissed Margaret when he left, and shook Hank's hand. The children asked him if he had to leave and he told them he had a lot of work to do. He put his hand on each of their heads, silently blessing them, then walked out the back door. As he was leaving Margaret slipped a small package in his hands, kissed him again, and closed the door behind him.

Down the road a ways, Joshua opened the package and saw a small jar of raspberry jam. Tears appeared in his eyes. "The poor never have enough for themselves," he thought, "but always have enough to give away."

It was only nine o'clock when he reached home. He put the jar of jam on the counter and took the figure of Moses and put it on a small stool in the kitchen, where there would be plenty of light and it would be all set up for his visitors. With a soft cloth he rubbed the wax veneer until it glistened in the sunlight. He looked at all the folds in Moses' robe to see if he had missed anything. No, it was perfect. All he had to do now was wait for the people to come and pick it up. He couldn't wait to see the look on their faces when they first saw it. Their first reaction would tell the story and reveal their true feelings.

He didn't have long to wait. He had just executed the finishing touches when there was a knock at the door. His heart fluttered. He knew he shouldn't be nervous, but he was. He wanted so much for the people to be pleased with what he had done for them. These people were special to him and so was Moses. He answered the door and was faced by four well-dressed people, three men and a woman.

"Shalom!" one of the men said to Joshua.

"Shalom alechem!" Joshua responded, to everyone's great delight and with an accent that was authentic.

"Where did you learn Hebrew?" the woman asked.

"I learned it a long time ago," Joshua replied simply, then welcomed them into his house.

The woman was very attractive and well-dressed. She was wearing a light blue skirt and blue silk blouse. She had soft black hair and an olive complexion that blended with her greenish-blue eyes. Her thin features were further refined by a delicately shaped nose, arched eyebrows, and soft, sensuous lips. She was beautiful. Whenever Joshua looked at her he seemed pleased. She held out her hand as she was introduced. Her name was Marcia Klein.

The men were, judging from appearances, all businessmen, well-dressed, sharp-looking. One was wearing a gray pin-striped suit. His features were thick and earthy, accentuated by heavy black-rimmed glasses. He was introduced as David Brickman. The second man was thin and looked like an intellectual. He was dressed in a light tan suit with a white shirt and bow tie. His name was Aaron Fahn. The third gentleman was meticulously dressed, wearing a dark blue suit, perfectly tailored, with a custom-made shirt and a dark blue tie decorated with gold fleurs-de-lis. The tie was held precisely in place by a gold tie clip with a diamond inset. His shoes were Italian imports, made of alligator skin. A stunning gold ring on his right ring finger sparkled with a brilliant sapphire. On each side of the sapphire were three small diamonds arranged in a triangle. The man introduced himself as Lester Gold.

"We can't wait to see our masterpiece," Aaron said enthusiastically. Everyone agreed. After shaking hands and exchanging pleasantries, Joshua ushered them into the kitchen, where the sun was still streaming through the window. As they entered the kitchen they were caught off guard, not expecting to see the statue there. But there it was, with the sun radiating the face of Moses as if he had just come down from the mountain. Marcia gasped with delight, "My goodness, that's beautiful!" then caught herself, as she had not intended to betray her feelings before she had made a thorough examination of the workmanship. But the surprise at coming upon the figure so suddenly had startled her, and she'd reacted before she realized it.

The reactions of the others were more measured. "I never imagined it would look like this," Lester said. Aaron looked at it carefully and showed obvious delight, then proceded to finger the nose, lips, and locks of hair. "This is a masterpiece," he finally decided. "I have never seen a work of art with such life-like qualities. I wouldn't be surprised if it moved."

The woman, who was without doubt an artist herself, looked at the statue more critically. She asked Joshua if the figure was done in one piece. Joshua told her no. He could not get a piece of wood wide enough. The woman looked for the seams in the arms but couldn't find them. "Where did you attach the arms?" she asked impatiently, unable to find them herself.

Joshua walked over to the statue, looked under a fold in Moses' robe, and found the seam with difficulty. The seam didn't show, and even after showing the woman, she still could not see it. She shifted her gaze to the nostrils and touched the ear lobes, which seemed soft. She knew they couldn't be—they were made of wood. She looked at the eyes and the details of the eyelids. They were carved to perfection. Satisfied, she stepped back and looked straight into Joshua's eyes and said, "All I can do is thank you for the remarkable piece of art you have sculptured for our hall. It is one of the most beautiful pieces of art I have ever laid my eyes on. It will be a treasure in our midst."

Joshua beamed his simple and unconcealed delight and thanked her.

"By the way, Joshua," Lester said to him, "are you Jewish, by any chance? With a name like Joshua and the feeling you put into the statue—you must be!"

Joshua smiled and answered cryptically, "Yes, I am very closely related."

"We'd love to have you visit our synagogue if you'd care to. You'd be most welcome," Lester assured him.

"I'd like that very much," Joshua replied, "but it's quite a distance from here and I walk."

"That's no problem," Aaron said. "I'd be more than happy to pick you up. How about tonight, so you can see the people's reaction to your masterpiece?"

Joshua was thrilled. "That would be wonderful," he responded excitedly.

"I'll pick you up at six-thirty sharp," Aaron promised.

"I'll be ready."

Lester reached into his pocket and took out an envelope. He presented it to Joshua. "I feel embarrassed giving you a check for only a hundred dollars for such a beautiful work of art. The wood alone must have cost most of that."

Joshua accepted the envelope and thanked the group, assuring them that he was very happy to have done this work for them. He then picked up the statue and carried it toward the front door as the group followed.

As they walked to the sidewalk each one took his turn admiring the figure, saying how impressed the rabbi would be when he saw it. Reaching the van, Lester opened the door for Joshua to place the statue inside. He stepped in and placed the figure carefully on the thick blankets covering the floor.

As he stepped back out Marcia put her hand on his arm and urged him warmly and emphatically not to miss the services that evening. Joshua looked at her, smiled, and said, "I'll be there."

After they exchanged good-byes the van took off and left Joshua at the gate of his cottage. He closed the gate and went inside, but only to emerge a few minutes later and walk up the street toward the grocery store.

The owner welcomed him and asked what he could do for him. Joshua ordered a variety of meats and groceries and vegetables and fruits. He also picked out an assortment of candies. The man tallied the bill, which came to $72.56.

While Joshua was taking the money from his pocket and counting it, the grocer put everything into bags. Joshua paid the bill and asked the man if he would be kind enough to deliver the food to the family down on the back road. He knew the people Joshua was talking about and told him they were very nice people and he would be happy to do him the favor. To save the people's pride, Joshua wrote a note and put it in one of the bags: "With grateful appreciation for all your kindness, please accept this small token."

The proprietor promised to deliver the order himself so no one would know about it. He'd have it down there within the hour. Joshua thanked him and left.

6

AARON ARRIVED PROMPTLY at six-thirty that evening, and Joshua was ready. His hair was neatly combed, with the semblance of a part on the left side, though his hair was too free to tolerate a perfect part. He had washed and pressed his pants and shirt, so he looked neat. He also wore a light sweater vest, which one of the women in the patch of houses on the back road had knit for him. It was brown, like the rest of his clothes, so he looked presentable, though no match for the elegantly dressed people who had picked up the statue earlier in the day. He was clearly a poor person by worldly standards. The sandals he wore were also plain but sturdily constructed to give good support to his feet.

Aaron parked in front of Joshua's cottage, right in front of the gate. As Joshua walked toward the car Aaron got out and met him on the sidewalk. He shook his hand and opened the door for him. Joshua seemed a little embarrassed by all the fuss, but accepted it graciously. It was a good twenty-minute ride to the synagogue, which was located in the city, but they had plenty of time to arrive before the service started.

It was a few minutes before seven when they got there. Aaron parked the car and the two men walked to the building together. They were cordially greeted by an usher who offered Joshua a yarmulke. He placed it on his head while the usher talked to Aaron. Aaron was obviously quite active in the congregation, which was clear from the greetings he got as he entered the vestibule.

Aaron introduced Joshua proudly as a friend and the artist who carved the figure of Moses for the hall—and, half-jokingly, as a potential member of the congregation. Everyone greeted him warmly.

Since it was almost time for the service to begin, Aaron brought Joshua into the synagogue proper. As Aaron had duties to perform, he asked Joshua if he would mind sitting by himself until he got back. He didn't mind at all. In fact, he felt right at home.

As soon as the rabbi entered, everyone stood and the service began. The rabbi welcomed everyone, especially guests from out of town, and in particular the special person who had designed the beautiful work of art for the congregation. A couple of people not too far from Joshua looked over at him and smiled warmly. Joshua blushed.

He became totally absorbed in the service, thoroughly enjoying the singing of the hymns, the psalms, which were so familiar and so precious to him. Being by himself, his voice stood out as he prayed unashamedly and sang with all his heart. He was not embarrassed or self-conscious, and when a few heads turned to see whose voice it was, he didn't even notice. His voice was a rich and mellow baritone, hearty and full of enthusiasm.

When the service ended and everyone filed into the vestibule on their way downstairs, a few people came over to Joshua and told him how much they had enjoyed his singing during the service. Joshua was really embarrassed but managed to thank them, blushing all the while. He didn't realize he was singing so loudly, he said. They told him he needn't apologize, his voice was beautiful.

In the vestibule the four people who had been at Joshua's house earlier in the day found him in the crowd and came over to rescue him. He was easy to pick out; everyone around him was well-dressed, while he looked like he just came in from the fields; and even though he had washed and pressed his clothes, he still was not what one would call elegant. In fact, he looked rather pathetic, though it didn't seem to bother him. He was not at all self-conscious about how he looked. No one seemed to care anyway. He was accepted for what he was and not for what he wore. And he was clearly a highly gifted individual who had a lot to give people. Those who knew him and grew close to him were proud of his friendship and cared little for what he wore. Besides, people were used to artists. They all seemed to dress strangely, so what he wore seemed quite normal for an artist. As a matter of fact, no one paid much attention to what he was wearing anyway. They were curious to see the sculpture, about which they had heard rumors all afternoon over the telephone.

Joshua's four companions flanked him as they walked downstairs together, telling him how impressed the rabbi was when he saw the figure. They were sure the congregation would love it.

When they entered the large hall they immediately spotted a group of people standing up front. In front of them was the figure of Moses, as if speaking to the crowd watching him, gesticulating and urging them with all the force of his mighty personality. As Joshua and his friends walked closer they could hear the comments. "What a powerful work of art!" "Do you think they really gave him as hard a time as his face betrays?" "I have no doubt they did. He was forever calling them names, like 'stiff-necked,' and 'hard-hearted,' and 'rebellious.' He certainly doesn't look like too patient a person from that statue."

The social committee had put out coffee, tea, and pastries on several tables in the room. The crowd began making its way to the food while some stayed on to look at the sculpture. At that point the rabbi came in with two women who were talking excitedly about something. One of the women, a Mrs. Cohen, was telling the rabbi she had been sitting near the visiting artist during services and had heard him saying his prayers and singing the hymns in Hebrew. The rabbi was skeptical, but the woman insisted and her friend agreed with her.

The rabbi tactfully ended the discussion by saying, "Perhaps he is Jewish. One never knows. If he is, I'll find out discreetly." That seemed to satisfy the women, and they settled down to a more relaxed dialogue as they walked closer to the statue.

As they approached Lester walked over to the rabbi, gently took him by the arm, and led him over to Joshua. The rabbi's face showed excitement, a departure from his normal composure. He had been pleased with the figure since he had first seen it earlier in the day, though he was overwhelmed with the power of the piece and did not miss the unambiguous directness of the message it conveyed. He could see it was not merely a representation of history, but carried a profound message to the modern Jewish community. He felt proud that the figure belonged to his congregation, and although some criticized him for erecting a "graven image," even in the social hall, he felt the figure's powerful message more than justified his decision. But as proud as he was of the statue, he did feel a certain annoyance, and, indeed, an embarrassment, that the statue should be delivering a message to his people and not just representing a plea to the ancients. However, his people were no different from the Hebrews of old and they, too, needed strong messages from above. Thinking of these things, the rabbi began to see in the statue all the messages he should have delivered but was afraid to, and his original annoyance over the statue's message was replaced with gratitude to the artist. At least by commissioning the artist the rabbi said through the artist's hands all the things he felt God wanted him to say. And his conscience felt soothed.

"Rabbi Szeneth," Lester said, "this is Joshua, the artist who carved the figure of Moses for us." Then, turning to Joshua, he introduced the rabbi as their esteemed spiritual leader. The two men shook hands.

"I am deeply grateful to you, Joshua, for the beautiful work of art you have created for our people. And you did create. It is not just a piece of wood, or even just a figure. It speaks loud and clear. I heard the message. I must admit that at first I didn't like what you said, but as I thought about it, I realized you were saying all the things I should have said but didn't have the courage to, and I am grateful. It is masterful," the rabbi said to Joshua.

"Thank you, Rabbi. You do me honor," Joshua said politely, then continued, "I want it to be a permanent testimonial of my love for my people."

"Your people?" the rabbi asked, surprised, remembering what the two women had been telling him.

"Yes, my people," Joshua answered, "I love them deeply."

"You are Jewish, then?" the rabbi asked.

"Yes."

"Then please come to our synagogue whenever you like and feel at home," the rabbi said, then quickly added, "I don't feel so bad now that the message in that figure came from one of our own."

Joshua chuckled as Rabbi Szeneth and the delegation accompanied him to the place where the statue was erected so they could all get a closer look. One lady glanced over at Joshua and, suspecting he was the artist, asked coldly, "Are you the artist?"

"Yes, I am," Joshua responded politely.

"Why does Moses seem so insistent? He looks almost desperate in his frustration."

"He was, after all, only a human," Joshua replied courteously, "and when you think of the task he had to accomplish, and the obstacles he faced daily for forty years, he couldn't have been any other way. What he endured would have broken a lesser man, so just looking frustrated isn't too unrealistic an expression, do you think?"

"I guess not, but it makes you feel almost guilty when you analyze it."

"Is that bad?" Joshua asked.

"Perhaps not, but when I look at a work of art I like to enjoy it. This one makes me feel uncomfortable. As a piece of art it is well done, and I'm sure most people will love it."

"I'm afraid many of our people are picking up the same impression I did," the rabbi said. "It certainly is not going to be ignored or be treated as just a decoration. And maybe it will be a constant sermon to all of us when we are tempted to stray from God's law."

By nine-thirty the social hour began to break up. Aaron came over to Joshua and asked him if he was ready to leave.

"I think so," Joshua replied, and the two men started to leave, saying good-bye to various people as they walked toward the front exit.

"What did you think of our congregation?" Aaron asked Joshua when they were leaving the parking lot.

"They seem like a friendly community," Joshua answered.

"Were you pleased with their response to your sculpture?"

"Yes, their reactions varied, as I thought they would. But I wanted to leave a lasting impression that would provoke a thoughtful response so the work would have a personal and lasting value for everyone. It is difficult, Aaron, for people to think in spiritual terms. The world of the senses is so vivid and so real. The world of the spirit is real to God, perhaps, but to human beings it is hard to believe it even exists. For someone to talk about it makes people feel uncomfortable, yet it is important that they be reminded of the spiritual world."

Aaron listened as Joshua spoke. He was captivated by what Joshua said, but also by the calmness of his manner. He wasn't critical of human behavior, but spoke as if the world of the spirit was very real to him. He moved with such ease through an area of thought that was a tangled jungle for most human minds. He let Joshua continue without even asking questions as he drove his luxurious automobile through the city streets and out into the country roads toward Auburn. The road looked like a long tunnel as the headlights cast beams far ahead under perfectly arched tree limbs.

The night was quiet. A cool breeze swept across the countryside as they drove along with open windows to breathe in the fresh air. Aaron was silent. Only Joshua spoke. Aaron was a worldly man, and Joshua mystified him. Aaron's father owned a steel factory, and Aaron, since childhood, had spent most of his time around the plant. Now he was president. His father had retired over a year ago and placed his son in charge of the whole operation. Aaron was a kind person; he spent much of his free time helping the rabbi with the many administrative chores around the synagogue. He was not a particularly spiritual man but donated money to various charities. His fascination with Joshua came from his inability to understand a man with the intelligence of Joshua who walked through life as if material things were worthless. He knew Joshua could have any position in life he set his mind to, but he was content being simple and having practically nothing in the way of worldly goods. This confused Aaron, who was taught at an early age the value of material things. He had position, bank accounts, stocks, real estate investments, and a happy family life, all that is really important to a man.

Joshua confused him because he had none of these things and didn't even seem interested in them. And yet he was happy and peaceful, which Aaron was not. Underneath all the material bliss and the good life he was living there was an emptiness, a gnawing void that gave him no rest. His money and investments were like a child playing monopoly. It was a game that fascinated him, and which, at one time, was exciting but now bored him. In quiet, lonely moments the thought that that was all there was to life frightened him. Perhaps that was why he enjoyed being with Joshua. He felt a certain peace when he was with him and a calming serenity that he could not find elsewhere. Aaron wished he could be like Joshua. He wished he had his peace. He felt good and clean inside, as if walking through a new atmosphere with a rarified, enriched environment.

"Joshua," Aaron finally said, breaking his long silence, "how did you become the way you are? Who taught you all the things you believe in?"

"Why do you ask?" Joshua questioned curiously.

"Because I can't understand how anyone could develop the vision of life that you have. It is so foreign to my way of thinking, and so different from the thinking of everybody I know."

"I experience what I believe, Aaron, so I know that what I believe is true."

"What do you mean, you experience it? How come I don't experience it?"

"Each person looks at life through a different vision. Three men can look at a tree. One man will see so many board feet of valuable lumber worth so much money. The second man will see it as so much firewood to be burned, to keep his family warm in the winter. The third man will see it as a masterpiece of God's creative art, given to man as an expression of God's love and enduring strength, with a value far beyond its worth in money or firewood. What we live for determines what we see in life and gives clear focus to our inner vision."

"Who taught you to think that way?"

"It is what I see. You could see it, too, if you could detach yourself from the things you were taught to value. They do not give you peace, nor do they give you lasting satisfaction. They leave you empty, and filled with a longing for something more."

"That's true, how do you know?"

"I know how man was made and understand what he really needs if he is to grow and find peace."

"Joshua, you are a strange man, but I really feel close to you. I would like to have you as a friend."

"I am honored, and I will treasure your friendship."

They had already arrived in the village. Aaron turned down Main Street toward Joshua's cottage. The streetlights were partially hidden in the foliage and the village looked quaint, like part of another age. The shadows hid from view all the modern additions to the village, showing only the shapes of buildings as they must have looked two hundred years before. There was a loneliness to the setting, and Aaron felt sorry for Joshua, living alone in the midst of everybody else's world but not being a part of all the joys and heartaches of family life. He couldn't help but feel alone.

7

THE NEXT MORNING Joshua lay in bed, propped up against his pillow, as he listened to the patter of raindrops on the roof. It was restful, almost musical, as it fell in measured cadence against the windowpanes. Joshua's mind seemed far away, and for the longest time he was completely absorbed in his thoughts, as if contemplating a vision of distant times and places. He left the house and walked up the main street to the diner.

Moe Sanders was walking toward the diner from the opposite direction. He was with Pat Zumbar and Herm Ainutti. "Hey, look who's comin'!" Pat cried out in a voice that shattered the early morning silence. Joshua couldn't help but hear, and since he was still almost a hundred and fifty feet away, he merely waved slightly and smiled at the unexpected recognition. As the men approached Moe greeted Joshua. "Good morning, men," he returned as the three men filed into the diner.

Part of the gang had already gathered, and the place was noisy with the clanging of dishes and silverware. The smell of frying bacon and eggs whet the appetite and put everyone in a good mood. "Look at Joshua's girlfriend beam now that Josh is here," Herm said jokingly about Mary, who owned the diner. Everyone knew Mary liked Joshua a lot. She couldn't keep it to herself, because every time Joshua came in she would get all flustered and blush. It was a dead giveaway, and there was no way she could hide it. Joshua was aware of it and smiled at her with a knowing twinkle in his eye.

She continued to blush and stood at the place where she knew Joshua was going to sit.

"Good morning, Mary," he said to her affectionately, then added quietly, "You look bright and pretty on such a gloomy day."

She blushed even more. "I guess I always brighten up when you come in. At least that's what everybody tells me. What'll you have for breakfast?"

Joshua looked up at the menu hanging on the wall above the stove and, after pausing a few seconds, gave his order. "I think I'll have pancakes and sausages, with orange juice and coffee."

Mary wrote it down and then put a cup of steaming coffee at his place. The others watched with feigned envy. "Boy, look at the service he gets. Privileged character," Herm said good-naturedly.

Moe reached over the counter and grabbed the pot of coffee. He filled everyone's cup, saying as he did, "I guess we'll just have to wait on ourselves if we want to get anything to eat." Before Moe finished a waitress came over and finished pouring the coffee. "If you guys were as nice as Josh, maybe you'd get special treatment too," she said as she poured the last cup.

It was only a little after seven, and a Saturday morning, so the diner was half empty. Pat's voice dominated the room, making everyone else's conversation a mere undercurrent. "Heard you were at the synagogue last night," he said to Joshua. "What were you doin' over there?" There was no offense intended. It was just the way Pat talked. Whatever passed across his mind automatically expressed itself.

Joshua had just taken a mouthful of hot coffee and almost choked on it over the abruptness of Pat's remark. The men laughed. "Yes, we had quite a time. You'd love it there," Joshua replied.

"I doubt it," Pat countered. "What were you doing at the synagogue?"

"I had been asked to carve a statue of Moses for them, so they invited me for the viewing. I felt quite at home. We're all Jews, spiritually, you know."

"I'm no Jew," Pat protested. "Maybe Moe is, his brother even looks like one."

Mary put the piping-hot pancakes and sausages in front of Joshua. She also put a few extra pats of butter with the order and winked, as if to say, "Don't thank me; they'll make fun." Joshua smiled back. He had a warm spot in his heart for this good-natured girl. But Mary's gesture didn't pass unnoticed. Moe, who was sitting right next to Joshua, spotted the action and immediately complained, "See that. She even gives him extra butter. All the special treatment. She wouldn't do that for us, and we've been coming here for years."

Mary just ignored the noise and went about her business.

Herm had been unusually quiet, but finally came to life. "You go to our church, don't you, Josh?" he asked.

"Yes," Joshua answered.

"I thought I saw you there, but I never saw you go to Communion, so I didn't know whether you belonged or not."

"I do go to Communion in my own way, which would be difficult to explain," Joshua replied.

Pat picked him up on that. "What do you mean 'in your own way'? Either you go or you don't."

Joshua laughed and tried to explain. Fortunately he was saved by the waitress bringing out Pat's breakfast. That distracted everybody for the moment, but Moe remarked that he had seen Joshua going to the Methodist church one Sunday.

Joshua nodded. "I feel at home wherever people sincerely honor my Father." Simple enough, and everyone seemed satisfied, but whenever Joshua said "my Father," it was so different from the way people spoke, it made everyone wonder. Joshua spoke those words with such deep affection, no one knew whether it was just a peculiar mannerism or whether he felt a special relationship to God. For the next few moments it was so quiet in the diner that all you could hear was the clashing of dishes and silverware. Everyone was busy eating.

When the gang had finished they filed over to the cash register and paid their bills. Joshua left a generous tip under his cup before he left. Then they walked outside.

The four of them walked down the street to the corner and took the turn to the back road.

"What possessed you to move out this way?" Herm asked Joshua. It seemed all they did was ask Joshua questions, but he didn't seem to mind.

"It's quiet and peaceful here, and the people are friendly," he answered honestly.

"You should be a politician," Moe said. "You know just what to say."

"You seem like such a happy person, even though you're all alone. Don't you get lonesome living by yourself?" Herm asked.

"No. I like being by myself. And I'm never really alone. People stop in all during the day and talk to me or ask me to make things for them. And besides, God is with us all the time, and He's real, though we don't think of that very much."

"God's with everybody, but it still gets lonely. When you finish work at night what do you have to look forward to but an empty house?" Pat objected. "Wouldn't it be nice if you had someone to cook for you and take care of you when you finish work at night?"

"Yes, I suppose, but I'm quite content, and I enjoy cooking my meals and eating in peace, and taking a walk across the meadow. The beauty of nature is endless in its fascination. And it's so peaceful. Wouldn't you like to be by yourself at times?"

"You're damn right I would," Pat said, "especially when my wife's after me for something I did or for shooting off my big mouth. But, no, she's good. I guess I got it made."

"You seem to be an intelligent fellow, Josh," Herm said, moving to a serious vein. "What do you think of religion?"

"What do you mean by religion? Do you mean the way it is or the way God intended it be? There's a big difference, you know."

"Well, the way it is, the way the churches run it."

"God never intended that religion become what it is today. Jesus came to earth to try to free people from that kind of regimented religion where people are threatened if they don't obey rules and rituals invented by the clergy. Jesus came to teach people that they are God's children and, as God's children, they are free, free to grow as human beings, to become beautiful people as God intended. That can't be legislated. Jesus gave the apostles and the community as a support to provide help and guidance and consolation. Jesus did not envision bosses in the worldly sense. He wanted his apostles to guide and serve, not to dictate and legislate like those who govern this world. Unfortunately, religious leaders model themselves after civil governments and treat people accordingly. In doing this they fall into the same trap that the scribes and Pharisees fell into, making religion a tangible set of measurable religious observances, which is legalistic and superficial. In doing this they become the focus of religious observance rather than God, and it is their endless rules and their rituals rather than love of God and concern for others that occupy the people's attention.

"Customs and practices and traditions then replace true service of God, and these become a serious obstacle to real growth in the love of God. If people take religious leaders too seriously, they become rigid in their thinking and afraid to think for themselves, and must always refer decisions to the clergy. Even as adults they will still cling to the religious practices of their childhood, and when even ceremonies and mere customs change they panic, because they have been lead to believe these things *were* their faith. With that kind of mentality all growth stops, because growth means change and holiness means an ever-deepening understanding of God and what he expects of each one of us. If a person is not open to the inspirations of the Spirit, because it goes beyond what priests allow him, then even the Holy Spirit cannot work in him and he remains stunted. What is worse, he frustrates the work that God wants to accomplish in him. That's why the prophets of old were such great men. They had the boldness to see beyond the limitations of human religious traditions and provide guidance to God's people. They had the courage to break out of the sterile rigidness of religious forms, and incurred the wrath of religious leaders who hated them for this, and persecuted them, even killing some of them in the name of religion. Religious leaders constantly fall into this pitfall of wanting to control religion and people's practice of religion, and not allowing people to think for themselves for fear they will lose control over them."

Joshua's companions listened intently, spellbound by the intensity and insight of this man who was ordinarily so gentle and calm. When Joshua finished they were very quiet, unable to add anything or even ask a question. Finally Herm broke the silence, saying to Joshua, "You really feel strongly about this, don't you?"

"Yes," Joshua answered, "because Jesus never intended that religion do the damage to people that it has. It is horrible how many religious leaders have persecuted and even had people tortured for their beliefs. Even God respects people's freedom, and faith is a gift. People must believe freely. The function of religious leaders is to set an example, to draw people to God by their own deep faith and by the beauty of their personal lives, not intimidate people into sterile external observance. That is not religion. That mocks true religion.

"True religion comes from the heart. It is a deep relationship with God, and should bring peace and joy and love to people, not fear and guilt and meanness. And worship has meaning only when it is free. God is not honored by worship that is forced under threat of sin or penalty. Nor is God honored by subservient obedience to religious laws devoid of love. God is pleased only by the free expression of the soul that truly loves him. Anything less is counterfeit and serves only the short-term needs of religious institutions."

The men weren't ready for such a discourse, but they were delighted to hear Joshua say what he did. In their hearts they believed what he said, but could never in a lifetime express it in the words he used. Moe reflected the feelings of the others when he told Joshua, "You should be a priest. We need to hear things like that. It is something we all feel, but we have never heard it expressed in church. In fact, I don't think any preacher would dare to speak like that. He'd be thrown out on his ear."

"Where did you get all your knowledge from, Josh?" Herm asked with almost respect in his voice.

"When you think about things and feel strongly, it is easy to express what you feel. Understanding God's love for us is something everyone should feel strongly about, and we should not allow anyone, even religious authorities, to take that from us."

The men were glad they took this walk with him. They had never talked like this with anyone before, and yet these were the things each of them thought about in the privacy of his own soul but never dared to share with anyone. They were delighted to hear Joshua speak so freely and unashamedly.

As the foursome started back to the village Pat asked Joshua if he'd like to come to the party he was having that night at his house. Joshua was delighted and readily accepted. Before long they reached Joshua's place, stopped at the gate for a few minutes, then broke up, each going his own way.

Joshua went into his house and, after relaxing for a minute, entered his shop and started to work. The sun was shining through the windows, bringing to life all the partially finished objects lying here and there around the room, some on the bench, others on little shelves, some resting on stools, or on the floor. Some were finished, though most were in different stages of production.

Since people were coming in shortly to pick up articles, Joshua knew where he had to start—the antique chair in the corner of the room, with the broken leg and the pieces missing from the back. The new leg and pieces were resting on the chair. He had made them at odd times during the week, when he wasn't working on the statue. They were easy to fashion, so they didn't take long. All he had to do now was sand them and glue them in place.

He finished the job by ten o'clock and set it aside. The next piece he took up was an old wall clock with beautifully carved molding around the sides, most of which was chipped or broken off. He stood the clock up against the wall behind the bench and wound it up so he could listen to the chimes. They were primitive but charming. They sounded almost like someone striking crystal. As the chimes played Joshua sat back on his stool and dreamily absorbed the mood created by the antique-sounding tones, his thoughts wandering off into a meditation on time and eternity and the ingenious invention of the clock to measure slices of time in an almost perfect relationship with the movement of the planets. He thought, with a twinkle in his eye, that few have yet grasped the reality that time is not real but only a figment, an illusion, that there is no past or future, only the present. The human mind invents the past because it can experience the present only in small, momentary slices. When the experience ends it is gone. To record the experience man invented time. We catalogue experiences and call them the past and place them in various time frames. To the human mind the future is a blank, a void. Though it is already present to God, it is not yet within the focus of man's experience, so it is called future. Will the mind ever be able to understand that the past is still present and that the future already is?

The chimes stopped and the abrupt silence broke Joshua's dreamy mood. He picked up the clock, looked it over, then set it on the bench and began to work on it. With a few deft movements of a tiny handmade saw, he cut off the broken decorations and laid them aside. He then drilled holes into the molding. The next step was more difficult. He had to recarve the broken pieces and make them look exactly like the damaged ones. It took time, but he seemed to enjoy the painstaking and tedious kind of work, which demanded perfection. One by one he recarved the broken pieces and drilled tiny holes in the back of each. Then, making equally tiny dowels, he dipped them in glue and inserted them into the holes. He then fit the decorations into place. It took a good part of the day, but the finished product was perfect, so perfect it was impossible to tell it had been repaired.

The day went by fast. Joshua interrupted his work only twice, once for lunch and again when an old couple came to pick up their antique chair, which turned out not to be an antique to them but simply one of the few chairs they still had in their house. They had sold off most of their furniture to pay bills, and this chair, along with a few other pieces of furniture, was all they had left. When they saw the chair all fixed their eyes widened with excitement. It was beautiful and sturdy. The old lady sat in it; it was solid and firm. Joshua smiled his own satisfaction. When the old man went to pay Joshua asked if they would do him a favor. He knew they were poor and didn't want to take any money from them, but he didn't want to hurt their feelings either, so he brought them out into the kitchen and asked the lady if she would teach him different ways to cook chicken. She taught him a couple of recipes and insisted on writing them down for him. While she was doing this the old man noticed the grill in the yard and gave Joshua a recipe he had for barbecued chicken. When they had both finished Joshua showed such obvious gratitude that, when he refused to take any money for fixing the chair because they had been so kind in helping him, they both felt as if they had done Joshua a favor and left the house happy. Joshua offered to carry the chair down to their house, but they wouldn't hear of it.

When they left Joshua watched them. They took turns carrying the awkward piece of furniture as they walked up the main street toward their house.

By four-thirty Joshua had finished for the day. It had been a long day and he had worked hard, and even if it was not hard work, it was tedious, and he was tired. The sun was still hot and high in the sky, so he decided to go and take a swim and maybe a nap. He had to go to the Zumbars' for supper, and as that would probably go on into the late hours, which he wasn't used to, he really should rest first.

8

THE WHOLE CREW was at the Zumbars' that night. Their small house could hardly contain the crowd, but that was no problem. They never stood on ceremony. If they wanted the whole gang over, they would invite the whole gang, and it was up to them to shift for themselves. They were used to "roughing it" at each others' houses. And this night was special. No one wanted to miss this occasion. Joshua had been too much of a mystery since he appeared in town almost three months ago. Though he seemed friendly enough, only a few individuals had had encounters with him, and he was known more by rumor than by hard facts about his real life. This party was a good chance to meet the real Joshua.

Joshua walked to Pat's house. It was a beautiful evening, a grand finale for a fickle weather pattern all day. Pat was standing on the porch talking to George Sanders, Herm Ainutti, and Charlie, the mailman, when Joshua approached. It was the mailman who noticed him first and cried out, "Hey, look who's comin'!" The others turned and loudly hailed his entrance, which embarrassed Joshua. He smiled and continued walking up to the house, greeting each one as they came over to welcome him. The mailman shook his hand, saying with a certain satisfaction, "Welcome, buddy," as if he had prior claim to his friendship, since he had been the first to make his acquaintance.

They all ushered Joshua into the house, where there was already a crowd. For a brief moment everyone just stood and stared. Joshua's sharp eyes scanned the crowd, locking the impression of each one in his memory. He had seen most of them before, at least the men. Most of the women were strangers. Pat was so proud of his guest that he swelled up like a peacock as he introduced each one to Joshua, who just looked deeply into the eyes of each as if peering down into their very souls and greeted them warmly with a simple hello.

This was not a sophisticated group. What you saw was what they were, nothing was hidden. They were down-to-earth, good-hearted people who had played together as children, studied together as students, and now worked and socialized together as adults. When they were at gatherings like this, there was no ceremony. People just stood up and walked around or went outside into the yard while eating or talking to one another. Some sat down to eat, but they were mostly the women. Most meals turned out to be buffet style whether they were planned that way or not. This particular one was planned that way.

Pat finally remembered to introduce Joshua to his wife, Minnie. She was a kindly, understanding woman, and was taller than Pat. Minnie also had a good sense of humor, and when her husband introduced her to Joshua as his wife she looked at Joshua and said good-naturedly, "Yes, for over forty years, and I don't know how I put up with it."

"What are you talkin' about? You got it made," Pat said in self-defense.

"I sure do," Minnie added.

Joshua smiled and said, "I can tell you two were made for each other."

"Let's get some food, I'm starved," Pat said as he ushered Joshua over to the table, where there were platters and serving bowls filled with all sorts of Italian pasta and meat dishes. Though not too many drank liquor in this crowd, they knew that Joshua drank wine, so they offered him a glass of homemade wine to see if he liked it. It had been made by a little man with a big soul, nicknamed Shorty. He used to be a boxer, and even though he was now in his sixties, he was still in good shape. He wasn't there that night, but had sent two bottles up for Joshua. Joshua tasted the wine, swished it around in his mouth, then looked at Pat and said, "Not bad at all. In fact, it's very good."

"You can thank Shorty for that. He wanted you to have it," Pat told Joshua. "You can take it home with you. Nobody here drinks it."

After allowing Joshua to talk to the women for a few minutes, the men started pulling him out into the backyard, where they were holding court. This was their big chance to ask Joshua all kinds of questions. Even though Joshua knew this was one of the reasons they were happy to see him, he realized they also had a genuine good feeling for him, so he didn't mind their intense curiosity.

"Josh, sit down here," Herm said as he motioned for Joshua to take the lawn chair next to him. Joshua walked over with the plate of food one of the women had dished up for him and sat down, trying at the same time to balance his dish and the glass of wine.

"Josh, tell the guys about your visit to the synagogue last night," Moe suggested.

"There really wasn't much to it," Joshua answered. "In fact, I felt very much at home. The congregation had mixed feelings about the statue I carved for them. Some thought the message conveyed by the figure was too graphic and critical of people of today. I suppose the work is vivid, but I intended to communicate a message and not just represent a dead figure from out of history. Most of the people seemed to like the work and they were very cordial and warm. They even invited me to come back whenever I liked, which I thought was very nice of them."

"It sure was," Herm said jokingly, "especially since they're not going to get rich on you."

"God never gave a penny to anyone, yet he enriches the whole world with gifts that cannot be calculated in terms of money," Joshua shot back none to gently. Herm seemed embarrassed over what he had said. He hadn't intended to hurt Joshua, but hadn't been able to resist making the remark.

"What do you think of the Jews, Josh?" Pat asked. "They still think they're God's chosen people. How long are they going to push that line?"

"They *are* God's chosen people," Joshua answered. "God has no favorites. He blesses all equally, but chooses everyone for a different work. The Jewish people were chosen for a special work, to be prepared for the coming of the anointed, so they would recognize and accept him when he comes and give him to the rest of the human family. That Jesus was born from the Jews is an honor that can never be taken from them. They still share that glory, a glory that they will one day realize. Unfortunately, Christians have not helped. By their cruelty and intolerance they have kept Jews away from Jesus and will one day have to answer for it."

No one had heard Joshua speak like that before. It was with an air of authority, and not like the congenial stranger they had come to know. But he was not offensive in what he said, nor in the way he said it, although he left very little doubt as to how he felt. The men, sensing this, backed off.

At that point a young man came walking up the path. He was a priest. He was wearing his clerical garb but no hat. He looked too young to be already balding, but he was still a good-looking man. Jim noticed him first and remarked, "Oh! Here comes Father Pat."

The crew turned and boisterously greeted the priest. As he approached he seemed a little unsteady. Pat got up and gave him his chair, telling him jokingly, "Here, Father, sit down here. You need it more than I do." Pat sensed the priest had been drinking and that he would feel more comfortable himself if the priest were sitting.

Father Pat sat down, thanking Pat as he did so. As soon as he sat back in the chair he looked over at Joshua, who was looking directly at him with a look that seemed to pierce his soul. The priest lowered his gaze momentarily, feeling a slight embarrassment in the stranger's presence.

"My name's Joshua," Joshua said to break the ice and make the priest feel more comfortable. As he did the two men reached out to each other and shook hands. "Father Pat," the priest said, "pleased to meet you."

Again their eyes met. This time the priest could not take his eyes off Joshua. It was as if he had been hypnotized. The priest's instinctive analytical sense saw something more in Joshua than just a mere stranger. He noticed the kindness in his eyes, and the sadness that came from being hurt, but a sadness unspoiled by bitterness or cynicism. He felt in his handshake an extraordinary strength that belied the apparent delicacy of his appearance. He had to force himself to keep looking at Joshua because he could tell Joshua's eyes saw more than just the surface. He knew Joshua was looking into his very soul, but he could not see criticism in his look. He saw a warm and gentle affection radiating from his glance and felt drawn to him immediately.

As the priest was analyzing Joshua, Joshua was doing the same thing to the priest. Priests can be a critical group, wary by experience, and frequently selfish, conditioned to be this way, perhaps, by the loneliness of their lives. Some priests are haughty, and look upon people as beneath them, as subjects to be kept in their place or told what to do. But Joshua saw none of this in Father Pat. On the surface he saw a man who liked to drink, but underneath a man almost overwhelmed and frightened by life, a man desperately lonely but struggling hard to observe the kind of life that was expected of him. Joshua could tell he sincerely loved people and enjoyed making them happy and doing nice things for them. Joshua had spotted him coming up the sidewalk long before the others had and noticed the children running over to him and grabbing his hands, happy to see him as he handed out little things he took out of his pockets. "Here was a real priest," Joshua thought, "a man after the heart of God, in spite of his drinking." Joshua's eyes, and the faint smile on his face, betrayed the love he immediately felt for this frightfully vulnerable man of God.

This whole exchange of glances took but a brief moment, which was unnoticed because everyone was too busy talking and vying for the floor.

"I'm glad you could come," Pat said to the priest. "We wanted you and Joshua to meet each other. What'll you have to eat, Father?"

"A glass of scotch with ice and soda," the priest said with a grin.

"Hell, I was going to get that anyway," Pat said, then added, "But what'll you have for a chaser—ravioli, lasagna, or sausage and peppers?"

"Lasagna sounds good," the priest answered as Pat entered the house, letting the back door slam behind him.

Father Pat Hayes was the assistant at the local Catholic church. He had come to town less than a year ago and almost everyone in town had taken to him immediately. His warm personality and engaging sense of humor put people at ease and they enjoyed being with him. Since they liked him so much, his drinking problem was easily overlooked. Father Pat was a far different kind of person from the pastor, who was a humorless, pompous man who could rarely say anything that didn't have a sarcastic edge to it. He was very conscious that he was pastor and thoroughly enjoyed being administrator over this rather widespread territory and every Catholic in it. He even treated Father Pat more as an altar boy than a highly intelligent professional with a much finer mind than his own. Father Pat's weakness left him vulnerable to chronic verbal abuse from the pastor, who seemed to be almost happy his assistant had a problem so he could give vent to his sadistic delight in humiliating him. The pastor treated the parishioners the same way. He was sole master of his parish and everyone in it. His sharp tongue kept everyone in his place. No one dared to cross him for fear of becoming the target of his cutting sarcasm. The spiritual state of the parish seemed to be of little concern to anyone except Father Pat. This was why the whole parish rallied around him, which totally exasperated the pastor.

Attending parish parties, like the one this particular night, was Father Pat's escape. Life in the rectory was intolerable. Supper was formal and joyless, and during each meal both sat in silence, and on the rare occasion when there was talk, it was about parish business. This was difficult for Father Pat. He came from a happy family and was used to good-humored banter. He wasn't a spoiled boy, so he learned at a young age how to get along with people. But no matter how hard he tried, there was no way he could develop a pleasant working relationship with the pastor. The fact that he was clearly more intelligent than the pastor didn't help matters.

Pat brought out the priest's supper and sat down near him on an old tree stump, which Minnie used as a planter. "How's our pastor?" Pat asked cynically. Everyone knew Father Pat's life must be hell, and even though he was loyal to the pastor and never talked about him to the parishioners, the people knew and joked with him about it. The priest would just laugh occasionally when someone hit the mark.

Joshua sat and listened intently to the conversation, picking up odds and ends and putting the pieces together to form a rather clear picture of the spiritual state of the Christian community. At one point George came over and asked Joshua what he thought of their parish. As usual, Joshua was honest and blunt.

"As I said this morning, Jesus' care is for people, not for the clergy's need for authority. Jesus preached a message of freedom, the freedom of God's children. Religious leaders should help people understand life and enjoy being God's children. They must resist the temptation to run the parish as a business and lord it over the people like the pagans do. Jesus never intended to start a business, but to lay the foundation for a closely knit family of people caring for one another. As it is, the Church has become a structure superimposed on the life of the people, and the people are not really allowed to be part of it. Their role is just to support the structure. In a real community of Christians the people are the heart of the community. They are allowed to live freely and plan their own lives as Christians, and to build up their own lives as God's people. The pastor is for them a gentle guide, offering advice and counsel and direction when needed. There is a genuine love that inspires a community like this. That is what Jesus intended."

Father Pat sat listening with a look of awe. When Joshua finished the priest asked him how he knew so much about the Church and the Christian life. Joshua just smiled. The priest told Joshua that what he said was beautiful but a dream that could never become a reality. "Priests are too stuck on their own authority to allow the people to be free and to function as mature Christians," the priest said. "There was one priest, a beautiful person, who tried to set up a Christian community styled after the pattern you just described, and the bishop himself took the priest out and replaced him with a priest who would get the people back in line. What the Church preaches and teaches is one thing, what the Church officials will allow is an entirely different matter. They become very nervous when they see the people having too much freedom to do things on their own. The Church is great on preaching justice and love, but they are also among the worst violators."

Father Pat usually didn't mouth off like that, but Joshua's insight into the life of the community had unleashed the priest's pent-up frustrations and he poured out, for the first time, his own feelings about the Church. The little group sitting around was taken aback but glad to see Father Pat expressing such strong convictions. He hadn't done that before, and people were getting the impression he was just a nice guy who liked to sip scotch and tell jokes. This outburst revealed a more serious side of his personality, a facet, perhaps, that expressed his real self, which was never allowed to surface in his work as a priest.

Joshua listened as the priest spoke and agreed that priests exist to serve the people, but they, too, frequently would rather rule them instead. Unfortunately people tolerate this because they are afraid of incurring the priest's wrath. The problem seems to be just the opposite with the Protestant churches. There the problem ministers face is too much control by the people, so the minister is often afraid to preach the real message of Jesus and compromises his ministry so he can keep his job.

The conversation gradually drifted to ligher topics. Father Pat told a joke about a contractor who was dying. The man's wife asked the parish priest to visit her husband in the hospital and try to put him into a more spiritual frame of mind. He certainly wasn't prepared to die. The priest went and talked to the old man. In the course of the conversation the priest suggested the man make a donation to the church in atonement for his sins. The church needed a stained-glass window. He even promised to allow the man to inscribe on the bottom of the window anything he liked. And this perpetual memorial would cost only ten thousand dollars, which, after all, wasn't much for a man of his great wealth. At that point the doctor came in and started making out the bill for taking care of the patient for the past two months. The bill came to almost fifty thousand dollars, at which the poor old man almost had a stroke. But realizing the end was near, and he couldn't take the money with him, he decided to oblige the two men.

Asking for his checkbook, he wrote the check for the doctor. Then, while writing the check for the priest, he reminded him of his promise to allow him to inscribe whatever he liked on the window. The priest reassured him. The old man then told the priest in a firm and steady voice just what he wanted: "In honor of Patrick J. Murphy, who died like Christ . . . between two thieves."

Everybody laughed at the priest's ability to poke fun at his own profession. For the rest of the evening the conversations stayed in a light vein. Joshua went inside and spent time talking to the women. They were thrilled at his interest in their families and felt proud when he praised them for the good job they did at keeping their families so close and preserving such a healthy spirit in the neighborhood.

Joshua left the Zumbars' at close to eleven o'clock. Father Pat was standing near the door when he left, his scotch in hand. He was in a jovial mood when he said good-bye to Joshua, promising to stop over to Joshua's house after his last Mass tomorrow. Then he told him, with a twinkle in his eye as he looked at the glass of scotch, that he could see Father Pat was deeply spiritual. The priest smiled good-naturedly at the subtle dig and watched Joshua as he walked down the steps to the sidewalk, wondering what kind of a man Joshua really was. His priestly intuition told him that he was not just a simple wood-carver. He'd find out tomorrow when he had a chance to talk to him alone.

9

THE SUN'S RAYS shimmered through the needles of the tall pine tree overhead, and the grass glistened with dew as Joshua walked through the meadow, deep in thought. Sunday morning was quiet in Auburn. No noisy traffic broke the peaceful silence of the Sabbath rest. Sunday should be that way everywhere so people could give their wearied souls a rest from the nerve-shattering noise of their workdays. The quiet of nature is God's tranquilizer.

From the village a melancholy church bell called out across the fields for people to come to worship. Joshua returned from the fields and walked down the main street to the Catholic church. He had been to the Presbyterian church the week before, which he found a very proper place and the people well-dressed and polite, although they weren't overly friendly. A teenaged boy had sensed Joshua's embarrassment and introduced himself to make him feel welcome. After the service the minister had politely suggested that Joshua wear clothes that were more formal to the worship service, since it was God's house. Joshua told him these were the only clothes he had and suggested God was more concerned about the adornment of his soul. The minister was a little annoyed at being preached to but said nothing and turned to the other people standing nearby.

In the Catholic church he got lost in the crowd. The sheer number of people blurred styles and fashions, and a stranger could remain a stranger in the sea of faceless people. Joshua walked in with the others, smiled at the elderly, distinguished-looking usher in the threadbare suit, and took a place in the last pew.

His eyes scanned the interior of the church, noting in a few swift glances every detail of the structure and decorations. He looked momentarily on the statue of the Virgin Mary and smiled ever so faintly, reflecting pleasure and understanding humor at the same time. He then knelt down, rested his elbows on the pew in front of him, and buried his face in his hands, resting his head against the tips of his fingers. He stayed that way the longest time, even after the priest began Mass. It wasn't until everyone sat for the sermon and the woman in front of him hit her head against his arms that he became aware of what was going on and sat down.

Father Pat was offering the Mass. He looked remarkably recuperated from the party and was speaking eloquently. He felt at home in the pulpit. He liked people and preached to them from his heart. He enjoyed sharing his own feelings about God and Jesus and about life. He seemed almost to caress the congregation with his warmth, and the people responded. There was hardly a person in the parish who didn't like this kindly, gentle man, except for a handful of individuals who seemed to delight in finding fault with every priest who came to town. But no one could criticize him for his sermons. They were masterpieces of clarity and simplicity. This particular morning he was talking about the carefree quality of Jesus' life-style and that the central point of Jesus' teaching was the freedom he came to declare to mankind. It was that announcement of freedom which amounted to a declaration of war against the religious structure of Israel that got him into trouble. No one felt comfortable with what he preached except the people. They loved him, and it would be no different if he came back today. He would preach the same message, and religious leaders would respond the same way, except they might be more subtle than resorting to crucifixion.

The priest noticed Joshua sitting in the back of the church and was briefly distracted, but not long enough for anyone to notice. He caught himself and continued speaking, every now and then looking over at Joshua, trying to see his reaction. The

priest went on to tell the people they should take this message of
freedom to heart and should enjoy being the children of God
and should feel free. They should trust God and believe Him
when he talks about the birds of the air and the flowers of the
field and not worry about what they are going to eat and drink
or what they are going to wear. The sermon was beautiful, and
everyone was moved by its simplicity. Even Joshua seemed to be
extremely pleased and slightly nodded his head in approval at a
couple of points.

The priest finished his sermon and went back to the altar to
continue the liturgy. Joshua watched the priest attentively and
was distracted only when the usher came by with the collection
basket. Joshua lowered his head and the usher passed him by.
During Communion time he knelt, and again became totally
absorbed in his thoughts.

At the end of Mass, Father Pat went to the back of the church
to greet the people. Whenever *he* said the Mass the crowd hung
around outside talking. As they walked past him they told him
how much they enjoyed his sermon and said how beautiful Jesus
must have been. When Joshua went past he shook hands with
the priest and, with a broad smile, congratulated him, telling
him, "One would judge, by your sense of intimacy with Jesus,
that you knew him personally."

"I think I do," Father Pat retorted, then reminded Joshua he
would be down to his place later on.

"I'll be waiting," Joshua replied.

A few ushers were standing around the priest. He introduced
them to Joshua. The men said they had heard a lot about him
but imagined him to be a much older man. They were happy to
meet him. After exchanging pleasantries they parted, Joshua
walking down the street while the others went back into the
church.

On his way home Joshua stopped at the bakery. He couldn't
resist the smell of fresh bread that filled the air on Sunday mornings. The baker was a high-strung individual but a hard worker.
He was sliding the huge wooden paddle back out of the oven.
On it were four fat loaves of freshly baked bread. He gave one to
Joshua, who picked up a bag and put the bread in it himself,
then paid the baker and left. When he got outside the store he

opened the bag and tore off a big chunk of hot bread and began eating it, tucking the rest of the loaf under his arm.

The rest of the morning went fast. Joshua enjoyed Sundays. He could walk in the meadow and watch the animals, who were no longer afraid of him. Occasionally he would take bits of food with him to pass out to them when they came up to him. He didn't walk too long this morning. It was already getting late.

When he got back to the house there was a frantic knocking on the front door. He opened it and was surprised to see Margaret, Hank's wife, carrying her little daughter in her arms. It was the little girl who always ran out to meet him when he walked down the back road. The mother was beside herself.

Joshua took them inside and asked the woman what had happened. Between sobs she tried to explain. She said her daughter was dying and pleaded with Joshua to help her. She knew he was a good man and God would listen to him. Would he please help her? The girl had been getting headaches and high fevers. The mother gave her aspirin, but it didn't help. She kept getting worse, sometimes becoming unconscious.

"Did you take her to the doctor?" Joshua asked.

"We have no money."

"What about the hospital?"

"We have no insurance either."

Joshua told the mother to sit down, taking the child from her and sitting down himself. He looked down at the girl, who could barely open her eyes. She looked up at Joshua and smiled faintly, then seemed to become unconscious. She lay almost lifeless in Joshua's arms, pale, her left arm hanging limp as Joshua held her close to him. He remembered her running out of the house in her underpants to greet him, grabbing his hand and holding it tightly. She really loved Joshua.

"Can you please help her?" the mother pleaded frantically.

Joshua looked at the girl, then looked up at the mother, who was sitting at the edge of her chair, tears streaming down her drawn cheeks. "Woman," Joshua said, "you have such faith. How could God not listen to you?"

Joshua couldn't stand seeing people in such hopeless straits. He told the woman to trust God and take her daughter back home. She would be better before they arrived there. "God has heard your pleas, and your great faith," he told her. "So don't worry. Your daughter will be well. Just give her a lot of liquids for a day or so until she feels like eating again. She'll be all right."

The woman had complete trust in Joshua. She thanked him and took her daughter in her arms and walked out the front door, carrying the child all the way up the street. As they disappeared around the corner the girl opened her eyes and looked up at her mother. "Why are you carrying me, Mommy? I can walk."

The mother cried for joy. "Are you sure, honey?" she asked the child.

"Yes, Mommy, let me show you."

The woman put the girl down and she stood up straight and firm, but she was still pale and weak. Margaret felt the child's forehead. There was no sign of fever. She asked her if her head ached. It didn't. The mother threw her arms around the child and cried out loud for sheer joy. Then the two of them walked down the back road together, holding hands.

It wasn't long after Margaret left that Father Pat came over. He was dressed in casual clothes, with a friendly grin on his face.

"Come on in, Pat," Joshua said, glad to see him.

"This is a nice little place you got," the priest said as he looked around.

"Nothing pretentious," Joshua responded, "just enough to suit my needs."

"I like it," the priest said.

"Have you eaten yet?" Joshua asked.

"No, we don't eat on Sunday at the rectory. It's the cook's day off."

"Will you have lunch with me?"

"Okay, I am hungry," Father Pat answered.

The two men walked into the kitchen. Joshua pulled a chair away from the table for his guest to sit down, then went about stirring the pot of chicken soup. It was much the same meal as when the mailman came except for chicken breasts, which he had roasting on the grill in the yard, and a bowl of salad.

Joshua served the soup, then the rest of the meal. The two men didn't waste much time getting into an involved discussion.

That was why the priest had wanted to come in the first place. Joshua poured two glasses of wine, which they sipped while eating. He left the bottle on the table in case his guest wanted more.

The two men enjoyed talking to each other. Father Pat was a ready talker and lost no time telling Joshua all the rumors about him in town, needling him when he finished the list. "You couldn't possibly be as bad as all the rumors I've heard. That's why I wanted to get to know you for myself."

Joshua laughed loudly. He knew he was the object of mystery and sort of enjoyed it. Not lost for words himself, he retorted with the same good nature, "You don't do too badly yourself, you know."

"Oh, don't I know it," the priest responded. "I guess I do keep them guessing. And my drinking doesn't help."

Joshua said nothing, just continued eating.

"I hear you have your own business, Josh," Father Pat said.

"Yes, it's not much. Just enough to pay my bills. I'll never get rich on it."

"What do you do?"

"I make things out of wood. Sometimes people bring in broken furniture. Sometimes they order pieces like lampstands or figurines."

"I heard about the statue of Moses you made for the synagogue. I thought Jews weren't allowed to have statues."

"They're not, but they thought it would be all right if they put it in the social hall rather than the sanctuary."

"I heard some were a little upset with the bluntness of the message in the statue," the priest said.

"I know, the rabbi told me as much."

"You know, Joshua, you're a strange fellow. You're not just a wood-carver. You have too much depth and understanding of things to be content to just carve wood. I almost get the impression you've been this way before," the priest said, looking intently into Joshua's eyes as he said it, trying to pick up the slightest change in facial expression. "You have such a beautiful attitude toward everything. When I was speaking about Jesus this morning in the sermon, I couldn't help but think of you. You seem to have picked up the real spirit of Jesus and adapted it perfectly to your own life. You're the only person I know who has done that. In most Christians, even good ones, their imitation of Jesus is just that, imitation. They zero in on one trait of Christ and practice that till it becomes almost a caricature. But you live his ways with such ease and grace. I don't think even he could be much different from you if he were to come back."

Joshua did show a trace of discomfort and started to blush.

"I embarrass you," Father Pat said. "I'm sorry, but I couldn't help telling you that because you are a living example of what I try to preach, and it's frustrating at times. When I met you I felt I had met the living ideal of what I had talked about so often. I wish I myself could be more like what I preach. I try, but it's hard."

"You're a good priest, Pat," Joshua reassured him, "but don't allow yourself to get discouraged. Everyone has imperfections. That's the way God made them, and as long as people are striving to love God and care for one another, they are pleasing to God. Perfection is more a process of striving than a state to be attained, so one's perfection is measured not by success in attaining a measurable goal but in attitudes constantly changing to ever more perfectly reflect the mind of God."

"That's what I like about you, Josh. You make even the most profound things simple. But what I can't understand is where you got such marvelous insight into things most people don't even give a damn about. Where did you learn it? Your whole life seems to be so finely attuned to God and nature that you walk through life as easily as a spring breeze floats through a forest full of trees."

Joshua continued to sip his wine. "I guess I just do a lot of thinking. I try to understand people and things and spend so much time alone that it gives me the peace and quiet to sort things out and put all of life together so it has meaning. That is the one thing most people don't take the time to do, and it is necessary if you are to find meaning to life."

"You know, Josh, I drink a lot. I wish I didn't, but I get so lonely, and living in the rectory with the pastor isn't easy. Sometimes I feel I'm not really cut out to be a priest, yet I feel so strongly called to the priesthood. I love the work. I love people. But I want so much to have a family and I feel that my whole spiritual life needs the support of a woman and a family if I am to grow as a person. I don't feel I have the gift of celibacy. I even have a friend I feel very close to and I feel guilty about it. Is it possible that God can give the call to the priesthood but not the gift of celibacy?"

"You have just answered that for yourself, Pat. Only the individual knows to what God is calling him. No one can dictate a calling or demand a gift that is not there. If God gives the call to the priesthood, but not the gift of celibacy, then others must respect what God has done and not demand more. Otherwise they will destroy what could be a beautiful work of God."

"But what if I know I have a call to the priesthood and also know just as strongly that I need to love someone who will love me and support me in my work? This need is so distracting that I cannot ignore it without it destroying me. It makes it almost impossible for me to do my work." Tears began to well up in the priest's eyes.

Joshua reached over and put his arm around the priest's shoulders and told him, "You are a good priest, Pat, and God has called you. You cannot compromise that. If my Father has not given you the gift of celibacy, that is his business, and your superiors should respect that. Tell the bishop and insist that he take you seriously and help you solve your problem. The Church must respect the way the Holy Spirit works, especially in the souls of priests, otherwise she will destroy her own priesthood. What Jesus has made optional, the Church should not make mandatory."

"But the Church will not allow priests to marry," the priest insisted, still pushing his point.

"Then you must struggle for change."

"But what about myself and my own situation? I want to be a good priest."

"Just try your best. God always understands if you try. Even if you fail, God still understands. But be careful not to shame your priesthood or damage the people's faith. If your conscience forces you to make a decision, God will understand. Doing the work of Jesus can be accomplished in many ways, and marriage is no obstacle to that work, and often, if a woman is spiritual, she can be a great help and inspiration. There are also many other

Christians who will need you and accept you. But do not be impetuous. Sometimes God works slowly and may want you to suffer the pain of loneliness right now so you can better understand the loneliness of others and be a better priest. It may be that in time God will free you from that pain, so be patient, Pat, and walk close to Jesus. When you are sad walk out into the meadow, and on the upper meadow you will find Jesus. He will meet you there. Talk to him and let him guide you. He promised, you know, and I promise you too."

"Joshua, I can't help but feel God speaks through you. You make me feel so much at peace. As I said before, for you everything is so simple. Even now you have answered something that has troubled me for years, and finally I see clearly. Thanks, Josh."

"I'm glad I helped," Joshua said.

By this time both were finished. Joshua started cleaning the dishes. The priest dried them. Afterward they went into the backyard. Joshua showed Pat the garden and pulled a batch of tomatoes that were beginning to ripen. He also picked some cucumbers and piled them in his arms as they both walked back into the house.

As Joshua was putting the vegetables into a bag, Father Pat asked him if he had any family nearby.

"My family have all passed on, I'm the only one remaining," Joshua answered casually as he continued putting the tomatoes into the bag.

"Josh, I hear you've been attending services at the various churches and I'm a little confused. I thought you were Catholic," the priest said curiously.

"I look upon all the churches as one family. I know God has no favorites. Religious leaders of each church feel their religion is the true religion. God doesn't view religion as structures. He loves people, and where people are trying sincerely to serve him and love one another, God is with them. God laughs at petty rivalries and ignores arrogant attitudes that make people think they are first in God's eyes. He looks upon all Christians as members of the same family who have never learned to get along, and who, like the apostles, are continually struggling for primacy. Each group of Christians expresses something different in what Jesus taught, but none of them reflects completely the spirit of Jesus.

"The Catholic Church shows a beautiful tenacity to the precise letter of Jesus' teachings, but it has missed the message of freedom that was so essential to Jesus' spirit, and it has done shameful things to enforce the observance of the letter of the law in its devotion to dogma. That was what the chief priests and the Pharisees did in their time. They failed to see the main thrust of Jesus' life, which was to free the human spirit from the theological prisons that religious leaders construct for people. Fidelity to the teachings of Jesus cannot be forced by threat of punishment. Jesus never wanted that. He wanted the human spirit to find him in freedom and to embrace him joyously and spontaneously.

"On the other hand, the other churches were wrong in tearing the body of Christ apart by their anger with Church leaders. They have been just as intolerant, even though they sincerely try to teach what they feel to be an important message of the gospel. Each of them, in their own way, stresses some aspect of Jesus' spirit, though they are frequently careless about things that Jesus was willing to die for. There is also an admirable love and spirit of caring and a simplicity among various Protestant churches that the others could do well to learn. That is why I feel free visiting all the churches. Would Jesus do any differently?"

"Joshua, sometimes I wonder about you when you talk like that. I still think there's more to you than just a wood-carver. Your vision far transcends the merely human mind. Joshua, who are you, really?"

"As you said this morning, you already know who I am. What more can I tell you than what I have said?"

The priest searched his memory in vain, trying to remember what he had said to him after Mass.

"One day you will understand," Joshua continued, "and your heart will rejoice."

At that point the priest started to leave and told Joshua he was going home to visit his mother and father, who were expecting him for dinner later on. As he started for the door Joshua handed him the bag of vegetables and told him, "Give these to your mother, I'm sure she can use them. She has a fine son. Your parents should be proud of you."

"Thanks, Josh. You're a good man and I appreciate your helping me. Have a nice afternoon."

The priest then left and walked out to his car, with Joshua, as usual, accompanying him to the gate. As he drove off Joshua went back into the house. He was tired. Last night's partying was unusual and he wasn't used to it. Today was busy, and even though he had enjoyed helping the poor distraught mother and entertaining the priest, it had been exhausting. Joshua fell down on his bed and in a few minutes was sound asleep.

10

DURING THE SHORT time Joshua had been in the village he had come to know a good number of people. He had, in his own way, become a celebrity, as almost everyone liked him and found his conversation stimulating. In a small village like Auburn you rarely come across exciting people, so Joshua stood out. His relationships with people were simple enough and uninvolved, but as he was friendly and outgoing, people easily engaged him in discussions about almost everything and found him knowledgeable about a wide range of subjects. And since religion is of almost universal interest, questions and discussions about religion came up frequently. It was about these matters that Joshua seemed to have the strongest feelings and spoke freely about whatever issues were brought up. But the things Joshua believed in so strongly, and which people found to be logical and sensible, were, as far as the current trends in religious thought were concerned, quite radical.

While most people found Joshua's ideas refreshing, and indeed beautiful, there were some of a more conservative bent who were deeply shocked, and even offended, by some of the things he expressed. His practice of attending services of different churches was beyond their comprehension. Some thought this to be an expression of liberalism, others thought it merely odd, and some wondered if it didn't show a lack of any strong religious convictions. The clergy, outside of Father Pat, had become familiar with Joshua more through rumor and occasional contact than by any serious encounter or dialogue. What they did see in him, or hear about him, they didn't particularly like. He came across as a free spirit who was more content to just shop around rather than commit himself to any particular church. They had heard he had carved a statue of Moses for a synagogue in the city and had even attended services there. At clergy fellowship meetings, when Joshua's name came up, he was the butt of jokes and wisecracks. It was reported that he was Jewish and might even join the synagogue. But it was surprising how well-known he had become in so short a time.

What was really troubling the clergy, however, were Joshua's freely broadcast convictions about religion. There were some well-placed lay people who were not happy with what Joshua had to say about the practice of religion in the churches, and because they were eager to ingratiate themselves, they were only too willing to bring tales back to their pastors. The reports made it look as if Joshua had criticized the pastors personally, which, of course, was not his way. However, it did serve to stiffen their attitude toward him, so for the most part they had already formed strong opinions of him without ever having met him or talked to him about any of these matters.

Joshua sensed this and realized there was nothing he could do about it. It wasn't the first time gossips had done serious damage to his work and reputation and ended up pitting the establishment against him. It is always that way with visionaries who are not afraid to think for themselves and dare to be different. They must be willing and prepared to endure misunderstanding and suspicion by those whose minds are too small to comprehend ideas that are beyond the ordinary. Their very existence is an annoyance and a threat to functionaries who are content to stick to the book without ever applying imagination to their work.

These were some of the thoughts Joshua was mulling over while he went about his work in the shop. But his meditation was broken by a knock on the front door. He put down his tools and went to see who was there. He was surprised to see two men, well-dressed, standing on the porch.

"Gentlemen, come right in," Joshua said to them cordially, then asked if he could do anything for them.

The men said they couldn't stay, just wanted to deliver a message. Would Joshua be kind enough to attend a meeting of the clergy association that was going to be held next Tuesday afternoon at two o'clock? Joshua said he would be very happy to attend. When he asked what the occasion was he was told that the clergy of the various denominations would like to talk to him. After delivering this message to Joshua the men left. Joshua went back to his shop to continue his work.

Interruptions in his work were becoming more frequent of late, and it was becoming increasingly difficult to finish his backlog of orders. As much as he disliked refusing work because of the joy his work brought people, he was beginning to let them know he could no longer keep up with the volume.

The week itself went by quickly, with nothing too eventful taking place other than a change in attitude on the part of some people who had previously been friendly toward him. He didn't know what had brought it about, but realized there was little he could do about it. He was still kind to them and acted no differently toward them than he usually did.

That Friday night he went to the synagogue as usual. His friend Aaron came and picked him up at exactly six-thirty. The people at the synagogue expressed a genuine warmth toward him and accepted him as one of their own. They did not know whether he was Jewish or not. It didn't matter. They liked him and treated him as a friend. After the first service Mrs. Cohen had told the rabbi that she had heard Joshua saying his prayers in Hebrew. The rabbi had promised to look into it, so he asked a close friend, Mike Bergson, to sit a discreet distance away from Joshua and listen to him. Mike was a Hebrew scholar and taught at the university.

At the service that night Joshua was aware of the man sitting in front of him, a little off to the side, and straining as if trying to listen to him. When the rabbi led the congregation, praying in Hebrew, only a few responded, Joshua among them. His voice was clear and unmistakable. After the service the man walked past Joshua, smiling at him as he did so. Joshua noticed him later talking to the rabbi, but was too far away to hear what he was saying.

When Joshua entered the social hall members of the congregation collected around him, forming their own little clique in the corner of the hall. The rabbi walked in with Mike Bergson. The two were still talking when Marcia, who had been a member of the statue committee, came over and stood near the two of them.

"Are you sure it was Hebrew he was speaking?" the rabbi asked Mike.

"Yes, Rabbi. I have no doubt about it. However, it is a form of Hebrew I am not familiar with. It seems to be a dialect of Hebrew no longer spoken, and if I wasn't afraid of seeming ridiculous, I would say it is Aramaic, the form of Hebrew spoken almost two thousand years ago. I can't imagine where he would have learned it."

In the meantime Joshua was busy speaking to his fan club. They had worked their way to the corner of the spacious room where there were sofas and comfortable chairs. Joshua was sitting in the rocking chair while the others formed a semicircle around him. The small group had come to know Joshua quite well, not only from the installation night, but from a talk Marcia had given to the sisterhood during the week describing the statue and discussing extensively the personality of the artist. She had done a good public relations job for him without even realizing it.

"Joshua, I know you are not a member of our congregation, but you showed such feeling in the figure you carved for us that we are convinced you are a deeply religious man," Mrs. Cohen, a plump, round-faced, middle-aged woman said to him.

Joshua merely smiled his pleasure at being accepted so readily by these people he loved so deeply. "You have all been very kind to me. You make me feel quite at home, as if I had always been part of your family," Joshua responded.

"When you carved that statue of Moses you expressed such deep religious feeling, I couldn't help but think you do a lot of thinking about God and religion. Would you share with us some of your thoughts?" It was a lady by the name of Mrs. Stern who asked Joshua that question, and it was a question that was right on target. This was just the opening Joshua needed to express his feelings about religion and what it should mean for people.

"I think it is important for people to realize that God's prime concern is people, not religious structures. They exist merely to channel God's word to people. But it is people that God cares about. He wants them to understand their lives and to find happiness. He wants nothing from them except that they allow themselves to grow. God's law is not a code arbitrarily imposed on people to restrict their freedom unreasonably. It was intended as a guide to happiness. Over the centuries religious leaders have twisted the law into a code that is irrelevant to man's nature and thereby restricts the natural freedom people should enjoy. This is what makes religion seem like a burden to people rather than something they should find joy and comfort in. This arbitrary restriction of freedom has given religion its bad name and, in fact, has given religion its name. The word *religion* means to 'bind up,' and that is just what God did not want to do. God created people to be free and to enjoy the existence he gave them. All that God wants is that we love him and love one another and in doing that, find happiness. It is all so very simple."

"That is beautiful," Mrs. Stern said. "I have never looked upon religion in that way before, yet God could not be any different than you just portrayed him. It is so simple when you look at life that way. You must really be at peace with yourself, Joshua."

At that point Marcia walked over and took a place in the circle directly in front of Joshua. He noticed her and smiled faintly. Marcia returned the smile. A man sitting next to Marcia by the name of Bernie Hauf asked Joshua a very pointed question: "Joshua, why do our people suffer so much?"

Bernie was a middle-aged man with strong features and eyes deeply set beneath his brow. He had known pain and sorrow in his short life and was always searching for answers. It wasn't the first time he had asked this question of guest speakers.

Joshua looked at him tenderly, expressing a warm affection for what he saw in the man. "Bernie," Joshua said, "you are still God's chosen people. Your destiny has always been tied up with God, who has used you to channel his blessings to mankind. But, as in times of old, when God was pointing in one direction and your people drifted in another, you suffered the pain of your alienation, so today when God points the way for your people and you go in all directions, many even denying his existence, God still lets you know he is concerned by allowing you to suffer again the pain of your alienation. You must remember, you are not free like other nations to choose your destiny. You belong to God in a special way, and you must allow him to guide you. When you realize that you will find an honored place among the family of nations."

Joshua's eyes moved toward Marcia. He couldn't help notice how beautiful she was. Her beauty was not only physical. Her mind was quick and alert, and beneath the genuine intellectuality of a highly cultured mind was a warmth and beauty of soul that was rare. Joshua instinctively loved her, and it showed in the way he looked at her. Again their looks met. Marcia did not look away, but tried to read what she saw in his eyes. There was a depth and a penetration in his glance that prompted her to turn away, but she would not. She was determined to understand him. She knew she was irresistibly drawn to him, though she could not understand why. She did not ordinarily react that way to men. Although she was capable of strong feeling, her career as an artist and a scholar so completely captivated her that interest in men proved little distraction. But Joshua was different. She seemed to find in him the personification of everything about her work that appealed to her. He was not just an artist, that was obvious. The way he carved showed a mastery of form and principles which had taken her years to master, yet she knew he did not learn these things from books or in a classroom. His understanding of nature and people and life forms revealed a knowledge that could not have been accumulated in one lifetime. His knowledge of people was too vast for his thirty years. Like Father Pat, Marcia had the distinct feeling he had been here before. His sense of history was too personal. It was experienced, not learned.

She saw in him the embodiment of everything to which she dedicated her life and could not help but be powerfully drawn to him. She also knew he was attracted to her, and although his eyes left her, she continued to analyze him. She could see by the way he treated people that he felt an intimacy with people that even members of families rarely felt. It was as if each person in some way belonged to him, as if he had known each one long before he met them. Each person's question he answered differently, as if he understood what each needed to hear, and each one responded accordingly. His mastery of the dynamics of group psychology was easy and graceful; he seemed to empathize with people's anguish in trying to understand life.

Marcia loved the way he handled people. The very simplicity of his understanding of life she found unsettling. As she thought of him she couldn't help but wonder what his personal life was like, what he did when he went home on a night like this to an empty house without even a telephone. He must be lonely. Why does he live the way he does? He is clearly not just in love with art or wood carving. He loves people too much to be contented with just that. What does he think of in the quiet of his thoughts in that empty house? Would he be terribly upset if she came to visit him some evening after he finished his work? At that moment Joshua looked at her. She felt he read her thoughts, and she blushed. But his look also seemed to say to her, "Come." In her heart she answered, "I shall."

All during this discussion Joshua had been talking. Now there was a lull. Marcia decided to ask a question. "Joshua, what do you think of God? This question has troubled me for a long time, and I never discussed it with anyone before. I am curious as to your feelings on the matter."

Joshua looked at her and took a few moments to compose his thoughts. How could he sum up in a few words his thoughts and feelings about a part of his life that was so intimate and so far beyond words to describe? "Marcia," he said, "before all else God is one. Moses stressed that point, and he was right. But it is important to understand that the unity in God's being is not like the unity in a human person. God is not human. God is unique and cannot be compared. However, God is simple, which is a part of his unity, but his simplicity is beautiful in that it can be seen in many facets and is capable of limitless expression. Every beautiful creation expresses some facet of God's beauty. Every prophet expresses something of God's presence. Jesus possessed in himself a unique reflection of God's infinite love for his people. Every delicate and powerful force in nature reveals a facet of

God's majesty. The vast expanse of space beyond the stars provides a hint of the unlimited comprehension of God's intelligence. And yet there is more to God than that.

"God's love is like the warmth of the sun, which touches every object in creation at the same moment, giving it warmth and light, and in touching knows intimately each one in the same instant. But God's love is also foolish, because he understands the difficulty we have in trying to grasp him, so he frequently manifests himself in ways we can understand, even at the risk of confusing us even more as to his identity. I think, Marcia, that you can best find God if you look within yourself. The most powerful revelation of God's presence and his love lies within you. If you take the time and talk to God, you will find him, and in finding him you will find the greatest joy of your life. He will reveal himself to you, and in possessing him you will understand all else."

"Joshua, that is beautiful," Marcia said, "but it is not easy to understand. I would like to talk to you about it again. I can see that you experience what you say and it brings you a lot of peace. That makes sense."

At that point a stocky man, an executive type, walked over to the circle. He had been watching and listening from a distance and seemed fascinated with Joshua. His name was Roger Silverman, another member of the synagogue's inner circle.

Roger stood near the outside of the circle and didn't ask any questions. He just wanted to listen. When the discussion group broke up Roger walked over and introduced himself. "My name is Roger Silverman. I already know you're Joshua. I've been hearing about you all week, and from listening to you talk I am quite impressed with your work and your involvement with people. I own one of the TV stations and would like to do a story about you if you wouldn't mind."

Joshua had mixed thoughts about publicity. Would it complicate his life and interfere with the limited purpose of his mission or would it provide good support for what he knew he had to accomplish? It didn't take long to decide. He calculated the advantages and disadvantages and made his reply.

"Where will the interview take place?"

"Wherever you feel most comfortable."

"As I have no car it would be difficult for me to come to the city."

"I will send the crew out to your place if that's all right with you."

"Fine."

"How about tomorrow?" Roger asked.

"You don't waste time, do you?" Joshua said with a grin. "Tomorrow will be all right. How about nine o'clock?"

"Okay, nine o'clock it is. The crew will be there right on time."

As Joshua and Roger were walking across the hall with a handful of people, the rabbi approached with Mike Bergson, who wanted to meet Joshua. "Joshua," the rabbi said, "I would like you to meet another good member of our congregation, Michael Bergson. He has heard some of your admirers talking about you and wanted to meet you."

"I am honored," Joshua said graciously as he held out his hand.

"I am the one who is honored," Mike responded. "The figure you carved for us is eloquent. Every time I look at it it speaks a different message. That says a lot for the artist who could put so much into a piece of wood."

"Thank you," Joshua said humbly.

"I must say, you also speak excellent Hebrew. I couldn't help but overhear as you were praying during the service. Where did you learn to speak so well?"

"I learned it from my family."

"You are Jewish, then?"

"Yes."

At that moment Aaron came over and offered to take him home. The conversation ended abruptly as Aaron had some business to discuss with the rabbi before he left with Joshua.

As many of the people were leaving they went out of their way to say "Happy Shabbat" to Joshua. Marcia said she would like to visit him some evening if he wouldn't mind. It seemed a bit forward, but Marcia was always independent and never ordered her life on the formalities of less independent women. Being involved in highly respected cultural and scholarly institutes, she felt comfortable with people so that what might seem forward to others was natural to her.

When Aaron finished talking to Rabbi Szeneth, he and Joshua walked out together. They still had a long trip home.

11

THE COTTAGE WHERE Joshua lived was no longer quiet and tranquil. People came to visit more frequently. Rumors spread about the dying girl who Joshua had cured. The television crew coming to town and stopping at Joshua's stirred enough talk for a month. He had become an instant celebrity. He was no longer the simple man who lived in the Van Arden cottage down the street. He was Joshua the sculptor and the man of vision whose ideas on religion and life had broken through to the big city. Orders for sculptured pieces came in large numbers, and his house was busy all day with visitors coming and going.

Even though he was trying to wind down his business, Joshua did commit himself to two large pieces because their influence would reach a number of people. They were works requested by two clergymen, one an Anglican priest by the name of Father Jeremy K. Darby and the other a pastor of a black congregation. His name was the Reverend Osgood Rowland. Oddly enough both men requested that Joshua carve a figure of Peter the Apostle, who was so warmly venerated by the early Christian community. Joshua told them that, although he was not taking any more orders, he would do these because of his own love for Peter and the influence the figures could have on so many people.

It was Father Darby who had approached him first. Joshua had been working in the garden, and was walking around the house with the hoe over his shoulder, when a highly polished black foreign car came rolling up to the front of the house. A chauffeur stepped out and opened the door for his passenger to exit. A huge hulk of a man flowed out of the back seat and pulled himself up to his full stature. He was a clergyman dressed in a gray suit and wearing a Roman collar. The man pompously strode over to the gate, which looked dwarfed in comparison to the man's huge frame. Joshua put his hoe against the fence and walked over to greet him.

"Is Mr. Joshua, the sculptor, at home?" the priest asked in an imitation Oxford accent.

Joshua extended his hand and, with a smile, said, "I am Joshua."

"You are Mr. Joshua?" the cleric responded with an almost hurt tone of voice. "But you are just a simple gardener. Surely there must be another Mr. Joshua who is the well-known sculptor?"

"I'm the only Joshua who lives here," Joshua responded. "I also carve wood. If I am the one you are looking for, I would be happy to assist you."

The priest looked over the simple surroundings and Joshua's very ordinary clothes. He seemed deflated.

"Well, if you are the only one, then you must be the one I am looking for. I had expected a distinguished man of the world with a certain elegance befitting his reputation," the priest said. "I am Father Jeremy K. Darby, rector of Saint Peter's Episcopal Church," he proclaimed as he put forward his hand for Joshua to do reverence.

Joshua, not knowing whether he was expected to shake it or kiss it, merely tried fitting his hand underneath it and held it briefly, then let go. The hand was listless, without character. Joshua felt a strange, creepy feeling in his stomach. "Would you like to come into my workshop?" Joshua asked courteously.

The priest bowed slightly his acquiescence and followed Joshua into the house. The chauffeur stood at attention near the gate. Joshua called to him and invited him too. The priest was taken aback by Joshua's violation of protocol, but as the chauffeur did not notice his boss's grimace, he accepted Joshua's invitation and came up to the house. Joshua extended his hand and gave his name, as the minister did not see fit to introduce a lowly inferior. "My name is Arthur, sir. I am honored to meet you," the man said with a real humility. The three men walked inside the house.

As Father Darby walked past the furniture he was careful to let nothing touch him, as if avoiding possible contamination. He looked around the room with disdain, questioning in his mind the ability of a man whose life-style bordered on poverty. Joshua was conscious of what was taking place but said nothing. They walked out through the kitchen and into the workshop. It was neat, but there weren't many carved pieces lying around and nothing to show off. The priest looked the place over, remarking, "Is this all you have? I thought I might see a well-appointed shop with the latest professional equipment and a room full of art work."

"Frequently real talent needs only the simplest tools to accomplish its work," Joshua said honestly and without sarcasm. "I do have all I really need."

The priest looked around and, seeing all he cared to see, turned back into the kitchen. "I hope I am not making a mistake in commissioning you to do this work for me," he said.

"I will do my best. What was it you had in mind?"

"A grand figure of the great Apostle Peter, a man for whom I have always felt a certain affinity and the greatest affection. He was the chosen leader of the apostles and was established by Jesus as the foundation of the Church. I envision him as a man of great proportions and equal dignity, not unlike myself, if I may be permitted to indulge in a little vanity."

"Yes, I can see there is a resemblance," Joshua told Father Darby with a smile, trying to be as serious as the comical situation would allow.

Joshua didn't dislike the man, but his mannerisms were annoying and, as much as he understood human nature, it was difficult for Joshua to converse with him because there was no way to break into the monologue. The priest's next remark was the payoff: "If you don't feel equal to the task, I would appreciate it if you would let me know now and I will look for someone else to do the job."

Joshua had no misgivings about his ability and assured the priest he could do the work for him. If he came back in a week, it would be ready for him.

As there was no further need for conversation, Father Darby turned and walked toward the door. "Come, Arthur," he said to his chauffeur. Joshua accompanied them to the door and walked up the path with them. The chauffeur made an attempt to exchange a final pleasantry, which Joshua did not miss, but as his employer made no similar gesture, he and Joshua just exchanged glances. The cleric did, however, manage a stiff "Good-bye, sir," before he walked over to his car.

As the car drove off Joshua picked up the hoe, which he had left leaning against the fence, and went back into the yard to finish his work in the garden. He thought about Peter for a long time, occasionally smiling to himself as memories crossed his mind. Yes, there were similarities between Peter and the priest. They were both pompous and taken up with themselves. They were both huge. But after that there was little else they had in common. Peter was a big man in other ways, too, which Father Darby was not. Peter had a big heart if not a big mind. Darby was cold and unfeeling. In his younger days Peter would have enjoyed having a chauffeur, but he was also the type who would have gotten just as much pleasure putting on the chauffeur's cap and taking the chauffeur for a ride.

During the course of these thoughts Joshua wondered how he should design the statue. He was almost tempted to use the priest as the model, but quickly dismissed the thought as mischievous. Peter certainly wouldn't appreciate it. Also, he wondered about the message the figure should project. Every work of art should have a message. Joshua thought for the longest time and, after tossing out a dozen ideas, finally decided just how he would carve the statue of the great Apostle Peter.

It was close to four when Joshua decided to take a walk up the road. It was a warm, sultry day, and he had been busier than he would have liked and needed to get away by himself for a while. Too many things were happening lately, and he had to sift through everything to see where it was all leading.

He walked up past Langford's place, but continued on so as not to break his meditation, stopping only occasionally to watch the birds playing in the trees or to look across the meadow and watch the wheat playing games with the breeze. As the gentle wind blew across the field of golden wheat it looked like flocks of sheep running through the meadow. He thought of people without a shepherd, then continued walking.

On his way back a small group of people confronted him. One of them, a woman, had spotted him from her window when he first started his walk. Like the Pharisees of old, she had been laying in wait for him and had found her chance. She called her cronies and they all gathered at the corner where they knew Joshua had to pass. The group didn't look sinister; it looked more like a casual meeting of friends. But this group had a purpose. They were middle-aged, mostly Catholic, intensely conservative, and deeply distressed about the radical changes taking place in the Church. Hearing Joshua speak on various occasions, and knowing his custom of attending different churches, Protestant as well as Catholic, their feeling about him bordered on something close to horror. He had spoken about Jesus coming to set men free, and that structured religions stripped people of the freedom God intended they enjoy. He was definitely not a healthy influence, and his lack of commitment to a particular church showed a real lack of religious conviction.

As Joshua walked down the road they came over and practically surrounded him, as if to prevent his escape. "We would like to speak with you, sir," spoke up a medium-built woman wearing blue jeans and a light blue print blouse.

"Would you like to come over to my house where we can be more relaxed?" Joshua asked calmly.

"No," the woman insisted, "what we have to say can be said right here. We are concerned about things we have heard about you and things that some of us have heard with our own ears and we don't like it."

"That is perfectly all right. I never felt that people always had to agree with me. They are free to do their own thinking," Joshua responded politely.

"You have been here in town for only a short time, and you have disturbed many of our people with your ideas and your unusual way of doing things," said another woman. "We are old-fashioned people from the old school and we are offended by what you said about our religion, about it depriving people of their freedom. You once made the remark that people who stick to the old ideas are incapable of growth, and that Catholics are stuck more on the external observances of religion than on loving God and their neighbor."

The silent pause after the woman's attack demanded an answer. Joshua looked at her and the others sympathetically. "Yes," he said, "most of what you said is true, but not quite the way you word it. Religion in the time of Jesus was not much different than it is today. Religious leaders may have had more power to punish people for violations of religious observances, but religious leaders have always felt that in some way they had a mandate from God to control people's lives, and even their thinking. When people don't obey they are made to feel they are disobeying God, and resisting God's grace, and jeopardizing their salvation. That is not healthy. God never intended that human institutions should have such control over people's lives. God made people free. They are his children.

"It is the function of the apostles and those who succeed them to guide the flock gently and to offer what Jesus taught. But it is not their place to dictate what people must believe or bully people into submission. That deprives people of their freedom as human beings. Nor should they demand more of people than God Himself. Religion is most beautiful when a person lives an ordinary life but motivated by a great love of God. Artificial practices imposed and added on as religion do not make a person religious or pleasing in God's eyes. That was the Pharisees' type of religion, which Jesus so vehemently rejected."

One lady remarked, "Well, I can go along with that. I always felt that we should be free to make our own decisions."

But another person took exception, saying the Church stands in the place of Christ, and what the Church teaches, man must obey.

Joshua admitted that the Church succeeded to the chair of Moses and the seat of Peter, as Jesus wished, but Jesus was also most insistent that his followers not imitate the practices of the Pharisees, who delighted in inventing elaborate practices for people to observe and transformed religion into observance of human traditions. When religious leaders do this they turn people away from God because people rightfully resent being forced to observe rules made by people and mandated as necessary for salvation. That is what Jesus was referring to when he told the apostles they should not partake of the leaven of the Pharisees, nor should they be like the pagan rulers who love to lord it over their subjects.

"Give us an example, sir," the same man insisted.

"Very well," Joshua agreed. "The Church demands that its members marry before a priest, otherwise the marriage is invalid. There is nothing wrong with marrying before a priest if that is what the couple choose. To demand it under penalty of invalid marriage and the stigma of immorality is another matter. If a couple marry without a priest, you say that marriage is invalid, and the couple lives in sin. They may be married for many years and have several children, but if one of them, at any time, walks away from that marriage, and the children, and comes with another lover to a priest, they can be married with the priest's blessing because the previous marriage was considered invalid.

"Or take a man who cares nothing for religion. He marries out of whim before a justice of the peace. Since he is a member of the Church, his marriage is ruled invalid. The same man marries five other women, and has children of each, then abandons each of them and all the children. He finally decides to marry a woman in the Church. This is easily arranged because the previous ceremonies were treated as if they never existed. It makes no difference that he left a flock of children behind. His new marriage is now blessed in solemn ceremony by the priest. Do you think this kind of legalism pleases God? It is the way the Pharisees conducted religion. Their laws and rituals were made with little reference to what pleased God.

"Or take the forgiveness of sins. Jesus intended this to be a great gift to bring peace to tortured souls. Religious officials turned that gift into a cruel nightmare that occasioned mental anguish for countless good but introverted people who found it psychologically impossible to lay bare their souls to another. Are they doomed to perdition because of this? It is this insensitivity on the part of Church officials that has taken the gifts of God and turned them into instruments of pain for people. Jesus intended forgiveness to be offered gently and with compassion, and not accompanied by humiliation from an impatient priest or in ways that would cause little children to urinate from sheer fright. What Jesus intended to be so casual and free-spirited they have encased in rigid rituals on scheduled times, as if the Holy Spirit worked on timetables dictated by humans."

The group was shocked by what they had heard. One or two listened with interest and were even inclined to agree. They had experienced similar happenings themselves, and knew Joshua was speaking the truth, but had never dared to criticize the priests or the Church for fear of committing sin. The others in the group were on the verge of rage. They had never heard anyone criticize their Church the way this man did. They had always been taught, and firmly believed, that the Church is the infallible voice of God.

"So what we have heard is true," retorted a stout, bespectacled man in his mid-forties. "You are hateful of the Church and you criticize her teachings and her laws."

"That is not true," Joshua shot back with fire in his eyes. "I love the Church, as Jesus loves the Church. It is his great gift to mankind, but there is a human aspect of the Church that needs constant correction and prodding to remain faithful to the spirit of Jesus. Mature Christians should not be afraid to speak their minds and out of real loyalty insist that the spirit of Jesus be followed. They are not servants in a household. They are the family itself, no less than those who like to rule. Jesus wanted his shepherds to be servants, not rulers, and the Christian people should not be afraid to speak. I say what I have said because I care that the Church be what Jesus intended it to be, a haven of peace, and a consoling beacon lighting the way, not a prison of the spirit or a sword that cuts and wounds."

What Joshua said did not smooth things over. They had never heard priests criticized this way before. Because it was done in the name of Jesus it was even more diabolical and cynical. He was evil, but in the guise of pretending to be a religious man. Either he was misguided or he was malicious in a devious and subtle way. One woman felt like slapping him in the face for his blasphemy. Another person expressed sorrow for the unhappy state of his soul and promised to pray for him. One of the men told him that he was a heretic and he would do all in his power to destroy his influence in the community.

One final question they had to ask him: "Why do you always go to different churches? Why don't you make up your mind and join one church?"

Even though the question was not well-intentioned, Joshua took no offense. He laughed good-naturedly, realizing that these people could never possibly understand. He answered simply. "I feel that Jesus loves people, not structures, and his people are not limited to Catholics or Methodists or Presbyterians. Wherever sincere people gather to honor God, God is in their midst, so I feel at home with them, whoever they are. Would you expect Jesus to do any differently?"

He was impossible. They couldn't make sense out of his reasoning. It was counter to everything they had been taught since childhood. They had to admit there was a certain beauty to the casual freedom he felt, but even that was dangerous because it was seductive. It was threatening to rigid concepts of faith and could weaken the faith of those already weak. His mentality would too easily appeal to the young, so they must keep their children away from him as something more dangerous than a disease. Their children already loved Joshua. That in itself was bad. They must never be allowed to go near him again. He could destroy their delicate faith. They didn't realize that he never talked about things like this to children. They couldn't understand. They were already free and beautiful, and he only wished the grown-ups could be more like them.

Joshua shook his head as they walked away, talking excitedly all the way up the street. As he watched he could see the long flowing robes of Pharisees and scribes. Their mentality was the same, only the setting was different—basically good people, but narrow and undeveloped, who must ultimately destroy what they cannot understand.

Later that evening the same group went up to the rectory and had a meeting with the pastor. Father Pat met them at the door and ushered them into the spacious living room to await the pastor's arrival. The young assistant was not one of their favorite people. He was too much like Joshua in his thinking, and it was only the good pastor's firm control that kept him straight. Father Pat knew they couldn't stand him, and the feeling was mutual. He had strange vibes about their coming to see the pastor and was curious about the purpose of their meeting. He knew it had something to do with Joshua, but wasn't exactly sure of their intentions.

However, after the pastor came and entered the room, closing the door behind him, it didn't take long before their loud voices revealed everything. It was not that Pat was eavesdropping. That was against his principles. But he couldn't help overhearing the whole conversation. His office was in the next room. The pastor's rising suspicions about Joshua gave easy play to what these people had to tell him. Pat was concerned. He knew no good would come from this. He felt torn. He loved Joshua but could do nothing to protect him from what he knew would come out of this meeting. He wished the pastor had invited him to sit in on the meeting so he could say something in Joshua's defense.

He himself knew that Joshua was harmless to a faith that was genuine. He was only a threat to a faith that was misguided and misdirected. He really loved religion and was deeply religious in a way that was authentic, even though he had none of the trappings of a pietistic person. Pat also realized that Joshua's understanding of religion was not blasphemous but, on the contrary, that he saw to the very core of what religion should be, an expression of people's healthy growth as human beings inspired by a deep love of God and humanity and all of God's creatures. As religion was, it was rarely healthy. But how could he tell the pastor that, because he wasn't healthy?

Joshua had eaten supper in the yard that night and, as usual, had entertained his four-legged guests. They were friendlier now that they were getting to know him. Even the skunk had become an accepted member of the group. But Joshua was not himself. Something was weighing on his mind, and he appeared depressed. The animals seemed to sense his depression and showed it, jumping all over him and pulling on his clothes.

But his mind was on other things. He was baffled by people. They find it so difficult to be tolerant or to open their minds to see another view of things. They cling so tenaciously to the things of their childhood, which they never dare to question. To hold to one's faith is one thing, but to hang on to mere traditional practices that do not really touch what Jesus taught shows a faith that is misdirected and also an insecurity and a fear that palsies any growth in real faith.

When Joshua finished supper and went back into the house, there was a rap on the door. He went to answer it and was shocked to see Marcia standing there. She looked ravishing in her kelly-green dress, which was soft and light and accentuated her sleek figure. Joshua's mood changed as soon as he saw her. His face relaxed and lighted up with a broad smile. The two of them embraced lightly and went into the house.

As he closed the door behind him he noticed a group of people walking down the street. It was the delegation just returning from the rectory. They had seen Joshua and Marcia embrace and the two of them go into the darkened house. Joshua only too well realized the implications.

Joshua was glad she had come. He was fond of Marcia and knew that she liked him, and he needed the comfort of a friend. It had not been a pleasant day, and Joshua could clearly see the way things were going. The future seemed ominous, and her coming was a welcome relief from the tension of the day and helped to dispel, at least temporarily, the gloom that had overtaken him.

As far as art was concerned, Joshua and Marcia had a lot in common. She was deeply involved in art and culture and philosophy and had so many questions to ask Joshua. She was probably not at all aware of how she really felt about him, and even though she may have originally been drawn to him for purely platonic reasons, each day the attachment became more intense. She found herself thinking about him frequently during the day and asking herself how he would feel about this or that idea or plan and wishing she could talk to him about it. Since she could not call him on the phone, the only way she would ever be able to enter into any kind of a relationship with him was if she came out to visit him. When she saw how happy he was to see her, she was glad she had come.

"Joshua, I hope you don't mind my barging in on you like this," she said in halfhearted apology.

"Not at all. In fact, nothing seemed to be going right today and I was feeling down. I'm glad you came."

"I know that you are an intense person," Marcia said, "and have profound ideas on many things. I treasure your opinions and the unique viewpoint you express. My own work is very demanding and I am asked for my opinion on a variety of topics. I don't feel adequate sometimes and I only wish I could discuss some of these matters with you. I know you could offer valuable suggestions. For example, the other day at the United Nations Culture and Art Committee meeting the question arose over political ramifications of the various types of art and culture. The Russian delegates felt that Americans were having too much influence on other peoples, thus affecting their political sympathies. They sarcastically suggested that American art is decadent and brings out the worst in people.

"My feeling is that the United Nations organizations should be a forum for the expression of each nation's feelings. If a people feel drawn to American art, or to Russian art, that is a good thing because it creates a bond between those two peoples. If another nation is unhappy about that, it is only because they feel threatened by people becoming attracted to a nation they oppose. But unless there is freedom of expression in the United Nations, how can it survive? Some Third World countries jumped all over me, and I left the meeting depressed. The meeting was an important one because we have to make a decision on what programs we are going to sponsor and fund for the coming year. Not being able to agree on something so basic was discouraging.

"I realize this is probably all new to you, and maybe out of your field, but I thought perhaps you might have some suggestions I could bring to the next meeting."

Joshua looked at Marcia, or, more precisely, seemed to look right through her. His thoughts seemed a thousand miles away. She wondered if he even heard what she had so carefully tried to express. Then, after what seemed an endless silence, he said to her, "Marcia, you are innocently involved in a struggle to control the human mind. What you propose as a way of uniting people is seen as a distraction from a dark and devious scheme to dominate the minds of simple people. You are dealing with forces that want to control people's thoughts by controlling their art and other forms of culture. Since these agencies are dominated by political considerations, you can't approach issues from a purely artistic or cultural prospective, but you must be as shrewd as a fox. My suggestion is that you propose the development of emerging art forms from one of the Third World countries that is neutral rather than lobbying for your own artists. If you do this, your opponents won't dare oppose you for fear of alienating emerging nations. Then, when your proposal is approved, you have won important allies and can plan more long-range goals with your newfound friends. It can all be done very nicely and discreetly, with no one realizing what you have in mind. In situations like this you have to have short-term and long-term goals to keep your opponents in the dark. You can accomplish more this way than by direct confrontations."

When Joshua had finished Marcia seemed impressed. "You are a lot less simple than you appear, Joshua. How does the saying go, 'Simple as a dove, and as shrewd as a fox'? I suppose that's the only way to outfox our opponents. It's worth a try. Now there is another question I want to ask you. It is more personal and I hope you don't mind my asking it."

Joshua nodded casually that he didn't mind.

"I don't know whether you realize it, but you have an extraordinary potential, not only as an artist, but also as a thinker and a philosopher. With the right connections you could have a devastating impact on society. I have already taken the liberty of talking about you to some of my friends, and they are anxious to meet you."

"Marcia, I feel honored that you think so highly of me. I am concerned about the healthy development of society, but each person is limited to the role in which he feels most comfortable. I don't look upon myself as one to influence the decision-makers of society but as a friend of ordinary folk, with whom I feel most comfortable."

"But, Joshua, you feel that way because you are so humble, and no one has ever pushed you to your full potential. I feel very close to you, and I can see that much of our thinking and feeling is identical. I really feel that, with the doors already open to me, we could do great work as a team. I know it's impetuous and presumptuous of me to intrude on your personal life like this, but I am very concerned about the problems of society, and we need men of vision like yourself to exert all the influence we can. I realize this is new to you, and you may not feel comfortable with it right now, but I do wish you would think about it and perhaps we could discuss it again."

"I promise to give it a lot of thought, and I would not be honest if I said it didn't have great appeal."

Having accomplished what she had intended by her visit, even though she had not succeeded, Marcia suddenly felt more relaxed. "I like your little house," she said as her eyes scanned the small living room. "It's a perfect setup for a bachelor, though it does look a lot more austere than I think you really are," she continued, trying to pry Joshua loose so he would reveal something about himself.

Joshua merely smiled at her playfulness. He liked that trait in Marcia so he went along with it and answered in equally playful fashion, "It is all I really need, and even though I would enjoy more artistic elegance and comfort, it serves a purpose in a practical way. I don't spend much time in the house anyway, so it never occurred to me to decorate the place. My dreams go a lot further than these four walls."

"You really dream?" Marcia said, surprised at this latest revelation.

"Of course, doesn't everyone? We would all love to see things different from what they are, and, being quite human, I am no different," he said.

"What do you dream about?"

"About people I meet, about things I would like to accomplish," he answered.

"I'm sure I never once entered one of your dreams," Marcia asked coquettishly.

Joshua smiled warmly. "Yes, I think of you, and I admire so many things about you. God has graced you with many gifts, and you are very dear to him because you allow him to use you as a partner in the work he has planned for your life. You are a rare person, Marcia, and I feel happy our paths have crossed."

She was hoping he would say something like that, and when he did her face lighted up. "I feel the same way about you," she responded. "I hope we can get to know each other better."

Marcia looked at her watch. It was getting late. She didn't want to wear out her welcome on the first visit. As she started to get up and leave she said to Joshua, "I hope you enjoyed your visit to our temple Friday night. The people feel close to you and look forward to seeing you. You don't know how impressed they were with your dialogue during the social hour. Are you coming this week?"

"Yes, I'll be there. It's just as enjoyable for me as it is for the people. I feel very much at home, thanks to all of you."

Marcia started walking to the door. Joshua followed, saying to her, "I'm very grateful for your visit. It picked up my spirits, and I will think over what you proposed."

As they were standing on the porch Marcia turned toward Joshua and tilted her head slightly, offering him an opening if he wanted to kiss her good night. He placed his hands on her shoulders and kissed her warmly on the cheek. She responded, embracing him and kissing him affectionately. They both walked up the path to the car.

A streetlight cast eerie shadows through the moving trees. Marcia stepped into her Mercedes, waving a last good-bye as she did so, and drove off.

As Joshua turned to walk back to the house he noticed the shadows of two figures across the street. They seemed to be two of the people who had accosted him earlier in the day.

12

By MONDAY MORNING gossip had spread all over town that a woman had stayed at Joshua's overnight. Though some disagreed and said they had seen a woman leave at a respectable hour, others denied it and insisted she stayed all night. When Joshua went to the store later in the morning, people were polite as usual, but he noticed a change. One woman, who was part of the group that had confronted him, was talking to another woman and every now and then would look furtively in Joshua's direction.

Joshua knew full well what was going on and that there was very little he could do about it. He was open and friendly as usual, and acted as if he was oblivious to all the undercurrents of rumors.

When he returned home he put away his groceries and went back to work. He finished up the little jobs and had already started work on Peter the Apostle. He had picked up special wood for the job, as he had to fit pieces together for a bas-relief. As the statue was more like a scene than a simple figure, he needed well-seasoned wood that wouldn't crack or separate when it was finished.

Later in the day he took a trip to the mill to get more wood. On the way he came across the children he had made the figures for. They turned the other way when they saw him. Joshua said hello to them, but they did not answer. He continued on his way and later returned home and spent most of the day working

on the figures. By late afternoon rough outlines were beginning
to appear.

On Tuesday he had his meeting with the clergy. It was held at
the social hall at the Presbyterian church. All the clergy in town
were there, including Father Pat. His pastor didn't attend these
groups. He felt the Catholic Church had the truth and there was
no point in fraternizing with ministers. The meeting started with
a prayer asking God's guidance on their work and petitioning
the Holy Spirit to use them as instruments of peace and love in
the community. Joshua bowed his head as they prayed.

"Joshua," the president of the group began, "we appreciate
your coming to this meeting. We feel it is important because
there has been considerable confusion since you came to town
and we would like to get some things straightened out before
the situation gets worse. We are concerned, first of all, with your
remarks about religion. From what I have heard you have been
critical of the way the churches practice religion. Is this true?"

"First of all," Joshua began, "I don't set out talking about
religious matters. People come and talk about many things, and
in the course of the conversation questions will come up about
religion. When they do I answer simply and matter-of-factly. In
fact, religion is not practiced the way Jesus preached it or intended it to be."

"Why do you say that?" Reverend Engman asked.

"Because religious leaders have imitated those characteristics
of Judaism that Jesus attacked so vigorously."

"Like what?" Reverend Engman continued.

"Like making religion an artificial observance of practices
contrived by religious leaders. Take the Christian denominations. It is not their following of Jesus that makes them different
from one another. It is the denominational practices that you
have created that make them different from one another and
keep them apart. This has brought ridicule on Christianity and
destroyed the united influence you could have on the world."

"I would agree to that," Reverend Engman responded.

But the others were not so agreeable. One of the ministers
asked him if he had any theological or scriptural training. He
had not. Where did he get his information from if he had no
training? The scriptures are quite clear to anyone who is willing

to read with an open mind, and history speaks for itself was Joshua's reply.

When the Presbyterian minister asked him why he went from one church to another and didn't join a particular church, Joshua replied, "I like to pray with all people who sincerely worship God. Each of your churches preaches a variation of what Jesus taught, but you have strayed far from his original message. Jesus prayed fervently that his people would be one, and you have torn it asunder with your bickering and petty jealousy. You have kept the Christian people away from one another and forced them to be loyal to your denominations rather than to Jesus. That is the great sin. You make null and void the teachings of Jesus and his commandment of love by forcing allegiance to your own traditions."

They were all stung by what he had said, and when Joshua finished there was an uncomfortable silence. In the course of the discussions that followed Joshua pointed out the history of each of their religions and their break with the body of Christ in order to start their own versions of what Jesus taught.

The meeting ended badly. The clergy were so angered by his stinging criticism of their denominations that it was difficult for them to be civil to him. They ended up by agreeing that Joshua would no longer be welcome in their churches until he made up his mind as to which religion he really belonged. Reverend Engman and Father Pat were the only two who did not go along with the consensus, and afterward they told Joshua privately that he was welcome in their church any time he wished to come. Father Darby had to leave the meeting early, so he was not part of the decision. Reverend Rowland did not attend these meetings, so he had no part in what took place.

Joshua walked home calmly, seemingly undisturbed. As soon as he got back to the house he continued working on his figures. He worked hard the rest of the day and the next few days, and by the latter part of the week he was well along on both figures. Though the subject of both statues was the same, the portrayal of each took an entirely different turn. In fact, the contrast was remarkable, as if the artist was delivering different messages through the different renditions of the same personality.

In the middle of the week the TV station aired the special program on Joshua. There were interviews with the artist in his workshop, scenes in the garden, and a beautiful pastoral scene of Joshua walking across the field with Joe Langford's sheep walking beside him. That was the first shot the camera crew took, because on their arrival Joshua was walking in from the meadow. It had not been staged, but it was so like him that it might have seemed so. There were also dramatic shots of Joshua carving intricate details of various figures. The highlight of the feature was the interview with Joshua himself in which he answered pointed questions about his life and his ideas. He was frank and honest as usual and became eloquent when speaking about religion.

When they tried to pin him down to which religion he belonged, he responded, "I feel very much a part of the whole Jewish-Christian tradition, and with the message that that tradition teaches. But that message has been fragmented and torn apart, so its clarity has been fogged by those who preach one message by their words and another message by their actions. I feel drawn to all those people who are trying to bring love and unity back into the human family, wherever I find them."

When asked about attending the synagogue services he answered that he enjoyed them and felt they were very much a part of Christianity because Judaism was the root from which Christianity sprang. His view of religion was stripped of all the fracturing pettiness that characterized most committed people's view of religion. He saw the overview of God's people trying in their own well-meaning ways to honor God and serve one another. He looked upon religion as people rather than as structures and saw no contradiction in being part of all believing people. It was very simple to him and, as one interviewer remarked, "an unusual point of view and quite beautiful."

When asked about the obstacles to unity among Christians, he was incisive and blunt. "Many religious leaders don't want it. They talk about unity and dabble in it, and feign attempts at oneness, but deep down they don't want to give up what they have so they postpone critical commitments to unity. They also contend that differences in belief are the great obstacle to unity. They say this because they presume purity of beliefs among their followers, which is false. People don't all believe what their leaders teach them, nor do all Catholics or Lutherans or Methodists believe the teachings of their bishops. Charity should be the first step to unity. Then, when people are worshiping together and working together as a Christian family, their love will make possible a unity of belief and a willingness to accept the guidance of Peter. There may still be some whose beliefs have strayed too far from Jesus' teachings. They will have to ask themselves where they really belong."

The whole interview lasted almost an hour and gave a fair picture of Joshua's life-style and a cursory glimpse into his unusual philosophy. The interview was well received and brought Joshua to the immediate attention of the religious leaders of Auburn. People from the synagogue thought it was a sympathetic portrayal of a sensitive, compassionate artist who was also a deep-thinking philosopher. They certainly did not consider him a theologian.

Christian leaders were divided in their reaction. Those whose denominations had little doctrinal content were impressed by his open-mindedness. Others found his mentality bordering on religious anarchy and a definite threat to simple believers. Father Pat said in his sermon the next Sunday that he thought Joshua to be a rare, authentically religious man and one of the few persons who truly understood religion.

There were some who thought Joshua was just another crackpot artist who was hooked on religion and had a big enough ego to peddle his own peculiar brand of it. Not too many took him seriously. Joshua became more the butt of jokes among the clergy than a serious threat.

The week passed rapidly and by Friday he was pretty well finished with the rough work on the figures and was well into the details. Friday evening Aaron came on schedule, and together the two men went to the temple. The evening was a happy one. People talked excitedly about the TV interview and congratulated Joshua on becoming a celebrity. They were proud he was their friend and exuded happiness for him. During the social hour he was more popular than the week before. His circle in the corner grew wider each week, and even the rabbi, who jokingly said he was a bit jealous, came over and joined the group. He and Joshua exchanged stimulating ideas, and, although they did not always agree, they respected each other and became very close. The rabbi whimsically remarked that night that he was even beginning to like the statue of Moses, and now that he was getting to know Joshua, could understand Moses better. Joshua laughed heartily.

Marcia's mother and father came to the synagogue that evening. Marcia introduced them to Joshua. They were proper, refined people. Joshua's casual dress didn't impress them, but Marcia had praised him so highly, they couldn't restrain their curiosity to meet him. It didn't take long for them to detect Joshua's innate refinement of personality, and they wondered, if he was not a rebel, why his dress was so casual and so unconventional. They came away with the distinct feeling they had met a person who seemed to walk through the world untouched and unspoiled by the greed and pettiness that poisoned the lives of so many. They sensed a purity and an innocence that was uncommon and realized their daughter had found a person much like herself. But the relationship confused them. They were practical people and could see nothing coming of it other than a broken heart.

On the way home Aaron and Joshua talked calmly and casually about a variety of topics and eventually came back to the same theme as the week before, Aaron's inability to feel the same way that Joshua did about life. Joshua told him he was too impatient. There really had been a big change in him over the past month, even though he didn't see it himself. This was the first time Joshua had seen Aaron's car not highly polished. Joshua laughingly said, "That's progress," to which Aaron replied, "I forgot about it."

Joshua told him he wouldn't have forgotten about it before, but now it wasn't that important to him. Joshua also heard, during the social hour, about Aaron hiring heads of poor families to work in his steel fabricating plant. Those incidents alone showed important changes in his life. We all have to be content with slow progress, Joshua reminded him. Human beings are like plants. They grow in stages and those stages can't be accelerated. In due time plants bear their fruit, and with human beings it is much the same. In the proper time and at the proper pace we grow into what God intends us to become. Events take place and strangers cross our path that force us to think. All these things God uses to teach us and suggest a different way of understanding things. So we grow, gradually, imperceptibly, under the subtle guidance of God's own spirit. Being conscious of our success is not important. The left hand shouldn't know what the right hand is doing. That can lead to vanity.

What Joshua said made Aaron feel better. He had done the things Joshua had heard about. He *was* a little less attached to his car. He even began to take little walks by himself and think about God. He found a real good feeling of peace when he withdrew into this world of the spirit. But he still felt he wasn't doing enough.

Joshua liked Aaron. He was a naturally good man with noble ideals, even if they weren't the same highly spiritual ideals that drove Joshua. These long weekend drives to the city and back had a big effect on Aaron's life. He never looked upon Joshua as belonging to a particular religion. Joshua was too big for that. Aaron saw him as a giant of a man whose life transcended denomination or religious affiliation. He was just a healthy person who had a supremely well-balanced view of life and whose relationship with God was well integrated into the fabric of his personality. To Joshua, God was like the air he breathed. It was so much a part of him that he didn't need to be aware of it. It was this carefree lightheartedness that had attracted Aaron to Joshua in the first place.

As he lay in bed that night Joshua's thoughts drifted across the centuries to the synagogue in Nazareth that he knew and loved so well. The whole scene passed vividly before his mind: the attendant handing him the scroll, the dead silence of the audience, the nervous reading of the text, "The Spirit of the Lord is upon me . . . to bring good news to the poor . . . to proclaim release to captives and sight to the blind; to set at liberty the oppressed, to proclaim the acceptable year of the Lord, and the day of recompense." It had been a hot, sultry morning, and the synagogue was packed. The air was tense. These were the people he had grown up with, and they were surprised at what they were witnessing. They weren't ready for it, and they resented it. "Is not this the carpenter's son? Where did he get all this from?" After a few brief moments the young preacher was being dragged bodily from the building. Only because of the confusion was he able to slip away and escape.

Tears came to Joshua's eyes as he lay there in the dark. "How different from the big-heartedness of the people at the synagogue this evening," he thought. These people responded in a way that was new and different from all his past experiences. He went to sleep feeling good, and grateful to his Father.

By Saturday morning the figures were taking shape. The one for Father Darby was almost finished. The one for Reverend Rowland was not far behind. Joshua spent the better part of the morning working on that one. Both figures were almost five feet high and wide enough to include considerable detail. Joshua worked assiduously, bringing meaning and messages out of the lifeless wood that were bound to cause conflicting reactions in the viewers. But that was what he wanted to do. Works of art that merely evoke admiration rarely stimulate the mind and have little effect on behavior. His work was, therefore, strongly suggestive, and no one walked away from his creations unmoved.

He worked late on Saturday and slept soundly that night. Early Sunday morning he walked down the back road to the Pentecostal church where Reverend Rowland preached. The building was a simple wooden frame structure. There weren't many people in the congregation; there weren't many black people in town. Some of their members came from a distance to attend services at this church, and they made great sacrifices to keep their community together.

When Joshua came walking up to the church Reverend Rowland warmly welcomed him and introduced him to the handful of parishioners standing with him. The minister asked Joshua how the statue was coming along. Joshua said it was coming nicely and should be finished by Friday. If he came late Friday morning, it would be ready for him. The man was delighted and made no attempt to hide his pride at the thought of having a figure of the Apostle Peter in his church. Even though statues were frowned upon, the minister managed to convince his people that Peter was a symbol of the rock foundation of Christianity and would be a constant reminder of the fundamentals of their faith in Jesus. The group felt all authority rested in the

Scriptures. The authority of religious leaders was merely human, and they were disinclined to place much authority in the Church. For them the Scriptures were the real touchstone of faith, not the Church. While this approach had its pitfalls in the confusion it occasioned over meaning of important parts of Scripture, and the splinter groups it gave rise to, the people themselves were simple and well-intentioned. Above all they took their faith seriously and were an inspiration to the rest of the community for the charity and honesty of their personal lives.

The service in the church was informal and joyful. The people sang and prayed aloud and gave touching testimonies to the wonders that took place in their lives when they gave themselves over to the Lord. Joshua was moved by the simple sincerity of the people. The minister welcomed the visitors and guests and singled out Joshua, the accomplished artist who was carving the figure of Peter the Apostle for their church. A lady prayed spontaneously for the Spirit to bless his hands, so he would put into the figure a message that would touch the hearts of everyone in the congregation. Everyone responded by proclaiming a loud "Amen."

After the service the people filed into the little hall that served at different times as classroom or meeting room. The friendly smell of coffee and pastry floated around the room, putting everyone in a congenial mood. A group of men gathered around Joshua and asked him how he liked their service. He was honest and told them of the thoughts that had passed through his mind during the service.

The Reverend Rowland also came over and told Joshua how happy he was to have him meet his people and that he was welcome to their service at any time.

The social hour ended and the group broke up. It had been a long session, almost two and a half hours in all. As Joshua walked home a handful of people walked down the street with him, then separated as they reached a corner, each going his own way.

Joshua spent the afternoon relaxing in his backyard. Pat Zumbar and Herm Ainutti stopped over with a friend they wanted Joshua to meet. His name was Woozie. That was not his real name, but it was what he had been called since boyhood so he still used it. He was shaped like Pat and could double for him in other ways. Woozie was earthy and practical, and his goals in life were simple. He had a gruff exterior but underneath was a kind man who would do anything for a friend. Joshua grinned broadly as he was introduced to him, as if he already knew all about him.

When the trio went into the kitchen Woozie eyed everything in sight. "You can tell a woman never touched this place," he commented. There was a coat of dust on practically everything, which was obvious to any visitor, though it was of little importance to Joshua.

"You really live alone?" Woozie asked, skeptical that a fellow as young and good-looking as Joshua really lived by himself.

"I'm never alone," Joshua countered, "but I am very contented living by myself. Some people can't live with themselves, and they find it impossible to imagine anyone else living by himself. When you are at peace you can enjoy the opportunity of living with your thoughts."

Woozie was interested in Joshua. "How come you moved up here all by yourself? You have to get away from someplace?" he asked Joshua as soon as they were all seated. "I can't understand why anyone would want to live in this godforsaken place," he continued.

"Maybe because people are so nice and friendly," Joshua shot back.

"That'll shut you up," Pat said to Woozie with a great belly laugh.

"You know, you're getting to be quite a celebrity," Herm continued. "I saw you on the television the other night. You should have been a politician, the way you handled the tricky questions. You looked right at home. Were you nervous?"

"Yes, a little. It was a new experience, but it gave me a good chance to say a few things I felt were important."

"You did a good job, even though I hate to admit it," Pat said.

"How come they put you on television?" Woozie asked.

Pat was quick to respond. "Because he's a good artist. He even carved a statue for a synagogue in the city. In fact, it's the synagogue Silverman belongs to, the one who owns the television station. I hear you've been going to the services every Friday night, Joshua."

"The people have been very gracious in inviting me, and I enjoy being with them. They are God's chosen people, you know."

"They were, you mean," Woozie interjected. "They had their chance when Christ came, and they blew it."

"They didn't all reject him," Joshua answered. "In fact, a great many of those who rejected him perished in the destruction of Jerusalem. Those who accepted Jesus took his advice and fled to the hills and were saved when the Roman armies came. The Jews of today are the descendants of Jews who lived throughout the Roman world. They never knew Jesus. Their descendants today are still God's chosen people. God never takes back what he gives."

The three men were surprised at Joshua's understanding of history. Even a historian would have been shocked at what Joshua just said because it revealed a knowledge of something historians would not have known.

Joshua took the men into the shop. It was cluttered with a variety of pieces in different stages. The two figures of Peter the Apostle stood out, and Woozie asked about them.

"They are both of Peter the Apostle," Joshua said, "for two different churches."

The men were impressed. Even Woozie, who prided himself on his ability as a craftsman, admired the perfect detail of Joshua's work.

13

JOSHUA WORKED HARD all the next week, trying to finish the figures of the Apostle Peter on schedule. Monday afternoon two boys from a local commune came to visit Joshua with a tale of woe. They and their friends had a little farm that they had been working. Their equipment was primitive and not in good shape. This morning, while they were working, a wheel on their wagon broke. They tried to fix it but couldn't. Would Joshua be kind enough to help them? They brought the wheel with them. Joshua looked it over and smiled. It brought back faint memories of so long ago, when he was just a young apprentice working for his father.

"Yes, I can help you," Joshua told them. "Come back tomorrow and it will be ready for you."

The free spirits left and talked about Joshua all the way home. He was freer than even they were, yet his life seemed so well-ordered, unlike theirs. They sensed a peace and a contentment in Joshua that they lacked, and also a joy that they had never known. Their simple life came from a discontent with society, and it didn't bring them the peace they thought it would. Joshua chose the simple life, obviously because it gave him the freedom to expand the breadth of his inner life. Externally his life and theirs were much the same. Internally there was a world of difference. They envied him.

Joshua worked on the wheel during the breaks in his other work. It was less tedious and even relaxing. He hadn't worked on a wheel in ages, and a train of memories flooded his imagination. Now and then a tear collected in his eyes as he thought of tender memories of long ago. They were good days, when he was just a boy learning about life. His mother was never far away, sometimes hovering over him like a mother hen, too protectively, as if some impending calamity would occur at any moment. His mother was a happy person, always humming to herself as she went about her household chores. He could hear her out in his father's shop. He remembered his father remarking one day, when they were carving an ox yoke, "How come your mother doesn't sing like that when we're around the house?" They both laughed. He remembered his mother forever trying to keep him away from bad companions. She never had much success. How many things have happened since then!

Joshua had to send for Woozie to help him finish the wheel. He needed the iron band welded. Woozie came and asked Joshua who the wheel was for. When Joshua told him he went into a tirade about those weirdos who don't know whether they are men or women. Joshua just listened and helped as Woozie welded the band on the wheel.

When Woozie left Joshua went back to the two figures. He had come a long way in the past week, and in another couple of days he would be finished.

The next day the boys and two of their friends came for their wheel. They talked with Joshua for over an hour, trying to understand something of his life. "You seem to have achieved in your own life something we struggle for constantly, but it always evades us, and that is peace and contentment. What is your secret, Joshua?" a tall, lean young man with full beard and overalls asked him.

"My peace comes from within," Joshua told them. "The simplicity of my life reflects what I possess inside. The simplicity of your life does not come from within. It is an escape from the world around you, a denial of what you have been a part of and been hurt by. I have no such problem in my life. I do not let myself be hurt by events. I realize all humanity is in a process of growing and, of necessity, will always be imperfect. It can never be any different. I understand that and accept it, and love people for what they are, and I find them enjoyable because our Father made them that way. Find God and learn to love people, and you will find the same peace and harmony with nature."

The young men were impressed, even though he criticized their values. They appreciated the insight. They thanked him for spending time with them, as well as for fixing the wheel. Each of the four fellows had a gift for Joshua. One was carrying a rooster under his arm, another a fat hen. One of the others had a jar of jam his girlfriend had made. The fourth had a basket of eggs and a small bag of flour he himself had ground. They were all deeply grateful to Joshua for what he had done for them. Joshua told them about Woozie welding the band. When they heard Woozie's name they were amused. They knew Woozie. They had had more than one encounter with him. They laughed over Joshua conning Woozie into doing a job for them. They took the wheel and left, rolling the wheel down the street as they went. Joshua watched them, smiling.

He went back into the house and worked zealously on the figures. He knew things about Peter no one else could ever imagine and incorporated them into the personalities emerging from the lifeless wood. Each figure was strikingly different, so much so that, although the features were perfectly similar, the character traits were so paradoxical that they gave the feeling of two different persons. That was the way Joshua had planned it. There were two distinct messages he wanted to express through these statues, and there was no mistaking them. Whether they would be understood by the two clergymen was another matter, and if they understood them, would they accept what they saw? But Joshua continued to work, chiseling away at all the fine details.

By Thursday afternoon he was finished with both of them. He sanded them down to a satiny smooth finish, then stained them with a deep color that brought out the rich grain of the wood. He then waxed them and set them aside. These were to be the last of the masterpieces Joshua was to create. His life was becoming increasingly complicated. His personal life was simple enough, but people would not allow his life to remain that way; their varied reactions to him were too intense. And there were some who did not feel at all comfortable with his presence in the community. They were determined to do all they could to get rid of him.

Joshua slept soundly that night, but dreamed strange dreams: of Nathaniel cynically questioning his origins, of James and John conniving for positions of authority, of Peter fearful of being identified with Jesus, and Judas meeting with temple officials. All the human weaknesses of the apostles that would forever be ingredients of those who shepherd his people. As they gave him trouble then, so the pattern would be repeated again. As long as people were human he would be too much for them to cope with. He complicated their lives too much, just by being himself.

Joshua woke up early. Birds were singing outside his window. He sat at the edge of the bed with his head in his hands. He was still tired. He had slept soundly enough, but the intensity of his dreams had drained him. He finally pulled himself up, dressed, and made breakfast. He didn't take his walk that morning. He puttered around his garden, harvesting the ripened vegetables, which had grown large and full. There wasn't much time left. He had planned his garden well, and was now picking what little was left of the first big crop.

While he was still working he heard a car pull up in front of the house and voices exchanging greetings. He walked out and saw the two clergymen coming up the path together.

It was Father Darby who spotted him first. He couldn't resist the remark that jumped out as he saw Joshua again with his garden tools, "Well, our famous artist has been working in the dirt again. I can't help but feel you would have made a better gardener than a sculptor. It seems you enjoy it more." The Reverend Rowland was shocked at the priest's behavior.

"The earth is where all life originates," Joshua countered, "and even the best of us can never be so proud as to believe we're above it. It is very much a part of us all." The black minister thought that was a fair rebuttal and justly deserved. The priest didn't accept it too graciously and his face showed his disdain.

Joshua walked to the porch and opened the door for the two men. Then, excusing himself, he returned to the living room carrying one of the figures. He left again to get the other one. When he brought it in the men were struck by the similarity of the features, but did not understand the wide difference in the bas-relief scenes. Neither had known what the other had commissioned.

The priest eyed the one he thought was his and admitted Joshua did not do a bad job—for a gardener. Joshua smiled at his attempt at humor.

"Gentlemen," Joshua said, "I was not expecting you to come together. It is a coincidence that both of you ordered a likeness of Peter. I tried to honor your requests and carve what I thought would be aspects of Peter's personality that would be of significance to your people." Taking the sculpture depicting Peter on his knees, caressing the head of a dying beggar, his three-tiered tiara lying disrespectfully on the ground, he lifted it up and placed it near the Episcopal priest. The man was horrified and deeply offended. "That is not the great Apostle Peter but some pious servant saint whom I do not even recognize," the priest said angrily.

"On the contrary," Joshua said, "that is Peter at his greatest. It was not part of Peter's personality to serve. He was born to rule, and that dominated his whole personality. As he grew spiritually to more resemble the Master, and realized his real role as the servant of God, he became much more humble in his attitude toward those he considered inferior. This figure depicts the moment in Peter's life when he had finally overcome nature and realized what Jesus meant when he washed the feet of the apostles and told them they should be the servants of God's children."

The priest was impressed with Joshua's logic, but unmoved by his explanation. He was still angered by what he saw, as if Joshua had hit him with a sledge hammer. The other clergyman was just as dismayed by the other figure, which he realized was his. He could understand the one Joshua had given to Father Darby, but this one was incomprehensible, with Peter standing in toga and stole, his left hand firmly gripping a shepherd's staff and his right hand gesturing with great force and determination to a crowd that included, obviously, the other apostles. It was everything about the Church that Pentecostals dislike, particularly the strong authority. Reverend Rowland was very uncomfortable with the scene. When Joshua placed it near him he was embarrassed.

"Joshua," Reverend Rowland said as politely as he could, "I think, perhaps, you have made a mistake with these two figures. It seems that Father Darby would be much more happy with this statue, and I love the message in the one you did for him."

"If each of you likes the other's statue," Joshua replied, "I have no objection, you may exchange them."

The two men exchanged statues. Reverend Rowland took out his checkbook and wrote out a check for the exact amount he and Joshua had agreed to, $100. Father Darby was surprised.

"Why is the sculpture you made for me so much more than the other one?" the priest asked. He had agreed to pay Joshua $135 for his figure. Joshua didn't charge the Pentecostal minister as much because he knew his congregation was poor, and it would be difficult for them to come up with much money.

Joshua looked at Father Darby with a trace of impatience. "Did we not agree that a fair price would be one hundred and thirty-five dollars?" Joshua asked him. "If you want to exchange costs between you that is your right, but that is between the two of you."

The priest was visibly angry, but was reluctant to show his pettiness in front of the minister, who, in his heart, he looked upon as inferior both professionally and socially. He merely told Joshua he would receive his compensation in the mail, as all his church bills had to be paid through the proper channels.

With that both men left, carrying their statues with them. Joshua accompanied them to the gate, where the chauffeur met his master and relieved him of his burden. The priest apologized to the minister for not being able to give him a ride, as there was not sufficient room in the car. Joshua watched both of them with an impish smile, as if he was aware of something no one else knew. He had carved those statues for a reason and that reason was not going to be frustrated, no matter how those two men felt about them. He went back into the house with a sigh of relief.

The workshop looked bare with the big carvings gone. Joshua went to work on several small pieces he still had left. When he finished them he set them aside. There weren't many left. It was almost three-thirty when Joshua finished the day's work.

It was Friday and Aaron would soon be over to pick him up. He quit early to prepare supper so he could be finished by the time Aaron came. While he was getting ready he was interrupted a number of times by people who came to pick up their pieces. They were all grateful for what he had done for them and for the reasonable prices. One man came in after the others had left. His name was Dick De Ratta. He had ordered a special piece as an anniversary present for his wife. He had liked Joshua ever since meeting him at the mill one day when he went to get some wood. The two would meet every now and then and talk about a whole range of things. Dick taught history at the university and practiced law. He was fascinated by Joshua's intimate knowledge of historical events and his ability to give unusual slants to events that differed radically from what was accepted by historians. Dick's respect for Joshua's judgment was such that he incorporated many of Joshua's interpretations of history into his courses. What Joshua said made sense and provided a better logic to the underlying social and political currents that criss-crossed through history. They seemed to provide the missing link between many heretofore unrelated facts.

Dick belonged to the Presbyterian church in the village. He was active in the congregation and, being a friend of the pastor, was privy to much of the "official" gossip around town. Joshua was a topic of that official gossip of late, and it had Dick worried. He was torn between loyalty to the inner circle of his parish and his friendship with Joshua, who he saw as very much alone in the community and quite vulnerable. Dick had heard things about Joshua he didn't like, but was confused as to what he should do about it. He finally decided to tell him in a way that would not violate his loyalty to his pastor and, at the same time, perhaps help Joshua.

"Joshua," he said, "I know you, and I understand your feelings about things. I know you share my own misgivings about religious leaders' abuse of authority. But you are in a much more difficult position than I am. I can talk about religion within a framework of history and disguise my criticism. When you express what you think it is looked upon as just that, an expression of your own personal views, and people judge you from where they're coming from. Most people do not have much understanding of things, and they are shocked by rumored versions of what you were supposed to have said. Unfortunately it gets back to the pastors, who are none too pleased with what they hear."

Joshua listened attentively. Dick was right. This was always the problem. Joshua spoke honestly, the way he believed about things, and few people had the experience necessary to understand him. But it was still important that he say it. At least people would be forced to listen and think about what he said. In due course it would have its effect, but unfortunately it would not be until after he was long gone.

"I know you are right, Dick," Joshua said, "and I appreciate what you're telling me. I've thought a lot about what I should do and say, and always come back to the same conclusion— nothing that I say will be heard or understood in the same way by those who hear it. But that is true of everyone's ideas. Mine are no exception. The difference is that what I have to say affects people's lives, their children's lives, and their relationship with God. They must have a clear understanding of these matters, so I really don't have much of a choice. In time, when the wind dies down and the chaff is blown away, the kernel will remain. But it will always be that the prophet is the first victim of his own message, and only later do people say, 'Oh, now I understand.' But he is already gone."

Dick listened in admiration of Joshua's insight and his cool courage in the face of approaching storms. It showed that this was not the first time Joshua had been through situations of this type. He turned his attention to the work of art Joshua had carved for him. It was a figure of a man standing near a fence playing a flute. Little children were looking away disinterestedly, while birds sitting along the top of the fence listened attentively. A woman stood near the fence looking admiringly at the man.

Dick recognized his family and couldn't help but laugh at Joshua's insight into the problems he was having at home. "Joshua, how clever," he said, "and perfect in every detail! How do you find the patience to work on such minute details? It would drive me to distraction, even if I had the ability."

Dick tried to pay Joshua for the work, but Joshua wouldn't hear of it. Dick had said it was his own anniversary present to his wife, and he wouldn't feel right if he didn't have some part in it at least paying for it. The love Joshua expressed in the work was itself a treasured gift to both him and Elizabeth. And he hoped the kids would get the message. Dick was so appreciative, he gave Joshua a big hug, and tears ran down his cheeks at the thought of Joshua understanding his family so completely and the affection shown in the carving.

He picked up the carving and shook his head in bewilderment as he walked toward the door with Joshua. They went outside together. Dick chuckled as he got into his car, thinking about what his wife's reaction would be when she saw the gift.

Aaron came on time. His car was washed and shining again. He did it just before he came because he knew Joshua would notice. Joshua was waiting on the porch and walked toward the car as soon as Aaron stopped. He was embarrassed whenever Aaron got out of the car to open the door for him. This way he could avoid all the fuss. "I'm glad you cleaned your car," Joshua said as he got in. "I couldn't imagine what it would look like after not being cleaned for two weeks."

Aaron laughed. "You're sharp, Josh. Why do you think I had it cleaned? I couldn't drive a fashion model like you up to the synagogue in a dirty car."

Joshua slapped Aaron on the knee. "I earned that one," he said good-humoredly.

On the way Aaron confided an interesting bit of information to his friend. A group of well-placed persons in the synagogue had approached the rabbi during the week with a proposition. Lester and Marcia and a few others were behind it. When Joshua asked him what it was Aaron beamed but said he couldn't tell him. It had to come from the rabbi. He just hoped that Joshua would be amenable to the proposal. Joshua didn't pry any further.

When they arrived at the synagogue they were, as usual, greeted warmly. Aaron left Joshua by himself and an unfamiliar man walked over and introduced himself. He heard Joshua had been coming to the synagogue each week and was warmly received. He didn't like it one bit. That was why he had come this evening. He and his family had been persecuted by Christians as long as he could remember, and he couldn't stand the thought of a Christian being welcomed so cordially by his people. He accused Joshua of a whole variety of charges, saying that he shared the guilt of all the people who had persecuted his people and killed them in the concentration camps.

Joshua pitied the man's tortured spirit and felt it would be cruel to counter him. Then, impulsively, to the man's utter disbelief, Joshua put his arms around him and hugged him intensely, asking him for forgiveness for all the meanness his people had done to his family and all other Jews throughout the centuries. The man was so overcome by the sincerity of Joshua's compassion that he broke down, threw his arms around Joshua, and cried like a baby. In a moment all the bitterness and rage had left his troubled spirit, and his body went limp with the release of years of pent-up hatred and sickness.

People who knew the man and had avoided him because of his bitterness were dumbfounded at the change that came over him in that brief instant. Everyone watched as the two men walked into the sanctuary, hand in hand. The incident was not soon to be forgotten.

The man sat with Joshua during the service and was shocked when he heard Joshua saying the prayers and singing the hymns in perfect Hebrew. After the service they walked out together. When Joshua's admirers gathered around him for their weekly conference, the man joined the circle and found Joshua to be a beautiful person in his understanding of human nature and his insistence that people will find peace only when they are ready to lay aside pettiness and prejudice, even those prejudices that have been consecrated through the passing of centuries. Only an open mind is capable of developing the attitudes necessary for peace. The things of this world cannot give peace; it must come from our ability to rise above material things and reach a point where we don't crave them. Even God's people must realize that each people is chosen by God to fill a different role in the destiny of the human race, and only by accepting other peoples as equal partners in God's plan can they hope to find acceptance by the rest of the human family.

These were bold ideas that Joshua put forward. But as strong as they were, some of the older men and women, who had suffered much in their long lives, were shaking their heads thoughtfully and knowingly. Where you want to find love and acceptance, you may first have to show love and acceptance, because love can be returned only when it is given. No one took offense at what Joshua said. They had come to know him and realized that what he said had great depth of thought and feeling and came from a profound understanding of life. Everyone was willing to listen to what he said, and many were inclined to agree.

One of Woozie's friends was at the service that night, a man by the name of Phil Packer, and his wife, Ada. They unobtrusively joined the little circle. They came over with Marcia, who was a friend of the family. During the discussions they did not take part, just listened. Marcia almost said something a couple of times, but realized her questions would have been of little interest to the others so she didn't ask them.

When the social hour was over Marcia introduced Phil and Ada to Joshua. They became fast friends. Phil was open and outgoing. He joked with Joshua right from the start. "How did a nice guy like you ever get to be good friends with Woozie?" Joshua laughed.

"Rather easily. With Woozie what you see is what you get. There's no guile, no deceit. There's no fine print, no hidden pages. There should be more people like him."

"You really like him, don't you?" Phil asked, not too surprised.

"Why shouldn't I?" was Joshua's simple return.

"Just testing. You're okay, Josh. You're my kind of man too. If ever I can do anything for you, just call, and I'll be there." When Phil said that, that was the seal of friendship. He and Woozie, and the Sanders and, in fact, the whole gang, were much the same in their code of honor. It was real. It was sincere and it was rugged love. Joshua thought of the apostles and the rough ways and shocking language when they thought Jesus wasn't listening.

While they were talking Aaron came over, waited till they stopped talking, then told Joshua the rabbi would like to see him. A broad grin lighted up his face, and when he noticed Marcia he winked, as if she would know what it was all about.

The rabbi's office was well-appointed. He was a scholar, and most of the books that lined his walls he had already read, not like so many who buy books for decoration. A russet-colored shag rug stretched from wall to wall. Deep maroon, velour-covered chairs flanked the rabbi's desk.

When Joshua entered the rabbi stood up and welcomed him. He offered a chair to Joshua and both men sat down.

"Joshua," Rabbi Szeneth began, "I appreciate your coming to see me. I know Aaron takes you home every Friday night so I won't keep him waiting. What I have to say won't take long, and I hope you will be able to oblige me."

Joshua listened as the rabbi continued, "Our people have come to love you over the past few months. They are very impressed with your little talks each week. They have never met a person quite like you, and I must admit, I share their admiration. You have been an inspiration to all of us. During the week some of my board approached me and asked if you could be allowed to speak to the whole congregation. I was happily surprised because the same thought was going through my mind, but I was a little reluctant to suggest it. I told the group there would be no objection and that I thought it was an excellent idea. They asked me to discuss it with you and ask if you would be willing. So, Joshua, my dear friend, I would be honored if you would accept our invitation to speak to our congregation at next Friday's service."

Joshua beamed his delight. Tears came to his eyes as his thoughts went back to a similar invitation so very long ago. "Rabbi, you have no idea what this means to me," Joshua said. "I am the one who is honored by your warmth and goodness. I would be more than happy to speak to our people next Friday."

"Is the notice too short? Do you need more time to prepare?" the rabbi asked.

"I need no time to prepare. I have been preparing for a longer time than you could imagine."

"Well, it's all set then, next Friday night." The two men shook hands, and the rabbi walked out with Joshua.

14

JOSHUA WORKED ALL day Saturday, finishing most of the remaining jobs. They were neatly arranged along the top of the workbench. Late in the afternoon, lying under the tree near the pond, he thought of the talk he was to give at the synagogue and smiled at the chain of recent events that had brought about this startling decision. He thought about the synagogue and others he was familiar with. They hadn't changed much through the centuries. They are still constructed much the way they used to be. Men and women sit together now. The scrolls are still enshrined in the ark, though they are not used anymore. Lectors read from printed versions. There are no scribes or Pharisees, or priests strutting around in flowing robes wearing broad phylacteries, looking like peacocks among the common people. But common people are not too common anymore either. He thought of the man who accosted him at the synagogue last night and reminisced about the man with the speech impediment from whom he had driven the devil. Devils were more visible in those days. Today they are subtle, disguised as advanced, compassionate thinkers who want to revolutionize society, sowing seeds of doubt about all that is sacred, or as religious leaders inciting their followers to hatred of their fellow man and even murder in the name of God.

Then he thought of Marcia, her work at the United Nations, and the good she was trying to accomplish among so many whose objectives were dubious. She stood out as a pure and innocent dove among a pack of vultures. Perhaps the beauty of her innocence would melt more hearts than the most devious political maneuvering. He thought of Mary of Bethany. Marcia was different, though they both loved with the same intensity. His feelings for both were the same.

Returning home, Joshua encountered a young boy walking off the porch. They met at the gate.

"Can I help you, young man?" Joshua asked.

"The pastor, Father Kavanaugh, wants you to come to the rectory. He wants to talk to you," the boy answered.

"Now?"

"No, he's busy now, and tomorrow he's busy. He'll see you on Monday morning at nine-thirty."

"Thank you, son."

The next morning Joshua went to the Episcopal church for Mass. Father Jeremy offered the Mass and spoke about the new statue of the Apostle Peter, which had been installed in the niche at the side altar. Joshua noticed the English flags all around the big church, betraying the denomination's focus of allegiance. He tried to pray, but found it difficult. The music distracted him beyond even his own power of self-discipline. The organist, Mr. Walls, pounded out in mechanical perfection two-hundred-year-old hymns from another continent and another part of history. The service was technically perfect, but worship rang hollow. Father Jeremy went on orating in well-cadenced elegance about the moving symbolism of the liturgy and how wise the Church was in incorporating artistic richness into the liturgy. It was a fitting tribute to the awesome majesty of God.

Joshua was glad when the Mass ended. The chauffeur met Joshua outside the church and made a big fuss over him, pointing him out to all his friends and introducing him as the artist who had carved the new statue. The people were nice to him, and congratulated him on his ability, and asked how he liked their church. Joshua told them the ritual was beautiful and he had noticed some people in church who seemed to be deeply absorbed in worship and felt they were the source of blessing to their community.

At that point Father Jeremy emerged and heard Joshua's remarks. Joshua turned and greeted him. The priest stayed where he was and merely nodded curtly, waiting for Joshua to come up to him, which he did not do. The priest turned and began talking to other people who were waiting for him. When the chauffeur saw the priest coming out of the church, he slipped away.

Joshua walked down the street. Some of his friends were leaving their churches and they stopped to greet him. Phil, the manager at the mill, came over and put his arm on Joshua's shoulder. "You're just the man I wanted to see," he said. "How about coming over to my house for breakfast?"

"Okay," Joshua replied, and the two men walked over to Phil's family, who were walking down the church steps. They all walked around the corner to the house.

When they went inside Phil took Joshua into the living room while his wife cooked breakfast. He had a few questions he wanted to ask Joshua. He hadn't seen Joshua lately and had heard all kinds of rumors. Was Joshua all right? How was his business? He hadn't been using as much wood lately and Phil was worried that he might be having problems.

Joshua was at a loss as to how he should answer. Yes, things had changed considerably of late. He had been very busy filling orders for people, but other aspects of his life were beginning to take precedence over his carving, and he wasn't taking any more orders.

Phil knew some people were making life difficult for Joshua and tried to reassure him that the majority of the people loved him and supported him.

Joshua told him he could read the signs of the times and could pretty well tell how events were shaping up. He told Phil not to be concerned, he was confident of the future.

The delicious odor of pancakes and sausage and bacon filled the house. Ellen, Phil's wife, called everybody to the table. Joshua went in with Phil and sat next to him at the table. The serious talk stopped, and after prayers everyone dug into breakfast. The hot coffee smelled good and tasted even better. The food disappeared as fast as Ellen could put it out. Joshua ate heartily, enjoying everything. He was glad there were so many good people who liked him and cared for him. It helped to dispel some of the gloom.

Ellen was a good woman. She had come from Germany as a young girl and still had a trace of an accent. Her ways were very much old country. The way she kept the house, the way she raised the children, even the way they dressed was in good taste but simple in an old-fashioned way.

Joshua talked to each of the children while they ate. They were not as demonstrative as the children on the back road, but they liked Joshua in their own way and were glad he had come to breakfast. Their father had told them so much about Joshua that they looked up to him as sort of a local hero.

The breakfast ended, and each of the children set about performing his and her chores. Joshua stayed a few minutes talking to Phil and Ellen, then went back home.

The rest of the day passed by slowly. Joshua didn't have the zest that characterized his carefree behavior of a few weeks before. He was still at peace. He still enjoyed his walks out past the Langfords'. He was still thrilled when a beautifully colored pheasant jumped up in front of him and flew off. But he seemed preoccupied with an inner world, where a drama was beginning to unfold. It was as if he was waiting for things to happen. He knew he could influence those events, but chose not to. He allowed himself to become an actor on a stage set by others.

On Monday morning Joshua went up to the rectory for his meeting with Father Kavanaugh. The receptionist greeted him cordially and took him into the office. It was a large room, well decorated, with a large mahogany desk at one end and high-back chairs along the walls. Behind the desk was a picture of the Pope, and on either side a picture of the bishop and the pastor. Off on the side wall was a large map of what appeared to be Auburn and its environs. Father Kavanaugh was sitting at his desk.

"Young man," the pastor started, "I have been hearing many things about you of late. You have quite a following for a person who has been in town for only a short time. One of the matters that has been brought to my attention is your discussions about religion."

"Could you be more specific?" Joshua asked.

"Yes. I have heard you have taken it upon yourself to teach religion, and from what I gather, a not-too-healthy version of

religion at that. Quite a few of my people are very disturbed
about it and asked me if I approve. I told them, of course, that I
did not approve and that I did not even know you. It seems also
that you have been telling people that religion today is not what
Jesus intended, and that religious leaders are not much different
from the religious leaders in Christ's day. Is that true?"

Joshua looked at the priest with compassion in his eyes and
answered simply, "Not exactly. I do not set out to teach religion, but when discussions get around to those topics I speak
freely about what I know. And, yes, it is true, Jesus never intended that religion become what it is today. Jesus was free and
preached to people that they are God's children and that, as
God's children, they are free. They are not slaves. Jesus also
intended that his leaders be humble men and allow people to
enjoy being free. Unfortunately not many religious leaders feel
comfortable with people being free but enjoy more exercising
their authority over the people. They like to make rules and laws
that burden people's lives and decree that, if they are not
obeyed, they sin and are liable to punishment by God. That is so
unlike Jesus."

The pastor was becoming uneasy and irritated by what Joshua
was saying.

"How do you know what Jesus intended?" the priest interjected.

"Aren't the Gospels clear in showing Jesus' attitudes on these
things?" Joshua asked calmly.

"What Jesus taught is one thing, but it's another thing for a
layman with no training in theology to criticize the Church's
practice of religion," the priest objected.

"I know what I say is true, and the Scriptures are solid evidence. You know that Jesus preached humility to his apostles
and told them they were to exercise authority with gentleness
and meekness. He even washed their feet to impress upon their
minds the importance of serving people, not ruling them."

"I don't like your attitude, young man, and I resent the way
you presume to preach to me. I also resent you talking to my
people, and I will not permit it."

"Who are your people?" Joshua asked caustically.

"You see that map on the wall?" the priest said, pointing to the large map. "All the people living in the territory marked out on that map are my people, and I have jurisdiction over them. No one is to speak to them without my permission."

Joshua was visibly angry. "They are not your people," he said sharply. "They are God's children, and as God's children they are free. It is shepherds like you who have stripped God's people of the freedom and joy they should experience as the children of God and returned them to the status of slaves, no longer free to follow their own consciences, or to listen to their inner voices, or even the voice of God. It is shepherds like you who are so taken up with your own authority that you resent people even talking to others about the things of God without your permission. It is men like you who have destroyed the good name of Jesus' message and have bound up people's lives in shackles and fear of punishment, not because you care for people, but merely to protect your authority. Jesus taught his apostles to love and to serve, but you have never loved your people because you cannot love in the normal way men love. You rule them and force them to serve you instead."

The priest was livid. He stood up and walked over to Joshua, who also stood up. The priest knew that Joshua knew him inside and out, although he had never met him. He was also afraid of him and, at this point, only wanted to get rid of him.

"Young man," the pastor said sharply, "this discussion is ended. I don't know what you are up to, but I cannot imagine it as anything good. I would prefer that you did not attend my church again. I do not see how you or my people could benefit from your presence. I intend to tell my people to avoid your company." With that the pastor ushered Joshua to the front door and went upstairs to his room, slamming the door behind him.

Joshua walked out and down the street. Some little children were playing in a vacant lot along the street. When they saw him they ran over and walked down the street with him, telling him about all kinds of trivial things that were important to them. Joshua forgot his own hurt and put his arms on the children's shoulders, telling them they should enjoy their childhood and not grow up before their time. "You are God's children," he told them, "and you are free. Let no one on earth take that freedom from you."

"We won't, Joshua," they responded, not really understanding what he meant, though the words would stick in their memories for years to come.

While Joshua was walking with the children Father Kavanaugh had gone to his room and paced back and forth, contemplating what he should do about this impudent fanatic. He certainly could not let Joshua get away with this unforgivable affront to his dignity. Since he could not control him himself, he would see to it that something was done. He reached for the telephone and called the bishop's office.

"What's the problem, John?" the bishop asked.

The pastor was enraged, and it showed in the stream of accusations he made against Joshua. "There is a man in our parish, a newcomer, who has a powerful influence over a great many of the people here. He has a thing with religion and is turning the people against the Church. If we don't stop him, he will undermine my position here and do irreparable damage to the faith of the people. I tried to talk to him in a nice way, but he insulted me and told me I was unfit to be a priest."

The bishop listened attentively, then, when the pastor finished, responded, "You are no doubt talking about Joshua."

"Yes, he's the one."

"What can I do?" the bishop asked.

"You might call him in and talk to him."

"What makes you think he would listen?"

"At least it will show him he can't get away with his impudence."

"And if he doesn't listen, then what do we do? His influence is not limited to Auburn, you know. We have already received a batch of letters from people all across the area as a result of his interview on television. He is fast becoming a celebrity."

"That's all the more reason to stop him now, before it is too late. Mark me, he's dangerous. If people pick up his ideas there's no telling what will happen to our churches. It's hard enough now getting people to come to church, and if his ideas take hold, our churches will be empty."

"Aren't you exaggerating, John?" the bishop asked. "Do you really think he is that important?"

"See for yourself, Bishop. If you talked to him, you might change your mind."

"But he is only a layman. We can't come down as hard on him as we could if he was a priest. However, if it will put your mind at rest, I'll see him."

When Joshua reached home after leaving the rectory he spent most of the day thinking. He took a walk out to the high meadow. The sun was hiding behind thick leaden clouds. The birds were quiet. Even the woods were silent. Joshua fell on his knees and sat on his heels, his hands folded tightly, resting on his lap. He looked out across the horizon, not seeing what his eyes saw but a vision of something far beyond the colors and sights of matter. He knelt motionless, transfixed, for almost an hour, as if his soul had momentarily left his body and only the shell remained. Tears flowed freely down his cheeks, then stopped. The sun played games with clouds as a single ray shone through an opening, lighting up Joshua's face, transforming his delicate features into radiant beauty. He knelt there still, in profound thought. Then his face relaxed, and tense muscles melted into peaceful calm as a faint smile hinted at messages only he heard.

15

LATE THAT AFTERNOON Father Darby received a phone call from the Reverend Rowland. He felt very uncomfortable with his statue of the Apostle Peter. He liked the art work, it was beautiful. He liked the message that spoke so clearly from the living wood, but he already knew that message. There was something missing, as if the figure had become dumb and no longer spoke. He felt uneasy having the figure in his church. Would the good Father consider exchanging statues again?

Father Darby was surprised by the call, but it saved him the embarrassment of having to make the same call. He, too, was having uncomfortable feelings about his statue. It fit only too well into his stately church, but, fitting in so well, it said nothing. It was as if his good friend, the Apostle Peter, refused to speak. The statue, too, had turned dumb, and just didn't seem in place in the church. He would be very happy to exchange it with his good brother. "I'll have my chauffeur drive us down right now," he said, referring to himself and his friend, the Apostle Peter.

In no time Father Darby was at the little church. He was surprised at the poverty of the minister and his family. This humble minister was a true Christian. The priest took the wood carving from the minister and gave him his. "Osgood," the priest said humbly, "I'd be honored if you and your family would come to my place for supper some evening this week."

"We would like that very much. My wife will be thrilled."

The chauffeur drove the car past Joshua's house. The priest was still angry at Joshua and resented his being right about the statues. He also felt an uncomfortable sense of guilt that Joshua should know him so well as to carve a statue like that for him. To make up for the insult, he had decided not to send the check for the statue, at least not right away. Now it bothered him that he hadn't, but he still couldn't get himself to relent.

They reached the church and went in to put the figure in place. When they had it positioned they stepped back and looked at it. It was a powerful and moving sculpture. It spoke with a force that would move the hardest heart. The dented tiara lying in the dust spoke powerfully of Peter's final triumph over nature and the conquest of grace. The face of the dying man Peter was attending struck Father Darby. He looked at it more closely. He looked again in disbelief. It was himself. He cringed at the thought of the great apostle on his knees caring for him. It was beneath him. And then he realized it really wasn't. Tears filled his eyes as the meaning of the statue hit him full force. The chauffeur was embarrassed and politely turned away so the priest wouldn't think he had seen. The priest knelt, not to the statue, but to offer a prayer, asking God to forgive him for his awful pride and to help him to be more like the real Apostle Peter, whom he loved so much.

The two men left the church. The priest took the chauffeur's cap and, like a true actor, opened the rear door of his Mercedes and gestured, with a flourish, for his chauffeur to enter. Arthur was embarrassed but obliged. The priest put on the cap, took the wheel, and drove the chauffeur home.

The week went by slowly. Joshua finished his work on the remaining figures and people came by to pick them up. These people loved Joshua. They had come to know him as a friend. They told him their problems. They shared with him the funny things that took place in their lives and they joked with him about events in town.

As people came and left over the next few days, they couldn't help but feel a sense of sadness for Joshua. He wasn't the same happy person who had come to town just a short time before. Oh, he laughed and joked with them as usual, but there was a melancholy that seemed to hang over his cottage. The shop was no longer filled with figures.

On Wednesday, Lester Gold came to see Joshua. He was a good friend of Aaron Fahn, who had told Lester practically everything he had learned about Joshua. Lester did volunteer work with a group of blind people and wondered if Joshua would accompany him on a visit to their meeting. He had told the blind folks about Joshua and about the figure of Moses he had carved. He had even brought some of them to "see" the figure, allowing them to run their highly sensitive fingers across the features and hands. They couldn't wait to meet Joshua. Would he come? That is, of course, if he wasn't busy. Joshua grinned. He was glad to see Lester. Aaron had told Joshua a lot about him and his family. Lester was now in the state legislature and was rising rapidly in the Democratic Party. He had just given a passionate speech in the Senate against the death penalty. Joshua was pleased when he heard that. How far Jews have come from the days of old, when the law and the death penalty were so much a part of life. Without realizing it, through the centuries they have absorbed the real spirit of Jesus, while Christians were so often inclined to abandon that spirit and return to the rigid strictness of the old law. It was a strange paradox.

Joshua told Lester he would be glad to go with him. He wasn't busy so it wasn't an imposition. He just asked for a few minutes to wash up.

A short time later the two men drove to the city. When they arrived at the meeting hall Lester took Joshua to the president of the organization and introduced him. The president, Thelma Bradford, was a woman with great dignity and a ripe sense of humor. Lester had told her all about Joshua and she knew, if she kept pestering Lester, she would get to meet him someday.

After introducing Joshua to the rest of the officers, Thelma asked Joshua if he would talk to the group for a few minutes. They were dying to meet him and ask him questions. Joshua consented and was led to the head of the room. After a short introduction he rose to speak. There were about a hundred people in the audience, men, women, and even some children.

Joshua scanned the audience. They knew where he was without seeing him. The room fell silent.

"My dear friends," he began, "and I call you that even though you have never met me, because I know you, and I know that you are special people. As Lester was driving me through the country on the way here, I looked across the fields and saw all the things you have longed all your lives to see. I thought of all the things that you do see, things which we who have sight will never see, and I realized the strange goodness of God. The vision of things that pass so quickly is indeed a fleeting vision and an illusion of real things. But the things that you see are the reality beneath the illusion. What you see is real. We see merely the appearances. And we are indeed to be pitied because so few of us ever find the reality beneath the lights and colors. Your vision pierces the surface and sees the substance of life, and you can much more easily see things the way God sees them. You have a role in life that is precious. You can share with others the visions of things you see, which others cannot.

"I realize the shock of not seeing is hard to accept, but if you can trust God, and know that he has a unique work for you to do for him, then you can understand the value of your role in life. You may be tempted to compete in areas where the sighted thrive, and that is your right, but there are unique contributions to humanity and to the understanding of life that only you can make because you have resources that others do not have. Listen to the voice of God, and do not be afraid. Let him take you by the hand and guide you. Let him be your staff, and the lamp at your feet. The world needs what only you can teach them. Find what that is for each of you, and you will find overwhelming contentment."

Joshua went on talking about other things, but that was the main thrust of his message. It was well received, and the people felt they had known him all their lives, his warmth so touched their hearts, like a soothing balm that nursed many hurts and bruises they had carried with them for years.

During the time after the talk they asked him a barrage of questions, about where he lived, where he was born, about his parents, and about his work as an artist, and where he learned to carve. He answered them all simply, with the same answers he gave others, but they saw more to him than other people did and realized that, in spite of his simple ways, there was more to him than meets the eye, and he was a very different kind of person. They wished they could get to know him better.

Informal and more personal conversations followed, and Joshua became acquainted with many of the people. Sensing his compassion, they told him of many of their trials and tragedies. He listened and encouraged each one. As he and Lester were walking toward the door afterward, a young girl in her twenties was introduced to Joshua. He talked to her for a few moments. She told him of her elderly mother she was caring for, and how difficult the situation was becoming, and that she was worried about the future. Joshua listened and sensed the impossibility of the girl's predicament. He talked to her briefly, and then reached out and placed his hand on the girl's head as he said good-bye, and told her to trust in God's goodness—he would not fail her.

"I do trust him," she replied. "He is my only hope."

When Lester and Joshua went out the door and were busy talking, they were unable to hear the commotion inside. The blind girl let out a scream that sent chills up and down everyone's spine, causing many to panic. "I can see, I can see. I could never see in my life before, but now I can see," she kept saying over and over. The crowd gathered around her and asked her what had happened. All she could say was, "I don't know. I was talking to the artist, and when he was leaving, he touched me. He touched me, and now I see."

Everyone was happy for her, as if they had been blessed just as much as she. They had felt that way since Joshua had begun speaking to them, and when they went home that afternoon they felt as if something wonderful had touched each of their lives.

Outside, Joshua and Lester kept talking as they walked toward the car, unaware of what had just taken place inside. It was private for those who were there, and Joshua did not want it to go any further.

By the time Lester dropped Joshua off in Auburn and returned home, his phone had been ringing constantly and his wife had a pile of calls for him to return. As he called each one they told him what had happened. They were so grateful for Lester bringing his friend to them. They would never forget what had happened that day.

When Lester had made his last call and hung up, he fell back in his green velvet armchair and cried out loud, "That fox, that consummate fox! He knew all along what was happening inside that hall and never let on. Wait until I see him on Friday night. I'll give it to him good," he said with a big laugh. But then his wife came in and sat down to talk to him. Several of the people had told her what had happened. She asked Lester what it all meant and what he thought of Joshua. They talked till well past midnight and couldn't wait until Friday night to hear what Joshua would say to a congregation full of Jews and a host of visiting rabbis. They were proud that Joshua was their friend, but they were beginning to have second thoughts as to his real identity. He was not just a simple wood-carver. There was much more to him than he let anyone know. They were just beginning to pierce the veil of mystery surrounding him.

When Joshua returned home he found a letter in the mailbox. Looking at the return address, he read, "Office of the Bishop," with the address beneath. He opened the letter and read it while walking into the house. It was a formal letter and from the bishop himself. "Dear Mr. Joshua," it began, "It has come to our attention that you have been expressing interest in religious matters and have shared your ideas with certain people in the parish community of Auburn. We would like to discuss this matter with you and have scheduled a meeting for this Friday morning at ten-thirty. We will expect you at that time." The letter was signed, "Cordially in Christ," followed by the bishop's signature.

Joshua saw through the unpolished attempt at formal protocol. He realized all too well not just the purpose of the meeting but how it had come about. "Obey them, because they occupy the chair of Moses" crossed his memory. He knew the bishop and the pastor were friends, and that the pastor must have insisted that something be done with him. Joshua did not like the arrogant way he was politely ordered to appear. There was no room for question, no consideration for any possible inconve-

nience to him. He was merely told what to do and was expected
to comply.

That evening Joshua went to bed early. He was weary, with a
tiredness far different from the kind that came from carving
wood for long hours. That was a satisfying tiredness. This was
the wearying fatigue of a harried man who was not allowed to
rest in peace. He slept soundly and woke, as he did every morning, as soon as the sun rose.

It was still early when he arrived in the village for breakfast.
The crew was at the diner and kidded him about all the rumors
going around town. He just laughed and commented, "Well, I
guess I'm finally accepted as one of the family, the way they're
all talking about me."

"You sure are," Moe said. "In fact, they're already arranging
your marriage, and it ain't to Mary either."

"Moe, I thought you were nice. You're being wise," Mary
said, then continued, "I don't believe a thing they're saying,
Joshua, and don't you pay any attention to it either. They'd
crucify Christ all over again if he came back here, and then
they'd be sorry over it two days later. They just like to talk, but
they're like dogs without teeth. They can't hurt you." Joshua
laughed and ordered his breakfast.

He returned home to finish the last of the figures. The people
who had ordered them picked them up in the early afternoon.
By two o'clock they were all gone and the shop was clear of
everything. Joshua looked around and thought of all the activity
of the past few months and how much fun it had been. He felt a
twinge of melancholy at the thought of how kind and friendly
the people had been and the good times they had had together.

He cleaned the house for the first time in weeks and tidied up
the yard. The two chickens had had the run of the place the past
few weeks because Joshua had been too busy to do anything
with them. He found a nest the hen had constructed and noticed three eggs in it. He decided to wait and see if they would
hatch. He cleaned the grill and wondered what he should have
for supper. The priest still hadn't paid him for the statue, so he
didn't have much money. What he got from the other statue
went for food and to pay for the wood. He reached in his pocket

and took out a handful of bills, totaling $175. He needed most of that for the rent, but still had a little money for food. Some people still owed him money for work he had done, but he wouldn't get that till next week. He wished Father Jeremy would pay what he owed him.

16

THE WALK TO the city took Joshua almost four hours. It was almost ten when he reached the outskirts. Now he had to find the bishop's office. It was a hot day and he was sweating profusely. After asking directions from several policemen along the way, he finally arrived at the bishop's place.

It was more like a modern office building than a traditional chancery. Joshua went inside and announced himself.

The place was cold and stiff. Joshua felt ill at ease and out of place. It was not his style and it brought back poignant memories of temple porticoes and flowing robes, and solemn clergy preoccupied with the same business of religion, and all its irrelevant legalities.

Joshua sat in the hall and waited. Priests and other functionaries walked back and forth looking very busy, going from one office to another. Joshua could hear conversations from each of the offices as they discussed the business matters of the diocese and the various parishes and agencies. They were very much involved in their work, and Joshua couldn't help but notice their deep interest.

Parish life was audited through this office, and financial reports were monitored with a fine-toothed comb. Monetary matters were, as in ages past, the prime occupation of religious leaders. There was no way to monitor spiritual matters anyway. That was God's business. Running the kingdom of God on earth was the noble task of ecclesiastics, and they thoroughly enjoyed this great work for God. Joshua shook his head in bewilderment. "How much they enjoy the business of the kingdom!" he thought. "If only they could become fired up with the same zeal for souls."

After waiting for almost half an hour, Joshua was finally ushered down a long corridor into the bishop's office.

The office was spacious. A deep red rug covered the floor. A golden coat of arms had been woven into the rug and looked impressive but commercial. A hand-carved desk stood at the far end of the room, and behind it sat the bishop. He stood when Joshua approached. They shook hands and the bishop gestured for Joshua to be seated. The bishop was a tall man, quite stout, and balding. His gold-rimmed glasses gave him a worldly appearance, and his mannerisms betrayed a refinement befitting his station.

As Joshua sat down his eyes scanned the ornately decorated room. Costly antiques placed tastefully here and there displayed one of the bishop's interests. A magnificent chandelier hung from the ceiling, its pendants sparkling as the sun's rays coming from a window bounced off various glass objects in the room.

The bishop thanked Joshua for coming and, as his time was valuable, got right down to business. "Joshua, I have heard many things about you the past few weeks. We have also received quite a few letters from people who are concerned about what you have been saying."

Joshua doubted very much what the bishop was saying. He knew full well the only reason he was here was because the pastor in Auburn had complained about him. Joshua also knew that, if people did take the time to write about him to the bishop, they would have said nice things, but the bishop found it difficult to let anyone know the nice things people said. It gave him a psychological edge.

"Where are you from originally?" the bishop asked him.

"Bethlehem, a little place with a lot of friendly people," Joshua answered.

"Oh, I know that community. I have some friends there. It's an-up-and-coming area," the bishop replied.

Joshua relaxed, knowing his response went right over the bishop's head.

"I have heard you like religion, and are a religious person, and enjoy talking about theological matters with people," the bishop said.

"I think you may have been slightly misinformed. I don't set out to talk about religion. I am not really interested in religious matters as you understand them. I feel strongly about God and I like people, and I am very much interested in people's relationship with God. That is different from the business of religion."

"But you have been talking about religious matters and things involving the Church, is that not true?" the bishop insisted.

"Insofar as Church people say and do things that affect people's relationship with God, yes," Joshua replied.

"What are some of your ideas about God?" the bishop asked.

Joshua looked at him and could see the emptiness of his spirit. Perhaps he was a good administrator, but there was very little spiritual depth in this man whose life was consumed with his position in ecclesiastical politics.

"How can one describe God in a few words?" Joshua said, almost bewildered over the uselessness of the question. "If you want to understand God, you have the full expression of the Father in Jesus. He is the living expression of the Father's love, unbegotten from endless time and born into this world in time to manifest God's love for all his creatures."

"What do you believe about Jesus' ideas about religion?" the bishop then asked, getting closer to the point.

"Jesus was not interested in religion as you understand it. For you religion is the passing on of finely chiseled doctrines and rigid codes of behavior. For Jesus religion was finding God and enjoying the freedom of being close to God—seeing Him in all creation, especially in God's children. Perfecting those relationships was Jesus' understanding of religion. In the mind of Jesus the Church's great concern should be to foster people's relationship with God and show people how to work together, caring for one another and building trust and love among the families of nations.

"Religion has not done that too well. Religious leaders have spent too much time and interest in setting up structures to imitate worldly governments. In running people's lives by law they have severely restricted the freedom Jesus intended his followers to have. Instead of inspiring people to be good, they have tried to legislate observances like the scribes and Pharisees. In running religion this way they have created more tensions and added to the barriers separating people from one another. Jesus intended that his message bring joy into people's lives, but too often religion has brought misery and guilt and made people see God as severe and critical."

"Where do you get your ideas from? Have you studied theology?" the bishop asked, trying to disguise his discomfort.

"I speak of things I know, and I know what I say is true. You also know that."

The bishop was irritated that this uneducated woodworker should preach to him, and it showed in his next question. "Have you been telling people that they are free of their pastor's authority?"

"I told them they are free, and that no one can take that freedom from them. If they feel their pastor deprives them of their freedom, they have made that judgment, not I," Joshua answered sharply.

The bishop began to realize he was not dealing with an illiterate. Joshua was shrewd, and the bishop couldn't help recalling the saying "Simple as a dove, but as sly as a serpent." He knew it would be futile to pry any more information out of this man without having a thorough examination by professional theologians and scriptural scholars. He saw that what Father Kavanaugh said was true. This man could be dangerous. If his popularity spread and his message of freedom took hold, it could cause a schism and severely damage the Church.

"The pastor in your church is very concerned about what you are teaching his people," the bishop continued, shifting responsibility for this meeting from himself to the pastor. He didn't want Joshua to think ill of him and tried to get on Joshua's good side. "I realize you are a learned man, Joshua, and beneath your simple ways you have a profound understanding of the things of God and a deep feeling for people. There should be more Christians like you."

Joshua said nothing, realizing the bishop was not being honest.

The bishop looked at his watch. It was almost lunchtime. He stood up, thanked Joshua for coming, and said that he had other appointments, ushering Joshua out.

As Joshua walked down the hall alone he walked past several priests and lay officials. He smiled hello, but they were too busy with their work to notice. He was famished from the long walk, and didn't have money to go to a restaurant, and the walk home would be long and hot.

As he left the chancery and was walking down the steps, he noticed a vendor selling hot dogs across the street. He reached into his pocket to see if he had any money. He had just enough to buy two hot dogs and a bottle of soda. The vendor was friendly enough, and Joshua talked to him while he ate his lunch. He then wished the man well and started on his long trip home.

In the meantime the personnel in the chancery were gathering in the dining room for lunch. When the bishop entered the chancellor met him and asked how he made out with that "oddball" from Auburn.

"He's a shrewd fox," the bishop told the chancellor. "John was right," the bishop went on, referring to Father Kavanaugh, "this guy is dangerous. We've got to get rid of him."

"How are we going to do that? He's popular, and the Jews love him. And if they suspect we're doing something to hurt him, it's going to seriously affect their donations to our charities," the chancellor suggested. He was used to carrying out unpleasant tasks that might tarnish the bishop's image and was quite adept at shrewd behind-the-scenes maneuvering.

"Call a meeting of the consultors for this evening," the bishop said. "But don't call Bob or John, they'll have conscience problems, and I don't need that. If they ask why they weren't called, tell them you weren't able to get hold of them. Don't take any excuses from the others. If they say they can't come, have them call me personally. I don't want to take the blame for this. It'll look better if the decision seems to come from them."

The chancellor skipped lunch and started making the phone calls. By the time lunch was over he had contacted everyone. Then he went back into the dining room, where the staff was relaxing after their meal. He told the bishop everyone had agreed to come. "Some of them gave me a hard time in the beginning, but when I told them they had to call you if they intended not to come, they gave in, even though it would mean changing their schedules."

The dining-room table in the chancery was the grand tribunal where personalities were discussed and reputations of priests made and destroyed. The chancery regularly reviewed the latest gossip about various priests, and as there wasn't any deep interest in the work the priests were doing as long as they were on schedule with the assessment payments, they enjoyed the pastime of discussing the latest scandals and rumors about priests. Most of the talk got back to the priests eventually and created deep resentments, which rarely surfaced. Priests knew which chancery officials said what about whom, and one day it would all erupt. Father Pat had always thought the comptroller was a good friend of his. Little did he know that everything he told his friend in secret became fodder for discussion at the chancery table.

The talk about Joshua was typical. There were rumors and jokes and casual remarks made about him, and the bishop and his staff were content to allow Joshua's reputation to be determined by these remarks. It showed the poverty of their concern for the real life of the community and the little value they placed on reputations.

In the meantime Joshua's walk back to Auburn was slow. He was tired from the long walk in the morning. The day was hot, and he hadn't eaten enough to give him the stamina for such a long hike. When he reached the outskirts of the city he rested under a fat maple tree in front of an old Victorian house. No sooner had he sat down than a crotchety man in his sixties came out of his house and, with a rake that he had picked up from the porch, walked over and told Joshua to get off his grass. Joshua assured him he would do no harm, but the man was in no mood to listen. He just raised his rake threateningly. Joshua picked himself up and walked down the sidewalk to a tree in front of the house next door.

Some kids were selling refreshments down the street and saw what had happened. One of the boys came over to Joshua with a tall glass of Kool-Aid. Joshua was sitting in a niche between the roots with his legs outstretched. His clothes were soaked with sweat. When the boy offered him the drink Joshua reached into his pocket, but the boy seemed hurt and said, "No, mister, it's free. You look sad, as if you've had a tough day."

Joshua thanked him, and took a deep draught of the refreshing drink, and sighed with great pleasure. The boy beamed his delight that he had given a stranger such comfort and sat down beside him. "What's your name?" he asked Joshua.

"Joshua," he answered.

"Where you from?"

"Auburn," Joshua said, almost too tired to talk.

"Do you work?"

"Yes, I carve wood."

"Don't mind that man next door. He's mean. He's always been mean. When I was a little boy he hit me with a stick for walking on his lawn. He hurt me too. So don't feel bad."

Joshua just smiled and said it didn't bother him. He was used to people like that. He reached out and put his hand on the boy's head and thanked him for the delicious drink, then got up and started on his way. "God bless you, Peter, and don't ever lose your kind feeling for people." The boy walked him as far as his Kool-Aid stand. As Joshua continued walking the boy watched him and wondered how he knew his name.

Not too far down the road a car drove past, stopped, and backed up. It was some of the crew from Auburn returning from work. They had finished a job and were going home early.

They were surprised to see Joshua walking along the road and were delighted to pick him up. Joshua was just as pleased. He had not been this tired for as long as he could remember.

That evening Aaron arrived at six-thirty sharp, as he did every week. Joshua ached all over and was limping slightly as he walked toward the car. Aaron asked Joshua what had happened. Joshua just laughed. "I'm getting old," he said. "I walked to the city this morning, and I'm just not used to those kinds of trips anymore." He thought back to long ago, of walks for days on end along rocky roads dry with dust, speaking in villages all along the way, with little time to eat or rest. But that was long ago.

"All ready for your talk?" Aaron asked as Joshua got into the car.

"I suppose. I had an unusual week and didn't get too much chance to think about tonight. I did get some time to think today when I walked to the city, so I suppose I'm as prepared as I'll ever be."

"Lester called me early today and told me all about what happened at the meeting of the blind people," Aaron said, thinking Joshua would follow up and tell him the whole story. But Joshua just kept looking out the window, as if it was all news to him. He merely said, "Yes, it was a nice little meeting. Those people have a lot of courage, but it will not go unrewarded."

Then Aaron asked him point-blank, "What happened to the young blind girl?"

Joshua thought for a long time. Aaron just waited. He wasn't letting Joshua off the hook over this one. When he finally realized he was trapped Joshua laughed and said, "Oh-h-h, Aaron, you and Lester are going to get the best of me yet. Why do you think I had anything to do with that blind girl?"

"It happened right after you put your hand on her head."

"Why would that have anything to do with it?"

"The coincidence is mighty strange. You touch her, and she immediately begins to see. And she had been blind from birth."

"I do admit I did feel sorry for her, and realized how impossible it was for her to care for her invalid mother, and I did pray for her. I guess it was quite a coincidence."

"You know damn well that was no coincidence, Joshua. Why don't you square with me? I thought by now we were friends," Aaron said in a hurt tone of voice.

That got to Joshua. He remembered words spoken long ago: "I call you friends because I tell you all things and keep nothing from you. You are no longer servants, but friends." If anything Joshua knew, it was how to be a friend. He felt bad; things were different now.

"Aaron," he said, "you are my friend, and you already know what happened Wednesday. It's difficult for me to talk about things like that. All I can say is that I am, and always have been, close to God, and He always hears me. Besides, that girl had great faith, and that had a lot to do with what happened."

Aaron seemed satisfied, but both men were quiet for a long time. Aaron felt bad for pumping Joshua and for using that event as a test of their friendship. He realized he had embarrassed Joshua, but Joshua's answer put him at ease and made him realize he understood. They looked at each other and laughed heartily over the incident, then talked about something else.

When they arrived at the synagogue the parking lot was full. There was an unusually large crowd filing their way up to the building. "Looks like you're pretty popular, my friend," Aaron said, looking at the crowd. "I have no doubt you will have them spellbound before they even know what hit them. And you don't even seem nervous. You certainly are a phenomenon," Aaron said good-naturedly.

"I really am a little nervous," Joshua told him. "I haven't done this in a long time, and I'm hoping this time will be different." Joshua's mind wandered far away and recalled many similar occasions, most of them pleasant. He thought of scribes and Pharisees. There were none here today. No institution, no structure in Judaism like the old days. The Church has assumed that role now. Too bad the Church didn't develop more like the synagogue. But Jerusalem had to be destroyed before that could happen.

The two men walked inside, mingling with the crowd. Aaron knew most of them, though tonight there were many strangers. People spontaneously greeted each other and introduced their friends. Lester and Marcia were waiting with Rabbi Szeneth. They greeted Joshua enthusiastically. They were ecstatic there were so many people. Even rabbis had accepted the invitation to come, and already there were a number of them in the crowd.

Marcia asked Joshua if he was nervous. She put her arm in his and held him tight, as if to reassure him. Joshua smiled and admitted he was nervous. He wanted so much for everything to go right. Marcia put a beautifully embroidered yamulka on his head, and over his shoulders she placed a prayer shawl that had belonged to her grandfather. It helped to cover his frightfully underdressed look. In fact, he looked quite attractive in his own rugged way.

The services started late, which was unusual for the rabbi, who was always most punctual. But people were still pouring in after seven o'clock so there was little else he could do but wait. Finally everyone was seated.

Aaron, Lester, and the rabbi walked with Joshua from the study out onto the platform and the service began.

Joshua was sitting on the left side of the ark, next to Rabbi Szeneth, who was sitting in the middle. After a silent prayer the rabbi began prayers and readings. Aaron then got up and read an appropriate text to suit the occasion. Joshua was shocked at the one he had picked.

"The spirit of the Lord is upon me," he read from the prophet Isaiah, and went on, "because he has anointed me. He has sent me to preach to the meek, to heal the contrite of heart, to preach release to captives, and to give sight to the blind; to proclaim the acceptable year of the Lord, and the day of visitation of our God, to comfort all who mourn."

Aaron closed the book and went to his seat. Joshua stood up and walked calmly to the lectern. Silence overcame the spacious sanctuary. Joshua put his hands on the lectern and gripped it firmly. The muscles in his strong arms rippled.

"My people," he began, then paused. The words resounded through the room. The people could not possibly imagine the full import of those words or who it was who said them. They could only sense the infinite tenderness with which they flowed from Joshua's lips.

The pause was only for a few seconds, but it seemed endless. He then went on, "Those words of Isaiah have more meaning today than they have had for centuries. God has not abandoned his people. He has been with you through all the joyful and tragic events that you have endured. You may have felt abandoned. You may have wondered what happened to Yahweh, who spoke with such tenderness in times long past and has been silent now for so many generations. You may have wondered what happened to the Anointed One he promised to send. You may have wondered if, indeed, you were still his chosen people, his bride he promised never to forsake or to cast off. You may even have felt as if you had been cast off when you were scattered among the nations and despised by the rest of humanity.

"But open your ears and open your hearts and hear me well. You have never been forsaken. Nor was God far away from you, even in your darkest hours. You are still his chosen. You are still his beloved, dear to his heart, and are still the apple of his eye.

"You may ask, 'Why did he treat us the way he did, and for so many centuries? Why was his voice silent and his powerful arm not outstretched to help us?' But I tell you, let the tragedies and the lonely wanderings speak for themselves. God gave your forefathers the key to understanding his signs and his messages. They speak no less clearly today than in ages past. Listen to them and hear what they say so clearly and so loudly. But more important, continue to trust God. What he promised he will carry out. What he has sworn to, he will fulfill. And though you may have walked from his paths, he will still be faithful.

"But you must not look for him and his salvation in the world around you. Nor will you find salvation in accumulating the goods of this world. You become what you love, and when you love the things of this world you lower yourselves to the level of those things. It is unworthy of you to crave them and set value on them as if they bestow upon you a dignity. They have value only as reminders of the world where God lives. To love them in themselves is to drink from the polluted well Jeremiah talked about.

"In spite of what you have suffered you have remained faithful. But it is important for you to remember that God is so far above you and his being is so far removed from anything you have ever experienced that you should not be shocked when he manifests himself to you. His love for you is so tender and so intimate that should he manifest himself to you in a way that is personal, in a way that expresses his desire to be present in your midst, you should not be scandalized. He is, as Isaiah said, your 'Emmanuel,' God in your midst. If this forces you to alter your understanding of the nature of God, then open your hearts and listen. Your minds must not be closed to a deeper and wider understanding of God than you may have known before. Though God is one, his oneness is far different from any kind of oneness you have ever known because he is unique. He is himself. His oneness is not like the oneness of man's nature. The sun is one, yet there is the source, the light, and the warmth of the sun, all one, but each a different facet of the one existence. Do not judge God by what you see in man. Even though man is, in a way, God's image, the image is reflected in man's soul. There is his soul, and his mind and his will, all distinct, but one."

As Joshua looked across the audience their faces were deep in thought, tears of understanding flowing down the cheeks of some. He went on, "You are destined and chosen, not just to bring material blessings to humanity but to be the instrument through which God will speak to people of all nations, helping them to come to a wiser understanding of Himself and his plans for mankind. Be true to that call, and never, never doubt that Yahweh is ever at your side. Do not try to find your Messiah or your salvation in a worldly kingdom. God alone is your Messiah, and only in him will you find peace and fulfillment of your long-sought destiny."

When Joshua finished there was a deafening silence, then the whole congregation arose and clapped their wild applause. Joshua beamed his joy and bowed slightly, acknowledging their response. They finally stopped and settled down. Joshua went back to his seat. Rabbi Szeneth shook his hand, as did Aaron and Lester, their cheeks wet with tears.

The rabbi walked to the lectern. "I must admit," he said, "that I do not know what to say. I could not help but feel, as our beloved friend was speaking, that I was hearing the voice of another speaking through him, and that what he said was not his own but a message sent through him. We have indeed been honored and privileged these past few weeks to know Joshua. Our lives are richer and more filled with meaning than ever before. We hope that, whatever the future brings, we will never lose the closeness and the love we have known on these Shabbat nights. May God bless our friend and be with him along whatever road he may travel."

The rest of the service moved along smoothly. At the end everyone filed out into the vestibule and down to the meeting room for their social hour. Joshua was a celebrity that night. They told him he was inspired, and they, too, felt inspired by his vision of God's people. They were impressed with his radically new concept of God's people and his plan for their lives. It would provide food for thought and discussion for months to come. They were, most of all, grateful to him for having given so much of himself to them. They were, for all anyone knew, strangers to him, and he had no responsibilities or commitments to them whatsoever.

Aaron and Lester hugged him affectionately. The rabbi kissed him on both cheeks and introduced him to his rabbi friends. They each expressed their evaluations of his talk, and even though they may not have completely understood what he was driving at, they thought his ideas came from a heart filled with love for people and gave them much to think about and search their consciences over. They promised to talk about his ideas when they returned to their own congregations.

Marcia came over and threw her arms around him possessively, and she kissed him, overjoyed at the success of his talk and the wild response of the people.

"Joshua," she said as she helped him take off his prayer shawl and yamulka, "I thought what you said was beautiful. You have to be inspired to talk about something so delicate among Jews and to say it in such a way that they not only did not take offense but applauded what you said and the way you said it. I was so proud of you. I can easily imagine God taking on a form that we could understand to assure us of his love. He has done it in the past. Jacob fought with him in the dark of night. Even Abraham saw God in the three strangers who came to visit him. I am so glad we have come to know you as a friend. We are all honored and proud of you."

Everyone socialized for the next hour. Many of the visitors were introduced to Joshua and told him they had heard many good things about him. The crowd in the hall was so large, it was difficult to talk in much depth about anything, or even to answer questions without being interrupted time and again. Finally the hour came to an end and everyone went home. Aaron, Lester, Marcia, and Joshua left together.

Aaron had listened intently to the talk Joshua had given in the synagogue and had some questions. "Joshua," he said, "when you were talking about the presence of God becoming manifest in a personal way, what were you driving at? I am sure most people thought what you said was beautiful, but knowing you the way I do, I see a lot more in your apparently simple remarks and I am intrigued by that particular statement. I wish you would elaborate."

"Aaron," Joshua responded, "I don't know who gives me a more difficult time, you or Lester. You are forever probing and questioning. Can't you take things on face value and just use them as reference points for your own meditation rather than have everything spelled out for you in detail?"

"With anyone else, yes, but with you, no. You speak in such riddles, you defy us to challenge you. I always knew there was more to you than meets the eye, and when you speak it is the same. There is more to you than meets the ear as well. So don't sidetrack me. What did you mean?"

Joshua laughed. "God is not limited in his presence. People are so frightfully rigid and limited in their understanding of things. Do you not realize that God can be present in many different ways? In whatever form he uses we should be careful not to prejudice ourselves and say, 'He can't come in that form, or in this form,' because if we do, then we reduce God to our own limited image, and in doing that run the risk of rejecting him if he comes to us in a way we don't expect. God may be one and he may be simple, but he can also manifest himself in many facets of his greatness. Look at the sun. The sun is one and it is simple. However, there is the sun itself, and there is the heat and the light that touches our lives. We know the sun when its rays disperse the darkness of night. A blind person knows the sun by its warmth. They are different, but they are expressions of the same being. It is the same with God. His oneness cannot be defined by our understanding of oneness."

Time passed quickly as they drove along. Marcia just listened, happy to be close to Joshua. She was content just looking at him when he spoke, trying to absorb all the meaning from his every word. In no time at all they were in Auburn. They drove down the street to Joshua's place. Joshua thanked them all for their kindness in coming so far out of their way to take him home and then got out of the car before Aaron got a chance to open the door for him. As he was getting out he put his hand on Marcia's and wished her good night. Lester jokingly remarked how dark

Joshua's house looked and suggested that Marcia should be his housekeeper. "I'd be delighted," she said, half joking, "but I don't think he'd want anyone around to distract him." Joshua smiled at Marcia, but said nothing. After telling Aaron he'd appreciate his picking him up next week, he said good night and went into the house.

17

THE NEXT FEW days were quiet. The workshop was empty, and Joshua took advantage of the lull to rest. The frenetic activity of the past two weeks had taken its toll on him, and he was glad he had no deadlines to meet, no schedules to keep.

On Thursday, Father Pat brought Reverend Joe Engman, the Methodist minister, and another priest friend of his to visit Joshua. His name was Al Morris.

Father Morris was a middle-aged man, good-humored, perhaps overly conservative in his thinking, but because he was so kind his parishioners loved him and overlooked his shortcomings. Joe Engman was a friendly, stocky man with curly hair. He was a good family man whose devoted wife, Mary, was his greatest inspiration. He had a ready laugh and was very open in his faith. Occasionally Joe would attend morning Mass, if Father Pat was saying it, and would receive the Eucharist, about which the priest never made an issue. The parishioners thought it was beautiful.

Joshua enjoyed Pat's two friends. They all had a good time helping him put the supper together, one making the barbecue sauce from ingredients he had brought with him, the other preparing the meat and another the salad from Joshua's garden vegetables. They laughed and joked as they reminisced over the events of the past few months. They kidded Joshua about taking the village by storm and stirring up a hornet's nest. He enjoyed their humor. They didn't talk about anything serious, they just had a good time.

After the party broke up Joshua went back into the house and went straight to bed. It was well past midnight, and he fell sound asleep as soon as he hit the bed. His last thought as he drifted off was the bishop. During the course of the interview the bishop had told him a number of times the things he was teaching were not really new. Joshua could detect a put-down. He also knew he had been the butt of jokes at the table after he left. Father Pat got some information about what happened and had passed it on to Joshua. He told Joshua it was too bad they didn't take the time to get to know him themselves rather than make decisions based on rumor and jokes. Pat was not a favorite of the chancery. His criticism of their pettiness and politics had gotten back to them. One night he had called them all phonies, accusing them of not really being interested in the Church or spiritual things but just public display and power. That was just before they transferred him to Auburn.

The consultors' meeting had taken place as planned. The bishop and the chancellor made believe they were asking the consultors' advice but shrewdly insinuated their own predetermined plan. The consultors perfunctorily fulfilled their accepted role and approved what was presented. It was decided that any handling of Joshua locally would meet with opposition, since he was popular, especially with the Jewish community. To antagonize them would be to jeopardize considerable contributions to the bishop's programs.

Since Joshua was docile, he could be counted on to cooperate, even in his own downfall. They decided to send a complaint to the Vatican telling about the spurious ideas of this man whose popularity was growing to such an extent that they feared the possibility of a schism. It was not true, of course, but it sounded intelligent, and as they knew which buttons to push to cause concern at the Vatican, they knew their strategy would work. It was decided the chancellor would write the letter and send it immediately, suggesting that, perhaps, a doctrinal proceeding might be held to look into these matters. This way professional theologians could carefully dissect Joshua's ideas and show him how uninformed and ignorant he really was and convince him he was over his head—dabbling in matters which were best left to the professionals who ran the Church.

Joshua found out from Pat what had happened and now all he could do was wait patiently. The drama was about to unfold. The stage was being set, and the actors were making last-minute preparations.

It didn't take long for the Vatican to respond. The bishop had contacts, carefully cultivated over the years. It was hardly two weeks later that Joshua received a very important-looking letter. Charlie, the mailman, couldn't just put it in the mailbox. This one had to be hand-delivered. He was dying to know what was in it. Not that Joshua would ever tell him, but he would at least see Joshua's reaction.

Joshua answered the door and smiled when he saw Charlie. Charlie couldn't hide his feelings, and it didn't take much for Joshua to guess what Charlie was excited about. As expected, Joshua invited him in, and they sat down and talked while they had something to eat. To Charlie's supreme disappointment, Joshua just took the letter from him and put it on the table, not opening it until Charlie left.

When he did finally open it it read:

Dear Mr. Joshua:

We have been informed by your bishop of certain religious matters you have been discussing and disseminating among the Christian people in your community and in other places. The bishop is quite concerned. Because of the serious nature of these matters and the doctrines involved, as well as our continued concern for the faith of the Christian people, we are requesting that you appear before this Congregation for a hearing. We hereby set the date for this proceeding as August thirteenth of this year of Our Lord, one thousand nine hundred and eighty-three, at 9:30 in the morning in the Palazzo del Sant' Ufficio in The Vatican. We hope these matters can be happily resolved to everyone's satisfaction.

> *Sincerely yours in Christ,*
> *Cardinal Giovanni Riccardo,*
> *Secretary,*
> *Sacred Congregation for the*
> *Doctrines of the Faith*

Joshua thought over the content and tone of the letter and its meaning. The bishop had told him he was impressed with him, and that there should be more Christians like him. Then why report him to Rome and demand an investigation? The memories of long flowing robes and broad phylacteries again crossed his mind and brought back a train of images, of men trying to hold on to power.

Joshua looked around for a pen and some paper. There was some good stationery left by the previous tenants, which Joshua found in an old desk. He sat down at the kitchen table and wrote a brief response.

> *Dear Cardinal Riccardo:*
>
> *I feel honored that I have been invited to come and meet with Peter. While I find it difficult to fully understand the purpose of the proceeding to be held on August thirteenth, I would be most happy to comply. However, I do have a problem. I am a poor man, and do not have the means to make a voyage like this. Even if I were to save what little I make, it would take me a very long time to save what would be necessary. If you could help me to solve this problem, I would be more than happy to cooperate.*
>
> > *Sincerely,*
> > *Joshua*

Joshua sealed the envelope and walked down to the post office to mail it himself.

From then on things happened rapidly. It was only ten days later that a messenger arrived from the chancery summoning Joshua to meet with the chancellor. He wasn't going to go through that routine again. He asked Father Pat to drive him. He was delighted and changed his schedule accordingly. On the way Joshua told him about the letter from the Vatican, which had surprised him, since the bishop had given him no indication that he was displeased with him but even seemed to approve. Pat just laughed.

He told Joshua what he had learned. "The bishop was ordered to pay your fare to Rome. Afterward he told the chancellor he'd be damned if he was going to give you a free trip to Europe so he made arrangements with a friend of his, who is captain of a tramp steamer, to take you on his ship and make you wait on tables to earn your fare. That ship is supposed to depart in just three days."

Joshua laughed. "That's going to be fun," he said.

When they arrived at the chancery Pat waited in the car while Joshua went inside. As Joshua entered the vestibule the bishop was walking across the hall. When they saw each other the bishop was caught unawares and looked sheepish, making believe he hadn't really notice him. The chancellor called Joshua in immediately. He was short, rather stocky, and balding none too gracefully.

When Joshua entered the room the chancellor was sitting behind his oversized desk. Joshua wanted to laugh at the sight. The chancellor almost disappeared behind the huge desk, and as the chair he was sitting in was extra large, to compensate for his short stature, Joshua could see his feet dangling a clear two inches above the floor.

Joshua walked to the desk and stood there, looking straight at the priest sitting insecurely in his high chair. The chancellor slid off the chair as he introduced himself and shook Joshua's hand. He told Joshua to be seated, then proceeded to tell him why he had been called.

"The bishop asked me to inform you that he had been requested to make arrangements for you to go to Rome and meet with officials of the Holy Office. Accordingly, he has very generously arranged for your trip with the captain of a very fine ocean liner. The captain will provide you with passage, and you in turn will earn part of your way by working in the dining room on board ship."

"I thought the bishop was impressed with me?" Joshua told the chancellor. "How come he praised me when I was with him, then a short time later I am summoned to Rome for an investigation? It doesn't make sense."

The chancellor could not look at Joshua. He told him he didn't know anything about that.

"When does the ship leave, and from where?" Joshua asked.

"This Friday morning. The name of the ship is *Morning Star*. The captain's name is Captain Ennio Ponzelli. The ship will be leaving from Pier Forty in New York at nine in the morning."

The priest then gave Joshua an envelope with all the papers he needed. The bishop had had to use his influence to get the passport, as there were so many unknowns in Joshua's life. They had used a picture taken of Joshua at the synagogue by a man who was a friend of one of the chancery staff.

When the chancellor finished he wished Joshua a good trip and saw him to the door.

Pat was sleeping when Joshua came out. When Joshua opened the door he woke up and rubbed his eyes. "This is always a good place to sleep," he said caustically.

Joshua smiled and commented, "The Church would function better if it were closed. Like Judaism, once Jerusalem disappeared, the spirituality of the Jewish people began to thrive."

"Well, what's the verdict, Josh?" Pat asked as they drove.

"I leave Friday morning."

"Did they tell you or ask you?"

"Told me, but I didn't object. I've been looking forward to this for a long time. I can handle myself, and there's nothing they can do without my permitting it, so don't worry, Pat."

"How about lunch?" Pat asked.

"Good idea, sounds like fun," Joshua replied.

"Where will it be," Pat asked, "the kosher deli or Gino's?"

"Let's try the deli. I haven't had kosher in ages." The remark went over Pat's head.

They drove around for a while just talking and looking at the sights, then headed for the deli. They were a strange couple as they entered the restaurant, but no one paid much attention. They sat down and ordered a beer while they decided what they would eat. Joshua felt right at home, ordered a Reuben sandwich on rye and another mug of beer. Pat ordered the same. They sat and talked about a thousand things while munching on their sandwiches.

It was almost two-thirty when they finished. They took a roundabout route back to Auburn. Pat was beginning to realize the implications of the events that were about to unfold. He asked Joshua if he would be coming back to Auburn after the affair in Rome. Joshua told him honestly that he didn't think so. What would he do and where would he go? Joshua liked Pat and answered him truthfully. His work was reaching its conclusion and his future was in his Father's hands.

Pat dropped Joshua off, then went back to the rectory. The pastor was furious. "Where have you been all day?" he demanded.

"In the city, at the chancery," he answered.

"What were you doing there? Never mind, it's none of my business. I want you to help the janitor in the cellar. He needs a hand bringing wood up for the bazaar."

"I'm sorry, Father, I have some important things to do that can't wait," Pat replied. It was the first time Pat had had the courage to refuse the pastor's orders.

Father Kavanaugh was enraged at the insubordination. "Do you know who you are talking to?" he demanded.

"Yes, unfortunately. To a man obsessed with a sense of his own importance who hides behind his priesthood to dominate other people. I'm sick of it. So leave me alone or I'll walk the hell out of here, and, with your reputation, you won't get a replacement."

Pat was angry because it was the pastor who had caused all Joshua's troubles. Rather than get in deeper, he went up to his room. The pastor was speechless. Like all bullies, he didn't know how to react when someone crossed him and showed he wasn't afraid of him.

What was so important to Pat was contacting all of Joshua's friends and letting them know he would be leaving in a few days. He wanted to at least give him a decent send-off, in spite of all those phonies who had done him in. He called Aaron and told him the whole story of what had happened. Aaron called Roger Silverman and Lester, and then broke the news as gently as he could to Marcia. She broke down and cried but got herself together and called the rabbi and a few other friends. Before the hour was over the whole Jewish community knew about what had happened. They were furious with the bishop. They had thought him a decent man and honorable. Now they knew. This would cost him a small fortune in donations.

After calling Joshua's Jewish friends Pat then called the Sanders and told them to pass the word around town that Joshua was leaving and that they were having a surprise party for him at his place on Thursday evening. He didn't tell them the whole story for fear of shaking their faith. They loved Joshua and could never understand how a religious leader could be so callous as to hurt anyone so good.

The party Father Pat was planning was to be in Joshua's yard. It was plenty big enough, and if the weather was nice they should have a great time. All the village would be able to see how much the people loved Joshua.

After Father Pat had called Roger Silverman, Roger called Larry Schwartzkopf, the news director, and told him to get a crew over to Joshua's place at five-thirty on Thursday night. "But that's almost air time," he protested.

"I don't give a damn if the President's coming to town, I want a crew over there at five-thirty," Roger insisted. He wasn't ordinarily that way with his men, but he was really disturbed over this whole matter.

Although there wasn't much time to prepare a party, the people loved Joshua so much that they would drop everything to make sure they'd be there.

After Father Pat had dropped Joshua off on their return from the city Joshua went into the house and surveyed the place, wondering what last-minute business he had to take care of. He had already paid the rent and told the landlord he'd be leaving within the week. There were still some vegetables left in the garden. He went out and picked them, intending to give them to his friends on the back road. The rest of the afternoon he spent doing little things around the house. After supper he walked up to the high meadow and just thought, planning his moves for the days to come.

The next day Joshua was at peace. Now that the future was decided and the course plotted, he rested in the assurance that everything was ready for the next act of the drama. He crossed over to the side road toward where the Langfords lived.

When he reached the place the children were playing back in the yard so they didn't see him. When he knocked on the door

Margaret answered. She was surprised to see him. "My goodness, what do you have there?" she asked.

"Just some vegetables from my garden, and a few chickens I
won't be needing anymore as I'm going on a trip. I thought you
might be able to use them. They're all special-grown and fresh-
picked," he said with a grin. After he put the bags on the table
Margaret kissed him and the two sat down to talk. She offered
him a cup of coffee, which he accepted.

Anxious over what he had just said, she questioned him further. He told her he was taking a trip to Rome. She was glad for
him but said she would miss him terribly. She promised the
family's prayers for a safe journey.

At that point the children came in carrying the chickens,
which were clucking and squawking angrily. The kids were
happy to see Joshua and asked if he had brought the chickens.
Yes, they were presents for them. Their mother told them about
Joshua's trip. They were glad for him and wished they could go.

Joshua didn't stay long. He told Margaret to say good-bye to
Hank, and after kissing her tenderly, he left.

When Joshua reached his house all was still quiet. The house
was empty and neat. It was early. Joshua packed a lunch, took a
towel, and walked out to the pond to take a dip. He stayed there
all afternoon.

It was around five when he returned and he was surprised to
see cars parked along the street and people standing around on
his front lawn. He was surprised to see all of his friends, some of
whom were carrying dishes of food or bottles of one sort or
another.

When he appeared around the corner they all turned toward
him and together cried out, "Surprise!" It was a surprise, and a
strange sight, all these people, so many of them not even having
met each other before. Joshua was baffled by the spontaneous
show of enthusiastic affection from such a large group of people
who just three months before had been total strangers. They
gathered around him. Some embraced him, some kissed him,
some shook his hand warmly. There must have been a hundred
people in all, and more were coming. Joshua spotted Aaron and
Lester, and Marcia and Rabbi Mike Szeneth, Father Darby and
his chauffeur, the Reverend Rowland and the Reverend Joe

Engman, all standing and talking together. Then he saw Father
Pat in the middle of the group, beaming from ear to ear. It
finally dawned on Joshua just what was going on. Pat had organized the whole affair. He just hoped he hadn't told everyone
the whole truth of what had happened. Joshua was concerned
for people's already fragile faith.

Walking over to the group, Joshua asked Lester what this was
all about.

"I guess you wouldn't have the slightest idea, would you,
Josh?" Lester said playfully.

Joshua looked Pat straight in the eye, and the priest broke
down and confessed what he had done. "Well, I didn't want you
to just disappear without saying good-bye to all these people
who love you so much. That would have been cruel, and knowing how sensitive you are to people's feelings, I knew you
wouldn't mind. So enjoy it and let them show you their love.
It's good for everybody."

Joshua realized they were right. He had never experienced
anything like this, except on that one occasion at Bethany so
long ago. But that was only a family affair. This was a grand
testimonial.

Joshua still had the towel over his shoulder and his hair was all
mussed up, so after smiling across to the crowd he excused himself and went inside to comb his hair and make himself more
presentable. Father Pat led the crowd around to the backyard,
where there was more privacy and the atmosphere more relaxing.

Some of the women were barging into the kitchen asking to
borrow things. Arthur, Father Darby's chauffeur, and Woozie,
and his friend Tony were busy trying to get a fire started in the
grill and they were looking for charcoal. When Joshua went out
Phil Packer confronted him. "Josh, you're like something from
another age. Don't you have anything modern? How are we
going to get this grill going?"

"Use Woozie's torch," Joshua replied. "If that doesn't work,
rub two sticks together. That's always worked."

At that moment Moe Sanders and his brothers came, all of
them this time, including his brother Freddie. Moe told Joshua
there was a television truck out in front and a reporter was look-

ing for him. Joshua went out front and they were all ready for him. The reporter had his pad in his hand and started firing questions at Joshua. What happened? How come this sudden turn of events? Is it true the bishop reported you to Rome and you're being investigated?

Joshua had to be shrewd this time. To be honest and truthful was one thing, to damage the Church or the people's faith was another. Out of a sense of loyalty to the shepherds of the flock, Joshua tried to put events in a light that would be more understandable. But the reporters saw that he was evading them so they zeroed in and asked him if what he taught was objected to by officials. Joshua told them that it was always difficult to agree on matters of belief:

"Church officials are concerned about order among the people, prophets are concerned about people's relationship with God. There will always be tension between the two. Only when officials try to suppress the voice of prophets is real damage done to people and to God's message. This tension would be lessened if spiritual leaders were as knowledgeable about spiritual things as they are about the worldly business of the Church. The real key to progress in the kingdom of God is not in legal structures but in allowing people to enjoy their freedom as God's children and to grow as individuals, not constrained by rigid laws that prevent growth. The Church has to get away from the role of universal moral policeman and judge of human behavior. She must learn to guide by inspiring people to noble ideals and not by legislating human behavior. The sheep will always flee when shepherds try to bully them. Human behavior must be free if it is to be pleasing to God."

"Is it true," the reporter asked, "that you have been summoned to Rome for official proceedings?"

"Yes."

"What have you said that is so wrong?" the reporter probed deeper.

"The words of Jesus and what they imply are never too popular. People get angry when they interfere with the way they are used to doing things. No one likes discipline, but, unlike other people, religious leaders see criticism of traditions or suggestions for change as attacks on doctrine. That is not necessarily true.

The Church must review its relationship with God and His people honestly if they are to remain faithful to their trust."

"What are some of the words of Jesus that are not being observed?" the reporter continued.

"Jesus preached poverty and humility. That is never popular so it is ignored. Jesus also preached gentleness and meekness among his apostles. That is also ignored. When it is criticized the criticism is resented."

"Is that why you are being called to Rome?"

"I don't know, I haven't been told."

"Didn't the bishop tell you when he was talking to you?"

"The bishop told me I was a good man and there should be more Christians like me."

"So you have no idea what their complaint is?"

"No."

"Since you are not a priest, can they order you around like this?"

"They presume jurisdiction over all baptized persons. I have no objection to meeting with Peter."

"Thank you, Joshua," the reporter said in ending the interview. Roger Silverman was standing nearby and told the reporter not to edit the interview but to televise the whole thing. The crew stayed around for a little while talking to people and getting their reactions to Joshua. They then left.

The people were watching Joshua. You could see the affection in their eyes. He had been in their midst only a few months, but he had captured their hearts. His quiet, unassuming ways, his sincere feeling for people, his concern for even the simplest, his gracious manner with rich and poor, the powerful and the lowly, attracted people to him like a magnet. He fascinated them and bewildered them. Who was he really? Was he just a wood-carver? Where had he come from? There were so many mysteries about him that it made people even more curious. But they loved him and now they were showing that love.

Joshua was gratified by the people's response. It made him realize how people could react to a shepherd who guided them the way Jesus intended. Father Pat was at home with all these different people. In situations like this he really shone. He liked people and he wanted this occasion to be special. All during the evening he didn't touch a drop of liquor. Pat Zumbar kidded him about it, and he told him that Joshua did so much for him, in helping him to understand himself and his work, that out of friendship he had sworn off the bottle. He no longer needed it. And it didn't go unnoticed by Joshua either, even though he seemed so occupied with others that it could have easily escaped him.

It had been arranged by Father Pat that no one would bring any gifts. Joshua would want it that way. It would also embarrass the poor. Only Father Jeremy K. Darby violated the agreement. He approached Joshua when he was alone and gave him two one-hundred-dollar bills, which he said was for the statue of the Apostle Peter. He also admitted it was a masterpiece of psychological insight. While he was talking he pressed into Joshua's hand a tiny gift-wrapped box, which he told Joshua not to open until he was on board ship. Jeremy was visibly shaken by the prospect of Joshua's leaving, but like a true Englishman he was not one to get emotional—no matter how he felt inside.

Joshua thanked him and looked deep into his eyes. Messages passed that needed no words, and Jeremy understood. He smiled and wished Joshua bon voyage.

Most of the activity during the rest of the evening centered around the grill. Everyone was either sitting on the grass or on the steps, or on whatever chairs there were available. They were all talking excitedly and in good humor as they got acquainted with their newfound friends. Pat Zumbar's voice could still be heard clearly above the rest. The Jewish people were more sophisticated than the other villagers but they were intrigued by their simple warmth and sincerity and many new friendships were made that night.

Marcia stayed in the background, though she was dying to know about Joshua's future. Only well into the evening did she finally approach him. She told him she cared for him deeply and would miss him more than he could imagine. Joshua told her he loved her and would think of her always. When she asked if he would be coming back he said he thought not, though he did not know what God had planned for him. He always left his future up to his Father. He told Marcia not to worry about her work. She was a light in darkness, and God would bring her work to fruition. What she had to offer mankind would stand out clearly, even when she seemed not to succeed. Success is measured in different ways. Her life's work would be a great success and would affect the lives of many people.

She told him she would pray for him every day and would never forget him. She doubted if there would be any other man in her life. He had made too deep an impression, and no one could ever take his place. She hoped their paths would cross again, but if they didn't she wanted him to have a little keepsake. She took his hand and pressed a gold medal and chain into his palm, asking him if he would wear it. It was her most precious possession, and she would be so proud if he would accept it. Joshua looked at it. It was a figure of the sun on fire, with a man standing in the middle of it. It had been given to her by an African king during a United Nations tour one year. The medal, for some reason, reminded her of Joshua. Joshua accepted it gratefully. Tears were beginning to well up in Marcia's eyes so she wished him well, kissed him affectionately, and walked back to her friends. Joshua watched her as she walked away. She was beautiful and rare. He did love her, and would never forget her.

The party went on until late in the evening. Then, as people had to get to work the next day, they began taking their leave and departed one by one, thanking Joshua for his friendship and wishing him well. Aaron, Marcia, Lester, their wives, as well as Father Pat and Reverend Joe Engman, were the last to go. Aaron mentioned to Joshua that Rabbi Szeneth's son, Michael, would be working on the same ship that he was taking to Rome. Aaron and Lester thanked Joshua for all that he had done for them. Not only their lives but the lives of many people would be affected by what he had taught them by his words and example. They would never forget him. Marcia looked at him sadly but said nothing. She just smiled and kissed him good-bye and left with the others. Joshua had tears in his eyes.

Reverend Joe Engman and Father Pat had earlier offered to take Joshua to New York. It was a good three-hour trip east by turnpike. Joshua was grateful for their offer. They were the last to leave with the Sanders and their buddies. Finally the place was quiet. Joshua went to bed, his work finished.

18

JOSHUA ROSE AT four-thirty, precisely as planned and without alarm. Father Pat and Reverend Joe Engman arrived at five-thirty, right after Joshua had finished breakfast. They had a cup of coffee with him, shared a few jokes, and started out. Joshua looked around the house with a touch of melancholy. He took a hammer and chisel off the workbench and gave them to Pat, and another set and gave them to Joe, without saying a word. He picked up his little pack containing all his worldly possessions and looked out the back window across the meadow. Through the slats in the picket fence he could see three sheep looking into the yard. He walked out the back door, over to the fence, and petted the sheep, affectionately pulling their ears like he always did, then went into the house and out the front door with his two companions. They saw tears trickling down his cheeks but said nothing.

The car rolled quietly out of the village. Most of the people were still asleep. The golden rays of a blood-red sun cut like lasers through the trees. It was chilly. Joshua was wearing his sweater. It was a perfect morning for a long ride. Down the country roads to the turnpike they went. In no time they were at the tollgate.

"Getting an early start today, Father?" the toll collector asked as he gave Pat the ticket.

"Yea, got a long trip ahead," Pat responded sleepily.

The trip to the city didn't seem long. Once they were fully awake the men talked all the way. They stopped at the service area near the last exit to get gas and another cup of coffee and a doughnut. Traffic in the city was not heavy yet and they arrived at the dock in plenty of time. The ship was all ready to leave. It was an old ship but presentable. As the three men walked up the plank to the deck the captain greeted them. He was a pleasant man, good-looking, and spoke with a refined Italian accent. He looked distinguished in his naval uniform. He presumed Joshua was the passenger, being accompanied by two clerics, so he asked for his papers. Joshua took them out of his pocket and handed them to him. He looked them over and welcomed Joshua coolly, then called a deckhand to show Joshua his cabin. Pat and Joe followed. Down the stairs to a back corridor they walked. The room was by itself. It was the only one left by the time the bishop made the arrangements. It was a room not ordinarily used. The deckhand opened the door and let the men pass into the room. It was small, but neat and freshly painted. There was one bunk, a chest of drawers, and a bathroom. They all laughed at Joshua's luxury apartment and went back upstairs together.

It was almost sailing time, so Pat and Joe said good-bye. It was a difficult parting for all of them. They had become close and had similar approaches to life. Pat told Joshua he would pray for him. Joe did the same. Joshua told them to be true to themselves and follow their convictions and not become discouraged because people did not understand them. Things that are of value are usually out of the ordinary. Same with ideas. To lead people you can't think the way they do. So don't expect them to understand. You are doing God's work, He will give the reward in good time.

The two men hugged Joshua and left the boat. The gangplank was lifted and the ship's whistle blew. Slowly the huge boat slipped away from the dock. From down below the men waved to Joshua. He waved back. He looked a sad, lonely figure all by himself on the big ship. That was the last his friends saw of him.

Joshua was assigned duties in the dining room. He was to report to the cook at six in the morning to set the tables for breakfast, then wait on people during breakfast. He would again come to the kitchen at eleven and do the same for lunch. Supper would be at six o'clock, so he would be ready at five to serve that meal. Otherwise, he was free.

When the sailor finished with the instructions Joshua walked back on deck and looked across the water toward the land. It was moving farther and farther away. A trace of melancholy passed over him as he thought of all the goodness and beauty he had found in so many of the people he met during his brief stay in Auburn. He thought also of the pastor and the bishop, and pitied them. Their lives were so shallow and empty. They had little to give people. He looked out to sea and wondered what the next few weeks would bring. Would it be pleasant or disheartening?

In no time it was eleven o'clock. Joshua went to report to the cook. He told him to put out the water and set the tables. He showed him where the serving dishes were and told him to bring them over to the counter so he could put the food in them. He then told him to cut the bread and put it in baskets. By that time the passengers were entering the dining room. They were friendly and asked Joshua his name. He told them, exchanged pleasantries, and helped them to their seats. The cook gave Joshua a serving towel to put over his arm.

"What's that for?" Joshua asked.

"In case you have to touch anything hot, or have to brush crumbs from the table, or open a bottle of wine and prevent it from dripping on the tablecloth."

Lunch went easily. There were only some twenty-five people in all, including the captain and his officers. Joshua was sharp. He watched and anticipated each little need, and if someone wanted something he would approach the person and courteously ask if he could help. The women, particularly, were impressed with the delicacy of his manners and how prompt he was in noticing when anyone needed something.

Supper was much the same. It didn't take long for some of the more observant of the guests to notice Joshua and the graceful dignity that flowed with such ease from his personality. They were tempted to ask him questions to learn more about him but decided against it, thinking it more courteous to respect his privacy. But as he became the topic of talk at the tables the curiosity deepened. By the second day of the voyage people were keenly aware that this was not just an ordinary ship's servant. There was a majesty about him even when he served that belied the simplicity of his appearance. Although it was not his place to talk to the guests, they could detect from the way he answered questions that he was highly intelligent. From conversations with him on deck between meals they got to know him more intimately and developed a respect for him that embarrassed them when he waited on tables. He sensed this and tried to put them at ease by telling them what nice people they were and how much he enjoyed waiting on them.

There was only one person who gave Joshua a difficult time. He was a rough, boisterous man who found fault with just about everything. Joshua tried hard to please him and, to the admiration of everyone, never lost his cool. The man seemed to become even more obnoxious when he noticed it didn't bother Joshua, who just smiled and ignored his remarks. The other guests were embarrassed for Joshua, but enjoyed noticing how little the man's manners bothered him.

On the third day of the voyage, while Joshua was sitting on deck with some of the guests, a tragedy occurred below. One of the cabin boys fell down the stairs. They took him into the sick bay and paged the doctor. He rushed down and examined the boy. His neck was broken, and there was little life in him. The doctor did what he could, but it was of no use. The boy died a few minutes later. The doctor examined the X-ray he had taken and found a fracture in two of the upper vertebrae. The boy's name passed quickly around the ship. His name was Michael Szeneth.

When word reached Joshua he said nothing, just excused himself from the little circle of guests and went below deck. As he walked along the corridor the captain was leaving the radio room. He saw Joshua but paid little attention to him until he noticed he was heading for the sick bay. Then he became curious. He watched him from a distance and saw him enter the room where the dead body lay. There was no one else in the room, and as Joshua had left the door half open the captain could see everything.

Joshua walked over to the table where the corpse was lying, lifted the sheet from the boy's head, and called out to him, "Michael, wake up!" Shivers went up and down the captain's spine. After a moment the boy's eyes opened. He looked at Joshua. "Sit up, Michael," Joshua told him. The boy did as he was told and sat up on the table. The captain was overwhelmed and didn't know whether to scream with joy that his friend's son was alive or to fall on his knees. The boy's father had been a friend for years, and he felt terrible about what had occurred. But now his joy was a thousand times greater than his grief, and he was thrilled beyond measure. Joshua, in the meantime, was telling the boy to eat a piece of bread he had just handed him. Michael asked what had happened. Joshua told him he was all right, that he should go about his work and not tell anyone about what had happened. Joshua then left the room and went back on deck as if nothing had happened.

The captain went immediately to the doctor and told him the boy was sitting up. The doctor said that was ridiculous, the boy was dead. The two men ran to the sick bay, and when the doctor saw Michael standing near the bed he was beside himself. He told the boy to get back on the table.

"But why? I'm all right."

"Sonny, you were dead. What happened?" the doctor asked.

When the boy said nothing the doctor insisted. Even the captain didn't feel he could tell the doctor what had happened. The doctor insisted on taking another X-ray. The X-ray showed nothing, no fracture, no trace of a fracture. He couldn't have made a mistake. He impatiently grabbed the first X-ray, looked at it, compared it with the second, and, with satisfaction in his voice, showed the captain. "There, his neck was broken. See. But what happened? How did it heal? I can't understand this."

The doctor released the boy and told him if he had any feeling of weakness or nausea to come back immediately. When Michael went upstairs he became an instant celebrity. Everyone wanted to know what had happened. Michael told them nothing more than what he himself remembered, about falling down the stairs and faint recollections of people gathering around him, but nothing more until he woke up. Did he see anything when he was dead? Did he hear any music or voices? Did he see God? The boy protested that he didn't know a thing until he woke up.

The captain didn't know what to do. He had to make a full report, but what could he put into the report? Should he tell just what he had witnessed? Who would believe it? But he had no choice. He could only write what he saw. If they believed it, all well and good. If they didn't believe it, that was their problem.

The doctor had more of a problem. He could not account for the few brief moments between his leaving the dead boy and seeing him standing up a few minutes later. The captain was no help, though later that night he confided to the doctor what he had witnessed. The doctor scoffed and was still at a loss as to what he should write in his report.

The incident happened in the middle of the afternoon. Captain Ponzelli was deeply affected by the event. He began to wonder about the real identity of this humble waiter who took such delight in serving the guests. The bishop had told him a few details about Joshua, but none of them seemed to fit the man he had come to know the past few days. He became nervous at the thought of Joshua waiting on tables, especially waiting on him.

The captain called Joshua to his quarters. When he arrived he offered him a seat and treated him graciously. "Joshua," he said, "I've decided to take you off dining-room duty."

"Why, Captain?" Joshua asked, concerned. "I enjoy waiting on the people. They are good people and I like doing things for them."

"Joshua, I saw what happened this afternoon. I know you and understand you better than I did. You are a lot different from what I had been told about you, and I really don't feel comfortable allowing you to do this menial kind of work."

"But Captain, that was my agreement with the bishop and I would like to keep my word."

The captain thought for a long moment. "All right, but I don't feel comfortable about it." Then he laughed as he thought of something. "I have an idea. I love to cook, but I never have a chance. How about me giving the cook some time off and you and I will do the cooking and serve the people ourselves? I usually do it one night of each voyage anyway."

Joshua laughed and agreed. So the captain called the cook in and told him his intentions. The cook was delighted. He didn't mind at all. So at four-thirty Joshua and the captain went down to the galley. Joshua got the tables ready as usual, and found things in the cabinet for the captain, while the captain went through the refrigerator and the pantry looking for things he needed for the meal.

For appetizers he decided on German-style fish in sour cream, fried wonton strips with soy-lemon sauce, and slices of tomato pesto tart. The next course would be artichoke mushroom salad remoulade and midwestern green salad. The main course would be Indonesian sate, a Southeast Asian version of kabobs, served with spicy peanut sauce and rice with turmeric. The dessert would be Gugelhupf cake served with apricot sauce and a variety of coffees.

The dinner started a little late, but no one minded. Word had gotten around that the captain was cooking so the passengers weren't expecting it to be on time. They were all delighted with the idea of the captain doing the cooking. And he really did look the part with his white apron and high chef's hat.

Joshua served the appetizers. The people raved about them. "The captain should stay on as chef," remarked the chef himself as he stuffed himself with wontons. The next course came out. The people couldn't get over the captain's flare for gourmet cooking. In fact, it was a stroke of public relations genius. The whole affair brought everyone closer together. When the main course and the big spread of desserts and coffees came out, that really impressed everyone.

When the passengers finished eating and Joshua had cleaned up the tables, the people just sat around in the dining room eating their dessert and sipping their coffee. The captain and his helpers all sat at the captain's table afterward, and ate their own supper. They were immensely proud of themselves, especially when the cook himself came over and praised them for the magnificent job they had done. "I couldn't have done better myself," he told them. They all laughed.

The whole atmosphere on the ship changed after that. Everyone seemed more relaxed and friendly. The crew, who ate in their own dining room, had the same food as the guests and they loved it. Their attitude toward the captain changed. They still respected him, but they now had a much warmer feeling for him, seeing that he could be so human. They showed their appreciation by doing many little extra things that weren't part of their duties.

Joshua could see a lot of goodness in the captain. That was why he was chosen to witness what he did. The next two nights the captain and Joshua did a repeat of the previous night but with different menus. The two men became close as they got better acquainted. The captain had not told anyone about the incident in the sick bay, except for the doctor. He was sorry he had told him. It upset the doctor, and he had been miserable ever since.

The incident also brought Michael and Joshua closer to each other. They shared a common secret. Michael, who knew the captain well, talked to him about what had happened and asked him what it all meant. The captain admitted he didn't understand it either and just felt that Joshua, for all his simplicity, was an unusual person who must be very close to God. Michael told him that he thought he was much more than that and proceeded to tell him about all the experiences at his father's synagogue in Auburn.

"You should hear him speak," Michael said. "He's inspired, I'm convinced. You should have seen what happened one night at the synagogue. This real nut from our congregation approached Joshua and lit into him for the way Christians have persecuted the Jews throughout history. Joshua just listened to him and then threw his arms around him. The two became friends immediately and walked into the sanctuary hand in hand. It was beautiful." The captain just listened, trying hard to understand and wondering why the bishop had shipped him off to Rome to be investigated.

The third day of the voyage passed without incident, though the sea was beginning to get rough. Joshua came down with a bad case of seasickness and had to miss lunch. He tried to make it, and even appeared in the galley, but when the cook saw him he called the captain. The captain ordered Joshua to stay in bed and had the doctor prescribe something to ease the nausea. "He can cure others, but he can't take care of himself," the doctor told the captain. Captain Ponzelli winced at the sound of those words.

The next day the ship was approaching the Azores. The weather was always unpredictable in this area, and Captain Ponzelli told the passengers that, if they were prone to motion sickness, they should see the doctor and perhaps take medicine to prevent nausea. The sea did become rough, and heavy dark clouds gathered over the horizon. The morning wasn't too bad, but by afternoon the waves were higher and heavy rains began to lash against the ship.

The captain called the radio room for a weather report. Heavy rains, severe winds. The waves were powerful and began rocking the boat. Even the gyroscopes had little effect. Sailors were securing everything that moved so nothing would be swept into the sea. Most of the people had gone to their cabins or to the recreation room, where *Return of the Pink Panther* was showing. Joshua stayed in his room and tried to rest. The heaving sea was too much for him.

By four o'clock the weather was much worse. The rains were beating against the ship with such force, you could scarcely hear anyone talking. The winds had risen to gale force, and radio warnings were telling ship captains not to leave port until the storm subsided. The captain worked his way to the front of the ship to be with the pilot. The pilot couldn't see a thing out the window. The ship was tossing mercilessly. At one point the captain lost his balance and fell against the wall, banging his head against an iron bolt. He mopped the blood off his head and put his hat back on over the handkerchief.

The waves were rising. They were already almost fifteen feet and still getting higher. The captain was beginning to fear the ship might not make it. It was an old ship, and had gone through many a beating before, but this was the worst and there was a limit to what the vessel could take. The pilot tried to steer the boat into the oncoming waves but the wind kept pushing the ship against them, which completely inundated the vessel, threatening to capsize it.

The captain looked out the windows for any indication of the storm letting up, hoping there were no other vessels on their course. Storms at sea make everyone feel helpless. A huge, powerful ship that glides like a sailboat during good weather is totally at the mercy of the elements as soon as the weather changes. It is tossed about like a helpless piece of driftwood. The most any captain can do is keep the vessel steady and prevent the passengers from panicking.

But Captain Ponzelli was becoming increasingly concerned. There were no signs of the storm letting up, and there was nothing more he could do. He sighed a quiet prayer and continued staring out into the wall of rain. He walked to the right side of the room and looked out onto the deck for any signs of damage. Nothing so far. It was hard to see clearly. He thought he saw something unusual. He looked again and could see the faint outline of a figure tugging on the railing as he pulled himself up along the deck. The captain gasped in disbelief. It was Joshua. What in God's name was he doing out there? One false move, one slip of the foot on that slick deck, and he would be swept into the sea. He started to open the window to scream down but realized it would be useless. What in hell was he up to? The captain just watched and kept what he saw to himself. He had come to love that simple, good-natured fellow and had enjoyed the happy times of the past few days. But why would he have to do a stupid thing like this? He said a silent prayer for the poor fool. What was he trying to do? Where was he going?

The captain stood there transfixed, watching breathlessly, as Joshua, soaked to the bone, worked his way up along the deck. Momentarily the wind shifted. The boat steadied itself for only a brief moment, allowing Joshua to stand up straight. He lifted his eyes to heaven and held out his arms as if giving command to the winds. His mouth could be seen screaming into the howling wind, as if he had gone mad. The captain felt pity for the poor fellow. Maybe this is what made the bishop nervous.

Suddenly the wind died down, the rain slowed, and the waves subsided altogether. The clouds began to disperse, allowing blue sky to appear and the sun to cast a bright ray through the opening in the skies. Joshua turned and walked back inside and disappeared below deck, into his room, to take a shower and dry off.

The captain covered his face with his hands, in awe at what he had just witnessed. The pilot thought he was praying his thanks that the storm was letting up. The captain told the pilot to go below and take a rest, he would relieve him for a while. The pilot thanked him. He sure could use a rest. He left and went below.

Left with his thoughts, the captain wondered about what he had just seen. He was more convinced than ever of the real identity of this humble, simple man. "But is it possible? Could it possibly be?" he wondered as the tears flowed down his cheeks at the thought that it could happen to him, unworthy as he was. His memory drifted far back into childhood, to when his uncle, a priest, told his family strange stories of things that took place in the lives of people with simple faith. But the captain was not a man of simple faith, at least he didn't think he was. He felt guilty he was not more religious. He thought of his uncle, who was now a cardinal at the Vatican. He would have to tell him all about this as soon as he landed. Perhaps he could tell him what it all meant. He couldn't wait until the ship reached port. He would call him immediately.

The pilot came back after his brief rest and thanked the captain.

"Did you get a rest?" the captain asked.

"Yes, and I was thinking about the storm and how fast it passed. I told the radioman. He said he couldn't understand how it could have cleared up here when he was still receiving severe storm alerts. There are storms and gale winds all around the area as far as the Canaries."

"I'm sure there are," the captain said simply, then left to find Joshua.

People were beginning to come back on deck when the captain came down. The sun was out and the air was beautiful. He asked if anyone had seen Joshua. Someone saw him soaking wet, a few minutes before, walking in the direction of his cabin. The captain went down below deck.

He could hear him inside singing an unfamiliar tune. He knocked.

"Come in."

The captain opened the door. Joshua was just taking his shirt off a hot pipe that ran through a space in the back of his closet. He put on the shirt and greeted the captain as if nothing had happened.

"Anything I can do for you?" he asked the captain.

"No, you've done enough already," was the captain's ready reply.

Joshua let the remark pass, not wanting to get drawn into the discussion that would inevitably follow.

"I just wanted to say thank you for what you did," the captain said humbly. Joshua just smiled at him with a strange, boyish smile as if it was nothing.

"Joshua, I don't know how to say this," the captain continued, "but I feel proud to have you on my ship. I really don't deserve what has taken place the past few days. But I know it will change my whole life. I feel bad about how it all came about, the investigation in Rome, the distrust of the bishop and the other authorities. I have an uncle in the Vatican. Maybe he can be of some help when you get there. I will give him a call as soon as I land and tell him to expect you. His name is Cardinal Giovanni Riccardo. He's a good man."

"Thanks, Captain," Joshua said, "I may need some help when I get there. I'm afraid they will have a difficult time understanding me. I don't have very high hopes."

"But how can they find fault with you? After all, it was you who started . . ." His voice trailed off before he finished, realizing he was on ground where he didn't belong. He had no right prying any further and knew Joshua wasn't going to open the door more than a crack. He had already heard and seen enough.

"But they won't have any idea, no more than you when I first set foot on your ship."

The captain blushed at the cool reception he had given Joshua when he arrived on board. Joshua reminded the captain it was almost suppertime and they hadn't prepared the food yet.

The two men walked out of the cabin, the captain asking Joshua if he was up to working in the galley after his last ordeal. Joshua looked at him sternly and reassured him how much he enjoyed waiting on the people. He hadn't had so much fun in a long time. Everyone has fun in different ways. He had fun making people happy.

"I suppose that's the way God is," the captain said with a grin. Joshua laughed at the captain's playfulness.

The dinner was late, but the people didn't mind. They spent an extra hour at the bar having cocktails and hors d'oeuvres and were just grateful the storm had ended. This was the last supper on board the ship and the captain outdid himself in spite of the strain of having guided the ship through the storm. The meal was a smorgasbord of all the guests' favorite dishes.

The dinner lasted till well past midnight. Since everyone was having such a good time, they turned it into the evening's recreation as well.

During the meal the doctor had been watching Joshua. He was more than curious. Besides, he had already had too much to drink and was determined to draw Joshua into a conversation.

When everyone was sitting around afterward he called Joshua over and pulled out a chair. After offering a drink, which Joshua politely refused, he asked him where he was educated. Joshua told him his education was extensive and he had the best of teachers, even though he had never gone to college. The doctor laughed at the flippant humor.

"You are quite an intelligent fellow," the doctor observed. "In fact, you have much more intelligence than most of the people in this room. You know, young man, what's your name, Joshua, you know, I haven't filled out the medical report on that boy yet," the doctor rambled on. "I'm frankly at a loss as to what I should put down. Perhaps you could help me."

"How can I help you, Doctor, you're the expert," Joshua remarked.

"I may be the expert, but there are some things that baffle me. And, I frankly admit, this is one of them. Do you believe in miracles, young man?"

"No."

The doctor was taken aback. He was expecting a pious lecture. "Then how do you explain what happened the other day?"

"A little thing like that stands out in your mind because you miss the much greater mysteries that take place continually every day. What happened the other day surprises you because it was unexpected. Look in the mirror when you go to your room tonight and you will see an evolution of wonders far more exciting than the healing of a broken bone and the revival of the spark of life. The whole course of each day is filled with endless wonder, which we take for granted because it all flows so smoothly as the ordinary course of life. But each tiny event, and each moment of time, is a miracle of creation."

"That's very poetic," the doctor commented, "but you presume it is creation. I take it then that you believe in God."

"No. We believe what we do not see. I know God is, just as surely as you know I am sitting here before you."

"What do I put down about what happened to Michael?" the doctor finally asked.

"Put down what you witnessed. It is very simple. It is because you don't believe what you saw that you are having trouble writing the simple facts," Joshua told him.

"I would be laughed out of the medical society if I wrote that down."

"But if it is true then you should be the one who is laughing at their ignorance. When you witness something beautiful you should be happy and proud, not ashamed and afraid."

"You're a strange man, Joshua. I don't know what to make of you. How did Michael get healed?" the doctor shot point-blank.

Joshua laughed. "When we pray God hears. When we need God grants. Faith is like the helpless look on the face of a deer in hunting season. God can't refuse."

"Joshua, I wish I had your faith, or whatever it is you have. You are so free and so happy. I don't believe in God. I guess I'm an atheist."

"No one who heals can be an atheist. Life just gets out of focus. You have become too used to seeing wonders slip through your fingers. When you take the time to put back together all the mysteries you have dissected, and stand back and take notice, you will see the reflection of God and His shadow passing by. Then you will have no more doubt. His healing power courses through your fingers every day, and you have never taken the time to sense his presence. You are God's hands. His very closeness has hidden him from you."

"Young man, you baffle me. I told you, you are smarter than most of the people here."

Joshua smiled and, after telling the doctor how much he had enjoyed talking to him, excused himself and left the dining room. It had been a long day, and, as free and casual as Joshua appeared, the day's events had drained him of every drop of energy. Tomorrow they would be arriving in Italy, and a new chapter would unfold. He needed his sleep.

When he reached his cabin and turned on the light, he noticed a little box that had fallen from the bag in which he kept his belongings. It was the present Father Darby had given him. He picked it up and opened it. Inside were two old Roman coins similar to the ones Jesus referred to when he made the remark "Give unto Caesar the things that are Caesar's, and give unto God the things that are God's." Joshua laughed. The priest had a good sense of humor. Joshua remembered the remark he had made on one occasion when talking to the priest about his church. He had said that in making the King of England head of the Church the bishops had not only violated the injunction of Jesus but betrayed their sacred trust and turned the kingdom of heaven over to Caesar.

19

THE *MORNING STAR* pulled into Ostia. It was late in the afternoon. The passengers stood along the deck, enchanted by the breathtaking scene, the ancient city rising from the shore. Houses seemingly sitting on top of each other. Beautiful pastel colors. The emerald green water clear to the bottom. A cool breeze sweeping across the water. The passengers were excited about landing so they could start exploring all the beauty unfolding before them.

The old ship dropped anchor. The captain said good-bye to the guests as they filed past. He shook Joshua's hand warmly, and at the last moment threw his arms around him and they embraced. Michael, who was standing next to the captain, did the same. They thanked Joshua for everything and wished him well. The doctor was going to Rome for a few days and asked Joshua if he needed a ride. Joshua was glad to accept. He didn't have much money and would have walked otherwise.

The ride to Rome was short. The doctor told Joshua he had thought a lot about the talk they had the night before and that he had written in the report the facts as they occurred. He felt good about it, though he wasn't sure what it all meant. He enjoyed the experience of meeting Joshua and doubted he would ever meet anyone like him again.

Joshua told him not to be hard on himself. He was a good man and, in time, the pieces of the puzzle would all fall in place and he would find peace.

The doctor left Joshua off near St. Peter's Square. After saying good-bye, Joshua took his traveling bag and walked off into the vast square, looking wide-eyed at the grandeur and splendor of Christendom's tribute to the majesty of God.

The piazza, with its massive statues of the saints along the top of the porticoes, seemed to reach out as if embracing the world, the gigantic basilica rising high in front of him, magnificent in comparison to the temple in Jerusalem. His thoughts wandered to similar porticoes, infinitely smaller, crowded with people and priests and Pharisees in flowing robes. The memory of the woman caught in adultery passed across his mind. Everything then seemed miniature when compared with the dimensions of this vast monument to God's glory.

He walked across the cobblestoned piazza to the basilica. People were wandering all around, looking here and there, trying to absorb all their eyes scanned. Black-robed clerics carrying briefcases dotted the open space. Joshua walked up the few steps to the entrance and went inside the vast sanctuary. He noticed the statue of Peter, with the toe worn down from being touched. He smiled. He looked up at the ceiling and stood there in ecstasy at the pictorial portrayal of the whole Bible. He walked around the aisles, noting every detail of every painting and statue. Organ music played as the organist rehearsed for a concert or Sunday service. Above the main altar a massive sunburst reflected the glory of heaven. The imagination and genius of man would be hard-pressed to improve on this representation of heaven to the human eye. The artists had done well in portraying God's majesty. "But," Joshua thought, "why do people try so hard to reproduce heaven on earth and have such a difficult time absorbing the message of the stable? They find more meaning in representing God's majesty and find more comfort in being surrounded by power and magnificence than in living the simplicity of the real message. They have missed the whole point of the gospel. Even when they preach poverty and detachment, coming from this setting it negates the sincerity of the message."

He walked out of the basilica and headed for the side street where he was to stay.

The apartment house was an old stone building with a heavy wooden front door protected by iron supports. Joshua walked in and introduced himself to the little old man who tended the desk. The man filled out some papers and gave Joshua the key to his room, which was around the corner and up a short flight of stairs. It was the only room at the head of the stairs. In fact, it was a dead end. Joshua went up the stairs and entered the room. It was small, just enough space for a bed and chair and a dresser. There was a simple bathroom with a shower. It was all he needed.

He put his bag on the chair and fell down on the bed to take a rest. He was finally here. Tomorrow morning he would have his interview. In a few seconds he was asleep. As he drifted off he thought of Auburn, and the simple people there; he thought of the synagogue and Marcia and Aaron. He missed them and felt homesick for all the memories he had left behind.

He rested for only half an hour, then got up, washed, walked out into the street, and wandered through the streets of Rome, watching vendors selling their wares, all charging different prices for the same things. He noticed little children, Christian children, in the center of Christendom, undisciplined, working at businesses no child should even know about. He was approached by exotically dressed girls inviting him to come with them. He was fascinated by the compact cars and mopeds speeding their way through narrow streets, miraculously missing little old ladies, frantically trying to cross the street. He saw robed clerics walking two by two, talking excitedly about the day's events. He was amused by the stately Protestant church with the bold sign in front, "Lux in tenebris lucet" ("A light shining in darkness").

A small restaurant attracted Joshua's attention. He walked over, looked at the prices on the menu in the window, which were a little high, but he was hungry so he went inside and sat down. A waiter wearing a black suit, with a white serving towel over his left arm, came over. Aware of Joshua's non-Italian features, he asked in broken English what he would like. A large dish of shell macaroni in marinara sauce and a glass of Frascati. The man took the order and returned with a small loaf of bread and a plate of salad.

Joshua looked around the room. There were pictures of Naples and Capri painted on the walls and small tables neatly covered with red and white checkerboard cloths. In the middle of each table stood a large Chianti bottle holding a lighted candle, which created a warm, congenial atmosphere. Two young lovers were sitting on the far side of the room in a corner talking intimately while they ate cannolis and sipped cappuccino. Joshua felt alone.

The waiter brought the steaming dish of macaroni and placed it before Joshua. He opened the bottle of Frascati, poured a little in a glass, and offered it to Joshua to taste. Joshua approved and the waiter filled his glass. Joshua thanked him, tucked his napkin into his shirt, and went to work on the gigantic pile of shells covered with red sauce. He was hungry and ate with gusto. The waiter brought over a bowl of grated cheese and placed it on the table.

Every now and then Joshua rested and sipped his wine. He enjoyed the meal and told the waiter how good the food was.

After he finished the macaroni he had just a cup of espresso, then left a generous tip, paid his bill, and walked outside. It was almost nine-thirty. He walked around the streets for a while, enjoying the colored lights and watching people in the sidewalk cafes, then went back to his apartment and went to bed.

The next day was hot and sultry. Car and truck engines replaced the birdsongs at sunrise. Joshua woke up early, washed, dressed, and went to a small restaurant for breakfast.

His appointment at the Ufficio was for nine-thirty. It wasn't far away, so he had plenty of time. After breakfast he walked to the entrance of Vatican City. Two brightly dressed Swiss Guards asked for his identification. The only identification he had was a letter from the cardinal. If he could show them the letter, that might do.

The guard looked at the letter, and allowed him to pass. He went up the stairs to the first office attended by a Christian Brother. Joshua told him who he was and why he was there. The brother made a phone call, then gave Joshua a pass and told him where to go, sending an attendant with him to escort him through the palace.

Outside the hall where the Congregation for the Doctrines of the Faith held its proceedings a guard was standing on duty, checking the papers of those entering. Joshua showed his pass from the Christian Brother and was allowed to enter. It was exactly nine twenty-eight. The officials were standing around talking to one another. The room had a high ceiling, with ornate marble molding. The floor was also of marble, with a large Persian rug in the center. A chandelier hung from the middle of the ceiling.

A long table ran along the front of the room. It was covered with a thick maroon velvet cloth. A large bishop's chair stood prominently at the center of the table. Legal-sized writing pads and some pencils were neatly arranged in front of each place.

When Joshua entered no one made any effort to welcome him. A few men turned and looked in his direction and then continued their conversations. Two bishops wearing red-trimmed black cassocks looked his way, stared at the odd sight, and continued talking. Joshua felt uncomfortable.

Exactly at nine-thirty a tall, aging cardinal in a black cassock entered the room. He was a courtly looking man with a full head of white hair, which made him look much younger than his seventy-five or more years. When he entered everyone took his place, the cardinal taking the chair reserved for him at the center.

There was a bench in the center of the floor about ten feet in front of the table. One of the clerics gestured for Joshua to take his place there. The cardinal began by offering a prayer, asking guidance from the Holy Spirit upon the serious work they were about to undertake. He prayed that they would conduct the proceedings with charity and justice and that truth would prevail. This prayer was directed in Jesus' name. Everyone responded, "Amen."

"Sir," the cardinal said as he looked at Joshua, "my name is Cardinal Riccardo. These are my colleagues. Their names are inscribed in front of their places. Would you kindly give us your full name and address?"

"My name is Joshua. Until recently I have been living in a little village in the United States. But I no longer live there. My present address is Via Sforza Pallavicini, Rome, Italy."

"What is your last name?" the cardinal asked.

"Joshua is my only name," he replied.

Realizing he was not going to get any further answer, the cardinal continued, "Joshua, we have before us extensive reports that you have been discussing theological matters with Catholic people belonging to certain parishes. Is this true?"

"I do not understand, Cardinal, what you mean by theology. I have never set out to talk about theological matters. I just work at my trade as a wood-carver. When customers come to visit me we talk. We talk about many things. We talk about people, about people's problems, about God, and problems they face in trying to do God's will. I am a simple man and talk very simply and honestly when people ask me what I believe."

"When you talk about God, and the things of God, and the Church, that is theology. Do you talk about these things?" Cardinal Riccardo asked.

"When people are concerned and confused about their religion and ask me what I think, I tell them," Joshua answered.

"What do you tell them?"

"I tell them that Jesus came to bring meaning into people's lives and that his message should give them peace and joy. They should not be confused and fearful and filled with guilt because of Jesus' message."

"Is that all you tell them?" a middle-aged bishop asked.

"No. People ask me what I think of religion as it is practiced today and I tell them honestly."

"What do you tell them?" the prelate continued.

"I tell them that religion is not something separated from life. It is their life, either well lived or badly lived. Jesus told people they are free and that they should enjoy their relationship with God and find joy and peace in their lives. But often Jesus' message is taught as a set of lifeless dogmas and rigid laws demanding observance under frightening penalties. That destroys the beauty of Jesus' message and frightens people away from God."

"You are referring to the Church when you tell people that?" one of the theologians asked.

"I am referring to those who teach Jesus' message in that way. The Church teaches beautiful things, but it is all on paper. The love of God is not preached the way it should be preached, nor is the beauty of Jesus' life preached to people, so they grow up without the comfort of knowing that God cares for them and accepts them as a loving father or mother accepts a well-intentioned but wayward child. The Church is supposed to be the living presence of Christ among God's children, but often all the people see is the aloofness and arrogance of ill-tempered shepherds who have little feeling for the people when they are hurting or when they have fallen."

"Are you saying all priests are that way?" a young, balding theologian asked.

"Of course not," Joshua replied. "There are some priests who give their whole hearts and souls to the genuine work of God but there are not too many. Far too many enjoy the prestige and honor of the priesthood and, like the Pharisees of old, enjoy places of honor in public and the power that comes with authority. They look upon people as subjects to be kept in place and told what to do. That is offensive, not only to people, but to God Himself. Even bishops enjoy acting like heads of state and have all but abandoned the local Christian communities, who are starving for direction and meaning to their lives as God's people and often are ruled by feelingless and arrogant shepherds who hurt the flock and do irreparable damage to God's people with complete immunity. That is because the Christian communities are not really important to the Church, which has become too preoccupied with the business of its far-flung empire of redundant charities. It is the function of religious leaders to inspire charitable works but not to abandon the Christian communities and set up their own massive operation. And it is the chief work of bishops to give guidance and direction to local shepherds but they spend little time sharing the burdens and problems of the Christian communities."

"To go a little deeper, Joshua," a shrewd older priest said, "do you feel this is just a peculiarity of certain individuals or the way the Church is structured?"

"I think it is probably both. Too many need power and authority to give meaning to their work. The spirit of authority seems quite deeply rooted in the Church and running institutions provides that feeling of authority."

"Are you opposed to authority?" the same priest asked.

"No, authority is necessary, but the proper understanding of authority is essential. Jesus' concept of authority is a radical departure from authority as the world understands it. Church leaders have been too eager to exercise authority as the world understands it rather than authority as Jesus taught it."

"You seem to know quite a bit about what Jesus taught and what he didn't teach," a nervous young theologian said sarcastically. "Tell us what kind of authority Jesus is supposed to have taught."

"Jesus taught that his apostles and shepherds should be like lights in darkness, giving light and inspiration to the flock and treating the flock, not as beneath them, as subjects to be ruled, but as brothers and sisters who need compassionate understanding and at times, rare times, firm admonition when they endanger others. That is different from looking upon people as subjects to be ruled by regulation and decree as civil officials do their subjects. There is no room for that kind of authority in the Church. It demeans people and creates a caste system, which is totally foreign to the mind of Jesus. Jesus could see this tendency in the apostles. That was why he washed their feet the night before he died, to impress upon their minds the lesson that they should be humble and not lord it over the flock but be servants of the flock. Not too many like to be servants."

Cardinal Riccardo was watching Joshua closely during all this interchange and saw the simple humility of the man and his total detachment from any spirit of argumentation. He did not appear to be in the slightest way opinionated but believed sincerely in what he said. But wasn't that true of all radical reformers? Their appeal to people was the very same sincerity. But Joshua didn't, for some reason, fit that mold. There was a genuine stamp of real understanding and caring that separated Joshua from radicals and malcontents. The cardinal's long years of experience taught him to see through people they were interrogating, but he felt the younger priests did not see what he saw in Joshua. To them he was just an intellectual opponent who had to be demolished or exposed as a fraud or a danger to Holy Mother Church. The old man did not at all like the turn the proceedings were taking. But there was little he could do, as everyone was free to express himself.

One of the bishops who had been listening directed a further question at Joshua: "Sir, I can see that you are deeply concerned about the Church. Is it your concern for people or your anger against Church leaders that prompts your remarks?"

The question was diabolical and Joshua knew it. It reminded him of the lawyers of old who delighted in setting traps. "I am concerned that the spirit of Jesus' love has been replaced by the law all over again."

"Do you feel that the Church has the authority to legislate and decree?" the bishop asked further.

"Jesus gave authority to bind and to loose, but it is an authority that is to be used widely and with solicitude for the flock. It was not intended to be exercised in an arbitrary manner or as the ordinary way of relating to the Christian people."

"Do you feel it is used arbitrarily?" the bishop asked.

"When one looks across history it is hard to conclude otherwise."

"But times have changed," the prelate continued.

"Circumstances may have changed, but the urge to control and dominate takes on different forms."

"You seem to subtly include the Holy Father in this blanket indictment," the bishop said.

"I have never met the Holy Father, but judging by the surroundings I have seen since I came to Rome, it is hard to see how the spirit of humility guides the lives of those who live here."

"Is that intended as a criticism of the Holy Father?" a priest asked.

"Not at all. I have never met him. I hear he is a good man and a dedicated apostle," Joshua said, carefully covering his tracks.

"You mentioned these surroundings. What are you trying to say to us? Do you feel these surroundings are out of harmony with the teachings of Jesus?" the same priest asked.

"You have said it. The houses people live in reflect their opinions of themselves. Jesus preached humility and simple living among his apostles and disciples. Even though those who live and work here did not build these buildings, they choose to live and work here and also live in a manner befitting these surroundings."

"Which means what?" the priest said caustically.

"That the style is little different from the palaces of kings and rulers of this world, which Jesus strongly warned against."

"You feel, then, that those living here, including the Holy Father, are living a life-style forbidden by Christ?" the priest asked.

"I do not presume to judge the way you live. Only you know whether you are true to what Jesus taught."

"But you state that anyone living or working in these surroundings of necessity lives a style befitting the surroundings. The Holy Father lives here and works here, so according to your own logic he is living a style of life out of harmony with the spirit of Jesus," the priest said triumphantly.

"You have said it, not I. A humble king can live in a castle and still be a humble man and unattached to his possessions. A humble successor to Peter can live here and, in spite of it, can still live humbly. But these very walls speak a message, a message of worldly power and authority. And that authority and power form the image of the person who lives here, so it is possible to give two messages, a real one and one not intended. That ambiguity is what confuses the people and clouds the purity of the message of Jesus."

Joshua was sharp. They couldn't pin him down to anything heretical or even rebellious. What was coming across loud and clear was that Joshua was highly critical of the way Church leaders lived and conducted themselves. There was no way he could avoid giving that impression, nor did he want to avoid it. He was here for a reason, and not just to joust or fence. He had a purpose, and that purpose would not be frustrated.

The questioning continued. "Did you, when you were back in your home town, talk about these matters to the people who came to visit you?" a bishop asked.

"No, there would have been no purpose to it."

"Did you tell the people that Jesus never intended that religion be taught the way it is today?" the same bishop asked.

"Yes."

"Did you tell the people that, as God's children, they are free and that no one can take that freedom from them?" the bishop continued.

"Yes."

"And did you tell them that their pastors were violating the teachings of Jesus by the way they ruled the Christian people?"

"No, that would confuse the people and would have been counterproductive."

"But you did tell the people that Jesus never intended that religion become what it has become today?"

"Yes."

"And in saying that you were telling the people that religion was not being taught properly. Is that not true?" the bishop continued.

"I did not say that," Joshua said calmly, indignant over the man putting words in his mouth.

"But it was clearly implied. What other conclusion can be drawn?"

"I did not say how religion came to be the way it is or who was at fault, whether it was parents or priests or teachers. And is it not true that many people do have false ideas of religion?" Joshua asked.

"We will ask the questions," the bishop reminded him sharply.

The younger men on the panel were becoming more and more agitated. The older ones had gone through these proceedings time and again, and they were all pretty much the same. They were immune to insinuations and implications. They were primarily concerned with whether a particular preacher was a threat to the faith of the people and whether his relationship with the Church and its leaders was hostile and ominous. The younger men were sticklers for the fine points of theology.

The young, balding theologian asked the next question. "Joshua, you mentioned before that the Church rules by legislation and decree. Can you give an example of what you mean by that statement?"

"Take the case of marriage. Jesus never said Christians had to marry before an apostle or a priest. Yet you legislate that if a Catholic does not marry before a priest, or marries before another without permission, the marriage is invalid and the couple live in sin. That is arrogant and denies people the freedom to make their own choice. Many people may have good reason for not wanting to marry before a priest. They may not be sure of their faith or their faith may not be mature. Or they may be conscious of the fact that they are not good Christians and a religious wedding would be a hypocrisy. How can you say that God does not accept their marriage or that they live in sin? It may be a beautiful gesture for a couple who are filled with faith and the love of God to make a commitment of their lives to each other in the presence of the Christian community and before a priest, but to force it is neither healthy nor inspiring, and when the lives of the couple are scandalous it is a mockery. Religion is beautiful only when it is free and flows from the heart. That is why you should guide and inspire but not legislate behavior. And to threaten God's displeasure when people do not follow your rules is being a moral bully and does no service to God. You are shepherds and guides, but not the ultimate judges of human behavior. That belongs only to God."

Everyone was shocked by what they heard. Even the cardinal winced but listened intently, realizing that he was not far from right. There really was no reason why the Church had to make such rigid legislation about marriage, and it does cause anguish in many lives. But he was on very dangerous ground, and this would do him damage.

"Are there other examples?" the same priest asked.

"Take the case of a married couple who are destroying each other. In the past you said they could not divorce. But now you say you will grant them an annulment so they may marry again. And you base your decision on the grounds that there was no real marriage and the relationship was destructive. And in the process you examine the intimate details of their sexual life and call in witnesses to discuss what they know of the couple's relationship. Yet you admit you do not give the annulment but merely decide there was no meaningful relationship to work with. Don't you think the couple already know that? And what is the benefit of priests monitoring the intimate details of people's lives? That's what the Pharisees did to maintain control over people and make them answerable to them for their behavior.

"And if a couple do not appear before you and divorce and marry again, you say they commit adultery. How can you say they commit adultery if they know in their hearts their previous marriage was unhealthy and was destroying them? Is it merely because you were not allowed to make the observation that their marriage was not workable? And how can you hope to maintain control over so many millions of relationships, and commit so many thousands of people to this work of such doubtful value, when there are countless millions of souls needing the Gospel preached to them and countless millions of Christians drifting away from God because of neglect? Is it not better to leave the judgment of the intimate details of people's lives to God and go about the work of bringing the message of Jesus to the millions who need to hear him?"

The logic was devastating. The panel had become very thoughtful while Joshua spoke, realizing there was much truth in what he was saying, and with no trace of arrogance or cynicism. His whole manner reflected a deep concern for the Church and for the work of the Church, which prompted the cardinal to ask the next question.

"Joshua, what is your idea of the Church?"

"The Church is the handmaiden of Jesus. It is his chosen partner in bringing God's love and his concern into the lives of people. It is his living presence throughout history. And it is because of this that it must take great pains to show the gentleness and the solicitude of Jesus for those who are hurting and not emphasize its legal and judgmental power, which serves only too frequently to frighten people and drive the sheep away from God."

The cardinal was impressed, though he said nothing. He was becoming tense over the way the proceedings were going and was showing his discomfort by wringing his hands in his lap. He was an old man and wasn't up to all this tense confrontation anymore. And Joshua was different from the rest. There was a goodness and a concern about him that gave meaning to what he said. He was not out to destroy or to tear down but to make people think, and that was a good thing.

One of the younger men questioned Joshua bluntly. "If you have such a high idea of the Church, why are you so critical?"

"Because I care," Joshua said wearily.

"If you care, why did you cause such turmoil in the place where you lived?"

Before Joshua could answer, the cardinal, who was mopping his face with his handkerchief, had some kind of an attack and fell over. His head hit with a resounding thud on the hard velvet-covered table. Everyone gasped. The two bishops on either side of him turned toward him, not knowing what to do.

Joshua quietly and calmly arose from his bench and walked to the table, leaning over and putting his hand on the cardinal's head and caressing his face and cheek. The cardinal's left arm was hanging limp; one side of his face was sagging and misshapen. He had had a stroke.

When Joshua touched him the cardinal could feel his hand caressing him and began to feel the life come back into his body and the paralysis leave his arm. At the same moment the young theologian came over in front of the table and pulled Joshua away, telling him, "Get away from him and get back to your bench," and pushing him as he did so that Joshua almost lost his balance.

By that time the cardinal was able to raise his head and saw what had happened. His eyes and Joshua's met in that brief moment, and the cardinal knew. The thought crossed his mind, "My God, is it possible? Can it be that history is repeating itself?" And the cardinal saw himself in the role of the high priest, and the young theologian as the high priest's servant slapping Christ in the face. He felt ashamed and powerless.

He had sensed something beautiful about Joshua. He had sensed his calm dignity that almost bordered on majesty, but now he realized everything. The other members of the panel were for adjourning the proceedings, but the cardinal insisted he was all right. He looked at Joshua as he said it, then lowered his eyes in shame. "The proceedings will continue," he said.

From that moment on the cardinal was for exonerating Joshua and tried in a number of subtle ways to sway the thinking of the panel. But it was of little use. The questioning went on into the afternoon, then, when everyone was satisfied with the information they had accumulated, the cardinal brought the proceedings to a close.

As they all walked out of the room the cardinal walked over to Joshua and thanked him. Joshua smiled and told him to tell no one. One of the bishops distracted the cardinal and they became involved in conversation so Joshua walked out alone. No one seemed very interested in him after the proceedings were over. Their interest in him was professional and detached, and the job was done, so they had no further care for him, not even if he was hungry or would like something to drink. He was just a case. It was another example of the almost inhuman approach to religion that had become the way of life for so many who had dedicated their lives to the pursuit of a career in religion. People were not important, but loyalty to the institution and efficiency in showing that loyalty was important if you wanted to get ahead.

Joshua was told by the attendant at the desk that if he was needed he would be summoned again so he should stay close to his apartment. Joshua walked out into the sun-drenched piazza and looked for a place to eat.

After lunch Cardinal Riccardo requested an audience with the Holy Father. It was very important. He was told he could see him at four-thirty in his library. He couldn't wait to tell him what had happened.

The Holy Father was congenial and listened patiently. "Holy Father," the cardinal began, "I am most distressed over what happened in the proceedings today. They were different from anything I have ever experienced. This man Joshua, as he calls himself, appeared to be a simple, uneducated man, but when we questioned him he showed a profound understanding of the things of God and an insight which, I am convinced, was inspired. I realize the report will show him to be critical of the way we run the Church, but I can see that in practically every point he makes there is a great wisdom, and perhaps we should listen to him. I also have the feeling the panel will decide against him, and I have a premonition that if we do it will be remembered in history as a dark hour for the Church."

The Holy Father watched the cardinal as he spoke. He had been around for a long time and had done his work well, but his age was showing. He had always been a compassionate man, but you can't run an institution like the Church on compassion.

There had to be order and discipline. When the cardinal finished the Holy Father told him he would read the report carefully before making a determination.

Cardinal Riccardo realized he was being put off and told the pope what had happened to him during the proceedings. He listened courteously and diplomatically expressed his thought that, even though it may be important to the cardinal, it was irrelevant to the proceedings and should not be used to prejudice his decision. Cardinal Riccardo had felt he could talk to the pope man-to-man, but the pope's legal conditioning was an immovable obstacle. The cardinal asked if the Holy Father would at least meet with Joshua and talk to him himself. The pope finally consented and thanked the cardinal for his concern. The cardinal returned the thanks and withdrew.

20

CAPTAIN PONZELLI HAD been trying in vain to contact his uncle in the Vatican. The secretary kept telling him the cardinal was busy with hearings and would contact him as soon as he was free. The captain was disappointed because he was hoping his uncle could be of some help to Joshua, never dreaming that it was his uncle who was chairing the proceedings against him.

Now that the proceedings were over the cardinal contacted his nephew and invited him over to his apartment. He didn't have much time to talk then, but he would be able to spend the whole afternoon with him the next day.

The next morning a courier appeared at Joshua's apartment house. He left a pass for an audience with the Holy Father. Joshua was delighted. The audience was for eleven-thirty the same morning. Joshua had over two hours before the audience so he decided to take a bus up to the Janiculan hill, overlooking Rome. It was hard finding the right bus, but once he did it took only a few minutes to wind its way up the streets to the top.

Joshua got off the bus, saw a food stand, and bought a candy bar. He walked along the sidewalk until he came to a place that provided a panoramic view of the whole city of Rome. The whole history of Christian civilization unfolded before him. The view was reminiscent of the Mount of Olives, overlooking Jerusalem. Only the dimensions were different. Many Jerusalems would fit into this scene. Joshua thought for a long time. He thought of the infant Church struggling to survive. He thought of the persecutions. He thought of the forced conversions of the pagans to Christianity and the heresies, the invasions, the rise in political power of the Church, the investigations into the beliefs of suspect Christians, the imprisonments, the tortures, the pope-generals leading armies into battle, killing other Christians. He thought of the proclamation of dogmas and the condemnation and excommunication of those who refused to believe. He thought of St. Francis and the many saints whose feet had trod this sacred ground. He looked at the magnificent sanctuaries spread out before him and saw the simple faith of people whose genius had raised these monuments to faith.

Joshua remembered days of old and the sad vision of his beloved city. "Jerusalem, Jerusalem, how often I would have gathered you together as a hen gathers her chicks under her wings, but you would not. And the days are coming upon you when your enemies will build ramparts around you and beat you to the ground, leaving not one stone upon another, because you have not known the day of your visitation." Joshua wept. Jerusalem . . . Rome . . . The one did not recognize him in the flesh. The other did not recognize him in the spirit. Both rejected him in different ways, unable to comprehend the meaning of his coming or the spirit of his message. The legal system of doctrines and morals he fought so hard against in Judaism, and which brought about the final events of his life on earth, resurfaced in the Church and replaced the living spirit of the good news. His grand mission to give a new understanding to human living, to breathe new hope into civilization, showing the world that to be Christian was different from anything it had ever known, and that the family of nations could see in Jesus' message a new bond of love that could unite all men into one, that vision was imprisoned and shackled in a bureaucracy that merely mimicked the forms and ways of worldly governments.

The vision faded. Joshua realized it was getting late. He walked back to the bus stop and boarded the next bus to the city. He got off not far from St. Peter's and walked to the Vatican.

The Swiss Guard recognized him but still waited for Joshua to show his identification, which this time was his invitation to the papal audience. The guard read Joshua's invitation and then allowed him to enter. He was ushered through vaulting corridors and around corners until he reached the room where the Holy Father was working. An attendant took him inside, telling him to kneel as he approached the pope.

"Kneel, what for?" Joshua asked, bewildered.

"That's the rule, sir," the man answered politely.

"I cannot imagine Peter wanting anyone to kneel down before him," Joshua said, half to himself.

As he entered the room the pope was sitting at his desk at the other end. He was dressed in a white cassock. His head was bare. When Joshua was halfway across the room the pope stood and walked around the desk to welcome him. He was gracious. The attendant again told Joshua to kneel and to kiss the Holy Father's ring. The pope held out his hand. Joshua took it and shook it with deep feeling. The attendant introduced the visitor.

"Holy Father, this is Joshua," he said as the two men shook hands.

"Hello, Joshua," the pope said cordially.

"It is a great pleasure to see you, Peter," Joshua said, to the pope's confusion.

After talking about little things the pope told Joshua he had received a copy of the transcript of the proceedings. "I must admit, I am not at all flattered or pleased by what I read. Cardinal Riccardo was impressed by many things about you, but he is a kindly and compassionate man. Why do you feel you must say the things you do, young man?" the pope asked Joshua.

"I say them because they are the things Jesus taught, and they should be a surprise to no one. In fact, I can't understand why it causes such consternation," Joshua replied calmly.

"Have you studied theology and do you have a degree in theology?" the Holy Father asked.

"No, I did not think I needed a degree to talk about the things of God. They flow as naturally from the human spirit as the air we breathe. As God's children they are our common heritage and, indeed, our very life."

"Son, you certainly do not lack self-confidence. I notice in the transcript you criticize the way we live and the surroundings here."

"I did not criticize. I was asked to comment and said honestly what I thought. Jesus taught the apostles to be humble and to live humbly and simply, not in the palace of kings, nor to rule like kings. You have changed greatly through the centuries, Peter, and it is not all for the good. Remember, it is by humility and meekness that you will win souls to God, not by rising above people in self-glory. Jesus also established twelve apostles, not one. Their identity has been overshadowed and all but lost. That is not right. Each apostle must be free to work with his own flock, and solve the unique problems of his own flock, with the different cultures and languages and understandings of life. The Spirit must be able to move freely and exercise His freedom in different ways and in different forms, and freely express Himself through a variety of gifts and not through sterile uniformity, which merely satisfies man's need for security."

The Holy Father was embarrassed by the audacity of this simple man's rudeness in giving him a sermon. He blushed and told Joshua his name was not Peter. He told him he had a lot to learn about life and about the Church, and if he was willing to learn, he should try to practice humility and care for his own soul rather than involving himself in matters that are above and beyond him. The Holy Father told him that in the future he should refrain from talking about these matters and follow the directions the Congregation would be sending him. It is behavior like his that can do untold damage to the Church and lead simple people away from God.

The pope then gave an eye to the attendant, who came over and gently took Joshua by the arm. Joshua told the pope that he had done much good for the Church, and that he would suffer much, but that he should not be discouraged because his sincerity would give him occasions to make great changes among God's people that would bring honor to God. As he was leaving Joshua asked God's blessing upon Peter and thanked him for the chance to meet with him.

The pope watched Joshua as he walked out, wondering about what kind of man could have the boldness to preach a sermon to the pope. Yet Joshua was, as Cardinal Riccardo said, a humble man and not really arrogant or cynical. The pope wondered as he watched Joshua walk down the long corridor.

At the same time Joshua was in audience with the Holy Father, Captain Ponzelli was just arriving at his uncle's apartment.

"Uncle, it is so good to see you. It has been so long," the captain said as Cardinal Riccardo welcomed him and the boy who accompanied him.

"I would like you to meet a friend of mine, Michael Szeneth. His father is a rabbi, and we have been friends for years," the captain said as he introduced Michael to his uncle.

"Welcome, my son. I have a friend here in Rome who is a rabbi. Perhaps we can meet him while you are here. Now, Ennio, my dear nephew, tell me all about yourself. What have you been doing since I saw you last? My sister told me you were coming to Rome, but unfortunately I have been so busy with proceedings, I haven't had much free time."

"Uncle, I have so many things to tell you, I don't know where to start."

"Before you begin," the cardinal interrupted, "let's go out to a little restaurant I know. It is more relaxing than this place, with phones ringing and secretaries interrupting."

The restaurant was just around the corner. As soon as they sat down and ordered light refreshments, the captain began to pour his heart out to his uncle. He told him about his friend the bishop asking him to do him a favor and take a certain fellow on board ship and make him work his way over to Rome by waiting on tables. The man had been summoned by the Vatican for a doctrinal proceeding. The man's name was Joshua.

"I obliged the bishop, took him on board, and assigned him to waiting on tables. Taking my cue from the bishop, I was cool to him, thinking he was a troublemaker. Two days into the voyage Michael fell down the stairs and literally broke his neck. The doctor examined him, found his vital signs weak, and tried to do what he could. But Michael died.

"We all left the sick bay. I went to the radio room to send a message. When I was coming out of the radio room I saw this young man, Joshua, walking toward the sick bay. I stayed at a discreet distance and watched to see what he was up to. He entered the room, leaving the door partially open, and walked over to the table where Michael's body lay. Then, lifting the sheet from Michael's face, he called out to him and told him to wake up. To my complete shock, Michael opened his eyes and sat up. I thought I would faint."

The cardinal listened intently as his nephew recounted the rest of the details.

"But, Uncle, that was nothing. Two days later the most extraordinary thing happened. We had this violent storm at sea. There were gale winds and heavy rain. The waves were tossing the ship around like a piece of driftwood. I thought surely it was going to sink. Looking out on deck from the pilot's window where I had gone to encourage the pilot, I saw a figure walking up along the deck. I couldn't believe my eyes. It was Joshua. I thought surely he would be swept into the sea. But as the ship steadied itself for a moment, he stood up straight, stretched his arms out as if commanding the storm, and yelled something that I could not hear. Immediately the wind died down, the rain stopped, the waves settled, and the sun came out. Uncle, ever since then, I couldn't help but think, could it be? Could it be?"

"Ennio. Hearing what you tell me, and knowing what I found out myself, I have no doubt. I wished you could have reached me before I got tied up with the proceedings. The man we interrogated was Joshua. It went badly. No one could understand him, and they were cruel. Even I added my share, and I feel guilty. Let me tell you what happened.

"During the middle of the proceedings I was beginning to become quite impressed with Joshua and felt bad for him and the way he was being treated. It began to bother me so much, I could feel myself getting sick. Then, all of a sudden, I collapsed. I fell forward, and my head hit the top of the table. I was not totally unconscious, but I was dazed. I felt my left arm hanging, but I couldn't lift it. The one side of my face was paralyzed. I couldn't even move my tongue. I realized I had had a stroke. I just lay there, unable to help myself. Then I felt a hand caressing my head and face. It was Joshua's. As soon as he touched me I felt power and life come back into my body. I lifted up my head and looked up at him. At that same moment one of the priests pushed him away and told him to sit down. I was shocked and could only think of the high priest and his servant. I saw myself in the same role, and I felt a shudder of horror pass through me.

"I directed the proceedings to continue and tried to help Joshua. But there was little I could do. There were too many on the panel, and I couldn't tell them what happened. They wouldn't have believed me anyway. I realized that I really wasn't supposed to do anything, that it was all part of a plan. I just felt bad I had to be part of it. Yes, Ennio, in answer to your question, I have no doubt but that it was."

Michael just sat and listened, thinking over everything he had heard and experienced. His own life would never be the same.

"Uncle, where is he now?" the captain asked.

"All I know is that he is staying temporarily in an apartment on Via Sforza Pallavicini. I am thinking the same thing as I think you are thinking. Let us go visit him and apologize for his rude reception."

The captain put down the money for the pastry and coffee and they left.

They arrived at the apartment house in a few minutes. The doorman bowed obsequiously when he saw the cardinal. "Your Eminence," he said, "I am honored. Can I help you?"

"Yes, is there a man here by the name of Joshua?"

"Yes. In fact, he came in before you and just paid his bill. He is walking up those stairs there now. His room is at the top of the stairs."

"Which room?" the cardinal asked.

"There is only one room there. It is his. It was really an old closet, but it was all we had left."

The three men went quickly over to the stairs and ran up. The door at the top of the stairs was open, and they could see shadows moving inside. Thank God they had caught him in time. They went to the room and knocked. No answer. They knocked again. Still no answer. They couldn't understand. They walked in and looked around. There was no one there. The bathroom door was open. They looked inside. There was no one. The room was empty.

Over on the floor near the bed were two sandals. In one sandal there was a gold medal with the figure of a fiery sun and a man in the middle of the sun. Michael recognized it as the medal Marcia used to wear. In the other sandal were two old Roman coins.

The men somehow knew they would not find him. But what a strange thing to find the sandals and the coins, the only mementos of a reality that only the three of them knew and could share only with each other, for who would believe them? They would give the medallion back to Marcia and the coins to whomever they belonged. The sandals were prized keepsakes, which they would forever treasure.

Epilogue

Cardinal Riccardo processed the report of the Congregation. The vote for censure was six to one. The cardinal read the details of the report. "The young man, Joshua, showed a distinctly hostile attitude toward authority, which if allowed to spread would do untold damage to discipline and faith. His criticism of bishops, and the highest leaders of the Church, could imply, if not immediately indicate, a defect of faith, which may be symptomatic of lack of belief in the scriptural or dogmatic foundations of the authority of bishops and even the Holy Father himself. His attitude toward members of the panel seemed to support this observation.

"The man's criticism of practices in the Church shows a lack of understanding of the realities of life and seriously questions the ageless wisdom and prudence of Holy Mother Church. The propagating of those ideas could seriously damage the faith and trust of the faithful. Although he seemed sincere, he was misguided and too angry to be of much good. Although his ideas do not appear to be heretical, they are so highly critical of Church practices and policy that it could be said that he does not have a healthy understanding of the nature of the Church or its role as the authority of Christ on earth."

The cardinal turned to the section on recommendations and censures. Joshua was directed to cease talking about these matters to the faithful under penalty of further censure. He was told that his attitude lacked the docility and humility that befits a Christian layman and that, in the future, he would do well to cultivate those virtues for the benefit of his own soul and the edification of his fellow Christians. And, since he was uneducated in matters of religion, he was unqualified to talk about these highly theological ideas he was circulating. He was also forbidden to discuss the sacred proceedings or anything that transpired during these same proceedings under penalty of excommunication. The report was signed "Cardinal Giovanni Riccardo."

There was an addendum to the report, which the cardinal himself wrote and in which he vigorously and bravely defended Joshua. He included this in the report as the minority opinion. The whole report, with the minority opinion, was delivered to the Holy Father. A copy was sent to the bishop of the diocese in which Auburn was located. In that copy the cardinal included a personal letter to the bishop telling him what had occurred at the proceedings and about what had happened to him personally. He told the bishop that he felt everyone involved in this matter had made a grave mistake and that they had not yet heard the end of it.

Captain Ponzelli also wrote a long letter to his friend Rabbi Szeneth and one to his good friend the bishop telling both of the events that had taken place on the voyage. The rabbi had already heard from his son, who, in his impressionable youth, had his own ideas as to the identity of Joshua. He had grown close to Joshua during the past few months and saw a striking similarity between what Joshua said and the Gospels, which he had begun reading since he left Rome.

Marcia also heard from Michael, who told her all that he had learned from the captain and the cardinal. Although she was deeply crushed over all that had happened, and sad that the medallion had been returned, she understood. She told Aaron and Lester, and her family, and other close friends of Joshua. She also told Father Pat, and as time went on, to keep the memory of Joshua alive, they would all meet and ask Father Pat to explain many of the things Joshua had said and done. On occasion they would read the Gospels together, feeling honored that they should have been graced with his presence during those beautiful moments in their lives. Word spread of the final days of Joshua, and the hearts of many were either soothed or grieved over what had taken place during that brief, bright summer in their lives.

Joshua
and the Children

In every age
There exist quiet heroes
Who, in their selfless devotion,
lay aside their own needs and comforts
and consecrate their energies and talents
to healing the wounds of a troubled humanity.
To these rare and often unhonored souls
this book is humbly dedicated.

Acknowledgments

No creation is the work of one person. There are so many who have contributed in ways great and small to this work that it would be impossible to even identify them. I would, however, like to express my singular appreciation to Lorraine and Lester Bashant, my sister and her husband, and also their son, Joseph, for their unstinting and tireless efforts in assisting me during the difficult time preceding the creation of this manuscript.

1

QUIET LAY UPON the meadow like a soft, green blanket. The sun, a globe of molten gold, shot laser beams across the fields and through the trees, burning away the early morning mist. The valley began springing to life. Rusty hinges of cottage doors squeaked open as farmers and factory workers slipped out into the narrow alleys to begin another day. The air was fresh and cool. A few friendly voices broke the stillness. A rooster crowed in the distance. A lone horse's hooves and wagon wheels clacked against the stone pavement. Peace reigned everywhere. If there were a heaven, its beauty and peace could not surpass the serenity of this countryside.

Michael Whitehead walked down the alley toward the main street on his way to work. "Good morning!" he yelled to his neighbor, Charlie Fellows.

"Good morning, Mike. It's too nice to work today. I'd rather be fishing."

Mike and Charlie had been friends since they were kids. They were inseparable. Mike was Catholic. Charlie was Presbyterian. It made no difference. Their families were close. Though they were not officially allowed to take part in each other's religious services, they were unofficially godfathers for each other's children. This did not sit too well with some individuals in town who wanted to keep everybody where they "belonged."

As the two men walked down the street together, a little voice called out, "Daddy, Daddy, you forgot your lunch again." It was Mike's daughter, Annie. She was only four and her father's pet. She and her brother, Pat, who was Charlie's godson, were running up the alley toward the main street, trying to catch up with their father.

As the two children reached the corner, barely a hundred feet behind the two men, an old beat-up car careened around the corner. A hand jerked open the window and tossed a grapefruit-sized object into the street just behind Mike and Charlie. It bounced and rolled away from the men and toward the children. The screeching tires were familiar sounds and almost always pre-saged some evil and violent act. The men reeled around, sus-pecting the worst. They saw the object and tried to warn the children, but it was too late. The thing exploded and hurled little Annie into the wall of the house on the corner, her father's lunch pail flying clear across the street. The boy, who was a few feet behind his sister, was somewhat shielded from the full im-pact of the explosion, but the force was so great, it lifted him off the ground and threw him to the stone pavement. His body was badly mangled.

Both men screamed in horror and disbelief. Instinctively, one man went to one child, the other to the other child. The girl was dead. The boy was in shock, unconscious, his left arm torn off and lying in the street a few feet away, his left leg cut in a hundred places and bleeding profusely. It would be a blessing if the child died. Mike cried like a baby, not knowing what to do with what remained of his son. Charlie told him Annie was dead and went to pick up the boy's arm. Mike made a tourniquet to control the bleeding from the stump, then picked up his son. Charlie carried the limp, lifeless body of the girl. The two men ran down the street as fast as they could to the doctor's house, praying that he would be home.

Joe Kelly, though everyone called him Tony, was a slow-mov-ing, peaceful man. He talked little, but his quiet, thoughtful gaze missed nothing. One could tell he had seen a lot and felt deeply about everything but revealed nothing of what he thought. As early as it was, it was unusual to catch him home. He began his rounds of the village early each day, long before he went to the hospital.

Charlie knocked on the door. It opened immediately, as if someone had been waiting. It was the doctor. He winced when he saw the bleeding child in his father's arms. He told the men to put the children on the two examining tables in his office. He checked the girl. She was dead. He examined the boy and checked his vital signs. He was alive, but barely. Joe Kelly had a rare genius for diagnosis. He was careful and sure and usually right.

"We'll have to get him to the hospital immediately. Bring the arm here," he ordered as he readied a large plastic bag full of ice.

The three men went out the door to the doctor's jeep. Mike sat in the back seat with his son on his lap as the vehicle backed out into the street and started down the main street. There wasn't much traffic, so the doctor didn't use the siren, as he liked to do during busy hours, but used his CB radio to call the emergency ward at the hospital, telling the nurse what he wanted ready as soon as he got there. They would also need Dr. Stern, the microsurgeon. Although he worked in the big city, he lived nearby, and with any luck they could get him at home. There was no time to spare.

Everything went with perfect precision at the hospital. Dr. Kelly's cool manner kept everyone else calm. Dr. Stern arrived and said little, just examined the boy, the arm, consulted with another doctor, and went to work. The operation took a good part of the day. By late afternoon the arm was reattached, and the boy was resting in the recovery room.

While the doctors worked on Pat, Maureen, beside herself, came running into the hospital. She had been told by a neighbor some of what happened, but it was all garbled. She raced to the hospital and demanded to see her children. The nurses tried to calm her, but when she saw the dead body of her baby lying on the table, her face gray, she wailed like a person who had lost her mind.

It was the first tragedy to strike the young couple, and it came upon them with such devastating fury that it was impossible to control the emotion.

"Did you see who did it?" Maureen asked through her tears.

"No, they looked like strangers," Charlie said. Mike half agreed, but secretly was sure he recognized one of the men.

"They were after us," Charlie said. "But the kids were right behind us, and the grenade bounced in the street and rolled right toward them. They didn't have a chance. But we'll find out who did it."

That was little comfort to a mother whose daughter was dead and whose son's life was hanging by a thread. Mike put his arm around his wife, trying to comfort her. "I swear on my grandmother's grave I'll find who did it. I won't rest until I bring the cowards to justice, even if I have to do it myself," Mike said, not fully realizing what he said.

Charlie felt guilty for what happened. He knew it was because of his friendship with Mike that they did this. Their sick minds couldn't stand to see the love the two had for each other and for each other's families. He found it hard to face Maureen. However, being a true friend, he stayed with them right to the end.

The three of them remained at the hospital all day. Charlie called work and told the boss what had happened and said they wouldn't be in. There wasn't much they could do. Charlie said little, his just being there, just being a friend, was a comfort, though the thought that just being a friend was what brought all this on. It wouldn't have happened otherwise. Mike and Maureen thought the same thing, but banished the thought immediately. Charlie was too good a friend and loved the kids as much as if they were his own.

Late in the afternoon, Pat opened his eyes, looked at the three hovering over him, smiled faintly, and went back to sleep. The simple sign of recognition reassured them. The three stayed until evening and lights-out. If the child woke up, he would be given medication anyway. Besides, arrangements had to be made for Annie's funeral.

2

Funerals are commonplace in towns where religious wars are rampant. But each death is new to each family, and the devastation is always total. Little Annie's funeral was the more tragic because even the killers didn't mean to kill and maim these little kids. Fanatics like that have no guilt; they have long since numbed their twisted consciences so their blind self-righteousness translates cowardly murders into heroism. It was just a sad mistake that the kids got in the way. And so the murderers even went to the wake with a whitewashed conscience, without the slightest twinge of pity for the broken and distraught parents, who had done nothing to deserve this senseless tragedy.

The wake went far into the night. The whiskey flowed freely and the tongues flowed just as freely. Friends came from all over. Relatives like Jack and Mary Behan had come a long way, so they slept at the Whiteheads' cottage together with other relatives, who came from the four corners of the country, some from across the border. Charlie's pastor, Rev. Russell Davis, a Presbyterian minister, came to pay his respects. He was a decent man, and though quiet and seemingly shy, he was boldly outspoken in his condemnation of the senseless violence that was rampant throughout the county, thereby infuriating the agitators. People could always count on him to do the decent thing, like coming to little Annie's wake, which also galled his critics. When the Whiteheads' priest, Father Elmer Donnelly, came in, the two clergymen shook hands warmly, talked briefly, and then prayed the wake service together.

The next morning the church bells tolled heavy, somber tones as they called everyone to church, reminding young and old alike that life is serious business and death is no respecter of age or person. Charlie and his wife, Barbara, sat in the front pew with Mike and Maureen. It took no little amount of courage for them to do that, as they now had no delusions as to how much hatred and poison their friendship stirred up in sick minds. They were more determined than ever to stand by one another, even if every last one of the family was killed. Situations like this may breed violence, but they also breed a depth of heroism that is rare in the ordinary course of events.

Father Donnelly was an old man, a saintly man, who had consoled many a grief-stricken parent in his parish. He had been pastor there for over thirty years and knew everyone better than their own relatives. He had baptized them, heard their sins, given them Communion, married them, counseled them, comforted them, and eventually buried them. He was really the father of them all, and they felt that way about him. Some wished he would do more to end the senseless hatred and killing that went on; others thought he was already too outspoken and should mind his own business and stick to religion and stay out of politics, as if politics should be exempt from morals and none of God's business.

The sermon the priest gave was simple but poignant, with the kind of strong, tough comfort that would come from a man whose heart had been broken a thousand times and whose concern went much deeper than mere pious sentiment. "Mike and Maureen, and my dear friends . . . It is easy to say 'The Lord gives and the Lord takes,' and 'God takes only the good young,' but there are no words that can bring comfort to a mother and father whose child has died such a senseless death, and another is critically injured. My own heart breaks every time something like this happens, for I have grown old knowing all of you and loving all of you as if you were my very own. I share your grief and your sleepless nights, and your troubled concern for the future and for your children's future. For Annie the trouble is ended, the pain is no more. She is with God, walking happily with the Good Lord and His Blessed Mother. The pain of her leaving is our pain. She is at peace and happy and safe in God's home. I used to be afraid to die. Lately, as the pain all around us grows ever worse, the prospects of seeing God do not appear so frightening, offering, as they do, the hope of liberation from the agony of living in this troubled world.

"However, we still live in this world, and our work is not finished. In the face of this senseless tragedy, we have arrived at a critical juncture in our lives. We can allow ourselves to live in hatred like those who killed little Annie, and add to the endless hatred we see all around us, or follow Our Savior as Christians and be like Him, who never allowed himself to take offense but forgave even those who plotted to destroy him, like they still do in our own day. 'Whatever you do to the least of my brothers and sisters, you do to me.' And in Annie's death, they killed Christ once again."

As the priest said those words he was distracted by two men in the congregation whose faces became distorted with a look that seethed with anger and guilt. And he knew that they were the ones who had killed the little girl. They were not total strangers. He had seen them around but did not know who they were or where they were from. He didn't remember them as children growing up in the town. They must be recent imports from someplace else.

Regaining his composure, the priest continued, "It is at times like this that it is not easy to be a Christian, and that is what should separate us from the rest of the world. 'An eye for an eye and a tooth for a tooth' may make sense to a heart that is filled with grief and to a feverish mind that can find no relief even in sleep, but forgiveness is the beautiful gift that Jesus gave us as the unfailing key to peace of mind.

"Over a hundred years ago in France, a butler attached to a wealthy family knew where the family kept all their wealth, hidden in a vault underneath the château. He methodically plotted to kill everyone in the family and steal the treasure. One night, when everyone was asleep, he murdered first the father and mother, and then, one by one, the children. Only the youngest escaped because he had heard noises and couldn't sleep. When he realized what was happening he quietly slipped out of his room and hid in a closet under a pile of clothes.

"For years he wandered the streets as an orphan, and later entered the seminary and became a priest. Eventually he was assigned to Devil's Island as a chaplain. One afternoon a convict came running in from the fields, frantically calling for the chaplain. 'There's a man dying out in the field, Father, come quickly.'

"The priest ran out with him and reached the dying man. Kneeling down beside him, he lifted his head onto his lap and asked if he would like to confess his sins. The dying man refused. 'Why, my son?' the priest asked. 'Because God will never forgive me for what I have done.'

" 'But what have you done that is so bad?' the priest continued. And the man went on to tell the story of how he had killed this whole family so he could have their money, and only the little boy escaped because he couldn't find him.

"Then the priest said to him, 'If I can forgive you, certainly God can forgive you. And I forgive you from my heart. It was my family you killed, and I am that little boy.'

"The convict cried and told the priest how he had been haunted all his life over what he had done, though no one else knew about it. Even the authorities never found out.

"The two men cried together. And, as the priest was giving the dying man absolution, the man died with his head resting on the priest's lap.

"My children," Father Donnelly continued, "that story is a true story, and has been the inspiration of my life whenever people have hurt me. It shows how beautiful and godly is the kind of forgiveness that Jesus taught. Trying to forgive like that has brought me much peace during my life, and I share that story with you in the hope that you may be able to follow in Jesus' footsteps and forgive those evil men who have done this horrible thing to your children, and find peace in your own souls. May the Good Lord fill your hearts with his peace and grant your other children a happy and peaceful life."

The priest continued the Mass, watching every now and then the two men he had identified during the sermon. They knew he was watching and lowered their eyes whenever he looked their way.

The Mass ended. The procession to the cemetery and the committal service was without incident. Mike and Maureen clung to each other during the prayers, and when it was over, thanked Father Donnelly for his comfort and support and asked him over to the house for refreshments with the family.

3

THE VILLAGE SQUARE was quiet in the early morning. Men had gone to work, women were at home doing their chores. Children were still not used to summer vacation. The sun was shining through the trees, lighting up the square with a fresh, warm glow. The mist that hung over the meadow at dawn had been burned away by the sun, but you could still smell manure and the fragrance of wet grass.

Three roads met at the square: Stonecastle Road, which came down the hill from the north; Downers Road, which came in from the east and snaked its way through the village, and Maple Street, which came in through the fields from the south. The square itself was small, about three times the size of a basketball court, but was the center of whatever activity took place in the town. At one time the square had been set with cobblestones, but lately these had been coated with cement—none too professionally, as the rounded tops of the stones were still evident. Lining the north side of the square was a row of buildings that had probably been built before the turn of the century, well over a hundred years ago. Most of them were brick. There was a general store, a meat market, a small apothecary shop, and, at the end of the row, a little tavern from which could be heard laughter and boisterous sounds at almost any time during the day or night. Hanging in front of the establishment was a faded wooden sign bearing the name "Almost Home," which the place was for many of its frequenters, though some never quite made it to their homes.

Across from the row of brick buildings, on the opposite side of the square, stretched a vast meadow where sheep and cattle and goats grazed lazily all during the day. A row of ancient maple trees separated the meadow from the square, and in front of the trees there was a stone wall that went the distance of the square. Other buildings lining the main street and what few side streets there were formed the village proper. Most of the people lived in cottages scattered on roads winding their way through the meadows.

There were four churches in town: Presbyterian, Roman Catholic, Anglican, and Wesleyan. The Presbyterian church was by far the largest, having most of the people in town as its congregation. It was located just north of the village on the hillside, and was impressive with its tall, pointed steeple overlooking the village and the surrounding countryside. The Catholic church was a small brick building located at the southern end of town and bordering on the meadow. It was more a chapel than a church. It was quaint and resembled an oversized cottage rather than a church building. Climbing roses clung to the front and sides of the building. At the one side of the church was the churchyard, lined with gravestones set in precise rows. On the other side was another yard used for parish socials. The Anglican church was a stately building constructed of imported stone, with dignified stained-glass windows. A bell tower stood next to the church. Its six bells, which were the pride of the parish, were exposed to view and could be heard at the far ends of the meadow. Surrounding the tower was a carefully manicured garden. The Wesleyan church was a small Tudor-style building just down the street from the Catholic church. It was surrounded by a white picket fence, with flowering shrubs placed discreetly at intervals both inside and outside the fence.

It was about ten o'clock. The waking village was still tranquil. The only sounds were the whistling of cardinals in a nearby bush, and the cawing of crows high up in a maple tree, and a child's voice calling a playmate. A lonely figure was walking toward the square from Stonecastle Road. He was wearing khaki pants, with a brown pullover shirt and sandals. He was of medium height, slim, with attractive features and wavy chestnut hair. His walk suggested a free spirit who seemed to have not a care in the world.

He entered the square and walked over to a bench near the stone wall that ran along the south end of the square. He sat down, took a handkerchief from his pocket and wiped his brow, then surveyed the scene as if planning a strategy. The village was just beginning to come alive. There were kids on bicycles delivering packages, other younger children coming from here and there, calling their friends to come and play with them. A girl who couldn't have been more than six years old came walking into the square carrying a bag of what must have been seeds or peanuts, and she was immediately deluged by an army of pigeons and birds of every description. They were obviously expecting her. She walked along the wall, throwing out small handfuls of food as she went, gradually approaching the bench where the stranger was sitting.

As she approached the stranger said hello to her, calling her by name. The girl was surprised.

"How do you know my name?" she asked.

"I have known you all your life, Jane. I can see you have a lot of friends."

"Yes, I feed them every day. Would you like some seeds to feed the birds?" the little girl asked the friendly stranger. She was surprisingly unafraid, although she had never seen the man before.

"Yes, I would like that very much." The man held his hand out as the girl poured some of the seeds into it. Immediately a pigeon landed on the man's hand and began to eat. Other birds flew over, but were not as bold as the pigeon. They landed on the ground and waited impatiently. The girl threw some seeds to them and they demolished them in an instant.

"What's your name, sir?" the little girl asked the stranger.

"Joshua," the man replied.

"Do you live around here? I've never seen you before."

"I just came into town. I'll be here for a while."

"Do you know how old I am?" Jane asked, then answered before Joshua had time to say a word. "I'm six years old, and I come out here every morning to feed the birds. Some of them come and eat out of my hand. I love those redbirds that hide in the bushes, but they won't come near me. See, there's one now." The girl pointed to a cardinal perched on a large maple branch hanging over the bench.

"That bird is called a cardinal," the stranger said, then asked, "Would you like him to come to you?"

"I'd love him to, but he never does."

The stranger looked up at the bird nervously dancing on the branch. He held out his hand with a few seeds in it and called the bird. The bird looked for a second, then flew over to the man's hand.

"Now, take some seeds in your hand and very slowly put your hand out," Joshua instructed the girl.

As she did so Joshua moved his hand ever so gently toward the girl's hand. When the bird finished the seeds in Joshua's hand, he paused, looked at the girl, then at Joshua, then made a timid move over to the girl's hand. Little Jane was thrilled. The bird finished the seeds and flew back up into the tree.

Jane was delighted. She loved those little redbirds, but they were always so nervous, they would never go near anyone. She never dreamed she would ever hold one in her hand.

"Thank you, Joshua," Jane said to the stranger, then asked him how he learned to do that.

"Oh, I guess the birds aren't afraid of me," he answered simply.

"But he came to you as soon as you called him," the girl persisted.

"Perhaps he recognized my voice," Joshua replied. That seemed to satisfy the girl.

"You are a nice man, Joshua," Jane said. "Would you stay here until I go and tell my friends about you? I would like them to meet you."

"Yes. I would like to meet your friends," Joshua responded.

In no time at all Jane returned with her friends, mostly girls, but also a few boys. Joshua was sitting on the bench, watching people as they went about their work. An old man smoking a pipe had just left him. The children said hello to him as they walked past him and approached the bench.

"Joshua, these are my friends," Jane said. "This is Mary, and Joan, and Nancy, and Patricia, and Eleanor, and Frances, and Meredith. And these are friends too," she said as she pointed out the boys. "This is Tom, and Mike, and Edmund, and Joe."

"I am very happy to meet all of you. It looks like you all are good friends. Joe, do you play that trumpet you are carrying?" Joshua asked.

"Yes," the little boy answered shyly.

"Would you show me how to play it?" Joshua asked him.

The boy was embarrassed to show off in front of his friends, but, seeing it meant so much to the stranger, he obliged.

Joshua watched intently. The boy played a few simple notes and asked Joshua if he wanted to try.

"Yes, I would."

Joe gave Joshua the instrument and watched the man put it to his lips. He blew into it once, then again, and again. Finally a note emerged, rather weak and sickly, but a note all the same. He tried again. A dismal, low-sounding grunt, like a sick cow. The children tried not to laugh. But Joshua wouldn't give up. He concentrated and tried again. This time notes came out firm and clear. He continued to experiment and after a minute or so was able to play something that sounded reasonably pleasant.

The boy offered to show him how to play other notes and a simple melody. Joshua watched and then tried again. This time he did better. The children all clapped and cried out, "Hurray! Hurray! Joshua can play the trumpet."

"Joshua," Joe asked as the man returned the trumpet, "do you live near here? We've never seen you before."

"Not far," Joshua said simply.

"Why are you here in our village?" Mary asked.

"I heard you are nice people here and I wanted to come and visit."

"Where will you stay?" she persisted.

"Wherever. I'm not concerned. The weather is nice and it is cool at night on the hill in the meadow. I can stay in that grove of trees up there," Joshua said as he pointed to the trees in the distance.

The children were amused at the casual unconcern of the man. But they had seen other strangers with no apparent roots wandering through their village, so they were not surprised.

"Will you be here in the square tomorrow?" Jane asked Joshua.

"Yes."

"Oh, good! I will bring my brother and his friends down to meet you," the girl added excitedly. "You'll like my brother. His name is Matt and he plays a guitar."

"I'm sure I will like him," Joshua responded.

The children said good-bye and promised to come back the next morning. They ran off, talking excitedly about their new-found friend. Simple little things were thrilling to these children who had few material things and managed to create their own fun and enjoyment out of each new event in their life.

4

WHEN JANE WENT home and told her mother about Joshua, her mother was upset that her daughter would be so forward with a stranger.

"But, Mommy," the girl protested, "it's not as if he's a stranger. He's so gentle. I felt he was my friend right away. There's nothing to be afraid of. Joey even taught him how to play his trumpet. And when he made funny notes and we laughed, he laughed too. He's really different. He's not like anybody I've met before. Come and see for yourself. He'll be in the square tomorrow."

All day the girl kept telling her friends about this man she had met in the square who called to the redbird in the tree and it came to him, and he let her hold the bird in her hand. "You have to come and meet him," she told everybody.

Joe went home and told his teenage brother Paul about Joshua and insisted he should come and meet him. Paul wasn't impressed, but to appease his brother, promised to come and meet the man the next day.

Later in the afternoon stories circulated around the village about an incident in the nearby city. It seemed a jeep filled with soldiers was patrolling a trouble-ridden neighborhood when someone threw a Molotov cocktail at the jeep and killed one of the soldiers. According to rumor, it was a teenager who threw the thing, but the soldiers, who were too occupied trying to save their burning companion, let the youth escape.

Whenever these incidents occurred everyone paid the price. The atmosphere became tense and people were jittery, watching for the slightest sign of trouble. Parents tried to keep their children off the streets and as near to home as possible. Added patrols rolled through the village as a warning to potential troublemakers.

Around suppertime a handful of not-too-steady individuals filed out of the tavern and wandered off in all directions on their way home. One of the men had to cross the field opposite the square. He was a ruddy-faced young fellow named Tim, who had a pointed face and a sharp, pointed nose and broad, thin lips. He was tall, and his long legs moved in almost disjointed steps, giving him an air of carefreeness, which was even more heightened by the double shots he had just had at the tavern. Whistling a tune as he ambled across the field, he was caught short as he passed the ancient oak that stood majestically in the middle of the field.

A figure was sitting under the tree eating what was apparently his supper. As Tim passed he waved a casual hello to the man and was caught short when the stranger responded by calling him by his name, "Good evening, Tim. It's a fine, cool breeze tonight."

Tim was shocked. "How'd you know my name? Who are you? I've never seen you around before."

"My name is Joshua. I'm just sitting here eating my supper. Would you like some?"

"No, thanks. How'd you know my name?"

"I could just tell when I looked at you," Joshua answered simply.

Tim was too curious not to stop and engage the man in some small talk. "What are you eating?" Tim asked.

"Some fish I just caught in the stream. Here, have a piece," Joshua said as he took a moist chunk from the little fire and held it out to the tall, skinny figure hovering over him.

Tim awkwardly and rather reluctantly accepted and ate it.

"Never ate fish like this before. Not bad. In fact, it's better than the way my wife cooks it," Tim said with a broad smile, then sat down on a log lying nearby.

"You look like too refined a man to be just wandering around shiftless. What do you do for a living?" Tim asked good-naturedly.

"Right now I'm sort of vacationing," Joshua answered simply. "I like people, and I enjoy visiting new places and meeting new people. You have a friendly town here, and I like your people."

"You might not have liked it if you had seen what happened the other day. Two little kids were blown up by some nuts driving through town. They intended to kill the kids' father and a friend for being friends. One is a Protestant, the other is a Catholic. They've been friends since childhood, and everyone thought it was beautiful that they stayed friends even when they grew up, everyone, that is, except a few nuts."

"That's sad. But I still think your people are nice people," Joshua insisted.

"Aren't you worried, traveling around so freely, that you might get caught up in some kind of police net or be suspect by one side or the other?" Tim asked, fishing to see where Joshua stood on these matters.

"No, that doesn't bother me. I don't concern myself with politics. They create artificial categories that are unreal, and divide people, and prevent people from thinking and living the way they want. Freedom is sacred."

As the two men were finishing their food, Tim asked Joshua where he intended to sleep for the night. Joshua said he would probably sleep in the field under the tree. Tim thought that unnecessary and invited him to stay at his house. Joshua accepted. The two men walked off together.

5

IT WAS NOT far to Tim's house, just across the meadow. Everyone was waiting impatiently for the head of the house to come home so they could eat supper. It had become accepted routine for Tim to come home late, not because the family approved, but because no one could do anything about it. Tim's shaky appearance didn't enhance his coming, and his bringing a total unknown with him added to the annoyance.

"Stella," Tim said to his wife, with a sheepish look on his face, "this is my new friend. I found him eating by himself in the meadow. His name is Joshua. He's a good man and doesn't have much use for politics, so everyone can relax. He's already eaten supper, but he might like something to drink." With that Tim went to the refrigerator and took out a beer and gave it to his friend.

Everyone eyed Joshua, not knowing what to make of him. He looked embarrassed, sensing the tension in the house. Stella felt his uneasiness, and being a kind person, she welcomed him with a cheerful smile and introduced him to all the family. There were four children in the McGirr family, two boys and two girls. Tim's mother also lived with them in the crowded bungalow.

The house was small. There was just a large kitchen that opened into a living room—really just one room divided by the difference in furniture—and three small bedrooms, one where Tim and Stella slept and the other two where the children slept. There wasn't much privacy. The grandmother slept in a bed against the wall in the living room. It was closer to the bathroom and more convenient for her. On nights when she couldn't sleep, she could slip out on the front porch and rock herself to sleep in the rocking chair.

Introductions over, the family sat down to eat. Everyone waited for Tim to say grace, which he usually forgot. This night was usual. He started to eat, saw that everyone else had their hands folded waiting for grace, then half choked on his first bite, which he didn't know whether to take out of his mouth or swallow.

"In the name of the Father and of the Son and of the Holy Ghost. Amen. Dear Lord," Tim prayed, "we thank you for the food we eat this evening and for my dear wife, who works so hard to prepare it, and for the children and for mother, who blesses us with her presence. We also thank you for our new friend, Joshua. May his presence bless our home. Bless us all with good health and grant peace to our land. We ask this in Jesus' name." Everyone responded with a hearty "Amen" and immediately attacked the food.

Conversation at the table was subdued because of the inhibiting presence of a stranger. Everyone was curious about Joshua. Who was he? Where was he from? Did he work? What was he doing in their village? Joshua answered simply and before long even the children were fascinated by his rare talent for conversation as he told of his experiences in the different places he visited recently and what the people were like in those places.

Tim tried to feel out Joshua about his feelings on the situation between the Protestants and the Catholics. Joshua's answer was simple: God's children have to learn to love one another. He wants his children to be one. Barriers are artificial. They make people believe they are different. God doesn't create barriers. People do. Beneath the surface there is little difference between those on either side. Once they stop hating, they will wonder why they were even fighting.

"My friend," Tim said, "I'm afraid you make it too simple. It's been going on for a long time."

"Time doesn't consecrate it," Joshua replied calmly, "nor does it justify what is happening. The causes were different centuries ago, and the issues today are not the same. They can be worked out by reasonable people. Fear and hatred should give way to understanding. The real damage today is to little children. They have a right to live and to grow up free of hatred. Parents who teach their children to hate destroy their own children and condemn them to go through life with tortured souls and twisted minds, never knowing peace in their hearts, the peace that Jesus wanted so much to give."

Tim and Stella had managed to keep aloof from the embroilments of the town and the city nearby. The kids worked their little farm during the school year and all summer. Milking the cows and goats, feeding the chickens and ducks, and tending the crops kept them busy and away from activities in the town and from other children. Their parents taught them early in their lives to avoid troublemakers and children who hang around in gangs. This served them well, as they were able to grow up free from the troubled feelings of so many of the children of their time. They were happy children, and it showed in the spontaneous way they laughed and reacted to life.

While everyone was finishing supper the two girls quietly cleared the table, and Stella filled a teakettle and put it on to boil, then cut up freshly baked soda bread and placed it on the table. Joshua had never tasted soda bread before and was eager to try it. Tim thought it would be a good idea to have the tea and bread on the porch since it was such a cool evening. Everyone agreed, so they retired outside. The soda bread was a treat. Even Joshua thought so and readily accepted a second piece when it was offered.

Tim's mother, Anne, was a pleasant woman in her late sixties who had a fine wit. She kept eyeing Joshua all during the evening, and when she finally thought she had him sized up, she opened up with her first remark. "Joshua, you're a fine-looking man, if I might say so, and too good a man to be living in this tough world. You look too refined to cope with what's going on these days. I hope no evil befalls you."

"Thank you, Anne," Joshua replied kindly. "I've experienced a lot and understand human beings quite well. They don't frighten me. My life is carefully planned by my Father, and no one approaches without his willing it. So I'm never afraid." It was a rather odd kind of response, which made everyone wonder, but no one felt comfortable enough to ask him to clarify.

As the sun set, directly across from the front porch, a beautiful golden glow spread all along the horizon. Swallows and nightingales could be seen silhouetted against the golden light as they glided gracefully across the vast ocean of cool evening air.

Stella offered to give up Tim's and her bedroom for the evening, but Joshua wouldn't hear of it. He was used to sleeping outdoors and asked if they minded his sleeping in the hammock on the front porch. He had never slept in anything like that before and thought it would be fun.

It wasn't long before they all retired. But before finally turning in, Stella peeked through the curtain to see if Joshua was comfortable in the hammock. He wasn't there. She looked around the porch and in the moonlight spotted him on his knees in the grass, sitting on his heels, with arms extended, deep in prayer. He looked so beautiful. She wondered who he really was.

6

JOSHUA WAS THE first one up the next morning, with the singing birds and the first rays of dawn. The air was fresh and clean. Joshua breathed in the clear, cool air in deep drafts, savoring each breath as it filled his lungs. A cock crowed. It reminded him of Peter long ago. What a sad night that was! It seemed like such a short time ago. Cows were mooing in the barn, calling the children to relieve them of their heavy burden of swollen udders.

Joshua walked about the farmyard, noticing everything. The animals fascinated him. The fields were carefully tended and showed how well disciplined the children were in following their father's instructions. It was mostly their job, as their father worked in an automobile factory in the city and had no mind for farming when he came home. He had worked the farm for years before he got his job at the factory, and had trained the kids to work with him since they were little children. They always enjoyed it, and now that they were older, and did practically all the work, they were allowed to keep for their savings accounts a good part of what they earned from the farm.

At the side of the barn was a fenced-off section where the sheep rested overnight. It was safer that way as there were still foxes roaming the hills and meadow. Joshua walked past the sheep. There was something about the sheep that always struck a sentimental chord in Joshua. He leaned on the fence and

257

watched them, the little ones with funny, shaky legs, keeping close to their mothers, looking back nervously over their shoulders, watching Joshua.

"Joshua, Joshua," a voice called out through the early morning silence, "are you still here?"

Joshua turned around and saw the youngest of the family, Christopher, on the front porch, an arm wrapped around a porch post, looking up and down the yard for him. Chris had a whimsical little face and a heavy crop of brown curly hair. He hadn't said a word all evening, just kept watching Joshua, absorbing everything about him, finally deciding he liked him. When he woke up Joshua was the first thing on his mind. He hoped he hadn't disappeared during the night. As soon as he dressed he ran out on the porch to find him.

"Here I am," Joshua called back, "down near the sheep pen."

Chris got tongue-tied all of a sudden and didn't know what to say. He just stood there, happy his friend hadn't gone.

Joshua walked up to the house. As he approached Chris froze, not knowing what to do but smile, which said everything he wanted to say in words but couldn't. He did get up enough nerve to tell Joshua that breakfast was ready. They went inside together.

Tim was all ready for work and was standing in the corner sipping a mug of steaming black coffee. Stella was frying eggs and ham. The children had brought the eggs in fresh from the yard while biscuits were baking in the oven. Grandma had just finished saying her rosary. Those prayers to the Mother of God had been her strength during the hard years after her husband had been killed by a Protestant fanatic almost fifteen years ago. In spite of it she managed to raise her children remarkably free from hatred and bigotry.

"Good morning, Joshua," Tim greeted his guest as Christopher ushered him quietly into the kitchen and sat him down at the table next to his place. At that point the other children, Pat and Tom and Ann, burst through the front door. They had just finished their chores at the barn. Everyone took his place, and Tim asked Joshua if he would say grace. He consented.

Taking a biscuit from the bread basket, he broke it in half, closed his eyes, and prayed, "Father, bless this family with your love and protection. Keep them from harm and let no evil touch them, for they preserve your love and forgiveness in a troubled land. Bless this food to nourish their bodies, and may your word nourish their souls as we cannot live on bread alone. Fill their lives with your joy and peace." Everyone responded with a thoughtful "Amen."

Joshua passed the two halves of the biscuit to those on his right and left and told each one to take a piece. Christopher was thrilled. He took a piece and passed it on.

"What a beautiful custom!" Grandma McGirr commented. "Where did you learn that, Joshua?"

"It was a custom in my family, and I added a new symbolism to it, to give it more meaning," he answered simply.

The McGirrs were happy people. Though they had suffered immensely from the bitter hatreds all around them, they remained free of spite and vengeance and exuded a carefree joy and lightheartedness that was infectious. It showed in a powerful way that another person's hatred does not have to fill the victim's life with hate unless he freely chooses to hate. The meanness of another merely provides an excuse to hate, but never a valid reason.

Because the McGirrs were happy people, mealtime was fun, even if Tim did come in late. Grandma was never pompous. As old as she was, and she was approaching seventy, she could still tell an old joke she remembered from years ago or poke fun gently at one of the children. They would go along with it and laugh. Joshua himself seemed pleased with this beautiful family.

Tim finished breakfast first and readied himself for work as Joshua, ready to leave with Tim, was finishing up. Everyone seemed sad at the thought of Joshua leaving. It was strange. They had only met him the night before, but there was something about this simple, gentle man that captured their hearts and they didn't want to lose what they found in him.

As Tim and Joshua walked out the door, Stella kissed Tim shyly and to Joshua extended her hand, which he shook warmly. The children stood by silently. Christopher had a tear in his eye but bravely held it back. Joshua thanked them all for their kind hospitality and rested his hand on Christopher's head as if in blessing. The two men started down the path toward the meadow. Everyone felt sad and wondered if Joshua would come to visit them again.

7

No SOONER HAD Joshua appeared in the village square than children started flocking around him, their curiosity aroused by the stories spread about him overnight. Even some of the older kids, curious and casual, hung around the square, talking in small cliques, feigning total disinterest in the little children's newfound hero.

Joe came back with his trumpet to show off a new tune he had been practicing all night. He couldn't wait to give Joshua another lesson. Another boy, Andrew, brought a guitar and waited patiently for his turn to show his skills.

"Joshua," Joe asked a bit shyly, "would you like to play my trumpet again?"

"Yes, maybe I can do a little better today," Joshua replied with a grin. Taking the shiny silver instrument, he put it to his lips and tried to play. Only a few sour notes belched forth. He tried again, and as his lips adjusted to the mouthpiece, the notes came clear and sharp. He played the tune Joe had taught him the day before, and then played a tune he had just made up, a happy tune with funny notes that made everyone laugh. Even Joe was amazed at how fast Joshua learned. He offered to give Joshua another lesson. Joshua agreed, and the child taught this grown-up stranger how to play other notes and another simple tune. The kids were surprised at the humility of this adult who would let a child teach him and thoroughly enjoyed learning from him.

Joshua had been noticing Andrew's patience while he waited for his turn with Joshua. "Andrew," Joshua called to him, "you are a patient little lad. Come here and let me see your guitar. Do you play it well?"

Andrew was beside himself with pride. "Yes, I think I do. Would you like to hear me play it?"

"I'd love to," Joshua responded with interest. The boy started to strum his guitar, and before long was lost in his music. The boy was good. He played a folk song, and the other children at first started humming, then began to sing. Before long they were all singing, even Joshua, once he picked up the melody.

It wasn't by chance that all the children gathering around Joshua were Catholic. Jane, the little girl who fed the birds, was Catholic, so her friends would naturally be Catholic. But it wasn't just her friends who came. There were others who had heard about this strange fellow wandering around. Any new activity was bound to arouse interest, the town being small and the amusements limited.

As Joshua was watching Andrew, so absorbed in his music, he noticed another group of children walking into the square. They looked no different from the children around Joshua, but they remained aloof and stayed off by themselves near the inn at the opposite side of the square. There were about ten of them and they were about the same age as the children with Joshua, which was on average twelve to fourteen years. In spite of their obvious curiosity, none of the children approached Joshua's group. They stood there, just watching, with a detectable look of envy at the fun Joshua's friends were having.

The group of older children, who had originally come to the square and kept to themselves, had gradually moved closer to Joshua's group and were now part of the chorus singing along to Andrew's accompaniment. Even though they were with younger kids, they had forgotten themselves and were really having fun.

The children must have been with Joshua the good part of an hour, then began to drift off in different directions until Joshua was left alone in the square. Resting on the stone wall, he looked up and down the square as if in deep thought, with no trace of the childlike playfulness of a few minutes before, but more like a military officer planning strategy for an upcoming encounter.

Then, with a determined look, he walked across the square and down the street, past a row of houses and shops, took a right turn at the last street in the town, and headed for the Catholic church. It looked pretty with all the roses in bloom. A man who appeared to be in his early seventies was on his knees working in the garden. Hearing footsteps approaching, he looked up and saw Joshua.

"Hello, young man," he said in a friendly voice. "Coming for a visit?"

"Yes, I thought I'd stop by. My name is Joshua," he answered.

"Are you new in town?"

"Yes," Joshua replied. "I've been traveling around the country and noticed what a quaint, friendly village you have, so I decided to stay awhile."

"I'm Father Donnelly," the old man said as he got up off his knees none too easily. Joshua stretched out a hand, offering to help him, but the old man made it on his own.

The two men shook hands, and the priest welcomed Joshua into his garden and automatically started showing him around.

"What a beautiful garden you have!" Joshua commented.

"Thank you," the priest responded, with a gleam of pride in his eyes. "Yes, I've been cultivating this garden for over thirty years now; it's like a little piece of heaven for me. I know I should be able to find God in the church, but for some reason I feel closer to him out here in the garden, so I spend most of my time here lately. It takes my mind off all the hurt around our neighborhood." A tear appeared in the old man's eyes. Joshua noticed and understood.

The priest had been there a long time. He was a member of every family, yet, belonging to none, he was very much alone. It was difficult getting too intimate with the people. A priest couldn't pick friends without others feeling left out, so he stayed pretty much to himself. God was his only real friend. Joshua knew that, so he came to visit.

Up to that point the old man, being distracted by his garden, hadn't looked directly at Joshua, but as he stood there talking to him he turned and looked into Joshua's eyes. He was immediately taken aback by what he saw in them—a look of intense compassion—and he had the strangest feeling this stranger could see into his very soul. The old priest's first impulse was to look away, out of embarrassment, but when he saw nothing critical in the man's eyes, he continued to stare.

After showing Joshua around the garden, the priest invited him into the church. It was a typical, old-fashioned country church, with rough-hewn wooden beams and rafters and almost life-size statues, which seemed to come to life as the red and blue and yellow lights from the stained-glass windows played tricks on the faces of the saints. The priest told Joshua he had bought the statues long ago with his own money. They were gifts to the people, simple reminders of the closeness of their sainted friends, telling them that they should be used as aids to prayer and to focus their minds on the things of the spirit, but never as objects of devotion in themselves, like a picture of a mother or a departed loved one.

Joshua was impressed with the simplicity of the church and told the priest he would like to spend a few minutes talking to God. The priest understood and said he would be working in the garden when he finished.

Joshua knelt and prayed. He was a beautiful sight, kneeling erect, with strong, delicate hands loosely folded, and his face relaxed and calm. You could sense the total absorption of his thoughts in a world to which no one else had access.

After a few minutes Joshua finished and walked back out into the garden. The priest was waiting, wiping his brow with a blue handkerchief. Standing there in his soiled black pants and wrinkled, faded white shirt, the old man looked more like the hired hand than the parish priest. He was glad the stranger had come along. He had distracted him from his troubled thoughts, thoughts over his own fast-approaching twilight and the events of recent days, which presaged no good for the future.

"Young man," the priest said, "would you like to have a cup of tea with me and a little snack? It's almost time for me to take a rest. I can't work long like I used to."

"Yes, I'd like that," Joshua answered cheerfully. The two men went into the parish house. The housekeeper, Marie MacCarthy, opened the door when she heard the footsteps approaching. As she welcomed Joshua, the priest introduced her, telling Joshua what a help she was, since he was getting too old to prepare his own meals, and he said, "She is a real angel of mercy to many in the parish. She even helps Protestants." Everyone chuckled.

The two men sat down.

"You've been here a long time, Father, haven't you?" Joshua remarked as he scanned the kitchen and noticed all the accumulated mementos hanging here and there around the room.

"Yes, sometimes I think too long," the old man answered rather wistfully.

"Why do you say that?" Joshua asked, concerned.

"Because there is so much hurt and anguish to life," the priest responded. "The burden on the heart gets heavier as you get older. Parents and family die, loved ones leave, children whom you have known from infancy grow up and come to pour their hearts out over their problems. And there are no little problems in our modern world. The problems today only God can solve. They are much too big for the human mind to even grasp, much less attempt to resolve. I go to bed every night with a heavy heart. I ache for each one in my parish; they have become more dear to me than my own family. The hurt is sometimes too much to bear." It all poured out as if the old man had been waiting for Joshua to come along. He could not talk to anyone in his parish this way. Indeed, who could he talk to like this who would ever understand? The tea ready, Marie poured a cup for each of them and put a newly baked loaf of soda bread on the table. The priest cut off a few slices and pushed the plate in front of Joshua.

"That is what makes you a good shepherd," Joshua said, trying to comfort him, fully intending all that the remark implied. The priest looked at him, wondering again about this stranger who seemed to know him so thoroughly, though they had just met.

Surprised, the priest asked him, "How do you know me?"

"Before you were born I knew you."

"But you are barely forty years old. How could you have known me?"

"Everyone knows in his own way. I have known you and have watched your work. You have labored hard and long for my Father's sheep, and you are dear to God. Don't be afraid."

"But I am afraid," the priest responded simply, overlooking all the other things Joshua had said. "There are troubles here and my own people are being drawn into them. There is another priest who comes into town stirring up the people. I've tried all my life to help my people to avoid hatred and to always forgive, but this man is undoing it all. I've told the bishop about him, but the bishop told me he can't do a thing with him. He's his own man, and the bishop is reluctant to censure him, feeling it won't do any good. And what is even more frightening, a bogus Presbyterian minister also comes through town agitating the Protestants. I have nightmares about the future."

Then the priest, realizing that he had just poured his heart out to a total stranger, remarked to Joshua, "Why do I tell you, a stranger, about problems I've never shared with anyone, not even the bishop?"

Joshua smiled. "Maybe because you feel you can trust me." They both laughed.

"Well, son," the old priest sighed, and picked up his cup and put it in the sink. Joshua did the same, and the two men walked back out into the garden. Marie stood at the door watching Joshua. She had heard the whole conversation and was wondering about this gentle stranger who seemed to understand so much.

Joshua thanked the priest for his kindness and told him God was pleased with the work he had done during such troubled times and would soon answer his prayers. The priest didn't pay much attention to what Joshua was saying, not having the slightest hint as to who he was. But he thanked Joshua for listening and welcomed him back whenever he wished to come. If he would like to come to supper, he would be most welcome anytime. Joshua thanked him and left.

The old man went back to his garden, watching Joshua as he walked up the road, thinking what a strange young man he was.

8

THE WALK TO the nearest city was invigorating. Joshua liked to walk. It was ordinary travel in his time, and he did a lot of thinking while walking. There were berry bushes along the way; he picked the juicy berries and ate them by the handful. They weren't very filling, but they were tasty and nourishing. Cars drove past, and every now and then someone would stop and offer him a lift. Joshua declined politely. Then, when he was almost halfway to the city, a car stopped and the driver offered him a ride. Joshua readily accepted, as if he had been waiting for this person all along.

He got into the car and the driver introduced himself. His name was John Hourihan, a sturdily built man in his forties, with thick, straight, jet-black hair. He was softspoken and said little during the ride, but he listened to Joshua, trying to analyze this stranger he had never seen before.

John was headmaster at a school in the city, and though he was Catholic he managed to persuade the trustees of the school to open its doors to children of all religions. It was a bold move for the time and place but it accomplished much in fostering a better feeling among the children for one another. John mentioned that some of the children from his school had been in the village square in the morning and told of a stranger they had met there, and that they were fascinated by him because he was different. Joshua asked if they were pleased with the stranger, and did his meeting with them make them happy, and did they like his guitar playing. John began to realize his rider may have been that stranger, so he asked him.

"Yes, it was I," Joshua replied simply. "I wanted to bring the children a little happiness. They seemed so heavy-hearted for such little children."

"Yes, it's sad," John commented, "to think that joy should be stripped from their lives even before they get a chance to live. That's why in my school we try to bring the children together in a relaxed atmosphere so they can get to know one another. We had problems in the beginning, and threats from some sick people, but things have been working out well. We have a good number of really good children, strong kids, the type who will be leaders one day."

They reached the city limits, and John asked Joshua where he wanted to be dropped off. Joshua told him near the city park.

"I don't know your name," John said to Joshua.

"Joshua," he replied, "just Joshua."

The park wasn't far away. John stopped the car and let out his passenger.

"Good luck, Joshua. Hope to see you again."

"Thank you very much for the ride. We will meet again."

Joshua walked down the street toward the park. John drove off, watching him through the mirror, still wondering about him.

The park was filling with people, and Joshua walked to the edge of the crowd. They looked intense, humorless. He had seen people like that before. He felt uncomfortable but walked on, mingling with a loose gathering of people who had entered the park with him. It was twelve twenty-five; the event was to start at twelve-thirty. A raised platform at the back of the tree-lined park was decorated with orange and white bunting and flags of various organizations. It was festive and dramatic in contrast with the greens and browns of the trees and lawn and the rather drab colors of the people's clothes. Many in the crowd were workmen on their lunch hour; others had come from a distance for the occasion, to hear this electrifying orator they had either heard before or heard about.

A stir rippled across the crowd, and a breathless silence ensued. A course-looking, bull-like man mounted the platform and was introduced as the great evangelist of their day, the Reverend John V. Maislin, to the wild acclaim of the crowd. After the seemingly endless applause, the speaker motioned for silence and began to speak:

"My good people, and I call you good because you have sacrificed your time and your lunch hour to be here with me on this hot summer day. You are here because you fear the Lord and you want to listen to the truth, the truth that sets us free, as the Lord has promised. We are in danger of losing that freedom, for the enemy is in our midst. He is right here mingling in the crowd with you today. He is the wolf in sheep's clothing, waiting for a chance to ravage and rape you good, God-fearing people. And that enemy is the Antichrist, the Pope, and his bloodthirsty emissaries, who are everywhere, trying to strip from you your freedom, your hard-won democracy.

"Democracy is the product of the Reformation. Rome had kept people enslaved for centuries, and would do so today if we let them. There are forces all around us today who would, if they could, strip us of our precious freedom. These are the secret collaborators of the Vatican dictators. Some of these evil and vicious people cloak themselves in the guise of Protestant bishops, as strange as that may seem.

"I speak to you as a friend. I stand between you and God and I speak to you from God. I have known God, and I speak to you as a prophet from God. I am concerned for you because of forces unleashed in the world today. Churches trying to unite is the work of Satan. It goes counter to all we stand for as Protestants. And everyone is falling for it, from the Archbishop of Canterbury to the Orthodox Patriarchs, who can't wait for the right time to team up with the Antichrist in Rome. That is because they are the leaders of churches that hate the Bible and teach their people the doctrines of men, the height of idolatry.

"I am warning you, my dear people, like the prophets tried to warn the Jews of old, that these enemies are all around us. Their followers are planning right now to strip your freedom from you and turn you back into bondage. We must fight them with every weapon at our disposal until we destroy the Satan in our midst."

A group of the preacher's henchmen had been watching Joshua all during the talk and could tell he did not approve of what their leader was saying. They walked over to him as he stood at the edge of the crowd and, confronting him, asked bluntly, "Don't you agree with the preacher?"

Joshua looked at them, unintimidated, and spoke very calmly. "God is love and what is of God never preaches hate. By their fruits you shall know them. The fruit of hatred is suspicion of one's neighbors, even of one's own family, and violence. Violence does not come from God. There is enough hatred and violence in the world without clergy preaching hatred. They are the true wolves in sheep's clothing, the true Antichrist, preaching the exact opposite of everything Jesus taught. Everyone is a child of God, and everyone is searching for God in his or her own way. People are not evil, and God's true shepherds preach love and forgiveness and forbearance in the face of injustice, never hatred and suspicion of one's neighbor. That is the work of the devil."

"You're a bloody papist, you bastard," said one of the hired thugs as he hauled off and hit Joshua straight in the jaw. Joshua looked at him calmly, unperturbed, like long ago when the servant of the high priest did the same thing.

The calm, fearless look in Joshua's eyes unsteadied the thug. He knew the stranger was not afraid of him, but for some reason, far beyond his retarded comprehension, he refused to react . . . and not from fear. The man felt a twinge of guilt, because he saw no hatred in Joshua's eyes, only pity. He walked away ashamed. His companion followed him.

People standing near were shocked but unsympathetic, because they were all of the same ilk, and they assumed that what the preacher's thugs did was totally justified though they didn't understand it.

Joshua now knew what he was facing. The battle lines were clear. A strategy was slowly taking shape in his mind.

He walked away from the crowd and started on his trek back to the village.

9

IT WAS ONLY a few miles back to the village. Joshua's jaw ached, but he tried not to pay attention to it. Not many cars were traveling in the direction of the village, but a farmer was driving his horse and farm wagon in Joshua's direction so he offered him a lift. Joshua hopped on the wagon and the two men rode down the highway.

"My name's Tommy. What's yours?" the farmer said in friendly fashion as he offered his hand to Joshua.

"Joshua," he responded.

"I saw what happened back there at the park when I was driving by. That preacher does the work of the devil. I'm Protestant myself, but I don't go for the likes of him and that crew with him. All they do is stir up trouble. Our village was friendly for years. Catholics and Protestants got along good until that fellow and his henchmen started coming to town, arousing fear and suspicion in people. I saw that fellow hit you back there. Why didn't you punch him back? You look strong enough to take care of yourself."

"Fighting has no meaning for me. Animals fight because they lack the intelligence to solve problems in any other way. For me it would have accomplished nothing. It's better to avoid those kinds of people," Joshua answered quietly.

"Where are you staying in town?" the farmer asked as he sucked on his pipe.

"No place in particular."

The farmer sensed Joshua was just one of those daydreaming wanderers and could see he was harmless, so he invited him to stay at their farmhouse. It wasn't much, but at least he would have a place to lay his head. It was lonely at the farm since their son left for America a few months before.

Joshua accepted.

Tommy was in his late sixties and was used to long hours of work each day. Even though it was only midafternoon, he had already done a good day's work and was on his way home after dropping off his produce at the market.

As the wagon approached the village a few of the children recognized Joshua and laughed with delight at seeing him on the old farm wagon, waving to him and calling him as the wagon rolled by.

Joshua waved to them. Two of the boys ran alongside the wagon, asking Joshua if he was going to be in the square the next morning.

"Yes, I'll be there. Bring your friends with you and we will have a good time."

"What was that all about?" Tom asked his rider.

"I've been meeting with the children in the village square. They are trying to teach me how to play the trumpet and a few other things. It's good for them, keeps them out of trouble."

The wagon continued through town, and the few people walking down the street waved hello to Tommy. He was a fixture in the neighborhood and everyone liked him and his wife, Millie. They were kind, gentle people who bothered no one and always lent a hand when someone needed them.

Tom did not have to steer the horse up Stonecastle Road. Old Willie knew the route by instinct. Even blindfolded he could travel the road from the farm to the market and back home. As they approached the farm the horse's pace speeded up. He knew his oats would be in a little pile at the entrance to the small corral.

Joshua helped Tommy unhitch the horse and unload the wagon. They went up to the house together. Millie met them at the door and relieved Joshua of some of the packages. Coming into the kitchen, Tommy introduced Joshua to his wife and told her all about the incident at Rev. Maislin's rally.

Millie was a thin, wiry woman in her early sixties. Her face was shaped like a leprechaun's which her quaintly pointed nose accentuated. When she smiled, as she did when her husband introduced her to Joshua, she radiated good humor and a jolly spirit.

Joshua had a good time that evening. Their supper was ordinary simple fare, but the good humor and happy spirits were in tune with Joshua's own free spirit. Tommy told Joshua about their pastor at the Presbyterian church and said he would like Joshua to meet him some evening, and if it would be acceptable to their guest, he would invite the pastor and his wife for supper.

Joshua thought that a great idea and said he would look forward to the occasion, as there were many things he would like to discuss with the pastor.

After supper Joshua insisted on helping his hosts with their tasks around the farm, and when everything was done they spent a few relaxing moments sitting on the porch enjoying the cool evening breeze and watching the birds gliding across the evening sky in the setting sun.

10

THE VILLAGE SQUARE was quiet early in the morning. The only people there were workers on their way to their jobs, lunch boxes in hand and a spring in their steps, some whistling happy tunes, some not so happy. Joshua greeted each one as he passed, and all without exception returned the good wishes. Before coming to the square Joshua had helped Tommy ready himself for his daily trip to the market, and after breakfast had ridden with him as far as the square.

Joshua sat on the wall, sometimes looking across the square, sometimes letting his gaze wander across the meadow. It was melancholy and peaceful this time of day. The shadows were long. The air was clean. The sun was soft. It was quiet. Joshua liked quiet.

It wasn't long after most of the workers had left the village that Jane walked down into the square to perform her daily ritual. All the birds in creation were waiting for her. As soon as she opened the bag they besieged her, one landing on her shoulder, another on her wrist. She scattered the seed along the pavement as she made her way toward Joshua. The flurry of flying birds distracted him. When he turned and saw the little girl walking toward him, he smiled.

"Good morning, Joshua!"

"Good morning, little one! Those birds surely do like you."

"That's because I feed them every day. If I didn't feed them, they wouldn't even come near me."

"They know you love them. You show them that by feeding them. During the summer it's good to skip some days, so they get used to looking for their own food. It's better for them. They need you more in the cold winter, when food is scarce."

"Joshua, do you think you can get the cardinal to come to me again?" Jane asked him.

They both looked up into the tree. He was there waiting, watching.

"Give me a handful of seed," Joshua said as he extended his hand.

He held his hand out toward the bird. After a little hesitation, the bird flew down, looked up at Joshua, then at Jane, and started to eat. The girl slowly took some seed from the bag and gently moved her hand closer to Joshua's, just like on the previous occasion. When the bird had finished the seed in Joshua's hand, he stopped, looked up, hopped onto Jane's hand, and started to eat. The girl was delighted and tried to contain her joy, so as not to frighten the nervous creature. When he had finished he flew back into the tree.

Children began filtering into the square earlier than usual. This time they were not the same children who had been with Joshua the day before. They were kids from the group who had stood at a distance and watched the others playing with Joshua. As they began to gather they looked over at Joshua talking with the girl. They wanted to approach him but were hesitant. Joshua noticed and made a friendly gesture toward them. They responded immediately by starting to walk across the square. Jane looked frightened. Joshua put his hand on her shoulder to reassure her and told her not to be afraid. "Stay here with me and don't be afraid," he said to her. She relaxed and clung close to her friend, though she wanted to run away at seeing all those strange kids coming. They were Protestants.

As the children began to encircle Joshua and the girl, Joshua told them his name and also introduced Jane. She tried to be friendly. The oldest boy in the group immediately took charge and introduced his friends. After giving the names of all the others, he introduced himself. "My name is John Clark." They all rather embarrassedly said hello.

John was about thirteen years old. He was not very tall, but was stocky and solid and had thick curly hair. He asked Joshua where he was from and why he had come to their village. Joshua answered, then asked them about themselves, and about school, and about their play. One of the children had a rubber ball. Joshua asked him if he could borrow it. The boy gladly gave it to him. Joshua took it and covered it with his hand. When he opened his hands a frog jumped out onto the pavement. The kids screamed with delight. One of the boys picked up the frog and gave it back to Joshua, asking him how he did it. Joshua smiled and took the frog. He threw it up in the air and it began to fly away. It had become a sparrow. After circling the square, and diving down toward the kids, the bird flew back to Joshua and landed on his hand. The children were beside themselves. They had heard about magicians but had never seen one in action.

At about that point the other group of children, who had been with Joshua previously, entered the square. They were surprised to see their friend playing with Protestant kids. At first they were offended. Joe felt the worst. He felt betrayed, but then remarked to the others, "He was our friend first. What difference does it make if the other kids like him too? Why should we stay away?"

Many of the children were reluctant to mingle with the Protestant group, but when Joe walked over the others followed. As they moved closer they saw what Joshua was doing and they, too, were fascinated. The bird had just flown back to Joshua and had landed on his hand as a rubber ball. Joshua took the ball and threw it over the heads of the children near him to Joe. When he saw it coming Joe quickly put his trumpet down and caught the ball. As he did it turned into a little rabbit. In shock, he dropped it, then stooped down, picked it up, together with his trumpet, and brought it over to Joshua. The kids had heard of magicians doing tricks like that but had never witnessed it. Was it an illusion? Was he just playing tricks with their imagination or was what they were seeing really happening?

Joshua continued playing with the children in this manner for the better part of an hour, coming up with an endless display of tricks, gradually drawing the children more and more into the action until, having forgotten themselves, they were all mingling and having fun together, something they had never done before—Catholics and Protestants playing and laughing and talking to one another and having a perfectly good time. It was unheard of. Before it all ended Joe was teaching one of the Protestant boys how to play the trumpet.

11

THAT NIGHT JOSHUA slept under the big tree in the meadow. It was a warm night with a delicious breeze, and no mosquitoes or troubling insects, so it was a perfect place to sleep. It was Joshua's chosen place of repose. He liked being alone at night, as in times past, when he would go off into the hills by himself, while his companions retired to their cozy, comfortable homes. "The birds of the air have their nests, the foxes have their dens, but the son of man has nowhere to lay his head." There weren't any tall mountains or big hills nearby, but the meadow was isolated and quiet, and it wasn't far from the brook that snaked through the fields, so it was a good place to gather one's thoughts and just relax.

The next day all the children gathered with Joshua. They were a little uncomfortable at first, but Joshua broke the ice by beckoning them all to come closer. After a few minutes they were all relaxed. He repeated some of the tricks he had performed the day before for the benefit of new kids the others had brought. Joshua asked each one his or her name, which, to the children's surprise, he was never to forget. He would even at times call by name children he had not met before, which really shocked them. The children didn't stay too long but said they would come back the next day if Joshua would be there. He said he would. After all the other children left, Joe stayed on at the square with Joshua, helping him to master the trumpet. When he left, a little after noon, he told Joshua to wait for him, he would be back. He did come back, a short time later, with a brown bag full of things to eat. Joe was thoughtful and noticed that Joshua didn't have much of anything and thought he might appreciate some things to nibble on when he got hungry. He was right. Had it not been for his thoughtfulness, Joshua would have gone to sleep that night with an empty stomach. Sitting under the tree in the restful quiet of the early evening, only a few feet from the rippling water, Joshua ate his supper, looking pensively toward the village square, dreaming about times past and things to come.

There was no one to be seen, either in the square or across the meadow. A few sheep wandered by, took a drink in the brook, looked over at the strange being sitting under the tree, and walked away. Joshua didn't bother to call them. He just watched. A cow crossed the stream, walked close to where Joshua was sitting, and mooed quietly. Joshua called the animal. She looked over, curious, and walked closer. Joshua held out his hand to the animal. The cow smelled the salt he was holding and came over and licked it out of his hand. Joshua petted her. She turned and walked away.

As the sun went down, Joshua looked across the horizon, and for a few brief minutes his lips moved as if in silent prayer. He lay down on the warm grass, and in a few minutes was in a deep sleep.

12

JOSHUA ROSE EARLY the next morning to the singing of the birds. He wandered across the meadow, drinking in the clean, fresh morning air, then headed toward the square and turned down Maple Street.

The streets were empty except for a few men who went to work early. As Joshua approached St. Mary's Church he saw Father Donnelly in his black cassock, walking through the garden, reading his morning prayers, and every now and then inspecting his roses.

"Good morning, Father," Joshua called.

"Good morning, son," the old priest replied in a cheerful tone, obviously glad, though surprised, to see Joshua so early in the day.

The morning Angelus bell was ringing, calling the people to prayer and announcing that morning Mass was about to begin.

"I'm just finishing my morning prayers. Would you like to read the last psalm with me?" the priest asked Joshua.

"Yes, I would. Which one is it?" Joshua asked.

"The Twenty-fifth." The priest intoned the first verse, " 'To you, O Lord, I lift up my soul. My God, in you I trust, and I shall not be shamed.' "

To the priest's surprise, Joshua took up the second verse without reading it in the priest's book: " 'Do not let my enemies laugh at me, for those who cling to you will never be defeated.' "

" 'Direct me in your truth, and teach me; for you are God my savior, and I look to you all the day long.' "

" 'The Lord is gentle and upright; he sustains those who are stumbling along the way.' "

The two men continued the ancient prayer, and while walking into the church Father Donnelly invited Joshua to stay for Mass, then went up to the sacristy to vest, leaving Joshua in the church.

He took a seat halfway up the aisle. There was a good crowd in the church, almost sixty people, quite a few for only a week-day service. They were mostly women, but there was a handful of men, even younger men, with strong, ruddy features. Many of the women were saying their rosaries, the men just kneeling, absorbed in their thoughts. Joshua knelt straight, with hands clasped. It was always a beautiful sight, watching Joshua at prayer. There was a calmness, a peace, a serenity, and a manliness about Joshua praying that would touch even the most cynical hearts.

The priest emerged from the sacristy and began the Mass. Morning Mass was brief, there were no long sermons like on Sunday. Father Donnelly did make a few comments on the Gospel, about the gentleness and understanding of Jesus. He went about every day doing good, healing, counseling, comforting, and nowhere, except in one place, does anyone ever thank him. In spite of the people's ingratitude, Jesus never stopped doing good. It is a lesson that his followers need today more than ever before. There is so much hurt and misery, and so many wounds to be healed. We have to adopt the forgiving nature of Jesus, who never allowed himself to take offense, so we can, each in his own way, reach out to heal the hurts all around us. It is our children who will ultimately reap the benefits of our goodness, because one day they will have a better world to live in.

At Communion time Joshua did not go up to receive the Eucharist. The priest noticed and looked down in his direction, quietly inviting him. He still did not go.

After Mass the priest brought his guest to the parish house and insisted he have breakfast with him. The two men enjoyed each other's company, and at one point Father Donnelly told Joshua he was welcome to come to Communion if he liked.

Joshua could see it was perplexing to the priest why this obviously good man refrained from receiving the Eucharist. "Father, did Jesus take Communion at the Last Supper?" he asked the priest.

"No, but that was because the Eucharist was the gift of himself to his followers," the priest replied.

"And so I share in the Eucharist in the same way. You will understand one day. I do believe in this beautiful gift of God."

It was too much for the old priest to grasp, but he was content to know that Joshua did believe in the Eucharist. He told Joshua that it was a beautiful thing he was doing for the children in the town. Joshua smiled and told the priest that children have the right to grow up happy and free of their parents' hatreds and prejudices. It is a terrible sin for mothers and fathers to teach their children to hate. It would be better if they were drowned in the depths of the sea than to go before God with that sin on their consciences.

"Joshua, I do worry about you. You are a kind man, and I wonder if you realize how complicated the troubles are here. What you are doing is beautiful. It goes right to the heart of the problem, but because it does it is so easy for you to make a mistake and give sick people the excuse they look for to commit some terrible evil. Be careful."

"My Father is with me in all I do and I will be careful. What I am doing is carefully planned and it will accomplish its purpose. My Father will not be frustrated."

When the two men finished breakfast, the priest told Joshua he had heard he had no place to stay. If that were true, he was welcome to stay in the parish house. Joshua thanked him but said it would be better for him to stay by himself, though he would appreciate it if he could stay at the parish house when it rained. He would very much like to be able to stay at a Protestant home on occasions, too, when the weather was bad. The priest offered to contact his friend Rev. Davis, the Presbyterian minister, and make the suggestion to him.

"I am sure he would be delighted for you to stay at his house. We have already had discussions about you, and I was supposed to invite you to dinner with us sometime soon."

"That would be fun," Joshua said.

"Before you leave, Joshua, you might want to use one of the bathrooms upstairs. Here's a bathrobe. You can leave your clothes outside the door and the housekeeper will wash them for you. They will be ready in no time."

The hot bath felt good. The clothes were cleaned and quickly ironed, so Joshua did not have long to wait. After thanking the priest and the housekeeper, he left. The priest walked him through the garden. The old man had found a friend in Joshua. As a result of his training in the seminary, he had never made friends with parishioners. It was not a good practice. He was father to all of them, so they all felt close to him because he had no favorites. Now that his own family were dead and what few living friends he had were so far away, life was lonely for this simple old man. And even though he was a holy man, it did not make up for the real human need for companionship. In finding Joshua he found in him a rare goodness that embodied all the ideals he had believed in and tried all his life to preach. Meeting this strange young man was perhaps the most rewarding experience of his life. He could talk to him about anything and Joshua would understand, and would have insights that went far beyond what his young years seemed to warrant.

Joshua walked down the street, and the priest wandered around his garden, smelling the lavender that bordered the rosebed.

13

THE CHILDREN WERE already in the square when Joshua arrived. They were all talking together, Protestants and Catholics. Joshua was happy. It showed on his face. One of the Protestant girls noticed it and remarked to him about it. "I am happy to see you all together," was Joshua's response. "It is the way God's children should be."

The crowd was growing too large to continue meeting in the square. Joshua suggested they walk out into the meadow and gather on the hillside. The kids were all excited with the turn this little adventure in their lives was taking. They scrambled over the stone wall and through the trees. Some walked around the wall and followed the path into the meadow. They gathered on the knoll looking toward the village, which was a good distance away. It was quiet in the meadow, with trees here and there sheltering birds of various descriptions, not unlike similar scenes of long ago.

Joe came up to Joshua and offered his trumpet. Joshua humorously played a simple melody Joe had taught him. It was obvious he didn't take his playing too seriously. The children enjoyed watching him. That was a lesson in itself, Joshua's relaxed, casual attitude.

Some of the other children brought musical instruments. Joshua suggested they get together and form a little orchestra and play for the group. At first they were a little embarrassed, but the idea was a good one, and after a while they were playing well together. Before long the other children were singing along with them. Joshua didn't know the songs at first, but before long he knew them all and sang right along with the children.

When the musicians stopped for a break, one of the boys asked Joshua if he would do tricks again for them, like the day before. The boy with the rubber ball offered his ball to Joshua. He laughed. The boy threw the ball to him and he caught it and threw it way up into the air. It started to fly away. The children looked up, trying to follow the bird as it soared through the sky. A thumping sound at the back of the group distracted the children nearby. They turned and saw the ball bouncing around the field. They looked up into the sky for the bird and couldn't find it. They were still mystified at what was really happening. Did Joshua turn the ball into a bird or was it just an illusion? Some of the kids asked Joshua what really happened. He wouldn't tell them. He just smiled coyly and said to them, "You see, things are not necessarily what they appear to be. Always watch what happens and try to understand. There are strange things in life that look attractive on the surface but underneath can cause you harm. Do not be taken in by nice words or deceptive ideas. Think about them in the quiet of your nights, and when you are worried talk to God and ask him for understanding. The devil still wanders around in sheep's clothing, trying to deceive God's little ones. Always be careful."

The children enjoyed listening to Joshua speak like this. He spoke so gently, not like parents and other grown-ups, who are usually harsh and dogmatic and critical with children. His words were soothing and tranquil.

A little girl, considerably younger than the other children, was standing close to Joshua. She was wearing a pink dress decorated with forget-me-nots. Joshua noticed her looking down at the ground. She seemed sad. He reached down, picked a wildflower that was only in bud, and handed it to the girl. Her eyes sparkled as the bud began to open up right in front of her eyes. The other children asked Joshua to do the same thing for them. Joshua laughed. He knew he had put himself into a predicament.

He told all the children to pick a wildflower in bud. They scampered in all directions, looking for the kind they liked. When they were ready Joshua told them to be very quiet and concentrate and really believe. One by one the buds began to open. Only one little boy's did not open. He was standing not too far from Joshua. When he saw that everyone else's had opened, he began to cry and tried to hide his tears. Joshua saw him and called him over. He bent down and put his arm around his shoulders and asked the boy his name.

"My name is Kevin."

"How old are you?"

"Seven."

"Why did your bud not open?"

Through his tears the boy told Joshua, "I didn't think it would happen, but now I know."

"Take the bud home with you and see what happens," Joshua told him.

"Will it open?"

"You will see."

Joshua then told the group to sit down on the grass in small groups. They did as he told them.

When they were seated and quiet, Joshua leaned against a huge boulder, half sitting on it, half leaning against it, and began to tell the children a story.

"A young boy dreamed of being a great musician. He practiced hours each day and thought of nothing else but becoming famous and very wealthy. He knew the kind of music people liked and the kind that would make him rich, so he learned to write and perform music that pleased people, and it was not always good music. It was music about pleasure and wordly games and revolution and drugs. Young people liked his music and it became the popular music of the time. He had left home and lost contact with his family, especially his younger brother, who had loved and admired and missed him very much. He, too, missed his little brother and thought about him on lonely nights when his friends were busy about other things. He wondered what had happened to him. He hadn't heard from him in so long.

"Not long afterward the older brother was invited to a surprise party, the kind he was accustomed to attending. There were many people there he didn't know, mingling among a handful of his friends. Late in the evening one of the guests started to read poems, poems like the lyrics in the musician's songs. They were not good poems, but cheap and immoral. Everyone was laughing and enjoying the poems, but laughing more at the young man who was reading them. He was drugged and strange-looking. His dissolute life had destroyed him as a man. The musician felt a strange sense of sadness but couldn't understand why. He asked one of his friends who the young man was who was reading the poems, and his friend was surprised he did not know. That is your brother. He has loved and admired you all your life and spent his whole life imitating what you write about in your music. The musician became sick and left the party in disgust. He had realized too late that he had used the beautiful gifts that God had given him to make money, and in the process had destroyed not only the lives of many people but the life of the brother he had loved so much. It never occurred to him what evil was until he saw what his music had done to this brother's soul.

"Fortunately, that was not the end of the story. The young musician left all his friends and went off by himself to repent. He prayed for God to forgive him and to heal his little brother's tortured soul. He promised that if God would heal his brother, he would write music about beautiful things, and about peace, and about things that would bring joy into this world of darkness and troubled hearts. God heard his prayer and healed his brother. The two became close friends, never again to be separated. The musician composed music that was to inspire millions of people and bring joy and harmony into a world torn apart by selfishness and ambition. The younger brother wrote the words for all his brother's music. And their lives were filled with the kind of peace and happiness that God gives to those who find Him and who bring his joy into others' lives.

"Each one of you is like that musician. You have rare gifts that God has given you, to bring an important message to those around you. God has given each of you something special that he wants you to share with others. You can see already the beautiful things God can work among you if you let him. A few days ago you were strangers. You never thought you would be friends. Today you are friends. You help each other. You teach each other, like Joe and his new friend playing the trumpet together. You share with each other. And you have a peace you never knew possible. That peace and that friendship can continue for many years and can change the lives of all around you, and can create a beautiful world for your children to live in. That is the beauty of God's love."

All during Joshua's talk the children sat spellbound, drinking in every word, some with tears flowing down their cheeks. When he finished they all stood up and spontaneously turned to each other and hugged one another, the only fitting conclusion to the touching story Joshua had just told them.

It was almost lunchtime when Joshua finished his story. He sent the children off and told them he would see them in the square the following morning. Joe and the friend he was teaching to play the trumpet accompanied Joshua across the meadow. Joe asked Joshua if he was talking about him in the story. Joshua told him that every individual has a decision to make, either to live his life for himself or to live his life as a partner with God. One day he will have to make that decision, and he should always remember that story.

As they approached the square Joe and his friend said goodbye to Joshua and sat down on an odd-shaped tree with an almost horizontal trunk. It was trumpet-lesson time for Joe's friend. Joshua continued his way through the square and up Stonecastle Road.

14

JOSHUA SPENT THE rest of the day by himself, wandering around the Protestant section of town, greeting people in his open, friendly manner. Many people in town already knew Joshua by reputation, so the people along Stonecastle Road recognized him from the children's description. Most were friendly, although some seemed wary.

The view from upper Stonecastle Road was magnificent. You could see for miles across the meadow, and on a clear day you could even see the ocean in the distance. Joshua walked out on a high knoll overlooking the village and the meadow and sat down on a rock to gaze out on the vast scenery before him. It was a peaceful spot, the kind that always appealed to him.

"Like that scenery, young man?" spoke a voice that startled Joshua and broke his silent meditation. He turned and saw a man dressed in a black clerical suit standing next to him. He was in his early fifties, thin, and, though a bit proper, radiated an affable kind of friendliness. Joshua assumed he was one of the village ministers.

"Yes, it's a beautiful site, and so restful. It's almost like a window into heaven," Joshua responded in friendly fashion.

"My name is Russell Davis. I'm minister at that church behind us across the street. I noticed you walking up the hill as I was coming from the post office. I think I already know you. One of my parishioners told me about you, the one who picked you up on the highway a few days ago. You're Joshua, aren't you?"

"Yes," Joshua replied as he stood up to shake the cleric's hand. "Word travels fast in the village, doesn't it?"

"Our place is small and there are few distractions, so every little event is news. Besides, you have become more than just an event. It seems the whole town is buzzing about you. I've heard from quite a few of my parishioners about what you have been doing with the children, and I think it's great. In fact, it seems almost miraculous. I hope it can continue. I just bumped into my friend Father Donnelly down at the post office. He told me you had been over to visit with him and said you would like to stay at the manse on occasion. I told him I felt honored, and I mean that, Joshua. You are more than welcome to stay at our home whenever you like. You are like a breath of fresh air to our village, and we are all so grateful for what you are doing for our children. Two of my own children are now among your "disciples" and they fill us in on everything you do. I didn't mean to interrupt your meditation, but I couldn't resist meeting you. In fact, I'm just going home for a bite to eat. I'd be delighted if you'd come home with me and have lunch."

Joshua did not get a chance to say much, but he was encouraged by the friendliness of the minister. "Yes, I would like that. I have to admit I am quite hungry."

The two men walked out of the little park, across the street, and up the long drive to the manse, talking excitedly about many things. Approaching the house, Joshua commented about how beautifully the minister kept his grounds. "You tend your gardens and lawns with such care. I'm sure it's a reflection of the care you have for your flock. The gardens are beautiful. Do you work them yourself?"

"Sometimes. I like to work in the garden, but I have all I can do to keep up with my people. We don't live in easy times, and I mingle with the people as much as possible, trying to help them steer a sensible course through all the troubles we have here. I'm sure Father Donnelly has already told you we used to have a peaceful village with Protestants and Catholics getting along well together until agitators came into town and started stirring up trouble and arousing suspicions and fears that had been laid to rest years ago.

"I don't know whether you've heard, but just a few nights ago there was trouble out on the coast, which, as you could see, is not very far from the village. I learned about it from Father Donnelly. No one has the straight story, but rumor has it that a boat full of arms landed and the Arab guerrillas who delivered the shipment had a young boy with them whose family lives in the vicinity. They were dropping him off to be picked up by his parents. While switching the cargo from the boat into trucks, the boy was careless and set off a small explosion, which left him blind. By the time troops arrived to investigate the reported explosion, the band had already slipped away. The boy himself had been smuggled back home and was being cared for secretly in the Catholic section of the city."

The inside of the manse was tastefully decorated with Queen Anne furniture and an assortment of antiques. Joshua admired the quality of the craftsmanship.

Hearing voices in the foyer, a woman came out to see who was there. The minister turned and saw his wife standing in the doorway and introduced her to Joshua. "Kathie, this is Joshua, the man the whole town is talking about. I just picked him up loitering in our park."

The woman walked over to the two men and Rev. Davis continued with the introductions. "Joshua, this is my loyal and devoted friend, Kathie. She is also my wife."

At that point his daughter came in, a young girl in her early teens, a pretty, quick-witted girl named Meredith. He introduced her to Joshua, who smiled a warm hello.

After exchanging courtesies, the girl left and the three went into the kitchen to continue their conversation over samplings of Kathie's cooking.

Joshua did not stay long at the manse, but the two men discussed issues that deeply concerned them both. They also made tentative plans for dinner with Father Donnelly. After Joshua left the Reverend Davis had the same peaceful and comforted feeling from his meeting with Joshua that the priest had experienced. He felt reassured and had the sense of being in the presence of a rare goodness that he had never experienced before. Kathie agreed and suggested they invite him over often.

15

JANE, THE LITTLE girl who first met Joshua, was feeling left out with all the excitement she had created among her friends over Joshua. She used to be able to meet him in the square while feeding the birds and have him all to herself, but he hadn't been there lately, so it was only among her crowd of friends that she got to see him. She was just one of a large group now, lost in the crowd. She felt hurt and hoped Joshua didn't forget her. She had hoped he would be in the square this morning when she went to feed the birds, but he wasn't. She was heartbroken and walked around the streets looking for him. He was nowhere. When he showed up later it was too late. The crowd of kids had gathered, and she couldn't even get near him. She had seen him later, after the crowd had broken up, as he was walking up Stonecastle Road. She wanted to follow him but didn't because that part of town was forbidden for Catholics. She just stood at a distance and watched him disappear from sight.

But the next morning she was all excited to see him in the square when she went about her daily ritual, which she had almost forgotten to do in her excitement.

"Joshua, Joshua," she called out to him, and came running over to him, with all the birds in creation chasing after their breakfast. When she reached him she lost her tongue and stood there speechless. Joshua bent down and reached out, holding her hands in his. He could see all the feelings running through her and tried to reassure her he hadn't forgotten her.

"It has been a long time since we talked," he said to her softly, "but I haven't forgotten you. I see you in the crowd with the other children, and I am happy you brought them all to me. I am your good friend always. I want you to remember that. You are very special to me—"

"But, Joshua," she interrupted, "there is another friend I want you to meet. His name is Patrick. He doesn't come with the others. He was hurt by a bomb and is afraid to go outside his house anymore. I told him all about you, and he wants so much to see you. Could you come with me to his house?"

Joshua smiled. "Yes, I think we could do that. Where does he live?"

"Not far, I'll show you. Come with me," she said as the two walked down the street.

She took her friend down Maple Street and, turning off the main street, stopped at a modest, whitewashed stone cottage.

"This is where he lives," Jane said, knocking at the thick wooden door. It was opened almost immediately by a young woman with reddish-brown hair. The woman looked tense and sad.

"Hello, Mrs. Whitehead," Janie said. "I brought my friend Joshua so Pat could meet him."

Still bitter over her daughter's murder and her son's incessant nightmares, Maureen was none too excited about letting a stranger into her house. "I've heard about you. What good can you do in this hell we live in?" she said cynically. "You can't bring my Annie back. And you certainly can't change these sick bastards, hell-bent on killing innocent children."

Jane was horrified at what came out of the woman's mouth. She was embarrassed for Joshua, who didn't seem the slightest bit upset. It was Maureen who was ashamed and shocked at her own behavior, and she apologized to Joshua and the little girl for her lack of courtesy and her emotional outburst.

"Please come inside. I can't imagine why I was so rude."

Patrick was sitting on the floor putting a puzzle together. When he saw Janie he got off the floor and walked over to her. "Hi, Janie!"

"Hi, Pat! I brought my friend Joshua to visit you. I told him you don't go out much."

The boy looked up at Joshua. Then he looked down at his heavily bandaged arm.

"Hello, Patrick! That is a good name you have. Patrick was a great man. Are you going to be like him?" Joshua asked the boy in an attempt to lighten the atmosphere and start a conversation with the boy.

"I don't think I could be like him. He was a saint," the boy responded.

"Everyone is called to be a saint, each in his own way," Joshua answered. "You are a very special boy, Patrick, and God has something very special for you if you listen to his voice."

The boy wasn't impressed, but he listened. (Someday it would have meaning. That's the way it is with children. They absorb everything and store it away. Later on it registers at a time in their lives when it will be needed.)

"What about my sister, Annie? I think she was special," the boy said, to everyone's surprise.

"Yes, she was special, and she had a special work to do for God. Her goodness and innocence live in everyone's memory, showing them the meanness of violence and the need for peace and love. She shared in Jesus' work, pointing the way to a better world. And as Jesus died so people could have God's love, so Annie died so others could have a better world. Her special work is now accomplished and she is with God, happy and in joy. Even though you can't see her, she is near you all the time, especially when you need her, and when you talk to her she hears you. She is like an angel, more beautiful than you can imagine."

"How do you know?" the boy asked, still needing reassurance.

"Because I've seen her," Joshua said bluntly.

"You've seen her?" Pat persisted, still not convinced.

"Yes. She is happy and knows everything about you."

"Where is she?"

"In heaven."

"Where is heaven?"

"Heaven is where God is, and God is everywhere, so heaven is everywhere, all around you."

"Why can't I see heaven?"

"Heaven is in a world beyond, just on the other side of a thin veil of time. If you could close your eyes and walk through that veil, you could be there. It is that close," Joshua said, more for Maureen's comfort than for the child's, realizing Pat could not fully understand. He was more impressed with Joshua saying he had seen his sister than by his description of where heaven is.

Maureen had tears in her eyes. She looked at Joshua, wondering about this strange man who could talk about heaven as glibly as a man could talk about his hometown, almost as if he had just come from there. It gave her an eerie feeling, but it also comforted her, hearing this man speak with such conviction.

While Joshua continued talking to the boy and Janie, the mother went to the stove to prepare a pot of tea, asking Joshua if he would like some, which he gladly accepted. She readied a glass of milk and some cookies for the children. Everyone was still standing. Maureen apologized for being so forgetful and offered Joshua a seat at the kitchen table. The children sat down on either side of him.

"Father Donnelly, our parish priest, talked about you at our women's club," Maureen said as she took the tea off the stove to let it steep. "Some of the women were concerned about you and what you were up to. He told them not to fear, that you were a good man and we could be comfortable letting our children be with you. I can see now. But I can't help but think you are very naive to think you can change things around here. There's too much hatred and fear."

"Fear comes from not knowing, and hatred comes from fear of being threatened," Joshua said calmly. "A willingness to understand is the first step in banishing fear. As understanding grows, fear diminishes, and hatred turns to trust. It can happen if people genuinely want peace. In these troubled times people owe it to their children to take the first step. It is unfortunate that men who pose as instruments of God are the very ones who are doing the work of Satan by preaching hatred and suspicion among God's children. They are the real satans, doing their father's work, but the people must not listen to them, because true men of God never preach hatred but try to heal and draw God's children together."

Joshua stayed only a few minutes longer after finishing the tea and cookies. Before leaving he placed his hand on Pat's head, and for a brief moment closed his eyes and prayed silently. Tears began to roll down the boy's cheeks. His mother asked him why he was crying.

"Because I feel so good. I feel so happy," the boy replied, not knowing what was happening to him.

Then Joshua left, with Jane following him.

"I'm glad you visited Pat," Jane confided to Joshua. "He's been very sad since he was hurt and his sister died. He doesn't want to play with anyone anymore. Your visit made him feel good."

Joshua thanked her for being a good missionary. Jane told him she had to go home, so she left abruptly and skipped down the street. Joshua continued in the direction of the square.

16

As THE DAYS went by Joshua's popularity with the children spread and the crowd that followed him grew larger with each passing day. The night after Joshua visited Pat's house was cause for the greatest joy. It was the first night the boy had been able to sleep undisturbed by haunting dreams and nightmares. It wasn't long afterward that the doctor removed the bandages from the boy's arm, and he was shocked to see that the arm seemed healed and there were no scars. X-rays showed no trace of any wounds or injury. He was at a loss to explain the phenomenon to the boy's parents. An even greater consolation for the parents was the fact that their son seemed himself and at peace again. They told the doctor about Joshua visiting their house and blessing the boy. The doctor said nothing. He did call in the other doctors involved in the case and let them examine the boy themselves to see what they made of the boy's condition. The surgeons were delighted with the boy's remarkable healing ability. The psychiatrist found it difficult to understand how the boy could have recovered from the trauma so fast. He was at a loss for an explanation but wondered if it might be just a temporary remission that could give way to a future relapse. Mike and Maureen also wondered. They had their own feelings about what happened but kept them to themselves. They were happy their boy was healed.

Sunday came and Joshua attended the Anglican church services. The people were surprised to see him there, but were pleased nonetheless. People were curious about him, as word had spread into practically every household in town. Most of the parishioners at Christ Church were friendly. Some were wondering what his ultimate agenda really was and looked askance at him, analyzing his every gesture and expression. The more astute realized this stranger had managed to captivate the total population of young people in their area—Catholics, Protestants, and everyone in between. Why? What was his purpose? Some were beginning to feel concern even if they didn't express it. Yet, he was a good man, and things the children brought back home about him were only good, and he was having a good effect on the way they were treating one another.

That Sunday afternoon another jarring incident occurred in the village. A Roman Catholic priest by the name of Father Jack Brown came into town and met with a group of Catholics outside the village. He was the one Father Donnelly had told Joshua about. His visits were clandestine, unlike the brash public demonstrations of his Protestant counterpart. The purpose, however, was the same—to arouse the people and incite them to violence as the only way they would ever have their freedom. They had been in bondage long enough. Peaceful means were not working. Violence was the only route. Joshua didn't make it to the priest's talk, but heard about it from Tim McGirr that afternoon when Tim passed Joshua on his way home through the meadow. Joshua was playing a little wooden flute he had made. Tim had just left friends he had stopped off to visit on his way home from Mass a few hours earlier.

The two men sat under the tree for the good part of an hour, talking about pressing issues in the village and the problems of the children. Tim could wax philosophical at times, and this was the time. After he had unwound his spool he invited Joshua to his house for dinner. Joshua accepted and they both walked across the field together.

On the way home Tim told Joshua all about Father Brown. He was a young man, not more than thirty-one, thirty-two. He was gaunt, nervous-looking, reminding one of a high-strung cat. When he spoke his eyes flashed with anger, an unforgiving kind of anger that could frighten people. Not many people listened to him, but those who did were fanatically loyal. He was an embarrassment to most of the Catholics here, who were decent people.

Joshua received a royal welcome this time when he and Tim reached the house, in contrast to the reception the first time he was there. By now his name had spread all over and he was a celebrity. Besides that, the kids missed him. They had all enjoyed his company the last time, but especially Christopher, who beamed now when Joshua came into the house, although he didn't say much.

Tim's mother had been saying her rosary on the front porch when the two came walking up the path. After she had greeted Joshua with a friendly hello, she continued her beads as Tim and Joshua went inside.

Joshua spent the rest of the day at the McGirrs', playing simple games with the kids and talking lightheartedly with the adults until well into the night. Christopher finally felt comfortable enough to ask Joshua if he would play a game of cards with him. They played a few games, until the others got jealous and started looking for attention. Then he went back to including the others in their games.

The McGirr children had heard about Joshua meeting with the children in town although they had not been there themselves. They asked Joshua if they could come too. Stella had some reservations, but when Joshua explained what happened at the meetings, she felt a little easier about letting the children go, even though it meant allowing them to mingle with children from troubled families.

The day began early at the McGirrs', so it was not too late when they turned in for the night.

17

JOSHUA LEFT EARLY the next morning, walking across the field and up to the meadow on the hill. On his way he stopped at his tree and picked up a bulky brown bag he had hidden there. It was a perfect start of a new day. The sun was warm, and the blue sky was undisturbed except for a few wisps of white floating like sailboats across a blue sea. Birds were singing, and Joshua felt the freedom of nature at peace, though he knew that underneath the surface of the peaceful calm were churning currents anything but peaceful.

He walked to the top of the knoll and surveyed the landscape. He could see almost as far as the ocean. A few small hills in the distance broke the seemingly endless sweep of the thick, deep green carpet that spread as far as the eye could see. Joshua sat down on the grass and it was warm. The sun had burned away the early morning dew. As he looked across the meadow he thought of Capernaum of long ago. This scene was not unlike the hillside up above the ancient city, though the meadow here was greener and the rolling hills more gentle. His prayer was a quiet prayer, mingled with memories, asking peace upon this troubled land of such simple, beautiful people. Joshua's mind saw clearly things far and things near. All was present to his simple but highly complex mind. He knew the way events were unfolding. He and his Father planned it this way. He could see the whole drama, piece by piece fitting into place, all the actors stepping onto the stage at the right time, as if on cue. But it wasn't all predetermined, as if people were just props. Each one's foreseen use of his freedom was carefully considered, providing material in planning the strategy for Joshua's visit to this little corner of the planet.

Joshua sat there on the knoll for well over an hour, most of the time just deep in thought. Suddenly, as if he had come to a long, thoroughly considered decision, he rose and walked through the square, down the street, and in the direction of the city. Children noticed him and ran to ask where he was going.

"To the city," was his reply.

"Can we come?"

"Yes, if you like, and if your parents give you permission."

Word passed rapidly. In no time Joshua's whole coterie of friends was surrounding him, curious as to where they were going and what they were going to do. It was a good five-mile walk to the city, and the thought of going there always thrilled the kids, no matter what the circumstances. They had no money, but these children had no need of money to have fun. They invented their own fun. Joshua admired this trait in them. The simplest little things made them happy.

As they walked along they noticed the bag Joshua was carrying. One of the children, Johnny, a tall, lanky, good-hearted boy who was walking next to Joshua, was dying of curiosity over what was in the bag. No longer able to contain himself, he asked, "Joshua, what do you have in the bag?"

Joshua smiled. "A surprise," he answered.

"What kind of a surprise?" the boy persisted.

By that time they were already past the limits of the village and were next to an open lot strewn with large boulders. Joshua walked into the lot, with the children following him, and told them to sit on the boulders.

There were about twenty-five of them in all, and when they were all settled Joshua opened the bag and emptied its contents on top of one of the rocks. It was a batch of simple flute-like instruments, obviously handmade.

"Where did you get all those piccolos?" Johnny asked him, wide-eyed with amazement.

"I made them," Joshua answered with a touch of pride in his voice. He had been carving them at odd times over the past week. They were easy to make, once you got the knack of it.

"Gee, they're neat. Do they work?" Johnny persisted, still incredulous.

"Of course they work," Joshua answered with a smile. "Here, Johnny, pass them out."

Johnny took a handful of the little instruments and gave one to each. The kids looked mystified, not knowing what to do with them. One of the boys, Nicholas, began to play his.

"It does work," Johnny said, startled at the happy notes that came out of the little gadget.

Nicholas had a similar instrument at home. His mother, Mary Catherine, had taught him as a young boy how to play it. Soon he was showing the other children how to play theirs. Before long all the children were making sounds, though none could be described as music.

Johnny got an idea when he saw what was taking shape. "Joshua, I have a drum at home. These things would sound great with a drum. Do you want me to go get my drum?"

"Yes, that would be a good idea."

Johnny ran home and was back in no time with the drum strapped over his shoulder, playing little rolls as he walked along. The other children were gradually getting acquainted with their instruments and the sounds were improving. In a little over an hour, with Nicholas guiding them, they were able to play simple melodies and at least have fun together. It was surprising how little it took to whip this little band into a ragtag fife-and-drum corps, not playing perfectly or with any polish, but with good high spirits.

When they had learned to handle the whistles sufficiently, Joshua headed down the road toward the city, with his band of troops behind him. As they walked along a few more children joined. Word of their coming had already preceded them, and as they approached the city, small crowds gathered along the way to greet them, curious to see this strange band of Catholic and Protestant children marching together and making happy music. Everyone was touched. As they passed the people clapped their approval, delighted to see these children playing together but harboring the sad feeling that it would never be allowed to last. There were just too many sick grown-ups who would not take kindly to these children having fun together.

Word had also spread to the fringes of the city that this stranger had managed to attract Catholic and Protestant children into a band of loyal followers who would follow him anywhere, like a modern Pied Piper. It was exciting, particularly in a land where there is little distraction from a monotony of life that can easily evolve into an unrelenting boredom.

On the group went, past the city line and into the city itself, preaching their unspoken message, shocking the whole populace with their bold violation of an ancient taboo that Christians of different labels were forever forbidden to be friends and doomed to permanent enmity. Joshua walked meekly in their midst, proud of these children who had become such loyal friends. The scene was reminiscent of a similar march on a Palm Sunday of so long ago.

By noon the band had reached the park, the same park where Joshua had stopped to listen to the preacher the week before. It was empty now, except for a few old men sitting around smoking their pipes and sharing stories of times gone by. Joshua walked over to the grass and the children followed. Tired, they sat down to rest.

Joshua approached Johnny, who was standing by himself, and quietly spoke to him. "John, the sandwiches you have in your drum, I would like you to quietly share them with the others."

The boy looked up at Joshua mystified and, with an embarrassed smile, asked him, "How did you know I have sandwiches in the drum?"

"John, just go ahead and share," Joshua said gently.

Johnny released the bands holding the drumhead in place and took out one of the two sandwiches and gave it to the boy nearest him. To Johnny's surprise, when he looked back inside the drum there were still two sandwiches. He took another one and gave it to one of the girls near him. Again looking back in the drum, he still saw two sandwiches.

Some of the children noticed the bewildered look on Johnny's face and, out of curiosity, came over to see what was in the drum—two sandwiches. They noticed, however, that as

Johnny took out one sandwich after another, there were still two sandwiches left. After he had finished feeding everyone, and even those who wanted seconds, there were still two sandwiches remaining in the drum.

Going over to Joshua, he asked him if he would like a sandwich. "Yes, I would," Joshua replied. "Thank you, John."

"Don't thank me, thank yourself. You're the one who made them."

Joshua smiled, blessed the children, and ate his sandwich. While they were all eating a little girl asked Joshua if he would tell them a story. The children, even the boys, liked Joshua's stories.

"All right. If you gather around me and sit quietly, I'll tell you a story."

The children gathered around in a semicircle on the grass and Joshua began. "A little girl was troubled because she felt she was not pretty and no one liked her. She spent many hours each day by herself, afraid to make friends. Other children were afraid to approach her because she was so quiet. Secretly they admired her because she was kind and never said anything hurtful about anyone. The shy girl watched all the other children laughing and talking and having fun and wanted very much to be part of their life. When she prayed she asked God to help her be happy and make friends. But she never heard God speak to her, not realizing that God does not have to use words to talk to us.

"One day, as the girl was leaving school, she saw a girl whom everyone considered beautiful and who had many friends. The shy girl told her how beautiful she was and how she envied her popularity. The other girl was surprised and confided to her, 'I wasn't always popular. Others thought I was vain and snobbish because I was pretty, and it was very hard for me to make friends. I went out of my way to be kind to others and talk to them even though they didn't seem anxious to talk to me. Gradually I made friends, and if I am popular today, it is because I have tried so hard and for so long to care for others and to make others happy when they are with me. Secretly I always admired you and wanted to be your friend, but I was afraid to talk to you because you are so quiet.'

"The shy girl was surprised and told her, 'I am not really that way. I am afraid of people because I think they are better than I, and I can't see why anyone would like me.'

" 'But we all feel that way,' the other girl said. 'It's part of being human.' That was a shock to the shy girl, who thought she was the only one who felt that way about herself.

"The next day at school the shy girl went out of her way to talk to the other children. She was thrilled to see how quickly they responded, and in a short time she had friends, friends who told her how glad they were she was their friend because so much goodness and joy come into their lives from knowing her.

"The point of the story," Joshua continued, "is very simple. First, God does answer our concerns. He speaks sometimes through things that happen and sometimes through others. On rare occasions he tells us in words or thoughts. The shy girl is like everyone. Every young person feels alone and unworthy. The key to making friends is to care. When we care we touch others' hearts and in our kindness heal their wounds. Kindness is the beginning of friendship."

All during the story the children sat spellbound. The way Joshua taught, the children listened, because it touched their lives. Joshua knew that children hurt just as much as adults, and if religion is to make sense to children, it has to deal with their very real troubles and concerns, not grown-ups' concerns.

When Joshua finished the children clapped. They enjoyed his stories. They were simple, and each one felt he was talking to them personally. And he was. He knew their hearts and knew their hurts. He also had his own understanding of what religion should do for people. It should reconcile people to their Father in heaven and heal wounds in people's hearts and in their lives with one another. Those who aid in that are truly religious. Those who refuse to reconcile and nurse hatreds are the truly evil people.

The picnic over, Joshua led his band of little disciples back home. The walk home wasn't as much fun, nor was the music playing as high-spirited, but each of the children had a chance to talk to Joshua alone as they took turns walking next to him along the way. Each one felt he or she had something special with Joshua, and they felt at ease talking to him about things they would never dare to share with anyone else. Joshua's effect on these children's lives was profound. They were still the same children with the same ways as before, but now they saw things differently and looked at one another differently. They had a vision of how beautiful their lives could be, whereas before their lives were boring and tense. They had been led into a whole new world, one that had always existed but had passed unnoticed.

Back in the village the children thanked Joshua for all the fun they had had and then scattered in all directions. They couldn't wait to tell their families what they had done and show them the piccolos Joshua had made for them.

18

THE REVEREND DAVIS and Father Donnelly had been trying to track Joshua down all day. The children they had asked to give him a message didn't know where he and the rest of the children had gone. His march to the city had been unannounced. Finally one of the children found Joshua as he was returning from his march.

"Joshua, Joshua," the boy called out to him. "I've been looking all over for you. My pastor, Reverend Davis, wants you to come over to his house tonight for dinner. The priest is coming too. I'm supposed to tell my pastor if you can come."

"Yes," Joshua said, "tell him I will be there. Did he say what time?"

"Five o'clock."

"Tell him I would be happy to come, and thank him, Edward," Joshua said casually.

The boy was startled when Joshua used his name. Even though he had been in the group with Joshua's friends almost every day, he had never spoken to him alone and was surprised he knew his name. The same thing happened to other children, which was another reason they felt so close to him.

It was after three. Joshua walked past the square and into the meadow toward the brook, his favorite spot, near the tree. There was a cool breeze sweeping across the meadow, a welcome relief from the warm sun that had been beating down on the marchers as they returned from the city.

Joshua sat down under the tree, closed his eyes for a few minutes, and rested before continuing across to a little pond he had discovered farther over in the meadow. It was fed by the brook as it came off the hill. Here Joshua could bathe, fish, and just relax.

At five o'clock Joshua arrived at the manse. Kathie and Meredith answered the door and welcomed him warmly. A few minutes later Father Donnelly arrived. They were both escorted into the pastor's study, a large, warm room with high bookcases lining the walls from ceiling to floor and filled with books, some antique, some quite recent, a few by modern theologians. On the pastor's desk were two books lying open, probably in preparation for next Sunday's sermon. In the center of the room, on a butler's table, was a plate of hors d'oeuvres that Meredith had made and a tray of wine and cocktail glasses. On the wall behind the desk was an old print of John Calvin in a beautifully carved maple frame.

"Joshua, my friend," Father Donnelly said as he entered the room, "I hear you had a busy day. Some of the children told me all about their march on the city. Did you conquer the big, evil Nineveh or was this just the first skirmish?"

Joshua laughed. He knew the priest had him figured out, at least as to his immediate intentions. "No, this was just the first scouting expedition. It went quite well. The children learned to play those little whistles with surprising speed. I guess it was their enthusiasm."

"And no doubt," the priest added, "a touch of magic from yourself. Speaking of magic, by the way, I brought a little rubber ball. I hear you can do marvels with these things."

Joshua laughed heartily. "I see the kids have been telling stories out of school."

At that point the Reverend Davis entered and momentarily interrupted the exchange. He welcomed the two of them, spotted the rubber ball, and quickly sized up the situation. "Oh, I see the word's gotten around about the magic rubber ball."

Father Donnelly picked up where he had left off. "I was just about to see what our magician friend can do with this thing," he said, tossing the ball to Joshua.

Joshua caught it, and as soon as it landed in his hand it disappeared. "I think you're playing tricks on me," Joshua said, looking at the two of them with an impish grin. "How did you do that?" he asked the priest with mock seriousness.

The old priest was mystified, and Joshua did nothing to clear up the mystery. They searched him and looked around the room, on the sofa and chairs, even got down on their hands and knees like two kids and crawled around looking under the furniture.

At that point Kathie walked in, and astonished at seeing the two dignified clerics crawling around on the rug, expressed her disbelief. "My gracious, what on earth are you two doing? How undignified!"

Joshua couldn't restrain his glee and just stood there saying to Kathie, "I can't imagine what's come over them. They seemed quite normal a few minutes ago. Do they always act like that when they get together?"

The two men were thoroughly embarrassed, realizing how silly they looked, knowing Kathie could in no way understand what they were doing and they could in no way explain. Joshua continued laughing as the two men composed themselves.

"Well, let's get on with the serious business," Rev. Davis said. "I know it's against our rules to have alcoholic beverages, but charity comes before all else, and I know you two could use something refreshing, so what can I serve you? I have almost everything in stock," he said, opening the carefully concealed panel hiding the liquor closet.

"I know you drink scotch, Elmer," he said to the priest. "Straight or with water?"

"A little bubble water and a little ice will do fine, Russ," the priest answered.

"Joshua, wine or a cocktail?"

Joshua hesitated a moment, then noticing a few bottles of wine, asked, "Do you have sherry?"

"I sure do. I just got it last week, my favorite," he said as he pulled out the cork and poured it carefully into a beautifully cut crystal wineglass. Its deep amber color sparkled in the glass.

Looking at his wife, Russ asked her, "Dear, what would you like?"

"What I usually have, thank you," which meant a tall vodka and tonic.

After serving his wife he poured his own drink, a glass of sherry, commenting, "I realize, gentlemen, this is not in our tradition, but Jesus said if you believe, you can do wonders. If Jesus could change water into wine, then, with faith, there's no reason I can't do the reverse. Though, I have to admit, I've been trying for a long time and it just doesn't seem to work, but I keep trying. I know my parishioners would be horrified."

Russ raised his glass in toast to their friendship and in blessing on Joshua's work with the children, which was the most courageous and noble deed he had ever encountered.

After the toast Kathie lifted the platter of hors d'oeuvres and offered them to the priest. He chose one, and as he raised it to his mouth he found himself about to bite into a rubber ball. Kathie almost dropped the platter in astonishment. Russ saw what had happened and laughed. The old priest, a little embarrassed at first over the unexpected shock, recovered and laughed at Joshua's remarkable sense of humor. The thought flashed across his mind of something Jesus had done two thousand years ago, telling Peter to go fishing and the first fish he catches will have two coins in its mouth, enough to pay the temple tax. From that moment the priest began to wonder.

"See, Kathie," Elmer said, "that's what we were looking for when you came into the room. Joshua made the thing disappear."

Joshua acted as if he had not the slightest idea of what was going on.

The priest put the ball in his pocket, took another hors d'oeuvre, and ate it hurriedly, before something happened to it. He then reached down in his pocket and felt something warm and furry. He tried to act nonchalant as he took the thing out of his pocket. It was a tiny rabbit. Everyone was delighted.

"Now, Elmer," Joshua said, "how did you do that?"

The priest offered the rabbit to Kathie, who politely refused it. Not knowing what to do with it, he put it on the mantel. The ball began to roll along the mantel, so he took it and put it back in his pocket, relieved.

Russ was watching the whole thing, trying to figure out what was happening. He could accept a magician's sleight of hand, but this seemed to go beyond that. What was happening? Joshua, still in the playful vein of having fun, was not about to destroy the illusion, or was it an illusion? He said nothing to clear up the mystery.

Finally relaxing, they all sat down and proceeded to get acquainted. It was really the first time the two clerics had had a chance to talk intimately with Joshua, and there were so many things they were interested in discussing with him.

At first they exchanged pleasantries, and then began to talk about the complicated present-day work of the clergy. It was no longer a simple matter of a nice Sunday service and an interesting Sunday-school program. Now it was the much more serious matter of facing the violent crises in society and helping the people to adjust to very painful and sometimes tragic situations in a way that was Christian. Each of these two men had had tragedies in their congregations. Russ's own brother had been murdered by Catholic fanatics. Elmer's closest friends had been murderd by Protestant extremists. The miracle in the men's lives was that they were still able to love and be Christian.

"I had a man come in the other day," Russ confided. "He told me he hated Catholics. As a child he had seen his grandfather murdered by Catholics and had to live with those terrible memories all his life. Now his daughter tells him she wants to marry a Catholic, and he's torn apart. They had a violent scene in their house the night she broke the news, and he hasn't slept since. He knows I have a reputation for being conciliatory, and he also knows my own personal tragedy and that my mother was a Catholic, but no matter what I said to him, I could not reach him. I didn't sleep well myself that night. Things are so different from what they used to be."

"You're right, Russ," Elmer agreed. "Things used to be so simple. I'm glad I don't have too many years left. My heart's been broken a thousand times with all this senseless tragedy and meanness. I don't think my heart can bear much more pain."

Joshua just listened and felt for these two good men who were trying under the most difficult circumstances to do the right thing and teach others to think straight and to forgive when tragedy struck their families. Both men were trying so hard to be responsive to the Spirit of God, and Joshua could add nothing new to what they already knew, but he felt constrained to offer some hope.

"An end is coming," he said with a finality that hinted of an awareness the others did not share. "It won't be long, and all your efforts will reap their harvest. Don't lose heart. My Father will never let your toil in his vineyard go unrewarded. And it will be a rich harvest. There will be deep hurt and loss, but for only a brief dark day, then a new life for all of you. And you will lead your people together in one family."

"Joshua, you dream," Elmer said.

"No, I speak of what I see and what I see is true, not darkly as in a dream, but clearly as I see it coming to pass in the full light of day. My Father's purpose will not be frustrated nor my mission to bring peace."

"You give me goose bumps when you talk like that," Kathie said to Joshua. "But I do have to admit that, from what I hear, you are surely working wonders with those children. I do hope it lasts."

"Never lose hope. It will happen. My Father's desire is for peace, not destruction. When troubles start do not be afraid and do not judge by appearance. As you have seen before in a playful way, truth is not always what it appears to be," he said with a grin.

The conversation then turned to lighter topics, and before long they were laughing and enjoying the fun of getting to know one another and, for a few brief moments, forgetting all about wars and tragedies. At one point Elmer said to Joshua, "You know, Joshua, you don't come across as a particularly religious person, and yet your attitudes and insights betray a depth of spirituality that could come only from unusual intimacy with God."

Joshua smiled. "I do not attempt to be religious. That has no meaning. To be perfectly human, as God made us, should be our goal. If we appear to be religious or pious, we've missed the point and our piety becomes a caricature and unauthentic. Real holiness is the natural growth of the human personality to its full maturity as an individual, and in the process, becoming a beautiful person. That is all that God wants of us. And since each individual is unique, and has a different task to accomplish in God's plan, each one has to grow differently, so holiness for each individual is different and has nothing to do with predetermined religious patterns and practices that mimic real holiness. Jesus lived in Nazareth for thirty years, and the kids he grew up with were shocked when he began to preach. They never looked upon him as particularly holy, and yet he was the holy one of God."

. Now it was Russ's turn. He was concerned about Joshua's long-term plan for the children. "Joshua, if I may run the risk of being presumptuous, what are you trying to accomplish in bringing the children together? You must realize it will never be allowed for very long. Yet, I sense you have already considered that and planned past it. And that precisely is my question. What do you have in mind when people try to stop you?"

Joshua became pensive. "Yes, I have considered the future. Naturally I am concerned, but I trust my Father and it is his will that nothing should happen to the children. What is taking place here will spread, and as it spreads no one can stop it because hatred is paralyzed in the presence of love.

"Adults are sick with hatred and unforgiveness. It is a disease that has no cure, because people who hate need to hate and resist a cure because it means an end to hatred, which they cannot give up. That is why only children can solve the problems you are facing. When children unite in a common goal, the adult world is powerless to stop them. Adults are always at a loss to deal with the innocence of children. I realize you must all be concerned about what I am doing, but do not be afraid. It is the only way."

"Joshua, you talk about 'my father.' What do you mean when you say that?" Russ asked delicately.

"God is my Father and your Father," he replied. "I could have said 'our Father,' but it is not the way we speak. I have always done the will of my Father, and I understand his ways and how events unfold. That is why I am not afraid for the children."

With all the talk, Kathie had a difficult time tearing the men away for supper. She had outdone herself in preparing the meal and couldn't wait to serve it: a rack of lamb, an array of tastefully prepared potatoes and vegetables, and an imported wine, which Joshua thought almost as good as the wine at Cana, but not quite as delicately aged.

The whole evening turned out to be a warm and comforting experience. The three found their guest to be an extraordinary man, so casually simple, but with an uncanny knowledge of events and people, which caused them to wonder about how such a simple and unassuming person could come upon such immense understanding. And all during the evening they felt a peaceful joy unlike anything they had ever experienced.

Before long it was time for the old priest to go home. They agreed to get together again sometime very soon. Russ and Kathie insisted Joshua stay at their house for the night. Somehow it did not seem right to just send him off to sleep in the meadow, so Joshua spent the night there in a warm bed for a change.

19

WORD ABOUT JOSHUA'S march to the city spread far. It wasn't just children who were fascinated. Grown-ups were interested, some out of curiosity, others for more obscure reasons, concerned no doubt about the long-term implications of something like this turning into a crusade. News reporters and other media people had heard about the march and were asking questions about this man Joshua whom everyone was talking about. Who was he? Where did he live? How do we contact him? Actually, Joshua would have been the last one to call his little hike a march. That had too many political implications, and Joshua was not political. He was concerned only that people care for one another and learn to live in peace as God's children.

Rev. Davis had gotten a phone call earlier that day from a reporter with the *Evening News* inquiring about Joshua. Russ told him what Joshua was doing, how he lived, what he thought of his attempts to unite the children, and the very favorable reactions of the adults in the area. When asked how he could contact this man, Russ told him he could come down and see for himself and get the story live. "He is around most all the time, if you really want to talk with him," he ended up telling him.

Joshua was in the square with the children, talking to Joe about his trumpet lesson, when the reporter arrived. The newsman parked his car off to the side of the square and stood on the side just watching and taking notes. Joshua noticed, and for a

315

brief moment the thought flashed across his memory of long ago when others used to take notes of everything he said and did. But this man was different. They didn't have newspapers or reporters in those days. This man could be an asset—in fact, a valuable means of accomplishing almost overnight what would take him by himself many months of hard work and travel.

Joe let Joshua practice for a few minutes. He had made remarkable progress since his first lesson and it was beginning to show. He could now play tunes that were a little less simple than the ones he first learned, and the children were impressed. Exercising his lip was a problem because Joshua never really practiced, and without practice there is no way to strengthen your lip to play the instrument with any degree of proficiency. What he did play was exciting enough for the children and that was all Joshua cared about. He had no illusions about becoming a concert artist.

The reporter watched Joshua with interest—how he noticed every child, letting nothing escape his eye, making sure each one received attention, and the personal way he treated each one. It was a lesson in psychology, and it was no longer just little children who were in the group. There were a number of older kids well into their teens for whom Joshua was obviously their hero. There was also a new boy who had come for the first time. He was different from the others, standing out because of his dark features and jet-black hair. A boy about twelve was leading him by the hand. On closer look you could see that the dark boy was blind. The two of them were standing near Joshua, who noticed them but said nothing.

After Joshua played the trumpet for a few minutes, he gave the instrument back to Joe and asked him to play for the children. He did. The contrast was dramatic. It was obvious that Joshua was no trumpet player. Joe's playing was superb. Even though a child, his mastery of the high notes and the trills was remarkable for a boy of his age. The children loved to hear him play. It was a high point of their get-togethers, and even Joshua enjoyed the boy's mastery of the instrument. What was beautiful, though, was the humility of Joshua. It was of no concern that a little boy could outshine him in front of all the others.

The routine this day was the same as every other day. The little personal engagements with various children, the entertainment, the storytelling, and Joshua talking individually with children who had things they wanted to share with him. The reporter stayed to watch the whole routine, and when most of the children had left, he walked over to Joshua and waited politely as he talked to the little blind boy and his friend. The two children looked toward the reporter, then stepped to the side, as if Joshua had told them to wait until the man left.

"My name is Brad Broyles," the man said, introducing himself to Joshua. "I'm a reporter for the *Evening News.* I must admit I am fascinated by the influence you obviously have on these children. Would you mind if I interview you?"

"Not at all," Joshua said graciously.

"How long have you lived here in the village?"

"Just a few weeks."

"Where are you from?"

"I travel here and there."

"What brought you to the village?"

"The thought of helping the good people here to find peace."

"Do you think you can do anything about it?"

"Yes, otherwise I wouldn't be here."

"Why spend all your time with the children when it's the adults who have the problem?"

"Because adults resist change, and once adults learn to hate, it is hard for them to forgive and lay aside their hatred. Children are the only hope of the future. If they can learn to love one another before they are taught to hate, then they will be able to grow up together as friends, and as friends there are no problems that cannot be solved."

"How do you intend to go about this?"

"As you have seen. Children like to see a world at peace, and they like to be friends with neighbors. It makes them feel secure and at peace themselves. You can see how well they get along, and it will spread."

"Do you think people are going to be happy with what you are doing?"

"It is clear many people already are pleased enough to let their children come each day."

"But there are others . . ." the reporter went on to say without finishing.

"There will always be 'others.' That will have to be their problem. The overriding interest of God is not perfect happiness or perfectly just societies in this world. It was not a just or perfect society in Jesus' day, and yet he was interested not in revolutions to resolve that problem, but in people focusing their vision on God and finding peace within themselves. If that message had spread, there would be just societies today. Turmoil in society is the expression of the torture within individuals. But few of his followers have ever taken Jesus seriously, so you still have a sick world, with his followers destroying one another. It is a scandal to unbelievers. That is God's real concern, the damage done to his creation by those who profess his name. And their wanton destruction of his children will not go unpunished."

Not getting caught up in the heat of Joshua's concern, the reporter continued, "But aren't you concerned precisely because of that?"

"My vision of the future is clear, and I am not concerned. I know what my Father has in store, and his intention is peace."

"Who is your father? You talk as if he is a politician."

"He is my Father and your Father. The world is his, and he cares for his children."

The reporter was unaccustomed to hearing people speak this way and was beginning to feel uneasy, but he still continued with his line of questioning. "How do the clergy accept what you are doing?"

"They have been supportive, as you already know," which unsettled the reporter, who was wondering how Joshua knew he had talked to the clergy.

The interview lasted a few minutes longer, after which the reporter thanked Joshua and left, but not before he interviewed the two children.

"What is your name?" he asked the blind boy.

"Acmet," he answered.

"That's a different kind of name. What nationality are you?"

"I am Arab," the boy answered simply.

"Do you live here?"

"Yes, I have lived here all my life."

"How old are you?"

"Nine."

"What happened to your eyes?" the reporter asked without any feeling.

"I had an accident and hit my head, but I am getting better," the boy said with a trace of fright in his voice.

"Do you like Joshua?" the reporter then asked.

"Yes, I do."

And the other boy added, "We all do."

"What is your name, sonny?"

"My name is Peter."

"How long have you known Joshua?"

"Since he came here. I met him the second day."

"Why does everyone like him so much?"

"Because he makes us feel good inside and happy, and he is kind and teaches us how to be friends."

"Is Acmet your friend?"

"Yes, we are good friends. I brought him to see Joshua because I thought Joshua might pray for him and make him see."

"Does he do things like that?"

"I don't know, but he healed a friend of mine whose arm was blown off by a hand grenade."

Joshua, in the meantime, had distanced himself from the three, anticipating what the children might say, and was too far away when the reporter turned to verify the story.

The reporter, having all the information he needed, thanked the children and left. Peter took Acmet by the hand and led him across the square to find Joshua. He was sitting on a rock at the edge of the meadow.

"Joshua," Peter said, "the reporter asked us questions. Do you think we will be in the newspaper?"

"Yes, I am sure you will."

"I can't wait to read it," Peter responded, to which Acmet agreed.

"Joshua, could you bless Acmet and make him see?" Peter asked hopefully.

Joshua said nothing, just thought for what seemed a very long time. Peter looked at him imploringly.

"Acmet, do you want to see?" Joshua asked the boy.

"Yes, I do, very much."

"Do you believe I can heal you?" he continued.

"Yes, Joshua, because you are a good man, and my parents said you are close to God. I know God will listen to you if you ask him. Please, Joshua, I want so much to be able to see again."

Joshua looked at the boy.

"Come here, Acmet," Joshua said.

Peter led his friend to Joshua's side. Joshua rested his hands on the boy's head, and with his thumbs touched his eyes. The boy stepped back and opened them, and his face began to glow with excitement and joy. "I can see, I can see," he screamed with delight. Turning toward Peter, he hugged him and cried with happiness.

Peter walked over to Joshua. With a happy smile he put out his hand and, in a very boyish, businesslike way, shook Joshua's hand, thanking him for healing his friend. "Joshua, I knew you would be able to heal him. You are always so kind to everyone. You are my best friend. Thank you."

"Yes, Joshua, thank you so much for helping me see," the little Arab boy said as he hugged Joshua. "I will never forget you."

The two boys ran off across the square, hopping with a joy they had never known, unable to wait to tell their families what had happened. Joshua watched them, smiling, then walked into the meadow.

20

JOSHUA SPENT THE rest of the afternoon at the coast, sitting on the rocks and meditating. God had programmed tranquilizers into nature, and Joshua knew how to draw serenity and calm from his Father's presence in His creation. It was just as important for him to take time alone as it was for him to be busy at his work. Indeed, it seemed to be the source of the remarkable orderliness and purpose that pervaded his whole life.

Meanwhile, the reporter had gone back to the office to write up his story and told his editor he expected something big to break eventually with this man Joshua because the political implications of what he was doing were just too explosive. In fact, various individuals in the city were already discussing Joshua's activities and assessing his motives. The pubs were beginning to hum with snide remarks about this fellow who had all the kids following him. Acmet and Peter had run home to tell their story. Acmet's parents were beside themselves with happiness and immediately set about discussing how to show their appreciation to Joshua for having healed their son. They asked the children where Joshua lived. They didn't know. They thought he might just live in the fields, because that's where he always seemed to be. Peter offered to look for him. Miriam, Acmet's mother, told him if he found Joshua to ask if he would honor them by coming to their home so they could thank him properly for what he had done for their son. This was remarkable. Joshua was not used to being thanked. It was also true of long ago. Only one example, and that was a stranger.

Peter set out, running down the street. There was no need to run, but the little fellow was that way, high-spirited and brimming over with life, never content for things to happen slowly, always trying to rush time so things would happen faster. Down across the square, along the path into the meadow, and to the pond, where he knew Joshua went sometimes. He was not there, but three kids were swimming. He asked them if they had seen Joshua. Yes, they had. He had passed by the pond a while ago and said he was on his way to the seashore.

Peter was crestfallen and disappointed, but, undaunted, he rested with the kids for a few minutes and then took off for the coast. He found Joshua sitting on a boulder just watching the water crashing up against the rocks beneath. He watched him for a few minutes, wondering why he came out here all alone, then walked out along the rocks to deliver his message.

"Joshua," Peter called. The roar of the water was overpowering. He called a second time. Joshua turned around and saw the little boy standing on the rocks not far behind him.

"Peter," he said, surprised, "what are you doing way out here?"

"I've come to deliver a message. Acmet's parents want you to come to their house so they can thank you for healing Acmet." He got it all out in almost one breath.

Joshua smiled. "They don't have to thank me," he said.

"I know, but they want to."

"Well, come over here and sit down and we will talk about it."

Peter jumped over the rocks and came to where Joshua was. He sat down on the rock next to him.

"Isn't the sea beautiful, Peter?" Joshua said to the boy.

"Yes, I've been out here before, once when I was a little boy. We came here for a picnic," Peter responded. "I come here with my friends sometimes."

"You can feel God's presence resting above the water. The sea looks so lifeless, but it is teeming with life. There are more living things in the ocean waters than there are in all the land. People don't understand the ocean and how important it is for them.

The future of human life on earth is in the vast ocean waters. They should be protected and kept pure and not used as a dump.

"I notice, Peter, that you are a very happy boy. You enjoy life, don't you?"

"Yes, but doesn't everybody?"

"Not really. There are many who are sad and many who are angry, and they don't know how to enjoy life. You are a rare happy person, like that swallow flying above the rocks over on the cliff," he said as he watched the swallow darting about in the water spray around the rocks.

"There was once a little boy very much like you. He liked to play and to have fun, and he brought happiness to everyone. God created him for a very special work and tried to send messages to this little boy so He could guide him, but the messages were never received because the boy was too busy to hear God's quiet voice. The boy grew up and went from job to job, not happy with his life. All his happy ways disappeared. One day he decided to take a walk into a quiet meadow just to think. He didn't even intend to pray. He had long ago stopped that. While he walked he felt the presence of God, and in his heart God talked to him, and the boy finally listened. From that day on his life changed. He had found his friendship with God, and God was able to use him to do beautiful things with his life. It is so important to take time to listen to the gentle voice of God. That is the way he guides you."

"Is that what you are doing here, Joshua?" the boy asked innocently.

"Yes. I enjoy coming into the presence of God. He guides me. He teaches me. He brings me peace. And I always walk away with joy in my heart. God made us to be his friends, not to walk alone.

"Let's get up and walk back home," Joshua said, rising from the rock where he had been sitting.

The two walked back across the fields and over the hills. As they approached the village Peter told Joshua he was going ahead to tell Acmet's family that he would come to visit them. "What time do you think you will be there, so I can tell them?" he said, trying to pin Joshua down.

"I will stop over later this evening, around eight. And thank you, Peter, for going all the way out there to give me that message."

"That's okay. I was glad to because I got a chance to talk with you. You're my friend, and I like being with you," the boy replied as he ran off.

21

JOSHUA HAD WANTED to stop off at Tommy and Millie's
house. He knew Tommy had been ill and was concerned for the
couple. Life was not easy for the elderly couple and Millie wasn't
up to caring for the farm herself. It was a frightening experience
when one of them got sick.

Millie was surprised to see Joshua when she answered the
door. She had just finished working in the barn and was busy
getting things ready for supper.

"Oh, young man, I'm afraid you've come at a bad time. Tom
is in bed sick, and I am running myself ragged trying to get
things done around here. I can't even offer you a decent bite to
eat. Though you're welcome to stay for supper if you like."

"No, Millie. Thank you for your kindness. I just wanted to
visit with Tom for a minute. I heard he was sick."

"How did you know? I haven't told anyone, and there's not a
soul who knows it," she said, bewildered.

"I just knew, Millie, and was concerned. I can't stay long."

"The ol' goat is in the bedroom," she said in feigned tough-
ness. "Go right in. He'll be glad to see you."

It was a simple bedroom, with a wooden chair, a dresser, and
a large bed filling most of the small room. On the walls were
pictures of old folks, no doubt Tom and Millie's parents, and
assorted relatives.

Tom brightened up when Joshua came in, really surprised to see him. He looked weak and drawn as he tried to gesture for Joshua to take the chair and sit down.

Joshua walked over to the bed and grasped the old man's hands in his own, telling him he was sorry that he was ill. Tom was just as shocked as Millie was to find that Joshua knew. Joshua wouldn't give him any more satisfaction than he gave his wife, and Tom didn't pursue it.

"Sit down there, young man," he said to Joshua. "It was real nice of you to come visit me. I sometimes feel I'm at the end of the line. I feel so weak. When I get sick like this I worry so much about my wife. Life is hard here, and I know she won't be able to take care of everything herself."

"Don't you worry about things like that. That's God's business. You just do your work and enjoy the time God gives you. Worry has never changed a thing. Trust God. He watches over you like a mother hen," Joshua said, attempting to reassure the old man.

"The doctor was out earlier today and said there isn't anything he can do for me. Told me just to rest and not get excited and make sure I stay in bed. My heart is worn out, I guess."

Millie came into the room with a cup of tea and a little dish full of cookies and placed them on the dresser next to Joshua.

"Thank you, Millie," Joshua said appreciatively.

The three of them talked for a few minutes, then Joshua got up to go. Before leaving he walked close to the bed and, reaching down, rested his hand on Tom's head and caressed the side of his face, telling him quietly, "Tom, be at peace. God has answered your prayers. You are well again."

The couple listened, not understanding. Tom felt what Joshua had said. He knew he was well again. A bit carefully at first, then spryly, he jumped out of the bed, and with tears flowing down his cheeks, he grabbed Joshua's hand and thanked him, then hugged his wife.

"Keep this to yourself," Joshua told them. "I don't want this to get around. It will complicate my work and create too much confusion." They were both quiet people and had no intention of telling anyone, though they treasured the experience in their hearts.

As Joshua was leaving the couple walked him to the door. Tom, in his nightshirt, stood on the porch waving to him like a little child as Joshua walked across the barnyard toward the road.

Joshua continued down the road toward the village, and crossing the square, he walked down into the Catholic side of town, the area where the Arab family lived. Peter had not told Joshua where his friends lived, and when the family realized that they wondered if Joshua would find them. Like many other unexplained things, Joshua knew.

He knocked at their door. The little boy answered, expecting Joshua's coming. He was wide-eyed with excitement when he saw who it was, and forgetting to invite him inside, Acmet ran into the house screaming, "It's Joshua, it's Joshua. He's here."

His parents, trying to act calm, walked out into the foyer and were embarrassed to see Joshua still standing outside. "Our sincerest apologies for our son not inviting you into our home," Acmet's father said. "He has been waiting all day for you to come and is so excited he can't contain himself."

"I understand. I am delighted by his childlike enthusiasm. It shows such simple innocence," Joshua replied.

"Please come in. I am Acmet's father. My name is Anwar, and this is my wife, Miriam. Our home is your home, as humble as it is. We are honored that you have come. It was presumptuous of us to invite you. We should have come to you, but we didn't know where you live and we wanted so much to be able to thank you properly for the wonderful thing you have done for our son. Please make yourself at home." The man guided Joshua to the living room. The house was unusually large by local standards, fashioned more after well-to-do people's homes of the Mideast rather than conventional homes of the area. There were Persian rugs scattered in all the rooms. The living room had a large fireplace and oriental antiques were placed discreetly around the room. The furniture was elegant French Provincial. Joshua looked very ordinary in such an opulent setting, and yet, at this point, he, and not the family's wealth, was the cause for all their happiness.

As soon as Joshua was seated the mother asked politely if Joshua had had supper. She asked in such a way that it was clear she hoped he had not and was delighted when he said he would stay. The father offered him a glass of wine, which Joshua accepted. After a few minutes everyone seemed more relaxed and Joshua seemed very much at home. That put the family at ease. It is so comfortable being in the presence of this gentle man, they thought, and yet there was much more to him than appeared on the surface. They could see an innate nobility and dignity about Joshua that belied the ordinariness of his dress. What a beautiful man! Joshua sat in his chair with an air that hinted royalty, yet it wasn't contrived. It was just his way. Even dressed in his poor attire, his natural dignity radiated. They were so honored to have this man in their home.

As they sipped wine the father asked Joshua about himself, and he could see that Joshua was more than just a run-of-the-mill Christian. "Joshua, my son has been talking about you ever since Peter introduced him to you. The children tell us all the stories. I just listen and develop my own ideas. From what the children say, if it is true, you are not an ordinary man. I have read the Gospels and I can see such precise similarities between the things that you do and say and what Jesus did and said that I can't help but feel . . . I won't have the presumption to ask, but your healing my son convinced me. Joshua, I want to let you know that my life and my family are at your service. Whatever we can do for you, we would be honored if you ask."

"Anwar," Joshua responded, "you are not far from the kingdom of God. The lights you have are not your own. It is my Father who has given light to your mind. You will honor me by following where God leads you. His Son is the Gate of Heaven, the Door to Salvation. Do not be afraid to follow where he leads. God's way is not a way of violence but a way of peace that he wants for his children. Those who honor that peace are truly God's children."

Anwar flushed with embarrassment, realizing Joshua knew of his family's clandestine arms shipments to terrorists. Meeting Joshua, he now saw everything clearly and in different focus, and he meant to reassure Joshua that things were no longer the same. "Joshua, I regret what has happened in the past. I felt, as did my family, that what we were doing was helping suppressed people, out of a feeling of solidarity, but I can now see destroying God's children is not the path that is pleasing to God. I assure you that things will be different. We will continue in our own way and with our abundant resources to work for justice for our neighbors. They are good people and have suffered much, just like our own people back home."

"Anwar, it is a noble work to sacrifice for justice. God did not intend to finish his creation. Much has been left undone, so men and women can fulfill their purpose on earth by channeling God's riches to one another. Hunger, poverty, and injustice exist because so many horde God's treasures for themselves and their families, or for political power, and the rest of the world goes starving or in dire want. It is not the will of God. It is the sin of those who refuse to share what God has entrusted to them. It is for such that hell exists, for they will be unable to bear the reflection of their own greed and selfishness in the face of God's infinite goodness and out of shame will forever choose to hide from God's love, preferring the company of those like themselves, totally self-centered and devoid of love."

Miriam interrupted to bring everyone into the dining room, which was adjacent to the living room and was spacious and richly adorned. Other family members appeared from all over, and by the time supper was served there were over twelve people in all, including some older relatives. Acmet asked if he could sit near Joshua. He was allowed. A whole array of imported Eastern foods was served, all of which Joshua enjoyed, feeling very much at home.

It was a new experience for Joshua to eat at the home of a Muslim family. The evening went well. Joshua heartily enjoyed the warm hospitality of this very grateful and gracious family. As the evening drew on and Joshua made as if to leave, the family insisted he stay, knowing, as everyone else did, that he had no place to call home. They provided a simple but nicely decorated guest room for him, and then, after sitting around talking until far into the evening, they all retired for the night.

22

JOSHUA'S BREAKFAST AT the Muslim family's home was reminiscent of breakfasts long past. The family was reluctant to see Joshua leave but were grateful that he would grace their home with his presence. When he was leaving Anwar slipped a small envelope into Joshua's pocket. Catholic people in the neighborhood were surprised to see Joshua leaving a Muslim home. The family was not looked upon kindly by most Catholics, who knew the nature of their political activities and the types of people who collaborated with them. They certainly knew Joshua had no sympathy for what they were doing, and after carefully considering it, surmised his visit had to do with Acmet's sudden healing, which the whole neighborhood knew about.

Jesus once made the remark "Be as simple as a dove, but as sly as a fox." Joshua lived that to perfection. There was a simplicity to everything he did. His purpose was pure and uncomplicated, but he was totally aware of the implications of even his simplest actions as he carefully plotted every little detail of the drama he was orchestrating. It gave one, if he or she chose to look, and if indeed they had the ability to understand, a rare glimpse into the beautiful way God's providence interacts with people's predictable use of their freedom to make decisions. Joshua's mastery of human psychology made it possible for him to predict reactions to everything he did; he could plan on those reactions to further organize his strategy. He knew precisely what would result from the newspaper story that would be coming out that evening. He would just wait calmly until it unfolded.

As he walked into the square Jane was just starting to feed the birds. The cardinal lately had even been coming closer, though not like when Joshua was there to call him.

"Joshua," she said to him as he approached, "I heard what you did for Acmet yesterday. That was nice of you to be so kind." She didn't fully realize just what he had done for the boy.

Joshua smiled and thanked her. "How are all your little friends this morning? There are more than usual."

"I noticed, and I'm going to have to get more food for them," she replied.

"Don't be concerned, little one," Joshua reassured her, "there is plenty of food for them in the fields. They know you like them. They don't need for you to give them a lot."

Joshua sat down on the stone wall. Jane came and sat next to him. "Joshua," she began by saying, "I heard my father and mother talking. They said you are a strange man, but a good man. They are happy at what you do for us kids, but they are afraid for you. Why are they afraid, Joshua?"

"Don't you trouble yourself about things like that, little one," he answered calmly. "Little children should be happy and not be burdened with troubles that give grown-ups heavy hearts. Enjoy being a child. Don't you worry yourself about Joshua. He is carefully protected in God's heart and no harm will touch him. Joshua is like a beam of light that comes from God to touch your lives and teach you love. Only for a moment will that light seem to go out, but do not be afraid. God will always be near."

The girl was reassured, understanding not a word of what he had said.

Children were entering the square, some coming from Stonecastle Road, others from the opposite direction, casually meeting in the center and greeting each other, no longer carefully but openheartedly, glad to be friends. There weren't many this morning. As Joshua found out, most of the children were going to the city with their parents to shop and to attend a local fair that took place each year at this time. Joe had to play at the fair and his friends went with him and his parents. The ones who came to visit with Joshua were older children, happy that the little kids were not around.

"Joshua, we heard what you did for the little Arab boy. How did you do that?" one of the boys asked.

"You have to realize that God is real," Joshua answered, "and he does care for all of you. When you understand that and let God into your life, you establish a bond between yourself and God. Your faith then can work wonders because the power of God moves freely through your life."

One of the other boys, a Protestant by the name of Robert, told Joshua his father was a politician in the city, that he didn't like what Joshua was doing and didn't want his son associating with him. The boy told his father that Joshua was a good man and he had no intention of not seeing him. A serious disagreement followed and the father stormed out of the house in the middle of supper and didn't come home until after midnight.

"Robert," Joshua responded in a casual, matter-of-fact tone of voice, "children should listen with respect to what parents say, but sometimes parents are more concerned with interests opposed to God's wishes. In those rare instances children must be willing to follow where God leads, even if it means upsetting parents."

"We all know," the boy continued, "that what you are doing is a good thing. The grown-ups here are really sick, and they won't let us live in peace. We have no quarrel with Catholic kids. They are just like us in many ways. You have taught us that and you have taught us to like one another. It is only our parents who don't want us to associate because it will get in the way of their own sick feuds."

Joshua listened attentively, then told the boy he had a great deal of courage and principle and should always follow his conscience.

The children didn't stay with Joshua very long that day. Sometimes just a few minutes to talk about things that troubled them was all they needed, then they would walk away at peace.

Joshua later found the little envelope the Muslim family had given him. It contained a short note thanking him again and telling him they realize he doesn't have much to live on, that they would be happy if he would accept this little token. Inside the note was a hundred-dollar bill. Joshua decided to eat at the tavern that evening. As it was still a few hours until suppertime, he walked up Stonecastle Road and wandered around the Protestant area. It was the nicer part of town. The houses were well kept, the streets nicely cared for, and the atmosphere tranquil. It was a pleasant place to live or even just to walk through.

He came across a blacksmith shop with an old, weather-beaten sign hanging over the doorway inscribed with the words "Charlie's Place." Joshua was curious. He stopped to watch Charlie working around the forge, fabricating things that might be needed on a farm or around the fireplace of an old cottage. The man, gruff but friendly, was well into his sixties.

"What's your name, young man?" he asked Joshua.

"Joshua. I guess you're Charlie."

"Yeah, that's me. And I guess you're the new fellow everyone's talking about. It's a nice thing you're doing with the kids. Wish you a lot of luck."

"Thank you, but that won't be necessary. It will work the way it's planned. I'm fascinated with your work. You really know your trade," Joshua commented.

I should. I've been doing this since I could crawl. I get tired lately. I have orders to get out today and don't have the energy to do this hard work anymore. Haven't been feeling well the past few days."

"Can I help? I'd like to if you'd let me. I used to do this kind of work and really enjoyed it."

The man was surprised at Joshua's pluckiness and immediately took to this friendly stranger. "Yeah, you sure can if you really know how. I could use a few minutes rest. You really think you can handle this thing?" he said, looking at the chain on the forge.

"Yes, I've done it before," Joshua answered as he proceeded to put on the thick leather apron hanging on the wall. In a few minutes he was handling the forge, the tongs, and the hammer and anvil as a professional, and starting to sweat just like a professional. The blacksmith admired his ease in handling the tools.

"You really do know how to handle those things," the man said to Joshua, surprised. "Wouldn't mind having you work for me. I could use some help the next few weeks. I got behind when I started feeling under the weather.''

"I'd like to give you a hand,'' Joshua said, then continued, "but it will only be for the next few weeks.''

"Suits me fine,'' Charlie said, more than happy to accommodate his new helper.

Joshua worked at the forge for almost two hours, then took off the apron and walked to the sink, cupped his hands under the running water, splashed his sweating face, and dried himself with the towel hanging on the wall.

"If you're serious about helping me, I'd appreciate your coming around the same time tomorrow, maybe an hour earlier. That's about the time I run out of steam.''

"I'll be here,'' Joshua said, like a young kid who had just landed his first job. He left the shop happy and walked down the street.

It was about six-thirty when Joshua entered the tavern. The bar was full, with ten or twelve men sitting around busily engaged in light chatter. No one paid much attention to Joshua. Tim McGirr was there but was busy and didn't notice his friend come in. The tavern was a quaint, nostalgic place, with pictures of famous and not-so-famous frequenters from the past. There were about a dozen and a half tables, neatly covered with green-and-white checkered tablecloths, arranged to the right of the bar and spreading down to the back of the room, where there was an open area reserved for any who liked to dance. The bar was ornately carved and looked as if it had been there for centuries. It probably had been. There were a few guests already seated, enjoying the ritual of eating out with friends.

A waiter came over and asked Joshua where he would like to sit. He said he preferred to sit near the window, so the man led him over to a table far enough away from the bar so that he could have some privacy and also a view of the square. Joshua seemed satisfied.

"Would you like something to drink before supper?'' the waiter asked.

"Yes, I would like a glass of sherry, dry,'' Joshua answered.

"Any particular brand, sir?''

"No, whatever you think is a good one. I'll trust your judgment."

Joshua sat and looked out the window. The square was quiet this time of evening. The declining sun painted soft shadows across the stone pavement. It reminded him of the square at Nazareth, except there was no fountain here where women could come to draw water and share news.

The waiter returned with Joshua's drink and a plate of crackers and cheese. Joshua spread his napkin, lifted his glass, and sipped the wine. He savored the first sip, enjoying its full flavor and bouquet, while the waiter prepared to take Joshua's order.

"What would you like for supper, sir?" he asked.

"I think I'll have ham steak, potatoes, and cabbage."

"And for dessert?"

"A piece of apple pie and a cup of coffee."

"Thank you. It should be ready in a few minutes."

Joshua sat looking out the window, lost in his thoughts as he sipped the wine, every now and then nibbling on the cheese and crackers. A boy came in and dropped off a few newspapers, which immediately circulated among the men at the bar, the bartender quickly grabbing one for himself. In no time the conversation switched to that stranger, Joshua. To their surprise there was an article about him in the paper. "Hey, look at this, guys, there's a story here about the village. It's got a picture of that stranger that hangs around with the kids and a long article."

"Read it!" one of the fellows yelled out.

"Hell, I'm not gonna read that thing in here. I can hardly see straight as it is."

The men started reading over each other's shoulders, and in no time the whole conversation at the bar centered on Joshua. Some were saying he was a good man, well-intentioned but a dreamer. Others said he had to be odd hanging around kids. One fellow, by the name of Matt, who had already had too much to drink, made the remark that he thought Joshua was a troublemaker and should keep the hell out of their affairs. "It's obvious what he's trying to do. He's out to screw up the whole works around here and undermine our cause. I think we should teach the bloody bastard a good lesson."

At that point Tim didn't like the way the dialogue was going so he added his comments. "You guys don't know what you're talking about. He's a decent chap. I had him over to our house one night and we had a long talk. The man's got one hell of a lot of courage if you ask me. It is obvious what he's up to, and I for one am glad. None of us has the guts to do what he's doing. I think the guy's a saint, and anyone who dares to lay a finger on him, I personally will break his bloody jaw. And that goes for you, too, Matt. You and your crew have caused enough trouble around here, and though no one will tell you to your face, we're all fed up with it."

Well, that did it. Tim, who had also put away a few, had crossed the line of barroom etiquette. Matt wasn't going to take that one sitting down, so, sliding off the barstool, he hauled off, catching Tim with a right to the face. Tim's mouth started to bleed. He flushed with anger. Tim hadn't been in a good fight in years, and this one seemed worth it. Joshua was such a decent guy, he was worth fighting for, so he swung and caught Matt on the jaw with an uppercut that sent him sprawling flat on the floor, half unconscious. The others were disappointed it had ended so soon. They had expected a little more excitement than that.

Joshua saw what had happened, and when Matt fell on the floor he went over and helped him up. Matt was ready to go after Tim again, but was shocked to see who it was helping him. Tim was just as shocked. Everyone was a bit embarrassed but invited Joshua to sit at the bar with them. He did.

"Joshua," Tim said, half proud of himself and half ashamed, "you're my friend, and I won't tolerate anyone attacking you."

"I appreciate that, Tim. Peter was that way a long time ago, and all it did was get everyone into trouble. There's nothing so bad it can't be discussed intelligently. And this is not the place to discuss serious issues. It is bound to end up in a fight."

One of the men shoved the newspaper in front of Joshua.

"See the article about you?" he said.

Joshua looked it over, but wasn't very interested. After glancing at it briefly he went back to talking with the men. "Matt is right," Joshua said, to everyone's dismay. Matt beamed. Joshua continued, "I am very concerned about the children. They are your children. You should be concerned about them too. It is cruel and callous to strip the joy out of little children's lives and instill hatred in their hearts that will fester till the day they die. If an evil person wants to destroy a child, the quickest and most vicious way of doing it is to teach that child to hate and to go through life suspicious of others. And here the terrible thing is that parents are doing that to their own children. I have come here to reverse that once and for all. I have come to free the children from hatred and teach them to love. I know full well where it leads, and I am not afraid. But I warn you solemnly, do not interfere with the work of God. You pride yourselves on being religious people. Truly religious people don't do the things that are done here in the name of religion. That blasphemes the name of God, just like others blaspheme the name of God by teaching their followers to hate others of God's children. It is sickness like this that poisons the world and makes peace impossible. Peace cannot exist as long as people enjoy hating. Hatred can end only when individuals choose not to take offense, can overlook the meanness and limitations of others, and understand the troubles that give rise to mean things. Few people grow to be that big."

Even though they were all half drunk, the men were touched by what Joshua said. They could see the goodness in the man's heart and had never heard anyone talk like that before. A couple of the men had tears in their eyes and were trying to hide them, embarrassed that they should become so emotional, though it was partly the effect of the alcohol. Matt had very mixed feelings. He could see the sincerity of Joshua, but, being involved himself, he couldn't justify what Joshua was doing.

The waiter came out with Joshua's supper and asked where he wanted to eat it. The men persuaded Joshua to eat at the bar and talk to them, and that's what he did.

While Joshua ate his supper the men questioned him about everything everyone else had questioned him about. Joshua answered the same as he had for the others. His answers made sense. Some liked what he had to say and liked what he was doing. Some disagreed. All were concerned about the final outcome, now more than ever since the newspaper had made it a public issue and the idea was bound to spread.

When Joshua finished his drink the men ordered another for him, but he declined graciously. "I enjoyed the one I had, any more wouldn't be the same." The men respected his wishes. They were enjoying this fascinating man. He was serious, but in a lighthearted, playful way that kept the mood light under circumstances that could have become heavy and argumentative.

One by one the men began to leave. Their families were patiently waiting for them to come home for dinner. Before long Joshua was left there with Tim and a couple of Tim's friends. They stayed until Joshua finished eating, then left with him.

"You know you're always welcome at our house for supper," Tim said to Joshua. "You don't have to stand on ceremony. Just pop in anytime. We would be delighted to have you."

"I know, Tim, and I do feel welcome," Joshua responded.

The men parted, going their separate ways. Joshua and Tim walked across the meadow together, Tim pressing Joshua to spend the night at the house.

23

IT WAS EARLY in the morning when Joshua came into the village. He headed straight for Father Donnelly's place, greeting people along the way. Everyone in town knew him by now. Some made comments about the article in the paper. Joshua just smiled and thanked them, continuing on his way.

The old priest had just finished Mass and was walking out of the church when Joshua came up the walk.

"Good morning, Father," he said with a respect for the venerable priest's age.

"Good morning, son," the priest returned. "I see you're a celebrity. That was quite an article they wrote about you in the paper. I read it with interest. I was surprised they were so sympathetic. Usually they're critical of everything, but they must have liked you to write the way they did. It will surely give a good push to what you're trying to do. Can you come in for a few minutes?"

"Yes, if you're not busy," Joshua answered.

"Not at all. Come right in," the priest said, ushering his friend into the parish house.

Marie was inside getting breakfast ready. She was glad to see Joshua and greeted him warmly. The two men sat down at the table in the dining room. It was small compared to the one at the manse, but the priest ate alone most of the time and didn't need anything spacious. There was a picture of the Pope on the wall and a smaller photo portrait of the bishop on another wall.

A crucifix hung on the wall above the buffet. The sun was shining through the windows and brightened up the room, which would have been dreary with the dark paneling and furniture. There were crystal lamps and vases and dishes placed here and there, all of good quality, some quite old. A small, aging photograph of an elderly man and woman rested on the buffet. The resemblance of the old man to the priest was striking. It was obviously his father.

"I hope you didn't mind my teasing you at dinner the other night," Joshua said to the priest.

"Not at all. I enjoyed it. It brought out a side of your personality I had not seen before. It was a good evening. Everyone enjoyed themselves. You seemed to be enjoying the evening yourself."

"Yes, I did. It is good to see the clergy having a good time together. Do the other clergy associate?" Joshua asked, concerned.

"No. They're a little stuffy, if I must say so. Russ and I became fast friends as soon as he moved here. The others get together occasionally. They are friendly enough, but are usually a bit distant. I think it's more their people who don't approve of their fraternizing. Things are too tense here, and they are afraid of being drawn into something they can't handle. So they keep their distance. Russ and I are always in the thick of things with our own people so we don't have much choice but to be in the middle of trouble. It's a blessing we are such good friends. It helps us to keep a steady rein on our people, most of them anyway."

"Most of them?" Joshua asked, surprised.

"Yes, there are some who are radical. They've been a thorn in my side all my life. They're not religious, but use religion as their front. Most of them haven't darkened the doors of the church since they were kids. That priest I told you about, they meet with him regularly when he passes through town. I guess he's the spark behind a lot of their doings. They get their arms from that Muslim family that lives in the neighborhood. I guess you know them. You helped their boy who was blinded when they were unloading a shipment of arms on the coast a while back."

"Yes," Joshua commented. "I was at their house the other night. They are nice people, and I think perhaps they may be changed in their way of looking at things."

"You may be right. The father came in to talk to me yesterday and asked if he could borrow a Bible. He had read the Gospels a long time ago and would like to read them again but didn't have a copy at home. I let him take mine. He said you reminded him a lot of Jesus."

Joshua blushed. The priest looked at him, curious, thinking hard about what the Muslim had said. He had wondered himself about Joshua, but didn't dare to entertain the thought. It seemed too preposterous. The thought, however, crossed his mind more and more.

Marie brought in the breakfast. The priest invited her to sit down and have breakfast with them. He knew how much she liked Joshua and would be thrilled just to be able to have the memory of having breakfast with him. At first she was reluctant, then she agreed, and sat across from Joshua. She was a bit embarrassed, but Joshua soon put her at ease, asking her questions about herself and her family. Before long she was telling him everything about her life. After a few minutes she excused herself, saying she had work to do.

Joshua and the priest continued their conversation, the priest wondering about the newspaper article and what it meant in terms of Joshua's strategy. "Joshua, I know you're aware that that newspaper story has already reached a lot of homes and by now has stirred a considerable amount of discussion. Not all of it is going to be favorable. You can expect strange people to be passing through here just to see what's going on and to figure out how they want to deal with you. You realize that, I'm sure. For every fifty people who may approve of what you're doing, there will be a hothead who will be driven to near apoplexy over it. I am so afraid for you and, I must add, also for the children."

"Elmer, don't worry about the children. They will be safe. Nothing will happen to them. Remember what it says in the Gospels, 'Not one of those you have given me will be lost'? Well, it applies here. Not one of the children will be hurt. So lay your fears to rest. I know my Father and he has willed it this way. It is the only way."

"Young man," the priest said, finishing his coffee, "I hope you're right. Still, be careful. I have work to do and I know you have your work cut out for you today, so we better get started."

They both got up from the table and walked through the kitchen to say good-bye to Marie. Joshua then left. Elmer watched him with a look of sadness in his eyes as he walked out through the rose garden. He was clearly concerned about the future and about this strange young man he had grown so fond of . . . and perhaps not without good reason.

Joshua arrived at the square around the same time as usual. Children were already waiting. Some had clippings from the newspaper they were excited to show him.

"Joshua," Peter called to him as he walked slowly across the square, "did you see the paper, and the article about you in it, and about me and Acmet?"

"I didn't read it all. What does it say? Tell me about it."

"No, Joshua, you have to read it. It's a good article," Peter insisted.

Joshua took the clipping from Peter and began reading it. The article started by describing Joshua, his appearance, his manners, and the effect he had on the crowd of children who followed him, then went on to say:

It is not difficult to see what this man Joshua is attempting to do, clearly the impossible. His strategy is faultless. The loyalty of the children, who literally follow him everywhere and hang on to his every word, is absolute. If what this man is trying to accomplish takes hold, it is capable of transforming the whole country. The march on the city a few days ago has already sparked children's interest in other places, and small groups of Catholic and Protestant children are associating with each other for the first time in their lives. The reaction of parents is mixed. Some think it is beautiful, some are troubled over it, radicals are clearly disturbed, realizing the movement's potential for undermining their cause, which can succeed only if they can pass on their hatred to the next generation. Whether this simple idealist's dream will be allowed to continue is the big question. Only time will answer that.

Then there was the little story about Peter and his blind friend, Acmet. The reporter did a good job of interviewing the two children.

When Joshua finished speaking to the children, they walked away. Two youngsters stayed. One was holding the other by the hand. I could see one boy was blind. The blind boy's name was Acmet. His friend's name was Peter. In talking to the boys I found that the blind boy was an Arab whose family was living in the village. Peter was waiting for Joshua to finish so he could ask him if he could cure his friend's blindness. Whether he ever did I was unable to find out. What was touching was the complete trust these children had in this man who was but a total stranger only a few weeks before. One boy was a Catholic, the other was a Muslim. The boy wasn't asking for anything for himself but for a favor for his Muslim friend. One could readily see how this simple stranger was capable of setting the world upside down.

Joshua gave the clipping back to Peter with the comment "The man did a good job writing the article. It should go far in helping to spread the good news. The article about you and Acmet was very well done. You should be proud of yourselves. Now you can see how unselfish love of others can touch people's hearts and inspire them to goodness."

The children were happy this morning. They were more interested in the picture the reporter had taken of the group standing around listening to Joshua, and trying to identify themselves in the photograph, than they were in the article.

Joe came up to Joshua with his trumpet tucked under his arm and looking very concerned. He asked Joshua what the reporter meant when he asked whether people would allow them to continue. Joshua tried to explain. "Don't you worry about that, Joe. That's God's business. We will do just what God wants, and he will see to it that the good he intends will be accomplished. It will go on until all that God intends is completed. No one can stop what we are doing. God will not be frustrated by mean people's schemes. That is definite. So there is no need ever to worry when you are doing good. God will see to its success. You must always trust God and have patience."

Joshua could explain the most profound workings of God's mind in ways that even these little children could understand. He had that knack of making sense out of religion so kids could find meaning and pleasure in it.

Joe had a little surprise for Joshua and for the group. His friend he had been teaching to play the trumpet was going to play for Joshua. The boy was a little embarrassed at first, then, after he started playing, forgot himself and played beautifully a piece from Haydn that Joe had been secretly teaching him. The boy made only one little mistake, which wasn't very noticeable. Everyone was impressed and clapped loudly when he finished.

Then it was Joshua's turn. He took the trumpet, put it to his mouth, and smiled, knowing full well he wasn't going to do nearly as well as the little boy. He started to play and played a simple melody Joe had been trying to teach him. He sounded better but still needed a lot more practice, Joe told him. Joshua agreed. He promised to try harder, especially when he saw that the kids really wanted him to play well. He hadn't taken his playing too seriously.

The children stayed with Joshua until noontime, then went home. Joshua went off into the meadow and wandered through the fields, thinking, relaxing, and contemplating nature, absorbing the presence of his Father in the beautiful world surrounding him. Sometimes Joe would bring him lunch, sometimes he forgot. This day he forgot. Joshua was unconcerned. At two o'clock he left the meadow and walked up to the blacksmith's shop. Charlie was glad to see him, relieved that he could take a break.

"That was quite an article about you in the newspaper. You're a real celebrity now." Joshua thanked him and just shrugged.

"All part of the day's work," Joshua said as he put on his apron. Charlie gave him a list of things he needed and asked if he minded if he went home for a while. Joshua didn't mind at all. He would have everything done when he returned. Joshua dived right into the work, hammering each piece into perfect shape and laying it aside, then going on to the next piece. He worked with a rare precision, using the tools with such an ease and care that when each piece was finished it looked like it had come out of a machine. By the time Charlie returned Joshua had made a whole order of door hinges, rims for wagon wheels, a number of horseshoes all ready for shoeing, and a fancy doorstop with a fine personal touch to it that fascinated Charlie.

Charlie couldn't believe Joshua was able to do all that he had done while he was away. "With help like that, I'll be caught up in a couple of weeks. I can't thank you enough, young man. Do you want your pay now or at the end of the week?"

"The end of the week is all right. I don't need it right now."

When Joshua left he was tired. He walked out across the field to the pond to take a swim and wash his clothes. The afternoon was hot, which made the water all the more refreshing. Afterward he fell sound asleep on the grass and didn't wake up until a flock of sheep came over to graze all around him. He sat up quietly so as not to frighten them, and when they came close he petted them, holding them affectionately by the ears. Then he got up and walked across to Tim's house to take him up on his invitation to dinner. Tim was thrilled, and so were the others. They, too, had read the article in the newspaper and couldn't wait to talk to him about it.

Joshua stayed there for the night. It was a happy ending to a fruitful day.

24

Each succeeding day became more complicated for Joshua, even as his work with the children became more enjoyable. The children and Joshua had grown close during the short time he had been in town, but as interest in what he was doing spread, people's involvement became more personal. Strangers came drifting into town from all over the country to get a glimpse of this unusual man and what he was all about. Some wanted to talk to him and spend time with him personally. Others were content to just watch and analyze. Some looked friendly. Others were clearly hostile. Two clergymen particularly, who had close ties to groups in the town, came to visit at different times, each with a band of local followers. One of the clergymen was a priest, a Roman Catholic; the other was a Presbyterian minister. The priest, Father Jack Brown, was the one Father Donnelly had warned Joshua about, whose clandestine activities were a cause of deep concern to the old priest. The other clergyman was the one Joshua had heard speak at the park a few weeks earlier. He was the kind of person everyone feared. Both men were fanatics, both filled with deep hatred and suspicions that they succeeded well in communicating to their followers.

On the occasion of Father Brown's visit, Joshua was talking to the children in the square. The priest and his handful of shabbily dressed cronies stood at a distance, just far enough away to hear all of Joshua's conversations with the children. The men's rage at seeing the Catholic and Protestant children having such a good time together was obvious. They never approached Joshua, never introduced themselves to him, just listened and took notes, then walked away, talking excitedly among themselves. As they walked out of the square the priest was silent. His sullen, tense features reflected the dark, ominous thoughts that were festering within.

The visit of the Presbyterian minister was similar. He came with his band of cronies, stood off at a distance, watching, listening, calculating, and wandering off like the others, deep in dark thoughts. Joshua noticed both groups when they came. A sadness crossed his calm features. While seemingly absorbed in talking to the children, his memories roamed across the centuries, recalling Pharisees and scribes in flowing robes sprinkled throughout crowds of his followers, listening, watching, calculating in just the same manner and with the same dark countenances worn by these men. It bode ill for the future. He realized there will always be those so stuck in their own narrow, myopic interests, whether it be theology or politics, that they feel threatened by people growing in love and understanding of one another. It is too threatening to their own narrow schemes, which can thrive only where there are clearly defined and impenetrable political or theological barriers. Their sick, disturbed personalities thrive on conflict, which can't cope with acceptance and understanding. While seemingly struggling for peace, they could never function once there is peace, and they become unglued at the prospect of imminent peace becoming a reality.

And now, as in the past, the serenity of Joshua's manner was unruffled in the face of churning tempests. His confidence in his Father's plans gave him all the assurance he needed to remain resolute in his purpose. The prospect of impending danger or even tragedy never became an overwhelming obsession. His trust in his Father's closeness was absolute, so all that the children saw amid the flurry of new activity in town was the same peaceful, tranquil, carefree man they loved. Everything went on as before. The children reflected in their behavior Joshua's own security.

In the afternoons Joshua went to the blacksmith's place, still helping him catch up on his work. Charlie was appreciative and offered to pay Joshua well, but Joshua declined to accept all he offered, saying he really didn't need that much. The old man was surprised, not offended, and looked upon Joshua's declining the money as a show of friendship, so he invited him to his house for supper, which Joshua readily accepted.

When Charlie saw how clever Joshua was at shaping the iron, he asked him to make some special pieces for himself, his wife, and his friends. Joshua was delighted to oblige him and spent three whole afternoons crafting imaginative articles that became a source of pride to the old craftsman.

Days passed. Mornings with the children were much the same. Strangers passed through the village, curious after reading the news article, eager to see with their own eyes if Joshua's project really worked. That was one thing no one could deny. It really did work, perhaps too well for Joshua's own good. Afternoons at the blacksmith shop were fun. Joshua had his own techniques and tricks for drawing, twisting, hammering, and shearing the hot iron into intricate and unusual shapes, giving the finished products an almost delicate quality.

One afternoon the Reverend Davis came down to watch Joshua. Charlie was one of his parishioners and he, too, had told his pastor about Joshua.

"You sure are a talented man, Joshua," Russ commented as he watched Joshua shaping the white-hot metal.

"This is fun," Joshua retorted. "It's the kind of thing everyone would enjoy doing. It's perfect for keeping in shape."

"Where did you learn how to do this kind of work?" Russ asked.

"Oh, I learned it a long time ago, growing up. I always enjoyed it but didn't do it for very long," Joshua responded without going into detail.

The minister picked up a finished piece that had already cooled, turned it over in his hand, looked at it from different angles, and remarked over the fineness of the workmanship.

"Thank you," Joshua said humbly. "Can I make something for you? I'm sure Charlie wouldn't mind."

"I'd like that," the minister answered.

"No, I wouldn't mind at all," Charlie said. "I enjoy watching him myself, and I've been doing it all my life."

While the two men watched Joshua took a piece of hot iron, put it on a flat surface, and started hammering it into shape, then reheating it, hammering it again, and carefully poking pieces out, forming an intricate pattern in the metal, then carefully shaping the delicate sections with the calipers and a stylus-like rod. In no time he had formed a beautifully designed trivet for Russ to give to his wife for use in the kitchen. When it cooled Charlie painted it for him. Joshua then proceeded to make a pair of bookends for the minister. Into the left bookend Joshua carefully carved with calipers a replica of the tablets of the Ten Commandments with a crack in them. Into the right bookend he carved the same tablets but in such a way as to take the form of a heart, symbolizing the New Law in Christ's love. The bookends looked almost molded they were so perfect. They were heavy, but with a finished and exquisite look about them.

"There, my good friend," Joshua said as he placed the cooled and painted pieces on the counter, "the old ways must go, the new way must take hold in people's hearts."

Russ was thrilled. Charlie was too. And so was Joshua. He was always happiest doing nice things for people.

Russ left, a little embarrassed nobody would take any money from him, but as he walked down the street he was like a child who has just been given a Christmas present.

When they closed the shop Charlie insisted Joshua come home with him for dinner so they could bring the special pieces home together. The house wasn't far from the shop, so they were there in no time, carrying big, heavy boxes full of things Joshua had made.

Charlie's wife, Margaret, had just come back from shopping and met them at the kitchen door.

"What do you fellows have there?" she said for conversation.

"A surprise," Charlie said as they all walked into the house together.

"I can't wait to see them," she responded.

Inside, she turned on the lights and made room for the boxes on the kitchen table. The men put them down and took a deep breath. The boxes were heavy.

One by one Charlie took the presents out of the boxes, giving Margaret hers.

"They're beautiful," she raved, thrilled with the delicacy of the pieces. "I have never seen work so fine, and Charlie's the best. He's always so busy making things for customers, he doesn't get a chance to make nice things like this."

"I couldn't do it even if I tried," Charlie admitted humbly. "Joshua's a master."

Joshua said nothing, just smiled, happy he had made the couple so happy.

The two men washed up and went out on the porch to rest while Margaret prepared supper. In no time Charlie was asleep, snoring. Joshua rocked back and forth in his rocking chair, taking in the scenery, resting his tired muscles. It was a warm evening, but a cool breeze drifted across the fields and through the yard. The sun was settling down over the distant hills, casting long shadows across the fields. Birds were flying frantically, catching insects in flight. There was a soft, golden glow in the atmosphere. It was quiet and peaceful.

Charlie woke up when Margaret called for supper. A little embarrassed, he apologized for going to sleep on his guest. Joshua laughed, not the slightest bit offended. The two men went into the house for supper. Margaret had the table set impeccably, wanting to make a good impression on their guest and also show her appreciation for all that he was doing to help her husband.

It was a simply prepared meal, potatoes and steak, which she had bought in the hope Charlie would be bringing Joshua home for dinner. The conversation at the table was simple. They were not intellectual people and their interests were limited to things happening around the village and how business had changed over the years. Fortunately the couple had put money aside when they realized the blacksmith business no longer had the demand it used to, and they could rest comfortably as business slowed.

After supper they all helped with the dishes, against Margaret's strong objections, then went out and sat on the porch talking and sipping tea until a little after sunset. At Charlie's insistence, Joshua stayed for the night.

25

THE EFFECTS OF the newspaper article were beginning to show. To the children in various places around the country Joshua was fast becoming their hero, although most had never seen him, had no idea what he looked like, or even who he really was. In places far from the village Catholic and Protestant children decided to ignore the ancient taboo of forced isolation from one another. A few groups of private school officials decided to open their schools to children of all religions. The response was immediate. Many people, just itching for the chance, began signing up their children. It took courage, but so many were so fed up with the incessant fighting and hatred, they were willing to try anything to bring peace back into their lives and prepare a better future for their children.

Follow-up news articles showed graphically how the movement was spreading, in little pockets at first, then to larger villages and towns, and even to the cities. No terrorist would dare violate children. It would show only too pointedly who the enemy really was and permanently seal their doom. Children even began going with their new friends to each others' churches, something unheard of. The clergy, even well-intentioned ones, became nervous over that but did not dare to say a word publicly. Politicians were either tongue-tied or speechless when interviewed by the press, not knowing how to react. They were trapped. To approve of what was happening would enrage their constituents, whose puppets they were. To criticize the chil-

dren's innocent show of concern would strip naked their bad
faith and secret meanness. They said nothing, but seethed inside.

Joshua's friends showed him the articles. He read them carefully, with a broad smile lighting up his face. "God bless the
children. Now if they would only start the same war against
drugs," Joshua mused, half to himself. "The children have the
potential to bring sanity and restore goodness to a sick world."

People from widely scattered places began coming to talk with
Joshua, a new kind of people, different from others who had
been coming. These were good people with social standing and
with resources. Some offered their help, some offered money.
Some asked what he thought they could do in their own way
back home. To each Joshua's answer was the same: "Work for
peace by rising above the pettiness of life and never taking offense. Be kind to those who are miserable. Show appreciation to
those who do good work. Respect the dignity of each person.
Heal wounds wherever you find hurt. Do whatever you can to
comfort those who are troubled. Replace anger and suspicion
with understanding. It doesn't take money. It take love and
concern."

Joshua's message was simple, just like himself, much like the
message taught so very long ago, a message that was never taken
seriously and yet had the potential to heal the world's ills.

One day two bishops came to town. Surprisingly, they came
together, one Roman Catholic, the other Anglican. They had
contacted their respective clergy in the village a day before to
announce their coming. They would like very much to visit with
this man Joshua if that could be arranged. They would also like,
out of courtesy, to visit with the other clergy in the village, since
they all had serious interests in common. Both churches made
hurried preparations to host both men jointly and provide for
their accommodations.

Father Donnelly took a rare walk down to the square to invite
Joshua up to the house to meet the bishops. The Anglican priest
invited the Wesleyan minister, John Cooke, and his wife, as well
as Russ and his wife and Elmer, to the parish house for the
dinner that evening.

Bishop Edmund Chalmers, the Anglican bishop, was a chubby, friendly man, with features that betrayed a life filled with troubles. The man had a broad respect from all decent-thinking people and a reputation for fairness. Bishop Charles Ryan, the Roman Catholic, was a tough-looking man who could have passed for a boxer, but a man who had a reputation for high intelligence and good humor, a man whose one ambition was to heal the terrible rift that plagued the country. The radicals of his own religion had little use for him. To them he was as dangerous as the enemy. The bishop said what he had to say and was totally unafraid of any possible recriminations.

Joshua's first contact with the two bishops occurred while he was talking with the children in the square. The bishops had stopped off first at Father Donnelly's place, left their car there, and walked down to the square, hoping to observe Joshua in action.

When they entered the square the children were just finishing their informal music session. Joshua was still trying to play the trumpet. The children were laughing good-naturedly at the mistakes he was making. It was all part of Joshua's lesson. When he finished he gave the instrument back to Joe, promising that one day he would give them a surprise. One of the older boys who had come recently played the guitar, making up songs for everyone to sing. One was about Joshua and his message of peace. Joshua sat down on the wall and listened as the children sang and the boy strummed his guitar.

When they finished he told them to be seated. Still sitting on the wall, he said to them, "See what beautiful harmony your lives are creating. That music is just an outward expression of the real harmony that is forming in your hearts.

"God formed you with tender love, and just like he loves and cares for you, so he wants you to have the same love and care for one another. When you choose to approach God alone he will say to you, 'Where are your brothers and sisters?' And if you have walked away from them and have not made them part of your life, then you go to God with your work unfinished. Your work on earth is to help form and perfect the family of God and, by sharing the gifts God gave you, fill up in the lives of others those things they lack. In that you will find your happiness on earth and earn your reward with God in heaven."

The two bishops were impressed with what Joshua said, and having picked up a sense of what his intentions were, they walked from the square back down to the priest's house.

Father Donnelly was picking roses to decorate the house when the two men arrived. Getting up from his knees with difficulty, he welcomed them and escorted them into the house.

"I am honored that you came to visit us. I hope you enjoy your little visit. Come right in. I assume your curiosity got the best of you and you took a walk to the square to see Joshua."

"Yes, we did," Bishop Chalmers answered. "And I must admit, I was quite impressed."

"As was I," Bishop Ryan added. "That man is quite an individual. I had the strangest feeling I was living in the midst of a real-life gospel story."

"That's strange," Elmer added, "because when he comes to the church to visit some mornings, I have the exact same feeling. The way he speaks, his tone of voice, his profound sense of peace, everything about him suggests that it couldn't be much different if Christ himself were right here. And I don't even feel guilty thinking that way."

In the house, Marie had anticipated their coming and had a snack already prepared for them. Elmer ushered them into the living room and seated them while Marie prepared to serve the refreshments.

The bishops did not take long to get around to the point of their visit. They wanted to experience Joshua firsthand and ask the local clergy for their sense of what Joshua was doing. Was it reasonable? Did it make sense? Or was it just a passing phenomenon that had no possibility of taking any real root?

Elmer answered those concerns emphatically. "No, I don't think this is just a flash in a pan. There's a depth and a sense of purpose to that young man that gives even cynics the feeling he knows he's going to succeed in what he has set out to accomplish. And he is brutally realistic. He knows full well that there are some who will be determined not to let his project continue, yet he knows in some way that nothing is going to prevent him from accomplishing what he has set out to do."

"And what is that?" Bishop Ryan asked pointedly.

"It is obvious. He has a long-range plan to short-circuit the violence that has become a disease in these parts. The route he has chosen is through the children. If he can get them to mingle and become friends, and can get this to spread, he knows it will succeed. I have to admit he's shrewd in the way he's going about it. He never does a thing to antagonize anyone. He's quiet, gentle, friendly, and, in the short time he's been here, knows half the town. He even cured a Muslim boy of blindness last week. The kid's father came in later and asked for a copy of the Gospels. I think we can feel quite safe with this fellow. I encourage my people to back him, and so does Russ Davis, the Presbyterian pastor. He thinks he's the greatest thing that's hit the country."

"What about the Anglican priest?" Bishop Chalmers asked.

"He hasn't said anything against him, but I really don't know how he feels personally about what he's doing. He's in a little different situation than Russ and myself. Our people are in the midst of things. His people are a bit more isolated."

"On the way down here Bishop Ryan and I were talking about making a public statement supporting what this man Joshua is doing in the hope that it can spread to the rest of the country. It might just work. If all the churches can work together on it, then it can happen that much faster. We want to get a feeling from yourself and the other pastors as to how you would feel about our support."

"I really can't speak for the others, but I think your support would be magnificent. It certainly can't do any harm, and it will reassure parents who might be concerned about letting their children become involved."

At that point the doorbell rang. Marie answered it and brought Joshua into the room. Everyone automatically stood up, not knowing why. Elmer introduced Joshua to the two bishops, and they all sat down.

"Our celebrity!" Bishop Ryan exclaimed. Joshua blushed.

"We were just talking about you, young man," the bishop continued. "Bishop Chalmers and I were impressed with the way you handled that rather large group of kids. Not too many could exercise that kind of control over children."

"I've always loved children," Joshua responded. "They are innocent and unspoiled, as they came from the hand of God. It is grown-ups who steer them in wrong directions."

"Joshua," Bishop Chalmers interjected, "why do you think your work with the children will succeed?"

"That's simple. It is the will of my Father, and his will will not be frustrated. He loves these people, and although they have been made to fear one another, they are all victims. They didn't create this situation. They inherited it and don't know any way out of it. The way I have chosen is the only way. It will succeed."

"Can we help?" Bishop Ryan asked.

"Yes, by encouraging others not to be afraid but to allow their children to reach out to others like they have here. In time they will learn to trust and become friends. They are the adults of the future. If they learn trust now, they will carry it with them through life."

It was all so simple. The bishops were glad they had come. They were glad Joshua had stopped by. They were grateful for the courageous work he was attempting to do and assured him of their support. Joshua excused himself and left.

The bishops had accomplished what they had come for and were anxious to visit the Anglican rector and meet over dinner with the others later in the evening. They got up to leave, thanking Marie for her hospitality, and walked to the door with the pastor. Elmer accompanied them to the car and said he was looking forward to dinner that evening.

J. Stanford Crist, or J.C., as his friends called him, had been rector at All Saints for over twelve years. He was tall, thin, scholarly-looking, and affable. His wife, Norma, not quite as tall, was round-faced and jolly. They were a happy couple and had survived in the village by keeping pretty much to themselves and becoming involved only in the lives of their parishioners, who had grown accustomed to their discreet, personable ways. Father Crist had taught in the seminary for over fifteen years before taking this assignment in the village. It was a pleasant assignment for a rector who could enjoy being a diplomat and had the discipline not to be drawn into the local politics.

If the rector was not overly warm in his relationships with the other clergy, it was not out of snobbishness but for the sake of his survival. It was his long-standing policy not to become involved in any relationships that would embroil him in the highly complicated tensions of the community, which could explode at any time and without warning. This uninvolvement was the reason he was still there after twelve years. His predecessors had not been as discreet or as fortunate. They had lasted only a few years.

The joint visit of the two bishops made Father Crist uncomfortable. He knew both of them by reputation, and his own bishop by close association on the seminary faculty, where he had been nicknamed "The Roman Rector of Canterbury." The two bishops were great friends and conferred on every decision each of them made. He strongly suspected why the two of them had come here together and did not like it one bit.

When the two bishops arrived in early afternoon, Father Crist met them at the door and welcomed them graciously. They congratulated him on the meticulous care he had obviously taken of the gardens and the buildings. Every rector should be as attentive to the surroundings of God's home. The comments were appreciated, and the rector conducted the two men into the parish house and introduced them to his wife, who was busy preparing a light midday luncheon for everyone.

After the formalities the priest showed the two men to their rooms upstairs, offering them the option of either staying upstairs to relax and freshen up before lunch or, if they preferred, coming down to the study to socialize. They said they would be down presently.

In the few minutes before lunch the socializing was more like shadowboxing. Bishop Chalmers asked Father Crist how he felt about Joshua. The rector had no strong feelings one way or another.

"Surely you've heard of him?" the bishop remarked rather caustically, revealing a long-standing tension between the two men.

"Of course I've heard of him, but I've made a point of not involving myself in politics around here."

"But from what I've gathered, this man Joshua is far from political. He seems to be a thoroughly dedicated Christian trying rather heroically, if I must say, to do a job that should have been done by the clergy long before this."

"You may look at it that way, Bishop, but I live here and I see things much differently. I see Joshua as a man who is totally political, maybe for religious motives and with good intentions, but political nonetheless."

Bishop Ryan felt it would have been better if he had stayed upstairs, feeling this was a private matter between the two Anglicans. Bishop Chalmers, realizing he had not put his best foot forward, tried to lighten the conversation without changing the subject, which he intended to pursue.

"J.C.," he said, adopting a more familiar tone, "I can see how he can be construed as political. His goal is certainly not going to endear him to radicals on either side, but how do you think the ordinary people view him?"

"Well, that may be a different question. My own people seem to like him. In fact, knowing that Father Donnelly and the Presbyterian minister have had him to dinner, my people have been pressuring me to do the same. I would like to meet him. He seems like a rather interesting chap."

"That might be a good thing, having him for dinner sometime. He does seem to deserve our united support," the bishop added casually. At that point they broke for lunch.

Norma's presence at lunch had a tempering effect on the conversation. The clerics did not feel as free to pursue the matter in front of the rector's wife. The occasion turned into a delightful social hour, which put everyone in a much better frame of mind to discuss more freely later on what the two visitors had on their minds.

In the afternoon the bishops retired to their rooms and rested, leaving the rector free to finish the work he had originally scheduled for the day. He was glad when they went upstairs.

26

By SEVEN O'CLOCK people were arriving at the parish house for dinner. Russ and his wife were unable to come. They were out of town for the day. Elmer, always promptly on time, was the first one to arrive. The two senior wardens and their wives came a few minutes later. They were all escorted into the study, which was cozier and more relaxing than the parlor. Father Crist was an excellent host and had everyone's drink already prepared, knowing from past parties each one's preference, except for Bishop Ryan, who said he would like a martini. Norma had made a huge tray of hors d'oeuvres, which she brought out and placed on a serving table strategically positioned for everyone's convenience.

Cocktail time was light and jovial. No one talked about anything heavy. Everyone just coasted into a warm, friendly mood that lasted for a good part of the evening and opened the way for a relaxed setting in which to discuss business later on.

The wardens and their wives had never met the Roman Catholic bishop before, though they had heard much about him in the news and had read some of his statements, which they agreed must have taken no small amount of courage to express. The bishop didn't think of himself as being terribly heroic. It was, he felt, just part of his job and something that he should do if he wanted to be able to live with himself. Whatever his motives, they still admired his strong stand on issues. That is the mark of a good leader, one of the wardens said in a not so subtle swipe at the rector's refusal to take a strong stand on issues they deemed important.

It was not lost on Father Crist or the others. Everyone was gracious enough to let it pass without comment. Elmer remarked it would have been nice to have Joshua at the dinner.

"That fellow sure does know how to handle himself, even socially," Elmer interjected. "You would think a person as single-minded as he is would be a bit gauche at social affairs, but not that one. He's as quick as a flash and has a playful sense of humor. You should see the tricks he can do with just an ordinary rubber ball. I don't know whether it's an illusion or something else, but he had us all acting like kids with what he did with the thing."

"Do you feel comfortable with what he's doing, Elmer?" Bishop Ryan asked.

"Yes, I do," the priest answered. "I feel comfortable with him because he's so methodical and circumspect. He makes you feel comfortable by communicating an uncanny sense that what he is doing is what God wants him to do. And he's not a disturbed person. He's very sane and very realistic. He talks about his work as being his father's will. It gives you a strange feeling when he talks like that, because you can't help but see the striking similarity between the way he talks and the way Jesus used to talk. Sometimes I even wonder . . . but then at times I feel it's not right to think that way."

The guests were so engrossed in their lively discussion about Joshua that no one paid much attention to the meal, though everyone was enjoying what they were eating and absentmindedly taking second helpings.

Norma would have felt slighted over her guests paying such little attention to what she had spent so long preparing for them except that they were all eating nonstop, which was the best show of approval because it was not contrived.

"The reason we are here," Bishop Chalmers remarked, "is to discuss what Joshua is doing. What that man has accomplished is having widespread consequences all across the country. There's something more than a mere natural phenomenon we are experiencing. If it is the work of God, as Joshua seems so convinced, then it behooves all of us, as religious and community leaders, to lend our support and make sure it takes hold. It may be the only chance we have to end this senseless scandal of Christians killing one another."

Everyone was quiet, looking furtively at one another, afraid to be the first to comment on the bishop's remark. To show support for his colleague, Bishop Ryan added his concerns: "Yes, this is something we all have to search our souls over. It is not right to let this total stranger stick his neck out to do something that should be the responsibility of us all. It shames us as Christian leaders to just stand by, secure in our own comfortable towers, and watch this brave fellow do what we should be doing, making efforts to resolve this problem, which has become a disgrace to our religion and an insult to Christ."

Elmer nodded approval. The senior wardens were also inclined to agree but were reluctant to embarrass their rector, who was already considerably uneasy over the direction the conversation had taken. He knew it was going to come around to something like this and was afraid of what concrete measures the bishops were going to pop on them.

One of the wardens, uncomfortable with the sudden lull in the conversation, asked the bishop what he had in mind.

That was the opening he needed and one that the rector shrewdly would not give him. "Something simple but practical. The people have to know where we stand. If we speak out in support of what Joshua is doing, then we lend credence to his work. That will have incalculable effects on those who are still on the fence. Bishop Ryan has a reputation for being judicious and outspoken. My own reputation is much the same, so people will listen. On the way down this morning we agreed to write a joint pastoral letter saying that we approve of what Joshua is doing and recommending the wholehearted support of all of our people. When we do this it is imperative that we have the support of our clergy here in the village, because the press will be looking for an immediate response from the local clergy. If you are not one hundred percent behind our statement, it will confuse the people and negate our own efforts. What I am trying to say is that we were hoping you could see your way clear to endorsing our expression of support."

No one knew what to say. Elmer had already given his support. The whole village knew where he stood on the matter, so he felt it was not his place to speak up now. Norma felt sorry for her husband. He was in the frying pan.

"Bishop," the rector finally said very slowly and in measured words, "I have spent my whole life trying to be careful, thinking it is the way expected of me. At times I felt I should be more forthright, but all in all my prudence has kept my people from becoming embroiled in the highly charged tensions in the community. For me to change now would not be in the best interests of my people."

"What do you see as the best interests of your people at a time like this, when the whole country is being torn apart? Security for our people is sometimes an interest we can ill afford when the country itself is being engulfed in a fratricidal war. Security under those conditions is merely an illusion. Everyone will be caught up in the conflagration if it burns out of control, and it will be the fault of those who could have done something and chose to protect themselves. With every killing the hatred multiplies by the number of people in the victim's family plus their friends. In time every family will be affected. It has to stop somewhere. Staying aloof is a luxury we can no longer afford."

The Methodist minister felt the same way J.C. felt. Why look for trouble? They had their flocks to think about. If other people were fighting, why should they become involved? Their strategy of noninvolvement had worked well for all these years, why change now? They admired Joshua for what he was doing, but that was his choice.

"If it works," John Cooke finished by saying, "all well and good, but if it doesn't, he can walk off and leave us all to clean up the streets."

The bishops hadn't come just to hear objections, and they were not going to leave until they had everyone's support.

"Gentlemen, I realize John and his wife are Methodists, and we are grateful he and his wife came this evening, and it is not our intention to preempt your superiors, John, but Bishop Ryan and I wanted to express to all of you in the village, out of courtesy, our intention of making a joint statement encouraging our people to act positively and together in this matter. And we feel it is important for as many as possible to be with us."

Father Crist agreed to consider the matter seriously and certainly would do nothing to show opposition. Elmer gave his wholehearted support. John Cooke expressed appreciation to J.C. for inviting him, and said he would work with him on the matter and that they would do jointly whatever they could agree on. With that expression of at least goodwill, the bishops let the matter drop for the evening and went on to discuss more enjoyable topics.

The evening ended amicably, and by the time everyone retired the bishops felt pretty sure they had at least a more solid support than when they came.

27

T HE BISHOPS LEFT the next morning with at least a tacit assurance that the rector would support their proposed statement. Russ had heard about the dinner the night before and felt more disappointed than ever that he had been unable to attend. He did call Bishop Chalmers and tell him of his willingness to give total support to whatever the two bishops might propose in their joint pastoral letter. The bishops spent the better part of the next two weeks drawing up the letter. Their advisers read it, made suggestions for minor changes here and there, and offered advice as to the timing of its release. A Friday was chosen for maximum press coverage and to allow the clergy to prepare comments for the following Sunday.

The pastoral letter received front-page coverage in the secular press and rave editorials from most newspapers. Some were highly critical, however, saying the bishops' ideas were unrealistic and might in the long haul occasion more harm than good. A surprising source of support came from youth groups of various denominations, praising the two leaders for their rare courage in taking such a strong position, and encouraging all their members to take the recommendations of the bishops to heart and reach out to young people of other denominations and form bonds of friendship and cooperation with those whose friendship had always been forbidden. A follow-up of Joshua's work was included in related articles in various papers.

The very day the statement was issued reporters appeared at rectory doorsteps in the village requesting interviews with the pastors of the different churches. To a man they were all supportive, even J. Stanford Crist, who issued a beautifully worded expression of support for the pastoral letter, praising the bishops "not just for the courage of their stand on this issue, but for the far-reaching implications of their joint statement in the whole area of ecumenical relations. The two men have, indeed, taken a giant step forward in making Christianity credible in a world that was fast losing hope." Everyone who knew the rector was impressed.

From the moment the pastoral was released, repercussions were immediate. It gave a notoriety and a credibility to Joshua's existence and his work with the children. Seeing the very positive results the letter was having aroused radicals on both sides. What they thought was a harebrained idea on the part of the oddball idealist now took on dimensions that threatened all their radical schemes. The main source of arms had been cut off when the Muslim family was converted by Joshua and they had become the most enthusiastic of his followers. Joshua was now seen as the most threatening of all their adversaries. What to do about it was fast becoming an obsession.

The radicals had no legitimate platform or vehicle for public expression to counter the massive and very positive coverage Joshua was receiving in the religious and secular press. To threaten children would turn the whole population against them and discredit them in the eyes of decent people everywhere. All they could do was hold hastily organized meetings to discuss strategy.

In the meantime, in the village, things went on as usual. People went to work, the children gathered with Joshua in the square or out in the meadow, strangers still wandered through town hoping to get a glimpse of this man who was turning the world upside down and, if they were lucky, spend a few minutes talking with him.

Rev. Davis met Joshua in the square one morning and invited him up to the manse for a chat. The pastoral letter had been out only two days. Joshua had not as yet seen it, nor the accompanying articles relating to him. It was of little importance for him to read them. In his uncanny foresight he had already anticipated the effects of the articles and the letter and was quietly planning his strategy to handle the problems he knew would be arising from them. He was aware of the secret meetings of the radicals. He was aware also of the limited number of options they had to counter the good things that were taking place all across the country. He was not concerned.

He went to the manse with the minister more for friendship than for any interest in seeing the articles, which Russ couldn't wait to show him. On the way they met the rector of All Saints. He was in a jolly mood, unusual for him.

"Good morning, Russ," Father Crist said. "I can't remember the weather ever being as nice as this for such a long stretch. I hope it lasts."

"J.C.," Russ responded, "have you ever met Joshua?"

The rector was taken back. Here was the man the whole town was talking about, and even he had offered to support, and, for the first time, he realized how ridiculous it was for him not even to have met him.

"Joshua, I'm embarrassed that I haven't made any attempt to get acquainted with you, but I am very happy that we finally got a chance to meet. My name is Stanford Crist. My friends call me J.C." Joshua smiled at the coincidence and shook the priest's hand.

"The bishops must think a lot of you to have issued their joint pastoral letter encouraging everyone's support of what you are doing. I know, I for one was a bit surprised at first over what I thought was their haste, but I have come to see that perhaps they may have a point. I finally decided to lend my own support, limited as it may be."

"In promoting worthwhile causes the contribution of each one is important," Joshua replied. "In these troubled times it is essential that everyone play his part. It lends solidarity to the undertaking and shows to radicals there is nowhere they can turn for support or even sympathy. God does not bless violence, nor is the maiming of innocent people condoned by God. Those who commit these evils will have to answer one day for their wanton treatment of God's children. They have completely ignored the Lord's counsels concerning injustice and have committed crimes that cry to God for vengeance."

The two men were taken back by the sharpness of Joshua's words. The rector blushed, thinking that Joshua was aware of his attitude of noninvolvement.

The men chatted briefly for a few more minutes about lighter topics. Father Crist invited Joshua to his house for dinner at his convenience. The men then parted, Joshua and Russ continuing on their way to the manse.

It was quiet at the manse. Russ's wife was not at home. The two men pored over the newspapers, noting the reactions of various editors to the pastoral letter and the tone of the news articles about Joshua's work with the children.

"Hey, Joshua, look at this little article!" Russ said excitedly as he showed the piece to his friend.

Joshua read it carefully. "Confidential Sources Reveal Radicals Consider Moves to Counter Children's Campaign." The article, hidden among advertisements on a back page, went on to spell out details of secret meetings that radicals on both sides were having in various parts of the country to offset the effects of the children's involvement in that very serious political issue.

This latest turn of events has put a crimp in the whole thrust of the issue and has taken the momentum away from the terrorists and placed the focus of activity clearly with the children. The scheme is considered by the radicals to be insidious and the greatest threat yet to their cause. Though they are stymied as to how to respond, they know that a response is imperative and at their meetings will be discussing the options.

Joshua said nothing.

"Well, what do you think, Joshua?" Russ asked, curious as to Joshua's reaction.

"It is natural for them to feel the way they do. They have to do something, because this makes them look ridiculous, and fanatics can't stand ridicule. There is, however, nothing they can do to stop this movement. It is God's will." Russ was impressed with Joshua's calmness and assurance.

After combing the papers for other items, Russ brewed a pot of tea and served it with some light pastry while they continued their conversation. Joshua did not stay long. He had to be down at the square to meet with the children. The two men finished their refreshments and Joshua left.

The children were waiting, more excited than ever on this day. Any of the parents who had reservations about Joshua changed their attitudes after reading the bishops' pastoral letter or hearing their pastors talk about it in church that Sunday. Many of the children were holding clippings from the papers for Joshua to read. When he came into the square the children, holding out their clippings, rushed to him and almost knocked him over. He took one of them, read it fast, and commented on it to the children. Since the children wanted him to have them, he took them and put them all together on the stone wall. He told them he would read them later in the day.

Practically all the children in the village were with Joshua now, even Acmet, who talked about Joshua to everyone. He was mesmerized by him, reporting to his family every detail of what Joshua said and did when he met with the children each day. Occasionally his family would come to the square and listen to Joshua speak. When they went home Anwar would get out his New Testament and read the Gospels carefully, comparing the things Joshua said with the things Jesus had said in the Gospels. He noted the striking similarity, not just in the words, but in the mannerisms and mentality of both. Even the name, Joshua, to a Semite, was striking in its coincidence.

The children, even the little ones, were now caught up in the importance of what Joshua was trying to accomplish in their lives. From listening to their parents speaking at home, and from sermons in the churches this past Sunday, they could sense that they were key players in a real-life drama, a drama that was affecting the whole country. They now not only loved Joshua deeply but felt a new pride in being part of his important work.

The entertainment part of the gatherings was becoming more polished. Knowing that they would be performing for the group each day, the musicians practiced for hours so they could really do a good job. It showed in the quality of their playing. Joe's friend showed marked progress. The guitar players had invited others to learn from them and they formed little ensembles, so they could play together and sound more professional. In each group there was a mixture of Catholic and Protestant children. Joshua still did his trumpet act each day, and each day showed only slight improvement. The children were beginning to think he played poorly intentionally so as not to upstage the children who worked so hard to play well. Joshua promised he would surprise them someday. That day, however, was not forthcoming.

Joshua had noticed a nice turn of events lately. When the group used to break up Catholic children would usually pair off with other Catholic children, and Protestant children would do the same. Now, when Joshua finished with the children, small groups of Catholic and Protestant children would go off together. It wasn't contrived, but spontaneous, showing that the friendships developing were beginning to take hold and show signs of becoming more permanent. Joshua smiled in happy satisfaction.

On this particular day Tim McGirr's little boy, Christopher, came with Peter and Acmet. He was all eyes, overcome with all the activity the other children had become accustomed to. He was enjoying the event and did not have to be very involved in order to be content. He wormed his way up to the front of the group so he could be near Joshua. Joshua spotted him and went out of his way to pay attention to him. Chris felt proud that he would single him out in that big crowd.

At the end of the session Peter and Acmet and Chris stayed to talk to Joshua. Joshua sat against the wall and listened. Peter was the one who always did the talking. Their three families were all having a party together and would like Joshua to come. The McGirrs had become friends with the Muslims only recently, when they heard about Acmet and how the family had grown so close to Joshua. Joshua asked him when they were having the party. It would be on the next Saturday night. He told them he would like very much to go. The three children ran off, delighted, as Joshua started out across the meadow toward the sea.

28

THERE WERE TIMES when the unseen activity surrounding Joshua was so intense that he felt a need to be alone, to digest all that was taking place, to prepare himself for what he knew was unfolding. Never had anyone so quiet and unassuming affected the lives of so many so deeply, by his mere presence, as did Joshua. It was almost as if he affected change in people's lives just by willing it, because on the surface of his simple life, it would be unimaginable that such ordinary things like talking to little children could have such profound and far-reaching repercussions. Perhaps that is the way it is with pure goodness. It is so rare that when it appears it reaches to the depths of good people's hearts and brings to life the goodness they have been unable to express. It also unleashes forces of evil that will always be threatened by the presence of goodness and feel an inexorable need to destroy it. It was the hidden conflict of these forces that Joshua sensed and had to deal with, thus his need to be alone.

The sea was rough when Joshua arrived at the coast. He walked along the rocks. The wind blew the salty spray against him. His long hair blew carelessly in the wind. His tall, slim, strong physique cut fine lines against the warm blue sky. He walked against the wind. It felt good after the trek across the hot meadow.

After a while the wind died down. Joshua walked out along the cliff close to the sea. Two large rectangular rocks, one lying partially on top of the other, formed a perfect seat. Joshua sat down, rested his elbow on his knee, and sucked a straw he had picked in the fields. The sea was growing calm. White-capped waves moved in measured cadence across the surface of the sea until they mysteriously disappeared as they neared the shore. Joshua watched. His thoughts wandered far away, his eyes looking out into the sea but seeing things far beyond in another world, the world from which he drew his strength, his Father's world. His prayer was quiet, deep, wordless. His gentle, peaceful features gave no hint of the hidden world that coursed through his mind.

Joshua stayed in that position for almost an hour, then stretched, yawned, and stood up. Two men fishing in a small boat waved up to him. They were coming to shore. As they landed on a sandy beach not far from where Joshua was walking, they called him and invited him to eat with them. It was late in the afternoon. The men had had a good day and were delighted to share their catch. Joshua picked some debris from around the shore, enough to make a good fire to roast the fish. With the fire going, the men sat down in the sand and introduced themselves.

"I'm George Cinney," one man said. "I came along for the ride because my friend always gets lost." George was a stocky, muscular man of about fifty-five, with taut features, weather-beaten from many years on the windblown sea. He was quiet but had a salty sense of humor.

"And I'm Ervin Farmer, 'Boots' for short." Boots was of medium height, sturdily built, with a round, ruddy face and wearing horn-rimmed glasses. He had a wary look in his eyes that easily broke into a winsome smile once he relaxed.

"My name's Joshua," Joshua said simply. They all shook hands.

"What are you doing out this way?" George asked Joshua.

"Just taking a walk to get some time to think," Joshua replied.

"Where are you from?" Ervin asked.

"The village," he answered.

"There's been a lot of talk about the village lately. You wouldn't be the one they're all fussin' about, would you?" Ervin inquired.

"Just might be," Joshua acknowledged.

"Read about you in the papers. You got a lot of spunk, son, if I must say. Wish you luck in what you're trying to do. It's been a long-drawn-out battle here for years. It's not going to end easy."

Joshua just listened without commenting.

The fire was getting hot. Ervin took a good-sized fish from the catch hanging off the back of the boat, brought it over to a flat rock, cut it open, and filleted it. It was a good fish, almost sixteen inches long, meaty and tender. Taking a little grate from a box, Ervin rested it on two rows of stones neatly placed on either side of the fire, then placed the two halves of the fish on the grate and waited for them to roast.

George busied himself with the other things they needed for the meal—a big loaf of homemade bread, which he took from the picnic box, paper plates, three bottles of beer, and some clean cloths for napkins.

The aroma of roasting fish and salt air whet the appetites of the three men and made the meal even more delectable. The men ate heartily, chatting, laughing, enjoying their picnic at the seashore. They were friendly men from a village miles away. Their boat had drifted down shore when the wind had risen. They had a good time making the best of it, and their generous catch of fish would cheer their ride back home.

When they had finished the men packed their gear, said good-bye to Joshua, and shoved off. Joshua started up the rocks on his way back to the village.

29

JOSHUA HAD HARDLY reached the village square when the sky turned black and ominous. A severe storm was imminent. Joshua picked up his pace and walked in the direction of Downers Road. Father Donnelly had invited him to stay at the parish house on occasions like this. No sooner had he reached the house when all the heavens broke loose. The rain came in torrents. Joshua thought of the men who were on their way back home from fishing. They lived up the coast. It was over an hour and a half ago since they had left. They should have made it home in plenty of time. At worst they were close to home, which was a fishing village, and there would be motorboats in the vicinity that could come to their aid.

Marie answered the door, surprised to see Joshua. Her face lighted up. "Hurry inside," she said, "before you get drenched. Your timing was perfect. One minute later and you would have been soaked."

Joshua went inside. Marie took him into the living room and called the pastor, who came down immediately.

"What a pleasant surprise!" the priest said.

"I decided to take you up on your offer," Joshua said. "That sure is some storm, and it doesn't look like it's going to let up anytime soon."

"No, it doesn't. Well, I can't say I'm unhappy it's raining, if that is what it takes to get you to come stay here at the house. Where are you coming from? You're all wet with perspiration."

"I've just walked back across the meadow from the sea. I took a walk out there to collect my thoughts and rest awhile. As I was about to leave two men who had been fishing pulled their boat to shore and offered to share their meal with me. It was kind of them. When we finished I walked back here. It was an enjoyable walk and a perfect day for it."

It was close to six o'clock. The priest was just finishing his office work for the day and would be able to spend time with his friend. He had hoped he would come and spend more time than he usually did.

"Joshua, you know where your room is," Elmer told his guest matter-of-factly. "There are towels and whatever else you need in the closet. Make yourself at home. If you want to take a little rest, you're welcome to it. I'll be in my room if you'd like to come in and chat awhile before supper. We won't be eating until eight o'clock. By then you should have worked up a good appetite. I'm going to have a little drink around seven if you want to wait until then. It's up to you. I want you to feel completely at home."

"I'll just wash up," Joshua responded, "and rest for a few minutes. Then I'll be in better shape to socialize."

"Whatever. I'll be in my room."

Joshua went upstairs and the priest went into the kitchen to tell Marie they'd be having a guest for supper.

The priest's bedroom was not too artfully decorated. An old brass bed that his mother had left him dominated the room. An antique dresser and a highboy, both of these pieces inherited, filled what little space there was left. A simple crucifix hung on the wall behind the bed. On the wall across from the bed was a picture of the mother of Jesus. In the corner between two windows was an armchair.

The room adjacent was the pastor's private sitting room. It was nicely furnished and a source of pride to the old priest, who loved to entertain his fellow priests and throw card parties for them at least once or twice a month. The men enjoyed coming to his place because it was so relaxing, the food so plentiful and well prepared, and the furniture so comfortable.

After washing and resting for a short while, Joshua went to the pastor's room. Elmer offered him a seat and the two men plunged into immediate conversation. There were a lot of things to talk about. Before they got serious, however, Joshua asked the priest about his family, where he was from, where his family lived now, and if he got many occasions to visit with them. The priest went into minute detail in relating many memories of his parents, how they instilled in him at a tender age a deep love of Jesus and his mother, which had been the source of his strength all his life. He had three brothers and two sisters. Two brothers were dead, the other living in another part of the country. Both sisters had moved to another country with their husbands. They came back to visit occasionally, but not often enough. He really missed them and hoped, someday, to surprise them with a visit.

Then it was the priest's turn.

"Joshua, you really are a mystery. For some reason I don't expect you will tell me where you are from, and for reasons I'm beginning to suspect, just like the Muslim man, Anwar. He was in to see me again the other day and asked if I had a book about Jesus' teachings. He wanted to compare them to the things he hears you teaching. He's quite taken up with you, as I'm sure you're aware."

The priest got lost in his own meandering and, to Joshua's comfort, forgot all the things he had intended to ask him. As it was seven o'clock, it was time for Elmer to release the creature and have their cocktail hour. He opened his well-stocked liquor cabinet and asked Joshua, "Well, young man, what will be your pleasure? I pride myself on having almost anything my guests enjoy."

"I think I'd like a sherry, dry, if you have it," Joshua responded.

"I sure do," the priest said with pride, taking out an unopened bottle of imported dry sherry.

After serving his guest the priest poured his own, a single shot of local whiskey with a little water. "I can't drink much anymore. I used to be able to have a couple before supper, but now if I take one, it is all I can handle. So I enjoy the one just as much as I used to enjoy two.

"Joshua, I have come to appreciate more and more what you have been doing in our village the past couple of months. It isn't just your working with the children. That's only part of it. It's the way you are, your personality, your ideas. You seem to be the very essence of the Gospels themselves, which I have been trying, in my own simple way these many years, to instill in the lives of the people. You are the epitome of everything I have tried to teach, and to meet this ideal so perfectly in you has touched my life almost miraculously. Your very presence has made my own faith come to life. For the first time I am not afraid to die and meet God. I feel in some strange way I have already met him, and I wasn't afraid. It brought me peace and not terror."

Joshua was touched by what the old priest said. For this good priest to have spent his whole life working for God and then to be frightened at the prospect of meeting Him didn't make sense.

"Elmer," Joshua said, "that is what people have done to religion. It is not what God wanted. Religious teachers so often miss the point of religion and dishonor God by teaching a God who is merciless and calculating and vindictive, which fills people with unbearable guilt that makes them afraid of God. That is not what God wanted. Jesus tried so hard to help people understand that God loves them as they are. He knows they are human. He made them that way and it is human to be weak and imperfect. God did not intend to make humans little gods. He created each individual to do a little job, to make their little contribution to help others and perfect his creation, and gave to each just what he or she needs to do that job. The rest of the personality is imperfect, but that's all right. The person will grow to become, in God's good time, what He wants that person to become. As long as people love God and care for others, they need never be afraid of meeting God."

"I understand now. I have met you and I am not afraid," the old priest said, not fully realizing the meaning of what he had said. Joshua smiled.

"That is the way the Church has taught religion for centuries, and it is hard to break from that mold," Elmer went on to say.

"Yes, that is unfortunate. The Church has assumed the role of Christ's stand-in, but has picked only the aspects of Christ's life that appealed to their need for power. The Church is the extension of Jesus' life in the world, but if it is to be effective, it must model itself on the way Jesus lived. Nobody was afraid of Jesus when he came to earth. They followed him everywhere because they knew he understood their anguish and their pain and looked past their failings. Sinners felt comforted in the presence of Jesus, and their lives changed in time. People don't feel comfortable with the Church because it has chosen to model itself on a legalistic, judgmental Christ molded in its own image. That frightens the sheep and drives them away and makes them afraid of God. The Church was intended to be the medium of Jesus' message, but instead it has become the message, and the living Jesus got lost."

It was time for supper. Marie called upstairs, telling the pastor everything was ready if they would like to come down.

The meal was simple. The old priest's diet had become more austere as he got older. Joshua wasn't too hungry, but enjoyed sharing a meal with his friends. When they began the meal, after they had said grace, Joshua took a piece of homemade bread, said a little prayer, broke the bread, and gave a piece to Elmer and one to Marie.

During supper the rain had stopped. Joshua and Elmer went outside to take a walk to the end of the village. The clean, newly washed atmosphere gave rise to a golden sunset. The two men stood on the roadside in silence, drinking in the changing colors of the sky reflecting across the meadow. The day had been a busy one. It ended well.

30

SATURDAY CAME FAST. Joshua spent the morning helping Charlie in the blacksmith shop. A few orders needed by farmers could not wait until Monday. Joshua was glad to help and had lunch with Charlie afterward.

That afternoon Joshua stayed out in the meadow carving little things out of wood, which he did often when there were lulls in his rather relaxed routine.

When early evening came Tim and Stella McGirr met Joshua at a crossroad in the meadow on their way to the Arab family's home for dinner so the three went together.

"You sure have changed things in the short time you've been here," Tim exclaimed to Joshua. "Who'd ever have dreamed I'd be going to an Arab's house for dinner? It was Father Donnelly who introduced me to them and we've become good friends."

"They are good people," Joshua remarked. "I think you will make good friends."

"Did you really heal their little boy of blindness?" Stella asked Joshua.

"It is faith that heals," Joshua answered. "The boy's family has deep faith, and it was rewarded by God."

"You know, Joshua," Tim said as they walked along the path, "people are beginning to develop strange ideas about you, like who you really are. I'm even beginning to wonder."

"People are so used to seeing meanness and pettiness that when a person acts normal and kind and caring, it is a shock and people begin to wonder. Why should what I do cause wonderment? Could anything be as simple as what I do?"

Tim wasn't talking about Joshua's life-style. He was asking about the extraordinary things that Joshua could do with such simplicity. Tim was too shrewd to shadowbox with Joshua. He'd wait until they were relaxed at dinner, then he'd press his point, when the others could come to his aid.

When they arrived Acmet answered the door. This time he was a perfect little gentleman, welcoming everyone and escorting them into the house, then announcing the guests' arrival to his family. Anwar and Miriam were most gracious in expressing their pleasure and immediately took them into the family room, where the rest of the family was relaxing. Everyone stood up and welcomed the guests when they came in. Then they all sat down to relax and enjoy refreshments before dinner.

A few minutes later Acmet's friend Peter came with his father and mother. They were all introduced and joined in the party. Peter's father, Jerry, was a comedian. He and Tim had been friends for years, and when the two got together they could entertain all night long. Peter's mother, Ann, was quiet, and said very little.

The dining room was splendid, with the vast table in the center of the room capable of seating almost twenty people. Costly accoutrements, some practical, some ornamental, filled the room. A large oil painting of a Middle East mountain village scene hung on the wall on the long side of the room. On the table, covered with beautiful linen, were expensive place settings, including sterling silverware. Two large platters of roast lamb rested on either side of the center of the table. Next to them were large dishes heaped high with saffron rice, boiled then fried so the children could have the chunks of crisp brown pieces scraped from the bottom of the pan.

Miriam seated each one strategically for the purpose of better conversation during the meal. Joshua she seated on her husband's right, with herself across from him. The others were scattered between members of her family.

Anwar offered to say a prayer before the meal. Everyone bowed his head. "Father in heaven, we have so much to be grateful for this evening. We have our health and our son whole again. We have the blessing of friends, new friends, who have given us so much love and companionship during this difficult time in our lives. You have given us Joshua, who has been a blessing to all of us, and who, by the beauty and simplicity of his life, has reflected into our lives the true presence of God and brought a new dimension to our own vision of life. We ask you to bless us all and to bless this food, which we gladly share in your honor. Finally, we ask you to bless this land with your peace," to which everyone responded with a hearty "Amen."

The children immediately asked if they could have the crispy rice from the bottom of the pan. Miriam said they would have to wait until the adults were served. The children knew that already, but it was their way of alerting the grown-ups that the crispy chunks were already spoken for so none of them would dare take those pieces, even if they were offered.

When everyone was served and the wine poured, the conversation picked up in earnest and before long the whole room was buzzing like a beehive. The room was large enough, and the table vast enough, for several conversations to be carried on at the same time. Anwar told Joshua about his talks with Father Donnelly and that he shared the priest's views about his work with the children, and also of his awareness of Joshua's striking resemblance to the man in the Gospels. Joshua just kept eating, saying nothing.

"Joshua," Anwar said, "you are not even listening."

"Yes, I am," Joshua returned. "I have heard everything you have said. I am at a loss as to what to say to you."

"How did you ever arrive at such a close similarity to Jesus? The coincidence is remarkable."

At that point all the other conversations stopped. Everyone turned toward Joshua.

"I wasn't aware," Joshua replied playfully, unwilling to let himself become the center of the conversation or to allow it to move along those lines.

"Come, my friend," Anwar persisted, "you are so much like him, it can't be by coincidence. It is either the result of years of imitation, which would certainly make you aware, or if you are unaware, then there is only one other possibility."

The man was sharp, and just as persistent to push his point as Joshua was to avoid it.

Joshua smiled, and then, to end the questioning, remarked simply, "We are all blessed to have the presence of God here in our midst this evening. May it be a true source of blessing to all of us, and may our lives be different from this day onward."

It was ambiguous, but it was not ambiguous to Anwar. It was the only way Joshua could respond. Anwar had the assurance he needed, and his life from that moment would radically change. He and his wife looked at each other knowingly and thoughtfully. It took awhile for the conversations to pick up after that. Everyone was digesting what Joshua had just said, each understanding it in his own way.

Tim asked Anwar what life was like back in his own country.

"Not much different from here. People don't vary much. At home you have the very rich and the very poor. If you are industrious, you can better your lot. Our family used to live in tents not too many years ago. My grandfather, Elie, was shrewd and started a small business, importing at first little items, then slowly developing his business into a big operation. With the troubles in the country it's hard to know who are your friends and who are your enemies. There is a lot of hatred in our country, just like here. The message of Jesus to forgive endlessly has never been a part of our culture. By the way, Joshua, not to change the subject, but maybe you can explain that to me. I am having a very difficult time with Jesus' injunction to forgive. Peter thought he was being generous in offering to forgive seven times, and Jesus said, 'No, not seven times, but seventy times seven times.' Don't you think that's a bit much?"

Joshua sat back, looked around at everyone, and very seriously said, "What Jesus was trying to do was not to issue an impossible commandment, but to offer the key to true inner peace. He came to bring peace to troubled souls and to show people how to live in a way that would not only lead them to God, but help them find a meaning to life that made sense. He was deeply concerned about people's inability to find peace. His secret, which he lived himself, was in forgiveness, a forgiveness so complete that it never even allowed itself to take offense. And that is the key to peace, personal peace and peace among peoples—do not allow yourself to take offense. Always try to understand why people say and do the things they do, the inner anguish that gives rise to those things, and then it is hard to take offense. Indeed, you can even pity them. You may be wary, so you can protect yourself, but you can still reach out and be a brother and sister to those people, never despairing of trying to heal their troubled, tortured souls. Jesus himself lived that way. He never took offense, and his last words were 'Father, forgive them, they know not what they have done.' "

"How beautiful!" Anwar said. "That does make sense—and for the first time."

The rest of the evening was much more lighthearted, with Jerry and Tim providing the entertainment, keeping everyone laughing until almost midnight. Even Acmet's grandmother enjoyed them, though she couldn't understand everything they said.

The party ending, everyone left. Anwar insisted Joshua again stay for the night. He accepted. Although it was a social evening, lives were deeply affected that night, and no one there would ever be the same.

31

FAR FROM THE village, in another part of the country, six men were meeting in a dingy, poorly lighted, smoke-filled tavern. One of the men was Father Jack Brown, dressed in jeans and a turtleneck pullover. The others were leaders in their subversive organization. The purpose of the meeting was to discuss the bishops' pastoral letter and what should be their organization's response to the bizarre turn of events caused by the meddlesome stranger in the village where all this activity had originated.

The group admitted that the move to organize the children was shrewd and could be severely damaging to their organization's plans, but not necessarily fatal if they countered with the right moves.

"We certainly can't go after the bishops," one remarked. No one disagreed.

"We definitely can't touch the children," another commented.

"However," a man with coarse, cynical features suggested, "we might do something that would frighten the kids, intimidate them, and then cause their parents to forbid any further involvement."

That suggestion seemed to have potential and was worth pursuing. They discussed various possibilities, one even recommending kidnapping some of the children. That was rejected because it would turn their own people against them. Finally, after much discussion, it was decided to observe a total hands-off policy when it came to the children. It could only backfire and arouse not just local but international repercussions.

Inevitably, the focus came around to Joshua. Who the hell is he anyway? He is, after all, only a stranger. No one has any ties to him, no personal loyalties, no attachment. The priest suggested they center their action against him. He was the one who started the whole thing. If they did something to him, there might be a stir for a while, but having no roots here, he would soon be forgotten. The children, having been deprived of their leader, would disband and forget the whole undertaking.

The suggestion appealed to everyone, but what action they should take was an issue not too easily resolved. One suggested roughing up Joshua but decided against that as being unproductive and something that would arouse the sympathy of the people. Besides, the media would use it to maximum advantage, making him even more of a hero. And he would still be around.

After a long lull in the conversation, one man calmly and slowly suggested, "Why not just eliminate him?"

"You mean really kill him?" another questioned, shocked.

"Yes, why not?" the man said coldly.

The priest, taken aback by the turn the conversation had taken, tried to make the point that it might not be the practical thing to do. "After all," he said, "the fellow isn't really evil and he means well."

The others jumped in immediately. "Hell, what do you mean, he means well? He's been out to destroy everything we've broken our backs over all our lives trying to accomplish," one man objected, to which the others agreed. The priest made a few other feeble objections but was overruled each time.

By the end of the evening they had all come to an agreement that Joshua had to be eliminated. As strongly opposed as he was to this solution, the priest finally gave his consent. The only question remaining was how this would be carried out.

"The fellow meets with the kids in the village square almost every day, though his schedule does vary," a man who lived in the village commented. "He almost always ends with them at noon, again in the square. So what we do should be done at that time." They all agreed to that—the action would take place in the village square at noon.

The next question to be settled was just what should be done. At that point a thin, wiry man said bluntly, "I think we should have one of our men from the village do the job. Two of them are excellent marksmen and would be better able to plan the details. No one would suspect them, seeing them around. If whoever does it uses a silencer, no one will realize what has happened. This will make for an easy getaway in the midst of the confusion."

"Good idea!" another man said.

The group had no problem with that suggestion. It was accepted. They knew just the one for it. That was also decided without delay. Whoever did it would have to make his own arrangements as to the details. They would contact him the next morning.

With all that business agreed upon, the group broke up in the early hours of the morning, not much after sunrise.

In another part of the country, on the following night, a similar meeting took place in the comfortable surroundings of a parish house. It was the house of the Reverend John V. Maislin. He had gathered the leaders of his pious hatemongers to determine what had to be done to end the farce of the busybody stranger in the village and stanch the flow of goodwill that was poisoning the atmosphere all across the country.

The scenario was much the same as the meeting the previous night, the suggestions similar, the objections parallel, and the conclusions identical. After all, there were few options available to counter an epidemic of goodness. Joshua had to be eliminated. The practical way was to assign a member living in the village to do the job. By eliminating him the cause of the problem would be eradicated, and the children would be panicked into abandoning the movement. Like the other group, they had to ascertain the daily movements of Joshua and determine when he would be in the village square. That was the only constant in his daily schedule, his appearance in the square when he finished talking with the children in the fields.

32

JOSHUA'S WORK WENT on uninterrupted each day, as if nothing was happening. His relaxed, serene manner showed no sign of anxiety or troubling worries. It wasn't that he was unaware. He was only too aware of just what was being planned, but such was his trust in his Father's closeness to him, he knew all would work the way his Father willed. So he faced each day unflinchingly.

After working with the children in the morning, he would help Charlie in the afternoon at the blacksmith shop. Charlie was almost caught up with his work, so he wouldn't be needing Joshua much longer. There was only one small change in Joshua's daily routine. He was staying longer in the fields with the children and not ending every day in the square. Only once or twice a week would he finish their gatherings in the square before sending them home for lunch. In the beginning Joe used to bring him lunch, but now the kids took turns, deciding among themselves who would bring his lunch the following day.

On the surface nothing really changed. Little things were happening that meant nothing to the children but whose significance Joshua understood only too well. A couple of children at different times would ask Joshua what he would be doing each day, and on following days, and if they would be ending their meetings in the square at noon. Joshua looked at the children with sadness in his eyes, troubled that calloused men would use innocent children as pawns in their dirty schemes, unconcerned that what they were setting up the children to do would scar them with guilt for life. Joshua was careful not to give the children any information, more for their own good than for his protection. The men would have to get their information elsewhere.

"Now run along, little ones," Joshua would say to them each time they came to question him, "and don't trouble yourselves with such things. Just be happy and be free and enjoy your play."

During the week a most unusual event began to take shape. A group of older kids organized an all-village soccer game, and rather than draw up teams from each side of town, they decided to divide the town down the middle so that each team would be half Protestant and half Catholic. When they told Joshua what they had done, and that the game was scheduled for the next week on Saturday, Joshua was overjoyed and proud over what these young people had done. They were also making a determined effort to encourage the whole town to come to the game. The game would be held on the field near the school. The kids personally went to the politicians and pressured them into coming, and although they all felt threatened politically if they attended, they ended up promising to come. The children even invited the police and the local contingent of soldiers that patrolled the area. No one could believe what was happening.

Each day the teams practiced diligently, each determined to win this unique and historic game. Naturally, Joshua was given a special invitation. He enjoyed seeing the young people planning and playing together and having a good time. It made him realize his movement now was irreversible. Once the children found each other in this way and with this depth of intimacy, and were fired, as they were, by an ideal they all cherished, Joshua knew it would not end and would survive well into the children's adult lives. He felt a deep sense of peace and satisfaction that a goal dreamed about for so many years for such basically good people was finally on the verge of fulfillment. All it needed was a catalyst to generate a chain reaction so that what was happening in the village would spread all across the country.

Joshua's meetings with the children were held each day as usual. In the afternoon they watched the soccer teams practice.

All the kids were caught up in the excitement. Even the parents picked up the children's enthusiasm.

By the time Saturday came the whole town was fired up and couldn't wait for the game to start. The field was packed. Even old folks and crippled people came. The clergy met on the way to the field and, in a heartwarming expression of solidarity and genuine friendship, stayed together during the game. Truly a miracle had been wrought, and, more than that, another miracle when the politicians showed up. They really had little choice. Everyone else in town was there. Their absence would have branded them. Townsfolk who had been at odds for years came walking out to the field together. Their children had become close friends, and the parents rather sheepishly found themselves socializing.

By two o'clock, starting time, the field was filled to capacity. The two teams, each named after its side of town, the Westside Tigers and the Eastside Rangers, came running onto the field to the loud applause of everyone, the little kids screaming, calling their friends' names.

The whistle blew. The Tigers brought the ball deep into Rangers' territory. One of the Rangers hit the ball with his head, driving it back across the center line into an open space. Another Ranger contacted and by good teamwork brought the ball almost to the goal, when a Tiger ran up behind him and broke the advance. The ball went back and forth furiously, cheered on by the excitement of the crowd as they shouted their support of their team.

It was almost fifteen minutes into the game when a Tiger kicked the ball from the right and drove it clear past the goalie. The Tiger fans went wild. It was a Protestant boy who made the goal. His teammates were beside themselves, the Catholic kids hugging him, which was touching for all the grown-ups to witness. Joshua clapped too. The people near him were wondering which side he was on. He applauded both teams when they did well.

By halftime the score was Tigers three, Rangers two. It was a hot day, the sun beating down fiercely. The kids kept wiping their faces, trying desperately to keep dry.

The second half was even more exciting than the first half. The Rangers tied the game shortly after the half began and held the tie for a good part of the period, until a teammate fumbled the ball only a few feet from his own goal when a fast-moving Tiger slammed it into the goal.

Soon after the game had started five strangers had appeared at the game, mingling with the crowd. They did not, however, come unnoticed. Elmer spotted them walking down from the road and immediately recognized them. He poked Russ and pointed them out. Russ turned and looked, but didn't have the slightest idea as to their identity or the significance of their presence.

"Don't you know who they are?" Elmer asked, surprised.

"No," Russ answered, "I don't have the slightest idea."

"They are officers in the radical Catholic underground, though I doubt if anyone around here would know them. I had a chance meeting with them years ago at a social affair and they were pointed out to me. I'll never forget them, though I doubt if they would remember me."

Word of the plot to assassinate Joshua had leaked out from the splinter groups that had planned it to the officials of the main underground organization, who were furious when they heard of it, furious that such a small outfit would dare do something with such shocking reverberations. These men had come down to the village on an intelligence mission to see firsthand just what was transpiring in the village and report back to the council.

People standing near them, knowing they were strangers, strained their ears to pick up pieces of their conversation. One of those townsfolk was Tim McGirr, and what he picked up was shocking. He couldn't wait until the game was over so he could tell his pastor what he had heard.

In the meantime, the game was moving fast. Two more goals were made by both sides by the middle of the second half, and the score, four minutes before the final whistle, was five to four. Every now and then Elmer would look furtively over at the strangers. Oddly enough, they had become interested in the game and found themselves taking sides, at times applauding a good play. Elmer noticed Tim standing in the crowd near them and was hoping he was discreetly eavesdropping.

With two minutes left, the Rangers scored another goal, tying the game. The roar of the small crowd was gigantic, louder than seemed possible for its size, the people's excitement spurring on the players to final heroic efforts to win the game for their team.

In the last thirty seconds the Rangers' youngest player, a boy by the name of Jay, who had not played all during the game, and who was put in at the last minute out of sympathy, was standing near the goal. A hard-driven ball struck him in the chest and landed practically at his feet. Half not realizing what he was doing, he kicked it. The ball went flying past the goalie and hit the post at an angle, then shot into the goal. The Rangers won. The whole crowd went wild. Teammates hugged Jay. He would be the hero for a long time. People ran out onto the field, mobbing their favorite players.

After a few minutes both teams worked their way together, forming a wedge, and moved through the crowd to where Joshua was standing by himself, watching all the fun the people were having. The kids had decided beforehand to do what they were doing no matter who won the game. They surrounded Joshua, picking him up and carrying him on their shoulders across the field. All the villagers clapped and shouted their joy and gratitude to this simple, unassuming stranger who had made this whole miracle possible.

The five strangers left the field shaken and confused, profoundly affected by what they had just experienced. Never had anyone dreamed that what was taking place would even be possible, and yet they were seeing it with their own incredulous eyes. And they could also see the imminent possibility for the fulfillment of their cherished dreams of peace in their land.

The game over, the people dispersed, going to their homes to celebrate. Some of the men went to the tavern to celebrate before going home. Tim was one of them. The clergy met at Elmer's. Since he was the oldest clergyman in town, he had invited them all to his place for a party. They picked up Joshua as they were walking across the field and insisted he come with them to celebrate. He good-naturedly went along with them, happy to celebrate the joyous occasion.

The players on both teams went to their homes to wash up and prepare for parties with their families and teammates. It was a totally triumphant day for the children. It made no difference who won the game. Their real triumph was a much loftier goal. They were now keenly conscious of their power to bring about radical change. Their lives would never again be the same. Joshua's work was done, indeed, well done, thorough to the last detail, showing the exquisite finesse of God's personal touch.

Elmer collared Tim on his way to the tavern and took him aside. "Tim," Elmer started by saying, "I noticed those fellows near you during the game. Did you overhear anything?"

"Did I overhear anything?" Tim responded, startled, sensing the priest knew something he didn't. He was now curious himself and decided to bargain with the foxy old pastor.

"Who are they, anyway?" Tim asked.

"Tell me what you heard first, then I'll tell you who they are," Elmer retorted, a little impatient at being trapped by his own move.

"Well, they didn't have much to say at first," Tim said, "but after a while they began to open up. One of the fellows made the remark 'You know, I can't believe what I'm seeing here today. I have to admit, I'm impressed. If this spreads, it could change the face of the whole country.' One of the others agreed. A third man added, 'Yes, and for the better. The bloody devils who are plotting to destroy it must be really sick. This stranger has accomplished single-handedly what we have been unable to bring about with all our efforts. Why would anyone want to destroy what is being done here? What I see here I've dreamed of all my life.'

"Only one fellow didn't seem to agree completely with the others," Tim continued, "but, you have to remember, what I'm saying is not exactly what they said. They were careful. I'm piecing together bits of the conversation, trying to give it to you in a way that makes sense. This other fellow had his doubts as to whether something like this could last, given the many years of hatred that have transpired. But even he admitted he was impressed. I couldn't help but wonder what they were talking about when they mentioned someone trying to destroy it all. What do you think they were talking about, Father?"

"I don't know," Elmer answered. "I'd give anything to find out."

"Father, you said you'd tell me who they were. Who were they, anyway?" Tim asked, his curiosity piqued.

"Tim," the priest confided to him, "they are officers in the organization. I suspect they must have gotten wind of something afoot and were sent to see things here for themselves and report back so the council could plan a response. The fellows you saw have a reputation in the group for being moderate and level-headed. They were sent for intelligence purposes, I'm sure. But I would like to know what's up."

"I can't imagine any rational person finding fault with what's taking place here," Tim said.

The priest agreed, but then commented, "There are some people who are so filled with hate that they can't tolerate goodness. It takes away their excuse to hate, and of necessity they have to see evil in innocence. . . ."

The priest prudently ended his thoughts at that point, not thinking it wise to say any more. But he was thinking about that radical priest who had his followers in the town, as well as others who had a reputation for being borderline cases.

"All we can do is pray," the priest ended by saying. The two men then parted, Tim going to the tavern, the priest catching up with the other clergy, who were waiting for him.

The whole village celebrated that night, not the victory of the Rangers, but the victory that filled everyone's heart with a peace and joy that could come only from God. Even the Muslim family, who had been at the game with everyone else, celebrated, inviting Jerry and Ann and Pete to their house for a party. Seeing the miracle that had taken place almost overnight, Anwar had decided to take his family back to their country in the Middle East and try to do the same thing in their family's village that Joshua had been able to accomplish in this village. He would discuss the matter with Joshua and seek his advice and his prayers.

33

THE FIVE STRANGERS at the soccer game reported back that very evening to their council. The consensus of the five was that Joshua was a simple, but obviously a very extraordinary, person to have managed to weld that whole village together into a totally transformed people. The men described the eerie sense of a presence at the game that was beyond anything human, but couldn't put their finger on what was responsible for it. They themselves felt the peace that the people in the village had come to know, and they could understand why everyone was so completely loyal to the man they called Joshua.

"Maybe the bishops are right for once," one of the men said. "Something has indeed happened to that village, and if it does spread, it can create the atmosphere we need to really effect the kind of change that will make sense and benefit everyone."

Another jumped in immediately. "But we have to find out what those bloody fools are plotting or everything will be just talk. They could destroy whatever good might come from this. Without realizing it, this fellow Joshua has set up everything we need to accomplish our own goals if we play it cool and plot our own strategy well."

The chairman asked if anyone had any more details on the plot. No one could offer anything. Their contacts were vague.

It was decided before the meeting ended to assign discreet individuals to ferret out exact details of the plot to assassinate Joshua and to use whatever means necessary to prevent it from happening. Whether it could be prevented depended upon the ability of the agents to pump enough information from their sources to be able to piece together the time, date, and the individuals involved. What the group did not know was that there were two distinct plots planned by two different groups. It would be almost two days later before they obtained that information. They needed to develop all new contacts to track down intelligence concerning the second group. With the uncanny and efficient network these men had, it was entirely possible for them to accomplish the task, given enough time. The problem was, they didn't have much time.

Both groups involved in the plots were well along in the planning of final details. They had both pinpointed the dates on which Joshua would be in the village square at noontime—only two days of the next week, Wednesday and Friday. They both separately decided that Wednesday would be too soon to get everything ready but that day could be used as a dress rehearsal, at least to determine Joshua's position in the square, how long he stayed at the spot before dismissing the children, the best vantage points, and the easiest and quickest escape routes with the least chance of detection.

That Sunday morning Joshua went to the Presbyterian church for the service. He could and did go to Elmer's church frequently because he had Mass every morning. The other churches had services only on Sunday, so he was limited as to when he could attend.

Russ was surprised to spot him in the back of the church. His sermon that day was on "Life as a Soccer Game." Joshua smiled a number of times at the clever way he took things that happened at the game the day before and applied them to the people's everyday life, and showed how beautiful life could be if everyone realized how much we all needed one another. He said that it is not how much we have done for ourselves that God will one day ask us, or the amount that we have accumulated for ourselves, but what we have done to better our brothers' lot and how much of the gifts God has given to us we have been willing to share with our hurting brothers and sisters that will concern God. "We have all made terrible mistakes by being afraid of our

Catholic brothers and sisters and cutting them out of our social and political and economic life, making it all but impossible for them to live. Hopefully, the beautiful stranger in our midst has forever changed that by giving us a vision that can translate into a whole new life for all of us, a life that can make us all feel good inside, and make our prayers to our Father meaningful and sincere, and bring down upon us the rich blessing of our common Father."

Joshua was clearly pleased, and told Russ afterward when they were having breakfast together in the manse. It was at breakfast that Russ asked Joshua if he was aware of anything untoward taking place. Joshua said simply that he knew some people weren't too happy about what his work was accomplishing and would try to stop it, but that could not happen because it was his Father's will that this work should not fail. Joshua's definitiveness in answering this way preempted any further discussion on the matter. He seemed to take every eventuality into consideration and discounted what seemed to others ominous and threatening.

Joshua spent the rest of Sunday with Russ and his wife. They had a relaxed, restful afternoon. For the evening they invited friends over for dinner and had a pleasant time just indulging in light talk and sharing stories about each of their lives. Joshua shared his insights into the personalities of some of the children who followed him faithfully.

At the end of the evening Russ invited Joshua to stay for the night, which he did.

Heavy clouds covered the sky all day Tuesday, but had passed by Wednesday. It turned out to be a beautiful day as Joshua met with the children in the meadow. They ended the morning by gathering in the square just before noon. Joe brought his trumpet and asked Joshua if he would really try to play well. He tried hard to teach him and felt bad that he hadn't succeeded. Joshua promised to take his playing seriously and took the trumpet from Joe. Putting it to his lips, he warmed up for a while and then started to play. What he played and the way he played shocked everyone. The kids sat there on the pavement in utter disbelief at the beautiful music that came forth from the instrument. He didn't play long, not more than two or three minutes, but the way he played brought tears to Joe's eyes and the eyes of many of the children as well. Joe's tears turned to a broad smile as he swelled with pride at having taught Joshua how to play the trumpet so beautifully.

When Joshua finished his face was flushed from the strenuous exercise. The kids clapped and applauded. Joshua smiled, thanked Joe for being such a good and patient teacher, and gave him back his trumpet. The kids all felt good that Joshua could play so well. They used to feel sorry for him.

"Joshua," Joe said, "I never dreamed you could play so well. I knew you were not playing seriously the other times, but this was beautiful."

Joshua just smiled.

It was a little after twelve when the group disbanded, going home for lunch. Joshua spent the afternoon at the coast, just thinking, praying silently, and gathering together his courage and strength for the crucial time ahead. He had supper that evening at the McGirrs and spent the night there, to everyone's great pleasure, especially Christopher's. The family was in rare good spirits. Even Joshua was lighthearted, playing cards with the kids and having a beer with Tim. When the children went to bed the adults sat on the front porch talking until late in the evening, when they all retired.

34

THURSDAY MORNING CAME. A mist from the sea hung over the fields. Chris was the first up, or thought he was. He wanted to spend time alone with his friend before the others crowded him out, like they usually did. To Chris's surprise Joshua was already up, sitting on the front porch watching the animals across the yard. A cock crowed, breaking the morning silence. Other animals were slowly coming to life.

Chris stood there, saying nothing.

"Good morning, Christopher," Joshua said, motioning for him to come and sit down next to him on the porch.

"See those fields, little one?" Joshua said. "One day they will be filled with trees, good trees to support your families and bring prosperity to your people. Ask your daddy to plant little trees with you. It will be a job just for you and him. When you are big they will be fully grown."

Chris said nothing, just listened and looked out across the fields, imagining a forest filling the meadow, something he had never seen. He liked the idea.

Joshua knew how hard it was for the boy to get his father's attention, and this would give him a chance to spend hours with his father all by himself as they planted the trees. Christopher looked forward to the project with excitement.

After a few minutes the house was buzzing with activity, with kids getting dressed and running about doing their chores in the barn, feeding the chickens and the other animals.

Stella was busy getting breakfast ready, the daily feast the whole family heartily enjoyed.

After breakfast Joshua prayed a blessing over everyone, hugged them all, then he and Tim left, walking across the fields together, Tim on his way to work, Joshua about his daily work.

"Joshua," Tim said as they walked along, "Chris told me about the tree project you have planned for the two of us. Although I can't help but feel I'm being conned, I like the idea. Why didn't someone do it years ago? It could have brought much needed income to our family. Chris will have fun working with me. He's forever trying to take me aside to do things with him, but I rarely have the time. I suppose I could come right home from work and spend the time with him before supper. It would be good for both of us to work on a project like that. I may not live to benefit from it, but the kids will reap the benefits long after I'm gone, and that's what counts. Yes, I think that's probably a good idea. Thanks."

"Your people have given much to humanity," Joshua said to Tim, "even to those who have tried so hard to destroy them and their loyalty to God. But nothing passes my Father unnoticed. It is now time for you to rebuild yourselves as a people. You have the resources. Use them."

"You do a lot of thinking, don't you?" Tim said to Joshua, then added, "The men at the plant have been talking about you more and more. At first they thought you were an odd fellow, but lately they've come around to appreciate what you have done for us all. Our children are much happier than they've ever been. To see all the kids in the village playing together, and even the grown-ups beginning to socialize, is truly a remarkable accomplishment. It is even affecting the atmosphere at work. Two Catholics were given promotions at the plant. That's been unheard of, and I mean big promotions, and the Protestants congratulated them, another first. It's all because of you, Joshua. I hope you realize that."

Joshua said nothing, just kept walking, a tear trickling down his cheek.

At the square the two men parted, Tim going to his job and Joshua down the street to Elmer's church. Men and women passing him along the way greeted him warmly.

The priest was in his garden as usual, praying his morning prayers.

"Just in time again, my friend," the priest said to Joshua as he approached. "I'm just saying the last two psalms. Want to join me?"

"Yes, I would," Joshua replied.

"I'm sure you know them by heart," Elmer said playfully.

Joshua smiled. The priest intoned the psalm "The Lord is my shepherd, there is nothing I shall want. He makes me to lie down in green pastures."

Joshua picked up the second verse of the Twenty-third Psalm: "He leads me beside still waters, and refreshes my soul.

He leads me in right paths for his name's sake.

Though I should walk in the valley of the shadow of death, I will fear no evil, for you are with me.

Your rod and your staff, they give me comfort.

. . . I will soon again dwell in the house of the Lord forever."

The psalm was apropos to the turn of events in Joshua's life, and the words fit perfectly.

The two men finished the prayers and went into the church for the breaking of bread, as the early Christians used to call the Mass.

Joshua sat in the back of the church, as he usually did, absorbed in his thoughts, resting in his Father's presence.

After Mass the two men went into the rectory for breakfast. Marie beamed when she saw Joshua walking in the door.

"Joshua," Elmer said as soon as they sat down, "you look calm and peaceful as usual. I assume everything is going well?"

Joshua knew the old priest was prying, but he was also concerned.

"Yes, everything is right on schedule according to plan," Joshua said simply.

The priest couldn't understand Joshua's calmness. He himself was anxious by nature and Joshua's serenity in the face of brewing storms totally baffled him.

"I have heard some things that worry me, and I can't help but be afraid for you. There were some strangers in town at the soccer game last Saturday. I know who they are and I can't help but be troubled as to their intentions. They have been involved in underground activities for years, and I'm sure their coming here has something to do with you. Tim McGirr was standing near them and overheard them discussing a plot involving the village."

"Father, don't worry yourself. Nothing will happen to the children. My Father's will is being accomplished exactly according to his plans. I know you are concerned. When events come to pass do not judge by appearances. Things are not what they appear. It is not the same as before. This is to teach the world a lesson in how far their hatred has taken them. Do not be troubled."

Joshua said all this to allay the fears of the old priest who had come to love him so deeply. There was no way, however, for him to understand then what Joshua was talking about, but it would be clear when it did come to pass.

Joshua stayed at the rectory a little longer than usual and was there when Anwar came to visit the priest. He was surprised to see Joshua and glad he was there. He had wanted to tell Joshua how meeting him had changed his whole life.

"Joshua," Anwar said to him, "I can't tell you what you have done for me. My life is completely changed. I see God differently. I see people, no matter who they are, or what they believe, as God's dearly loved children. I see the life of each human being as a sacred creation of God, to be loved and respected, and never, for whatever motives, to be desecrated. And to atone for the terrible things of the past, I am going back to my own country and work with the children there, the way you have here, to teach them to build a better life for the future. It is the first time in my life that I feel I have a purpose."

Joshua listened, and when Anwar finished he said very solemnly, "Anwar, the troubles there are not the same as here. They are much more complex. You must remember that and consider it when you plan your work. You must be very careful and pray each day. Let God guide your every step. You cannot do that work alone. You do not have the understanding. No human does, so listen to the gentle voice of God each step along the way. With your new faith and your new direction, your friends will be wary. Respect where each one is coming from.

Do not try to change their beliefs. That's God's business. Just be a light in the darkness and a warm fire in a cold night. People will see your goodness and will come to see God's light shining through you. There will be those who hate goodness and will try to harm you, but do not be afraid. You and your family will be protected from above. No evil will touch you. Go there in peace."

Anwar was deeply touched by the prophetic insights of his gentle friend and reassured by his words. They were obviously from God. Although he was determined to go back home, he was burdened with fears about his family and their safety. Joshua's words had a profound effect on him, as if God himself were talking to him. He felt a strange calmness when Joshua had finished.

Father Donnelly was also impressed with what Joshua had said to Anwar, but said nothing.

Joshua excused himself, saying the children would be waiting for him. They all embraced and said good-bye. Joshua left. Anwar stayed to talk to the priest.

In the meantime, the men assigned by the underground council were frantically trying to track down leads in a last-minute attempt to frustrate the plots to assassinate Joshua. The only detail they could pin down was the date on which the plot would be carried out. The nature of the plot and the exact time were still unknown. They continued pursuing leads all day long. It wasn't until late Thursday morning that they found out the two plots were to be executed at the exact same time. What that time was they still had no idea.

While all this feverish activity was taking place, Joshua met with the children as if nothing was happening. There was no noticeable change in his manner. He joked with the children and was perhaps a little more affectionate and playful than on other days. Joe's Protestant friend played the trumpet as usual and did an excellent performance for a boy who had been taking lessons for such a short time. The children sang along with the guitar players, expressing the joy and exuberance that Joshua had brought into their lives. It was an unusually happy day, although it must have had a certain gloom for Joshua, knowing with his uncanny knowledge the dark events swirling all around him.

Pete and Acmet sat in the front of the group, right near Joshua. During a break Pete asked Joshua, "What is the matter?"

"Why do you think something is the matter, Peter?" Joshua asked him.

"Because I feel you are sad, and it makes me feel sad," the little boy replied.

"Don't you worry, Peter. God always takes care of us. We all have our work to do, and we must face each day bravely, knowing that God is always by our side. Even out of things that hurt he brings good. Never be afraid when you are doing God's work."

"I hear people talking," Peter said. The boy had an unbelievable ability to pick up information from people's casual, loose remarks and put things together. "I hear people talking and I can tell something is going to happen. Isn't it?"

"Whatever happens is part of God's plan, so we shouldn't worry. Much good will come from it. Hurt is only temporary. The good that comes from it is endless. Memories of good things and those who love us will always be precious. No one can take those from us. Always treasure those memories and share with others the beautiful things you have experienced, like you did with Acmet. Because you cared, God healed him. And remember, I will always love you and be with you."

"Joshua," Peter said, attempting to find out just what was wrong, "if something happens, will you leave us? And if you leave us, where will you go?"

"If something happens, little one, I will return to my Father," Joshua answered.

"Can I come with you?" the boy persisted.

"Not now," Joshua said, "but when your work is done you will come, so always be strong and be loyal to God's wishes."

"I will miss you if you go," Peter said with tears in his eyes.

"I will always be near you. When you talk to me I will be by your side and even in your heart," Joshua said, trying to console his little friend.

Acmet listened intently to the whole conversation and was himself feeling sad at what he had heard. Joshua looked at the two of them, took them in his arms and held them close, then told them to go and play and think happy thoughts.

After the break the children reassembled for a little story before being dismissed for the day. When they were all seated on the grass, Joshua began his story.

"A good and kind king had a vast kingdom. The people of the kingdom fought among themselves over who was the most favored of his subjects. In their jealousy they grew to hate and despise one another and even made laws to destroy each other. They went so far as to set up separate parts of the kingdom, forbidding each other to cross the others' boundaries. They taught their children also to hate one another. The king was badly distressed over all the hatred that poisoned his kingdom and destroyed the peace and joy he had so carefully planned for his subjects. The subjects had no idea how angry and sad the king was over all of them and the way they treated one another. The bitterness lasted for centuries, and not knowing what else to do, the king sent his son to visit the kingdom and heal the divisions.

"When the son came he was sad to see how terrible was the anger and meanness the people had for one another. The adults showed no willingness to heal the wounds, so the son decided to work among the children, especially when he saw how sad and lonely they were. He would bring them the peace their parents rejected. The son met with the children every day and taught them how to have fun together and care for one another.

"When evil men saw the children were beginning to love one another, they became angry because it was destroying hatred throughout the land and undermining their power and evil schemes, which could thrive only where there is hatred and suspicion. In their fury and spite over the son's goodness, they plotted to destroy him and the work he was doing. They tried but they could not harm him, because it was beyond their ability to touch him.

"When the children saw the terrible things those evil men tried to do to the son whom they had come to love, they were determined to carry on the son's work and make sure his mission to bring peace to the kingdom would succeed. They carried his message far beyond the boundaries hatred had built and they reached children everywhere.

"As time passed the children were able to do what for centuries the grown-ups were unable to accomplish—to bring peace to the kingdom, because they had learned that to have peace there must first be love and caring for one another."

The children sat through the story spellbound. Joshua's calm, soothing voice added to the magic of his storytelling. When he finished they all clapped, though they had not fully realized the meaning of his story.

When the story ended Joshua dismissed the children and walked up Stonecastle Road to the hill overlooking the fields and just sat there for the longest time, absorbing the quiet and beauty of the landscape. He had finished his work with the blacksmith and wasn't needed there anymore, so he had the rest of the afternoon to himself, which he spent walking through both parts of town. He met the Wesleyan minister, a venerable old man, as he was taking his daily walk. They had a long talk as they walked through the village together. Joshua had been in his church on one or two occasions and had spoken with him briefly, but not having many people in his congregation, they were not very involved in the events that embroiled others.

After walking through the Protestant area Joshua wandered through the Catholic part of town, greeting people along the way, stopping to talk to old folks on their way to church for a visit or workingmen on their way home from work. Some of the children were playing along the way. He stopped to chat with them and moved on.

It was almost six o'clock when he went down to the Almost Home Tavern for supper. When he sat down some of the men came around the table to talk with him. They all knew him by now and enjoyed being in his company. They talked mostly about the soccer game and praised Joshua for the job he had done with the kids. When the waiter came with his supper the men were polite enough to let him eat in peace. After finishing he spent a few minutes with them, talking to them at the bar and encouraging them to continue the beautiful work the children had started. The men felt things would be different from now on, since everyone had finally found each other. Joshua left and went out into the meadow, lighted a fire because it was chilly, and spent a good part of the night absorbed in prayer.

35

FRIDAY MORNING CAME with a severe thunderstorm that passed through the meadow near the coast but bypassed the village. It lasted only fifteen or twenty minutes, then turned into a glorious, sunny day, with a blue sky as light as silk and the air as fresh as the first day of spring.

Joshua spent the morning walking through the meadow thinking, feeling, and praying to his Father. He knew the day would go well, but he was concerned for the children. It would be a difficult day for them and he wanted assurances that his Father would keep them in his care. He had grown fond of these children who had been so open, so accepting, and so willing to commit their young lives to his mission.

It was late in the morning when all the children had assembled in the meadow. The routine was the same as on other mornings, and Joshua was the same as always. The children took turns providing the entertainment for the group.

At the same time, in the nearby city, members of the underground council were meeting to discuss the latest intelligence concerning the plot. They had found, after working all night, that the two separate plots were to be executed in the village itself. They still could not pinpoint the times, though the men knew they had to take place some time on this day. It was crucial to find out immediately if they were going to be able to stop them. The chairman decided to dispatch a contingent to the village to survey the area and make whatever on-the-spot decisions were necessary to abort the plots. The others were to continue to check out leads.

After the children assembled in the meadow, Joshua met them on a little knoll that provided a view of the whole area. Everyone seemed in a lighthearted mood. It was such a beautiful day. How could they feel otherwise? A little before noon the children took their break. Joshua told them to reassemble in the square. After a few minutes of meeting with their friends and socializing, Joshua started toward the village. The children followed.

Arriving at the square first, Joshua sat on the wall and waited for the children to reassemble. Once they had all gathered and were seated on the pavement, Joshua stood up and began speaking to them in unusually tender language.

"Little ones, you are truly blessed by God. You have been chosen to do a special work for him. The grown-ups have grown weary and tired of the heavy burden of solving life's problems. A new way has to begin. You have been chosen by God to start on that way. You can see what your love and your caring has already accomplished in the village. You have been able to transform the whole community. Where before there was hatred and suspicion and fear, now there is love and friendship and trust. The secret is to love and never to take offense. Always try to understand the tortured anguish that drives people to do the mean things they do, and it will not be hard to forgive. Let your love conquer all obstacles and slowly your message will spread throughout the world. Even the shepherds are following the little sheep and have spread your message of love and peace to other parts of the country. You are especially loved by my Father and by myself as well. He has entrusted you with a love that is rare and has called you to set fire upon the earth. You must treasure that love and keep that fire alive in your hearts."

As Joshua said those words he crossed his arms on his breast, and in an instant his face became distorted with pain. Blood gushed from his hands, and he began to fall backward against the wall.

A little girl saw what happened and jumped to her feet and screamed. Another shot struck her in the head. She fell to the ground, lifeless. The marksman saw through the telescope what had happened, saw the girl fall to the ground, and was overcome with grief. It was his own daughter.

With his last bit of strength, Joshua fell to his knees, saw the girl lying there in a pool of blood, stretched out his bloody hand, and touched her. The gaping wound immediately healed. The girl opened her eyes, dazed, looked at Joshua, and smiled.

He smiled at her and fell to the ground.

The children panicked and screamed, not knowing what to do. The strangers sent to foil the plot, realizing what had happened and that they were too late, left immediately. Villagers came from all directions, rushing into the square. Women cried, looking frantically for their children. As men stood around the body of Joshua someone ran for the clergy. In no time Russ and Elmer were there, kneeling beside the body of the saintly stranger they had come to love. Elmer, who was always so controlled, burst into tears, crying, "Joshua, Joshua, our beloved friend, who was so gentle he could not harm even a broken flower! How could they do this? How could they?" The two men prayed over him, asking God "to bring him safely home far from this world of hatred and meanness. He was too good to live in our midst."

The doctor came, turned over the body, and, opening the shirt, examined Joshua. When the children saw the wounds in the heart and the wounds in the hands, one of them yelled out, "Look, it was God. It was Jesus. They killed God all over again and he was our friend. See what their hatred has done."

The children wept uncontrollably. When they saw Joshua heal the girl they all knew finally who Joshua really was, and everything he had said the past few days was now beginning to make sense, though they were too overwhelmed with grief to think about it.

The doctor asked some of the men to carry the body to the funeral director's house, but the older boys insisted on doing it, so the doctor let them. They reverently picked up the dead body of their friend and carried it across the square and down the street.

In no time reporters converged on the village, asking questions of everyone—clergy, bartenders, parents, children, Charlie the blacksmith, everyone who had anything to do with Joshua.

Loaded with information, they went back to their offices to prepare their stories for the evening news and the next editions of the paper.

Elmer and Russ went to visit the other clergy and told them what had happened and suggested they all work together on a burial service for Joshua. They all agreed to do whatever they could. Since no church was large enough for everyone to fit, they decided to have the service in the ruins of an old monastery chapel outside the village, off in the meadow. It was a beautiful old building, even though part of the roof was gone and it was not clean. When word spread where the funeral was to be held, the whole town turned out to clean up the building and ready it for the occasion.

The funeral director cleaned the body of Joshua. It was decided he should be buried in his own clothes. Marie, Father Donnelly's housekeeper, took his clothes and washed them, so they would at least look clean.

It was decided that they would have the burial the very next day. It was Saturday. So deeply had he touched their lives that the whole village mourned that night like they had never grieved before, and they had not even known this man just a few months before. None of the children slept that night. Even crying all night didn't relieve their grief and the pain they felt over the loss of their friend who had taught them to love and to forgive. They prayed that God would forgive the ones who killed him.

36

THE NEXT MORNING the whole village gathered at the funeral director's house and waited for the clergy. Having heard the news on the radio and seeing it on the television, children and adults came from faraway places for the funeral. Television crews came; reporters were everywhere.

When the clergy arrived the procession started. Teenagers acted as pallbearers, carrying the open coffin of their friend, every now and then looking down with tear-filled eyes at the body lying so peacefully in the coffin. John, the boy who played the drum on the march to the city, played muffled drumrolls through the village and across the meadow. It was mournful and heartrending as the procession meandered along the path through the meadow to the old church.

At the church the procession stopped, and the people stepped aside for the pallbearers and the clergy to pass through. Russ said the entrance prayers at the door to the church. Inside the church, the clergy together conducted a simple, dignified, but emotionally powerful service. Elmer had been asked to give the homily. It was brief but to the point, the kernel of which went as follows: "God sent into our midst a beautiful gift, a gift so precious that only innocent children were able to appreciate his value and draw him to their hearts. In the brief time he was among us the lives of our children changed forever, and not only their lives, but the lives of all of us as well. By the simple goodness of his life he taught us the beauty of values we preached but never experienced. Our village will never be the same. By showing a caring and accepting love for all of us, this simple stranger—only God knows who he really was—has taught us in a powerful way the basic truth of all religion—that we are all the children of God, belonging to the one family that he created. If we are to please him, we must begin from this day, never again to look upon our neighbors as strangers or as enemies but as one family. There can never again be divisions among us if we are to live in a way that is pleasing to God. This lesson has been burned into our hearts over the past few months by this good and gentle man. It is, I suppose, inevitable that the presence of goodness itself will never be allowed to exist in our midst except for a brief moment, until evil men, stung by the searing indictment of their own meanness, must rid themselves of a presence they cannot tolerate. It was true the first time, and it is no less true now. We do, however, have the beautiful memories of the goodness of Joshua forever branded on our minds and on our hearts, and the personal love he has shown for each one of us. There was no person who met him who did not become aware that they were totally and unconditionally loved by God, no matter what their faults or peculiarities or, yes, even their sins. We have all been blessed by God in his presence, and out of gratitude we cannot let his martyrdom pass in vain. We must carry on the message of his life until the love that he has shown us is spread far from the ruins of this decaying church into a new world that will share God's own vision of humanity as one family, all trying to understand their Father in their own limited and feeble way. And in ending all we can say is . . . 'Good-bye, dear friend. You have touched our lives forever.' "

By the time the priest finished there wasn't a dry eye in the church. Indeed, everyone's heart was breaking with grief. The words expressed in the homily were exactly what everyone was feeling, and it showed in the outpouring of tears, even those of strong men who had never cried before.

The Eucharist that morning was the most meaningful of their whole lives. He had been with them each day, without their realizing who he really was, and now all of them, regardless of denomination, were uniquely one in this sublime Presence that expressed so beautifully their new oneness in life.

All during the service the guitarists, the singers, the boy Joe taught to play the trumpet provided the music, playing things they had played so many times before. At one point they all played the pipes Joshua had given them the day of the march. At the end Joe and his friend played taps. While Joe played from inside the church the other boy was stationed out in the field and played the echo of each phrase, until the last note trailed off in the distance. It was heartrending and people cried uncontrollably.

After the service the clergy led the people in silent procession past the coffin for one last view of the body to pay their respects. As each one passed, looking sadly into the crude wooden box, the reaction was the same, from the clergy to the children. Their faces became ashen, their look one of shock and then joy. The coffin was empty.

Outside the church the children gathered and started talking. "You see," one of them said, "it *was* Jesus. He even rose from the dead again."

Another added, "Yes, and he was our friend. He came to teach us a message and show us how to love, and they killed him."

"But what he taught us won't die," Peter said.

"That's true, and we have to make sure his message is carried out," one of the girls mentioned.

"What do you think we should do?" an older boy asked, half thinking out loud.

"I got an idea," said a boy whose father had been a close friend of the radical priest.

"What's that?" another asked.

"There are some who resisted right to this day and didn't even come to the church. Some are Catholics, some are Protestants. Why don't we get together and exchange parents?"

"How are we going to do that?" a girl asked.

"Just sit on each other's doorsteps until they take us in," answered the boy who made the suggestion.

Some didn't think it was a good idea, but the kids whose parents were resistant, and may have even been part of the plot, wanted to do something heroic to atone for what their parents had done. They thought it was a great idea and decided to do it.

"Suppose they don't take us in?" one girl questioned.

"We'll just sit there until they do, even if we have to starve. They will eventually be shamed in front of the rest of the town if they don't take us in. Then, when they change their attitudes, we'll go back home."

The kids didn't realize it, but reporters were standing behind them all during the exchange, jotting down everything the kids said. It would be in every newspaper in the country before the day was out, creating tremendous pressure on the recalcitrant parents. As it turned out the marksman, whose bullet struck his own daughter and whom Joshua healed, was so conscience stricken after seeing Joshua touch and heal her, he became the kids' best ally, telling all his cronies secretly what had happened. With his help, the kids' strategy would work.

When the little girl had gone home on that Friday afternoon, her father was not there. During the commotion in the square he slipped out to the meadow and buried the rifle deep in the ground. He sat in the field and cried like a baby, overwhelmed by the terrible evil he had done.

His eyes were bloodshot and his face had a tortured look when he arrived at his house and walked into the kitchen. The family, together with a houseful of neighbors, was all astir, excitedly questioning the girl about what happened in the square. She didn't remember very much. Her father was silent and passed unnoticed in the confusion. He looked at his daughter, closely scrutinizing the side of her head where the bullet struck. There was not the slightest trace of a wound. He couldn't even let her know what had happened. He simply stood around, dumb and outwardly emotionless. He was usually considered odd anyway, so no one thought his behavior any stranger than usual.

At Joshua's funeral the girl's father had sat with his whole family. At times during the service he cried uncontrollably, which made his family wonder; previously, he had shown nothing but anger and suspicion over the work the stranger carried on with the children.

After the funeral, he went off with his cronies and told them all that had happened. They could see how broken up he was over what he had done and were afraid he might betray them all in his grief. He told them they had nothing to fear, but still managed to shake their consciences. Reluctantly, they went along when he insisted that they cooperate with the children's plan to exchange parents. They were more afraid of what he might do if they didn't go along with them.

Children all across the country, fired up by the news stories and the television coverage, were more determined than ever to carry on the message of this simple man whose coming was so unobtrusive and whose presence was so brief, but whose extraordinary love and caring changed the lives of all who accepted him.

John Hourihan's ecumenical school became more popular than ever, forcing its board to initiate double class sessions to accommodate the increased enrollment.

The two bishops who authored the pastoral letter gave sermons on Joshua that Sunday. They held a joint service in the Anglican cathedral honoring Joshua and his work, and encouraged people not to fear drawing closer to one another in a unity that could only be pleasing to God.

But most remarkable of all was that almost overnight the children throughout the land came to dominate the political life of the country, and they did it in the spirit and gentle ways of Joshua. Politicians and activists were shamed into cooperating with the programs and suggestions advocated by the young people, whose influence in society was universal and profound.

A new day had dawned, a new spirit spread throughout the land, and it all seemed to have happened because of the simple, unassuming goodness of one gentle stranger who knew only how to love.

Joshua
in the Holy Land

*This book is dedicated to those rare individuals
who have been able to rise above self-interest and
personal ambition to bring the presence of God and His peace
into our troubled world.*

Acknowledgments

I would like to express my sincere gratitude to Peter Ginsburg, my agent and good friend, for his continual support and valuable assistance. I would like also to express my appreciation to the staff at Macmillan: Barry Lippman, the president; Bill Rosen, the publisher who personally did a most sensitive job in editing this difficult manuscript; Bonnie Ammer, Judy Litchfield, Richard Dojni, Norm Adell, Pat Eisemann, Patrick Sadowski, Susan Richman, Marie Marino, and Melissa Thau for their professional expertise and friendship, which I shall always treasure. The artists who designed the jacket deserve special praise for their thought-provoking portrayal of the essence of the story. The copy editors and proofreaders have my heartfelt thanks for their painstaking work. And not to be forgotten are my dear friend Elie Zambaka and his family, whose deep commitment to their faith has been a constant inspiration, and also my dear friend Monsignor Tom Hartmann, for his insights and constant support.

1

A BLAZING SUN BEAT upon the desert sands, painting strange images across an overheated horizon. A lonely figure walked with determined step along a trackless path toward his destination. His loose brown pullover shirt, his tan pants, his sandals seemed out of place in the desert. Only his desert head-gear seemed to fit the scene. He was humming a light tune as he walked briskly along, looking here and there as if for something to distract him from the monotony of the barren wasteland.

Off to the right a young lamb staggered along the top of a dune, confused and obviously lost. The man walked toward the frightened animal, bent down, cuddled its head between his hands, and rubbed its ears gently. The animal didn't resist, merely looked up at him as if pleading. Picking up the lamb, he placed it on his shoulders, and continued on his way.

Hills of sand stretched endlessly on every side. How could anyone find his way in such a place, with no reference points? But the wanderer pushed on, knowing precisely where his steps were leading as if he had lived here all his life. Over one more sand dune, then another, and finally in the distance, an oasis: tall palm trees shooting majestically from the sand, tents spread like giant mushrooms around a pool of cool water that glistened like an emerald in the setting sun.

An old man sat pensively on an Oriental rug before a fire, with legs crossed, smoking a water pipe. His face was thin and taut, his fingers gnarled and tough like leather. The stranger approached him, and bowing, greeted him in Arabic, "Salaam aleichem, my friend. My name is Joshua. Wandering through the desert I found this lamb walking aimlessly. I thought it might belong to your family, so I am leaving it with you."

With that, Joshua took the lamb from his shoulders and placed it on the ground. The lamb spotted a little girl about nine years old and immediately ran over to her. The girl noticed it and screamed in delight.

The old man turned toward Joshua, eyed him critically, looking deeply into his eyes, and introduced himself. "My name is Ibrahim Saud. These are my family," he said as he proudly motioned with a sweep of his arm toward the hundred or so people milling around the camp. "I am grateful to you for bringing back my granddaughter's lamb. It is her pet and has been lost since early morning. She has been crying all day. I would be honored if you would stay and eat with us. It is getting dark, and the desert is treacherous. Sleep here for the night. It will be safer."

Children were walking timidly toward Joshua from different directions. When he noticed them, he turned and smiled. Gradually they walked over and surrounded him and the old man.

Speaking in Arabic, Joshua asked their names. The girl who owned the lamb told Joshua her name was Miriam.

"That is a beautiful name," Joshua told her. "It is my mother's name."

"Is your mother beautiful?" the girl asked as she kept stroking the lamb in her arms.

"Yes, she is very beautiful," Joshua answered.

"Where did you find my lamb?" she asked. She eyed Joshua from head to foot, noticing how different he looked.

"Not too far away, just over that hill and the next one beyond," Joshua responded.

"Was he looking for me?" she continued.

"He was looking everywhere but could not find you," Joshua reassured the girl, to her delight, then continued, "Couldn't you tell how glad he was to see you?"

"Yes, he means more to me than anything in this world," she told him. "He was my birthday present. My grandfather gave him to me."

"Isqar, your look tells me you have a thousand questions to ask me," Joshua said to a boy who kept staring at him.

"Yes," the boy replied, surprised that the stranger knew his name. "Where were you coming from, and where are you going? People don't just wander around the desert. The nearest bedouin family is miles away from here, and you aren't one of them."

"I am just passing on, stopping here and there wherever I am welcome," Joshua told the boy.

"Where are you going?" the boy went on.

"Visiting places I remember from long ago," he replied.

"From long ago?" Isqar said, surprised. "You're only a young man. How could you have been here long ago?"

Joshua laughed. "I may be older than I look."

As Joshua continued talking to the children, a wiry young man whose face was bronzed and wrinkled from constant exposure to the sun approached the old man.

"Father, that man is not one of us," he blurted out angrily. "He's a Jew. How can you show kindness to an enemy? How can you share with him our family hospitality?"

"My son," the old man said calmly, "I don't know he's our enemy, and he doesn't look very Jewish to me, though I suppose you are right. His accent is Jewish. Do you have any reasons that would convince me he is our enemy? He did return the child's lamb. He did not even ask for a favor in return. When you grow as old as I am, my son, you will see things the young cannot see. This man is not an evil man, nor is he an ordinary traveler. Allah walks in his shadow. As soon as I looked into his eyes, I saw the presence of God."

"In a Jew, Father?" the young man protested.

"Allah does not see Jew or Arab," his father answered. "We are all formed by the hand of God, fashioned in God's heart. Whoever opens his heart to His goodness, Allah blesses them with His presence. And this man is close to God. There is no evil in him. It is when we hate we drive God from our heart, and become like broken tools. Then we begin to do the work of Satan. Now, go, Khalil, my son, and leave me in peace. Your anger troubles me deeply."

Others in the family, just as curious as the children, began to encircle Joshua, asking him all kinds of questions. They were all wondering what a Jew was doing wandering the desert full of Arab bedouins.

Joshua took their questions good-naturedly, laughing at their last concern. "I walk through the world as a pilgrim. I have no hatred in my heart. I see a child of God in everyone I meet. My innocence threatens no one. Where I see hurt, I heal, if the heart is open to God's healing. Where there is no room for God, I walk on."

"You're a strange man, pilgrim," one man said. "Where are you going?"

"Passing through," Joshua replied, "wandering through places I remember from long ago, remembering the events that happened here."

"You are heading in the direction of Jerusalem. To visit Jews?" the man continued.

"To visit whomever I meet along the way. To bring God's message of peace," Joshua answered patiently.

"Do you think people will listen to your message of peace, pilgrim?"

"Yes, people want peace. Only sick people thrive on hate. Someday, however, when fathers learn to love their children more than their hatreds, then peace will come."

Khalil overheard Joshua's comment but said nothing, merely smirked cynically.

Miriam's lamb left her side and walked over to Joshua and started nibbling at his toes, which were exposed between the sandal straps. Joshua bent down and picked up the lamb. Everyone was surprised that the lamb took so easily to a stranger.

"See," Joshua said, "the lamb makes no distinction. Neither does God." The animal relaxed in Joshua's arms.

The old man had been listening to everything that transpired, and smiled as the lamb fell asleep in Joshua's arms. He called out to his wife, who came immediately.

"My husband, you called?" she asked.

"This stranger has found our child's lamb," the old man said to his wife. "Prepare a place for him at supper. He will be our

guest tonight. Prepare a bed for him as well. It is not right that
we send him out into the darkness of the desert."

The woman shot a furtive glance at Joshua, who was watching
her. She left and disappeared into one of the tents, with some of
the women following her. They were all curious about this
stranger. She could tell them nothing more than her husband
told her, and that he would be a guest for the night. The
women, too, were surprised that the sheik would welcome a
Jew.

The supper turned into a celebration. After the sun set, a cool
breeze swept through the camp. Lamps hung on poles lighted
up the oasis, creating a festive air. Simple instruments, most
handmade, were used for the music. One woman played pan-
pipes that held the whole family spellbound. Men danced spontaneously with one another. Some of the more friendly ones
even grabbed Joshua to dance with them, which he did and
enjoyed immensely. The fragrance of meat heavily laced with
garlic cooking on a huge spit filled the atmosphere. Wine flowed
freely.

When the party ended, everyone was ready for sleep. In no
time, a vast chorus of snores broke the silence of the cool desert
air. Everyone slept soundly.

In the middle of the night, the quiet was shattered by a child's
piercing scream. Lanterns and flashlights were turned on in
every tent. A little girl was crying uncontrollably, pointing to
two tiny punctures on her arm. With his flashlight one of the
men found the snake slithering out from under the tent. Running outside, he clubbed the viper with a shepherd's crook. It
was a deadly snake whose bite was almost always fatal, especially
for a child. Bedouins feared these deadly creatures more than
their worst enemy. They struck without warning in the dark of
night when no one could see them. People went to sleep at
night in fear, wondering and praying about these snakes that
wandered unseen and unheard in the darkness.

There were no doctors in the camp, and no medicines that
would help. Without hospital care the girl would surely die. But
the nearest hospital was a two-hour journey by camel. One old
four-wheel truck wouldn't be much faster, even if they could
find their way in the dark.

Awakened by the commotion, Joshua walked over to the tent where the girl was still screaming. Her arm was turning redder each minute and was extremely painful. Women wailed, and children cried in fright, afraid to walk on the ground in the dark.

As Joshua entered the tent, the girl's father was asking everyone if they had any experience with such a thing, or any medicine that might be a cure for the deadly bite. No one could help. The old man was standing next to Joshua, who seemed so calm. "Joshua, on your travels, have you learned of anything that might save our little girl?" Ibrahim asked his guest.

"Once, a very long time ago, I came across a family who carried medicine with them as they crossed the desert," Joshua said. "Has no one here any medicine?"

"No one," the old man said.

"Then trust God to heal her," Joshua said quietly.

A woman nearby laughed cynically.

"Young man, I have faith. I trust Allah, but would He heal a snakebite?" Ibrahim said to Joshua, not questioning but wondering if God would concern Himself with a matter so trivial to Him.

"Nothing in a child's life is trivial to God. He loves you and cares tenderly for you. A child's life is not a little matter. It is precious to God. If you trust Him, He will help your child," Joshua said reassuringly.

"I do trust in Allah," Ibrahim said, "and I also know that you are a holy man. I could tell the moment I met you. Can you help? Is there something you can do for our child?"

"Do you believe strongly in God?" Joshua asked.

"With all my heart," the old man answered, to which the whole family boldly assented. "We believe in Allah. Do you think He will help our child?"

"Just trust Him." Joshua walked over to the girl, who was sitting on her mother's lap, and touched her badly swollen arm, saying simply, "Little one, be well."

Immediately, the swelling went down, and the pain ceased. The two bite marks disappeared, and the girl relaxed and slowly stopped crying. Her mother hugged her frantically, almost smothering the little girl between her breasts.

The whole camp was overcome with awe. Ibrahim's initial respect for Joshua was more than vindicated. He thanked Joshua profusely and pledged his family's eternal gratitude. Joshua tried to downplay this display of his powers, attributing it to God's care and the family's faith. After a few minutes the camp was quiet again, as everyone retreated to their tents. Khalil was the only one not impressed. He was sulking in the corner of the tent, more angry now than ever that a Jew could be an instrument of God, and that his family now owed a debt to a Jew. The old man noticed the look in his son's eyes and grew sad.

The rest of the night was long, as everyone found it difficult not to imagine creeping things crawling through their tents. Joshua fell asleep immediatcly, to the amazement of everyone in his tent.

As soon as the sun rose, the camp came back to life and in no time was buzzing like a hive of agitated bees. People looked at Joshua with almost a reverence, which only his lighthearted humor was able to dispel. The little girl had no trace of the snake-bite and was busy playing with her friends. After their breakfast of various cheeses and fruits and coarse bread and strong, sweet coffee, Joshua prepared to take leave of his new family. Though they had known him but a few hours, they had already learned to love him as one of their own.

The old man kissed Joshua on both cheeks and hugged him like an old friend. "Joshua, you are welcome in my family at any time. You have saved the life of our little child. My whole family is in your eternal debt. Should you ever need us, we will give our lives for you." The sheik removed a gold coin from deep inside his robes. "Only twelve such coins have ever been minted. Twelve coins for twelve saintly men. Wherever you go among Arab people they will respect this medal," Ibrahim told Joshua. Joshua accepted the gift, and read the words inscribed on the face: "Forever our friend. May Allah protect him," and on the reverse, "Sheik Ibrahim Saud." The old man placed it around Joshua's neck and kissed him.

"May God bless you, my friend, and your whole family for your kindness to me," Joshua said gratefully. "I shall never forget you. And I know that one day our paths will cross again. Till then, may God walk in your midst."

Miriam ran over to Joshua and threw her arms around him. Joshua bent down and hugged her.

"Thank you, Joshua, for finding my lamb, and bringing him back to me. I will never forget you."

Joshua walked out of the camp into the desert. A teenage boy ran out to him. "Joshua, Joshua, I want you to have this," the boy shouted, holding out a container of water.

"This is my favorite canteen. I've had it since I was a little boy. I want you to have it. It's full of cold water. The desert is hot and you will need it."

Touched by the boy's thoughtfulness, Joshua thanked him and, caressing his face, blessed him. "God will richly reward you, Isaac, for your kindness."

Joshua walked off. The boy stood there watching him as he disappeared over the hill, surprised that he remembered his name. Everyone knew he was walking toward Jerusalem, and wondered.

2

JOSHUA PUSHED ONWARD in spite of the heat and hot,
coarse sand that washed through his bare toes with each step.
This was the way it used to be, he remembered; territory so
familiar from long ago, isolated villages little changed through
the centuries, though the original ones were now buried deep
beneath piles of sand and rubble. The people were still the same,
hardened by the harshness of life, but hospitable and kind,
mostly Arabs now, but no different from the Jews of old. People
are not much different from one another. Events and circumstances condition their behavior, and most humans respond pre-
dictably when subjected to the same treatment.

Joshua's path out of the desert took him into the Judean hills.
Passing ancient Beersheba, he wandered through the rolling
hills of Shephilah and stood above the famous site where Goliath
and the Philistines encountered Saul's army of Israelites. Standing on the hill of Socoh, Joshua surveyed the bowl-shaped Valley of Ela and could easily envision David walking boldly across
the valley to meet the Philistine giant. He could see David carefully aim his slingshot at the laughing Goliath and watch it strike
him squarely on the forehead, thus winning the day for the
Israelites. Leaving this, Joshua approached the site of ancient
Emmaus, now called El Qubeibeh by the local inhabitants, and a
Sabbath day's journey from Jerusalem along the western slope
of the Judean hills.

Walking into the village he saw a crowd of villagers gathered around a cow or a steer that had just been slaughtered or had been hit by a careless driver passing through town. The towns-folk were busy dividing up the carcass and carrying off portions in wheelbarrows. Flies were everywhere and almost completely covered every chunk of meat.

As Joshua passed by, most were too busy to notice him, but one man standing off to the side looked over as he passed and in shock commented, "Hey, there's a Jew walking down the street."

Everyone stopped, all noise ceased. Every head turned toward Joshua. The same reaction as that of the bedouins the night before: stunned disbelief that a Jew would dare walk in their midst. A few laughed, some made insulting remarks. Taking their cues from the grown-ups, the children picked up stones to throw at the intruder.

Joshua made no move to defend himself, but instead called each of the children by name, "Ismael, Iqbal, I met your friends Ahmed and Isaac in the desert last night. They told me all about you and said what good friends you have been."

The boys were shocked and ashamed and dropped their stones, and just stood there as Joshua approached.

"Why would Ahmed and Isaac talk to you, a Jew?" the boys questioned.

"I stopped in their camp last night, and their grandfather extended hospitality," Joshua answered calmly.

Iqbal noticed the canteen Joshua was carrying, and excitedly pointed it out to Ismael. "Look, he's carrying Isaac's canteen."

"How did you get that water container?" Ismael asked angrily, suspecting foul play.

"Isaac gave it to me as I was leaving the camp this morning," he replied.

By that time, some of the men had walked over to Joshua and the boys. "What are you doing here, Jew?" one of them asked bluntly.

"I am just a pilgrim passing through, visiting places I remember from long ago," Joshua answered patiently. "I bring no harm to anyone, just peace and Allah's blessing to those oppressed."

"You're a strange man, pilgrim!" a rather thoughtful man interjected, disarming his companions and shifting the conversation to a more friendly tone.

"What sites are you looking for?" the same man continued.

"There was a house here I stopped at many years ago, long before your time," Joshua replied.

"Which house?" another asked.

"A house by the side of the old highway that passed through here on the way to the sea," Joshua answered.

"There is no highway passing through here to the sea," another middle-aged man said sarcastically.

"There was at one time," Joshua said, looking straight into the man's eyes.

"And you visited someone here then, I suppose," a fat man said, laughing.

"Yes, they were relatives and good friends. The highway went right past the side of their house," Joshua replied matter-of-factly.

By then the men were beginning to think this stranger had something missing upstairs, and they all began to laugh at him.

"Don't be too quick to laugh," said the thoughtful one. "Up near the church are the remains of an old Roman highway that used to go from Jerusalem to Jaffa, on the seacoast. And in the back of the church are preserved the ruins of an old house that once stood there. The priest told me the whole story one day."

The man was one of those strange paradoxes in the Holy Land, a Christian Arab, and remembered the Bible stories his priest had told the people so many times.

"How would you know about that place?" the man said to Joshua. "Are you Christian?"

"Yes," Joshua replied simply.

"But you're a Jew!" the man answered, confused.

"Yes, and you are an Arab. Which kind of Christian is more surprising, a Jew or an Arab?"

The man laughed.

"I will show you the place, if you like," the man offered.

"I would like that," Joshua answered gratefully.

The two men walked off, with a couple of the others following close behind. Most of the others went back to their dead animal and continued dividing it among themselves.

As they approached the church, Joshua was struck by the beautiful rose garden surrounding the courtyard in front of the church. An Arab man was conscientiously tending the bushes with great pride. A priest in Franciscan robes had just emerged from the church and was walking down the stairs to the courtyard when Joshua and his companions approached.

"Salaam aleichem, Daoud," the priest said in friendly fashion.

"Salaam, Father," the man replied, and Joshua followed suit.

"What can I do for you?" the priest asked.

"This man just came into town and wanted to see a house he used to visit, a house that sat next to the highway," Daoud told the priest.

The priest was caught off guard and seemed mystified.

"My friend, Daoud, there are no houses like that around here," the priest said.

"What about the one in the church, Father?" Daoud asked.

"What about it? This man certainly couldn't have visited friends there. That house hasn't been lived in for centuries, almost since Jesus' day."

"But Father, how did he know it was here?" Daoud pushed further.

"What was the house like, young man, the one you visited?" the priest said to Joshua.

"It was a small house with tile floors," answered Joshua, going on to describe the tiles in exact detail.

"Have you ever been in the church?" the priest asked.

"No, I haven't, Father," Joshua replied.

"Amazing! You have described the house so perfectly, and yet you have never been in the church. Come, I will show you," the priest said as he guided the group into the back of the church.

There in the back left-hand corner was the house Joshua described. Joshua turned and looked at the remains of the house, deeply absorbed in his thoughts. A red cross on the wall placed there by the earliest Christians marked the site as one authentically associated with Jesus' life. The men stood there a few min-

utes watching Joshua as his eyes passed along the tile floor and
scanned the stones in the wall.

"Who was it you were visiting here, young man?" the priest
asked Joshua.

"A couple I met along the way. They were relatives," Joshua
answered.

"What were their names?" the priest persisted.

"Clopas and Simeon," Joshua said.

"Where did you get Simeon from? He is not mentioned in the
Gospel story. Have you ever read the Gospels, Joshua?" the
priest continued.

"No," Joshua replied.

"How, then, do you know the story?" the priest asked, baffled.

"It is not a story. It is a memory I treasure," Joshua answered
calmly, as the three men exited the church.

The priest did not know what to make of this odd pilgrim and
the things he said, so he concerned himself no further.

Outside the church were the ruins of the old Roman highway,
constructed of black tufa stones neatly laid next to one another.
Grass had grown between the stones and all around them. Only
sections of the road were exposed, but enough was visible to
delineate what were clearly the remains of a very ancient highway. Joshua looked at the stones and followed the road with his
eyes toward Jerusalem, remembering clearly that late-afternoon
meeting with the two disciples who were on their way to Emmaus, and his playful encounter with them as he met them at the
crossroad and hid his identity from them.

The whole story of Joshua visiting this house, and his knowledge of the existence of the highway, was not only baffling, but
totally incomprehensible to the priest, who could only surmise
that this stranger must have at some time or other visited the
church as a young boy, and confused the details of his experience in his mind over the years. Daoud, however, wondered
about Joshua and how he knew so much about the house when
he had not seen it in God knows how long.

The priest shook hands with the two men and wandered off
toward the garden where he began conversing with the gardener. Joshua and the Arab walked to the gate of the com-

pound. Daoud gave Joshua a little piece of paper with his name and address on it and said he hoped their paths would cross again. After talking a few minutes, the men parted, going their separate ways.

Joshua continued on his journey toward Jerusalem, detouring through Bethany first before approaching the city.

Bethany was still only a small village on the eastern slope of the Mount of Olives, not more than a mile and a half from Jerusalem. Joshua walked around the site of Mary and Martha's house and the tomb where Lazarus was buried. The original buildings were no longer to be seen, but the tomb was still there, the oddly constructed sepulcher with its twenty-some steps down into the burial chamber. Joshua was tired when he reached the spot and sat down near a well to rest. Again he caused a stir as the local inhabitants recognized him as a Jew. However, this time one of them noticed the gold medallion around his neck and was curious to see it. Their attitude immediately changed when they saw the sheik's name on the reverse of the medal. Then they couldn't do enough for him, even inviting him to their home for refreshment.

The lunch the people prepared for Joshua was light. The people were poor but generous in sharing their meager fare with this stranger, who was a friend of their relative. They asked Joshua how he came to know the sheik, and Joshua recounted for them the events of the previous day. The sheik had helped their family when they were in need, and now they were only too glad to show hospitality to a friend of the sheik's. Joshua promised to relay their kindness to the sheik when he saw him again, which he assured them would be soon. Joshua knew his path and the path of the sheik would cross again very soon and that the sheik's family would become a part of his life in the weeks to come.

"Where are you going from here?" one of the men asked Joshua.

"To Jerusalem."

"Do you have family there?" the man asked.

"No, I go on a mission of peace," Joshua answered.

"We have family in Jerusalem," the man continued. "Let me give you their names and their address. They are good people.

Tell them you stayed with us and also tell them what we had for lunch. They will smile and then they will open their hearts to you. They are a big family and have done well in their lives. They are closer relatives of the sheik than our family, but we are all one, and will help you in whatever way we can. Go in peace, Joshua, and may Allah bless you."

"May Allah bless your family as well. I am grateful for your kindness," Joshua said as they parted and he walked down the road toward Jerusalem.

As Joshua wended his way along the hot, dusty road, a road traveled so many times, a flood of memories swept across his mind. The road to Bethany, which crested at the Mount of Olives, opened onto the glorious panorama that was Jerusalem with its magnificent golden-domed temple and crenellated battlements and turrets and surrounding countryside. Every place Joshua looked brought back memories, of a man and twelve companions sitting on the hillside admiring the beauty of Herod's temple, a wonder of the ancient world, and a tearful prophecy that it would all come to a bitter end because its priests failed to recognize the day of Yahweh's visitation. How vivid the memory of that briefly triumphant procession on the first Palm Sunday when the vast crowd of ordinary Jewish folk sang their hosannas to the son of David, acclaiming him as their king.

At the top of the Mount of Olives a handful of shabbily dressed Arabs was hawking postcards, handmade wooden whistles, and other cheap articles. An old man was offering a camel ride to tourists. They were gentle people trying to eke out an existence from the pennies they made, while official government tour guides were shunting their tour groups away, promising better prices and more attractive objects in "official" stores.

Joshua watched, and his face turned red with anger. Taking a batch of postcards and other objects from the children, he began offering them to the tourists at the fringe of the group. "These people are poor. They need your help," he said. "They are good people trying to earn a living. Help them."

The tour guide was furious but dared not create a scene and just stood there while Joshua sold practically everything in sight except the old man's camel.

When the tourists left, the old man walked over to Joshua and, thanking him profusely for his courage, asked him his name. He was surprised a Jew would be so concerned.

"Things have changed lately," the old man said. "Time was when we could conduct our business undisturbed and modestly support our families on what little we made. Even Israeli soldiers would stop and buy things from us. But things are not the same now. Little things like this, mean and petty things, create anger and resentment. You would think they would understand. They were once treated this way themselves."

"Don't let it trouble you, my friend. This, too, will pass," Joshua said to him. "Don't let it poison the children's minds. Their untroubled souls are more important than a few shekels."

The children thanked Joshua, and he moved on down the slope, pausing for a few moments to contemplate the tomb of Zechariah the prophet, slain by priests right near the altar itself. The whole hillside was a vast cemetery where many a historic figure was buried, including Absalom, David's rebellious son, who was buried in a vault along the roadside below. The path Joshua trod was the same one the Son of God traveled on the first Palm Sunday, and the spot where long ago he wept over his beloved city, "Jerusalem, Jerusalem, you who have stoned the prophets and murdered those who were sent to you! How often I would have gathered you together as a hen gathers her chicks under her wings but you would not have me!" And then he cried, surprising the apostles who were not accustomed to such outbursts of emotion from their master.

As Joshua stood lost in memory, a young female Israeli soldier toting an automatic weapon over her shoulder tapped him on the arm. "Sir," she said, "could you tell me, what is this site? What is its historical significance?"

When Joshua turned toward her, she saw tears in his eyes.

"It is not a famous historic site, just a place of memories," he replied. "One day Jesus sat here on this rock looking across the valley at the temple and the beautiful city, and in prophetic vision, saw that it would one day be destroyed by Roman legions, exasperated by the people's constant rebellion."

"Are you familiar with these other sites, sir?" the girl asked Joshua.

"Yes, quite familiar," Joshua answered.

"Would you mind being our tour guide? We are all friends who have a few hours free and decided to visit historic sites but know nothing about them," the girl confided in him.

"That's all right. Not too many people know the details of their history. I would be glad to explain them to you. These sites here, except for the cemetery, are of more interest to Christians than to Jewish people. The path here going down the hillside is the path Jesus walked many times. One time when the crowds saw Jesus coming down the path on a donkey, the sight reminded them of the prophecy of Zechariah: 'Shout, O daughter of Jerusalem; Behold, your king comes to you. He is triumphant and victorious, lowly, and riding upon an ass, sitting upon a colt, the foal of an ass,' and they pulled olive branches off the trees and began to hail him as the son of David, and their king. As the procession approached the temple, the chief priests were furious at seeing their people acclaiming Jesus and demanded that it stop. It was on that day the religious leaders decided to put an end to it all. His popularity was too threatening."

Joshua's audience listened intently with eyes riveted on the walled city across the valley dominated by the Mosque of Omar. But in place of the mosque the group envisioned the ancient temple.

"On the left is the old cemetery where countless good people are buried," Joshua continued. "Following the words of the prophet Joel, many pious Jews insisted on being buried here because they believed it would be here that the souls of the just would be gathered on Judgment Day. That tomb up there to the left is where the prophet Zechariah is buried. He was murdered by the priests between the altar and the temple.

Walking down toward the bottom of the road, they reached a garden filled with ancient olive trees, some measuring over four feet in diameter. "Those trees," he said, "are over two thousand years old. If they could speak, they could tell a thousand stories.

"This is the spot where Jesus came with his apostles after celebrating the Passover for the last time. It was here he was betrayed by Judas and arrested by the temple police. They had to do this dark deed at night because the people would never have allowed it had they known.

"Over there to the left is the Valley of Hinnom, Ge-Hinnom, where human sacrifice was once offered to Moloch. King Josiah was so distraught when he witnessed the event, he ordered the place to be used from then on as a perpetual dump. Rubbish has been burning there for centuries, and the place has become a living reminder of the eternal fires of hell, and believed by some to be the very entrance to hell. No one dares go near the place after dark."

By the time Joshua finished his narrative, the group had reached the end of the path that opened onto the highway. A bus was waiting for the soldiers. They thanked Joshua for his tour, and some insisted on keeping in touch with him. A woman captain named Susan gave him her calling card and said if there was anything any of them could do for him, just to let her know. Some of her friends joshed her for being so forward; they could tell she liked Joshua. They all hoped they would meet him again on their next leave, so he could continue his guided tour.

Joshua said good-bye and started across the Kidron Valley toward Jerusalem. Entering the city through the Dung Gate, the ruins of Caiaphas' palace, he found that his memories became unusually sharp. The cold air that last night, the fires in the courtyard of the high priest, the servants standing around, and Peter and John there in their midst, and Peter's loud mouth, all filled his memory in vivid recollection. The trial before the high priest. The slap in the face by the high priest's servant. Incarceration for the night. All the sad memories of that historic evening warred in his mind.

Not far from Caiaphas' palace was the building where Jesus and the apostles celebrated the Last Supper, the Seder meal, and where, for the first time, the Eucharist had been offered.

Working his way through the city with its smells and noises and strange sights, he found himself at the Temple Mount. Gone was the temple, gone all the familiar sites. Arabs milled around the plaza in front of the grand mosque, one of the holiest shrines in Islam. Again, the same reaction on the part of Arabs toward Joshua on finding him in their midst, and even in the precincts of one of their most sacred shrines.

An elderly man approached Joshua and, seeing his apparent unawareness of the incongruity of his presence there, politely suggested that he move on before something happened. Joshua thanked him politely, telling him he had come to worship his Father. He asked if the man would accompany him into the mosque. Perplexed, the man obliged.

The inside of the holy place was covered with intricately designed ceramic tiles and columns surrounding the whole inner space. Hundreds of Persian rugs of every design and size covered the floor. Men were on their knees with hands folded and bowed to the floor as they prayed. Joshua knelt and assumed the same posture, then sat back on his heels and, resting his folded hands in his lap, closed his eyes and was soon lost in prayer.

The old man knelt near Joshua and occasionally looked over at him out of the corner of his eye. He was impressed by what he saw, and after a while just knelt back himself and watched Joshua, who was motionless for over half an hour.

After looking around admiringly at the beautiful interior, the two men walked outside.

"Young man," the Arab said, "I have never seen anyone pray like you before, and you are so young. You pray as if you really were talking to God, or perhaps listening."

"God is always close to us, and wants so very much to be part of our life. He always listens and speaks to us when we approach Him, though most people find it hard to believe that God cares," Joshua replied. "So many people pray just because they have to, not realizing what a joy it can be."

The two men stood outside the mosque, unaware that they had become an attraction, and the topic of conversation to passersby. After a while the two men parted. Joshua wandered through the streets, working his way down to the remains of the Western Wall, where he stood looking, reminiscing, and in deep thought, for the longest time.

Approaching a middle-aged man in a long black coat and beard, he attempted to strike up a conversation, but the man was too engrossed in his thoughts to notice and walked past Joshua. Joshua smiled, shaking his head in wonderment. Off to the left archeologists were working on a dig. Curious, Joshua walked along the edge of the roped-off site. The workers were friendly, as if thrilled to share their findings. Most of the workers were Jewish students from the United States, working on advanced degrees in archeology.

"Where are you from, stranger?" one of them asked Joshua in a friendly tone, as he kept digging and scraping.

"From nearby," was Joshua's simple reply.

The men were busy conferring with one another over objects just unearthed and chatted with Joshua only between their own conversations. Joshua was content to just watch, impressed with their patience and excitement over the apparently insignificant things they uncovered, each of which had great meaning to them.

Leaving the site, Joshua walked across to the gate through which he had previously entered, and turning right, walked down the steps to the Pool of Siloam, where once a blind man had been given back his sight. Originally incorporated within the walls of the city, it was now just a shallow stream flowing from the mouth of the tunnel. Children were playing, some swimming in the cool waters of the stream. Farther downstream were lush gardens fed by the stream, in ancient times called the Garden of the Kings.

Joshua walked toward the gardens where a dozen men were working.

"Salaam aleichem!" he said to them as he approached.

"Aleichem salaam!" a few of them returned.

"A beautiful farm you have there, one of the best I have seen," Joshua told them.

"Thank you. We are fortunate here to have the stream flowing through the land. Our crops never thirst for water," one of the men replied, as Joshua walked closer.

"My name is Jakoub," the man said as he offered his hand to Joshua.

"And mine is Joshua," he returned as he shook his hand.

"It is a hot day today, Joshua. We have been working here since morning, but it is a joy to see the vegetables grow. We are fortunate," Jakoub said, mopping the sweat from his brow.

Noticing the medallion around Joshua's neck, the Arab remarked, "That medallion you have around your neck, I have seen only a few others like it, specially made by my uncle, Sheik Ibrahim."

Joshua smiled. Everything was unfolding as planned. "Yes, this was made by your uncle. He gave it to me yesterday," Joshua told him.

"May I see it?" the gardener asked.

"Yes," Joshua said, as he removed it from his neck and held it out to Jakoub.

It was the same simply designed medal Jakoub had seen before, given by his uncle to a few extraordinary people for whom he felt profound gratitude.

"You must be a very special person, Joshua, for the sheik to honor you the way he did. And I can tell you are not one of us, so my uncle paid you a rare honor. And did you eat with the sheik's family?"

"I did, and I stopped at your cousin's home in Bethany as well. They offered me some of the pepper sauce the sheik had given them. I never tasted anything so hot," Joshua replied, and went on to describe the meal.

Jakoub laughed loudly and said, "Just like uncle. He makes that pepper sauce himself and gives jars to all the family. Most of us can't eat it, it's so hot. The sheik is like a father to all of us. I am glad you found your way to my home. As the sheik's nephew, you do me honor by visiting here. I also am in your debt for whatever kindness you showed my uncle. These are all my relatives here working with me. I will introduce them to you. We are almost finished for the day and will be leaving shortly. You must come home with me and tell me why you have come. We will help you in whatever way we can."

As the men picked up their tools and came together before starting home, Jakoub introduced them to Joshua. They, too, recognized the medallion, but discreetly waited until later to question Jakoub about it.

3

JAKOUB'S FAMILY WAS large. He and his wife Shareen had three daughters and five sons. Four of them were married: two living nearby and two living in Nazareth. The ones living nearby were home visiting. Their other children ranged from fourteen to eight. Their house was a well-built rambling home of stone and stucco, with enough space to create a comfortable atmosphere.

On entering the house, Jakoub stunned everyone as he introduced Joshua. They just were not accustomed to their father bringing a Jew into the house, and what was even more shocking, introducing him as a friend. Once Jakoub had Joshua tell them the story behind the medallion, however, everyone relaxed, and the evening proceeded happily.

It was cool that night, so the family decided to eat outside in the courtyard. The meal, while painstakingly prepared, was not fancy, but tastefully put together from meats and vegetables grown and raised on their modest farm.

Joshua relished the meal as was clear from his expressions, and congratulated Jakoub on the excellent wine he had produced from local grapes. He was hungry after the day's journey and was grateful for this family's kindness to a stranger who was not even one of their own.

After supper, which lasted until past midnight, the family scattered. Jakoub took Joshua aside, and the two of them talked far into the night.

"Joshua, you are an unusual man," Jakoub said, once they were alone. "I watched you at table tonight. You talked to each one of the family; even the little children you treated with respect. They wanted very much for you to stay over so they could spend time with you in the morning. I trust you will honor our family by sleeping here with us."

"It is I who am honored," Joshua replied. "Yes, I would like that. My work is finished for the day, so I would be only too happy to stay with you."

"Joshua, you mentioned you had a purpose in being here," Jakoub continued. "May I ask what it might be, because, out of loyalty to the sheik, I would like to place myself and my family at your service."

"It is sad seeing all the violence and hatred that infects our people's lives," Joshua started by saying. "Everyone wants peace, but no one knows where to start or whom to trust, and people are afraid not to hate, for fear of letting down their defenses. I would like to reach out and make friends with good families on both sides and, in time, bring them all together in a special closely knit community of Jewish and Arab families."

"That's a dangerous goal, Joshua. You'll be lucky not to be assassinated, like some of our noblest people who tried to reach out and make friends with Jews. Fanatics looked upon them as traitors and informers," Jakoub responded.

"I know that, but I am not afraid, my friend," Joshua responded calmly. "God's work cannot be abandoned because of fear of fanatics. Evil people can only kill the body. They cannot touch the soul, and that is what counts. Your family is a good family, Jakoub, and you could be a powerful instrument of Allah in assisting in this work. It will ultimately be successful and will bring God's peace to your people, and to all people. There are many Jewish people of goodwill who will also be willing to sacrifice themselves to bring peace to this troubled land. Working together, we will be able to forge a powerful alliance that can create the pressure needed to promote peace. Will you work with me?"

"I have no choice, Joshua. The sheik has committed his whole tribe to support you. I will be by your side, and my family will as well," Jakoub assured.

The next morning before breakfast Joshua spent time with the children, telling them stories and playing tricks that kept them spellbound. After breakfast, he thanked the family for their warm hospitality and departed.

Walking across town, he ended up in the business section of Jerusalem and stopped at Ben-Yehuda Street, a quiet oasis in the midst of all the downtown hubbub. People were sitting around tables neatly placed along the sidewalks on both sides of the street, on which no vehicles were allowed.

Joshua sat down at one of the tables and ordered coffee. Two Israeli soldiers on patrol were casually sipping coffee at the next table and unobtrusively keeping an eye on everything that happened on the street.

One of them recognized Joshua from seeing him wandering around the day before and started a conversation with him.

"You really get around, young man," the soldier mentioned casually, though gently prying for information. "It isn't every day you see a Jew wandering in the vicinity of the mosque, much less stopping in to pray. I noticed you up on the Temple Mount yesterday near the mosque. Are you a tourist on holiday?"

"Yes, I suppose you might say that. I enjoy visiting all the beautiful sites," Joshua responded in friendly fashion.

"I think some of my friends bumped into you on the hill yesterday while they were touring the sites around the old cemetery," the other soldier remarked. "They were quite impressed with your description of the sites over there."

Joshua laughed and thanked him for the compliment.

"If you are going to be around later this afternoon, you may see them. They're scheduled to patrol here on the next shift. They'll be glad to see you," the same soldier said, rising from the table with his buddy and walking off with automatic rifles slung over their shoulders.

As they left, Joshua spotted two men on the opposite side of the street discreetly turning their backs as the soldiers rose and turned in their direction. Joshua had seen them, the same two men, the day before on the Temple Mount. They reminded him of the scribes' and Pharisees' spies of old. He was to see these men and others like them more and more in the days to come. They were certainly not tourists or businessmen or even casual townsfolk strolling for exercise. They were men with a purpose, and with his uncanny sense of people, Joshua knew only too well that that purpose was dark and threatening.

Finishing his coffee, he rose and walked down the street, admiring objects in store windows all along the way. At the corner he turned up the street, then crossed over, discreetly looking back to see if he was being followed. The same two men were not far behind, appearing to be window-shopping.

Joshua slipped around the next corner and disappeared. It would serve no good purpose, he thought, to let his life become an open book to that kind of people. His mission was too important . . . and too easily misunderstood.

For a person who was supposedly a stranger in the city, Joshua knew exactly whom he wanted to see and where they lived. Continuing on his jaunt, he worked his way to the government office buildings and sat on a bench nearby. A middle-aged man left the building and approached the bench where Joshua was sitting.

"Daniel, I have something to discuss with you," Joshua said as the man was passing the bench. "You are on your way to the parking lot. Do not drive your car today. It is not safe."

The man looked at Joshua as if he were crazy.

"Why are you telling me this, and how do you know? And how do you know my name?" the man asked in rapid succession.

"You are a good man, Daniel, and your vision of peace is upsetting people who are bent on evil. You are frustrating their schemes."

"Who are you?" Daniel asked.

"My name is Joshua, and I would like to work with you on your plan for peace," Joshua answered simply.

"Thank you, but I hardly know you. I do appreciate your interest. We shall see," the man said.

"I will be around. We will find each other," Joshua said, then walked off.

Toward evening Joshua found himself back on Ben-Yehuda Street, and just as the soldiers told him earlier in the day, found his friends on duty patrolling the street. They immediately recognized him walking up the street, but being on duty were not as sociable as the day before.

"Joshua, our tour guide!" one of them exclaimed. They both greeted him warmly, chatted briefly, telling him how much they enjoyed his tour.

"If you are going to be here after we finish our duty," one of them said, "some of our friends are meeting us and we can spend some time together. We are not supposed to fraternize while we are on patrol."

"I understand. That would be nice," Joshua replied. "Yes, I will be here, and will enjoy spending time with you."

It was cool later in the evening. The street was filled with visitors sitting at tables all along the street, sipping a variety of coffees and other drinks and eating Greek pastries, creating a happy, friendly atmosphere. The two soldiers came by as they promised and soon afterward their comrades, six in all besides Joshua, including the colonel, Aaron Bessmer, a physicist, and the captain, Susan Horowitz.

They were all glad to see him. After ordering their coffee and pastries, they sat back and jumped into their conversation. Aaron began, "Joshua, I heard about your escapade this afternoon. You have been in town only a day and you have already got yourself into the thick of things. We had to send a bomb squad to Daniel Sharon's car. Do you realize you actually saved his life?"

Joshua answered simply, "Yes, I could see he was walking into trouble. I am impressed with the efficiency of your intelligence and how you put all the pieces together."

Aaron laughed. "There's not much happens here we don't know about. Our existence depends on it."

"How did you know his car was booby-trapped?" Aaron asked, half as a friendly question and half as part of an investigation.

"Some things I just know," Joshua answered. "As soon as the man walked toward me I could see the danger he was in. I knew he was a good man, so I felt I should warn him."

"Had someone told you about the bomb?" Aaron asked.

"No, I wasn't aware of anything until that moment. But when I saw the man, I knew clearly," Joshua replied.

The captain interrupted. "Aaron, I'm surprised at you. You are interrogating our friend as if he were a suspect. We are grateful, Joshua, you saved our friend's life."

"I've known of Daniel and his family for a long time," Joshua said. "What he is trying to accomplish is admirable, but he exposes himself to risk from people who do not want peace and are threatened by people working together."

"Joshua, I am amazed you are so familiar with what's happening around here," Susan said.

"Anyone who is concerned should be vitally interested in those who are making an effort to bring peace to our troubled land," Joshua replied. "With all the blessings God has showered on this land, people still have never learned to respect one another as God's children. That is the great evil."

"Well, I don't think God has anything to do with it," one of the others named Nathan interjected. "In fact, it's the religious people who cause much of the problem. I gave up religion myself precisely because of all the hypocrisy. I feel if there is a God, He has to love everybody. It is stupid to think that God would create a race of people and then pick sides and show favorites. He would want them all to get along. During the wars chaplains on both sides prayed that God would help them destroy the enemy. It doesn't make sense. Everyone expects God to be on their side while they kill one another. That has to be offensive to God if He's real."

Susan agreed. "I don't share your lack of faith. I still believe in God," she said, "but I've only come across one rabbi who made sense. He seemed to have faced all these issues honestly himself, and discussed them freely with the congregation. He used to be Orthodox but they kicked him out. I heard him in a Reform synagogue in Tel Aviv. He really renewed my faith in God."

Aaron listened intently to the other two and watched Joshua's reaction. He was just listening. "My family's been here a long time," Aaron said. "Long before all the trouble started. In fact, for years my folks were partners with an Arab family in a business venture. We are still friends, but we had to dissolve the partnership because people made it so difficult to operate. My sister

Rebecca is married to one of their family, and we all get along famously."

"My family is Orthodox," one of the others named Samuel contributed. "They feel that we are still God's chosen people, and should be totally separated from the Arabs. In fact the won't feel comfortable until all the Arabs are driven out of the land. They just don't feel good about others living in their community."

"That's really racist," Susan said sharply.

"It may be racist, but that's the way they feel," Samuel retorted. "Their families have seen a lot of persecution and injustice in their day. Besides that, they feel God gave them this land and it rightfully belongs to them."

"How is that any different from Hitler with his idea of the pure Aryan race?" Aaron added.

"Come now, Aaron, there's a big difference between the two," Samuel shot back.

"Yeah, we use God to justify it," Aaron said bitterly. "I have a problem with the religious approach to our troubles. I'm not religious, but I know our history well, and I believe God had a purpose when He called Abraham and when He led our people out of Egypt, and sent prophets to guide them. There was an objective to their being isolated in this land, so God could prepare them for something special. For many centuries God was involved with them, as our religious books record. But then it ended. The prophecies ended. Our Bible ended. It is as if what God intended was accomplished. For people who say that God's chosen purpose is still continuing among us, I fail to see it. Where is the evidence?"

"What do you think, Joshua?" Susan asked. "You've been sitting there thinking deeply during all this exchange."

"We are still God's chosen people," Joshua responded, "but times change and needs change. When a people are chosen by God, they are chosen for a reason, as Aaron indicated so beautifully. They gave to the world a whole new civilization that they can still affect if they so choose, or they can live in the ancient past and withdraw from modern life as some do. But the people will always be special to God and have a special mission. All

God's children are special for different reasons. For one people to feel that they are the only ones loved by God is not good. God loves all His children. The situation here in our land is different now from what it was in the distant past, and all the people here must learn not to cut themselves off from each other, or look upon the others as intruders, but to be responsible for one another, and to care for one another, and to get along as one nation. It is the only way life can exist in this land. Any other way is self-destructive and offensive to God."

"Well put!" a quiet fellow named Reuben chimed in.

"Joshua," Susan started, "tell us something about yourself. Where are you from? And what do you do?"

"I was born not far from here, in Bethlehem," Joshau answered casually. "I live simply. I am deeply concerned about our inability as a people to solve the problems we face, and I walk from place to place trying to encourage people to think differently."

"Like what, for example?" Aaron asked.

"Like what we were talking about before and about what you said, Aaron," Joshua replied. "It is a fact that Arabs and Jews share this land. It is not that one is good and the other evil. Each is trying to live life in peace. Many good people live here but feel threatened by the other, and not without cause. There has been much hurt and pain inflicted by both sides. Neither is innocent, so neither should stand self-righteous as if their hands are unbloodied. The meanness and pettiness has to stop, and we have to cut a new road, a new path of decency and tolerance and kindness to one another. It will not be simple, nor will it bear fruit immediately. Just as it took time for the hatred to take root and spread, so it will take time for the kindness to take root. But with patience and a willingness to forgive, in time the atmosphere will change. I go from place to place sowing the seeds of kindness and goodwill. Some listen and respond. Some resist. But with patience we will succeed."

"You seem so confident and so casual about it, Joshua," Susan commented.

"It is the only way to be," Joshua replied. "A program like this, by its very nature, is a long, tedious process. It has to be the work of a lifetime, not of a day. We may not reap the fruit tomorrow, but our children will live to enjoy the fruits of peace and goodwill. I am confident it will succeed, so I am patient."

"You talk to Arabs, too?" Reuben asked.

"Yes. How can we solve the problems if we do not talk to them?" Joshua answered.

"Aren't you afraid?" Reuben continued.

"We can't afford to be afraid when important work has to be done," Joshua rejoined. "It is God's work and God takes care of those who work with Him. We can never be afraid. It is only those who can kill the soul we should fear."

It was not just talk, it was the way Joshua lived. His Father was always real to him, so he walked through danger unafraid.

"Joshua, that medal around your neck," Susan noted. "It is beautiful. Where did you get it, if I may ask?"

Taking off the medallion, Joshua handed it to her. Turning it over, she read the back of the medallion, " 'Sheik Ibrahim Saud.' You know him?" she asked, shocked.

"I met him one night and helped his family when they were hurting," Joshua answered. "He was grateful and gave me the medallion as a gift."

"You must have done him a huge favor for him to give you this. He has committed his whole family to you. That man is like Abraham. He has family everywhere. It seems half of Jerusalem is related to him. He is one powerful friend to have, Joshua, I hope you realize that," Susan assured him, returning the medallion.

"We have been trying for years to get him to work with us, but he has always been wary of our intentions," Aaron said.

"What kind of work, Aaron?" Joshua asked.

"A group of us," Aaron replied, "have been trying discreetly to reach out to certain decent Arab families and form an alliance of like-minded people to create a healthier atmosphere in our country. Daniel Sharon is one of us. That's why they tried to kill him. There is no reason why we can't all work together and do things together, socially and in other ways. The sheik would be a great help, but for some reason he stays aloof. Yet he's a good man, a decent person."

"That is a noble goal," Joshua agreed. "As I wander around I will gather those who are interested. It is someting we can all work on together."

"How long do you think it will take you to gather your friends, Joshua?" Aaron asked.

"Give me a few days," Joshua answered.

"Good. Then we will meet here in three days, same time," Aaron said decisively, and everyone assented.

4

THE NEXT THREE days Joshua wandered around the city and its environs, meeting people, searching out those who would be open to his message of peace. On the third day he stopped at the Church of the Holy Sepulcher, the traditional site of Calvary and the Tomb. It was now under the protection of various ecclesiastical groups who were constantly feuding for control of the sacred site.

When Joshua arrived at the church, the tomb was open to view but Calvary was encased in marble walls which made the site of the Crucifixion inaccessible except for a foot-wide hole at the top of the marble staircase, through which a pilgrim could reach down and touch the ground which was Calvary.

Approaching the tomb, around which a small crowd was standing, Joshua waited in line for his turn to enter. Just as his turn came, it was time for the scheduled change of jurisdiction. The Catholic Franciscans were guarding the site during the day. Now it was being turned over to Greek Orthodox. Something occurred between the two groups that occasioned a heated discussion. They had almost reached the point of fisticuffs as Joshua was entering and accidentally bumped into him, shoving him into the barricade, where he lost his balance and fell.

Angered, Joshua arose, and looking at the group of them asked them pointedly, "Are you people Christians or hoodlums? If you can't conduct yourselves with dignity and charity, it would be better to turn the site over to heathens. They would show more respect."

Both groups were highly incensed at the stinging indictment and physically ushered Joshua out of the shrine, telling him that if he couldn't come with a better attitude, he should stay away from this sacred place. On this, at least, they could agree.

An old Franciscan friar with white beard and rustic walking stick saw what had happened and walked over to Joshua.

"I am sorry, my son," the old priest said to him. "It is a shame priests can't conduct themselves with charity. They are a disgrace and a scandal. This has been going on for centuries, and it seems it will never end."

"Religion is a game with these people," Joshua said, "and competition their liturgy. They are in love with their churches and their traditions, not God. Their rituals are hollow praise, and God would turn a deaf ear were it not for the simple faith of pious people who come here with reverence. It would be better if these buildings were never built, so people could be inspired by the uncluttered simplicity of the sites themselves."

"Sit down here, young man, and talk to me," the old priest said as he sat down on the bench near the wall. "My name is Father Ambrose Boyd. What is your name?"

"My name is Joshua," he responded.

"Don't be offended by what happened," the priest said by way of apology. "We are not all that way. Most of the priests who come here are pious men completely dedicated to these shrines. A few are feisty, and they cause all the trouble. They are an embarrassment to our community. I came here years ago in an attempt to sow seeds of peace in this troubled land. It has been a difficult road. Now I am old and see more meanness and hatred than ever."

"I have come for that same reason," Joshua said. "Gather your friends together and work with me. Together we will accomplish much."

"I have all kinds of strange friends," the priest said, "even Orthodox priests like the ones in there. They are not all political like those fellows. Some are decent men, though they stay more with their own, and don't mingle. We meet regularly and pray together, even in our Lord's own language. I have other friends

who are Arab and Jewish Christians, a quiet little group. These
are the best of all, the cream. I would like you to meet them
sometime."

"I would like to. We must all work together if there is to be
peace," Joshua told the priest.

"I am old. My work is done," the priest complained.

"Your work is not done, Father. The best is yet to come,"
Joshua reassured him.

"What can I do?" he asked Joshua.

"Keep preaching your message of peace," Joshua told him.
"Soon we will all come together and show the world how beautiful it is for brothers and sisters to work in harmony."

"I must go and take a rest; I tire easily. Thank you for taking
the time to talk with me, young man. I enjoyed it very much,"
Father Ambrose said. Then he rose and said, "Good-bye."

"We will meet again, Father," Joshua responded.

On the afternoon of the third day Joshua left the city for Bethlehem, just a few miles away. As it was late in the day, he did not
walk the whole way to Bethlehem, but slept in the hills that
night in a grove of olive trees, with the roots of a tree as his
pillow. The canteen given to him by the Arab boy came in good
stead, as the days were hot and in the hills there was no water.

The next day, Joshua reached Bethlehem. The town proper
was, as then, small, with a massive shrine church hovering over
the traditional site commemorating Jesus' birth two thousand
years ago, and surrounded by Orthodox and Catholic convents.
A vast square in front of the entrance seemed to shrink the small
portal, intentionally designed that way to keep hostile soldiers
from riding their horses into the sacred shrine.

The area surrounding Bethlehem was no longer a little hamlet
out in the hills. It had become a sprawling community ex-
tending far beyond its original boundaries and home to over a
hundred and fifty thousand people, mostly Arabs. There was a
university in the village now, run by Christian Brothers, educat-
ing not just Christians living in the area but Muslims as well.
Christian Arabs and Muslims had lived together in peace in this
community for decades.

Joshua walked through the town, talking casually to people he met along the way, paying special attention as always to the little children.

As he was sitting in the village square around noon, a tall, thin man approached him, and in friendly manner introduced himself. "My name is Naim," he said, with a broad smile that betrayed a perfect set of white teeth. He held out his hand for Joshua to shake.

"I am Joshua," Joshua responded, as the two men shook hands.

"I have a little business here," Naim said. "We carve wooden figurines out of olive wood. Your face looks very much like one of our carvings, so I had to say hello to you."

"I passed your store. You have good people working for you," Joshua said.

"Thank you," Naim replied. "Yes, we try to hire honest people. They are all Arabs, some Christians, a number of Muslims. They work well together."

"That's the way it should be," Joshua remarked. "You have made a good contribution to peace."

"I try to do my little part," Naim answered with a touch of pride. "I know it is not much, but it shows how people can work together. They all live here in the village or roundabout and are good neighbors to one another. We have had peaceful relations here for a long time. Some of our people used to be members of the Knesset. Lately, however, relations are strained; we feel a kinship and a loyalty to our brothers who are hurting in other areas of the country. It didn't used to be that way, but each government is different and treats the Arab population differently. Some day, perhaps, some day, we will learn to respect one another."

Joshua told the man of his concerns, and before they finished speaking, Joshua had another follower, glad to be part of his undertaking. The man liked Joshua and invited him to stay at his house and meet his family, which he did.

The next day, as Joshua was walking through the village, he noticed the two men who had been following him in Jerusalem now tailing him through the streets of Bethlehem. He walked past the town, out into the countryside, and wandered through the Shepherds' Field. Sheep and goats had grazed there for thousands of years. Their shepherds had never been well treated by polite society. In fact, they were despised by religious people for not keeping the law.

Joshua thought of the events of so long ago when angels appeared to shepherds telling them of Jesus' birth. Shepherds were the first to show the newborn honor, the first to welcome him. Others had no room for him, or showed no interest. The walk through the hillside held, perhaps, the most tender of memories for Joshua. Joseph had tried so hard to make events surrounding the birth joyful and comfortable, but all he could find was a smelly stable. To Joshua, things like that were unimportant.

Leaving the field, Joshua began his trip back to Jerusalem. That night he met his friends at the cafe on Ben-Yehuda Street. They were dressed in ordinary clothes and were glad to see him.

"We haven't seen you around, Joshua," Susan began. "I take it you have been busy."

"Yes, there was much to be done, and much has been accomplished," he replied. "One of the details I thought important was a place for us to meet. The manager of the Seven Arches is very enthused about our work and offered to let us use their facilities for meetings."

Aaron was surprised, but delighted. He then brought the group up-to-date on their accomplishments so far. Daniel Sharon wanted Aaron to thank Joshua for saving his life and said he would thank him personally when he met him. He then explained that their network of friends was still small but excited about the prospect of doing something tangible that would have some positive effect on the community. They were all happy about Joshua's contacts with Arab people who were interested in working with them to promote peace.

Joshua told them of the people he had met and of their willingness to come to a meeting.

"Joshua," Samuel said in an almost unbelieving tone, "how could you possibly have persuaded those Arabs to agree to come to a meeting, something we have tried in vain to do for months, even with our best show of goodwill?"

Joshua smiled and replied, "Perhaps it is due to their allegiance to the sheik. Whatever, they are committed to work with us and are waiting for us to set the date."

"Aaron," Susan said, "I think we should tell Joshua about his shadows, or we may all end up with a surprise we can't handle."

"Joshua," Aaron said, "I don't know how to tell you this, but you are being followed by intelligence people. They work on their own, and are totally independent of us. We have no control over their activities. You will really have to be careful."

"I realize that already," Joshua replied, not too terribly concerned. "I have seen them on a number of occasions. It is a problem I have always had. We need not worry. This mission will not fail. What we are doing is God's work."

"I wish I had your confidence," Nathan interjected. "Every attempt in the past to get Arabs and Jews to work together has come to a miserable end. There are just too many people whose interest it is to keep the two sides enemies." Nathan was a young man in his early twenties, bright and quick-witted, with curly brown hair and an infectious laugh.

"We have to trust God to be with us," Joshua replied. "Prayer would help. With our Father's help, it is possible. Without Him it won't succeed."

The group decided that they should work out the details of their first meeting at the Seven Arches Hotel. Joshua told them to expect close to thirty Arabs for that meeting. These thirty Arabs were willing to test the waters at the first meeting, and then to commit themselves and their families, if they felt comfortable after this meeting. The date was set for the next week, depending upon available space, which Joshua assured them would be no problem. The group then broke up, with Aaron taking Joshua to his house to meet his family.

Aaron's family lived in a well-to-do section of town, in the hills outside the city. Their house was not large but pleasingly designed, and well-appointed inside. Aaron's wife, Esther, was tall, with long, straight black hair, and dark blue eyes, appearing at times to be almost violet. Her smooth olive complexion made her look far too young to be the mother of three children.

Esther welcomed Joshua warmly and told her husband to bring him into the kitchen. She was preparing food for the next day.

"I am thrilled to meet you, Joshua," Esther said as they entered the kitchen. "You are all Aaron has been talking about since the day he met you. You certainly made an impression on him. He doesn't usually fuss over people."

"Well, now you can see for yourself, I am just a simple man," Joshua answered.

"Not so simple, Joshua. There is something about you that made me take notice as soon as you walked in," Esther told him. "You have such a tranquil bearing."

"Thank you, you flatter me," Joshua replied.

"Joshua, how about a glass of homemade wine, the best in the country?" Aaron boasted as he offered his guest a glass.

"Sounds good. Homemade is always the best. It's alive," Joshua responded, picking up the glass Aaron had poured for him. Aaron poured a glass for his wife, and for the children and himself, then they saluted "L'chayim" to one another.

"Esther, this man is absolutely amazing," Aaron said, as soon as he swallowed his first mouthful. "Do you know what he has done?"

"I don't have the slightest idea," Esther replied.

"He got a whole group of important Arabs to join with us in our movement," Aaron told her. "Something we haven't been able to do in over two years of hard work." Then, turning to Joshua, he asked, "How did you ever do it?"

"Oh, I merely hypnotized them. Then, when they were completely in my power, I told them they had to come. It was so simple," Joshua said flippantly.

"Come, now. You know it wasn't an easy task," Aaron pressed him. "What did you say to them?"

"Everyone wants to live in peace, so I just convinced them that if they really cared, they had to make their own contribution to peace, not just wish it," Joshua answered simply.

"When we get them all together, how shall we handle it? That's going to be the touchy part," Aaron said, concerned.

"Let me handle the groups. I can guide them gently and they won't be suspicious of me," Joshua offered.

"Sounds like it might work. They trust you already and will be more willing to listen to you than to any of us. Do you think the sheik will come?"

"I think he might come for the first meeting out of courtesy. Then, if he feels comfortable, he will bring others to future meetings," Joshua said confidently.

One of the children, three-year-old Mirza, had worked her way over to Joshua and asked if she could sit on his lap. She was round-faced, with big, black eyes. Joshua chuckled and said he would be thrilled if she would. Climbing up, she wiggled her way into his lap and sat there with a look of pride, as Joshua cradled her in his arms. Her two brothers laughed, so she stuck out her tongue at them. Her brothers, Moishe, a skinny, nervous eleven-year-old, and David, a playful, happy seven-year-old, were always in trouble for teasing their baby sister, who could do no wrong. This time they really asked for it when David made the wise remark, "Moishe, she likes Joshua so much, maybe we'll be lucky and he'll kidnap her."

"David, I hate you, I hate you," was their sister's immediate response.

Joshua assured her with a hug that he would never do such a thing and that he would send a special angel down from heaven just to protect her, so that no one would ever harm her.

David was peremptorily shipped off to his room and told to get ready for bed. Not long afterward the other children followed, which left Aaron and Esther in peace with Joshua. They stayed up late sharing thoughts they never imagined they could share with anyone.

"Joshua, if I am not being personal, where do you sleep?" Aaron asked almost apologetically.

"Usually out in the hills, where it is quiet, and I can just lie under the trees in an olive grove and look up into the sky. It is peaceful. On cool nights, I light a fire and sit and think, and talk to my Father, then fall asleep."

"You really feel close to God, don't you?" Esther asked.

"Yes, He is always close by. I draw my strength from Him and also my vision. He is the reason for my confidence in the future," he responded.

"Joshua," Aaron said, "I had the strangest feeling the first day we met, when you were describing the sites across the Kidron, that you had personally witnessed what you were narrating. I immediately felt a kinship with you and knew I could trust you."

"These places have always been dear to me, every stone and every path, and every brook. They should be precious to every child of Israel," Joshua replied. "Yahweh's presence has always hovered over this city, and everyone, Jew and Arab, should feel it is their home, and not a place of endless conflict, like it is."

"I mentioned earlier that my sister is married to an Arab," Aaron said. "His family has lived here for generations. They are really saintly people and often talk about feeling the presence of God in this city. It is a real spiritual home to them.

"Joshua, if you like, you are more than welcome to stay here with our family, rather than sleep out in the hills at night," Aaron said to him.

"Your offer is generous," said Joshua, "but it is better that I stay alone. It is the way I have always been, and I feel at home under the stars. My Father feels very close when I'm alone."

It was late when they retired. Bringing an extra towel to Joshua's room, Aaron rapped on the door, impulsively opening it, and caught Joshua kneeling near the window wrapped in prayer, unaware that Aaron had even entered the room.

Aaron left the towel on the chair nearby and quietly withdrew, with the image burnt into his thoughts.

5

EVERYONE ROSE EARLY the next morning. Aaron had to be at the office for a special briefing, so breakfast was rushed. After breakfast, Joshua left and continued on his way. He wanted to meet the old Franciscan priest who was so kind to him earlier that week. The man's sincerity and wide circle of friends could be a great asset in the present venture.

Joshua met him in the same place as before. It seemed the priest spent much of his time of late in the precincts of the sacred shrine, meditating on the life of Jesus and the ways of God, and trying to show kindness to pilgrims of whatever race or belief.

"Father Ambrose, I was hoping I would find you here," Joshua said as he met the old priest sitting on a chair meditating. "I have been thinking much about you since our last visit. We are planning a meeting at the Seven Arches and we would like very much for you to come with your many friends. All your prayer and hard work is coming to fruition. I hope you can make it."

The old priest was thrilled. He could see that his work was not ended. He did still have a purpose. His brown eyes twinkled with a new life. "My son, I am glad you did not forget me. I have been praying for you since your unfortunate visit here last week. I will be happy to come to your meeting. I will contact all my friends. I am sure they will want to come as well."

The two men went over to the site of the tomb, and the priest escorted Joshua inside, explaining important information about the history and archeology through the centuries. Joshua was indeed impressed, and the priest was delighted he could provide him with a personal tour.

With almost a week before the meeting at the Seven Arches, Joshua decided to leave Jerusalem and wander far up north, to Tabor and Nazareth and Cana on his way to Capernaum, and on his return trip to the shrine to the prophet Elijah on Mount Carmel. Nain, as in days of old, was still sparse—simple houses with round stone ovens dotting the field just off the highway. A mournful dirge and the image of a brokenhearted mother still sparked memories . . . memories of a man, once dead, now stretching his arms to the heavens. The long distance of time seemed to have little effect in erasing the vivid recollections so full of meaning.

Tabor loomed high over the village.

Reaching the top of Tabor, Joshua walked the rocky perimeter, surveying the valley that surrounded the huge rock that thrust seemingly to the clouds. Here was a perfect vantage point to scan massive military operations forming far below. Long ago, Peter, James, and John were lifted from their senses in seeing Jesus conferring with Moses and Elijah. Overwhelmed, Peter offered to build a shrine to commemorate the event.

As Joshua walked the hilltop, lost in memory, two reconnaissance jets zoomed overhead.

Nazareth was no longer the little village of previous times. It was now a major city in the north with a mixed population of mostly Muslims, with Catholics, Orthodox, and various Protestant groups, and a large Jewish community, all living in their own sections of town. Joshua's memories as he walked into the city were mixed. His previous visit here had been, he thought, his last. The townsfolk had tried to kill him. But it had not always been that way. There were pleasant memories, too, of childhood and his youthful years. He walked past the spot where once his house stood, no longer there. Sights, sounds, and smells of old filled his senses as he remembered a thousand details of life so long ago. Walking down the street he could see his mother on her way to the well from which people were even now drawing water. He stopped to drink the cool, fresh water he once drank daily, and drew so often for his mother who, it seemed, was always working, or worrying about him. Memories of his foster father's workshop filled his mind, and the many hours spent there helping him, and the sad day when Joseph died, leaving him and his mother all alone. Tender memories, so vivid!

The new basilica dedicated to the coming of the Word of God in human flesh, a massive structure built to accommodate huge crowds, dominated the city. Underneath in the crypt was the reason for the building. There, dramatically displayed for pilgrims to see, were remains of the home where Mary lived when the angel appeared to her, and next to it a small shrine built by the earliest Christians, with the telltale red cross marked on the wall, and the words in Greek, "This shrine was built to honor Mary, the Mother of Jesus, by her family and friends." On another slab of stone from the earliest Christian period were marked the words, "Jesus, Son of God."

Joshua tried in his imagination to strip away the stone, the glass, and the steel and picture the scene as it had been, as he remembered it so well. It was a simple house, like so many others in the village. His grandmother and grandfather, a learned priest, lived there and were always thrilled when he came to visit them, bringing them presents he had just made—a chair or a bench or a small cabinet. His mother seemed so young at the time, just a child herself, so full of laughter and joy, in spite of the harshness of life and the priest's prophecy that her life would be pierced by seven swords. He remembered being in love with his mother. She was the most beautiful woman he had ever seen. His Father couldn't have given him a better mother, though she worried about him too much, and to his child's way of thinking, was overly protective. His foster father, Joseph, was a good match. His love for Miriam was so tender, bordering almost on veneration. He knew she was special to God; she was special to him as well. He treated her accordingly.

As Joshua was pondering all these memories, a nun walked past with a group of Arab children, explaining to them the story of the place, which roused Joshua from his reveries.

Exiting the building, he wandered through the town. It was far different from the way he remembered it. Walking back down the street to the well, he sat down on the stone ledge that flanked the fountain, as if waiting for someone.

After a few minutes, a man in his early forties passed. Joshua caught his eye, and nonchalantly said, "Shalom." The man returned the greeting, and something made him stop and walk over to Joshua.

"You seem so at home sitting here, yet I can tell you are a stranger. It is as if I should know you, but I don't. May I ask your name, sir?" the man said to Joshua.

"Yes, my name is Joshua. I'm just traveling and stopped for a rest. May I ask your name?"

"My name is Samuel."

"That's a good name. Great men carried that name," Joshua responded.

"Yes, I know. I try to live up to it," the man returned.

"The mood is so peaceful today. The air is quiet, the breeze so gentle. It is too bad people can't have the same peace inside. It would make for a much better world," Joshua said.

"I have lived here all my life and have never known peace," Samuel replied. "It seems someone is always stirring up trouble. If they don't have a reason, they invent one. I would give anything to see peace in our country."

"Samuel, follow me and I will lead you to peace," Joshua said, to the man's surprise.

"Follow you? Follow you where?" Samuel asked, confused.

"I have come to bring peace, and God's help will make it possible. Find your friends and bring them to me, and I will lead you to peaceful waters," Joshua continued.

"You are a strange man, Joshua. But there is something about you that commands my respect," Samuel answered. "Where will we find you?"

"I will wait here for you," Joshua told him.

It was not long before the man returned with his friends, over a dozen of them, all curious to meet this strange man.

After they had all been introduced to Joshua, they walked to a quiet area, and Joshua spoke to them. "The reason the world has no peace is that people have no peace inside themselves.

How can people give peace if they have not found peace themselves? Peace means disciplining what is unruly and harmful within ourselves. It means overlooking hurt and insult and forgiving those who offend you. It means reaching out to God and allowing Him into your soul, where He can become your friend. When God is within you, then you will have peace. Bringing peace to the world means bringing God into the hearts of others. It cannot be otherwise. You cannot have peace without God. You are His children, and you will always be troubled as long as you are orphaned from God. I have come to help you find your heavenly Father."

The men listened intently, not knowing what to think. They had never heard a man talk like this before. He was different, yet his words touched their hearts deeply, and they were moved.

"We will follow you, sir," one of them said, and to a man the others agreed. "Where will we meet with you?"

"In Jerusalem," Joshua replied. "On the Mount of Olives, next Wednesday evening at seven o'clock. There will be others, good people, all searching for peace."

"I will be there," Samuel promised, "and the others as well. Shalom."

"Shalom," Joshua returned. And they departed.

Joshua walked through town, toward the spot where the ancient synagogue stood, the place where he had worshiped as a child and a young man, the place where he learned his lessons about God and the Torah, and the history of his people. At the spot, now covered over with tons of debris and a modern building, he stood and remembered his last visit. He had just begun his public ministry, filled with enthusiasm. Word had gotten back to Nazareth that he had been preaching and working miracles in Jerusalem, and the townsfolk were jealous. On his return, his neighbors invited him to speak in the synagogue one Saturday.

It was with fear and trepidation that he started reading the scroll that was handed him: "The spirit of the Lord God is upon me; because the Lord has anointed me to bring good news to the humble; He has sent me to bind up the brokenhearted, to proclaim liberty to captives, sight to the blind; to proclaim the year of the Lord's favor, and the day of recompense from our God."

Putting down the scroll, he looked across the packed meeting room and quietly announced, "This day, this prophecy has been fulfilled in your very sight. No doubt you will say to me, physician, cure yourself. Work here among your own the miracles we heard you have been working for others. And I cannot, because you have no faith in me."

He hardly had time to speak another word when confusion broke loose in the synagogue and the townsfolk ended up physically dragging him outside to the edge of the town where they intended to throw him. But wriggling away, he escaped, never—he thought—to return.

Tears welled up in Joshua's eyes as he recalled those sad memories. How different from these simple folk today who hardly knew him, yet trusted him so openly! His own who had grown up with him could find only scorn for him. And he had so much he wanted to share with them.

Joshua turned away and walked toward Cana on his way to Capernaum, though things were vastly changed in the hamlet, even to its name, which was now Kfar Kana. There were hints of sights and places as they once were. The scene of the wedding party rose in his mind with all the fun and dancing and meeting of old friends. Miriam's worries about the wine dissolved with the sudden appearance of a hundred and fifty gallons of excellent vintage. The revelers had already gone through the sixteen-year supply prepared by the bride's father. At Capernaum, Joshua was surprised to find that Peter's house was still standing, not intact, but recognizable. It was the oddest-shaped house in the whole country. Being Peter's could it be anything but unusual? Not far away was the shore where he stood on that early morning after the Resurrection, calling out to the apostles as they fished in vain. There was a little chapel on the spot now, commemorating the event. Joshua stopped at one of the seaside restaurants and bought a roasted fish sandwich and took it with him down along the shore where he sat and ate his supper, dreamily looking out across the sparkling Sea of Galilee, reminiscing over all the memories of times long gone.

As twilight approached he headed up the hillside that rose abruptly from the lake and found a quiet place nestled in a clump of trees overlooking the sea, where he settled down to prayer. Then he lay down, resting his head against the root of a tree, and fell sound asleep.

Sunrise on the Sea of Galilee is spectacular. Vast waters, as far as the eye can see, unlike the oceans, calm, unruffled, sparkling in the orange and yellow brilliance rising from the distant shores. Joshua sat, resting against a tree, soaking in the beauty of the sunrise as it unfolded, thinking that, as breathtaking as it was, it paled in comparison to the beauty of heaven. And yet to his human eye and all his human emotions, the constantly changing colors in the rising sun fascinated him, inspiring a deep sigh. "If people only took time to enjoy the endless beauty my Father has placed in His creation for their enjoyment and contemplation!"

Joshua had many memories of Capernaum, this cosmopolitan community that catered to every describable foreigner passing through for trading or financial purposes. The beautiful synagogue built by a Roman centurion, whose servant Jesus had restored to life, was no longer there, though remains of a later synagogue survived. Its mere presence stimulated memories, the huge crowds who followed him everywhere, from dawn to sunset, their enthusiasm when he first appeared on the scene, and their gradual disillusionment as he showed no interest in assuming power and frowned on accumulating material possessions. Promising them his flesh and blood as the food of their souls was the last straw. He could have sidestepped the crisis, saying it was only symbolic, but he repeated and emphasized even more, "My flesh is real food and my blood is real drink and unless you eat my flesh and drink my blood you have no life in you." What he didn't tell them was how he would do this so it would not be ridiculous. His miracle of the loaves and fishes the day before gave them more than enough reason to believe that if he promised something he could carry it through. But instead they turned their backs on him, shaking their heads and muttering, "This is a hard saying, who can accept it?" as they walked away, never to return.

His discouragement and sense of failure at the time came back to him with a sharpness that revived the same moods all over again. He remembered leaving the area and wandering through the pagan lands up north to calm his troubled soul.

Thinking these things, he left Capernaum and traveled west to Mount Carmel. He was fortunate to be given a ride most of the way, as the Plain of Esdraelon was barren and monotonous, though filled with history as the great battlefield of times past, and the supposed site of the Armageddon, the final battle between good and evil.

Reaching the outskirts of Haifa, Joshua walked up the highway to the top of Mount Carmel, and arrived at the Carmelite monastery a little before supper. A priest by the name of Elias Friedman met him at the entrance. He was a hero in the Jewish resistance in Warsaw and had eventually become a priest and was transferred by his order to Mount Carmel. His greatest dream now was to become an Israeli citizen, which so far had eluded him.

"Shalom," the priest said in greeting.

"Shalom aleichem," Joshua replied, then continued speaking in Hebrew, to the priest's delight. From then on they both spoke in Hebrew. The monk invited Joshua into the church and showed him around, explaining all the details of the history of the place to him. He was surprised to find that Joshua was even more familiar with historical details than he was.

"Many Jewish people have been coming here to our monastery, curious about our history and also curious about Christianity. In fact, we have had so many Jewish people, particularly military, coming here on their day off, that we have had to schedule tours in Hebrew several times a day.

"But, I don't speak to them about Christianity. That is a mixed bag with so many of our people having tragic memories of the cruelty of Christians through the centuries. The churches haven't done justice to Jesus' message either by the way they lived or by the way they complicated his teachings almost beyond recognition.

"What I do is talk to them about Jesus; he was one of ours, you know, and what he was all about and how our people loved him and followed him everywhere, because he spoke directly to their hearts. It made sense to them then, and it makes sense to our people now. People today are no different. They too are looking for what Jesus had to give. But they don't want all the baggage and pettiness of a church with its politics and legalism. They have had their fill of that in their own religion. Jesus' philosophy is something we can handle, something we Jews can be proud of. That's what I talk about and it makes good sense."

Joshua just listened as the high-spirited priest poured out his ideas. "It makes good sense what you say," Joshua told him. "Our people are searching. The old ways no longer have meaning to so many of them. They feel it is tied in with a concept of mission that has passed them by, and does not seem relevant to everyday life in a modern world.

"I have talked to a number of soldiers. I know they don't believe in God, but their lack of faith is not in God as He is, but in God as others have conceived Him and presented Him to them. This god they reject. The fact that they come here shows they are not without faith. They are still searching. You do them a service by presenting to them a Jesus who is reasonable and caring, and a God who is gentle and caring. They need to know they are loved."

Father Elias invited Joshua for supper. Joshua was only too glad to stay. He was introduced to the other priests. Some were friendly; the others gave the impression they couldn't care less. After supper, Elias brought Joshua down to the shrine of Elijah, the founder of their order.

"Some laugh at us for claiming the prophet Elijah as our founder, but he really was. The Bible talks about Elijah founding a school of prophets. They always existed here on Mount Carmel. When Jesus came, the hermits on Carmel accepted him and always had a special affection for his mother. She may have visited here. When the Crusaders came to the Holy Land, they found the monks living here and admired their way of life. We are still here after surviving all kinds of persecutions. Come, I will drive you down to the shrine of Elijah. It is only a short distance down the road."

As their car exited the parking lot, Joshua noticed the two shadows who had been tailing him across the street from the monastery trying to remain hidden behind a tree.

"That building across the street belongs to the monastery," Elias told Joshua. "Years ago the government took it for a barracks and a radar post. It overlooks the Mediterranean and can scan practically the whole country."

Joshua was impressed with the shrine of Elijah, and the spot where Elijah slew the four hundred priests of Baal and single-handedly, with God's help, brought the whole nation back to the worship of God.

"This shrine is still popular with our people," the priest said. "It is one of the rare authentic sites in our history. Jewish people love to come here, and often bring bus loads of children with them. It is a powerfully inspirational experience."

Joshua stood there looking up at the bigger-than-life statue of Elijah. The statue itself tells a story, and makes an indelible impression.

As the two men were admiring the statue, three reconnaissance jets thundered overhead, shaking the ground beneath them. "Someday, maybe, we will have peace," the priest sighed.

"That will happen only when people decide they want it," Joshua added. "Peace has to be everybody's business."

"I would like to do more for peace, but an individual doesn't even know where to start," Father Elias complained.

"I meet many people who are concerned and want to do something about it," Joshua told him. "Many of them are Arabs, some are Christian, many are Jews. If you like you can work with us. We are forming a little community."

"Where do you meet?" Elias asked him.

"We are meeting on the Mount of Olives at the Seven Arches Hotel," Joshua told him. "The manager was kind enough to offer us space. You are more than welcome, if you would like to come. Bring a few of your friends, too, if you like."

"I'll be there," the priest promised, then continued his narration about the history of Mount Carmel.

6

J OSHUA TRAVELED ALONG the coast, stopping at Caesarea and Tel Aviv, where he picked up more allies, then worked his way back east to Jerusalem. The trip was for the most part uneventful, until he reached Tel Aviv. There he spotted the two agents who had obviously been following him all across the land.

It was in Tel Aviv that Joshua met Bernard Herbstman, a thin, balding rabbi with blue eyes who headed a Reform synagogue— the same rabbi Susan had boasted about a few days before. How they met was bizarre. Joshua had decided to take a walk through a Hasidic neighborhood on a Sabbath afternoon. As if that wasn't bad enough, he was carrying a small backpack with his belongings. Some of the people were offended that he should be so bold as to walk through their quarter in violation of the Sabbath. Not having any of the trappings of a Hasid, it seemed only too obvious that he was intentionally challenging their laws and their beliefs. Perhaps he was. Joshua had always been bothered by the nonsensical rules concocted in the name of religion, which stripped the joy out of life and turned God's children into caricatures. Besides, it gave God a bad name, which to Joshua was really offensive.

Whatever his motive, the residents took offense and confronted him. The discussion became heated, more so since Joshua was so cool and unperturbable.

"You know our laws and our customs. Why do you violate them and insult us by invading our neighborhood?" one man said heatedly.

"I do not come to insult anyone. I come to visit a friend," Joshua retorted.

"One of us?" the man said, shocked. "Where does he live?"

"On the other side of the neighborhood," Joshua answered.

"Why didn't you walk around the neighborhood, so we wouldn't have to see you?" the man asked indignantly.

"Because it doesn't make sense. It's almost a mile longer," Joshua answered.

Trying to prevent Joshua from continuing, the two men stood in front of him, and soon others came to their aid, refusing Joshua passage through their neighborhood.

"You people think you are honoring God by acting like this," Joshua said pointedly. "Instead, you make of God a fool like yourselves, living a way God never commanded, paralyzing people's minds, and forcing people to live in fear and bondage."

At that point Rabbi Herbstman, who saw the confrontation from his car window as he drove down past the entrance to the neighborhood, stopped and approached the group and tried to mediate. They insulted him, saying he wasn't even a Jew, since he belonged to a Reform synagogue.

"Mister," the rabbi said to Joshua, "come with me. I have a car. I will drive you where you want to go. Come with me, these people are unreasonable. You can't talk to them. They'll end up stoning you. I know them. They live in another world."

Realizing that he was getting nowhere, Joshua left with Rabbi Herbstman. He drove him where he was headed, and in fact he knew the people. They were Hasidim, but they were good friends. The family was also friends of Aaron Bessmer, who had insisted Joshua visit them when he came to Tel Aviv.

When they opened the door and saw the rabbi, they welcomed him with open arms. He then introduced Joshua to them, and they all retired to the yard for refreshments.

"Aaron told us about you, Joshua," said Moshe, the man of the house and Aaron's good friend. Moshe was a rotund and jolly fellow. "And we had sort of a premonition of your coming.

We just got a phone call from a friend at the other end of the neighborhood, telling us about a stranger creating a scuffle over there. My wife made the remark, 'I wonder if that's Aaron's friend, who's supposed to come to visit us. It sounds like him.' And sure enough, here you are."

Everyone laughed.

"Rabbi, it is a real honor having you visit us. We don't see you that often," Moshe's wife, Rose, said.

"Thank you," the rabbi answered. "But you have to admit, you almost have to have a visa to get in here. Fortunately, I know the back way and have a car. Today I was on an errand of mercy, otherwise I wouldn't have been driving over this way."

"I hope you can stay awhile. Lou and Toby are coming with friends of theirs, Forrest and Katherine. They said Forrest is Jewish somewhere in his background, but I think she's joking. Tom said he's a brilliant man, supposed to have fed half the Jewish population of New York with his kosher chickens years ago. Toby and Lou would love to see you, Rabbi—you have to stay," Moshe said to his friend. "In fact, we have a nice spread prepared for them, ready since yesterday, of course."

"Of course," the rabbi said with a knowing smile.

"Joshua," Moshe said, "you have a reputation for being quite a mystery man. Tell us, what brings you up this way?"

"I guess I've been on assignment. I'm sure Aaron has briefed you on what we are doing," Joshua replied.

"Yes, he's all fired up about it, thanks to you. He's even got us committed to coming to Jerusalem for the meeting next week. Bernie will have to come, too. This will be right up your alley, Bernie," Moshe said to his friend.

"What's it all about, if you don't mind my asking before you sign me up?" the rabbi said.

"Not at all," Rose said. "Aaron's been involved with a group of people trying to promote peace. They haven't had much luck except with other Jews. They've been trying in vain for years to interest leading Arabs, but without success. Then, along comes Joshua and snags a sheik and all his family to join forces. We are having a meeting in Jerusalem this coming Wednesday night. It could be the beginning of great things, especially with Joshua here involved."

"Sounds like it might work. At least it has potential with the kinds of people involved," the rabbi said. "They certainly aren't just a group of do-gooders. Yes, you can count me in. I'll bring some of my people with me. There are some government officials in my congregation I can count on."

Lou and Toby and their friends Forrest and Katherine finally arrived. They were charming people, though not the type to become involved in peace movements. As they all settled down to the festivities, Joshua became the center of attention, as if they had known him all their lives.

"We have a priest friend in the States who is very interested in Joshua," Lou said, then looking at Joshua, continued, "He would like your kind of message. We will have to tell him all about you when we go back."

"I'd like to meet him someday," Joshua responded.

"Joshua, where are you off to from here?" Rabbi Herbstman asked.

"Jerusalem."

"I'm driving to Jerusalem tomorrow, so if you don't mind staying over at my house, you can ride with me if you like," the rabbi said.

"That's better than walking," Joshua responded. "I appreciate your hospitality."

Later in the evening when the party broke up, Moshe promised to come to the meeting on the next Wednesday. Joshua bid his friends shalom, and he and the rabbi left together.

"They are fine people," the rabbi said to Joshua, "so different from most of the people who live there. I'm surprised they stay. They don't have too many friends in their neighborhood."

"I can understand that," Joshua replied. "Yes, they are exceptional people and have caught the genuine religious spirit. God intended the Sabbath to be a day of joy and recreation and a time to visit with family and friends. Religious people have turned that beautiful gift of God into a nightmare, booby-trapped with endless restrictions. These people understand its real meaning and truly enjoy it. Visiting them was fun."

The next day Bernie and Joshua drove from Tel Aviv to Jerusalem. It was less than an hour's ride, but in that time the two men became fast friends as they shared many ideas about God, about religion, about peace. When they arrived in the city, Bernie was surprised when Joshua asked to be dropped off at Ben-Yehuda Street. He expected to drop him off at his residence. When Joshua told him he had none, Bernie said, "You mean you are homeless!"

"I suppose if you want to say that, but it is by choice," Joshua replied.

"You're a mystery, Joshua," Bernie said in bewilderment.

The rabbi left Joshua, promising to be at the meeting. Joshua wandered the neighborhood until his friends gathered later on. He obviously had much to tell them, giving them the names and addresses and phone numbers of everyone who had committed themselves. Their staff would contact each one and provide them with all necessary details. Aaron again surprised Joshua with his efficiency by informing him that he knew of his latest confrontation with the Hasidic group in Tel Aviv.

Joshua merely laughed. "You amaze me, Aaron. It happened only yesterday afternoon. I thought you were supposed to be relaxing on the Sabbath and not doing any work."

"We never relax, you know that," Aaron quipped. "We also found out that your two friends have been following you every place you went."

"I know. I saw them in Haifa on Mount Carmel," Joshua told him.

"By the way, you are not too bad yourself," Susan remarked. "You rattled off all those names and addresses and phone numbers without even referring to a note."

Joshua smiled. "Some things you don't forget," he commented.

"We will contact all these people, then hope they all show up next week," Susan said. Then they all sat back and relaxed while they enjoyed their refreshments. "Joshua," Susan said quietly, "why don't you say a prayer with me over the food and ask God to bless me?" A little embarrassed at being singled out, he agreed and said a beautiful prayer. "Father, we thank you for one another and our friendship. Bless this delightful food which you have given for our pleasure. Bless the work to which we have committed ourselves. May our efforts bring peace to our people and draw them closer to you. And Father be always by our side and in our hearts." The others answered, "Amen." Then they enjoyed each other's friendship, sharing notes over all that had transpired since they were together last.

7

Aaron, SUSAN, AND Joshua were the first to arrive for the meeting at the Seven Arches. The evening was blessedly cool, a night when people wouldn't mind going out. Long before the scheduled time, people of all kinds began filing into the hotel. All Joshua's newfound friends came, every one of them, Arabs, Jews, Christians, priests, imams, Rabbi Herbstman. In time the spacious room was filled. The last to arrive was the sheik, Ibrahim Saud, with a retinue of important family members from all across the land. Joshua met him at the door and the two men embraced and kissed each other on both cheeks. Aaron and his friends were amazed. When Sheik Ibrahim entered the room, everyone stood and began to applaud. The sheik was taken aback by all the attention but composed himself and responded with a pleasant smile of appreciation, then took his seat with everyone else.

The meeting was called to order by Daniel Sharon. Daniel Sharon's family were old Jewish pioneers who had settled in Palestine early in the century, early settlers who had befriended their Arab neighbors and developed many solid friendships among many local Arab residents. In fact, Daniel's sister was married to an Arab, a pious man who attended Jewish services as well as services at the mosque. Daniel, together with a number of others, had been trying to foster better relationships among all the peoples in their communities. Their greatest opposition, however, came from militantly religious people who felt he was undermining their culture and their religious ideals by fostering the integration of people with different religions. Daniel began by introducing himself and the others in the core group, last of all Joshua.

"I must tell you, my friends, I owe my life to this man," Daniel said. "Last week Joshua was a total stranger to me. I met him for the first time on the street and he warned me not to take my car home. I went back into my office at the government building and had my car checked. It had been booby-trapped. I don't know how he knew about it. I don't even know how he knew me. He himself was a stranger here in town until the very moment we met on the street. But I shall be forever grateful to him for saving my life.

"I would like now to turn the meeting over to Colonel Aaron Bessmer, who has dedicated so much of his time and talent to bring peace to our land. Aaron is a highly respected military officer on the general staff, and is totally dedicated to peace. Colonel Bessmer."

"Thank you, Dan. I am glad you are still with us. I must admit I am overwhelmed by the number of people and the composition of the group here this evening. The story Dan just told you is true, and I must admit, as a military officer, I was a bit skeptical about Joshua when I heard about the incident of Dan's car, and wondered just how Joshua knew about the bomb. But over the past couple of weeks I have learned not to be surprised about anything that this man might know or do. The success of tonight's meeting is due largely to him, who has no car, no telephone, not even a home or a bed to sleep in, yet he traveled the length and breadth of this land touching people's hearts and, like a magnet, drawing them to this meeting.

"I know the many things I would like to say to you all. But, being who I am and what I am, my words might not be understood in the way I mean them. Since so many of you are here tonight because of Joshua, I would like to introduce him and let him speak to you. He has captured in his person the dream we all aspire to.

"Joshua, would you please step up here and speak to this wonderful group of people?"

Everyone applauded as Joshua approached the microphone. Aaron shook his hand warmly and then sat down.

"My friends, your presence here this evening is impressive. We are Jews, and Arabs, Christians of all sorts, men and women, and even some children. I am grateful to all of you for coming. It took a bold leap of faith and trust in the future to come here. It was not an easy decision, and one for which many will demand an explanation, an explanation that cannot be easily given, and even less easily understood. I admire you for your courage and for your love and concern for your children's future. That is really what is at stake here: the kind of life we are willing to bequeath to our children.

"Aaron mentioned I have nothing. That is true. I need little, a little food perhaps, and water, a few clothes people give me, and my Father in heaven takes care of the rest. I walk without fear. I am not odd, and I am not a freak. I just enjoy being free. I care about my people, and you are all my people because you are all the beloved children of God, and we all belong to one another. I feel just as much a part of Sheik Ibrahim's family as I do a part of Aaron's family. God is not Arab or Jew or Christian. He is the Father of all. He has bestowed different gifts and different lights upon all of you, not to make you proud and elite and alien to one another, but that you might share with one another those special gifts.

"We live in a troubled land. We are all Semites. We are all the children of common ancestors. We are closer to one another than most other tribes and races on this earth. Yet we live in fear and distrust of one another. It is not right. It is not healthy. And it is all so unnecessary.

"We are all here tonight because we realize that, and at great personal risk we have decided to do something about it. Before all else it is important for us to realize that God is not pleased with hatred and distrust, and He abominates terrorism, which destroys the living temples of His presence in the world. No excuse can shield those perpetrators from the awful judgment of God.

"And we all must remember, there is only one God. There is not a god of the Christian, and a god of the Jew, and a god of the Muslim. There is one God, who is Lord and Father of us all.

He looks upon all of us as His children, and we must have enough faith to see each other through God's eyes, and to show understanding and concern for one another.

"It is not easy to reverse the trend of fear and suspicion that has been our heritage, but that trend must be reversed. We can start here. It will take time, and discipline. We can teach our children to love and care for one another. Religion should not be a divisive force, as it has been for so many centuries. True religion is the living expression of God's wisdom and love, and a truly religious person will reflect that wisdom and love of God to all he or she touches and will be a powerful source of peace and goodness to everyone. No one need fear a truly religious person, because he carries in his heart the living presence of God, and blesses everyone he meets.

"So our movement starting here tonight has to start with God. He is the only bond who can unite us. This should be our first lesson, to find again our Heavenly Father, and allow Him to come into our hearts, so we can begin this noble journey toward peace. The people who manage this beautiful hotel have graciously offered us their facilities for our meetings. We will meet again next week. I hope you will all feel comfortable enough to bring your families. May you all have a safe journey home."

Joshua received a standing ovation which lasted for a full five minutes before Aaron could begin his closing remarks and dismiss the group.

Sheik Ibrahim approached Joshua after the meeting and thanked him for touching his life so deeply. The sheik assured him his whole family would be solidly behind him. He then asked Joshua if he would mind if he looked upon him as his family's imam, to which Joshua said he would be honored.

Other people Joshua had called during the recent weeks came up to him and told him how impressed they were with what he had to say. They said he seemed transformed as he spoke and seemed to radiate the wisdom of God Himself. And to think they had looked upon him as just a simple wanderer when they had first met him. Many left with tears in their eyes and a new feeling of hope in their hearts.

The old Franciscan priest was there with a good number of his friends, including an Orthodox priest. Next to him sat the monk from Mount Carmel and also Rabbi Herbstman, who was deeply touched by what Joshua said. These all came over to Joshua after the crowd had thinned out and expressed their thanks and admiration. The old priest said that when he closed his eyes during the talk, he thought he was hearing Jesus speak.

Daniel Sharon made a warm gesture of gratitude to Sheik Ibrahim for coming to the meeting. The sheik told him it was out of loyalty to his friend, Joshua, that he came. He then told Daniel that he too was blessed by Joshua's goodness and related the story of his granddaughter, the lamb, and the miraculous curing of the snakebite. Both men went home wondering about this man who could touch people's hearts and even their lives so intimately.

After the meeting broke up, Aaron, Dan, Joshua, and their original group went over to Ben-Yehuda Street for refreshments and debriefing. Aaron leaned back contentedly and observed, "What we saw tonight is the beginning of a wholly new community composed of Arabs, Jews, and Christians."

Joshua just listened, thoughtfully weighing everything, happy at the blessed changes in so many hearts.

8

THE NEXT DAY Joshua walked through Jerusalem. The old section was so much as he had remembered it with all the smells and sights and haggling over prices in the markets along the streets and back alleys. As he walked along, he was again conscious of being followed. Walking around the corner and up a side street, he looked back and saw two men among the pedestrians walking up the street, the same men he had seen everyplace else. He also noticed, following in the distance behind the two men, a boy. He had seen the boy on one other occasion at the sheik's camp. Now he was certain the young fellow was following the two men, though so far in the distance they would never have suspected it. He recognized the boy as one of the sheik's grandsons and wondered what he was doing in Jerusalem.

Joshua knew the two shadows had nowhere near his stamina, so he decided to give them a good day's exercise. The next few hours he wandered all through the city, going up to the Temple Mount and visiting the smaller El-Aqsa mosque. There he stayed, praying for almost an hour while the two men stood out in the blazing sun, each ruing the day he took the job. The young boy positioned himself in the crowd at the other end of the square, waiting, watching.

The day finally ended uneventfully. When Joshua left the mosque, he continued his walk through the city, then worked his way over to Bethany, where like old times, he spent the night.

The two men disappeared. The boy went home and reported to his father what had transpired during the day.

The next day over lunch, Susan remarked to Aaron and a few of their friends how well the meeting had gone the night before. "Do you realize," she said, "that all those people Joshua got to come were total stangers to him just a week ago? How did he know he could trust them? How did they know they could trust him? How did he know where to find them? They are from all over the country. He couldn't have done any better if he had the intelligence service working with him. And for some strange reason, they are already completely dedicated to him."

"I noticed that myself," Samuel remarked. "The sheik looks at him with almost veneration. I think he would do anything for him."

At that point Daniel Sharon came into the cafeteria and sat down with the others.

"Continuing last night's debriefing?" he said.

"Just about," Aaron answered. "We were remarking how uncanny it was that Joshua could so easily have picked all those people to come to last night's meeting in so short a time, and he never even knew them before."

"Well, I found out why the sheik is so committed," Daniel said, with an evident note of triumph in his voice.

"Why is that?" Susan asked.

"Joshua saved his granddaughter's life," Daniel replied.

"How so?" Samuel questioned.

"Well," Daniel continued, "the sheik and I talked after the meeting last night and compared notes. I told him about the car incident, and he told me about Joshua visiting their camp at the oasis. During the night a viper bit his granddaughter, and the whole family was beside themselves, unable to get the girl to a hospital at that time of the night. Well, it seems Joshua ended up curing the girl. Even the bite marks disappeared. Needless to say, the whole family was overwhelmed. The sheik is convinced that Joshua is a prophet of some kind and he and his family are totally committed to following him. He even asked Joshua if he would be his family's imam. Imagine that, and they all know Joshua is a Jew."

"How did he cure her?" Susan asked.

"It seems he just touched her and told her to be well and she recovered immediately," Daniel replied. "The sheik attributes it to his being so close to Allah. And if the sheik and his family feel this way about him, who knows what all the others experienced when they met him? After what happened to me last week I would believe anything he told me."

"Yet he seems so normal and so down-to-earth," Aaron remarked. "He doesn't seem especially pious or religious. He's just ordinary, like us."

"I guess that's what's so beautiful about him," Susan added. "You feel you've known him all your life."

"Well, he's got the Mossad standing on their heads," Aaron interjected. "They don't know what to make of him. Gus, my friend over there, told me they are baffled by his continually meeting with Arabs of all sorts, and they all know he is a Jew. They are convinced he is up to something, but they can't put their fingers on it. He seems innocent enough on the surface. His objectives remain a mystery. They have him on continuous surveillance, but he eludes them."

"I think he is just a good man with few needs who has found peace within himself and wants to help others find peace. I think it is as simple as that," Samuel added. "I think he is a rare, innocent individual who is authentically holy and has nothing of the self-righteous about him. If that's subversive, then our world is no longer fit for good people to live in."

"Susan thinks he's special, too," Aaron said flippantly.

"Aaron, you're being wise," Susan shot back at him. "I think he's a very unusual person, but a bit too unworldly for me. I admit I do have a deep admiration for him."

"We all do," Aaron added as everyone finished lunch and started back to work.

That same afternoon Joshua was taken by some of his Arab friends to visit the sheik, who had requested a meeting with him. His family had moved to a site closer to the villages where grazing was better.

"Salaam, my saintly friend," the sheik said as he welcomed Joshua and kissed him with all due ceremony.

"Salaam, my dear friend," Joshua said returning the greeting. The family were all excited at seeing Joshua again, the children especially, who ran over to him and grabbed his hands and his clothes. Joshua spoke with them briefly until the sheik ushered him into his tent where they could talk privately.

After small talk while they partook of light refreshments, the sheik came to the point of their meeting.

"Joshua," he began, "I must tell you I came away from your meeting the other night deeply moved. It is only recently, now that I am an old man, that I have begun to think along the lines on which you spoke. You touched me by your ability to rise above pettiness and hurt and find goodness in people who might have been your enemies. That is a new thinking for me, and I find it hard to comprehend. Could you explain to me why you can feel that way?"

"Ibrahim," Joshua answered, "you are a good man, and you are trying sincerely to find the kingdom of God. But you look in the wrong direction. God's thoughts are not our thoughts. We look at people and measure their worth and their goodness in their relationship to ourselves. God as a loving Father sees the intrinsic goodness in each of His children. People are not evil. They are easily hurt and they hurt back, because of pride and because of fear. It is to protect themselves. It is not because they are evil. Some have been so deeply hurt and damaged they strike back at everyone indiscriminately. They become deranged.

"A person who is close to God learns to see others through God's eyes. As your prophet writes so frequently, 'Allah is all compassionate.' He sees the hurt and the anguish, and the reasons why people do hurtful things. God tries always to heal. The closer a person comes to God, the more that person reflects His healing love. Anger and vengeance have no place in a soul where God dwells, only forgiveness and understanding.

"You ask why I can feel this way. Since my beginning, God possessed me. I have always been a clear vessel of His love for His children. When people do hurtful things, I see their hurt and I seek only to soothe their hurt and heal their wounds. Since my life is in my Father's hands I cannot be threatened, so I fear no one. They cannot hurt me, so I feel no need to strike out and destroy. It is a goal all God's children should strive for. It is the key to peace."

"Joshua, I think that is the reason I love you," the old man said. "You are so pure. Evil has never touched your soul. Only God can feel the way you feel and, as much as I respect you, I do not think I can rise to those heights of holiness.

"I used to hate, when I was younger. It is hard to see our people who lived here for over a thousand years be driven into camps behind barbed wire and treated like animals. But I know that hatred is not good for the soul, so I have risen above the hatred that once possessed me. However, I still cannot forgive, and to love is impossible. Yet I see the damage my past hatred has caused in my family. My son is consumed with hatred. I am afraid. I spend many nights without sleep fearing the future.

"I know that forgiveness is the only way to peace. My people are unable to forgive. The Jews are unable to forgive. What do we do, kill each other until no one is left?

"Your way, Joshua, is the only way to peace. That is why I admire what you are doing. You are the only one who has been able to gather our people and the Jews and the Christians together to talk to one another.

"I am an old man, Joshua, and it is hard for me to change, but I want to do what is good for my children and my people. I assure you of my own and my family's support for what you are doing."

"Ibrahim, you are not far from the path of godliness. In time you will reach what you are striving for," Joshua assured him. "We cannot change overnight what has taken a lifetime to cultivate. In time we will rise above the pettiness of being human and reach across the chasm of ignorance and hatred to embrace those who are fearful and hostile. When that happens, the children will reap the harvest."

When the two men finished talking, Joshua left and was driven back to the city. The sheik did not tell Joshua that he was being followed by the two intelligence people and that he had instructed his grandson to follow the two men and report back to him anything that should happen. Joshua already knew it.

Joshua also knew that the sheik's son Khalil was plotting with Arab radicals to ambush and assassinate him for trying to bring about peace. Joshua knew the old man sensed something, and it was breaking his heart knowing his son was up to something evil. The sheik was also overwhelmed with guilt that he had instilled the hatred in his son that was now bearing such bitter fruit. That is the paradox of hatred, that it destroys the children of those who nourish it, a poisoned heritage to one's own off-spring.

9

THE NEXT MEETING of Aaron and Joshua's group, the Children of Peace, took place as scheduled, at the Seven Arches Hotel. This time, however, the crowd was so large the hotel was unable to accommodate it, so the meeting had to be held outdoors. The manager was more than gracious in offering the assistance of his staff to facilitate all the changes necessary, like moving the speaker system outdoors and rearranging all the chairs. Not only did the other members of the sheik's extended family come to the meeting, but relatives and friends of people Joshua had invited to the first meeting. Rabbi Herbstman brought a sizable number from his congregation. A large contingent of Arab Christians came all the way from Ramallah, a city with an Arab Christian population of over fifty thousand, and many others from Nazareth. They had all come to hear the speaker who had held the people at the last meeting spellbound. His reputation had spread far and wide.

He did not disappoint them. After the usual introductory comments and recognizing of important personages in attendance, Aaron turned the meeting over to Susan, who introduced Joshua to the newcomers. Resting his folded hands on the lectern, he began:

"My friends, it is not by chance or by circumstance that you are here this evening. The spirit of God has touched each of you. You are special and have been called. You all have realized, each in your own way, and by your own experiences, that peace in our land is long past due. If there is to be peace, it must come from the people. Leaders forever find reasons to postpone peace and at times to upset the peace. Peace is not always in their best interest. If people want peace, they must seize the peace.

"But it will not come without hard work.

"We are all children of a common Father, a Father who loves you with a love beyond understanding, a love that is so tender that He watches over you day and night, not with a critical eye, but with a mother's love, protecting you each day from a thousand dangers. Even though tragedy sometimes strikes, through sickness or human cruelty, your Father is always nearby to heal your wounds and offer His love if only you open your hearts to Him."

As Joshua was speaking, he could see diverse groups spread throughout the audience. He spotted Khalil's terrorist friends and also the two detectives who were tailing him day and night. Sitting together was a group of Hasidim, curious as to what this man was teaching, whether it would strengthen their oneness as a people or threaten the purity of their goals. They listened intently. Joshua's memory soared back through history and saw Pharisees all over again, Pharisees in modern, well, not-so-modern dress. He wondered if he could reach them or if they were like their ancient counterparts, frozen in their thoughts, like automatons in lock step, unable to think in any way other than the way their leader told them they could think. Joshua sensed their minds were already closed. He could see opposing forces already beginning to take shape, as they had once, long ago. This time, though, he knew things were different.

"We live in difficult yet exciting times, times in which each individual can make his or her mark on history. We cannot face the future with fear, we must face it boldly. We cannot look to a future with total isolation from the world around us. We live in a world fashioned by God in such a way that we all need one another as members of a family. Isolation is a refusal to love, a rejection of others around you. It calls forth the bitterest feelings of resentment and recrimination, because it is a self-righteous rejection of your neighbor whom God said you should love. Isolation is foreign to God, who wants His children to love and help one another and build up a community of shared concern and mutual enrichment. Religion that regards as evil contact with others whom God created is not a religion that has come from God. It creates an infection in the community. It causes its members to withdraw their love from the community around them. It creates a vacuum that becomes filled with resentment and alienation and draws upon itself recriminations and hostility.

"If there is to be peace, it must begin in the hearts of each one of us. It must become a way of life, a seed that grows like a beautiful flower spreading its fragrance throughout the whole garden.

"Peace cannot grow where there are angry and hostile thoughts. Peace must come from a mind that is pure and gentle and free from meanness and suspicion.

"Peace can flow only from a soul that sees the goodness in others and is willing to excuse and repair their faults.

"Peace must be loving parents' first gift to their children, the soil in which the most beautiful gifts of grace can then flourish.

"Peace flows from the heart of God and like a soothing balm bathes the soul it touches in its delicate perfume.

"If you want peace, open your hearts to let God enter. Do not be afraid of Him. He wants nothing from you. He wants only to give you His love and His peace and His freedom. When you leave here this evening, do not go alone. Walk home with God in your heart, and bring Him home to your families. Teach your children to open their hearts to Him, so they can find Him early in their lives and not make the mistake so many make in looking for Him when their lives are almost over."

All during Joshua's talk the audience sat spellbound. No one had ever heard anyone speak like this before. Each heart was filled with a peace and a lightness it had never experienced. The audience was reluctant to leave and wished Joshua would continue speaking.

When the talk ended, Aaron got up and after a few business items suggested that, since there were so many people from Galilee, it was only fair they have their next meeting in Galilee. Joshua suggested the hillside outside Capernaum overlooking the Sea of Galilee as the site. They set the date and decided it should be in the afternoon. The people were to bring their own lunch. The meeting broke up with everyone hugging each other. Some Jews and Arabs had never hugged each other before. It brought many tears of joy and forgiveness, and a sense of wonder at how simple it could be.

The next day Joshua went to the Temple Mount and prayed in the Mosque of Omar. Many of his friends were there worshiping. Afterward they gathered outside and spoke freely with him. Some of their neighbors joined in, anxious to meet the man they had heard so much about. It was a new experience for the Temple Mount to witness Arabs and a Jew talking in so friendly a manner, and openly.

As the group broke up, Joshua sat down and looked across the square, reminiscing. This had once been the sight of the glorious temple built by Herod, with its beautiful golden roof and frieze work, and rich marble and other stones rare to the area, and delicately designed porticoes surrounding the vast courtyard. Here, long ago, the Son of God spoke often. Here, Jewish people by the hundreds would gather to listen to him, and be mesmerized by His teaching and touched by his healing of the troubled and the crippled. The priests and politicians were furious at his boldness in daring to meet with the people right at the very seat of their power. He called them "whitewashed sepulchers so nice to look at on the outside, but on the inside full of filth and dead men's bones," and excoriated them for stripping the joy out of people's relationships with their heavenly Father and for "laying heavy burdens on people's shoulders and not lifting a finger to lighten those burdens." Hypocrites he called them. They were stung to fury at his audacity and beside themselves because the common people loved him.

And here it was that one day a group of Pharisees dragged a woman found in adultery through the crowd and flung her at the Teacher's feet, demanding he tell them whether they should follow Moses' command to stone such a one to death or ignore Moses' law and let her go. Disgusted he turned his back and ignored them. When they persisted, he turned and said, "If that is the law, then stone her to death, but let him who is without sin among you cast the first stone." When they picked up stones to kill her, he knelt down and began to write in the dust, looking up at each one, "Oh, yes, I know all about you," and then proceeded to write their secret sins in the dirt. When they saw what he was doing they dropped their stones and slinked away.

Standing up, he said to the woman shivering at his feet, "Is there no one to condemn you, woman?"

"No one, Lord."

"Neither will I condemn you. Go and sin no more."

Joshua sat there wrapped in memory. It seemed like just yesterday. And he wondered how the Pharisees were able to find someone committing adultery, and only the woman at that. It will always be an enigma how merciful is God and how unforgiving sinners are toward other sinners.

Sitting there, watching people walking back and forth, mostly Arabs and small groups of tourists, Joshua wondered why his group couldn't also worship together at this site. But then he realized that what is important to his Father is not the place where people worship but what is in their hearts. With that thought Joshua rose and left the site, wandering through the streets of the old city, talking to people, comforting the sick and the elderly as he passed by their ancient hovels. He was becoming a common sight in the neighborhood, and people found themselves looking forward to his passing through. There were even rumors of desperately ill people being cured as he passed by and touched them.

Every street had a hundred memories. This was his beloved city. Arriving at an intersection, he noticed a sign on a stone wall, VIA DOLOROSA, the Way of Sorrows. Looking one way down the narrow street he recognized the approach to the Roman soldiers' quarters. Here the Son of God was held prisoner during his trial and here he was beaten by the soldiers. In the opposite direction, the street ascended slowly. Along the street were stations, the stops on the way to Calvary venerated by pious disciples through the centuries.

Joshua stopped at the spot where he met his mother, who had been waiting for him as he stumbled along on his death march. She had been used to pain and suffering ever since the priest Simeon prophesied that her son "was destined for the rise and fall of many in Israel and her own soul a sword would pierce." But the pain he saw on his mother's face that day was almost too much for him to bear. She, of all his disciples and loved ones, was the one pure innocent soul who was totally possessed by God since her very beginning and had never harmed a creature. To see her in such pain and torment was indeed a keen agony. His one comfort was that he would appear to her in three days and her joy then would be endless, and the pain would be no more. Tears welled up in Joshua's eyes. He walked on, and then out of the city, around to Siloam, where he visited his friends farming on the banks of the brook.

They had been at the meetings and were impressed with this simple man. Now they felt honored that he would come to visit them in their fields while they were working. They offered him a cup of water from the brook. It was cool, fresh water. The last time Joshua passed through he was a stranger. Now he was a friend and they treated him as such. They wanted him to stay with them, but he was on his way to visit some of the people farther down the valley. They knew he was going there to visit the poor. They gave him a sackful of vegetables from the field to bring to them. Then he filled his canteen in the stream and continued on his way.

He had made the remark two thousand years before, "The poor you will always have with you," and here he was visiting them in their hovels centuries later. They didn't care that he was Jewish. They saw only a man full of love and genuine concern, and they opened their hearts to him. He had nothing of value to give them in any material way, but what he gave them was a sense that a saintly presence was touching their lives and they felt not only honored, but touched by the grace of God's presence. Joshua stopped at the home of the poorest and gave them the bagful of food. They were grateful and insisted he stay and have something to eat with them, which he did. They had others staying with them, neighbors whose simple homes were bulldozed a few days before. Joshua spent some of the time sitting in an open yard talking to the children, telling them stories and playing tricks for them.

The father of the family was named Mohammed. His wife's name was Iffat. They had five children, aged four to sixteen. At the supper table, Mohammed poured his heart out to Joshua, telling him of the cruelty of the military and the harsh way they treated the people. The homes of their neighbors who were staying with them were mistakenly destroyed in retaliation for an ambush in which two soldiers had been killed. But it was others who were responsible for the ambush. These people were innocent.

Joshua listened. It was the same complaint his people had had long ago when the Romans occupied their land. They treated the Jews the same way.

"The problems will resolve themselves in time," Joshua said. "For now, bear with it for your children's sake. They will be the only ones to reap a harvest of bitterness. We must all work together with others of goodwill and put endless pressure on political leaders to give justice to your people. It must be done peacefully."

"It is easy to talk like that," Mohammed complained to Joshua, "but when you have to live this way day after day, it is demeaning and makes one ashamed in front of his own family."

"Anger and vengeance is no solution," Joshua said calmly. "It hardens everyone and turns even the good and well-intentioned against your cause. With your neighbors and friends you must continually present your cause. As your numbers grow, the pressure mounts, and good people will see the justice of your cause and mount their own pressure. In time it will have its effect. Even now you can see that good people are willing to work for peace, even among the soldiers. So you must have patience but constantly work for peace and justice."

"When people are hurting, it is hard to have patience," Iffat said.

"I know," Joshua answered, "but discipline tempers the frustration and cools the burning coals. It is the only way."

When the supper ended, Joshua asked Allah's blessing on the family and left, walking down through the village speaking to the people as they sat in front of their houses, playing cards or solving the world's problems.

As night began to fall, Joshua walked up into the hills and, resting under a spreading olive tree, shared the day's experiences with his Father, then fell into a deep sleep.

The next day Joshua spent wandering through the area sightseeing and talking to people he met along the way. Every place he went he noticed the same two men following him, and the Arab boy in the distance. Or rather, boys, for now there were two Arab boys; it seemed they were taking turns.

That night Joshua met his friends Aaron and Susan and the others on Ben-Yehuda Street. They had their usual dessert and coffee and talked about the vast progress made within the past few weeks, and how everyone was looking forward to the "picnic" up in Galilee. They were happy to share with Joshua that a good number of their friends in the army would be coming with them, impressed with what had been happening the past few weeks. They wanted very much to be part of it.

"You don't know what a breakthrough that is, Joshua," Susan commented. "These are people who have been hardnosed over peace issues, and used to laugh at Aaron and myself when we talked about such things. I suppose we shouldn't be surprised, even my parents don't really approve of what I am doing. By the way, Joshua, my parents would love to meet you. Do you think you might come over to our house, sometime?"

"Yes, whenever you like," Joshua answered.

"You sure it's your parents, Susan?" Aaron quipped with a broad grin.

"Don't be wise, Aaron," Susan shot back. "I'd love to have him, too, but it was my parents who asked."

"Joshua, how do you keep so calm and so relaxed with the uptight people you mingle with all day long?" Samuel asked. "I watch you and you don't seem to have a nerve in your body."

"Oh, I guess it's just that I know people and what is in their hearts, and they know I care and they trust me, so I can feel comfortable working with them," Joshua answered simply.

"I'm amazed," Samuel said, as he sipped his cappuccino.

"Joshua," Aaron said, "I don't know how you intended to get up to Galilee, but if you like you are more than welcome to ride with me. My family and I will be going up the day before."

"That's very thoughtful of you. I appreciate it. It would be a long walk," Joshua responded.

The group broke up before long. As they were leaving, Susan arranged to pick up Joshua the next evening and bring him to her house for supper, so her parents could meet him.

The next day went fast, and toward evening Susan promptly met Joshua and took him to her home. She wasn't dressed like a soldier this time. Her outfit was simple yet tasteful, and her hair had been done that very day. Susan's parents were dignified people in their early sixties. They had seen much heartache and misery in their lifetimes, and it had scarred them but not embittered them. Her father's name was Moshe. He was a tall man, with a full head of white hair, steel blue eyes, and a slightly aquiline nose. He had the elegant grace of a man who might be a diplomat. He was affable and had a keen sense of humor.

Susan's mother was dressed like the cook she was that evening. When Joshua arrived, she was in the kitchen cooking, perspiring over the hot stove. She gave the impression of being a strong woman who had had to make many hard decisions in her life and was quite capable of handling any difficult situations that might present themselves. As she held out her hand to greet Joshua, he could tell by her strong grip that here was a woman like the ones written about in the Bible, a strong woman well capable of managing her affairs.

They soon sat down and relaxed, and after simple refreshments, had their supper. Susan's parents knew their daughter was very taken with Joshua, and they were curious to know all about him, where he was from, what he worked at, what was his goal in life. Joshua smiled at the simplicity of their questioning and answered them as well as he could. What could he say? His origins were incomprehensible, he had no family, he had no job. He went about talking to people. It seemed to add up to nothing that any mother would want to see her daughter involved in.

The fact that he was changing the whole face of the nation by doing nothing of apparent significance would never show on a resume, because all he did was talk to people. The fact that he was Susan's hero could not be translated into anything of any substance. But he was likable enough, and so they decided to enjoy the evening and let the future take care of itself.

It turned out to be a pleasant evening. Before the evening was out, both Susan's mother and father were totally enamored of this lovable dreamer. He had to stay for the evening. There was no way they were going to send him out to sleep under some tree somewhere. So he stayed for the night. He and Susan stayed up late, sitting in the garden enjoying the coolness of the night and sharing dreams. Susan knew Joshua liked her and was thrilled he would share his thoughts and dreams with her. She in turn poured her heart out to him, at one point resting her hand on his as she explained all she had been trying to accomplish with her peace project and how nothing had come of it until Joshua appeared that day on the Mount of Olives. Her whole life's dream began to come to life, and it was so beautiful that he was part of it. They sat talking until late, then Susan showed him to his room. Tomorrow would be a long day.

10

PEOPLE STARTED GATHERING around Capernaum late in the morning. Some came early to sightsee, others as part of their vacation, the bulk just for the meeting that afternoon. Aaron had business to attend to in Nazareth, so Joshua and Aaron's family had the thrill of riding in a military vehicle.

Joshua walked among the people who were already gathering for the occasion. He seemed so ordinary, so casual, without the slightest air of self-importance, that it was easy to overlook him, and so he fast became lost in the crowd. By afternoon, Aaron had everything organized to the last detail, and committee members were ushering people to the area outside the city where the event was to take place. Joshua smiled. It was not the first important sermon preached on this hillside.

At two o'clock the program started. People were sitting all over the hillside, which was in an isolated area, the ancient Tabgha, which sloped gently along the lake, providing the effect of a theater setting. It was quiet and peaceful overlooking the golden wheat field at the foot of the hill and the calm waters of the huge lake shimmering in the sunlight.

People had come from all over the land: from the hill country near Lake Huleh, and from Haifa and Mount Carmel, from Nazareth and Tsipori, from Nablus and Ramallah, and many from Jerusalem, and a large contingent from Bethlehem and the surrounding hill country. Desert people were also there, invited by Sheik Ibrahim. There were Jews and Arabs and Christians of all descriptions. And not to be forgotten, the two shadows who had followed Joshua everywhere. They arrived at Capernaum in a van with eight others who spread out and mingled with the crowd. Susan was the first to notice them and alerted Aaron, who made a mental note of their presence.

Joshua asked Aaron if he would have the people settle on the ground in groups of about fifty or a hundred so he could walk through the crowd afterward and talk to the small groups while they were eating their lunch.

The organizers stayed on the lower area, with the idea that the sound would rise more easily, and they could be heard without raising their voices, as they had only the battery-run speaker system hooked up to a truck. Daniel Sharon estimated there must have been between three and five thousand people. Never in their wildest dreams did they imagine anything like this could happen.

Daniel was the first to speak, and as he approached the microphone, he was overcome with emotion, and tears flowed freely down his cheeks. He looked at Joshua and it all dawned on him. Daniel had read the Gospels as a college student and it then seemed so idyllic, so simplistic and unrealistic. Now he saw it all happening before his eyes. It seemed like a dream. When he looked over at Joshua and saw him standing there, he knew. The Gospel story was being relived all over again and it was still so idyllic, so simplistic and so unrealistic, but it was happening, and so the tears.

It took him a while to compose himself, and then he began, "My brothers and sisters, never would I have dreamed that I would be addressing in my lifetime an audience like this, of Arabs, Jews and Christians, and calling them all brothers and sisters. Even a few weeks ago, if anyone had told me this could happen, I would have laughed at them. But we are here and it is so beautiful. I would like to start our simple program this afternoon with a song. We are privileged to have with us today an unusual man. He spends his life bringing love and joy into others' lives with his music and his friendliness. Many Arabs and Christians as well as Jews already know him, for he travels from village to village just loving people and hugging them and playing music for them. His name is Shlomo.

As soon as his name was mentioned, everyone seemed to know him, and a thunderous applause arose from the crowd. Shlomo arose and approached the microphone with his guitar. "The song I would like to sing for you today is one I composed last night after Daniel Sharon told me I had to come here. He didn't know that I intended to come anyway. The song God inspired me to write down is named "In God's Family There Are No Strangers." I will play it once and sing it, then I would like all of you to hum it the second time. The third time around I would like everyone to sing together, loudly and clearly.

With that he began his song. It indeed was inspired.

In God's Family there are no strangers,
Only brothers and sisters.
We walk down each other's streets and never say "hello."
We pass each other's houses and never stop to visit.
We hurt and pain and wound each other,
So often without cause, not even knowing why.

In God's Family there are no strangers,
Only brothers and sisters.
But today, things are different.
We have all found our Father,
And we are no longer strangers.
A new life has sprung among us, a new day has dawned.

A new hope has arisen,
Because in God's Family there are no strangers,
Only brothers and sisters.
And we are one and we are one, ever more only one.

When Shlomo finished, Daniel thanked him, then introduced Aaron, who was also deeply moved by the sight of all these different people on a hillside by the Sea of Galilee. He thanked everyone for their sacrifices in making not only the long journey to Galilee, but the long journey in faith and trust in one another to make this day possible. He finished by introducing Susan, who was one of the original organizers of the group. He apologized to the more fundamental Arab people present, but since

Susan was the dreamer who helped initiate this whole program, he felt it would be wrong not to allow her to take her rightful place at this assembly. He then introduced Susan. Almost everyone applauded.

"My dear friends," she began, "and I know now that we are friends, I will not take much time, because I know why you are all here. It is not because of me, nor is it because of anything any of us has done. It is because of one man, a man who was, until a few weeks ago, a total stranger. Even today none of us knows very much about him, but we have all come to love him dearly. No one even knows where he lives. Indeed he seems to have no place to lay his head, and I find myself lying in bed at night worrying about him, wondering under what tree he sleeps and on what hillside. Many of you have already met him, not just at our meetings, but as he walked through your villages, quietly, lovingly, touching your sick and your troubled. I know for certain the lives of many have been changed by his touch, as well as by his words. When I first met him, I thought he was a simple man. As each day passes, I see his beautiful life unfolding and realize that in our midst is a person who has been sent to us, I feel, for only a brief moment, to pass through our midst as one of us, but as one who carries in his soul the brilliance of God's own light, and the passion of God's own love, to show our blinded minds a new way, and our sick hearts a new love, to make it possible for all of us to dream a new dream of a future together as indeed a new family of God, sharing a common purpose to build a whole new nation together and show to the world how beautiful it can be for brothers and sisters to live together in harmony. This man I now present to you. Joshua, please come forward."

Joshua approached the microphone with a serene smile and a casual demeanor and looked across the crowd. It was so familiar. As of old, "He felt sorry for the people, they were like sheep without a shepherd." Looking at a small group with crutches and walkers, he addressed the crowd:

"We have come here battered and bruised and hurting, not because of something God has done, but because of what we have done to one another. I saw two little children this morning. One was blind and the other was crippled. They were playing together and laughing and having fun, as children should. One was an Arab, the other a Jew, but they didn't know that, they were friends. The Arab child had been shot in the head by a soldier's bullet, the Jewish child wounded by a terrorist's grenade. But they were too small to know hatred, and vengeance was still foreign to them. They were just friends playing together and sharing their cookies and candy.

"It has been said, 'You shall not kill,' but I tell you, evil does not begin with the soldier's bullet, or coward's grenade. Evil is conceived in the human heart. That is the great sin, because it assaults the temple of God's presence within one's soul and drives God from that soul. In the hate-filled heart Satan makes his home, because hatred is the foul air where Satan thrives. It is the nourishment of sick minds. Satan cannot exist where there is love. If someone asks me, 'Is my child possessed by the devil?' I will ask that person, 'Have you taught your child love?' In that you have your answer.

"I can see so many of you have heavy hearts, and so many worries. Stop worrying. Look at the world around you, the warm sun, the vast blue sky, the air so fresh and clean, the water teeming with life, and the wheat ready for the harvest. It is all yours, it is the expression of God's love for you. Look at that flock of swallows. They are so free. They don't worry about their next meal. They don't worry about the winter. Your heavenly Father cares for them. You are worth more than all the flocks of birds and all you do is worry, as if you never had a heavenly Father to care for you. Stop worrying. He is more like a mother than a father and looks over you not to find fault or to accuse, but with tender love. Indeed, call Him 'Abba,' 'Daddy,' because that is what He is to you. He will care for you, He will heal your wounds if you give Him a chance. He will prepare you for the future. You are concerned with tragedy. There will always be tragedy. That does not come from God, but when tragedy strikes, He is closer than ever because He knows you need Him. And in His home all wounds are healed and all pain is taken away, and there the joy and peace is endless. So do not be afraid of those who can kill the body, but only of those who can destroy the soul, because when the body dies a new and more beautiful life begins. I know because I came from there, and I have seen what my Father has prepared for those who love Him."

The vast crowd, spread out across the hillside, sat there spellbound, hanging on every word, many with tears in their eyes, and filled with a peace they had never known before.

When Joshua finished, the whole crowd rose and applauded wildly. That wasn't what he was looking for, but he accepted it as a spontaneous expression of their appreciation for what he had given them, something they had been starving for all their lives and had never received.

The crowd eventually settled down, and Daniel spoke to them, giving them instructions for the next item on the agenda, which was lunch. Joshua had spoken for well over an hour, and the crowd was hungry. While they ate, Joshua walked among them, talking to them in small groups, families pouring their hearts out to him with problems plaguing them, others asking him to pray for them, others asking him to touch their little children and bless them, just as of old.

Susan had been trying to get his attention, because he had forgotten to eat, and she thought he must be hungry and tired after that long talk. She ended up bringing lunch to him, so he could eat it while he moved among the people.

Father Ambrose Boyd was there with a group of his friends, including three Orthodox priests. Rabbi Herbstman and his wife were also with him, as well as Father Elias Friedman, all having a good time. In the group next to them were a dozen Protestant Pentecostals who had heard of Joshua's reputation and were anxious to meet him and hear him speak.

Joshua moved unobtrusively toward the men who had been following him all over the land and did not let on he had the slightest idea he knew who they were. They looked sheepish as he approached and asked them their names and what city they were from, and about their families. They answered briefly and gave no more information than was absolutely necessary. People around them sensed they were strange, but Joshua did not betray them.

During lunch Shlomo played the guitar and sang a medley of songs for the crowd. Some they knew and sang along with him.

After lunch, Aaron spoke of the practical steps the group might take to promote peace. One of the steps was writing letters to the officials of opposing sides and telling them strongly how they felt and how important it was that they take definite steps toward peace. They should also encourage their friends to become part of the movement, and if possible to attend the next meeting, which would be held on the hill outside Bethlehem. The date was set for that meeting and everyone was welcome and encouraged to come. Joshua then spoke for a few minutes, and the crowd departed. It was a totally successful day. Daniel, Aaron, Susan, and the others on the committee were beside themselves with how well Joshua's message was received and how friendly everyone was toward one another. Sheik Ibrahim came up to Joshua afterward and thanked him in the name of his family and said he had never felt such peace in his heart in all his life. He asked Joshua if sometime they could all meet on the Temple Mount. If he was willing, the sheik would talk to his friends in charge of the mosque and other leaders of the Arabic community and pave the way. Joshua thought that would be a splendid idea, since it was happening so spontaneously.

By six o'clock the hillside was empty, and perfectly clean. Aaron and his comrades decided to stop off with Joshua at a restaurant and have a little something to eat before they made the journey back to Jerusalem. It turned into a quiet but happy celebration.

11

ONCE BACK IN Jerusalem, Aaron insisted Joshua spend the evening at his house. It did not take much persuasion as they were all tired from the journey. The children were told to get ready for bed. They asked Joshua to tuck them in and tell them a story, but they were sound asleep before he finished.

Aaron and Esther stayed up late talking to Joshua, sipping cordials as they relived the events in Galilee earlier in the day.

"Joshua," Aaron started, "I can't get over the ease with which you handled such a tense and suspicious crowd. Weren't you nervous?"

"What was there to be nervous about?" Joshua replied. "Everyone there came for the same purpose, with the hope that this time, perhaps, they might set out on a solid path to peace. People are sick of war, of hatred, and of living under siege. They feel guilty they can't give something better to their children than guns and bitter memories that poison their future. They came ready to listen."

"How do you think they left?" Esther asked. "People have been so disillusioned in the past and are so tired of empty words and promises that it is hard to imagine them being optimistic about anything. I know they felt good after your talk. So many told me of the peace they felt when you were speaking. They said they had never felt that way before. Do you think it will last?"

"With God's grace," Joshua answered, "and our continuing efforts, we can forge a way to peace. But Esther, remember, peace is a full-time job. It doesn't just happen. People's minds must be conditioned to thinking peace. That is what is difficult. Anger stirs up suspicions and fosters isolation. That isolation sends out messages, such as 'I don't want to have anything more to do with you,' which is itself offensive because it affects the innocent as well as the guilty and generates more hostility. So we have to keep people talking and encourage them to make the effort to be friendly. Friendliness also feeds off itself and generates corresponding good feelings. Peace cannot grow in a vacuum. A climate of peace must be cultivated.

"And it has to start with the children. It is a terrible evil to teach children to be suspicious and to hate. Our people have to put past evils behind them and look afresh to the future. Their children have a right to be happy, and they have a chance only if parents don't instill their own hatred and prejudice in their minds. Every child should be allowed to start life free of suspicion and with a happy outlook. So, yes, I think what people found today will have a lasting effect, if we keep up our own efforts and pray."

"Why do you say 'pray'?" Aaron asked, with an almost cynical grin. "I never saw much value in praying. I've seen too damn much of it in pious people who use it as a mask for meanness."

"Come now, Aaron, you know not everyone is like that," Joshua replied with disappointment in his voice but fully appreciating Aaron's past unpleasant experiences. "God has the same problem you have with people. But real prayer is valuable. It is inviting God into your life and sharing your life with Him, and even more important, listening to Him as He guides you. When prayer is sincere, God listens, and He can move hearts just as easily as He can cause the wheat to grow and the trees to bear fruit. With His help our task will be much easier. Without His help an army of psychiatrists could not change these people's hearts. Do you think that what happened in Russia was just an accident? Mikhail Gorbachev came from a prayerful family. On the backs of the pictures of Lenin and Stalin in his family's living room were icons of Jesus and Mary. He is a man of deep faith, and knew he had a destiny from God to lead his people to freedom. In six months he dismantled an empire which had stood for seventy-five years. And he did it peacefully."

"How do you know that?" Aaron asked impetuously, thinking he had finally caught Joshua off guard and was about to trap him into revealing something about himself.

"It is easy to pick up information these days with communication being so instantaneous," Joshua responded. "Gorbachev himself told the priests who arranged for him to meet the pope that he had a faith which he got from his mother. He also told them he knew he had a destiny that would not fail."

"You mentioned Jesus," Aaron said. "Do you believe in him?"

"Aaron, how can a Jew not see beauty in him? He is part of our history. His life and goodness reflected Yahweh's presence in a way that is unparalleled in all of our history. What others have done to His message does not diminish his beauty or his greatness. Our people should be proud he is one of us."

"Joshua," Esther said, "when I was watching you speak to that crowd today, I have to tell you, you reminded me of the stories I heard about Jesus. And I thought he couldn't have been much different. Even the setting was striking in its similarity."

"Well, I'm tired," Aaron finally admitted, "and unlike you two, I have to work tomorrow."

"Chauvinist!" Esther shot at him as he picked up the glasses and headed for the kitchen.

They were all tired. It was almost two o'clock, the edge of a new day.

The children beat the alarm clock and woke everyone early. The first thing they did was look for Joshua to finish the story for them. They knocked on his door and pushed it open. Joshua was on his knees facing the open window, deep in prayer. He didn't hear the children. They discreetly tiptoed back out and closed the door quietly.

"Abba, Daddy," the little one said as she entered her father's room. "Joshua is on his knees praying."

"How do you know that, little one?" Aaron asked.

"Because we saw him," David answered. "We went into his room to ask him to finish the story he started last night. But we didn't disturb him. We walked back out and closed the door. He didn't even know we were there."

At the breakfast table, the two little children fought to sit next to Joshua. Who could deny them? They made him promise to finish the story after breakfast.

Esther passed around the bowl of fresh figs. "I know they're not quite in season, but we got some from friends back from vacation."

Joshua immediately thought of the fig tree on the road to Jerusalem from Bethany, the one he cursed because it looked so promising but bore no fruit.

After breakfast Joshua took the three children out in the yard and finished the story.

"Last night I told you about the very special donkey. He was just an ordinary donkey, like all children are ordinary, but he had a special job, just like each of you will have a very special job to do when you get older. I told you about how this donkey was trained for his very special job and then one day he was sold to a holy man called a prophet. From then on the donkey used to carry the prophet everywhere. Sometimes the prophet would fall asleep on the journey. Any other donkey would have stopped to graze or to lie down, but not this donkey. He continued on the journey and when the prophet woke up he found himself just where he wanted to go. But how did the donkey know? Can you tell me that, David?"

The little boy shook his head.

"After many years, the donkey grew old, but still he carried the holy man wherever he wished. But the prophet was growing old, too. And on one journey, while they were traveling along a deserted road, the prophet became ill, and falling forward, rested his head on the donkey's neck.

"The donkey knew the old man was sick, and what do you think he did? He walked off the road and took a very dangerous path through a valley and hills that sheltered robbers and thieves. However, the donkey was smart, and he cared for the burden on his back, so he cleverly took a path that circled around behind where the bandits usually waited in the rocky hills and avoided them.

"Not far from the hills was a village where a kind old doctor lived. The donkey was born in that village and, though he never talked to anyone, he knew things about everyone there. He remembered just where the doctor lived and carried his friend to the door of the doctor's house and banged on the door with his hoof until the doctor answered.

"After lifting the old prophet from the donkey's back, the doctor carried him into his house and examined him and put him in bed. After a few days under the doctor's watchful care, the prophet regained his strength and was able to continue on his journey.

"No one even realized what the donkey had done, and no one even thought to thank him. He could tell no one about it, and no one ever knew how the old prophet found his way to the village and the doctor's house. But the donkey didn't care whether anyone knew or not. He loved the old prophet and needed no thanks and no applause. He was simply glad he was able to save his friend's life.

"When you get older, perhaps the most important accomplishments of your life may go unnoticed or unappreciated, but that's all right. You didn't do them to be appreciated, or to be noticed. You did them for God from the goodness of your heart, to brighten other people's lives or to make the world a better place to live in. And that is what will always make you precious in God's eyes."

"Joshua," David asked, "if no one knew about the donkey's story, how did you find out?"

Joshua laughed loudly, surprised at the child's sharp mind, and told them someday they would understand.

When Aaron left for work, Joshua asked if he would drop him off in the city. The kids didn't want him to leave. He hugged them and said good-bye.

No sooner had Aaron left Joshua on the street than the two intelligence people picked up his trail again. It was a mystery how they knew where to find him. And just as surely, an Arab boy was not too far off, always in the crowd, and always pushing his bicycle should he need it. The two boys now took turns watching out for Joshua, so it didn't look obvious they were following someone.

If the men thought they were going to follow Joshua this day, they had another thought coming. Joshua spotted an Arab riding a camel. Sensing the man was headed in the direction he was going, he asked him for a ride.

"I'm going to Jericho," the man said.

"I know. That's where I'm going," Joshua responded. "Would you kindly give me a ride?"

"I'd be happy to," the man said.

As the man nudged the camel to sit, Joshua mounted and the two men rode off, to the utter despair of the two agents. The boy laughed to himself, seeing how upset the men were. But it didn't take them long to recoup, and in a matter of minutes a military vehicle appeared. The men boarded and tried to catch up with the camel. It had disappeared, vanished like a puff of smoke. Where could they have gone? There was nothing along the highway on either side. Driving farther down the road into the valley, they found the camel again, but there was only one man riding it. Joshua was gone.

Joshua had asked the man if he would drop him off in the desert, so he could walk to the hills; the man obliged him. Joshua immediately set out for the rocky cliffs overlooking Jericho. The boy had followed along the road on his bicycle to where the highway opened onto a wide stretch of desert where the boy had no cover. However, he knew the men had only one way back to the city and that was this same road, so the boy climbed up on the rocks and just waited. He could see the vehicle in the distance and the camel as well. A long way off to the left he spotted a lone figure crossing the desert. It had to be Joshua. The boy chuckled at his uncanny shrewdness.

The men in the vehicle questioned the camel driver for a long time, apparently getting nothing from him, because they turned back and tried to find tracks on either side of the highway. By now the boy could see Joshua was a good distance into the foothills. There would be no way they could catch up with him. The men finally decided he had gone in that direction but it was futile to try to follow him, so they turned back to the city, no doubt to report to headquarters and let their superiors decide what to do. They at least knew where their man was, and they could catch up with him at any time.

The boy followed the vehicle until it reached headquarters.

That night Joshua spent in the caves on the side of the rocky escarpment. Here was the place where he retreated long ago to prepare for his ministry. Here was the place where he was tempted by Satan. The site was totally barren and empty of life other than a few animals and birds who made their homes in the rocks.

Walking along a narrow ledge for almost five hundred feet, Joshua had found a cave and entered. It was the same cave where long ago he had spent forty days and nights fasting and praying. This time, too, he spent the night praying. As the sun was setting, Joshua could see for miles, far across to the city of Jericho, and down along the northern end of the Dead Sea.

The events that took place there were so real. The blind beggar by the roadside crying out, "Jesus, Son of David, have mercy on me," and jumping up and down like a child when he saw the light of day for the first time; and the diminutive chief publican, climbing out on the branch of the sycamore tree so he could see Jesus when he passed by, and his delight when Jesus stopped and called him by name and invited himself to his house for supper.

The next morning on waking up, he got up and looked out across the valley. The sun was rising and turning everything a reddish gold hue. In imagination Joshua could see all the kingdoms of the earth Satan had promised for one act of devil worship. He could also see the loaf-shaped rocks the devil tried to nudge him into miraculously turning into loaves of bread, but to no avail. In the dark of night Joshua prayed for all his new friends, and for peace.

It wasn't until the next day the two intelligence men with four others left headquarters and started out after Joshua. This time the Arab boy was ready. He had a motorized bicycle. He also brought lunch, a pair of binoculars, and a two-way radio to contact a contingent of friends whom he had mobilized in case the men should try to do something to Joshua. The boy sensed a drama was about to unfold.

The men scoured the hills for almost four hours. The Arab boy spotted Joshua nearby as he was approaching the highway. The boy laughed to himself. Joshua had eluded them again and would be well on his way into the city before the men could catch up with him. This simple man was making a fool out of these intelligence people. It was as if he knew beforehand every move they would make and adroitly sidestepped them, leaving them wringing their hands in frustration. The boys relayed brief, cryptic messages to one another, telling each one along the way what had happened, then signed off.

Joshua was aware of the boy's presence but betrayed no sign of recognition. He did not go back to Jerusalem, but headed up into the hills and worked his way to Ein Kerem. Even though the land had changed over the centuries, Joshua remembered every road and pathway and had no difficulty finding the village.

Ein Kerem was an ancient town tracing its origins far into the Bronze Age. In the time of Jesus, it was where John the Baptist was born and grew up. It was roughly five miles from Jerusalem, in the Judean hill country, not far from the main government buildings in Jerusalem. Ein Kerem was also the place where Mary visited her elderly cousin Elizabeth, already six months pregnant, and felt her child leap within her at the approach of the mother of her Lord. Mary was at the time herself only a few weeks pregnant. For centuries Ein Kerem had been inhabited by Muslims and Arab Christians. Recently they have been replaced by Jewish settlements.

Joshua walked through the town, remembering the ancient sites, and visiting familiar places like the church which sheltered the remains of Zachary and Elizabeth's house. His real purpose in coming there, however, was not to sightsee but to visit close friends of Aaron and his companions and interest them in his campaign for peace, a herculean task.

Joshua stayed for two days in the town, watching, waiting for the right moment and for the right person, much like his one-man invasion of Samaria long ago, when his contact was the disreputable woman at Jacob's Well who had been married five times. She became his emissary to the Samaritan community.

The day after his arrival, an incident occurred as Joshua was wandering through town. A truck came plowing down the main street when a child thoughtlessly chased a ball out into the street and was struck by the vehicle and thrown up on the sidewalk. Joshua witnessed the incident.

People, hearing the screeching brakes, began to converge on the scene. Two construction workers coming out of an alley were the first to reach the child lying there unconscious, her head covered with blood. Joshua calmly walked over and bent down, quietly caressing the girl's face and head with his hand, as if wiping away the blood. As he did so, the girl slowly opened her eyes and looked up at him. He arose and continued on his way, leaving the two men and the others just arriving to care for the girl.

Word spread of what had happened. Some said the girl was dead and this stranger brought her back to life. Others laughed at the idea and said she had only fainted. The two construction workers told the parents the bare details and left it up to them to believe what they wished. The fact that there was no trace of a wound when just a moment before the stranger touched her the girl's head had been covered with blood said all that needed to be said. Whatever had happened, their daughter was well. But the stranger was nowhere to be found.

It was the next day, as Joshua was sitting on a bench along a sidewalk in the shopping district, that a shopkeeper named Anna recognized him as the man who had healed the little girl.

"Aren't you the one who helped that little girl yesterday?" the woman asked.

"Yes," Joshua answered simply.

"Was she dead?" the woman continued, trying to solve the mystery.

"That is of little importance. She is well now. That is all that matters," Joshua replied politely.

"What did you do to heal her?" the woman persisted.

"I did nothing more than what you saw," Joshua responded.

The woman went back into her store and phoned the family of the little girl. They came up the street immediately and found Joshua still sitting on the bench, watching people as they went about their business, with such harried looks on their faces, seemingly beset with so many heavy burdens.

It was quiet time, and some stores were closed for the afternoon.

"Sir," the little girl's mother said to Joshua, "are you the one who helped our daughter?"

"I saw her lying there on the ground and I went to see if she was all right. She is all right, isn't she?" Joshua said simply.

"We know you are just being modest," the girl's father said. "Whatever you did, you gave our daughter back to us and there is no way we can adequately express our gratitude to you. Would you please honor us and come to our house? We would like our daughter to meet you. Oh, by the way, my name is Elias and this is my wife Sarah."

"Shalom," Joshua said in reply. "I am Joshua. Yes, I would like to meet your little girl."

Anna, the shopkeeper, who was just closing her store, came over to the three of them. Sarah turned to her and hugged her for being so thoughtful in calling her.

"Anna, thank you so much for finding this wonderful man for us. I'd given up hope of ever meeting him, as nobody seemed to know him. Won't you please come down to the house with us now that your store is closed?"

"Yes, I'd like to see Ada, she is such a lovable child. I'm so glad she is all right," Anna said, obviously delighted. The four of them walked down the street.

Elias and Sarah lived in a modest home, one of the older ones in town. When they entered, the little girl met them at the door.

"Joshua, here she is, here is our little Ada, whom you saved yesterday. Isn't she a beautiful child?" Sarah said as she ushered everyone into the living room.

"Ada, this is Joshua, the man who saved your life yesterday when you were hit by the truck," the mother told the girl.

Joshua reached out and rested his hand on the girl's head. She looked up into his eyes and smiled but did not recognize him.

After they all sat down, Sarah served refreshments.

"Joshua," Elias said, "since yesterday our phone has been ringing off the hook, people wanting to know who this stranger was who saved Ada's life. And we couldn't even tell them. We want you to know we will all be eternally grateful to you for your kindness. You must be very close to God. The two construction workers told us all the details. They certainly were impressed. They've already spread your fame throughout the neighborhood. And even they couldn't tell people your name."

Joshua just laughed.

As much as the family pressed Joshua to tell them whether the girl was dead, Joshua would not answer. The rumor the two men spread around town was that the girl was so badly injured she had to be dead. You could tell her skull was cracked. There was no way she could have survived that blow.

All that Joshua was concerned about was that the girl was now all right, and everyone should be grateful to God for giving the child back to them.

Finally, the family pursued the matter no further, and Sarah set about preparing for supper. They decided on an early meal to accommodate their guests. Anna had to get back to work, and Joshua had other things to do before the day ended.

By the middle of supper, Ada began to warm up to Joshua, though she still did not know what everyone was talking about, or what had happened to her. As she was sitting next to Joshua, he could talk to her quietly and at one point dipped a piece of bread into the sauce on his plate and gave it to the girl. After dinner he gave her part of his dessert. Now they were good friends.

Conversation during the meal centered mostly on Joshua, who he was, what he did for a living, where he came from. Joshua told them about his friends and the community that was forming among the Arab and Jewish people. Elias and Sarah were curious though not particularly interested, until he mentioned Aaron Bessmer's name. Then they brightened up and told Joshua they knew his relatives who lived not very far away, indeed, just down the street. In fact, Elias promised to call them after supper and see if they couldn't stop over afterward, if that was acceptable to Joshua.

Joshua's mentioning the involvement of military officers in their project seemed to bless it, and the others began to show

more interest. Also since the movement seemed to mean so
much to Joshua, they felt, out of gratitude, they should at least
show some willingness to listen and, perhaps, even help in some
limited way. Anna was very excited about the idea and said she
would talk it up with all her customers, though she doubted if
there would be much interest among those living in the settlements.

After supper, Anna left for her store. Elias called Aaron's relatives, Simon and Mildred Rose, who said they would be delighted to meet Joshua, about whom they had heard so much.
They lived only two blocks away, in a simple dwelling like so
many others in the settlement.

Although Aaron was not their favorite relative because of his
close association with Arabs, they were all proud of him because
he was a military hero and had brought honor and fame to the
whole family. They were cordial mostly, however, because of
their friendship with Elias and Sarah, who, like Mildred, belonged to the temple sisterhood.

After initial conversations, the topic came around to Aaron,
since it bothered the family so much. "As for me," Mildred said,
"I couldn't care less whether the Arabs even exist. I hope they
drive them all out of the country."

"Mildred," Joshua said, "you are a religious woman, and you
try to please God. Do you think it is pleasing to God for religious persons to harbor hatred for people of a different race or
religion?"

"I don't know whether it is pleasing to God or not, but I
know how I feel, and I can't forgive Aaron for what he is doing!"

"The ultimate judgment of God," Joshua answered, "will not
be based on whether we are a chosen race or not, or on how we
as Jews treat one another, but on how we treat all of God's
children. If we say we love God whom we cannot see and turn a
deaf ear to the desperate cries of anguish and deprivation all
around us, we cannot expect God to welcome us into His home
when we face Him on Judgment Day. Don't be too hard on
Aaron. He and his family have gone through painful experiences
that have brought him to where he is. He is merely trying to do

his part to make life bearable for people. We can't continue living this way."

"You may be right, but everyone is filled with hatred around here," Mildred said, annoyed with this stranger preaching to her.

"That is precisely why it has to stop," Joshua said, pressing his point. "A community can't exist with everyone filled with hatred. That is what hell is. Your children deserve better than that. They have a right to grow free of suspicion and fear and hatred. We owe them that."

Mildred was not about to admit that Joshua was right, but she had to admit that he made sense.

"I take it you and Aaron are good friends and work together on this project," Mildred said.

"Yes, we have come a long way, and much goodwill has already been generated. You and Simon might even like to come to our next gathering to see what it is like," Joshua said with tongue in cheek, but serious nonetheless.

"Simon can go, but I really have no interest," she said.

"In fact, I think I might like to go," Simon interjected. "It will be good to see Aaron again anyway. We were always good friends. When do you meet next?"

"We will be meeting on the Temple Mount next Wednesday evening," Joshua answered.

"The Temple Mount?" Elias said, shocked. "You'll end up with a riot."

"No, it will be a beautiful event," Joshua replied. "Sheik Ibrahim Saud is making arrangements with the officials at the mosque for all of us to gather there. They have a great respect for the sheik. Don't you think that will be an event worth seeing?" Joshua ended by saying, not without a trace of humor.

They all agreed it would be extraordinary if it happened, although it was impossible to imagine something like that taking place.

As it was getting late, Elias, Sarah, and Joshua rose to leave. Even though the conversation was a bit heavy, it dealt with matters on everyone's mind, and in a friendly way, so it turned out to be a fruitful introduction for Joshua. He had accomplished his mission, with the help of fortuitous events and kind people, a beautiful example of the delicate way God brings people and events together to accomplish His carefully laid plans.

Joshua slept out in the fields that night. He had many things to discuss with his Father.

12

THE NEXT DAY Joshua went up to Jerusalem. When he arrived, the city was in turmoil. A group of Arab students had been arrested and the Arab community was protesting. People were roaming the streets looking for trouble. As Joshua entered, Arab children were throwing stones at soldiers walking down the street. One of the soldiers turned his automatic rifle on the children, felling two of them. The others fled in panic.

Joshua rushed over to the children lying in the street. The soldiers came over and grabbed him, ordering him to leave. Joshua looked at them with anger flashing in his face, and said bitterly, "You wouldn't have done this to your own. Why do you do it to these children? They are no less God's children than Jews. You will answer to God for this."

The soldiers were shocked and ashamed that one of their own would say that to them.

Joshua knelt down beside the children, and placing his head against their chests, listened for a heartbeat. There was none. Placing his hand on the children's heads, he prayed quietly. The soldiers, thinking he might be a doctor, just stood watching. An eerie silence hung over the empty streets. People peered furtively from their darkened windows. The soldiers, becoming nervous with the ominous silence, cast glances in every direction, as if expecting trouble, then looked down at Joshua and the children. They were stunned to see the children open their eyes and look up at Joshua. He took each of them by the hand

and helped them sit up, then lifted them to their feet and told them to go home and behave themselves and keep out of further trouble.

The soldiers stood there in dumb silence, not knowing what to make of this odd Jew. Joshua looked at them in anger and walked away, leaving them standing there in the middle of the street. Arab people in houses adjacent to the street were now jeering at the soldiers, shouting "Shame! Shame!" for having shot little children. Many of the people, frightened by the noise in the street, had come to their windows just before the soldiers shot the children and had witnessed the whole incident. In a matter of minutes the episode spread like fire through the Arab community. When the soldiers reported the incident to head-quarters, Aaron found out about it and couldn't wait to see Joshua and get the whole story straight from him.

Even though the soldiers did not know the man's name, Aaron knew it could only have been Joshua who would have done such a thing.

Joshua's popularity among the Arab community had now reached a new high. People were beginning to wonder who he really was. They knew he was a Jew, but the man clearly stood above the common herd of humanity by his sheer greatness of soul and manifested in his caring for people an uncommon sense of goodness that separated him from Jew and Arab and Christian yet made each of them feel he was a part of them.

Only those who had a stake in continuing the internecine conflicts were developing a hatred of Joshua that bordered on frenzy. Some people are so filled with hatred and need for vengeance that peace is like a poison that threatens to heal their tortured souls. That is the last thing they could even think of allowing. Joshua's effect alone on people of every description was capable, given the occasion and the time, of bringing about that peace. He seemed simple enough, but his simplicity was to these diseased minds a carefully calculated strategy to disarm the unwary and seduce people into thinking peace was possible. Merely bringing people to that state of thinking was a step toward peace. That could not be tolerated.

It was only two days later when this fact became very clear. Joshua had been visiting friends near the Pool of Siloam. He had dropped off some packages he thought the poor families in the area might need. Walking back up the hill above the pool, an isolated area, he was accosted by five men, Arabs. As he approached, they rushed him, pulling out knives, attempting to stab him. Joshua spotted them just in time and slipping behind a tree, picked up a large stick lying on the ground and fended off their attack, striking one of them in the head and jabbing another in the stomach, then knocking the knives from the hands of two of the others. He was then face-to-face with the last one, who lost his nerve when he was standing there alone with Joshua.

It was Sheik Ibrahim's son, Khalil.

What he could not accomplish with four accomplices, he was too cowardly to accomplish by himself. The majesty of Joshua's bearing awed him, and the look in Joshua's eyes was a look the man would never forget. It was a look of anger and a frightening threat of impending judgment, yet a look filled with an unbelievable compassion. In an instant it drained the strength and energy from the man. He turned, ashamed, and fled like a beaten dog.

The incident did not go unnoticed. Joshua's faithful young friend was watching from a distance and saw what had happened. That night he would have to report it all to his grandfather.

Joshua continued up the hill, using the stick to help him up the steep ascent. He was clearly troubled by what had just taken place, and his expression, which was ordinarily calm, became serious and distressed. The concern was not for himself. He knew he could control whatever situation might arise. His concern was for Khalil. He was not an evil man. He had been trained to hate from infancy. How could he not hate? Joshua could see clearly the fate that now awaited the man. The boy would tell his grandfather, the sheik, what had taken place. The grandfather would become enraged at the audacity of his son so flagrantly violating the family's honor and the sheik's orders concerning Joshua. The penalty for such an affront to authority was death by hanging.

Joshua spent the whole rest of the day preoccupied with the situation. That night he slept little. Far into the night he was still on his knees talking with his Father, asking His guidance. It was only a little before dawn when he finally lay down on the ground and, resting his head on the root of an ancient olive tree, fell into a deep sleep.

The next day he rose early and, after having breakfast at a little shop in the city, started out for the sheik's camp. Joshua knew the trial was already taking place while he was on his way, and by the time he would arrive, the young man would already have been convicted and condemned. Son or not, the family's honor and, what was more, the sheik's honor had been shamelessly violated. Such a crime could not be tolerated. As much as it broke the old man's heart to have to pass a sentence of death on his own son, it was his responsibility to his authority and to the tribe that he not cave in to sentimental feelings and fail to execute his duty to Allah and to his family. His son, his own flesh and blood, had attempted to assassinate not just someone who had become a dear friend of the family but one for whom the sheik himself had vowed protection and the enduring loyalty of his family. The shame and humiliation the sheik felt over the perpetration of such a crime by his own son devastated the old man. There was no alternative. The son had to die.

Joshua knew what the outcome would be. He hoped he could bring some comfort to the family and mediate the crisis that had overtaken them.

Joshua arrived a little before noon. The atmosphere in the camp was somber. People were gracious and wished Joshua peace, but no one seemed happy. Even the children who were normally jovial and in high spirits seemed depressed and listless. They weren't even playing.

The sheik was in his tent. Joshua asked if he might see him. Naturally, the answer was yes. Joshua had immediate entree to the sheik whenever he should wish to see him. Joshua entered the tent. The two men exchanged salaams and the kiss of peace. Then, after the sheik gestured for Joshua to be seated, they sat and immediately began sharing with each other what was on their minds.

"My dear friend," the sheik began, "I cannot begin to tell you how ashamed I am that you have been so insulted by one of my family, and what is the greatest indignity, by my own son. A thousand apologies, and I know that that is not enough. I must tell you that we have just held court before you arrived, and my son confessed his guilt. He will be executed tomorrow morning by hanging."

The old man was so ashamed that he found it difficult to look directly at Joshua but forced himself to keep a steady gaze. Joshua looked at him with no anger, or sense of insult, but with a look of deep concern which was disconcerting for Sheik Ibrahim.

"You do not look pleased, my brother, that I have decided to execute my own son to offer satisfaction for what he attempted to do to you," the sheik said, confused.

"Sheik Ibrahim," Joshua said calmly, "you have become a beloved brother to me, and dearer to God than you could imagine. I realize what the men tried to do yesterday. But they could not hurt me. My Father would not allow it. Your son's soul is eaten up with hatred. He was not born that way, my good friend. He was taught to hate. He was merely being faithful and obedient to what he has been taught since childhood. Because his teachers have changed as they grew older does not mean that he will lay aside what was instilled in him for a lifetime."

The sheik lowered his eyes in shame. He realized Joshua was referring to him and the way he had brought up his son. The sheik, as he grew older, had realized the futility of hatred and vengeance and changed his whole outlook, especially since meeting Joshua, which confirmed his new vision of life. But the son still carried on faithfully the lessons he was taught.

Joshua went on, "To sentence your son to death is to deny your son can be saved. No human being has the right to terminate the life of one whom God has created. That right belongs to God Himself. In days gone by, people presumed they had the right from God to destroy other human beings, but my Father has given that right to no one. It belongs to Himself alone. Your son, Sheik Ibrahim, is not an evil man. If he can be exorcised of his hatred, he will do much good, and one day you will be proud of him. I know what plans God has in store for him. I beg you, my dear friend, to grant me this request and spare his life, so God may continue to work in his life."

The sheik was shaken by what Joshua said to him and felt guilty that in condemning his son, he was condemning himself as well, because Khalil was a product of his teaching and also of the sick environment in which they all lived. There was a long silence. A ray of hope passed across the sheik's mind at the possibility that he might not have to execute his son, but what about his own pride at rescinding his order of execution? If it were someone else's son, he would not back down. He would lose face with the rest of the tribe if he pardoned his son. His people would never respect him again. The sheik expressed these concerns to Joshua, who listened patiently and understood.

"Sheik Ibrahim," Joshua continued, pressing his plea, "if you pardon him, that is one thing. If I request you in front of your family, that is another thing."

"You would request me to pardon someone who attempted to assassinate you?" the sheik asked, the full import of Joshua's plea finally striking him. "That is difficult for me to understand. Forgiveness is not a virtue we are taught. You are so different from all of us, Joshua. Your ways are so beautiful. I wish I could have learned your ways from my youth. Our lives would be very different now. But how would you ask for this pardon?"

"I would ask that you assemble your family who are present here in the camp," Joshua replied. "You would then have your son brought before the whole family. I would at that point talk to your family, expressing to them my convictions and my feelings, and then present my request."

"Joshua," the sheik said, "I don't think I would do this for any other being alive. But since I have such respect for you, and since you are the person offended, I think it only right that I grant your request. I will call the family together immediately."

Getting up from his pillows with Joshua's help, the old man walked out of his tent and told his assistant to call the family together for a special meeting. Everyone was to come.

It was only a matter of minutes before everyone assembled. Last of all, Khalil, with hands bound behind his back, was led by two men into the front of the assembly. The sheik called for everyone's attention and introduced Joshua, who had asked to speak to the family.

Joshua rose and stood in the center of the huge semicircle. "My friends," he began, "I am no stranger to you anymore. I have been honored by Sheik Ibrahim in being made a member of your family. I know you are all aware of what happened yesterday. It is unfortunate. What your brother has done is not his fault alone. He lives, as do all of you, in a climate of hatred and revenge. It has become a way of life, and acceptable. But it is not God's way. It is not even reasonable. And it must come to an end if your people are to survive. Since I was the person offended yesterday, I have a right to express what I judge to be a legitimate request. I know your brother has been condemned. No matter what he has done he is still a child of God. No man has the right to take the life of God's children. It is the ultimate admission of despair, that there is no more hope for one whom God created out of infinite love. As long as God exists, there is always hope for even the most unfortunate of His children. It is for God to decide when He will take back the life He has given them. I know that my Father's work for your brother is not yet finished. He is to accomplish things that will one day make all of you proud. Now, he is a bound criminal condemned to die.

"I am aware of what the men attempted yesterday. They may have thought they were doing a good deed for a just cause. I do not agree. It is never a just cause to violate an innocent person. I do not approve of their evil deed. But I do forgive their sin, and I ask my Father as well to forgive them. And since the time is long past for us all to start forgiving one another if there is to be peace in this world, I ask my dear friend, Sheik Ibrahim, to pardon your brother so he may come to know God's forgiveness and find peace in his troubled soul. May God's peace be upon you all."

Finished, Joshua stepped back and waited for the sheik to respond. The crowd showed no emotion, just sat silently, intently. The sheik arose and walked over to Joshua.

"My people, my friend Joshua, my imam, I speak with a heavy heart, indeed, with a broken heart. What Joshua has said is true. We all share the guilt in the eyes of Allah. But evil must be punished. Joshua asks us to forgive. I must admit I do not understand this forgiveness. We have not been taught forgiveness. It is a strange teaching for all of us. But listening to Joshua speak I could see for the first time the beauty and the greatness of a man who can forgive. It makes him most Godlike. Khalil has committed a terrible evil. I cannot forgive him for that, though Joshua can find it in his heart to forgive him. Out of honor for Joshua who has already done so much, not just for our family, but for our people and for the cause of peace, I listened respectfully to his request to pardon the offender. While I cannot find it in my conscience to pardon such a heinous offense, I will change his sentence. The sentence of execution is revoked, but in its place, the offender will be banished from our family forever. He is not to be present in our midst, nor contact any of our family here present from henceforth. If he shows sorrow for his evil deeds and changes his ways, we will consider his situation at a time in the future to be determined by myself. The offender has one day to prepare for his departure. The meeting is over. The family is dismissed."

Khalil broke down sobbing like a baby. Still bound, he came over to Joshua and fell down on his knees, thanking him for his forgiveness, expressing his sorrow that he had such hatred in his heart, asking Joshua to pray to Allah to take the hatred from him. Joshua lifted him up and untied the straps that bound him. "Get up! You are forgiven. Be freed from the hatred that binds you!"

Khalil arose and looked into Joshua's eyes with gratitude and peace. Tears streamed down his face as he turned and walked away. The sheik watched from a distance, hoping he was witnessing a change in his son, then walked back into his tent with a heavy heart, thinking he would never see his son again.

Khalil was led back to his tent. A few friends came over to him expressing their relief and their sorrow for him. Most just ignored him. Joshua went to the sheik's tent and thanked him for his benevolence, then took his leave, promising that one day he would be proud of his son. As a parting remark, the sheik assured Joshua that all arrangements had been made with his friends at the mosque for the next meeting to take place on the mount. Joshua thanked him, then left.

13

JOSHUA'S DEFT GENIUS at avoiding unwanted intrusion into his privacy left the Mossad agents stunned and unable to account for his whereabouts over the previous twenty-four hours. Nor did they have the slightest clue as to where he was, or how he eluded them. So his reappearance in Jerusalem after leaving the sheik's camp was a further embarrassment. His disappearance not only intensified their suspicions and increased their own insecurity but put added pressure on their superiors to initiate some immediate action concerning him. There were no longer two agents assigned to track Joshua, but four. He, of course, was immediately aware of their change in tactics. He was also aware that the sheik had assigned two other grandsons to follow the agents, sensing some imminent and dramatic turn of events.

Indeed, Joshua's carefully laid plans were beginning to come together, and he was determined that nothing would frustrate what was so painstakingly planned. The scheduled meeting of Aaron's new "community" was to take place the following week. The Mossad had decided to execute their own plans concerning Joshua before then. Joshua was keenly aware of all the plotting, but he gave not the slightest hint that he had any idea of all the undercurrents. His ability to modify circumstances that threatened those plans became marvelously clear during the next few days.

Since the last meeting Aaron had appointed key leaders of small groups from various geographical areas and divided among them the list of all those who attended previous meetings, as a safe method of rapid and secure communication within the new organization. News of the upcoming meeting circulated in this way overnight; it would later prove to be an effective method of communicating with this vast group without using any of the news media, thereby avoiding unwanted attention and depriving obstructionists of an opportunity to create mischief.

That night Joshua met with his friends on Ben-Yehuda Street. They had not seen him in days and were excited when they spotted him walking down the street toward the cafe.

"Well, good friend," Aaron shouted as Joshua approached the table, "you certainly have a lot of explaining to do. It seems we can't leave you out of our sight for a minute without you getting into all kinds of predicaments."

Joshua just chuckled as he sat down next to Susan.

"Yes," Susan added, "and you have the Mossad agents tearing their hair out. We heard about you eluding them in the desert a few days ago. Even with the electronic surveillance equipment in their van they couldn't track you. You're uncanny. How did you avoid them?"

"And our own men at headquarters have been frantic over the incident with the Arab children," Aaron added. "What happened there anyway?"

"What did you hear?" Joshua asked him.

"We interrogated the soldiers involved. They were young fellows. It was the first assignment on patrol for one of them," Aaron said in an embarrassed attempt to excuse them, then continued, "When the Arab kids began to throw stones, he panicked. It's no excuse, and I'm ashamed, but more important, Joshua, what happened to the children?"

"They are all right," Joshua answered briefly.

"We know they are all right now," Nathan said, "but what condition were they in when you found them? We got two stories. The soldiers said they were slightly wounded. The Arab residents in the area said they were dead."

"Just thank God they are all right now," Joshua said, trying to pass over the subject.

"You are being evasive again, Joshua," Susan interjected. "Tell us what really happened. Even if the children were only wounded, after you touched them they got up and walked away with no trace of any wounds. Where were they hit?"

"They each had several wounds. It was an automatic," Joshua answered. "Why do you keep pressing? It should be obvious that God wants peace here and shows how interested He is in it by healing wounds."

Catching on to Joshua's ambiguous way of answering certain things, Simon broke in with the comment, "Well, I guess you just gave us our answer. You certainly have a subtle way of evading issues and couching facts. I can understand why the Mossad have a time with you. Not even their computers can figure you out. Talking to you is like playing a chess game. Every move is a maneuver."

Changing the subject, Aaron brought up the topic of the next meeting. The sheik had also informed him of the mosque officials' permission to use the square in front of the mosque for the meeting. They were at first concerned about the danger of a riot, but when the sheik assured them that there was no possibility of anything like that taking place, they accepted his judgment and gave their permission.

"How many do you think will be coming?" Aaron asked Joshua, as only he had a handle on the Arab community and their growing interest. Aaron also heard from his relatives in Ein Kerem that a good number of people from there would be coming as well.

"There should be quite a few more than last time," Joshua said confidently. "We are growing into a good-sized community."

"Of Jews, Moslems, and Christians," Susan said with ill-concealed pride. "Whoever would have dreamed of such a thing happening even a few months ago?"

"Yes, it is beautiful what can happen when people try to sense what God wants and open their hearts to His voice," Joshua said, making sure he got the point across as to who really deserved the credit for all the beautiful events taking place.

Aaron and Sheik Ibrahim had decided that the following Thursday would be the date for the upcoming meeting of the

whole group. Extensive plans were not needed, though the
mosque officials agreed with the sheik to set up an efficient
sound system to accommodate the huge crowd that was expected.

Aaron wanted Rabbi Herbstman to meet the mosque officials
in an attempt to prepare dialogues for the future. The rabbi was
not only an intelligent man, he was bighearted and almost totally devoid of prejudice and racial or religious pettiness. Joshua
also liked him and trusted him.

After talking a while longer, the group broke up. Knowing
that the Mossad had plans, Joshua decided it was best for him to
accept Aaron and Susan's invitation to stay with them for the
next few days. In fact, even Nathan and Samuel invited him to
stay at their places as well. This protected Joshua from the Mossad for at least twelve hours each day for the next week. So when
they left the cafe, Aaron took Joshua home with him.

The next morning the children squealed with delight when
they found that Joshua was in the house. During breakfast they
vied to sit next to him, and after breakfast he had to play games
with them, which he did until Aaron took him down to the city
on his way to work.

In the city, Joshua was again trailed by the agents and the
ever-present Arab boys, who must have started out each morning tracking the agents as they left headquarters, because wherever the agents were, there were the children. They were dog-
ged in their persistence and in their determination to let nothing
happen to Joshua. He had by now become their hero. Still,
Joshua never let on he had the slightest idea he was being followed, or knew what was going on, though he was aware of
their every move.

During the next few days, he knew it would be safer if he
spent the time in more heavily populated Arab neighborhoods,
where the Mossad would have to be much more discreet. So he
visited several of Sheik Ibrahim's relatives on the back streets of
Jerusalem, one family in particular whom Joshua knew would
ultimately play an important role in the community once the
peace movement was well on its way. Their names were Majid
and his mother Jamileh. They belonged to a respected and well-
to-do family in the neighborhood. They were also good friends

of another family that would play an important role in the peace movement, Elie, Soad, and Mathilde Zanbaghe, a brother and two sisters originally from Iran. Soad's husband, Siavosh Avari, was an engineer who had very well placed connections in the palace of the King of Saudi Arabia. Mathilde's husband, William, was also an engineer with other valuable contacts. Elie Zanbaghe was a genius at public relations and should have been a diplomat, but his most valuable asset at this time was his unique interest in the Jewish people and his rare insight into the complex issues facing the two hostile communities whose lives would be permanently and inextricably entangled. His feeling was that at some point they would all have to learn to get along with their neighbors if they wanted to thrive. They couldn't count on distant outside forces to protect them forever.

Joshua visited these people over the next three days and laid the groundwork for the roles they would be playing in the not too distant future. At their first encounter with him, they were impressed. They had heard of him from relatives. The sheik had previously contacted them to become involved, but they were not in town at the time. Now, having met Joshua and been told of the venture, they were enthusiastic to cooperate in whatever way they could. Joshua visited them during the day and later on met with Aaron and Susan and the others in the evening. He had already discounted events that were to happen the next week and was planning stategy for months down the line.

His vision was penetrating. He saw everything in very simple terms and refused to let human complications blur that vision. His steps were, accordingly, logical, methodical, and uncomplicated, like an artist who, with a few deft strokes, projects a powerful image on a piece of paper.

On Friday night, Aaron, Esther, Joshua, and the children went to the synagogue. Rabbi Herbstman had been invited to speak to their congregation, and Aaron thought Joshua would enjoy listening to him.

They arrived early, as Aaron wanted to introduce Joshua to his friends. Some had already heard of him. Surprisingly, a good number of Aaron's friends from military headquarters were present. Some were faithful attendants, but some came just for the occasion to hear Rabbi Herbstman.

The services were ordinary, except for the music. A guest musician from the United States, Joseph Eger, together with a few friends, provided the music for the ceremony. The rabbi was a thin man in his fifties, clean-shaven, with thinning and slightly graying hair and penetrating brown eyes. When he rose to speak, the sanctuary which was filled for the occasion fell completely silent.

"My dear friends," he began in a quiet, gentle voice, "I came across a strange man a few weeks ago on a Sabbath morning, walking through, or rather attempting to walk through, a Hasidic neighborhood in Tel Aviv. He was carrying a backpack and a canteen. As you can imagine, he might as well have been carrying a hand grenade, with the explosion that took place. Needless to say, he did not get very far, when I spotted him and extricated him from what could have been a tragic situation.

"It made me think, and I have done a great deal of thinking since then. So often we approach our religious situations from political or legal or cultural angles and will fight to the death over things that really have nothing to do with God. Even the Sabbath. Yahweh originally intended the Sabbath as a protection for slaves so that their owners could not work them to death. It was a day of rest and a time to have fun at family gatherings. It was religious leaders who thought that people were having too much fun on their day off and then turned the Sabbath into a legal nightmare, filled with endless prohibitions.

"What we have all lost in our religious focus, whether we are Jews, Moslems, or Christians, is how God feels about important issues in our lives. We have, in the course of our lives, deified our own political interests and prejudices, and even our own religions, so that God is no longer an entity to be even considered when we are making important judgments. We have effectively made Him irrelevant, because His values could too easily upset our carefully laid plans.

"We Jews worship God. Christians worship God. Moslems worship God. It is the same God, the same Intelligent Being. If He is alive and created us with tender love, then it seems only logical that He would want more than anything else that we love one another and would be delighted if we were to gather together and worship Him together. Yet what do we do—we kill one another, thinking we are doing God a service. But that is not the God for whom we are doing the service. We have made our religions and our cultural heritage God, and then kill in the name of that God whom we have created. It is the ultimate blasphemy.

"I saw a man last week playing a guitar. He was a Jew, but he was playing his guitar and singing songs for a crowd of Arabs. They were dancing and singing with him as he played. I stood there with my mouth wide open in wonderment. "How beautiful!" I thought. And I cried, as I thought that God must be smiling. That was real religion, and I am sure God was pleased.

"What would be so evil for Jews and Moslems and Christians to gather together and pray to our God whom we all say we worship? I am sure it would please God if we were to find common goals and work together, and if we could plan our lives together, and work together as one people. Our ancestors lived in Spain for half a millennium under Islamic rule, and they treated us humanely. Why can't we treat their descendants humanely today? Why can't we live side by side in peace and prosperity and as one people work together for the common prosperity of our nation?

"There is someone here in our midst this evening. I say this not to embarrass him, but because he had touched my life and the lives of many others as well. He is also a Jew, but he wears a medallion given to him by an Arab sheik, who reveres him so much he has even asked him to be his family's imam. How unusual, how unorthodox, yet that wise old sheik has finally, in his old age, found a rare religious man who understands God and truly speaks in God's interest and in God's name. So, for that sheik, it was not unorthodox for him to want this Jew to be his imam. It was an honest admission that, after searching for a lifetime, he finally found God in the teachings of a very rare Jew.

"This Jewish man mingles so casually and so gently among Arabs and Jews and Christians alike. Of late we have been gathering by the thousands to be with him and to listen to him. He truly interprets for us the ways of God and in the beauty of his own life shows us how simple our life as a people can be if we can only learn to forget our past hatreds and suspicions and reach out to one another and find each other as children of God.

It has to first happen among our own, whether we be Orthodox or Conservative or Reform or Hasidic. We have to be convinced that God is not pleased by walls of hostility we build between ourselves. If we want to really practice God's religion, we must start by learning how in God's name to love one another. Then we can reach out to others and bring them into our sphere of love and concern."

Before he ended, the rabbi invited everyone to the Temple Mount the next Thursday to gather with the others for their scheduled meeting.

The congregation was quiet, not just during the sermon but afterward. It was a powerful message, but one that no one ever expected to hear in a synagogue. Joseph Eger, off to the side with the other musicians, repeatedly nodded his approval all during the talk and couldn't wait for the service to end so he could tell the rabbi how much he appreciated his words.

Joshua also smiled throughout the talk and congratulated the rabbi during the social afterward. Even Aaron felt good about religion that night.

The next few days were quiet days, pauses in the busy schedule of hectic meetings and personal encounters. Joshua's quiet time was not at night in the hills, but in secluded spots here and there in Arab neighborhoods. Whenever he wanted to be alone, he unobtrusively eluded the agents and could usually snatch an hour or two of privacy before they finally caught up with him. The Arab children, however, seemed to be more ubiquitous than the agents, and Joshua rarely escaped from their seemingly ever-present eyes. On one occasion, Joshua had found a secluded spot on the hill above the Hinnom Valley. The spot was shrewdly picked by Joshua. He reached it by walking up the hill through terraced alleyways between the houses of Arabs, where the Jewish agents would be most reluctant to follow. The children, however, had no such difficulty. The spot was near a Greek monastery. Joshua ate his lunch there and after resting knelt and, sitting back on his heels, folded his hands in his lap and for almost an hour was in deep thought. The children just watched him. At first, they did not know what to make of it; then they realized he was praying. He was totally absorbed. All they had ever witnessed were people praying in front of others on a prayer rug, or Jewish people at the Wailing Wall. Joshua's prayer was different. There were no body movements, no loud expressions, just total concentration and a beautiful peacefulness as if he were in the very presence of Allah Himself. The children were deeply impressed.

Thursday came around rapidly. People began gathering on the Temple Mount, or to the Arabs, Haram es-Sharif (the noble enclosure), at first timidly. This was forbidden territory for Jews. The officials of the mosque went out of their way, out of deference to Sheik Ibrahim, to make the visitors feel welcome. Indeed, Jewish people were the first ones to arrive, and they were most cordially welcomed by Muslim officials.

Aaron, Susan, Daniel Sharon, and the others arrived early to help with preparations. Sheik Ibrahim sent several of his lieutenants to help with whatever needed to be done. The sheik himself came just before the ceremonies were to start. With his advanced age, it was becoming difficult for him to travel and attend affairs like this. Joshua arrived in the midst of a large contingent from Tel Aviv and Galilee who had arrived by bus at almost the same time. He was already lost in the crowd.

The program started at two o'clock. The sheik was asked to offer a prayer at the beginning and say a few words. Standing before the microphone, dressed in white robe and Arab headgear, he appeared fragile. Though he was little more than five and half feet tall, he looked tall and dignified. His white beard was neatly trimmed for the occasion. His green eyes carefully surveyed the vast crowd. More than eight thousand people almost half-filled the huge esplanade. The prayer the sheik offered was touching. The few words he said were simple but direct.

"My people, my friends, salaam! Shalom! This day is the dream of my old age. I have known poverty and I have known wealth. I have known love and I have known hatred. I have dreamed dreams and I have endured nightmares. I have seen children born and I have seen my children die. In the fading years of my life on this earth, I have learned much, but sadly, oh, so late. Had I in my youth the wisdom of my old age, I would have lived a different life. Hatred is an illusion. Hatred is the poison that destroys the dreams of innocence and turns the future into a living hell. It is the cancer that destroys our children.

"It is not like old men to talk about love. But only recently have I learned how to love. I have learned it from a Jew. I know he is a special person. He wandered from the desert into our camp one night and returned a lost lamb, my granddaughter's pet. He ate with us and stayed the evening with us. Wonderful things happened that night that changed my life. He taught us in a few hours how to love. Love is the answer to our problems here, not hatred, not revenge, but love. You can see what love has done for us all in just a few weeks. Look around you. We are Jews, Moslems, Christians, men, women, children, soldiers, politicians, even religious people. Look at where we meet, on this holy mount. This is the first time in all of human history that Jews and Muslims and Christians have met in this place together in the name of Allah, in the name of Yahweh, in the name of God. It is love that has brought us here. It is the work of God. What the future holds has to be bright, because God is our light and our inspiration. I may not live long, but being here today has given me hope for my children and for all our children. May God bless us all! Salaam! Shalom!"

After the sheik's words, Shlomo was asked to lead the group in singing as he did on the previous occasion. After the song, Aaron introduced Daniel Sharon, who spoke of the progress that had been made since the last meeting. The numbers had been growing steadily, and the influence of the group was beginning to be felt in high places. People had been asking what they could do in a practical way to create a better world. Daniel suggested that the purpose of the gatherings was not to tell people what they should do specifically, but to help people realize that there was much they could do, and that they should not be afraid to take whatever steps they felt inspired to take and attempt whatever good they were able to within their own circumstances and field of influence. They could contact their group leader if they had any questions. They in turn could always contact Aaron or Susan or one of Sheik Ibrahim's assistants.

Aaron and Susan then took their turns speaking, with Susan introducing Joshua. For some this was the first time they had seen Joshua, although they had heard so much about him. When he got up to speak, his appearance was disconcerting. He looked ordinary, but there was a dignity about his bearing that immediately set him off as someone very special.

"My friends," he began, "much has happened since our last gathering. God always makes things work for the good of those who love Him, and so many good things have happened to make this day possible. The goodness of the religious officials of this beautiful house of worship has made this gathering today memorable and historical. We are all deeply grateful to them for their kindness and their trust. It must please God very much to look down on what is happening here. And this is just the beginning.

"Cynics say it is impossible for our people to live together. From a human point of view, it may be true. But we forget there is a God, and a God who cares, a God who is the Father of us all and who loves us with the tenderness of a mother. It is His desire that we learn to find one another and reach out to one another in love and compassion.

"I saw a little Arab boy the other day run out into the street in front of a speeding car and pull a Jewish girl to safety. It was a beautiful sight seeing the two of them hugging and crying tears of joy. The families of those two children will be forever close.

"But walking through your streets day after day, I see so much pain, so much fear and anguish. Why are you so anxious? Why are you so afraid? Don't you know that God loves you and watches over you? I know you worry about your children. I know you worry about your jobs, and about your health. It is natural to worry, but it is of little value. You say God will not protect your children from a terrorist's bomb or a soldier's gun. You don't realize how many of your children God has protected from terrorists' and soldiers' guns and bombs. Had He not, many, many more would have died. Even those who died are at peace with Him, living a life of happiness you could never imagine. And they are still close to you, like the angels are to one another.

"Your Father in heaven wants you to enjoy the life He gave you here on earth. He has given you all you need to be happy.

Much of the hurt and pain comes not from God, but from people's abuse of His gifts, especially free will. It is such a special gift, but one which ties God's hands, because He has more respect for the freedom He gave you than people do. Once given God does not take back. Freedom can so easily be misused and is so often used to hurt others. Injustice and meanness are not from God. God spends much of His existence picking up the pieces of broken humanity, caused by the meanness and cruelty of others, healing the hurt caused by selfishness. There is more healing in the world than you could even dream of. God channels His healing power through the gentle hands of caring doctors and nurses, but many wounds He heals Himself in the quiet of the unknown, where He touches your hearts and souls.

"Trust Him. He loves you tenderly. Do not be afraid to turn your lives over to His care. There are so many beautiful things God wants to accomplish through your lives. So let Him draw you into His life so He can work through you. Once you let Him into your hearts and learn to reach out to one another, and break the isolation that separates you, you will find peace, and in that peace find all the resources you need to provide lavishly for the needs of one another.

"If only you can learn to get along and help each other, and work together, this little country will become the showplace and the model for all the world; she will be the light unto the nations. The whole world will see how beautiful it is for brothers and sisters to live in harmony.

"The past has many hurts and injustices. As painful as it has been, it is the past. It must be forgotten. It is today that is important. And we must start now to create the climate for peace. Take your olive branches and wave them through your streets. Give them as tokens to one another. And learn to love. Let your leaders know your feelings. They are the obstacles to peace. They thrive on conflict. They cannot afford to have people love each other. They must know your sentiments and feel the pressure of your concern. From this day, know that you are God's children, brothers and sisters to one another. May God's peace reign in your hearts and may you be blessed in one another. Salaam, shalom!"

The vast group sat on the pavement all during the talk, in breathless silence, hanging on to every word that fell from Joshua's lips, reminiscent of times long past when on these very sites huge crowds gathered to hear him speak. When he finished, the crowd stood up and spontaneously applauded him, many people turning toward one another and hugging and repeating Joshua's last words, "Salaam, shalom." In no time the whole crowd was embracing people who were complete strangers. The sheik walked up to Joshua and embraced him, kissing him three times, saying to him, "How beautiful, how beautiful, my son! God truly abides in your soul and speaks through your lips. We are indeed blessed."

Aaron waited until everyone settled down. Then after a few final perfunctory ceremonies, and another song led by Shlomo, the crowd was apprised of the next meeting and told they would be informed as to its whereabouts. Until then they were encouraged to initiate whatever gestures of goodwill might inspire them and to pray for one another and for peace.

In spite of the large numbers, the crowd dispersed in an orderly fashion and left the esplanade spotless. Afterward, Aaron and his colleagues met with the mosque officials and introduced them to Rabbi Herbstman. They talked briefly and made arrangements to have dinner together in the near future. The officials had heard Joshua's talk and, when they were introduced to him, told him how deeply touched they were by the profound simplicity of his understanding of God and wondered where he learned such beautiful sentiments.

In no time the mount was empty, except for a handful of Arab people walking around and praying. In the distance were the sheik's four grandsons, doggedly faithful to their duty of watching over Joshua. Aaron, Susan, Daniel, Nathan, Simon, and Sheik Ibrahim with his assistants walked off together, with Joshua in their midst. The sheik insisted they join him for supper at the Seven Arches. They enthusiastically accepted.

That night Joshua spent at Nathan's. They lived out in the country, in a large home. His family was very wealthy, and everything in their house showed remarkably good taste, the artwork, the furniture, the garden, and even the dishes. They kept kosher, and Joshua respected their attachment to the old ways, though his own life-style was far from traditional.

Nathan's parents were in their early seventies, warm people and sensitive. They showed a delicate respect for each other, which was not put on but quite natural and spontaneous. Joshua felt immediately comfortable in their presence. As it was late in the evening when Nathan brought Joshua home, they did not spend much time talking. Nathan showed Joshua to his room, and they all retired.

After breakfast, Nathan brought Joshua back into the city and dropped him off on Mount Scopus, where he visited the campus of the university. He had hardly arrived when the Mossad agents appeared, and far behind them on their bicycles at scattered intervals the Arab boys, always among other people. How the agents tracked Joshua's whereabouts was a mystery, whether through contacts on campus or from knowing he had stayed at Nathan's house the evening before and merely followed him to work the next morning.

When they arrived, Joshua was talking to a group of students. The agents, four of them this time, exited their van and walked up into the campus and surrounded Joshua, ordering the students to leave immediately. Grabbing Joshua, they marched him off to the van and promptly sped away.

One of the Arab boys saw what had happened and immediately alerted the other three on his portable phone.

"They have Joshua," Ali said. "I'm following close behind." Ali rode down the street past the campus's main entrance. The other boys caught up, and together they chased the van on its circuitous route through the city's heavy traffic. Around corners, down side streets, through alleys they went, and after almost thirty minutes of tortuous driving ended up in a sleazy part of town with poorly kept houses and odd-looking people. Parking the van in an alley, the agents dragged Joshua from the van, his hands tied behind his back, blindfolded. Entering the back entrance to an old house, the agents dragged him upstairs into a dirty old room with just a mattress, a few wooden chairs, and a lamp. Pushing him into the chair, two of the men left to check the rest of the building to make sure it was secure.

When they returned, they began interrogating Joshua. They asked him his true identity, where he had come from. As he had no identity papers, or papers of any kind, they were even more baffled. They tore the canteen off his shoulder and threw it in the corner of the room, then removed the blindfold.

Joshua refused to answer any of their questions.

"You have no right to touch me or question me. I have done nothing wrong."

"You will answer all the questions we ask either willingly or by whatever means we need to pry it out of you," one of the agents said, smacking Joshua across the face and pushing him against the back of the chair.

Joshua remained silent. One of the men slapped him again, as the other repeated the questions.

In the meantime, the Arab boys, realizing they were in a Jewish neighborhood, pulled yarmulkes from their pockets and put them on their heads. They had met down the street from the house where the agents had taken Joshua. Ali had already planned a strategy if something like this should occur. He decided not to tell his grandfather. It would be too upsetting for him. He sent two of the boys, instead, to Colonel Bessmer's office at military headquarters with all the details and with orders to give the colonel the phone number of Ali's portable phone.

Ali positioned himself across the street from the van, but before doing so he picked up two old nails and a chunk of broken glass lying in the gutter and stealthily worked his way into the alley and under the van, where he proceeded to push the nails into two of the van's tires and put the glass under a third, with the idea that there would most likely not be more than two spares inside. He then went across the street and three houses down and, sitting on a rock in a vacant lot, waited and watched, whittling a piece of wood to while away the time. The other boy, Mahmoud, sat on the steps of an old house up the street and started to read a paperback he had taken from his pocket.

Over an hour went by and nothing happened. No one left the building. The portable phone was ingenious. The small battery pack fit into the boys' pants, and the microphone and receiver were patched into their shirts so they could talk without holding anything in their hands.

Finally, Aaron called Ali. He was very upset but spoke in a calm, cool voice. "Ali, your friend here has just told me the story about you following Joshua and the agents. Where are you now?" Aaron asked.

"We are in a seedy part of town," Ali answered, and then described the section and the name of the street, as well as the house where Joshua was being kept.

"This is dangerous business you're in, Ali," Aaron warned him, "and I don't want anything to happen to any of you. So be careful! I'm sure you and your friends are all street smart, but be extra watchful now, because they are going to be on the lookout for anything suspicious. Act as if you are a part of the neighborhood. Don't appear to be too observant. I will have a special patrol sent down there to keep an eye on things. Don't give them any sign of recognition. If the Mossad make any move, inform me immediately."

"Colonel, I don't think they are going anyplace," Ali told him. "I put nails in two of their tires, and a sharp piece of glass under a third. They're stuck here, which means that one or two of them are going to have to leave on foot to get the tires repaired. That's over a mile away."

"Good job, Ali," Aaron responded, laughing loudly at his ingenuity. "You didn't tell your grandfather about this, did you?"

"No, he would be too upset. And he's an old man. It would hurt him."

"Good. Sit tight. My men will handle everything from here on. Should anything come up unexpectedly, call me immediately, and when they find out about the tires and take them away for repairs, let me know right away," Aaron said as a final instruction. Then, after giving Ali his special number, he hung up.

Inside the house the agents were still questioning Joshua, trying to pry out of him his full name, his place of birth, his reason for being in Israel, where he lived, who his family were, what were his reasons for meeting with Arabs and especially those who were suspect. Joshua, as on a similar occasion long ago, kept silent and answered not a word. This made the agents furious, and they began to beat him. His face was now full of blood, and he was retching violently from the blows to the stomach. Still, though tears flowed down his face, he spoke not a word, just gave them an icy stare.

Within an hour, a military jeep went by with four men in it. Shortly after, another jeep went by as if patrolling the neighborhood. The boys acted as if they knew nothing, but one of the soldiers, an officer, looked in Ali's direction and gave a slight gesture of recognition. Ali showed no reaction, just watched.

Every fifteen or twenty minutes the jeeps went by as if by routine. Almost two hours went by and still no action. Then, just before noon, two agents came out and entered the van. As they were backing out of the driveway, two of the tires popped, then the third. The van sank to the ground. The men got out of the van and looked at the tires and lost their cool. They let out a stream of foul language and then started to remove the tires. They had only one spare in the van. That they put on, but they had to take the others away to be repaired. As soon as the two men started rolling the tires down the street, Ali called Aaron. Within five minutes three jeeps came, filled with troops. Ali told the officer in charge they had taken Joshua up the back stairs of the house to the right of the van. Four of the men went up the back stairs, and four went up the front. The others stayed on guard.

They had no problem finding Joshua. His captors were shocked and tried to show their identification, but the soldiers acted as if they thought them just kidnappers, and as two soldiers held the agents at gunpoint, the others freed Joshua and led him out of the room and down the stairs to the jeeps outside.

Meanwhile, the soldiers on guard opened the hood of the van and disconnected the wires and the radio and were ready to leave when the rescue team appeared. They had to practically carry Joshua out of the house and into the officer's jeep, he was so crippled with pain. Then the contingent sped off.

Ali already had Aaron on the phone and was giving him a description of the operation as the soldiers pulled out. Aaron then told Ali and his friend to leave the neighborhood immediately, as if what had happened was of no concern to them.

By the time the soldiers arrived at Aaron's place, he was already there waiting for them, together with a doctor friend of his from headquarters, in case Joshua needed medical attention. They helped Joshua from the vehicle and led him into the house.

"Bring him into the bathroom, so we can clean him up," Aaron ordered. "Those brutal bastards will pay for this," he said in undisguised rage. "Did any of you recognize the agents?"

"No," was the unanimous answer.

"Well, I'll find out, and also who ordered it. They'll have hell to pay."

By the time Esther arrived, the only evidence of violence was the bloody towels lying all over the bathroom. Joshua was pretty well cleaned up. The doctor examined him. His face was red from the slapping, his nose was swollen, and his left eye was partially closed. Other than that, there were no signs of serious injury. But the doctor grimaced when he took hold of Joshua's hands to examine them and saw marks under the fingernails.

"What did they do, put needles under your fingernails?" the doctor asked Joshua, in a tone of disbelief.

Joshua looked at his fingers but said nothing. It would only incite more anger if he told them all the details.

"Those sadistic bastards!" the doctor said angrily.

"Do you want to lie down and rest?" Aaron asked Joshua.

"No, it's not necessary. There's no damage done, it's just painful," Joshua replied as they all moved into the living room. Aaron congratulated the soldiers on a masterful piece of work in rescuing Joshua and also praised the shrewdness of the Arab kids for the neat job they did. He then dismissed the soldiers.

"Well, it's certain now. From now on, Joshua goes nowhere without a bodyguard," Aaron said with strong determination.

Esther brought out a cup of hot tea and a couple of aspirin tablets, insisting that Joshua take them to ease the soreness.

"Thank you, Esther," he said as he took the tablets and washed them down with the tea.

"After you finish your tea, you are to go in and lie down and get some rest," Esther ordered. "I'll be your nurse, and I guarantee you will never have had such good care. I'll have you back in shape in no time at all."

"She's tough, Joshua," Aaron said, "but you couldn't have a better nurse."

After finishing the tea, Joshua did as ordered and went to bed. He almost fit into Aaron's khakis, a little baggy, but otherwise a pretty good fit. Aaron called the office and had two special army agents assigned to guard his house. When they arrived, he went back to work.

14

JOSHUA SLEPT THROUGH supper. Esther let him sleep, as he needed the rest to heal his bruised body. It was not until the next morning that he woke, surprised he had slept so long. The children were standing outside his door wondering if they would see him before they left for school. When they heard his footsteps, they were excited.

Joshua's face was bruised, and he had a black eye. The children felt sorry for him and hugged him, telling them how much they loved him and hoped he would be all right.

"Don't worry, little ones," he assured them, "I look worse than I really am. With your mother's good care, I'll be better than ever in no time."

"You're still alive," Aaron said to Joshua as he walked into the kitchen.

"Yes, thanks to you and all the others," Joshua replied.

Aaron could not help but laugh when he looked up from his paper and saw Joshua's black eye. Joshua laughed, too.

"It will go away in a few days," Joshua said good-naturedly. "At least I feel much better this morning. I am grateful to you and your men for what they did. They were soldiers at their best."

"The Arab boys made it easy," Aaron said. "They had everything under control. They really are street smart, those kids. They had been following you around for weeks, didn't you know it?"

"Yes, but I didn't let on," Joshua answered. "They really are sharp little kids. The sheik's trust in them was well placed. They did a good job."

As Joshua sat down at the table, Esther bent over and kissed him.

"That was a powerful cup of tea you gave me last night. I never slept so well or so long in my life," Joshua said to her.

"It wasn't the tea," she answered. "It was the beating you took from those hoodlums. Your body was in shock. But thank God, you look better this morning, except for your black eye."

After breakfast, the guards arrived to watch the house and protect Joshua. Aaron had already told the Arab boys that he would take over Joshua's security and they would not have to watch him any longer. The boys were somewhat disappointed but proud of their accomplishment and happy to be able to be kids again.

Aaron asked if Joshua wanted to come into the city with him, but he declined. During the day, he took walks through the neighborhood, talking to people. The guards followed him everywhere, always at a discreet distance out of respect for his privacy. Some of the neighbors knew Joshua from talking to Aaron and Esther. A few invited him into their homes for a cup of coffee and biscuits, though their real reason was to get acquainted with this stranger who had had such a remarkable effect on so many people's lives in so short a time.

The black eye and the swollen nose disappeared after a few days. By then Joshua could not wait to get started on his daily rounds. There was so much to be done.

Father Ambrose, the old Franciscan priest at the Church of the Holy Sepulcher, had been to all of Joshua's talks and had brought with him a host of friends of every description and religion. He had also met up with Father Elias Friedman, the Carmelite monk from Mount Carmel. The two had become good friends and had been corresponding. Joshua wanted to meet with some of these people again privately. So the first item on his agenda was the Franciscan monastery, and a visit with Father Ambrose.

The priest was at home and was excited when the doorkeeper told him there was a man named Joshua who would like to visit with him.

"Joshua, Joshua," the old priest said on entering the room. "How many times I have thought of you! How many times I had wished I could talk with you, but had no way of knowing where to find you. And here you are."

Father Ambrose grabbed both of Joshua's hands in his own and welcomed him cordially to their monastery.

Joshua was also glad to see him and told him how appreciative he was that the father brought all his friends to the meetings. "Father, you are a good shepherd. Your sheep are the kind of flock Jesus would have gathered around him, sheep of every description. It was good to see them in the crowd. I am also glad you got to meet Father Elias, the Carmelite. You have much in common. Help him; his life is not easy."

"Yes, my people were so happy they could hear your talks," Father Ambrose said. "You touched all of them deeply, even those who had been insisting they did not believe in God."

"I noticed that your friends come from different parts of the country," Joshua said. "Do you think you could encourage them to bring our message to others in their communities?"

"Joshua, they have already been doing that in a limited way. But I am sure they would be happy to do even more, especially if they knew that you requested it. By the way, my young friend, do you know there are two men following you? One of the friars noticed them as you were coming up the walk to the monastery."

"Yes, I am aware," Joshua replied. "Colonel Bessmer assigned them to protect me. A rather unfortunate incident occurred last week, and the colonel wanted to be sure I was protected in the future."

Since Joshua did not offer any further information, the priest did not pursue the matter, but asked him if he would like a tour of the monastery.

"Yes, I would like that." The old priest gave Joshua the grand tour of the spacious building. He was particularly proud of their chapel where the friars chanted their prayers and offered Mass every day. The tour ended in the refectory, the community dining room, where a few friars were sitting around a table, having a snack.

Father Ambrose pulled out a chair and told Joshua to be seated while he went to get the coffee and donuts from a nearby serving table. Sitting down, the two continued their conversation. Joshua made the priest feel his work in this world was not yet done, and even though he was on in age, the most important work of his life was about to begin.

After their snack, the priest brought Joshua over to the Church of the Holy Sepulcher for a relaxed visit to make up for his previous unpleasant experience at that sacred site. They did not stay long but passed through the church, taking a quick glance at the mementos of events long past.

When they finished, Joshua meandered over to Siloam to visit his friends, who were as usual tending their fields. He talked with them for a few minutes, bringing them up-to-date on happenings and in general letting them know he was thinking of them and hoped to see them all at the next meeting.

The next day a strange thing happened. A phone call came for Joshua at Aaron's house. Esther was the only one home at the time, and as Joshua was not there, the caller would not give his name, but said he would call back. That night he did call back. It was Khalil, the sheik's son. He wanted very much to talk to Joshua. Could he meet with him? After talking briefly, Joshua said he would meet with him the next day at the park on the east side of Jerusalem.

They met as planned. Khalil was already there when Joshua arrived. He was alone and sitting on a bench, sad and in deep thought. As Joshua approached, he arose and timidly extended his hand. They shook and sat down on the bench.

Seeing that the young man was on the verge of tears, Joshua put his hand on his shoulder in an attempt to steady him. Joshua was aware of the profound change that had taken place in the man's tortured soul.

As they sat there, Khalil unburdened his heavy heart, telling Joshua everything about his life, with a total confession of all the hateful things he had done even from his childhood. Joshua just listened.

"Joshua," Khalil said, "I have not slept since that morning in my father's camp. To be sentenced to death by your own father, when I had spent my whole life following the way he raised me, was a blow I could not bear. Then to be allowed to live but cut off from everyone I ever loved made the anguish all the more unbearable. And the realization that you could forgive me and even talk my father into letting me live has caused me nightmares. I have thought so often of suicide, then in the darkness of my tortured soul I would see your face, and the kindness in your eyes told me I was really forgiven, not just in words, but that you meant it and you really cared for me. I felt such peace. I was sure you were there by my side, so real I could touch you. Such peace and calmness I had never known before. You seemed to tell me I am not evil or worthless trash. I had the strange, eerie feeling that Allah was telling me He loved me. Gradually all the hatred and poison poured from my soul and your words at my father's camp came true, 'Go in peace, you are free.' Who are you, Joshua? So ordinary, so common, yet in your look and your touch I see and feel God."

Joshua just listened. When Khalil finished, he lifted his head and tried to look at Joshua. Tears streamed down his cheeks.

"You are precious to God, Khalil, and now that your soul is at peace, God will work great things through you," Joshua told him.

"What is it God wants me to do?" the young man asked.

"Don't worry about that now. What is important is that you open your heart to God. In time He will let you know what you are to do and you will have no doubt. In the meantime, enjoy the peace of being close to God, and let Him work in your soul healing you and teaching you new ways and a new understanding. He will put a new heart in you and a new vision."

"Joshua, I know what you are trying to accomplish. Can I be your disciple?" the young man pleaded.

"Yes, that you can be. But my Father has other work for you to do. Be patient and let Him speak to you in the quiet of your soul."

The darkness left the man's face, and a peaceful smile appeared. The two men stood up and embraced, Joshua resting the young man's head on his shoulder. Khalil thanked him for saving his soul and walked off.

Joshua stood there for a few moments, his eyes following the figure down the street as if following him into the future. A tear glistened in his eyes as he turned and walked up into the hills to enjoy the peaceful quiet of the warm afternoon.

Later that day he visited Sheik Ibrahim's camp and spent the next few days with him. The sheik was surprised but honored to see him. After supper the first night, Joshua and the sheik walked outside the camp for privacy and talked about many things. His son Khalil was forever on the sheik's mind.

"Joshua, have you seen my son, Khalil?" the sheik asked Joshua bluntly. "I worry so much about him. I stay awake nights wondering where he is and what he is doing, and if he is all right."

"Yes, my friend," Joshua said, "I have seen him. It was only this morning. Be at peace, your son is a changed man. You would be proud of him. Do not give up on him and do not stop loving him. My Father has beautiful things in store for your son. What had been twisted and tortured is now pure and innocent. He will be from now on an instrument of God. You can be proud. Understand why it is not wise to despair of any of God's children. God works in ways that are unfathomable to humans."

"Joshua, you have brought peace to my soul," the old man responded. "I cannot help but be responsible for what has happened to that boy. He was always a good boy and so very loyal to me. I think he loved me more than all the others. He was like a mirror of myself, and in condemning him, I knew I was condemning myself. He was everything I taught him."

"That is a problem parents have with their children," Joshua said. "They realize their mistakes too late, then flail themselves with guilt, rather than know that God understands their shortcomings and wants to help. He loves His children and will heal their deepest wounds and bring beautiful things out of the most twisted souls, if parents will only learn to trust Him to repair their mistakes. God's love is like snow on the mountain trails. In the fall the trail is filled with mud and dung from the passing of many animals. Then the snow falls, covering the tracks, and in the springtime the trail is filled with beautiful wildflowers."

"Joshua, you breathe such peace and goodness," the sheik said. "I am an old man, and I have never met anyone like you in my long life. Thank you again for being a part of our family and for teaching us so many inspiring lessons."

15

THE NEXT MEETING of the Children of Peace took place almost three weeks after Joshua's kidnapping. In the time between meetings, small groups were organizing throughout the land in Jewish and Arab communities. In some places the groups were mixed and even included Arab Christians of various denominations. Jews of every kind were represented, including quite a few Orthodox and a sprinkling of Hasidic Jews. Most of the Jews coming to the meetings were either Reform Jews or Jews who would not consider themselves religious. Father Ambrose's group was a motley assortment that met regularly at the monastery. The spirit and feeling among the people was so high that it generated enthusiasm among others in their communities, so that the groups were constantly growing in numbers.

Because of the large crowd expected, it was decided to hold the next meeting in an out-of-the-way place on the road down from Jerusalem to Jericho, just outside the city.

When the day arrived, people came in what looked like caravans of old, but with buses and cars and trucks rather than camels.

Aaron and Esther and their children took Joshua and Nathan along with them. On their way down to the site, Joshua's memory jumped across time and a smile crossed his face. Aaron, noticing the smile, remarked, "Joshua, what's the secret? Share it with the rest of us so we can enjoy it, too."

Joshua chuckled. "I can't share this one with you, Aaron. Coming down this road just brings back memories of long ago. It seemed like yesterday. I couldn't help but smile."

Nathan, who was sitting next to Joshua in the backseat, and was an avid reader of religious books, remarked quietly, "A man was going down the road from Jerusalem to Jericho and he fell among thieves . . ." then stopped and left the ball for Joshua to pick up.

Joshua turned, looked surprised, then smiled on noticing the impish grin on Nathan's face. Aaron thought Nathan was talking to himself and said nothing. As no one else in the car saw any connection, the matter was dropped.

As they drove along, all one could see was an endless train of cars and buses. People were flocking from all over. Approaching the field, Aaron commented about the good number who had already arrived and were busy greeting others as they came. Many had become friends over the past months and were glad to see each other, especially those who lived in faraway places. The group was melding nicely into a well-knit family. It was inspiring to see Moslems and Jews and Christians hugging one another, genuinely glad to see each other. Some even exchanged gifts and other tokens of friendship with people they had become particularly fond of.

Susan's genius for organizing was the key to the smooth running of the whole operation. She was at the site early with her assistants and already had matters well under control. She had thought of every possible eventuality, even the need for doctors or nurses in case of accident or a sudden illness.

Buses were now arriving from all over the Holy Land. Aaron and Susan, together with Jamileh and Charli and a few others, had spent days trying to find the right spot, with a large flat place for parking and a gently rising hillside so the crowd could spread out. The place they found was a natural amphitheater.

As the crowd was growing, a small contingent of Arabs came walking from the parking lot over to where Joshua was standing. They were young people, about thirty of them in all, ranging from twenty to thirty years of age, not at all like most of the people who came to the meetings. These were tense, nervous fellows who could be intimidating, as if they had mischief up their sleeves. Many of them looked out of place with their sullen, insecure expressions, in contrast to the happy, enthusiastic air of the rest of the crowd.

As they approached Joshua and the group he was talking to, Joshua turned and looked at them, surprised and happy. It was Khalil and his friends. Khalil beamed from ear to ear as he embraced Joshua and introduced his friends to him.

"Joshua, these are my friends," he said. "I know they don't look like much, but we have been together for a long time and I talked them into coming to listen to you."

"Thank you, Khalil," Joshua said, as he shook the hand of each of them and seemed to know each one's name, which stunned them.

Joshua then introduced Khalil to those standing by, and as Aaron and his friends were coming to get Joshua, he introduced Khalil and his friends to them as well.

"This is Sheik Ibrahim's son, Khalil," he said to Aaron and Susan, who were standing next to him. They gave them a warm welcome and told them to feel at home and assured them that everyone was a friend.

When most of the crowd had assembled, the program started. It was much the same as the previous gatherings, but people did not come to be entertained but to share peace and goodwill and to hear Joshua's powerful messages.

Aaron introduced Soad Avari, a distant relative of the sheik's, whose husband Siavosh was well connected in Saudi Arabia. She was invited to speak out of respect for the many members of her family who were represented in the group. Her family was totally committed to Joshua and was planning to take steps to make all Joshua's dreams practical. Soad spoke of the profound effect Joshua had had on their family and their whole community. If only there had been someone like Joshua among them years ago, the terrible tragedies of the present might never have taken place. What was needed was an entirely new way of looking at life and, indeed, a new understanding of God and how He relates to His human creatures. They had all been living as if there was no God, and even those who professed religion were filled with hatred for those who were the slightest bit different from themselves. "Joshua has given us all a new and beautiful vision of life and helped us to see that no one is a stranger," was the way Soad described Joshua's effect on people.

Shlomo was again invited to lead the singing. This man was so unassuming and self-effacing, and expressed such sincere love for everyone, no matter what their religion or race, that everyone loved him and looked forward to his performing at each gathering. The Arab children were particularly fond of him. He always singled them out and showed them special affection. In his spare time he was teaching Arab children to play the guitar and make up their own songs.

Aaron introduced Joshua this time, and to Joshua's embarrassment, revealed some remarkable things about him.

"The first time we all met Joshua, we were on a three-day furlough. Susan, Nathan, Samuel, myself, and some others bumped into him on the Mount of Olives. Not knowing much about the sites, we asked this stranger who seemed to be knowledgeable, and he kindly explained them to us. He seemed so ordinary. When we said good-bye, it never occurred to us we would ever see him again.

"Now that he has become one of us, each day we learn more and more about him. His life is like a rose unfolding. This past week some tragic events occurred, and our friend was severely injured. What was remarkable was that he showed no trace of anger or hostility for those who perpetrated the vicious act. He showed us all in a very graphic way that he not only preaches to us, but lives what he preaches. Indeed, in getting to know him the way we have, he seems to be utterly incapable of taking offense at anything anyone does to him. I know what I have said embarrasses him, but I felt it proper to tell you. We have all had clergy preach pious things to us, only to be disillusioned to see that it was mere words they themselves never practiced. We have for our beautiful teacher a man whose words are his very life. To watch him each day is a living sermon. I tell you this so you can feel confident that you are not following someone who just says pleasant things, or a captain who merely sends his troops into battle, but one who leads them into the thick of the fight and is an inspiration to all.

"Joshua," Aaron said, turning toward him, "I know I have caused you to blush, forgive me. I wanted everyone to know how proud we are to have you as our teacher. Now, please come forward and speak to us."

"Aaron, you are without shame," Joshua said as he stood at the podium. "You make ordinary things seem so dramatic, you almost had me believing you. I am grateful to you, Aaron, and to all my friends who have helped me. You are truly good friends."

Then, turning toward the vast crowd spread out before him, Joshua began to speak. "My dear friends, I have heard recently of the many wonderful things you have been doing in your communities. You have been practicing all the things we have been speaking about, and you can already see the rich harvest you are reaping. Your goodness and love has spread like a fire in dry grass. Old relationships have been renewed, new friendships have been cultivated. People who were once unfriendly or hostile have responded to your genuine expressions of concern and interest in them and have now become your friends.

"Of late I have come across so many hurting people, and so much pain. I know you all endure hurt and pain and struggle with difficulty to understand it. I know life must be very confusing for you. But it is not senseless. There are patterns and reasons, though you may not be able to see them. It is important for you to know that your lives are not just an accident of circumstance or the products of random forces at work in the universe.

"Each of you is a masterpiece of God's creation. You were made special and are precious to God. He works each day quietly, calmly, within you, weaving together the apparently disconnected strands of your life. Your youth was a preparation for your life later on. As you grew older, each moment was part of the carefully planned training that God was putting you through, each day building on another, each of you being drawn along a path different from everyone else, because each of you is unique and special to God, with a special mission to accomplish for Him in this world, and a special message to preach through your life.

"There will always be pain in life and hurt. You cannot grow without it. Pain and suffering are the dark strands weaving through the tapestry of your life, providing the shadows that give depth and dimension to the masterpiece God is fashioning within you. Athletes embrace stress and pain as they prepare their bodies for the contest. You are made strong and refined through your hardships and struggles. They are not a punishment for sin. They are the necessary ingredients of life if you are to grow in God's image. If God is to mold the human clay of which you are made into something that resembles Himself, that process cannot help but be painful.

"So be patient! Know that your pain is not in vain, nor is it a punishment. God is too big to pick on people when, in their weakness, they fall. When you do things that are hurtful, God, like a kind father, or more a tender mother, makes adjustments in your life to remind you that your actions are hurting others or yourself and prompts you to make changes. But God is never cruel. He accepts you where you are and is very patient as you turn ever so slowly back to His love. He weaves everything, even your sins, into good when you reach out to Him.

"Your life is really like a tapestry. You look at one side and see all the disconnected and loose ends, and say, 'What a mess my life is!' God sees the finished product on the other side and sighs, 'How beautiful you have become!'

"So don't be discouraged or lose hope. Trust your Father in heaven. He loves you more than you can imagine. Call him Abba. He is truly your Daddy, so tender is His love for you.

"He watches over your every deed, not to find fault or to judge, but because He cares. This may seem impossible, that He could be fully aware of every detail of your life, but look upon the mind of God as the sun rising in the morning. Its rays penetrate every detail of creation in a single moment. God's mind is like that sunshine, touching and penetrating all of creation in an instant. In this way He can guide and enlighten you with His wisdom and inspire you with His love.

"And do not be afraid to turn your children over to Him. He is their Father and created them for a reason. He is more concerned that they accomplish the purpose for which He created them than you are and is determined they will carry out His plan. So entrust your children to Him. He will not disappoint you.

"May His peace and blessing go with you each day and guide you in His own way, and along His own paths, and may you always know that He is near."

When Joshua finished, there was no applause at first, just silence as everyone was in deep thought. Then the vast crowd stood up and gave a thunderous ovation, much to Joshua's embarrassment.

Susan walked up to Joshua and hugged him, herself deeply moved by what she had just heard, tears rolling down her cheeks. Joshua kissed her tenderly on the cheek and stepped aside as she took the microphone.

When the crowd finally quieted down, she spoke.

"My dear friends, I really can't speak after that. Nothing more need be said. But a few words are in order. All of us who worked to prepare this day are most grateful to you for the sacrifices you all made to be here today, in spite of the boiling heat. Should you need anything, we would be more than happy to be of assistance. You can pick us out, as well as those who generously volunteered to help us, by the red armbands we are wearing. If we break now for our little picnic, we can continue in about an hour."

During the break, Joshua mingled with the crowd, talking to small groups and individuals. He seemed so ordinary and so casual, yet people were in absolute awe of him, as he looked at them and touched them so deeply that their lives would never be the same. As he spoke to them, each one had the same eerie feeling: "This man knows me. I just know it. When he looks at me I can tell he is looking down into the very depths of my soul and knows all about me. Yet he is not critical. He seems to be telling me, 'I know all about you, everything. I see your hurt and your struggle, and I understand. Do not be discouraged and do not give up. God loves you as you are, and I love you and want you to be my friend. I am your friend, and I will always be with you.' "

Each one felt the same way, and the realization changed their lives.

Then he would move on, briefly entering others' lives, bringing them healing and peace. Though all were touched profoundly, only they knew it. All the others were totally unaware of the profound change taking place throughout this vast crowd. A woman came up to him at one point excitedly holding up her large thermos container. Because of the heat of the day, her family had been drinking from the container since they arrived. Then she had noticed that they must have drunk three times the capacity of the container and it was still full. Joshua smiled and told her to keep it to herself. But then others noticed the same thing, and others, and still others, and before long pandemonium broke loose. But by that point, Joshua was nowhere to be found.

He had quietly slipped away until the snack time ended, then appeared with Aaron and the sheik and the others as the next session was about to begin. By then the crowd had calmed down.

The real climax of the day was the morning session. The afternoon was routine. Joshua spoke once more, briefly, then the crowd was dismissed. They had been instructed to contact their representative in the Knesset to work diligently for peace and in whatever way they could to pressure the prime minister and his cabinet to lay aside their hard-line platform and open their hearts to the misery and fear all around them, among their own people, and particularly in the ghettos, the refugee camps.

The crowd dispersed in a surprisingly quiet and orderly fashion. Joshua mingled among the people right to the end, leaving afterward with Sheik Ibrahim and Aaron and some of their families. Susan, Samuel, Nathan, and Daniel Sharon left with them and retired to the beautiful estate of Soad Avari's brother Elie for an evening meal and to rest.

That night was a most rewarding experience for everyone. Soad and Siavosh and Mathilde and Bill and Elie, and their friends Charli and Jamileh and Majid, shared plans they had for Joshua's dream of everyone working together. It was a generous undertaking brought about by a strange twist of fate. Both of these families were friends of Khalil, through their sons who had grown up together. After Khalil's conversion, all he would talk about was Joshua and the beautiful work he was trying to accomplish. Before long the two families became totally dedicated to Joshua's work and were avid Joshua disciples. Siavosh had already contacted his friends in Saudi Arabia and had traveled there to discuss with them his proposal. It was to develop a series of factories in various places with the intention of providing employment for both Arabs and Jews and whoever else needed work. The factories would contain research and development laboratories as well as training schools. The plants would have state-of-the-art equipment and would manufacture high-quality electronic products and then market them in the area and throughout the Middle East, gradually raising the living standards of all those affected. Their friends in Saudi Arabia at first laughed at the idea, thinking it was a joke, then when Siavosh pushed the proposal, they began to take it seriously and sat down to discuss it with him. He had to familiarize members of the royal family with the movement that Joshua and his friends had started and how widely it was spreading throughout the country. As hard as it was for them to believe, they were finally convinced that as a business venture, and as long as it would help Arabs, it might be worthwhile to give it a try. They had lost fortunes on other less honorable ventures. This might just be something that could take hold and do some good for people for a change. It certainly would generate goodwill.

Charli and Jamileh had also contacted relatives in Lebanon to ask for their help. They insisted that Charli come and discuss the matter with them personally. He was to do that within the next week.

The sheik was impressed at the generous spirit of these people, and he offered his help. He was not as rich as the royal family, but his resources were considerable, and he wanted to make his modest contribution. Though he lived simply and still enjoyed the simple nomadic life, the sheik had a reputation as the wealthiest man in the country. At times, members of various royal families would go to him for short-term loans when secrecy was imperative.

The evening ended on a high note. No one could really believe all that had transpired ever since they had all become friends. Friends with high ideals working together can truly change the world. As the sheik and his family were leaving, the sheik took Joshua aside and quietly asked him if he had seen his son of late. Joshua could see the anguish in the man's heart.

"Yes, my friend," Joshua assured him. "As a matter of fact, he came to the meeting today with a large group of his friends and introduced them to me. Also, remember Soad Avari who spoke today? You know her family well. It was your son who interested her family and a considerable number of others in joining our group. He has done much for us. Be at peace, Sheik Ibrahim, your son is a changed man, and my Father is blessing his life because of your kindness in forgiving him and the great sacrifice you have made. Let your heart be at peace. You will soon be very proud of him."

"Thank you, my dear, dear friend," the sheik said, with grateful tears in his eyes. "I know you and Allah are very close, and that both of you watch over him. I am again indebted to you." With that the sheik walked down the path to the family's limousine that was waiting for him, and they drove off.

When the others left, Joshua stayed with the Avaris for the next few days and helped them formulate their grand undertaking.

16

IN THE DAYS that followed, the country was churning with activity. Much to the satisfaction of Aaron and the original organizers, the highly charged members of the Children of Peace, now deeply loyal to Joshua, were ready to carry out careful directions in laying a road for peace. A movement like this could easily get out of hand and become the tool of fanatical activists which would not affect its intended goal but merely polarize the society and add another layer of hostility.

But with Joshua's gentle leadership and the depth of his spirituality, his guidance spilled over into his followers, and they went forth armed with his peaceful spirit and deep sense of forgiveness for past wrongs. Government leaders began to feel the heat. Calm heads in the military also saw value to this new movement that seemed devoid of radical activists and operated with a coolheaded leadership. Only some of the Mossad felt distrust for the movement. They could not get a handle on it and contain it. They were still smarting over their debacle of a few weeks earlier and were angry over the protective guard Aaron and his friends had thrown around Joshua. Aaron had also, in the meantime, cleverly worked out an agreement with friends in higher places to restrain the Mossad and order them to leave Joshua in peace. They agreed, but Aaron's office would have to assume complete responsibility. With this he had no problem.

Newspapers were picking up the story and tracked down Aaron for an interview. Aaron contented himself with merely stating that a few friends of his had been trying to make some gesture to foster peace but had been getting nowhere. Joshua seemed literally to come out of thin air as an answer to their prayers. Almost single-handedly he forged together this whole movement by the beauty of his teachings and the sublimity of his messages, as well as the healing charisma of his personality. Soon Moslems and Jews and Christians were streaming to the gatherings from all over the country to listen to him. His message of healing and reconciliation appealed to everyone. "We are all sick of fighting and hatred," Aaron related to the reporters. "Only fanatics on both sides have the stomach to continue. And if we turn our country over to them, we will never have peace, because their sick minds feed on hostilities. It is a way of life with them. They are so filled with hatred and suspicion; conflict is their only relief."

"Where can we find this Joshua?" one of the reporters asked.

"He will be here tomorrow," Aaron told him. "You can come back and interview him then. I am sure he will be only too happy to meet with you."

The reporters left. Only one returned the next day, a Greek Jew by the name of Elias Seremetis. Joshua was there, and graciously acceded to his request for an interview.

"What is your full name, Joshua?" the reporter asked him.

"Joshua is all you need. That is what everyone calls me and that is what I go by," Joshua responded.

"Where do you live?" Elias asked him.

"I have lived in this land all my life, and wander from place to place," he answered simply.

"Don't you have a home?" the reporter continued.

"No, I have never needed one. Everyone is so kind to me," Joshua answered.

"Do you work? Do you have a job?" Elias asked.

"Yes, I bring a message of peace and good news to the people. Don't you think that's a full-time job?" Joshua answered, to the dismay of the reporter, who began to twist his long handlebar mustache.

"Yes, I can see that could be a full-time job if someone really took it seriously," Elias answered with a trace of embarrassment and cynicism. "Is it true the Mossad tried to stop your activities and even tried to kidnap you?" the reporter asked.

"You seem to have more information than I do. Why don't you tell me about it?" Joshua responded shrewdly.

"Isn't it true that Mossad agents kidnapped you?" Elias pursued.

"In truth, I can't say. The men didn't have any signs on them. They were strangers. Others may know who they were. But they didn't give me their names, so I really have no way of identifying them. Anyway the episode is over and we have since passed on from there. The significant thing is the profound desire the ordinary people have for peace. It is a shame leaders don't respond to the people's desires and establish a program of reconciliation which will bring all the people together the way God intended and create the climate where they can work and live side by side in peace. There is no room or justification for social or racial isolation in this complicated modern world. All God's children must realize they are the children of one Father and must work and live together in harmony. It was a beautiful testimony at our people's previous gathering to see Jews and Moslems and Christians meeting and praying together on the Temple Mount. To drive people out and then worship God by yourselves is a blasphemy against God and could not possibly make your worship pleasing to Him. These are lessons our people, Jews and Arabs, must learn to live by if there is to be peace."

"Don't you think this is just a bit naive?" Elias asked him.

"All dreams are simplistic and naive until you begin to put them into practice," Joshua answered. "Then you see how realistic they can become when there is goodwill to resolve the problems. Dreams are naive and simplistic only to the fainthearted and the cynics."

"Where do you intend to go with this movement, which obviously has considerable potential for either good or evil, depending upon your agenda?" the reporter asked.

"By its fruits you can tell," Joshua replied. "The people are being guided into a way that will lead to peace. It is inevitable. But prodding and pressure are necessary to instill courage where needed. In this we will not rest until all is accomplished."

The interview went well. The reporter, at first skeptical of Joshua's intentions and political skills, ended leaving deeply impressed, if not converted.

Later that week a frightful tragedy took place, which grieved Aaron and all his inner circle. Charli Mouawad had gone to Lebanon as planned. While he was there a vicious shelling occurred in the village he was visiting. A shell struck the house next door. People in neighboring houses escaped, but Charli went into the shelled house to rescue the trapped survivors, pulling six of them to safety before another shell struck, which killed him. His family was devastated when they received the news. Charli's mission, however, was not in vain. The people he saved were the family of those who were considering investing their money in Charli's venture. Out of gratitude they contacted his family and promised even more money than they had previously intended to give and said they would like to play a more active role in the project to help make it a reality as a memorial to Charli.

The episode was a sad note in the peace project that in all other aspects was flawless. The funeral for Charli took place in Lebanon. His family had a funeral Mass for him in Jerusalem, which Joshua, Aaron, Susan, and many of the others attended, an unusual sight, which would have been unheard-of only a few months before. Jewish friends even brought food for the family as well as mementos. The tragedy brought the group closer together than ever. Joshua assured the family that Charli's death was not in vain. He died as a martyr of charity, precious to God, and was now at peace with Him in paradise.

The next few weeks were on the surface uneventful, though ferment was growing everywhere. Then Elias's interview with Joshua hit like a bombshell. There were still millions who had not heard of the movement. The news story spread awareness of the movement everywhere, interesting many more people. Aaron's committee of key Jewish and Arab people was besieged with phone calls and inquiries, most excited in their enthusiasm about what they could do for peace. The inquiries came from both Arabs and Jews.

The effects of the news story, however, were not entirely positive. While the notoriety gave greater momentum to the movement, it also aroused the ire of the meaner elements in society, provoking them to plot countermeasures, furious at the thought that these "liberal activists" should dare attempt to bridge the chasm between Jews and Arabs. Hardly two weeks after Charli's death a strange thing happened.

A phone call came for Joshua at Aaron's house early one evening. The caller spoke in Arabic. Joshua answered in perfect Arabic, to Aaron and Esther's surprise. After the phone call, Joshua seemed sad.

"Joshua, what is the matter?" Esther asked, concerned.

"It is something I have to attend to. No need to be alarmed," he said to reassure her.

"Aaron, would you call Sheik Ibrahim?" Joshua asked. "I must talk with him."

Aaron called the sheik, then gave the phone to Joshua, who explained the phone call he had just received. The sheik agreed to meet him and promised to leave immediately.

"Aaron, would you drive me to the city? It is very important," Joshua asked.

"Of course, but what has happened? I am very concerned," Aaron asked.

"Aaron, there are some things I cannot share even with you who are so close to me. Life is not simple. Things that appear simple are not really simple, but are like threads in a finely woven tapestry with more ramifications than we could anticipate. God is aware of all of them and makes provisions for every contingency, even the most minute. Something tragic is about to happen, but you will get a rare glimpse into the beautiful ways of God. That is why I called Sheik Ibrahim."

"Joshua, you baffle me," Aaron complained. "Only months ago you were a stranger. Now you are part of my life, and I still do not understand you any more than when you were a stranger. I can't fathom this mind of yours."

"Don't fret over it, my friend," Joshua told him. "You will put the pieces together one day, and it will make sense. I do appreciate your trust."

Before they left the house, Aaron contacted his staff officer and had him send an armed guard to follow them down the highway toward the city. Not feeling comfortable with this whole affair, he also left instructions for the guard to follow them to the site and reconnoiter the place when they arrived.

It was an out-of-the-way place where Joshua directed Aaron, down near the dump in the Kidron Valley. As they arrived, the sheik was also arriving. Aaron ordered the guards to fan out and survey the area. Then, walking to the site the person on the phone had directed them to, they came to a ditch covered by a clump of low-growing shrubs. As they approached they could hear moans. Pushing aside the brush they found a figure lying in the ditch, badly beaten and bleeding profusely.

Aaron and Joshua went down into the ditch and gently lifted the body out of the hole onto soft ground. As soon as they placed him on the ground, the sheik cried out, "My son, my son! Khalil, my son!" The man fell to the ground and bent over the battered body of his son. Khalil's hands were tied behind him, and a note was pinned to his shirt. Pulling off the piece of paper, the sheik began to read it. It was clearly intended for Joshua.

"To the devil's son, and Satan's followers: Let this be a warning to all other traitors who turn against their brothers and collaborate with the despicable Jews, the enemies of our people. Death to traitors. Hell and eternal fire."

The note was signed "The soldiers of Allah."

Blood was pouring from Khalil's breast. He had been carefully stabbed to bleed to death slowly, with perfectly perverted timing so as to be alive to cause more pain to those who found him. The bizarre spirituality of fanatics "dedicated" to a loving God. That had to be the ultimate insult to God.

"Father, Father," Khalil said to his father as he reached out to touch him. The three men were kneeling by his side.

"What happened, my son?" his father asked.

"When I told all my friends about Joshua, many of them decided to follow him. They came to the last meeting and were touched by Joshua's words and his kindness. The others were angry and swore to punish me. They wanted me to tell them where they could ambush Joshua, but I wouldn't betray him.

They beat me and I still would not tell them. I was supposed to be bait, but when they saw the armed guards they fled just as you came."

"We must get him to the hospital immediately," Aaron said.

"No, I won't make it. They made sure of that," Khalil said with weakening voice.

"Joshua, can't you do something to save my son?" the old man said imploringly.

Putting his arm around the sheik, Joshua told him, "Ibrahim, it is not my Father's will. My Father has called your son home. This very night he will be in paradise. Your son has given his life for peace, and for God. He is truly a martyr. Let God take him home. You will be with him soon and you will see the honor my Father will bestow upon your son."

"I love you, father," the dying man uttered faintly. "I always tried to be true to you."

"I know, my son, you have been my special one, always loyal to me since you were a child. Now it breaks my heart to see you broken like this."

"That's all right, father. I know God is calling me. I see His light, and I already know His peace. He is beckoning to me."

"Good-bye, my son," the old man cried through his tears. "I will be with you soon."

"Thank you, Joshua, for giving me back to God and to my father," the boy said.

Joshua bent over him, saying quietly, as he kissed him on the forehead, "Go in peace to paradise, Khalil. You will be welcomed with great joy."

Kahlil's hand fell from his father's grasp. His father closed his eyes and kissed him.

Aaron called the guards down. They took Khalil's body to their van and drove off to the hospital.

Joshua embraced the sheik and held the old man's trembling body. He stepped back and looked into Joshua's eyes.

"Joshua," the sheik said, "I know all those boys who did this to my son. In the past, I would have had all of them killed. But now I feel no revenge, only pity for our troubled land and our people. And I know that is what my son would want. You have worked more miracles among us, Joshua, than you will ever know. And I do look forward to being with my son. Again you are right—I am deeply proud of him."

Joshua and Aaron both accompanied Sheik Ibrahim up the hill, assisting him as his feeble limbs faltered. Aaron invited the sheik to stay at his house. He declined. Joshua offered to go back home with the sheik. The old man thanked him but said he needed to be alone with his family. If Joshua would say a few words at the funeral, the family would be honored. Joshua nodded his willingness to do so.

The drive back to Aaron's house was long and sad.

"I can't help but feel for that òld man," Aaron said. There was something touchingly beautiful about that cruel tragedy. How did you know what would happen there tonight, that you should call the sheik?"

"Some things you just know, my friend," Joshua answered.

"But you had to know that the boy would be there, and you also had to foresee the circumstances," Aaron continued. "Joshua, you are a mystery. I won't ask anymore, because I know you won't answer anyway. But what happened tonight was beautiful, as heartrending as it was. I feel honored to have been included."

"The sheik is a remarkable man," Joshua said. "He has seen much in his lifetime and has come a long way to understanding the mind of God. It was a difficult thing for him not to want revenge on his son's killers, especially knowing who they were. That is true godliness."

"I don't know whether I could have done the same. I was never taught to think that way," Aaron replied.

"Neither was the sheik," Joshua responded. "This represents a radical change for an old man who was just as militant as all the rest in his younger years. Maybe that is why he can forgive, because he understands them. It was a great comfort to know his son died such a hero's death. That healed a broken heart."

"Joshua, I hope there's no more tragedy," Aaron said. "It might scare people off, especially if they have families."

"It should be quiet for a while," Joshua said to reassure him. "There are many people in our family now, and you have to expect some incidents. It's a mark of success."

"Joshua, do you really think there is a heaven?" Aaron asked.

"Aaron, you could never imagine the beautiful things my Father has prepared for those who love Him," Joshua replied. "The beautiful things in this world are hints of the beauty of God's home. I do not think there is a heaven. I know there is a heaven, just as truly as you know there is a world all around you. God's creative power is not limited to the crass material things of earth. God has created things you would never dream of. One day you will see."

Not feeling comfortable on this territory, Aaron shifted gears. "How do you think our movement is going? Do you think we will attain our goals?" he asked.

"It seems we are moving in that direction," Joshua said. "The people have taken hold of the message and are carrying it in the right places. I have no doubt it will work."

Back home, Esther met them both at the door and could not wait to hear all the details of what had happened. Joshua said little. Aaron gave a detailed account of the whole episode, telling with tears how touched he was at the love between the sheik and his son, and what a beautiful ending to such a tragic life. Aaron found himself consoling both himself and his wife by telling her the old man probably didn't have much time left and would be with his son again soon. Esther looked at Joshua tenderly.

He just smiled.

17

THE FUNERAL FOR Khalil was carried out with simple dignity. Although there were moments of traditional oriental wailing, there was an unusual note of joy that surrounded the ceremony. Sheik Ibrahim himself shed only a few tears and seemed strangely at peace during the whole affair, which set the tone for the rest of the family. People had come from all over the Middle East for the funeral. There were even representatives from royal families. The service was held at the Mosque of Omar. Aaron, Susan, Nathan, Daniel, and Samuel were present, as well as many other Jewish members of their organization who admired the sheik. Even the men who killed Khalil had the nerve to come. Whether it was from guilt or from curiosity or whatever other motive, they were there.

Joshua was asked to speak after the Imam delivered his sermon. Joshua's talk was very brief and delivered in beautiful, flowing Arabic.

"My dear people," he began, "few children have known such pain and anguish as this young man. His life was a tortured existence. Yet few will ever bring to their loved ones, and to the world around them, such a legacy of peace and hope for the future. This boy died at the hands of sick people, who will never know till they meet God the evil they have done." As Joshua said this he looked directly at the men who killed Khalil. They tried to stare him down but finally lowered their eyes in shame.

Then he continued, "The circumstances that led to his murder, and the moments surrounding his death, were so filled with heroism and godliness that his passing was precious even to God. The peace and joy that hovers over this assembly today is a striking testimony to the conversion that transformed Khalil's life into a herald of peace, which gives a new hope to all the people in our land. Few children have brought such hope to their parents in their last moments of agony. For parents to know that their son died in the arms of God is a rare blessing few can hope for. Khalil's parents have had that joy as well as the joy of knowing they will soon be reunited with their son. The beautiful way God brings good out of what appears to be evil and tragic! For those who believe, death is not a pitiful end. It is the beginning of a new and wonderful life.

"Everyone wonders what God is like. Khalil now sees Him. Everyone wonders what heaven is like. Khalil now walks through the streets of heaven, sharing with his new friends the joy and happiness of being in God's presence. This is a happy day for this young man. His pain is ended. He is now in a world of peace and endless joy. So while we mourn our loss, we rejoice in his happiness. That is the way it should be for those who have faith. Take heart and have faith. Your future is a little brighter because of this young man's sacrifice. Salaam."

After the ceremony, the sheik asked Joshua, Aaron, and their comrades if they would honor him by coming to his family's home where they intended to celebrate their son's going home to God. "This is a new practice for an old man, but I can truly say that I do rejoice in my son's death, or to be more positive, in his going home. I have you to thank for this, my young imam," the sheik said, as he patted Joshua's arm.

They all left together. The celebration that took place that day was a precedent devoid of all remorse and vengeance or any trace of bitterness. The last moments of Khalil's life more than atoned for his troubled past and brought great honor to his whole family. It would be talked about for years to come.

In time word passed through the whole organization. Letters of condolence poured in to the sheik's family from all over the Holy Land, from Jews and Arabs and people of all beliefs. When everyone heard the story of this Arab boy's refusal to betray

Joshua and his consequent martyrdom, it brought the group closer together than ever and even more determined to force a mind for peace on the stone-hearted leaders.

Then a strange, unexpected twist occurred, which made everyone pause.

The whole Arab community knew the identity of the men who killed Khalil. Joshua's Arab followers also knew and saw them frequently in public and never turned them in. The murderers were aware of this and were beginning to realize they had done a terrible deed and felt a profound shame, caused mostly by Joshua's community not betraying them. They also realized the sheik must know, yet he hadn't ordered their execution. Their confusion and guilt was a terrible punishment. To have to associate publicly with people who knew the mean thing they had done, yet were kind to them, was becoming almost unbearable. They even felt uncomfortable in their own homes, as many of their family members were followers of Joshua, and knew what they had done. Joshua's spirit of forgiveness was more devastating than a death sentence or a public flogging.

It was hardly a week after Khalil's funeral that the organization sponsored a rally for peace. It had been in the planning for weeks, unbeknownst to Aaron and his colleagues. The planners intentionally left them uninformed because of their positions in the government. Consequently, when they were called on the carpet, they could say in all honesty they knew nothing about the rally. It was an event that sprang spontaneously from the people's frustration with the way events were shaping up in the country.

Secretly, Israel's president was happy over the rally. He was trying, though without results, to encourage a more open and humane policy on the part of the government. The prime minister and his cabinet were furious. There had been rallies before, but this one represented such a cross section of society that one could say it truly represented the feelings of the vast majority of the populace, Jews and Arabs alike, something previously unheard-of in the country.

What was significant was the apolitical nature of the rally. All the banners and posters were simply marked, "We want peace, We want peace." No conditions, no other demands, just the statement of fact from the people themselves, a message that demanded to be heard, and accepted, and acted on.

A counterrally was organized a few days later by radical conservatives, but their fanaticism and bizarre appearance made them look more like a farce than a serious contribution to civilization. If government leaders identified with that group it showed dramatically how out of touch with reality they really were.

Events were accelerating now, and a host of undertakings were launched. Contacts with people in high places made it possible to get the buildings under way for the development projects that would provide jobs and needed products for consumers as well as income for the country. There were not many Arab-run operations like this in the land. Initial resistance was overcome because of the caliber and reputations of the persons sponsoring the projects. In a matter of months they were off the ground, and after a slow start, production mushroomed. Majid proved a master in organizing production lines and had his family's factory running like a top in no time at all. The Avari-Zanbaghe plant was much larger and under the shrewd management of a family friend, Ben Lautenschlager. Production was way ahead of schedule. Elie's contacts throughout the Middle East and other places brought in lucrative contracts for finished products from both operations. Employment increased, with Jews and Arabs working side by side and enjoying it. The sponsors were so happy with the results even from a business point of view that they began planning for other factories in the near future in other areas of the country.

These and other projects were quietly taking place while the organization was busy gaining new recruits and developing more awareness centers throughout the country, applying pressure on Arab as well as Jewish hard-liners. It was this balance sprung from genuine concern and care for people that made the movement so effective. Its strategy was being executed with almost military efficiency.

Joshua was spending his time behind the scenes but still active by keeping in touch with key friends in the movement, advising, focusing, counseling, prompting his followers to be careful not to take sides on issues but to show genuine concern for people everywhere so no one could accuse them of being divisive or political or partisan. "Peacemakers," he said, "must love everyone and not pit one segment of society against another or they will not be worthy to be called the blessed children of God."

Occasionally Joshua would take trips to Mount Carmel to visit Father Elias Friedman and talk to the many people who came out of curiosity to visit the sacred shrines there. Being a loyal Jew, the priest took care to instill in his Jewish visitors a deep reverence for their religious traditions. He was also thrilled to see Joshua visit their monastery and spend time with the monks.

Joshua also visited, with Aaron and Esther and the children, Rabbi Herbstman in Tel Aviv. Attending his synagogue, Joshua felt very much at home. Bernie's talks were about God and about those things that were of genuine concern to God. His relentless endeavor was to develop a deep spirituality in the hearts of his flock. Joshua also enjoyed his keen, quiet sense of humor that had the congregation rolling with laughter in the midst of the most serious talk on spirituality. "All holy people should have his humor," Joshua told Aaron and Esther as they were leaving the service one Friday evening.

One day as Aaron was taking Joshua and his family for a ride, they drove through the Plain of Esdraelon, the site of so many historic battles. Aaron made the flippant remark, "If your crowds get any larger, we may have to have our future meetings here in the ancient battlefield, with all its connotations for the Armageddon."

"You jest, Aaron," Joshua replied, "but the next crowd is going to be so large it might not be a bad idea to consider this place. We don't have many options left."

"Are you serious?" Aaron asked.

"I expect there might be somewhere close to thirty thousand people at the next gathering," Joshua answered. "People are getting desperate for peace and are beginning to feel this is their last chance. They are ready to cooperate with whoever will seriously work to end the conflict and the constant tension."

"Maybe this might be a good place to meet," Aaron said. "There is plenty of space. Susan will hate making preparations for a site this far away. But you are right, we may not have a choice."

As they drove along, Aaron suggested to Joshua that he organize his followers into a more permanent community. The movement was now widespread, and it was obvious the people were coming back not just because of their interest in peace but because they were starving for the kind of spiritual sustenance Joshua was giving them.

"You really have to organize them into something more permanent," Aaron told him frankly. "They will not leave you, Joshua. If we found peace tomorrow, these people would still come after you. We are truly your disciples now, and you are really God's presence for us. We need you; in fact, the whole world needs what you have to give."

Joshua listened thoughtfully, saying nothing for the longest time. Then, finally, he answered, "Aaron, I have taught you and Esther and Nathan and Samuel as well as Susan and Daniel and Rabbi Herbstman and Father Elias many things while we were together on private occasions. I also met with Elie and Soad and Mathilde and Sheik Ibrahim and taught them many things I did not teach the others. You have all been well prepared. Father Elias is well trained and well prepared to give guidance where there are questions. I leave it to all of you to pass on my message and to spread it to others. I will always be by your side and in your hearts. Do not be afraid of the future. Leave that to my Father. That is His problem. Let today take care of itself."

"What are you saying, that you're leaving?" Aaron replied. "Joshua, I can never figure you out. Can't you ever answer a question in a way I can understand? You're impossible."

"Oh, Aaron, stop worrying! Why can't you just enjoy today and be happy we are all together right now? Tomorrow will take care of itself."

It was not that Joshua had not anticipated the problem. The group was growing to such proportions that it was becoming impossible to meet the way they had been. Joshua realized this and was quietly grooming his closest friends to carry on his message long after the present problems ceased. But he saw no point in creating a problem within the group before their peace project was completed. That would still take time, as the truly powerful people on either side lacked the grandeur of soul or the wisdom of spirit to rise above the petty squabbles of infantile feuding in order to reach out and offer a compromise based on a workable partnership rather than an icy standoff at borders waiting for a pretext to pounce on one another. A partnership, Joshua knew, was the only compromise that made sense. The Arabs had the money. The Jews had the technology and the expertise. Why not work together in joint development and business ventures, like the two projects already started?

The peace movement was a plum for the opposition party, who had been pushing for peace in season and out of season. It was only blunders on the part of Arabs that had thrown them out of office years back. But now the climate was ripe again. This put extraordinary pressure on the present government to come up with something other than a mere gesture for peace. The prime minister held a special meeting of his cabinet. Hardliners under pressure become more irrational and intransigent than ever, and this time they were no different. The prime minister, afraid of losing his job if he gave in to demands for peace, was in a state of paralysis. Unwilling to lose the support of the radical right, he could offer nothing of any real value to the people. In his heart he would like to be the champion of peace with dignity and strength but was not willing to sacrifice his political office to accomplish it. The meeting ended in anger with no decision.

Outside, the demonstrations were larger and more persistent with each passing day. What the prime minister did not realize was that if he had the courage to make a sensible decision in spite of the radicals, he would not have to worry about his job. He could count on the vast support of the people who would be behind him all the way. This way eventually his government would fall and new elections would sweep him back into power with a strong mandate for peace with dignity and solid defense. Everything was in place for a new government to form lucrative technical, industrial, and agricultural partnerships with Arab residents and Arab investors from neighboring countries. From there on the potential was mind-boggling. The natural markets for goods made in the Holy Land were Arab neighbors. With these markets undeveloped, the country could survive only with the help of goodwill offerings from friends.

The peace movement had forced a stalemate with the government. No one could predict what turn events would take. Aaron apprised Joshua of the situation and asked if he had any insights into what would happen next. Joshua's answer as usual was unsatisfying. "Be patient, everything unfolds in due season."

The demonstrations never let up. Day after day, incessant chants for peace were enough to unnerve the most calculating and calloused politician. Joshua did not even ask Aaron for information, nor did he read the newspapers. He met with the sheik, Aaron, and his friends on a daily basis, talking to them about the future, sharing with them his vision of God and the love the disciples should have for one another, and encouraging them to be towers of strength to the people as time went on. The sheik felt honored Joshua picked him in spite of his old age to be part of his inner circle. Each of those he picked had imbibed Joshua's spirit fully and were well prepared to carry on that spirit.

The time came for the next gathering. Everyone was fired up for this one. The Plain of Esdraelon was out of the way, but since people were coming from all over, and the country was small, it was no more than an hour's ride from even the farthest places.

On the way there, Joshua told the story to Aaron's children and the sheik's grandchildren of the great battle that took place during the reign of King Zedekiah in the time of Jeremiah the prophet. Hundreds of chariots and tens of thousands of soldiers lined up on either side of the battlefield and met head-on. Thousands lay dead and wounded in the field, a tragic waste of human life, and all because the people cut God out of their lives and chose to live independently of Him and worship gods of their own fashioning. The children's vivid imaginations had no trouble filling in all the details. The vast plain that stretched before their eyes provided a dramatic panorama for replaying the whole battle scene from beginning to end. Joshua answered their endless questions, leading one of the children to ask him, "How do you know so much about the battle—were you there?"

Joshua answered whimsically, "Yes, right there watching the whole thing."

Susan and the others, including Soad and Jamileh and Elie, had arrived and were busy organizing the volunteers when Aaron and Joshua drove up. The acoustics people had come the day before and set up the complex sound system and tested it out. They stayed overnight in the organization's rented trailer to protect their equipment.

People had been encouraged to come in buses to ease the parking burden. They were arriving in a continual flow. Many were newcomers and were anxious to meet Joshua, who made himself readily accessible. Crowds flocked around him right up until the program started. His easy ways and unassuming manner put everyone at ease. People felt they had known him all their life and remarked at how comfortable he made everyone feel. It was almost like talking to a long-lost friend.

The format for the program was the same as the previous ones. There was nothing grandiose, nothing of the theatrical. People did not come to be entertained. They came for a purpose. They came for peace, peace within their own hearts and peace in the world in which they lived. Joshua, they knew, had the key to that peace, and they came to hear him and follow him.

Joshua's effect on people was so profound, it didn't take long before they began to wonder about him and who he was. Charismatic personalities affect others at a level that is almost mystical, causing people to attribute to them characteristics that transcend the merely human. Joshua's effect went beyond even that, especially after word circulated about the two children shot in the street, and the Arab girl hit by the speeding car, and the incident of the drinking water at the last gathering. People would approach Joshua just to touch his clothes, or to have him touch their children, or themselves. Many said they were healed after Joshua touched them, some from physical ailments, others from emotional problems. Whether this was true or imagined is not possible to ascertain, but what was true was that his followers' love of him knew no bounds, whether they were Jews, Moslems, Christians, or whatever.

Those closest to Joshua, however, had their own ideas about Joshua. Nathan, supposedly so cynical, had discussed the matter over lunch with Aaron and Daniel, with whom he worked. Nathan had been watching Joshua like a hawk and noticed little things about him that eluded the others, like Joshua's ability to understand things before they happened. He concluded this from noticing that Joshua was never really surprised at anything new or surprising that occurred. He also noticed Joshua calling people by name before he was introduced to them. Joshua's intimate identification with biblical sites fascinated him. He had also caught Joshua a few times at prayer, his whole being completely transformed. He had no doubt but that Joshua was truly communicating with his Father, and his Father was answering him. He himself felt he was on sacred ground just being there. It was an eerie feeling. Aaron, too, had incidents to contribute, really intimate ones culled from the hundreds of little things Joshua did during the long time spent at his home. Daniel also had his ideas. He never got over Joshua's warning him about the car bomb.

All in all the little circle, although they could not put together what they felt about Joshua, sensed there was something sacred about his presence and felt that God had, for some precious purpose, placed him in their lives. They all felt honored and privileged that he should be so specially close to them and their families.

By noontime, the gathering crowd was already approaching thirty thousand, and there were still more coming. Concerned about possible disorder, Aaron had asked Joshua over a week before if he should assign troops to be present just in case. Joshua just laughed and said not to worry. There would be no disorder.

The program began a little late. Shlomo was present again and only too happy to provide the music. This time, however, he had a partner, a blind Arab singer, a girl named Fatima. She had been blinded by soldiers' bullets when troops raided the refugee camp where her family lived. She had a rich soprano voice that rang with such pathos and sincerity that it touched the hearts of everyone. Sheik Ibrahim was there on the platform with the other members of Joshua's inner circle. Though appearing sad and pensive, he sat with great dignity. Soad and Jamileh and Elie sat near him. Off to the side of the platform was Elias Seremetis, with his camera, taking shots of all the important people present, and every now and then twisting his long waxed mustache.

Finally, Joshua was introduced. The applause was thunderous. When he rose to speak, he looked so unpretentious and unassuming. It was as if he were not even aware that this whole crowd would do his slightest beckoning.

"My dear people," he began, as was his custom, "we have grown from such humble beginnings. Those who dreamed this vision long ago, Aaron and Susan and Daniel and Nathan and Samuel, and those who responded so willingly, Sheik Ibrahim and his family and friends, all deserve our respect and our gratitude for what has taken place during the past several months. It is truly the work of God. You yourselves are no small part of what God is accomplishing in your midst. It is a beautiful work.

"We have watched from a distance what you have been doing and how you have conducted yourselves. Your behavior has been beyond reproach. I myself am proud of you.

"I know you all carry many burdens. Many have lost parents and children in the terrible slaughter of times past. Many of you are newcomers to our land and have left behind family and dear friends. I know your pain and your loneliness and the trials you face even here. Some of you are without a home and unemployed. Many of you nurse old and painful wounds. Others have been victims of cruel injustice right here in your own lands. I feel your hurt in my own heart and carry the pain of your anguish. I have watched you grow to rise above that pain and let it go. I have seen you reaching out to others who were hurting, trying to ease the burden of their pain. In doing this you forgot your own anguish, and opened your hearts to receive God's blessing and the comfort of His presence within you. You have grown immensely in the spirit of God.

"You have also freed yourselves from bitterness and hatred and in the beautiful spirit of God's forgiveness have befriended one another in a truly sublime expression of divine love. This has not been easy, nor will it be easy in the future. But do not lose heart. Even when your gestures of goodwill are not appreciated, do not take offense. Continue to do good. You are not doing good for praise or for appreciation. You are doing good because goodness is a part of you and you are expressing what is within you. Never weary of doing good and never tire of forgiving. Goodness will win out in time.

"In your demonstrations, you have been quiet and restrained. Continue that way. Words and loud noises are of little value. Your silence is deafening. Your peacefulness touches hearts and opens minds. Never resort to bizarre behavior or illegal acts. They tarnish the simplicity and the purity of your message and distract people from your true purpose. They create other issues and polarize those who would otherwise support you.

"Know that God is always by your side and in your hearts. Love one another, my dear friends, and know that I will always be with you. When you love one another, my Father and I will come and live within you and bring you peace. Keep high your ideals. Teach your children to love. Do not pass on to them your hurts and your grief. They cannot bear it without damaging their lives irreparably. Teach them to be free and not be afraid to trust.

"My faithful friends Aaron, Susan, Nathan, Samuel, Sheik Ibrahim, Soad, Jamileh, Father Elias, Rabbi Bernard, Elie, Mathilde, I have spent many hours with them, teaching them, guiding them. They are your teachers. Listen to them. They will not lead you astray.

"There are among us today four very special young men. They are very special to me. They do not know that I knew, but I did know, that they saved my life. They were assigned a very difficult mission by their grandfather, Sheik Ibrahim. They were assigned to watch me so nothing would happen to me. They did their job well. I was not supposed to know about it, but I did. I was aware of their presence every moment, and I am deeply grateful to these four heroic young men. Daoud, Najah, Ali, and Mahmoud, please step up here and let me thank you.

The boys looked up at their grandfather as if to ask for permission to go forward. He was beaming from ear to ear and shook his head, signaling them to step up. When they reached the platform, the crowd drew their breath in awe at seeing four little boys, hardly fifteen years old, who had such a frightening assignment. Joshua hugged each of them and gave them a present, a figurine he had carved, a perfect replica of himself, as a symbol that he would never forget them and did not want them ever to forget him. The boys blushed, and as the sheik stood up, they walked over to him and he kissed each of them. The people clapped for almost three minutes while the boys went back to their places.

Joshua continued with his talk. "My message to you today is: stay the course. Continue on your way and do not lose heart. You are doing the work of God, and He will not allow you to fail. That is certain. Your work is likened to a wise man who was growing old. His time was running out and he was concerned about his children. Times were bad and the old man had little left to provide for them. The old man's neighbors were miserable people and he could not trust them to be kind to his children when he died, even though their children were his children's playmates.

"The wise old man called in his own children as well as his neighbors' children and sat them down. Taking a sack out of the closet, he confided to them a secret. In the hills not far from their home was a very large field which he owned. The old man opened the sack and took out a handful of nuts that looked like acorns. 'You see these nuts?' the old man asked. 'Well, listen to me. I have nothing to give you but these. And you, my neighbors' children, are like my own. Each day I will give each of you a bag of these nuts. You are to go up into the hills and plant them. The next day I will give you more. And each day after that until the sacks are empty. And you are to keep this secret to yourselves.'

"Years later, the wise old man died. The neighbors were mean to the old man's children and tried to turn their children against them. In time the neighbors died, and the children were left alone. Being poor and having nowhere to earn a living, the children said to one another, 'Remember the wise old man, our father, how he gave us the bags of nuts to plant? Let us go to see what has happened to them.' They went up to the hills overlooking the valley, and to their surprise, there before their eyes was a vast forest of tall, beautiful, and rare trees, stretching as far as the eye could see, a rich treasure that would make them all extremely wealthy. However, in order to gather that wealth they had to be forever friends and work together on a piece of land that before was useless.

"And that, my friends, is the way it is here in our land, like the treasure the wise old man gave to all his children—to reap the treasures you must work together. May the wise old Father's peace and blessing be always in your hearts and may you always love one another. Salaam, shalom."

The vast crowd was stunned at the tone of finality in Joshua's message and stood for a moment in silence, then let out a thunderous ovation which lasted for over five minutes. Aaron had a difficult time quieting the crowd. In fact he had a difficult time calming himself. Strong man that he was, the tears kept rolling down his cheeks each time he approached the microphone to speak. No one else on the platform could help him as they were all crying as well. Whatever it was that Joshua said, it touched them all profoundly, and they could not restrain the force of their feelings. The whole vast crowd was just as deeply shaken, and spontaneously began to shout out, "Blessed is he who comes in the name of the Lord, Hosanna, Hosanna, Hosanna to the son of David." Never had they heard anyone speak the way this man spoke, and it touched the very core of their being.

During the break, Joshua mingled with the crowd. They clung to him as if he were to disappear. When he looked into each one's eyes, his look spoke volumes and healed many wounds and changed many lives. They could see in those eyes the love of God. In spite of their past lives for which they had long repented, and what they thought of themselves, they knew God loved them. That realization alone brought powerful healing.

As Joshua walked through the crowd, many asked if they would see him again. He told them not to worry, they would see him again, and that it was important for them to nourish the good relationships they had struck with all their new friends, and that they should help one another, particularly during difficult times. God was pleased when people lived like a family and not in isolated existences, because people needed one another.

The remainder of the session was routine. Instructions were given to the group before they left, and they were encouraged to be persistent in their efforts for peace, not become frustrated or tempted to resort to desperate means. Their most powerful asset was their unit and calm persistence and their unblemished behavior. They must let no one draw them off guard into illegal or violent acts. Help one another, care for one another. That was the bond that cemented the whole group together into a family. No one was a stranger.

18

THE RAPID GROWTH of the movement around Joshua was so dramatic it could not but cause concern among settlers in the occupied areas. They soon began to organize counterdemonstrations and attempted to draw Joshua's disciples into a confrontation, but to no avail. Aaron, Susan, and the sheik had appointed leaders whom they could trust for their prudence and patience and assigned them to lead the various groups around the country. They were a great influence in keeping the crowds calm at times when hostile instigators tried to start a brawl or bait Joshua's followers into doing something violent or illegal, in an attempt to discredit the movement. But the people's discipline was unshakable.

The meeting on the Plain of Esdraelon was the last of the big assemblies. The crowds were just too large. The members in various parts of the country now met in their own smaller groups, with their group leaders to guide them. Joshua had trained the leaders well in the quiet, private sessions he had with them. He was so casual about it, they did not even realize they were being trained for anything. However, by the time he had finished with them, they had so thoroughly absorbed his spirit, they were well prepared to go out and mold the people into a Joshua-like way of thinking and a Joshua-like way of acting. The people's own fond memories of the words of Joshua still moved their hearts and kept the fire alive and the memory of him fresh.

Aaron saw Joshua less and less. Nathan and Susan and the others were constantly calling Aaron to ask where he was, but he could give them no answer. Even the sheik did not see him, except on rare occasions. More and more word was coming back to Aaron and the others that Joshua had shown up in Tel Aviv or on the West Bank or in Haifa.

One such incident occurred while Father Elias was meeting with his group in Haifa. He had a large contingent of Joshua people in the area. They were not only a loyal group consisting of Arabs, Jews, and Christians, they were also a very influential group, who had powerful contacts within the Knesset and even in the cabinet. As they were meeting on this particular occasion, there was a knock at the door. When one of the people answered, they were shocked to see Joshua standing there. Of course they were thrilled that he came but were surprised that he even knew of the meeting. They immediately ushered him inside and properly seated him in a place of honor before continuing the meeting, then afterward invited him to speak.

"I have not come to give you a speech," he said, "but merely to encourage you in the new life you are living. The peace venture is only a temporary issue. The important thing is that you do not lose sight of the fact that you are now a new people, a new family. I am happy you have Father Elias to guide you. Trust him and accept his guidance. He will teach you all you have to know to find your way to God and to preserve your unity as a family. And remember I will be with you always, so do not lose heart."

After speaking briefly, while people were busy talking to one another, Joshua just seemed to have walked through their midst and slipped out of sight.

On another occasion, Rabbi Herbstman was telling Aaron how Joshua had shown up at a meeting he was having in Tel Aviv. He was at first stunned, though on thinking it over, realized he should not have been shocked because that was just the way Joshua did things, unannounced and spontaneously. Aaron, curious as to the time and the date, asked Bernie when it was Joshua had made his appearance. When Bernie told him the exact time, Aaron was silent. "What's the matter, Aaron?" Bernie asked him.

"What you have just told me is strange, because I got a phone call from Samuel who was holding a meeting in Ein Kerem at the same time and the same day, and he said Joshua stopped in to visit with his group. I don't know what to make of it."

"Are you sure it was the exact same time?" Bernie asked.

"Yes, I am certain," Aaron replied, baffled as to what was happening. "Next time I see Joshua, I'm going to pin him down and ask him point-blank. I feel we are friends enough for me to be blunt with him and for him to be honest with me. This is the most uncanny thing I have heard of in my whole life, and me a physicist. Imagine trying to tell someone about this. They would think I'm an idiot who has lost his screws."

"There is something very special about that man, Aaron," the rabbi said. "I don't know what it is, but I have the strangest feeling when I am in his presence. I don't know how to say it, but I feel there is something sacred about him. Yet he is so human and so natural, and so much fun to be with."

"I know, and to think that he sleeps in our house," Aaron responded. "I've wondered more than once."

The other groups around the country had similar brief visits from Joshua. He was always pleasant and friendly. If they doubted their senses when they saw him, touching him convinced them he was real. His message was always similar, though varying at times according to the needs of the group.

Finally Joshua showed up at Aaron's door. He must have known he was in for a thorough grilling, because as soon as Aaron answered the door, Joshua greeted him with a broad grin and commented on how busy Aaron had been of late.

"You're darned right I've been busy, trying to track you down," Aaron shot back, half in humor and half in bewilderment. "I hear you've got a new trick lately, being in two places at the same time. Joshua, you push our friendship to the ultimate limits. I can't keep up with you."

"Aaron, don't be so upset. You know with all that has to be done, I can't check in with you over every move I make. You have to know I'm trying to accomplish the impossible already, and it can't be done in just ordinary ways. Relax and just enjoy the fun. Well, are you going to make me stand out here all night or do you think you might invite me in?"

"Oh, I'm sorry, Joshua. You distracted me. Come right in. We were just sitting down for supper. Esther said she thought you might stop by, so she made some extra. Apparently a woman's intuition can get a better handle on you than my military training."

"Joshua's here!" the children cried out in unison, as they ran out to greet him. "We missed you, Joshua. We're so glad you're back."

"Yes, Joshua's here," their father answered. "At least the children are glad to see you."

Joshua realized this was all Aaron's ironic sense of humor. He was actually happier to see Joshua than anyone. He was just feeling sad that Joshua's time with them seemed to be coming to an end, and the thought of it hurt.

As the family was well into the meal, Aaron told Joshua some good news. "I've been waiting for weeks to tell you this, but I couldn't find you. Elie's brother-in-law, Siavosh Avari, came to talk to me. His family is very pleased with the progress of the factories and not only are they planning to build others, but they have a remarkable idea. Siavosh and Elie came over to test it on me. Their family is very close to King Fahd. Inspired by Joshua's idea of working together, they thought maybe they would make an appointment for an audience with the king and lay a proposal before him. Saudi Arabia and the other Arab countries, with all their oil money, are having a difficult time developing their countries. Our country on the other hand is always broke but has the genius and technology everyone needs. It is a natural complement. They need one another. With the success the Zanbaghe-Avari factories have been having, Siavosh and Elie thought they would try to interest the king in a joint venture with our country. It would be the salvation of the Arab people within our borders and would force everyone to work together and act as neighbors for a change."

"I think that is a wonderful idea," Joshua said, excited about the proposal. "When are they meeting with the king?"

"Sometime this week, I think," Aaron replied. "They had no trouble arranging for the audience. Sheik Ibrahim is a personal friend of King Fahd, and he is going with them."

"Well, that is something we will all have to pray over, because there will have to be considerable face-saving all around," Joshua responded. "It certainly does make a lot of sense."

The weeks that followed saw a continual buildup of support for the peace movement. The pressure on the prime minister increased accordingly, so did demands for further settlements on the West Bank. It was only the restraining power of Joshua's teachings that prevented the situation from exploding into open violence.

Siavosh, Elie, and the sheik returned from their visit with the king and were enthusiastic as they relayed the whole story to Aaron, Susan, and the others. The king had listened and sat very thoughtfully through the entire proposal. His brow furrowed several times as he thought of what it would take for him personally to enter into such an enterprise. At the end he said he would like to talk it over with some of his close allies whose counsel he could trust and whose support would be critical. The sheik's presence made it difficult for the king to say no outright and prompted him to consider the whole proposal in depth, since the sheik thought it worthwhile.

The king did have a difficult problem with the undertaking. He could not see himself dealing directly with these people who were treating his Arab brothers and sisters so harshly. He reminded his guests that the Jews in Spain had prospered under the Moors, and "now look how they treat our people. It is very difficult for me to even consider helping them."

"But Your Majesty," Sheik Ibrahim assured him, "you will be nicely forcing them to undertake a venture that will make it possible for our people to live in dignity and to play a major role in the future of the country. That has all kinds of potential. And you will be looked upon as the savior of our people. Not only will you be helping our own people immediately, you will be the catalyst for bringing prosperity to Arabs throughout the whole Middle East."

The king began to see some merit to the idea and admitted the proposal had some interesting long-term ramifications. He promised to consider the matter without delay and let them know his answer within the week. After their audience, the king invited his old friends to have lunch with him. Later in the afternoon they returned home.

The group's reaction was one of delight. The possibilities were mind-boggling. Joshua himself was optimistic. But they still had to wait for the king's reply.

To their surprise they did not have to wait long. Hardly a week after their audience with the king they received a request from King Fahd to come back and meet with him again. They wasted no time and were there by the next day.

The king had talked with his advisers and with other Arab leaders. They liked the idea, because it was a positive way of helping Arab people directly, but they thought it would be out of place for the king to be directly involved. After much thought and a couple of sleepless nights, the king came up with a solution. They would use their well-respected contacts in Holland to act as intermediaries. This would save face for everyone and make it possible to get the projects off the ground.

The remaining problem was this: Who would make the initial contacts with Jewish officials? The sheik offered to approach the prime minister and inform him of the king's interest in meeting with him. The king thought that a good idea and suggested that for follow-up one of his personal representatives could then meet with the prime minister or his representative. With that much decided upon, the three men returned home to share their good news.

The sheik met with the prime minister, and after a long and tedious session, the prime minister agreed to receive a representative from King Fahd. The meeting took place a short time later, and after a full two days of secret talks with top advisers, the prime minister decided to go ahead with the project. He knew the proposal would infuriate his radical right supporters, but this time he could afford to ignore them, because this proposal was so far-reaching and would be of such massive benefit to the whole country he could survive without their support. He knew the whole population would ultimately support him on this one.

The king was humble enough to agree to the trip to meet with the prime minister and sign the agreements. The day of the signing was kept a secret, so there was no time for any opposition groups to mar the day with raucous protests or worse. The evening television carried the story, and within hours the whole country was in a frenzy. Most people could not believe it. Joshua's people were ecstatic. The sheik was an immediate national hero. Aaron and Susan and their colleagues were no longer suspect but were invited to dinner at the prime minister's home. The radical right were beside themselves with rage. For them it was treason and spelled total rejection of everything they held sacred. Just the thought of having to exist side by side forever with Arabs and to see them as equal partners in society, in business, in every aspect of life was a humiliation so monumental they could not even conceive of it as being possible. To these fanatics, the insidious betrayal by the government was tantamount to giving official recognition to the Canaanites of old, whom, to their way of thinking, God had ordered to be eliminated.

Needless to say, they brought about the fall of the government. The prime minister anticipated this, and new elections were scheduled. The prime minister won by a comfortable majority, which put the radical right forever out of the picture. Joshua was unsurprised. He knew that no society can long survive with people like that. They have no worthwhile contributions to make to civilization. They put society in deep freeze and muzzle creativity and innovation and obstruct decent people from solving the dreadful problems facing our civilization.

Negotiations now had to be conducted with the money people. The Dutch intermediaries were seen almost daily meeting government officials and bankers as details of the complex financing arrangements were being made. Siavosh and Elie and the Mouawads attended all the meetings as they would be the prime agents for setting up this whole operation throughout the country.

The agriculture minister was in heaven at the newfound international position he held. It was his assignment to work with the Saudis in sharing the imaginative techniques for making the desert flourish. A multitude of new jobs was created which gave hope to highly trained engineers and doctors and technicians pouring into the country from Russia, who previously were wandering the streets all but homeless and hopeless.

The whole country, in fact, had a new life and a new hope. People could not believe that such a cataclysmic undertaking could happen almost unnoticed and overnight.

The radicals on both sides were unhappy. They would always be there. Sometimes Joshua got the feeling they were born that way and were that way as children. Political or theological principles had nothing to do with their behavior. Their problem was purely psychological and should they one day find their way to heaven, their response would probably be pretty much the same, negative and critical: "Oh, is this all there is, God? What a disappointment!" Then, Joshua thought, they would begin to spell out in detail all the things God could have done in designing heaven.

19

DURING ALL THIS flurry of activity, Joshua was nowhere to be found. Aaron called all over the land. No one had seen him, not the sheik, nor Father Elias, nor Samuel, nor Susan, nor Rabbi Herbstman. No one. If anyone should have gotten the credit for this completely peaceful overthrow of a society, it was Joshua, and he had vanished. Aaron was furious. Even Esther, who was ordinarily imperturbable, was upset. She wanted more than anything to see him bask in the glory that was rightly his. Apparently that was unimportant to him. Even the Mossad had a change of heart and had half their home-based force scouring the country looking for him. He was nowhere.

Then one day a band of nomads coming in from the Negev stopped off to pay their respects to Sheik Ibrahim and told him of this strange group of Jewish and Arab children trekking through the desert, retracing Moses' steps. They were with a young man they called Joshua. He was dressed in ordinary shirt and khaki pants and was wearing desert headgear. A gold medallion hung around his neck, and he was carrying a canteen and a backpack. He looked like a Jew.

The sheik quickly asked in what direction they were heading. The travelers could not tell him for sure. It seemed they had just come from the hills and were traveling northeast.

Sheik Ibrahim immediately had a courier deliver the information to Aaron. There was little Aaron could do but wait until Joshua returned and then hope he would contact someone. On second thought he decided to send someone to catch up with him and stay with the group until they reached the city or wherever they were heading. At least they would have him within their grasp and would know his whereabouts. This way they could pick him up and meet with him on his return.

Two days later, Joshua showed up, invigorated and relaxed after his trip through the desert. They all met on Ben-Yehuda Street. He seemed totally unconcerned about what was taking place throughout the country, to the exasperation of everyone.

"Joshua," Samuel said, with a tone of disbelief, "don't you realize all the things that have been taking place around here the past few weeks?"

"What things?" Joshua asked calmly.

"Why, the whole country is in turmoil and all because of you, and you take off for the desert with a bunch of kids," Aaron said, beside himself in his inability to understand this man.

"Joshua," Esther told him quietly, "King Fahd accepted Siavosh and Elie and the sheik's proposal. The prime minister also accepted it. The government has fallen. New elections have been held, and the whole country has come to life with all the new construction projects. Our agriculture experts have gone to work in Saudi Arabia to set up farms throughout the desert."

"I think that is marvelous," Joshua said simply. "But what does that have to do with me?"

Exasperated at such total detachment, Nathan asked impatiently, "Well, isn't this what you were aiming at all along?"

"My sole aim was to encourage people to reach out to one another and treat each other as friends and open their hearts to God so He could guide them in the way of peace," Joshua answered.

"Well, this is how the people responded to your messages," Aaron said. "They took you seriously and accomplished a miracle. Aren't you excited about that?"

"Of course I am, Aaron," Joshua replied, "and I am also glad that my work is coming to a close. My part is done. The rest is up to yourselves entirely. And you will do a good job."

"What do you mean, coming to a close?" Susan said, with an air of annoyance and sadness. "You can't just drop out of sight after leading these people to the brink of revolution. Where do you intend to go?"

"Susan, my work is done. The revolution you speak of flows from the change in people's souls. It will not disrupt society. It will bring only peace. The people know what to do and where to go from here."

"You mean you are just leaving us?" she persisted, with tears in her eyes.

"I must go back to my Father," Joshua answered. "But don't be concerned. I will be with you always. You are very special to me. You are all my dear friends. I will always be by your side. Trust me. You will see me again. And we will all be happy together."

"Where are you going?" Esther asked.

At this point Nathan was growing impatient and interrupted the conversation with the remark, "Are you people so thick you don't realize yet what has been taking place in our midst? Joshua isn't just someone who happened to come in off the desert. I've been watching him for months now and I think I pretty well have him figured out. Read the old Gospels and see what you come up with. Then you won't need to ask any more questions. You will have the answers. Right, Joshua?"

"My Father loves you all in a very special way," Joshua told the group. "He saw your frustrating attempts to make a difference here and knew how difficult it was. He made His presence known to you in a powerful way to show you the path and bless your efforts. That has been accomplished now, and I must go."

"What about the children?" Esther asked. "You can't just leave them. They have grown so fond of you and are so attached to you."

"I will see them and talk to them. They will understand better than yourselves," he said. "I would also like to meet with our little group once more. They have all been so loyal."

Aaron agreed to make the arrangements.

After the meeting broke up, Joshua went home with Aaron and the next morning spoke to the children, telling them that he had been sent to do a job and now he had to leave.

"You are going back to God, aren't you, Joshua?" Mirza said bluntly.

"Yes, little one, my work is done," Joshua replied. "But I have something special for each of you." Wrapped in tissue were three wood-carved figurines just like the ones he gave the four Arab boys. "I want you to keep these as a reminder that I will always love you and watch over you."

The children were thrilled to receive the beautiful figures, and they took turns hugging and kissing Joshua.

After breakfast, Joshua blessed the family and, promising never to be far from them, left and walked down the street. Watching him till he disappeared, the whole family hugged one another, sobbing, and walked back into the house.

The meeting Aaron arranged for the others in the group took place only a few days later, where it all began, on the Mount of Olives. Aaron hosted their last supper at the Seven Arches. It was a repetition of the scene in Aaron's house. They were all brokenhearted to learn that this was the last they would see of their friend. But they realized his work was done, and they had to carry on the beautiful legacy he had given to them. The parting was tearful, but they were comforted by his promise never to be far from them. They could not understand how, but having such confidence in his words based on past experience, they trusted that if he made a promise he would keep it.

As they talked, church bells rang in the distance, a voice called out over loudspeakers beckoning Moslems to prayer, and a lone shofar announced the Sabbath. The coincidence reduced the group to silence. The setting sun cast its golden rays across Jerusalem. All eyes turned toward Joshua, who stood silently with a vision of the future, a tear in his eye, and a smile on his face. The impossible dream had come true.

Honest expression of goodness can dissolve hatreds, dissipate suspicions, allay fears, and transform ancient enmities into warm friendships. When that happens, no one can predict the forces that are unleashed upon society. When people saw the good generated by the factories and other projects spun off by the Joshua people, everyone was caught up in the enthusiasm. The phenomenon was indeed so simple that people could not help but wonder why someone did not think of the idea sooner.

Though the idea may be simple, leading people out of a dark jungle of entangled, hate-filled emotions is a task that is beyond human capability. But once accomplished, the consequent events appear simple indeed.

The days that followed were filled with frenzied activity, as more factories were planned, conducted, and put on line. New housing was also needed. No more ghettos as in the past, but housing where people of wide differences were to live in the same neighborhoods. Only a handful objected. Those benefiting from the new housing were highly enthusiastic.

While some neighboring countries were slow to approve of the developments, decent people everywhere could not help but admire the vast changes that had taken place. The country was no longer a pariah, but truly the spearhead of a movement of cooperation that had the potential in time for bringing about the economic and cultural resurgence of the whole area.

Joshua's friends still met on a regular basis, no longer in peace demonstrations, but in much smaller groups with their leaders, who would discuss with them the many messages Joshua had given them. They kept alive Joshua's vision and told stories about this simple, wandering teacher, who by his love of God and belief in human goodness had changed forever the lives of the people who met him and listened to him. His goodness would live on in the hearts of those who followed him and would be passed on to the children, who were fascinated by the stories their parents told about him.

Not long after all these happenings, Sheik Ibrahim died. His funeral was carried out in elegant style. He wanted only a simple service, but the massive outpouring of affection from all the people necessitated a service that allowed for everyone, Jews, Arabs, and Christians, to weep and mourn their loss in a way that did honor not only to the sheik and his family for all that they had done but also to themselves for having risen above pettiness and vicious racial strife to bring about the transformation of their whole society. Before he died, the sheik requested of Aaron that his nephew, Jakoub, who lived on the farm in the Kidron Valley, might be appointed to his place in the Joshua community. Aaron was happy to accommodate him.

The story of Joshua and his brief sojourn among a tragic people may seem like a dream or a fantasy, and to some unreal or simplistic, but a dream is often nothing more than reality shorn of cynicism. Dreams have in the past come true where goodwill and determination overcame the obstacles and cleared the way for a new reality.